"A BROAD, COMPELLING STORY . . . A LONG, SATISFYING LOOK AT HELL AND SALVATION. . . ."

—*Publishers Weekly*

SWAN SONG

On the edge of a barren Kansas landscape, a man called Black Frankenstein hears the cry . . . "PROTECT THE CHILD . . ."

In the wasteland of New York City, a bag lady clutches a strange bejeweled ring and feels magic coursing through her . . .

Within an Idaho mountain, a survivalist compound lies in ruins, and a young boy learns how to kill . . .

In a wasteland born of nuclear rage, in world of mutant animals and marauding armies, the last people on earth are now the first. Three bands of survivors journey toward destiny—drawn into the final struggle between annihilation and life!

THEY HAVE SURVIVED
THE UNSURVIVABLE.
NOW THE ULTIMATE TERROR BEGINS.

"DISTINCTIVE AND ENGROSSING . . . McCAMMON COMBINES GRITTY REALISM WITH MAGIC . . . YOU'LL WISH THERE WERE MORE [OF *SWAN SONG*]."

—*Rave Reviews*

Books by Robert R. McCammon

Baal
Bethany's Sin
Blue World
Boy's Life
Gone South
Mine
Mystery Walk
The Night Boat
Stinger
Swan Song
They Thirst
Usher's Passing
The Wolf's Hour

Published by POCKET BOOKS

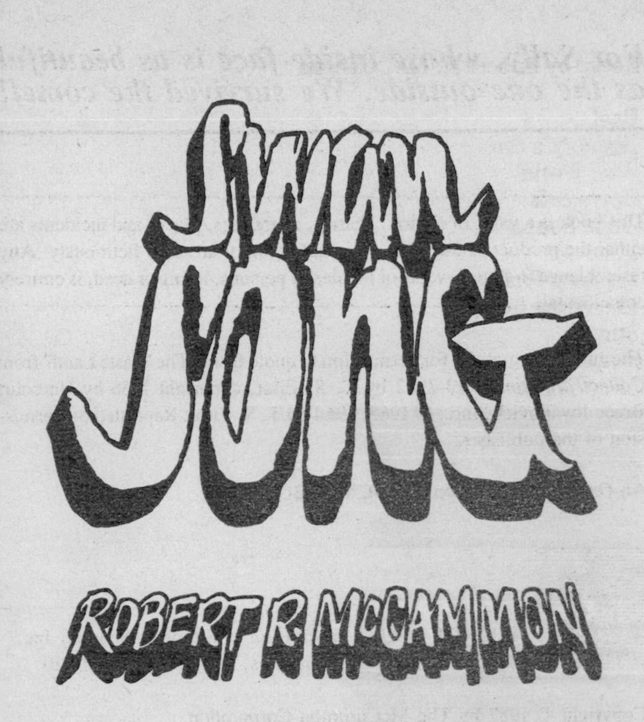

POCKET BOOKS

New York London Toronto Sydney Tokyo Singapore

For Sally, whose inside face is as beautiful as the one outside. We survived the comet!

The authour is grateful for permission to quote from "The Waste Land" from *Collected Poems 1909–1962* by T. S. Eliot, copyright 1936 by Harcourt Brace Jovanovich, Inc.; © 1963, 1964 by T. S. Eliot. Reprinted by permission of the publisher.

An *Original* Publication of POCKET BOOKS

POCKET BOOKS, a division of Simon & Schuster Inc.
1230 Avenue of the Americas, New York, NY 10020

ISBN: 0-671-74103-9

First Pocket Books printing June 1987

15

POCKET and colophon are registered trademarks of Simon & Schuster Inc.

Printed in the U.S.A.

BOOK ONE

ONE
The Point of No Return

Once upon a time / Sister Creep / Black Frankenstein / The spooky kid / King's Knight

One
July 16
10:27 P.M. Eastern Daylight Time
Washington, D.C.

Once upon a time we had a love affair with fire, the president of the United States thought as the match that he'd just struck to light his pipe flared beneath his fingers.

He stared into it, mesmerized by its color—and as the fire grew he had the vision of a tower of flame a thousand feet tall, whirling across the country he loved, torching cities and towns, turning rivers to steam, ripping across the ruins of heartland farms and casting the ashes of seventy million human beings into a black sky. He watched with dreadful fascination as the flame crawled up the match, and he realized that there, on a tiny scale, was the power of both creation and destruction; it could cook food, illuminate the darkness, melt iron and sear human flesh. Something that resembled a small, unblinking scarlet eye opened in the center of the flame, and he wanted to scream. He had awakened at two in the morning from a nightmare of holocaust; he'd begun crying and couldn't stop, and the first lady had tried to calm him, but he just kept shaking and sobbing like a child. He'd sat in the Oval Office until dawn, going over the maps and top-security reports again and again, but they all said the same thing: *First Strike*.

The fire burned his fingers. He shook the match out and dropped it into the ashtray embossed with the presidential seal in front of him. The thin thread of smoke began to curl up toward the vent of the air-filtration system.

"Sir?" someone said. He looked up, saw a group of strangers sitting in the Situations Room with him, saw the high-resolution computer map of the world on the screen before him, the array of telephones and video screens set in a semicircle around him like the cockpit of a jet fighter, and he wished to God that someone else could sit in his seat, that he was still just a senator and he didn't know the truth about the world. *"Sir?"*

He ran his hand across his forehead. His skin felt clammy. Fine time to be coming down with the flu, he thought, and he almost laughed at the absurdity of it. The president gets no sick days, he thought, because a president's not supposed to be sick. He tried to focus on who at the oval table was speaking to him; they were all watching him—the vice-president, nervous and sly; Admiral Narramore, ramrod-straight in his uniform with a chestful of service decorations; General Sinclair, crusty and alert, his eyes like two bits of blue glass in his hard-seamed face; Secretary of Defense Hannan, who looked as kindly as anyone's old grandfather but who was known as "Iron Hans" by both the press corps and his associates; General Chivington, the ranking authority on Soviet military strength; Chief of Staff Bergholz, crewcut and crisp in his ubiquitous dark blue pin-striped suit; and various other military officials and advisors.

"Yes?" the president asked Bergholz.

Hannan reached for a glass of water, sipped from it and said, "Sir? I was asking if you wanted me to go on." He tapped the page of the open report from which he'd been reading.

"Oh." My pipe's gone out, he thought. Didn't I just light it? He looked at the burned match in the ashtray, couldn't remember how it had gotten there. For an instant he saw John Wayne's face in his mind, a scene from some old black-and-white movie he'd seen as a kid; the Duke was saying something about the point of no return. "Yes," the president said. "Go on."

Hannan glanced quickly around the table at the others. They all had copies of the report before them, as well as stacks of other Eyes Only coded reports fresh off the NORAD and SAC communications wires. "Less than three hours ago," Hannan continued, "our last operating SKY EYE recon satellite was dazzled as it moved into position over Chatyrka, U.S.S.R. We lost all our optical sensors and cameras, and again—as in the case of the other six SKY EYEs—we feel this one was destroyed by a land-based laser, probably operating from a point near Magadan. Twenty minutes after SKY EYE 7 was blinded, we used our Malmstrom AFB laser to dazzle a Soviet recon satellite as it came over Canada. By our calculations, that still leaves them two recon eyes available, one currently over the northern Pacific and a second over the Iran–Iraq border. NASA's trying to repair SKY EYEs 2 and 3, but the others are space junk. What all this means, sir, is that as of approximately three hours ago, Eastern Daylight Time"—Hannan looked up at the digital clock on the Situation Room's gray concrete wall—"we went blind. The last recon photos were taken at 1830 hours over Jelgava." He switched on a microphone attached to the console before him and said, "SKY EYE recon 7-16, please."

There was a pause of three seconds as the information computer found the required data. On the large wall screen, the map of the world went dark and was replaced by a high-altitude satellite photograph showing the sweep of a dense Soviet forest. At the center of the picture was a cluster of pinheads linked together by the tiny lines of roadways. "Enlarge twelve," Hannan said, the picture reflected in his horn-rimmed eyeglasses.

The photograph was enlarged twelve times, until finally the hundreds of intercontinental ballistic missile silos were as clear as if the Situations Room wall screen was a plate glass window. On the roads were trucks, their tires throwing up dust, and even soldiers were visible near the missile installation's concrete bunkers and radar dishes. "As you can see," Hannan went on in the calm, slightly detached voice of his previous profession—teaching military history and economics at Yale—"they're getting ready for something. Probably bringing in more radar gear and arming those warheads, is my guess. We count two hundred and sixty-three silos in that installation alone, probably housing over six hundred warheads. Two minutes later, the SKY EYE was blinded. But this picture only reinforces what we already know: the Soviets have gone to a high level of readiness, and they don't want us seeing the new equipment they're bringing in. Which brings us to General Chivington's report. General?"

Chivington broke the seal on a green folder in front of him, and the others did the same. Inside were pages of documents, graphs and charts. "Gentlemen," he said in a gravelly voice, "the Soviet war machine has mobilized to within fifteen percent of capacity in the last nine months. I don't have to tell you about Afghanistan, South America or the Persian Gulf, but I'd like to direct your attention to the document marked Double 6 Double 3. That's a graph showing the amount of supplies being funneled into the Russian Civil Defense System, and you can see for yourselves how it's jumped in the last two months. Our Soviet sources tell us that more than forty percent of their urban population has now either moved outside the cities or taken up residence inside the fallout shelters. . . ."

While Chivington talked on about Soviet Civil Defense the president's mind went back eight months to the final terrible days of Afghanistan, with its nerve gas warfare and tactical nuclear strikes. And one week after the fall of Afghanistan, a twelve-and-a-half-kiloton nuclear device had exploded in a Beirut apartment building, turning that tortured city into a moonscape of radioactive rubble. Almost half the population was killed outright. A variety of terrorist groups had gleefully claimed responsibility, promising more lightning bolts from Allah.

With the detonation of that bomb, a Pandora's box of terrors had been opened.

On the fourteenth of March, India had attacked Pakistan

with chemical weapons. Pakistan retaliated by a missile strike on the city of Jaipur. Three Indian nuclear missiles had leveled Karachi, and the war was deadlocked in the wastes of the Thar Desert.

On the second of April, Iran had unleashed a rain of Soviet-supplied nuclear missiles on Iraq, and American forces had been sucked into the maelstrom as they fought to hold back the Iranians. Soviet and American jets had battled over the Persian Gulf, and the entire region was primed to blow.

Border wars had rippled across North and South Africa. The smallest of countries were depleting their treasuries to buy chemical and nuclear weapons from arms brokers. Alliances changed overnight, some due to military pressure and others to snipers' bullets.

Less than twelve miles off Key West, a trigger-happy American F-18 fighter pilot had sent an air-to-surface missile into the side of a disabled Russian submarine on the fourth day of May. Cuban-based Russian Floggers had come screaming over the horizon, shooting down the first pilot and two others of a squadron that arrived as backup.

Nine days later, a Soviet and an American submarine had collided during a game of cat-and-mouse in the Arctic. Two days after that, the radars of the Canadian Distant Early Warning line had picked up the blips of twenty incoming aircraft; all western United States air force bases had gone to red alert, but the intruders turned and escaped before contact.

On the sixteenth of May, all American air bases had gone to Defcon One, with a corresponding move by the Soviets within two hours. Adding to the tension that day was the detonation of a nuclear device in the Fiat complex in Milan, Italy, the action claimed by a Communist terrorist group called The Red Star of Freedom.

Incidents between surface ships, submarines and aircraft had continued through May and June in the North Atlantic and North Pacific. American air bases had gone to Defcon Two when a cruiser had exploded and sank, cause unknown, thirty nautical miles off the coast of Oregon. Sightings of Soviet submarines in territorial waters increased dramatically, and American submarines were sent to test the Russian defenses. The activity at Soviet ICBM installations was recorded by SKY EYE satellites before they were blinded by lasers, and the president knew the Soviets saw the activity at U.S. bases before their own spy satellites were dazzled blind.

On the thirtieth of June of the "Grim Summer," as the newsmagazines were calling it, a cruise ship called the *Tropic Panorama,* carrying seven hundred passengers between Hawaii and San Francisco, had radioed that they were being stalked by an unidentified submarine.

That had been the final message of the *Tropic Panorama.*

From that day on, American naval vessels had patrolled the Pacific with nuclear missiles armed and ready for launch.

The president remembered the movie: *The High and the Mighty,* about an airplane in distress and about to crash. The pilot was John Wayne, and the Duke had told the crew about the point of no return—a line beyond which the plane could not turn back, but had to keep going forward, whatever the result. The president's mind had been on the point of no return a lot lately; he'd dreamed he was at the controls of a disabled plane, flying over a dark and forbidding ocean, searching for the lights of land. But the controls were shattered, and the plane kept dropping lower and lower while the screams of the passengers rang in his mind.

I want to be a child again, he thought as the other men at the table looked at him. Dear God, I don't want to be at the controls anymore!

General Chivington had finished his report. The president said, "Thank you," though he wasn't sure exactly what Chivington had said. He felt the eyes of those men on him, waiting for him to speak, to move, to do anything. He was in his late forties, dark-haired and ruggedly handsome; he had been a pilot himself, had flown the NASA shuttle *Olympian* and been one of the first to walk in space wearing a jet pack. Contemplating the great cloud-streaked orb of the Earth, he'd been moved to tears, and his emotional radio transmission of "I think I know how God must feel, Houston" had done more than anything to win him the presidency.

But he'd inherited the mistakes of the generations of

presidents before him, and he'd been ridiculously naive about the world on the eve of the twenty-first century.

The economy, after a resurgence in the mid-eighties, had tumbled out of control. The crime rate was staggering, the prisons packed slaughterhouses. Hundreds of thousands of homeless people—"The Ragtag Nation," as the *New York Times* called them—roamed the streets of America, unable to afford shelter or cope mentally with the pressures of a runaway world. The "Star Wars" military program that had cost billions of dollars had proven to be a disaster, because it was realized too late that machines could only work as well as humans, and the complexity of the orbital platforms boggled the mind and broke the budget. The arms brokers had fed a crude, unstable nuclear technology to Third World nations and mad-dog leaders thirsting for power in the seductive and precarious global arena. Twelve-kiloton bombs, roughly the strength of the device that had decimated Hiroshima, were now as common as hand grenades and could be carried in a briefcase. The renewed riots in Poland and the Warsaw street fighting the previous winter had chilled United States–Soviet relations to below zero, quickly followed by the collapse and national disgrace of the CIA plot to assassinate Polish Liberation leaders.

We are on the edge of the point of no return, the president thought, and he felt an awful urge to laugh, but he concentrated on keeping his lips tightly sealed. His mind was grappling with an intricate web of reports and opinions that led to a terrible conclusion: the Soviet Union was preparing a first strike that would utterly destroy the United States of America.

"Sir?" Hannan broke the uneasy silence. "Admiral Narramore has the next report. Admiral?"

Another folder was unsealed. Admiral Narramore, a gaunt, wiry-looking man in his mid-sixties, began to go over the classified data: "At 1912 hours, British recon helicopters off the guided missile destroyer *Fife* dropped sonobuoys that verified the presence of six unidentified submarines seventy-three miles north of Bermuda, bearing three hundred degrees. If those subs are closing on the northeastern coast, they're already within strike range of New York City, Newport News, air bases on the eastern seaboard, the White House and the Pentagon." He gazed across the table at the president, his eyes smoky gray under thick white brows. The White House was fifty feet above their heads. "If six were picked up," he said, "you can rely on the fact that Ivan's got at least three times that many out there. They can deliver several hundred warheads within five to nine minutes of launch." He turned the page. "As of an hour ago, the twelve Delta II-class Soviet subs two hundred and sixty miles northwest of San Francisco were still holding their position."

The president felt dazed, as if this all were a waking dream. Think! he told himself. Damn you, *think!* "Where are our submarines, Admiral?" he heard himself ask, in what might have been a stranger's voice.

Narramore called up another computer map on the wall screen. It displayed a line of blinking dots about two hundred miles northeast of Murmansk, U.S.S.R. Calling up a second map brought the Baltic Sea onto the screen, and another deployment of nuclear subs northwest of Riga. A third map showed the Russian east coast, a line of submarines in position in the Bering Sea between Alaska and the Soviet mainland. "We've got Ivan in an iron ring," Narramore said. "Give us the word and we'll sink anything that tries to break through."

"I think the picture's very clear." Hannan's voice was quiet and firm. "We've got to back the Soviets off."

The president was silent, trying to put together logical thoughts. The palms of his hands were sweating. "What . . . if they're *not* planning a first strike? What if they believe *we* are? If we show force, might it not push them over the edge?"

Hannan took a cigarette from a silver case and lit it. Again the president's eyes were drawn to the flame. "Sir," Hannan replied softly, as if speaking to a retarded child, "if the Soviets respect anything, it's force. You know that as well as every man in this room, especially since the Persian Gulf incident. They want territory, and they're prepared to destroy us and to take their share of casualties to get it. Hell, their economy is worse than ours! They're going to keep pushing us until we either break or strike—and if we delay until we break, God help us."

"No." The president shook his head. They'd been over this many times, and the idea sickened him. "No. We will *not* deliver a first strike."

"The Soviets," Hannan continued patiently, "understand the diplomacy of the fist. I'm not saying I think we should destroy the Soviet Union. But I do believe—fervently—that now is the time to tell them, and decisively, that we'll not be pushed, and we won't let their nuclear submarines sit off our shores waiting for launch codes!"

The president stared at his hands. The knot of his tie felt like a hangman's noose, and there was sweat under his arms and at the small of his back. "Meaning what?" he asked.

"Meaning we intercept those goddamned submarines immediately. We destroy them if they won't turn back. We go to Defcon Three at all air bases and ICBM installations." Hannan looked quickly around the table to judge who stood with him. Only the vice-president glanced away, but Hannan knew he was a weak man and his opinion carried no weight. "We intercept any Soviet nuclear vessel leaving Riga, Murmansk or Vladivostok. We take control of the sea again—and if that means limited nuclear contact, then so be it."

"Blockade," the president said. "Wouldn't that make them more eager to fight?"

"Sir?" General Sinclair spoke in a folksy, down-home Virginia drawl. "I think the reasonin' goes like this: Ivan's got to *believe* we'll risk our asses to blow him to hell and back. And to be honest, sir, I don't think there's a man jack here who'll sit still and let Ivan throw a shitload of SLBMs at us without gettin' our own knock in. No matter what the casualty toll." He leaned forward, his piercing stare directed at the president. "I can put SAC and NORAD on Defcon Three within two minutes of your okay. I can send a squadron of B-1s right up to Ivan's back door within one hour. Just kinda give him a gentle prod, y'see."

"But . . . they'll think *we're* attacking!"

"The point is that they'll know we're not afraid." Hannan tapped a stalk of ash into his ashtray. "If that's crazy, okay.

But by God, the Russians respect insanity more than they respect fear! If we let them bring nuclear missiles to bear on our coastlines without lifting a finger, we're signing a death warrant for the United States of America!"

The president closed his eyes. Jerked them open again. He had seen burning cities and charred black things that had once been human beings. With an effort he said, "I don't . . . I don't want to be the man who starts World War Three. Can you understand that?"

"It's already started," Sinclair spoke up. "Hell, the whole damned world's at war, and everybody's waitin' for either Ivan or us to give the knockout punch. Maybe the whole future of the world depends on who's willin' to be the craziest! I agree with Hans; if we don't make a move right soon, a mighty hard rain's gonna fall on our tin roof."

"They'll back off," Narramore said flatly. "They've backed off before. If we send hunter-killer groups after those subs and blow them out of the water, they'll know where the line's drawn. So: Do we sit and wait, or do we show them our muscle?"

"Sir?" Hannan prodded. He glanced again at the clock, which showed fifty-eight minutes after ten. "I think the decision belongs to you now."

I don't want it! he almost shouted. He needed time, needed to go to Camp David or off on one of those long fishing trips he had enjoyed as a senator. But now there was no more time. His hands were gripped before him. His face felt so tight he feared it would crack and fall to pieces like a mask, and he wouldn't want to see what lay underneath. When he looked up, the watching and powerful men were still there, and his senses seemed to whirl away from him.

The decision. The decision had to be made. Right now.

"Yes." The word had never sounded so terrible before. "All right. We go to"—he paused, drew a deep breath—"we go to Defcon Three. Admiral, alert your task forces. General Sinclair, I don't want those B-1s over one *inch* of Russian territory. Is that clear?"

"My crews could walk that line in their sleep."

"Punch your codes."

Sinclair went to work on the keyboard console before him, then lifted his telephone to make the voice authorization to Strategic Air Command in Omaha and the North American Air Defense fortress in Cheyenne Mountain, Colorado. Admiral Narramore picked up the phone that instantly put him in touch with Naval Operations at the Pentagon. Within minutes there would be heightened activity at the country's air and naval bases. The Defcon Three codes would hum through the wires, and yet another check would be carried out on radar equipment, sensors, monitors, computers and hundreds of other pieces of high-tech military hardware, as well as the dozens of Cruise missiles and thousands of nuclear warheads hidden in silos across the Midwest from Montana to Kansas.

The president was numb. The decision was made. Chief of Staff Bergholz adjourned the meeting and came over to grasp the president's shoulder and say what a good, solid decision it was. As the military advisors and officials left the Situations Room and moved to the elevator in the outside hallway the president sat alone. His pipe was cold, and he did not care to relight it.

"Sir?"

He jumped, turning his head toward the voice. Hannan stood beside the door. "Are you all right?"

"A-OK." The president smiled wanly. A memory of his glory days as an astronaut had just flashed by. "No. Jesus Christ, I don't know. I think I am."

"You made the correct decision. We both know that. The Soviets have to realize we're not afraid."

"I *am* afraid, Hans! I'm damned afraid!"

"So am I. So is everyone, but we must not be ruled by fear." He approached the table and paged through some of the folders. In a few minutes, a young CIA man would be in to shred all the documents. "I think you'd better send Julianne and Cory to the Basement tonight, as soon as they can pack. We'll work out something with the press."

The president nodded. The Basement was an underground shelter in Delaware where the first lady, the president's seventeen-year-old son, ranking cabinet members and staff people would—they hoped—be protected from all but a direct hit by a one-megaton nuclear warhead. Since news of the carefully constructed Basement had leaked to the public several years before, such underground shelters had started appearing all over the country, some dug into old mines and others into mountains. The "survivalist" business was booming as never before.

"There's a subject we need to talk about," Hannan said. The president could see his own face, weary and hollow-eyed, reflected in the man's glasses. "Talons."

"It's not time for that yet." His stomach had knotted. "Not nearly time."

"Yes. It *is* time. I think you'd be safer in the Airborne Command Center. One of the first targets would be the roof of the White House. I'm going to send Paula to the Basement, and, as you know, you have the authority to send whomever else you want there. But I'd like to join you in the Airborne Center, if I may."

"Yes. Of course. I want you with me."

"And," Hannan continued, "there'll be an Air Force officer aboard with a briefcase handcuffed to his wrist. Do you know your codes?"

"I know them." Those particular codes were among the first things he'd learned after taking office. An iron band of tension gripped the back of his neck. "But . . . I won't have to use them, will I, Hans?" he asked, almost pleadingly.

"Most likely not. But if you do—*if* you do—I want you to remember that by then the America we love will be dead, and no invader has ever, or will ever, set foot on American earth." He reached out and squeezed the president's shoulder in a grandfatherly gesture. "Right?"

"The point of no return," the president said, his eyes glazed and distant.

"What?"

"We're about to cross the point of no return. Maybe we already have. Maybe it's way too late to turn back. God help us, Hans; we're flying in the dark, and we don't know where the hell we're going."

"We'll figure it out when we get there. We always have before."

"Hans?" The president's voice was as soft as a child's. "If . . . if you were God . . . would you destroy this world?"

Hannan didn't respond for a moment. Then, "I suppose . . . I'd wait and watch. If I were God, I mean."

"Wait and watch for what?"

"To find out who wins. The good guys or the bad guys."

"Is there a difference anymore?"

Hannan paused. He started to answer, and then he realized he could not. "I'll get the elevator," he said, and he walked out of the Situations Room.

The president unclasped his hands. The overhead lights sparkled on the cuff links he always wore, embossed with the seal of the president of the United States.

"I'm A-OK," he said to himself. "All systems go."

Something broke inside him, and he almost cried. He wanted to go home, but home was a long, long way from this chair.

"Sir?" Hannan called him.

Moving as slowly and stiffly as an elderly man, the president stood up and went out to face the future.

Two
11:19 P.M. Eastern Daylight Time
New York City

Whack!

She felt somebody kick the side of her cardboard box, and she stirred and hugged her canvas bag closer. She was tired and wanted to rest. A girl needs her beauty sleep, she thought, and she closed her eyes again.

"I *said* get outta there!"

Hands grabbed her ankles and hauled her roughly out of the box onto the pavement. As she came out she shouted in indignation and started kicking wildly. "You bastard sonofabitching bastard lemme alone you bastard!"

"Shit, lookit that!" said one of the two figures standing above her, outlined in red neon from the sign of a Vietnamese takeout restaurant across West Thirty-sixth Street. "He's a woman!"

The other man, who'd grabbed her ankles above her dirty sneakers and hauled her out, growled in a darker, meaner voice, "Woman or not, I'm gonna stomp her ass."

She sat up, the canvas bag holding her worldly belongings clutched close to her chest. In the red wash of neon, her square-jawed, sturdy face was deeply lined and streaked with street grime. Her eyes, sunken in violet-tinged hollows, were a pale, watery blue and glinted with both fear and anger. On her head she wore a blue cap that she'd found the day before in a split-open garbage bag. Her outfit consisted of a dirty gray printed short-sleeved blouse and a baggy pair of brown men's trousers with patched knees. She was a big-boned, fleshy woman, and her stomach and hips strained against the coarse material of her trousers; her clothes, as well as the canvas duffel bag she carried, had come from a kindly minister at the Salvation Army. Under the cap, her gray-streaked brown hair hung untidily around her shoulders, parts of it chopped off here and there where she'd taken scissors to it. Stuffed into her canvas bag was a melange of objects: a roll of fishing line, a tattered bright orange sweater, a pair of cowboy boots with both heels broken off, a dented mess tray, paper cups and plastic eating utensils, a year-old copy of *Cosmopolitan,* a length of chain, several packages of Juicy Fruit chewing gum and other items buried in the bag that even she'd forgotten were there. As the two men stared at her—one with menacing intent—she clutched the bag tighter. Her left eye and cheekbone were bruised and swollen, and her ribs hurt where she'd been pushed down a flight of stairs by another indigent woman at the Christian Shelter three days before. She'd picked herself off the floor, stalked up the stairs and knocked two teeth out of the woman's head with a roundhouse right.

"You're in my box," the dark-voiced man said. He was tall and skinny, wearing only a pair of blue jeans, his chest shining with sweat. His face was bearded, his eyes filled with shadow. The second man, shorter and heavier, wore a sweaty T-shirt and green Army surplus pants pocked with cigarette burns. He had oily dark hair, and he kept scratching his crotch. The first man prodded her in the side with the toe of his boot, and she winced at the pain to her ribs. "You *deaf,* bitch? I said you're in my fuckin' box!"

The cardboard box in which she'd been sleeping lay on its side amid a sea of oozing garbage bags, a symptom of the garbage strike that had clogged Manhattan's streets and gutters for over two weeks. In the suffocating heat of one-hundred-degree days and ninety-degree nights, the bags had swollen and exploded. Rats were having festival days, and mountains of garbage lay uncollected, blocking off traffic on some streets.

She looked dazedly up at the two men, the contents of a half bottle of Red Dagger percolating in her stomach. Her last meal had been the remnants of chicken bones and the scrapings from a discarded TV dinner. "Huh?"

"My box!" the bearded man shouted in her face. "This is *my* place! You crazy or somethin'?"

"She don't have no sense," the other one said. "She's crazy as hell."

"Ugly as hell, too. Hey, whatcha got in that bag? Lemme see!" He grabbed at it and yanked, but the woman emitted a loud howl and refused to give it up, her eyes wide and terrified. "You got some money in there? Somethin' to drink? Give it here, bitch!" The man almost tore it from her arms, but she whimpered and hung on. Red light sparked off an ornament around her neck—a small, cheap crucifix attached to a necklace made of linked gemclips.

"Hey!" the second man said. "Looky there! I know who she is! I seen her panhandlin' on Forty-second Street. She thinks she's a damned saint, always preachin' to people. They call her Sister Creep."

"Yeah? Well, maybe we can pawn us that trinket, then." He reached to tear the crucifix off her neck, but she turned her head away. The man grabbed the back of her neck, snarled and balled up his other hand to strike her.

"Please!" she begged, about to sob. "Please don't hurt me! I got somethin' for you!" She started rummaging through the bag.

"Get it out, and hurry! I oughta bust your head for sleepin' in my box." He let her head go, but he kept his fist poised and ready.

She made little weak whimpering noises as she searched. "Somewhere in here," she muttered. "Got it somewhere."

"Put it right *here!*" He thrust his palm at her. "And maybe I won't kick your ass."

Her hand closed around what she was looking for. "Found it," she said. "Sure did."

"Well, put it here!"

"Okay," the woman replied; the whimpering was gone, and her voice was as tough as sunbaked leather. With one blurred, smooth motion she withdrew a straight razor, flicked it open with a snap of her wrist and slashed it hard across the bearded man's open hand.

Blood jetted from the gash. The man's face went white. He gripped his wrist; his mouth contorted into an O, and then the scream came out like the sound of a strangling cat. At once the woman was on her stocky legs, holding the canvas bag in front of her like a shield and swiping again at the two men, who tumbled back into each other, slipped on the garbage-slimed pavement and went down. The bearded man, blood streaming down his hand, came up holding a piece of wood studded with rusty nails; his eyes gleamed with rage. "I'll show you!" he screamed. "I'll show you right *now!*"

He swung at her, but she ducked under the blow and slashed at him with the razor. He staggered back again and stood looking dumbly at the line of blood that leaked from his chest.

Sister Creep didn't pause; she turned and ran—almost slipping in a pool of ooze, but regaining her balance—with the shouts of the two men ringing out behind her. "Gonna get you!" the bearded one warned. "I'll find you, bitch! You just wait!"

She didn't. She kept going, her sneakers slapping the pavement, until she came to a barrier of a thousand split-open garbage bags. She crawled over it, taking the time to pick up a few interesting items, like a broken salt shaker and a soggy copy of *National Geographic,* and stuff them into her bag. Then she was over the barrier, and she kept walking, the breath still rasping in her lungs and her body trembling. That had been close, she thought. The demons almost got me! But glory be to Jesus, and when he arrives in his flying saucer from the planet Jupiter I'll be there on the golden shore to kiss his hand!

She stood on the corner of Thirty-eighth and Seventh Avenue, catching her breath and watching the traffic pass like a stampeding herd of cattle. The yellow haze of garbage fumes and automobile exhaust stirred like the stagnant matter atop a pond, and the wet heat pressed in on Sister Creep; beads of sweat broke and ran down her face. Her clothes were damp; she wished she had some deodorant, but the last of the Secret was gone. She looked around at the faces of strangers, daubed the color of wounds in the glare of pulsing neon. She didn't know where she was going, and she hardly remembered where she'd been. But she knew she couldn't stand on this corner all night; standing out in the open, she'd realized a long time ago, brought the demon X rays jabbing at your head, trying to scramble your brains. She began walking north, her head ducked and her shoulders hunched, in the direction of Central Park.

Her nerves were jangling from her experience with the two heathen who'd tried to rob her. Sin was everywhere! she thought. In the ground, in the air, in the water—nothing but rank, black and evil sin! And it was in people's faces, too, oh, yes! You could see the sin creeping over people's faces, hooding their eyes and making their mouths go crooked. It was the world and the demons that were making innocent people crazy, she knew. Never before had the demons been so busy, or so greedy for innocent souls.

She thought of the magic place, way over on Fifth Avenue, and her hard, worried frown softened. She often went there to look at the beautiful things in the windows; the delicate objects displayed there had the power to soothe her soul, and even though the guard at the door wouldn't let her pass she was content to just stand outside and stare. She recalled a glass angel in the window once—a powerful figure: the angel's long hair was swept back like holy, glittering fire, and her wings were about to unfold from a strong, sleek body. And in that angel's beautiful face the eyes shone with multicolored, wonderful lights. Sister Creep had journeyed to look at that angel every day for a month, until they replaced it with a glass whale leaping from a stormy blue-green glass sea. Of course, there were other places with treasures along Fifth Avenue, and Sister knew their names—Saks, Fortunoff's, Cartier, Gucci, Tiffany—but she was drawn to the sculptures on display at the Steuben Glass shop, the magic place of soul-soothing dreams, where the silken sheen of polished glass under soft lights made her think how lovely Heaven was going to be.

Somebody jostled her back to reality. She blinked in the hot shout of neon. Nearby a sign announced Girls! Live Girls!—would men want dead ones? she wondered—and a movie marquee advertised *Born Erect*. The signs pulsed from every niche and doorway: Sex Books! Sex Aids! Boom Boxes! Martial Arts Weapons! A thunder of bass-heavy music came from a bar's doorway, and other pounding, discordant rhythms strutted from speakers set up over a strip of bookstores, bars, strip shows and porno theaters. At almost eleven-thirty, Forty-second Street near the rim of Times Square was a parade of humanity. A young Hispanic boy near Sister Creep held up his hands and shouted, "Coke! Poppers! Crack! Right here!" Not far away, a rival drug seller opened his coat to show the plastic bags he was carrying; he yelled, "Getcha high, you're gonna fly! Do it deep, cheap cheap cheap!"

Other sellers shouted at the cars that slowly drove along Forty-second. Girls in halter tops, jeans, hot pants or leather slacks hung around the doors of the bookstores and theaters or motioned for the drivers to pull over; some did, and Sister Creep watched the young girls being swept away into the night by strangers. The noise was almost deafening, and across the street in front of a peep show two young black men were grappling on the sidewalk, surrounded by a ring of others who laughed and urged them on to a higher level of violence. The burning hemp aroma of pot floated through the air, the incense of escape. "Switchblades!" another vendor yelled. "Blades right here!"

Sister Creep moved on, her gaze warily ticking back and forth. She knew this street, this den of demons; she had come to preach here many times. But the preaching never did any good, and her voice was drowned out in the thunder of music and the shouting of people with something to sell. She stumbled across the body of a black man sprawled across the pavement; his eyes were open, and blood had pooled from his nostrils. She kept going, bumping into people, being shoved and cursed at, and the neon glare all but blinded her. Her mouth opened, and she shouted, "Save your souls! The end is near! God have mercy on your souls!"

But no one even looked at her. Sister Creep plunged into the swirl of bodies, and suddenly an old, gnarled man with vomit on the front of his shirt was in her face; he cursed at her and grabbed for her bag, yanking several items out of it and running before she could get a good swing at him. "You're goin' to Hell, you sonofabitch!" she shrieked—and then a wave of freezing cold gnawed at her bones and she flinched. The image of an onrushing freight train bearing down on her streaked through her mind.

She did not see who hit her, she simply sensed that she was about to be hit. A hard, bony shoulder thrust her aside as easily as if her body had turned to straw, and in the second of contact an indelible picture was seared into her brain: a mountain of broken, charred dolls—no, not dolls, she realized as she was flung toward the street; dolls had no insides to burst through their rib cages, no brains to ooze from their ears, no teeth to grimace in the frozen rictus of the dead. She hit the curb and a cab swerved to avoid her, the driver shouting and leaning on his horn. She was all right, just the wind knocked out of her and her hurt side throbbing, and she struggled to her feet to see who'd hit her such a blow, but no one was paying her any attention. Still, Sister Creep's teeth chattered from the cold that clung to her, there on the hottest night of midsummer, and she felt her arm for what she knew would be a black bruise where that bastard had collided with her. "You heathen shitass!" she yelled at nobody in particular, but the vision of a mountain of smoldering corpses lingered behind her eyes and a claw of fear clutched at her stomach. Who had that been, passing on the sidewalk, she wondered. What kind of monster dressed in human skin? She saw the marquee of a theater before her, advertising a double feature of *The Face of Death, Part Four* and *Mondo Bizarro.* Walking closer, she saw that the poster for *Face of Death,*

Part Four promised Scenes From The Autopsy Table! Car Wreck Victims! Death By Fire! Uncut And Uncensored!

A chill lingered in the air around the closed door of the theater. Come In! a sign said on the door. We're Air Conditioned! But it was more than the air conditioner, she decided. This was a dank, sinister chill: the chill of shadows where poison toadstools grow, their ruddy colors beckoning a child to come, come take a taste of candy.

It was fading now, dissipating in the sultry heat. Sister Creep stood in front of that door, and though she knew that sweet Jesus was her mission and sweet Jesus would protect her, she knew also that she wouldn't set foot inside that theater for a full bottle of Red Dagger—not even *two* full bottles!

She backed away from the door, bumped into somebody who cursed and shoved her aside, and then she started walking again—where, she didn't know, nor did she care. Her cheeks burned with shame. She had been afraid, she told herself, even though sweet holy Jesus stood at her side. She had been *afraid* to look evil in the face, and she had sinned yet again.

Two blocks past the forbidding theater, she saw a black kid toss a beer bottle into the midst of some overflowing garbage cans set back in the doorway of a crumbling building. She pretended to be searching for something in her bag until he'd passed, and then she stepped into that doorway and started looking for the bottle, her throat parched for a sip, a *drop*, of liquid.

Rats squealed and scurried away over her hands, but she didn't mind them; she saw rats every day, and much bigger ones than these. One of them perched on the edge of a can and squealed at her with furious indignation. She tossed a cast-off tennis shoe at it, and the thing fled.

The smell of the garbage was putrid, the smell of meat that had long since gone bad. She found the beer bottle, and in the murky light she rejoiced to see that a few drops remained. She quickly tilted it to her lips, her tongue struggling into the bottle for the tang of beer. Heedless of the chattering rats, she sat down with her back to the rough brick wall. As she put her hand to the ground to steady herself she touched something damp and soft. She looked to her side; but when she realized what it was, she put her hand to her mouth to stifle a scream.

It had been wrapped up in a few pages of newspaper, but the rats had chewed that away. Then they had gone to work on the flesh. Sister Creep couldn't tell how old it was, or whether it was a boy or a girl, but its eyes were half open in the tiny face, as if the infant lay on the edge of sweet slumber. It was nude; someone had tossed it into the heap of garbage cans and bags and sweltering filth as if it were a broken toy.

"Oh," she whispered, and she thought of a rainswept highway and a spinning blue light. She heard a man's voice saying, "Let me have her now, lady. You've got to let me have her."

Sister Creep picked up the dead infant and began to rock it in her arms. From the distance came the pounding of mindless music and the calls of the vendors on Forty-second Street, and Sister Creep crooned in a strangled voice, "Hushabye, hushabye, little baby don't you cry. . . ." She couldn't remember the rest of it.

The blue light spinning, and the man's voice floating through time and distance: "Give her to me, lady. The ambulance is coming."

"No," Sister Creep whispered. Her eyes were wide and staring, and a tear trickled down her cheek. "No, I won't . . . let . . . her go. . . ."

She pressed the infant against her shoulder, and the tiny head lolled. The body was cold. Around Sister Creep, the rats chattered and squealed with frustration.

"Oh God," she heard herself say. And then she lifted her head toward a slice of sky and felt her face contort, and the anger flooded out of her as she screamed, *"Where are you?"* Her voice echoed off along the street and was drowned by the merry commerce a couple of blocks away. Sweet Jesus is late, she thought. He's late, late, late for a very important date, date, date! She began to giggle hysterically and cry at the same time, until what came from her throat sounded like the moaning of a wounded animal.

It was a long time before she realized that she had to move on, and she could not take the infant with her. She wrapped it carefully in the bright orange sweater from her bag, and then she lowered it into one of the garbage cans and piled as much as she could on top of it. A large gray rat came close to her, baring its teeth, and she hit it square with the empty beer bottle.

She couldn't find the strength to stand, and she crawled out of the doorway with her head bowed and the hot tears of shame, disgust and rage coursing down her face. I can't go on, she told herself. I can't live in this dark world anymore! Dear sweet Jesus, come down in your flying saucer and take me with you! She leaned her forehead against the sidewalk, and she wanted to be dead and in Heaven where all the sin was blotted clean.

Something clinked to the sidewalk, ringing like notes of music. She looked up; her eyes were blurred and swollen from crying, but she saw someone walking away from her. The figure turned the corner and was gone.

Sister Creep saw that several coins lay on the pavement a few feet away—three quarters, two dimes and a nickel. Somebody had thought she was panhandling, she realized. Her arm darted out, and she scooped up the coins before anybody else could get them.

She sat up, trying to think what she should do. She felt sick and weak and tired, and she feared lying out on the street in the open. Have to find a place to hide, she decided. Find a place to dig myself a hole and hide.

Her gaze came to rest on the stairs across Forty-second Street that descended into the subway.

She'd slept in the subway before; she knew the cops would run her out of the station or, worse, haul her off yet again to the shelter. But she knew also that the subway held a warren of maintenance tunnels and unfinished passageways that snaked off from the main routes and went deep beneath Manhattan. So deep that none of the demons in human skin could find her, and she could curl up in the darkness and forget. Her hand clenched the money; it was enough to get her through the turnstile, and then she could lose herself from the sinful world that sweet Jesus had shunned.

Sister Creep stood up, crossed Forty-second Street and descended into the underground world.

Three

10:22 P.M. Central Daylight Time
Concordia, Kansas

"Kill him, Johnny!"

"Tear him to pieces!"

"Pull off his arm and beat him to death with it!"

The rafters of the hot, smoky Concordia High School gymnasium rang with the combined yelling of over four hundred people, and at the gym's center two men—one black, one white—battled in a wrestling ring. At the moment, the white wrestler—a local boy named Johnny Lee Richwine—had the monster known as Black Frankenstein against the ropes and was battering him with judo chops as the crowd shouted for blood. But Black Frankenstein, who stood six feet four, weighed over three hundred pounds and wore an ebony mask covered with red leather "scars" and rubber "bolts," stuck out his mountainous chest; he gave a thunderous roar and grabbed Johnny Lee Richwine's hand in midair, then twisted the trapped hand until the young man was forced to his knees. Black Frankenstein growled and kicked him with a size thirteen boot in the side of the head, knocking him sprawling across the canvas.

The referee was scrambling around ineffectually, and as he stuck a warning finger in Black Frankenstein's face the monster shoved him aside as easily as flicking a grasshopper; Black Frankenstein stood over the fallen boy and thumped his chest, his head going around and around like a maniac's as the crowd screamed with rage. Crumpled Coke cups and popcorn bags began to rain into the ring. "You dumb geeks!" Black Frankenstein shouted, in a bass boom that carried over the noise of the crowd. "Watch what I do to your hometown boy!"

The monster gleefully stomped on Johnny Lee Richwine's ribs. The young man contorted, his face showing deepest agony, while the referee tried to pull Black Frankenstein away. With one shove, the monster threw the referee into the turnbuckle, where he sagged to his knees. Now the crowd was on its feet, paper cups and ice flying, and the local policemen who'd signed on for wrestling arena duty stood nervously around the ring. "Wanna see some Kansas farmboy blood?" Black Frankenstein bellowed as he lifted his boot to crush his opponent's skull.

But Johnny snapped to life; he grabbed the monster's ankle and threw him off balance, then kicked his other leg out from under him. His thick arms windmilling, Black Frankenstein hit the mat with a force that made the floor shake, and the crowd's noise almost ripped the roof off.

Black Frankenstein cowered on his knees, his hands up and pleading for mercy as the young man advanced on him. Then Johnny turned to help the injured referee, and as the crowd shrieked Black Frankenstein bounded up and rushed Johnny from behind, his huge hands clasped together to deliver a hammerblow.

The frenzied screaming of the fans made Johnny Lee Richwine whirl around at the last instant, and he kicked the monster in the roll of fat around his midsection. The noise of air expelled from Black Frankenstein's lungs sounded like a steamboat whistle; he staggered around the ring with drunken, mincing steps, trying to escape his fate.

Johnny Lee Richwine caught him, bent and lifted Black Frankenstein's body on his shoulders for an airplane spin. The fans hushed for a second as all that weight left the mat, then began to shout again when Johnny started twirling the monster in the air. Black Frankenstein bawled like a baby being spanked.

There was a noise like a pistol shot. Johnny Lee Richwine cried out and began to topple to the mat. Leg's busted, the man who was called Black Frankenstein had time to register before he flung himself off the young man's shoulders. He knew very well the sound of popping bones; he'd been against the boy's trying an airplane spin, but Johnny had wanted to impress the home folks. Black Frankenstein slammed into the mat on his side, and when he sat up he saw the young hometown wrestler lying a few feet away, grasping at his knee and moaning, this time in genuine pain.

The referee was on his feet, not knowing what to do. Black Frankenstein was supposed to be stretched out, and Johnny Lee Richwine was supposed to win this main event; that's how the script went, and everything had gone just fine in the run-through.

Black Frankenstein got up. He knew the boy was hurting bad, but he had to stay in character. Lifting his arms over his head, he strutted across the ring in a torrent of cups and popcorn bags, and as he neared the stunned referee he said in a quiet voice very much different from his villainous ranting, "Disqualify me and get that kid to a doctor!"

"Huh?"

"Do it *now!*"

The referee, a local man who ran a hardware store in nearby Belleville, finally made a crisscrossed waving motion that meant disqualification for Black Frankenstein. The huge wrestler made a show of jumping up and down with rage for a minute as the audience hooted and cursed at him, and then he stepped quickly out of the ring to be escorted to his dressing room by a phalanx of policemen. On that long walk, he suffered popcorn in his face, a pelting of ice and spitballs, and obscene gestures from children and senior citizens alike. He had a special fear of grandmotherly old ladies, because one had attacked him with a hat pin a year before in Waycross, Georgia, and tried to boot him in the genitals for good measure.

In his "dressing room," which was a bench and locker in

the football squad room, he stretched as many of the kinks out of his muscles as he could. Some of the aches and pains were permanent, and his shoulders felt as tight as chunks of petrified wood. He unlaced his leather mask and looked at himself in the little cracked mirror that hung inside his locker.

He could hardly be called handsome. His hair was shaven right to the skull to allow the mask a good fit, his face marked by the scars of many ring accidents. He remembered exactly where each of those scars had come from—a miscalculated turnbuckle blow in Birmingham, a chair swung too convincingly in Winston-Salem, an impact with the edge of the ring in Sioux Falls, a meeting with a concrete floor in San Antonio. Mistakes in timing caused real injuries in professional wrestling. Johnny Lee Richwine hadn't been balanced well enough to support the weight, and his leg had paid for it. He felt bad about it, but there was nothing he could do. The show must go on.

He was thirty-five years old, and the last ten years of his life had been spent on the wrestling circuit, following the highways and county roads between city auditoriums, high school gyms and country fairs. He was known in Kentucky as Lightningbolt Jones, in Illinois as Brickhouse Perkins, and in a dozen states by similar fearsome aliases. His real name was Joshua Hutchins, and tonight he was a long way from his home in Mobile, Alabama.

His broad, flat nose had been broken three times and looked it; the last time, he hadn't even bothered to get it set. Under thick black brows, his eyes were deeply set and the pale gray of woodsmoke. Another small scar looped around the point of his chin like an upside-down question mark, and the hard lines and angles of his face made him resemble a war-weary African king. He was large to the point of being freakish, a curiosity that people stared at when he walked the streets. Ridges of muscle bulged in his arms, shoulders and legs, but his stomach was dissolving to flab—the result of too many boxes of glazed doughnuts consumed in lonely motel rooms—but even carrying a spare truck tire of fat around his midsection, Josh Hutchins moved with grace and power, giving the impression of a tightly coiled spring about to burst free. It was what remained of the explosive force he'd commanded when he was a linebacker for the New Orleans Saints, many years and a world ago.

Josh showered and soaped the sweat off. Tomorrow night he was due to wrestle in Garden City, Kansas, which would be a long, dusty trek across the state. And a hot trip, too, because the air conditioner in his car had broken down a few days earlier, and he couldn't afford to get it fixed. His next paycheck would come at the end of the week, in Kansas City, where he was to participate in a seven-man free-for-all. He got out of the shower, dried off and dressed. As he was putting his gear away the match's promoter came in to tell him that Johnny Lee Richwine had been taken to the hospital and that he'd be okay, but that Josh should be careful leaving the gym because the hometown folks could get a little rough. Josh thanked the man in his quiet voice, zipped up his traveling bag and said goodnight.

His beat-up, six-year-old gray Pontiac was parked in the lot of a twenty-four-hour Food Giant supermarket. He knew from the experience of many slashed tires not to park any nearer the wrestling arena. While he was so close to the market, Josh went inside and emerged a few minutes later with a package of glazed doughnuts, some Oreo cookies and a jug of milk. He drove away, heading south on Highway 81 to the Rest Well Motel.

His room faced the highway, and the rumble of passing trucks sounded like beasts prowling the darkness. He turned on the "Tonight" show, then took off his shirt and smeared Ben Gay on his aching shoulders. It had been a long time since he'd worked out in a gym, though he kept telling himself he was going to start jogging again. His gut was as soft as marshmallow; he knew he could really get hurt there if his opponents didn't pull the kicks and punches. But he decided to worry about that tomorrow—there was always tomorrow—and he put on his bright red pajamas and lay back in bed to consume his snack and watch the tube.

He was halfway through the doughnuts when an NBC News bulletin interrupted the celebrity chatter. A grim-looking newsman came on, with the White House in the background, and he began talking about a "high-priority meeting" the president had just had with the secretary of defense, the Armed Forces chief of staff, the vice-president and other advisors, and that sources confirmed the meeting involved both SAC and NORAD. American air bases, the reporter said with urgency in his voice, might be going to a higher level of readiness. More bulletins would break in as the news was available.

"Don't blow up the world till Sunday," Josh said through a mouthful of doughnut. "I've got to collect my paycheck first."

Every night the newscasts were filled with the facts or rumor of war. Josh watched the broadcasts and read the newspapers whenever he could, and he understood that nations were jealous and paranoid and downright crazy, but he couldn't fathom why sane leaders didn't just pick up their telephones and talk to each other. What was so tough about *talking?*

Josh was beginning to believe the whole thing was like professional wrestling: the superpowers put on their masks and stomped around, roaring threats and swinging wildly at each other, but it was a game of macho, strutting bluff. He couldn't imagine what the world would be like after the nuclear bombs fell, but he knew it'd be pretty damned hard to find a box of glazed doughnuts in the ashes, and he surely would miss them.

He had started on the Oreos when he looked at the telephone next to the bed and thought of Rose and the boys. His wife had divorced him after he'd left pro football and become a wrestler, and she had custody of their two sons. She still lived in Mobile; Josh visited them whenever the circuit took him down that way. Rose had a good job as a legal secretary, and the last time Josh had seen her, she'd told him she was engaged to be married to a black attorney at the end of August. Josh missed his sons very much, and sometimes in the arena crowds he glimpsed the faces of boys who reminded him of them, but the faces were always yelling and jeering at him. It didn't pay, he knew, to think too much about people you loved; there was no point in driving the hurt too deep. He wished Rose well; sometimes he longed to call her, but he feared a man would answer.

Well, he thought as he opened another cookie to get at the creamy stuff, I wasn't cut out to be a family man, anyhow. No, sir! I like my freedom too much, and by God, that's just what I've got!

He was tired. His body ached, and tomorrow would be a long day. Maybe he'd call the hospital before he left, find out about Johnny Lee Richwine. The boy would be smarter for what he'd learned tonight.

Josh left the set on because he liked the sound of human voices, and he slowly fell asleep with the package of Oreos balanced on the mound of his stomach. Big day tomorrow, he thought as he drifted off. Gotta be mean and strong again. Then he slept, snoring softly, his dreams filled with the noise of a crowd shouting for his head.

The devotional came on. A minister talked about beating swords into plowshares. Then the "Star Spangled Banner" played over scenes of majestic snow-capped mountains, wide, waving fields of wheat and corn, running streams, verdant forests and mighty cities; it ended with an image of the American flag, stretched out and immobile on a pole sunk into the surface of the moon.

The picture froze, lingered for a few seconds, and then static filled the screen as the local station signed off.

Four
11:48 P.M. Central Daylight Time
Near Wichita, Kansas

They were fighting again.

The little girl squeezed her eyes shut and put the pillow over her head, but the voices came through anyway, muffled and distorted, almost inhuman.

"I'm sick and tired of shit, woman! Get off my back!"

"What am I supposed to do? Just smile when you go out drinkin' and gamblin' away money *I* earn? That money was supposed to go for the rent on this damned trailer and buy us some groceries, and by God you went out and threw it away, just threw it—"

"Get off my fuckin' back, I said! Look at you! You look like a worn-out old whore! I'm sick to death of you hangin' around here givin' me shit all the time!"

"Maybe I oughta do somethin' about that, huh? Maybe I oughta just pack and get my ass out of here!"

"Go on, then! Get out and take that spooky kid with you!"

"I will! Don't you think I won't!"

The argument went back and forth, their voices getting louder and meaner. The little girl had to come up for air, but she kept her eyes tightly closed and filled her mind with her garden, just outside the window of her cramped bedroom.

People came from all over the trailer court to see her garden and to comment on how well the flowers were growing. Mrs. Yeager, from next door, said the violets were beautiful, but she'd never known them to bloom so late and in such hot weather. The daffodils, snapdragons and bluebells were growing strong, too, but for a while the little girl had heard them dying. She'd watered them and kneaded the soil with her fingers, and she'd sat amid her garden in the morning sunlight and watched over her flowers with eyes as blue as robin's eggs, and finally the death sounds went away. Now the garden was a healthy blaze of color, and even most of the grass around the trailer was a rich, dark green. Mrs. Yeager's grass was brown, though she hosed it down almost every day; but the little girl had heard it die a long time ago, though she didn't want to make Mrs. Yeager sad by saying so. Maybe it would come back when the rain fell.

A profusion of potted plants filled the bedroom, sitting on cinder block shelves and crowded around the bed. The room held the heady aroma of life, and even a small cactus in a red ceramic pot had sprouted a white flower. The little girl liked to think of her garden and her plants when Tommy and her mother were fighting; she could see the garden in her mind, could visualize all the colors and the petals and feel the earth between her fingers, and those things helped take her away from the voices.

"Don't you touch me!" her mother shouted. "You bastard, don't you *dare* hit me again!"

"I'll knock you on your ass if I want to!" There was the sound of a struggle, more cursing, followed by the noise of a slap. The little girl flinched, tears wetting her closed blond eyelashes.

Stop fighting! she thought frantically. Please please please stop fighting!

"Get away from me!" Something hit the wall and shattered. The child put her hands over her ears and lay rigidly in bed, about to scream.

There was a light.

A soft light, blinking against her eyelids.

She opened her eyes and sat up.

And there on the window screen across the room was a pulsing mass of light, a pale yellow glow like a thousand tiny birthday candles. The light shifted, like the swirls of an incandescent painting, and as the child stared at it, entranced, the noise of the fighting got quieter and far away. The light reflected in her wide eyes, moved over her heart-shaped face and danced in her shoulder-length blond hair. The entire room was illuminated by the glow of the light-creature that clung to the window screen.

Fireflies, she realized. Hundreds of fireflies clinging to the screen. She had seen them on the window before, but never so many and never all blinking at the same time. They pulsed like stars trying to burn their way through the screen, and as she stared at them she no longer heard the awful voices of her mother and "Uncle" Tommy. The blinking fireflies commanded all her attention, their patterns of light mesmerizing her.

The language of light changed, took on a different, faster rhythm. The little girl remembered a hall of mirrors at the state fair, and how the lights had reflected dazzlingly off the polished glass; now she felt as if she were standing at the center of a thousand lamps, and as the rhythm became faster and faster they seemed to whirl around her with dizzying speed.

They're talking, she thought. Talking in their own language. Talking about something very, very important . . .

"*Swan!* Honey, wake up!"

. . . talking about something about to happen . . .

"Can't you hear me?"

. . . something bad about to happen . . . real soon . . .

"SWAN!"

Someone was shaking her. For a few seconds she was lost in the hall of mirrors and blinded by the flashing lights. Then she remembered where she was, and she saw the fireflies leaving the window screen, rising up into the night.

"Goddamn bugs all over the winda," she heard Tommy say.

Swan pulled her gaze away from them with an effort that

strained her neck. Her mother stood over her, and in the light from the open door Swan could see the purple swelling around her mother's right eye. The woman was thin and haggard, with tangled blond hair showing dark brown roots; she glanced back and forth between her daughter's face and the last of the insects flying off the screen. "What's wrong with you?"

"She's spooky," Tommy said, his thick-shouldered body blocking the doorway. He was stocky and unkempt, with a scraggly brown beard covering his angular jaw, his face thick-jowled and fleshy. He wore a red cap, a T-shirt and overalls. "She's fucked up in the head," he said, and he swigged from a bottle of Miller High Life.

"Mama?" The child was still dazed, the lights blinking behind her eyes.

"Honey, I want you to get up and put your clothes on. We're leavin' this damned dump right now, you hear me?"

"Yes, ma'am."

"You ain't goin' nowhere," Tommy sneered. "Where you gonna *go?*"

"As far away as we can get! I was stupid to move in here with you in the first place! Get up now, honey. Put your clothes on. We want to be out of here as soon as we can."

"You gonna go back to Rick Dawson? Yeah, you go on! He kicked you out once before, and I picked you up! Go on and let him kick you again!"

She turned toward him and said coldly, "Get out of my way or, so help me God, I'll kill you."

Tommy's eyes were hooded and dangerous. He drank from the bottle again, licked his lips and then laughed. "Sure!" He stepped back and made an exaggerated sweeping gesture with his arm. "Come on through! You think you're a goddamned queen, come on through!" She looked at her child with a glance that urged her to hurry and walked past him out of the bedroom.

Swan got out of bed and, clad in her nine-year-old-girl-sized Wichita State University nightshirt, hurried to the window and peered outside. The lights of Mrs. Yeager's trailer next door were on, and Swan figured the noise had probably awakened her. Swan looked upward and stared open-mouthed with awe.

The sky was filled with waves of moving, blinking stars. Wheels of light rolled across the darkness over the trailer court, and streaks of yellow fire zigzagged upward into the haze that obscured the moon. Thousands upon thousands of fireflies were passing overhead like galaxies in motion, their signals forming chains of light that stretched from west to east as far as Swan could see. From somewhere in the trailer park a dog began to howl; the noise was picked up by a second dog, then a third, then from other dogs in the subdivision across Highway 15. More lights were going on in the trailers, and people were stepping outside to see what was happening.

"God A'mighty, what a racket!" Tommy was still standing in the doorway. He bellowed, "Shut the fuck *up!*" and then finished the rest of his beer with one angry gulp. He fixed Swan with a baleful, bleary-eyed gaze. "I'll be glad to get rid of *you,* kid. Look at this damned room, all these plants and shit! Christ! This is a trailer, not a greenhouse!" He kicked over a pot of geraniums, and Swan flinched. But she stood her ground, her chin uplifted, and waited for him to leave. "Wanna know about your mama, kid?" he asked her slyly. "Wanna know about that bar where she dances on tables and lets men touch her titties?"

"Shut up, you bastard!" the woman shouted, and Tommy spun around in time to stop her swing against his forearm. He shoved her away. "Yeah, come on, Darleen! Show that kid what you're made of! Tell her about the men you've been through, and—oh, yeah, tell her all about her daddy! Tell her you were so high on LSD and PCP and God knows what else that you don't even *remember* the fucker's name!"

Darleen Prescott's face was contorted with anger; years ago she'd been a pretty woman, with strong cheekbones and dark blue eyes that communicated a sexual challenge to any number of men, but now her face was tired and sagging, and deep lines cut across her forehead and around her mouth. She was only thirty-two, but looked at least five years older; she was squeezed into tight blue jeans and wore a yellow cowgirl blouse with spangles on the shoulders. She turned away from Tommy and went into the trailer's "master bedroom," her lizard-skin cowgirl boots clumping on the floor.

"Hey," Tommy said, giggling. "Don't run off mad!"

Swan began to take her clothes out of the dresser drawers, but her mother returned with a suitcase, already full of gaudy outfits and boots, and shoveled as much of Swan's clothes into it as would fit. "We're goin' right *now!*" she told her daughter. "Come on."

Swan paused, looking around at the roomful of flowers and plants. No! she thought. I can't leave all my flowers! And my garden! Who'll water my garden?

Darleen leaned down on the suitcase, pressed it shut and snapped it. Then she grasped Swan's hand and turned to go. Swan had time only to grab her Cookie Monster doll before she was pulled out of the room in her mother's wake.

Tommy followed behind them, a fresh beer in hand. "Yeah, you go on! You'll be back by tomorrow night, Darleen! You just wait and see!"

"I'll wait," she replied, and she pushed through the screen door. Outside, in the steamy night, the howling of dogs floated from all directions. Banners of light streamed across the sky. Darleen glanced up at them but didn't hesitate in her long stride toward the bright red Camaro parked at the curb behind Tommy's souped-up Chevy pickup truck. Darleen threw the suitcase in the back seat and slid under the wheel as Swan, still in her nightshirt, got in the passenger side. "Bastard," Darleen breathed as she fumbled with her keys. "I'll show his ass."

"Hey, lookit me!" Tommy yelled, and Swan looked. She was horrified to see that he was dancing in her garden, the sharp toes of his boots kicking up clumps of dirt, the heels mashing her flowers dead. She clasped her hands to her ears, because she heard their hurting sounds rising up like the strings of a steel guitar being plucked. Tommy grinned and capered, took off his cap and threw it into the air. A white-hot anger flared within Swan, and she wished Uncle Tommy dead for hurting her garden—but then the flash of anger passed, leaving her feeling sick to her stomach. She saw him clearly for what he was: a fat, balding fool, his only possessions in the world a broken-down trailer and a pickup truck. This was where he would grow old and die without letting anyone love him—because he was afraid, just like her mother was, of getting too close. She saw all that and understood it in a second, and she knew that his pleasure at destroying her garden would end with him, as usual, on his knees in the bathroom over the toilet, and when he was through being sick he would sleep alone and wake up alone. But she could always grow another garden—and she would, in the next place they went to, wherever that was going to be.

She said, "Uncle Tommy?"

He stopped dancing, his mouth leering at her and a curse on his lip.

"I forgive you," Swan said softly, and the man stared at her as if she'd struck him across the face.

But Darleen Prescott shouted, "Fuck you!" at him, and the Camaro's engine fired like the roar of a cannon. Darleen jammed her foot down on the accelerator, laying rubber for thirty feet before the tires caught and rocketed them out of the Highway 15 Trailer Park forever.

"Where are we going?" Swan asked, cuddling Cookie Monster after the noise of the shrieking tires had faded.

"Well, I figure we'll find us a motel to spend the night in. Then I'll go by the bar in the mornin' and try to get some money from Frankie." She shrugged. "Maybe he'll give me fifty bucks. Maybe."

"Are you going back to Uncle Tommy?"

"No," Darleen said firmly. "I'm through with him. He's the meanest man I've ever known, and by Christ I can't understand what I ever saw in him!"

Swan recalled that she'd said the same thing about both "Uncle" Rick and "Uncle" Alex. She paused thoughtfully, trying to decide whether to ask the question or not, and then she drew a deep breath and said, "Is it true, Mama? What Tommy said about you not knowing who my daddy really was?"

"Don't you say that!" she snapped. She riveted her attention on the long ribbon of road. "Don't you even think such a thing, young lady! I've told you before: Your daddy's a famous rock 'n' roll star. He's got blond, curly hair and blue eyes like yours. The blue eyes of an angel dropped to earth. And can he play a guitar and sing! Can birds *fly?* Lord, yes! And I've told you time and again that as soon as he divorces his wife we're going to go out and live in Hollywood, California. Won't that be somethin'? You and me on that Sunset Strip?"

"Yes, ma'am," Swan said listlessly. She'd heard that story before. All Swan wanted was to live in one place for more than four or five months, so she could make friends she wouldn't be afraid of losing, and go to the same school for a whole year. Because she had no friends, she turned all her energy and attention to her flowers and plants, spending hours creating gardens in the rough earth of trailer parks, boarding houses and cheap motels.

"Let's get us some music on the radio," Darleen said. She switched it on, and rock 'n' roll blared from the speakers. The volume was turned so loud that Darleen didn't have to think about the lie that she'd told her daughter time and again; in truth, she only knew that he was a tall, blond hunk whose rubber had broken in mid-thrust. It hadn't mattered at the time; a party was going on, and in the next room everybody was raising hell, and both Darleen and the hunk were flying high on a mixture of LSD, angel dust and poppers. That had been when she was living in Las Vegas nine years ago, working as a blackjack dealer, and since then she and Swan had lived all over the west, following men who promised to be fun for a while or taking jobs as a topless dancer wherever she could find them.

Now, though, Darleen didn't know where they were going. She was sick of Tommy, but she was afraid of him, too; he was too crazy, too mean. It was likely he'd come after them in a day or so if she didn't get far enough away. Frankie, at the High Noon Saloon where she danced, might advance her some money on her next paycheck, but then where?

Home, she thought. Home was a little speck called Blakeman, up in Rawlins County in the northwest corner of Kansas. She'd run away when she was sixteen, after her mother had died of cancer and her father had started going crazy on religion. She knew the old man hated her, and that's why she'd left. What would home be like now, she wondered. She imagined her father would drop his teeth when he found out he had a granddaughter. Hell, no! I can't go back there!

But she was already calculating the route she would take if she did decide to go to Blakeman: north on 135 to Salina, west through the sweeping corn and wheat fields on Interstate 70, north again on arrow-straight country roads. She could get enough money from Frankie to pay for the gas. "How'd you like to take a trip in the mornin'?"

"Where to?" She clutched the Cookie Monster tighter.

"Oh, just somewhere. A little town called Blakeman. Not much going on, the last time I was there. Maybe we could go there and rest for a few days. Get our heads together and think. Right?"

Swan shrugged. "I guess," she said, but she didn't care one way or the other.

Darleen turned the radio down and put her arm around her daughter. Looking up, she thought she saw a glimmer of light in the sky, but then it was gone. She squeezed Swan's shoulder. "Just you and me against the world, kid," she said. "And know what? We're gonna win out yet, if we just keep on sluggin'."

Swan looked at her mother and wanted—wanted very badly—to believe.

The Camaro continued into the night along the unfolding highway, and in the clouds hundreds of feet above, living chains of light linked across the heavens.

Five

11:50 P.M. Mountain Daylight Time
Blue Dome Mountain, Idaho

A gunmetal gray Ford Roamer recreational vehicle climbed the narrow, winding road that led to the top of Blue Dome Mountain, eleven thousand feet above sea level and sixty miles northwest of Idaho Falls. On both sides of the road, dense pine forests clung to harsh ribs of stone. The RV's headlights bored holes in a low-lying mist, and the lights of the instrument panel glowed green on the drawn, tired face of the middle-aged man behind the wheel. In the reclined seat beside him, his wife was sleeping with a map of Idaho unfolded on her lap.

On the next long curve, the headlights hit a sign on the roadside that said, in bright orange luminescent letters: PRIVATE PROPERTY. TRESPASSERS WILL BE SHOT.

Phil Croninger slowed the RV, but he had the plastic ID card they'd mailed him in his wallet, so he kept going past the forbidding sign and onward up the mountain road.

"Would they really do that, Dad?" his son asked, in a reedy voice, from the seat behind him.

"Do what?"

"Shoot trespassers. Would they really?"

"You know it. They don't want anybody up here who

doesn't belong." He glanced at the rearview mirror and caught his son's green-daubed face floating like a Halloween mask over his shoulder. Father and son closely resembled each other; they both wore thick-lensed eyeglasses, had thin, lank hair and were slight and bony. Phil's hair was threaded with gray and was receding rapidly, and the thirteen-year-old boy's was dark brown, cut in straight bangs to hide the height of his forehead. The boy's face was a study in sharp angles, like his mother's; his nose, chin and cheekbones all seemed to be about to slice through his pallid skin, as if a second face were underneath the first and on the edge of being revealed. His eyes, magnified slightly by the lenses, were the color of ashes. He wore a T-shirt done in military camouflage colors, a pair of khaki shorts and hiking boots.

Elise Croninger stirred. "Are we there yet?" she asked sleepily.

"Almost. We should see something pretty soon." It had been a long, tiring trip from Flagstaff, and Phil had insisted on traveling at night because, by his calculations, the cooler temperatures were kinder on the tires and boosted gas mileage. He was a careful man who took no chances.

"I'll bet they're looking at us right now with radar." The boy stared toward the woods. "I'll bet they're really taking us apart."

"Could be," Phil agreed. "They've got about everything you can think of up here. It's a terrific place, wait'll you see it!"

"I hope it's *cool* in there," Elise said irritably. "God knows I didn't come all this way to cook in a mine shaft."

"It's *not* a mine shaft," Phil reminded her. "Anyway, it's naturally cool, and they've got all sorts of air-filtration systems and safety stuff. You'll see."

The boy said, "They're watching us. I can *feel* them watching us." He felt under his seat for what he knew was hidden there, and his hand came out with a .357 Magnum. "Bang!" he said, and he clicked the trigger toward the dark woods on his right. And another "Bang!" to the left.

"Put that thing down, Roland!" his mother told him.

"Put it away, son. We don't want it out in the open."

Roland Croninger hesitated and grinned slyly. He pointed the gun at the center of his mother's head, pulled the trigger and said quietly, "Bang." And then a "Bang" and a click of the trigger at his father's skull.

"Roland," his father said in what passed for a stern voice, "stop kidding around, now. Put the gun away."

"Roland!" his mother warned.

"Aw, heck!" He shoved the weapon back under the seat. "I was just having some fun! You two take everything too seriously!"

There was a sudden jolt as Phil Croninger planted his foot on the brake pedal. Two men in green helmets and camouflage uniforms were standing in the middle of the road; both of them were holding Ingram submachine guns and had .45s in holsters at their waists. The Ingram guns were pointed right at the RV's windshield.

"Jesus," Phil whispered. One of the soldiers motioned for him to roll down the window; when Phil had done so, the soldier stepped around to his side of the RV, snapped on a flashlight and shone it in his face. "ID, please," the soldier said; he was a young man with a hard face and electric blue eyes. Phil brought out his wallet and the ID card and handed it to the young man, who examined Phil's photograph on the card. "How many coming in, sir?" the soldier asked.

"Uh . . . three. Me, my wife and son. We're expected."

The young man gave Phil's card to the other soldier, who unclipped a walkie-talkie from his utility belt. Phil heard him say, "Central, this is Checkpoint. We've got three coming up in a gray recreational vehicle. Name on the card's Philip Austin Croninger, computer number 0-671-4724. I'll hold for confirmation."

"Wow!" Roland whispered excitedly. "This is just like the war movies!"

"Shhhh," his father warned.

Roland admired the soldiers' uniforms; he noted that the boots were spit-shined and the camouflage trousers still held creases. Above each soldier's heart was a patch that depicted an armored fist gripping a lightning bolt, and below the symbol was "Earth House," stitched in gold.

"Okay, thank you, Central," the soldier with the walkie-talkie said. He returned the card to the other one, who handed it to Phil. "There you go, sir. Your ETA was 10:45."

"Sorry." Phil took the card and put it away in his wallet. "We stopped for a late dinner."

"Just follow the road," the young man explained. "About a quarter mile ahead you'll see a stop sign. Make sure your tires are lined up with the marks. Okay? Drive on." He gave a quick motion with his arm, and as the second soldier stepped aside Phil accelerated away from the checkpoint. When he glanced in the sideview mirror again, he saw the soldiers reentering the forest.

"Does everybody get a uniform, Dad?" Roland asked.

"No, I'm afraid not. Just the men who work here wear uniforms."

"I didn't even see them," Elise said, still nervous. "I just looked up and there they were. They were pointing those guns right at us! What if one had gone off?"

"These people are professionals, hon. They wouldn't be here if they didn't know what they were doing, and I'm sure all of them know how to handle guns. That just shows you how secure we're going to be for the next two weeks. Nobody can get up here who doesn't belong. Right?"

"Right!" Roland said. He had experienced a thrill of excitement when he'd looked down the barrels of those two Ingram guns; if they'd wanted to, he thought, they could've blown us all away with a single burst. One squeeze of the trigger and *zap!* The feeling left him amazingly invigorated, as if cold water had been splashed in his face. That was good, he thought. Very good. One of the qualities of a King's Knight was to take danger in stride.

"There's the stop sign," Phil told them as the headlights hit it, dead ahead. The large sign was affixed to a wall of rough, jagged rock that ended the mountain road. Around them were only dark woods and the rise of more rocky walls; there was no sign of the place they had come from Flagstaff to find.

"How do you get *inside?*" Elise asked.

"You'll see. This was one of the neatest things they showed me." Phil had been here in April, after he'd read an advertisement for Earth House in *Soldier of Fortune* magazine. He slowly guided the Roamer forward until its front tires sank into two grooves in the earth and triggered a pair of latches. Almost immediately, there was a deep rumbling sound—the noise of heavy machinery, gears and chains at work. A crack of fluorescent light appeared at the base of the rock wall; a section of it was smoothly ascending, like the door of the Croninger garage at home.

But to Roland Croninger it looked like the opening of a massive portal into a medieval fortress. His heart had begun to pound, and the crack of fluorescent light reflected in the lenses of his glasses grew wider and brighter.

"My God," Elise said softly. The rock wall was opening to reveal a concrete-floored parking deck, its spaces filled with cars and other recreational vehicles. A row of lights hung from a gridwork of iron beams at the ceiling. In the doorway stood a uniformed soldier, waving Phil to come ahead; he eased forward, the grooves guiding the Roamer down a concrete ramp and onto the parking deck. As soon as the tires had disengaged the latches again, the doorway began to rumble shut.

The soldier motioned Phil along to a parking place between two other campers and made a gesture with a finger across his throat.

"What's that mean?" Elise asked uneasily.

Phil smiled. "He's telling us to cut the engine." He did. "We're here, gang."

The rock doorway closed with a solid, echoing *thunk,* and the outside world was sealed off.

"We're in the army now!" Phil told his son, and the boy's expression was one of dreamy amazement. As they got out of the Roamer two electric carts pulled up; in the first one was a smiling young man, his hair sandy brown and clipped in a crewcut, wearing a dark blue uniform with the Earth House insignia on his breast pocket. The second cart carried two husky men in dark blue jumpsuits and pulled a flat luggage trailer like those used at airports.

The smiling young man, whose white teeth seemed to reflect the fluorescent lighting, checked the information on his clipboard to make sure he had the name right. "Hi, folks!" he said cheerfully. "Mr. and Mrs. Philip Croninger?"

"Right," Phil said. "And our son, Roland."

"Hi, Roland. You folks have a good trip from Flagstaff?"

"A long trip," Elise told him; she gawked around at the parking deck, figuring that there were well over two hundred cars. "My God, how many people are here?"

"We're about ninety-five percent of capacity, Mrs. Croninger. We figure to be a hundred percent by the weekend. Mr. Croninger, if you'll give these two gentlemen your keys, they'll bring your luggage along for you." Phil did, and the two men began to unload suitcases and boxes from the Roamer.

"I've got computer equipment," Roland told the young man. "It'll be okay, won't it?"

"Sure will. You folks just hop aboard here and I'll take you to your quarters. Corporal Mathis?" he said, addressing one of the baggage-handlers, "Those go to Section C, Number Sixteen. You folks ready?" Phil had gotten into the front passenger's seat, and his wife and son in the back. Phil nodded, and the young man drove them across the parking deck and into a corridor—concrete-floored and lined with lights—that angled gently downward. A cool breeze circulated from an occasional strategically placed ceiling fan. Other corridors branched off from the first, and there were arrows that pointed to Sections A, B and C.

"I'm Hospitality Sergeant Schorr." The young man offered his hand, and Phil shook it. "Glad to have you with us. Are there any questions I can answer for you?"

"Well, I've taken the tour—back in April—and I know about Earth House," Phil explained, "but I don't think my wife and son got the full impact from the pamphlets. Elise was worried about the air circulation down here."

Schorr laughed. "Not to worry, Mrs. Croninger. We've got two state-of-the-art air-filtration systems, one on-line and one backup. The system would power up within one minute of a Code Red—that's when we're . . . uh . . . expecting impact and we seal the vents. Right now, though, the fans are drawing in plenty of air from outside, and I can guarantee you that the air on Blue Dome Mountain is probably the cleanest you'll ever breathe. We've got three living areas—Sections A, B and C—on this level, and underneath us is the Command Center and Maintenance Level. Down there, fifty feet below us, is the generator room, the weapons supply, the emergency food and water supply, the radar room and the officers' quarters. By the way, we have a policy of storing all incoming firearms in our weapons supply. Did you happen to have any with you?"

"Uh . . . a .357 Magnum," Phil said. "Under the back seat. I didn't know about that policy."

"Well, I'm sure you overlooked it in the contract you signed, but I think you'll agree all firearms should be localized for the safety of Earth House residents. Right?" He smiled at Phil, and Phil nodded. "We'll code it and give you a receipt, and when you leave us in two weeks you'll get it back cleaned and shining."

"What kinds of weapons do you have down there?" Roland asked eagerly.

"Oh, pistols, automatic rifles, submachine guns, mortars, flamethrowers, grenades, antipersonnel and antivehicle mines, flares—about everything you can think of. And of course we keep our gas masks and antiradiation suits down there, too. When this place was put together, Colonel Macklin wanted it to be an impregnable fortress, and that's exactly what it is."

Colonel Macklin, Roland thought. Colonel James "Jimbo" Macklin. Roland was familiar with the name through articles in the survivalist and weaponry magazines that his father subscribed to. Colonel Macklin had a long record of success as a 105-D Thunderchief pilot over North Vietnam, had been shot down in 1971 and had been a POW until the end of the war; then he'd gone back into Vietnam and Indochina looking for MIAs, and had fought with soldiers of fortune in South Africa, Chad and Lebanon. "Will we get to meet Colonel Macklin?"

"Orientation is at 0800 hours sharp, in the Town Hall. He'll be there."

They saw a sign reading SECTION C with an arrow pointing to

the right. Sergeant Schorr turned off the main corridor, and the tires jubbled over bits of concrete and rock that littered the floor. Water was dripping from above into a widening puddle, and it wet all of them before Schorr could brake the cart. Schorr looked back, his smile slipping; he stopped the cart, and the Croningers saw that part of the ceiling the size of a manhole cover had collapsed. Exposed in the hole were iron bars and chickenwire. Schorr took a walkie-talkie from the cart's dash, clicked it on and said, "This is Schorr, near the junction of Central and C corridors. I've got a drainage problem here, need a cleanup crew on the double. You read me?"

"Read you," a voice replied, weakened by static. "Trouble *again?*"

"Uh . . . I've got new arrivals with me, Corporal."

"Sorry, sir. Cleanup crew's on the way."

Schorr switched off the walkie-talkie. His smile returned, but his light brown eyes were uneasy. "Minor problem, folks. Earth House has a top-line drainage system, but sometimes we get these minor leaks. Cleanup crew'll take care of it."

Elise pointed upward; she'd noticed the jigsaw of cracks and patches in the ceiling. "That doesn't look too safe. What if that thing falls in?" She looked wide-eyed at her husband. "My God, Phil! Are we supposed to stay here for two weeks under a leaking mountain?"

"Mrs. Croninger," Schorr said in his most soothing voice, "Earth House wouldn't be at ninety-five percent capacity if it wasn't *safe.* Now I agree, the drainage system needs work, and we *are* getting it in shape, but there is absolutely *no* danger. We've had structural engineers and stress specialists inspect Earth House, and all of them gave it the okay. This is a survivalist condominium, Mrs. Croninger; we wouldn't be here if we didn't want to survive the coming holocaust, right?"

Elise glanced back and forth between her husband and the young man. Her husband had paid fifty thousand dollars for membership in the Earth House timesharing plan: two weeks every year, for life, in what the pamphlets called a "luxurious survivalist fortress in the mountains of southern Idaho." Of course, she believed the nuclear holocaust was coming soon, too; Phil had shelves of books on nuclear war and was convinced that it would happen within a year, and that the United States would be driven to its knees by the Russian invaders. He had wanted to find a place, as he told her, to "make a last stand." But she'd tried to talk him out of it, telling him that he was betting fifty thousand dollars that nuclear disaster would happen during one of their two-week timesharing periods, and that was a pretty crazy gamble. He'd explained to her the "Earth House Protection Option" which meant that, for an extra five thousand dollars a year, the Croninger family could find refuge in Earth House at any time, within twenty-four hours of the detonation of an enemy-fired nuclear missile within the continental United States. It was holocaust insurance, he'd told her; everybody knew the bombs were going to fall, it was just a question of when. And Phil Croninger was very aware of the importance of insurance, because he owned one of the largest independent insurance agencies in Arizona.

"I suppose," she finally said. But she was troubled by those cracks and patches, and by the sight of that flimsy chickenwire sticking out of the new hole.

Sergeant Schorr accelerated the electric cart. They passed metal doorways on both sides of the corridor. "Must've cost a lot of money to build this place," Roland said, and Schorr nodded.

"A few million," Schorr said. "Not counting loose change. A couple of brothers from Texas put the money into it; they're survivalists too, and they got rich off oil wells. This place used to be a silver mine back in the forties and fifties, but the lode ran out, and it just sat here for years until the Ausleys bought it. Here we are, just ahead." He slowed the cart and stopped in front of a metal door marked Sixteen. "Your home sweet home for the next two weeks, folks." He opened the door with a key affixed to an Earth House insignia key chain, reached inside and switched on the lights.

Before she followed her husband and son over the threshold, Elise Croninger heard the sound of water dripping, and she saw another puddle spreading in the corridor. The ceiling was leaking in three places, and there was a long, jagged crack two inches wide. Jesus! she thought, unnerved, but she stepped into the room anyway.

Her first impression was of the starkness of a military barracks. The walls were beige-painted cinder block, decorated with a few oil paintings. The carpet was thick enough, and not a bad color of rust red, but the ceiling seemed awfully low to her. Though it cleared Phil's head by about six inches, and he was five feet eleven, the apparent lack of height in the suite's "living area," as the pamphlets had called it, made her feel almost . . . yes, she thought, almost *entombed.* One nice touch, though, was that the entire far wall was a photographic mural of snow-capped mountains, opening up the room a little, if just by optical illusion.

There were two bedrooms and a single bathroom connecting them. Sergeant Schorr took a few minutes to show them around, demonstrating the whooshing toilet that flushed upward to a tank, he said, that "delivered the waste materials to the forest floor and so aided the vegetation growth." The bedrooms were also of beige-painted cinder block, and the ceilings were made of cork tile that presumably, Elise thought, hid the latticework of iron beams and reinforcing rods.

"It's great, isn't it?" Phil asked her. "Isn't this something?"

"I'm not sure yet," she replied. "I still feel like I'm in a mine shaft."

"Oh, that'll pass," Schorr told her amiably. "Some of the first-timers get claustrophobia, but it wears off. Let me give you this," he said, and he handed Phil an Earth House map that unfolded to show the cafeteria, the gymnasium, the infirmary, and the arcade game room. "The Town Hall's right here," he said, and he pointed on the map. "It's really just an auditorium, but we figure we're a community down here, right? Let me show you the quickest way to get there from here. . . ."

In his bedroom, the smaller of the two, Roland had switched on the bedside lamp and was scouting a suitable electrical outlet for his computer. The room was small, but he thought it was okay; it was the atmosphere that was important, and he looked forward to the seminars on "Improvised Weapons," "Living off the Land," "Governments in Chaos," and "Guerrilla Tactics" that the pamphlets had promised.

He found a good outlet, near enough to the bed so he could prop himself up on pillows while he programmed the King's Knight game on his computer. In the next two weeks, he thought, he was going to dream up dungeons and monsters to roam them that would make even an expert, jaded King's Knight like himself tremble in his jambeaus.

Roland went to the closet and opened it to see how much room he had to store his stuff. The inside was cheaply paneled, a few wire hangers dangling from the rod. But something small and yellow suddenly flitted like an autumn leaf from the back of the closet. Roland instinctively reached out and caught it, closing his fingers around it. Then he walked over to the light and carefully opened his palm.

Lying stunned in his hand was a fragile yellow butterfly with streaks of green and gold along its wings. Its eyes were dark green pinheads, like gleaming emeralds. The butterfly fluttered, weak and dazed.

How long have *you* been in there, Roland wondered. No telling. Probably came in on somebody's car or camper, or in their clothes. He lifted his hand closer to his face and stared for a few seconds into the creature's tiny eyes.

And then he crushed the butterfly in his fist, feeling the body smear under the power of his grip. Zap! he thought. Super Zap! He sure hadn't come all the way from Flagstaff, he told himself, to share a room with a fucking yellow bug!

He dropped the mangled remnant into a wastebasket, then wiped the iridescent yellow sparkle from his palm onto his khakis and went back to the living room. Schorr was saying goodnight, and the other two men had just arrived with the luggage and Roland's computer gear.

"Orientation at 0800, folks!" Schorr said. "See you there!"

"Great," Phil Croninger said excitedly.

"Great." Elise's voice delivered the jab of sarcasm. Sergeant Schorr, smile still locked in place, left Number Sixteen.

But the smile disappeared as he stepped into the electric cart, and his mouth became a grim, rigid line. He turned the cart around and raced back to the area where the rubble lay on the floor, and he told the cleanup crew that they'd better move their asses to patch those cracks—and this time *keep* them patched—before the whole goddamned section fell apart.

TWO
Burning Spears

The man who liked movies / Judgment Day / The greeter / Underground boys / Discipline and control makes the man / Charter

Six
July 17
4:40 A.M. Eastern Daylight Time
New York City

"He's still in there, ain't he?" the black woman with orange hair asked in a whisper, and the Hispanic boy behind the candy counter nodded.

"Listen!" the boy, whose name was Emiliano Sanchez, said, and his dark eyes widened.

From beyond the faded red curtains that led into the auditorium of the Empire State Theater on Forty-second Street there came a laugh. It was a sound someone with a slashed throat might have made. The sound of it grew louder and higher, and Emiliano put his hands to his ears; the laughter had reminded him of a locomotive whistle and a child's shriek, and for a few seconds he was back in time, eight years old and living in Mexico City, witnessing his kid brother being struck and killed by a freight train.

Cecily stared at him, and as the laughter rose in volume she heard a girl's scream in it, and she was fourteen years old and lying on the abortionist's table as the job was done. The vision was gone in an instant, and the laughter began to fade. "Jesus Christ!" Cecily managed to say, whispering again. "What's that bastard *smokin'?*"

"I been listenin' to that since midnight," he told her. His

shift had started at twelve and would continue until eight. "You ever hear anythin' like it?"

"He alone in there?"

"Yeah. Few people come in, but they couldn't take it neither. Man, you shoulda seen their faces when they come out! Give you the creeps!"

"Shit, man!" Cecily said. She was the ticket-seller and worked in the booth out front. "I couldn't stand to sit through two minutes of that movie, all them dead folks and such! Lordy, I sold that guy his ticket three shows ago!"

"He come out, bought a large Coke and buttered popcorn. Tipped me a buck. But I tell you, I almost didn't wanna touch the money. It looked . . . greasy or somethin'."

"Bastard's prob'ly playin' with hisself in there. Prob'ly lookin' at all them dead, messed-up faces and playin' with hisself! Somebody ought to go in there and tell him to—"

The laughter swelled again. Emiliano flinched; the noise now reminded him of the cry of a boy he'd once gut-stabbed in a knife fight. The laughter broke and burbled, became a soft cooing that made Cecily think of the sounds the addicts made in the shooting gallery she frequented. Her face was frozen until the laughter went away, and then she said, "I believe I've got things to do." She turned away and hurried to the ticket booth, where she locked the door. She'd figured that the guy inside the theater was going to be weird when she saw him: He was a big, husky Swedish-looking man with curly blond hair, milk-white skin and eyes like cigarette burns. As he bought his ticket he'd stared holes through her and never said a word. Weird, she thought, and she picked up her *People* magazine with trembling fingers.

Come on, eight o'clock! Emiliano pleaded. He checked his wristwatch. In a few minutes, *The Face of Death, Part Four* would be ending, and Willy, the old drunk of a projectionist, would be changing the reels upstairs for *Mondo Bizarro*, which showed bondage scenes and such. Maybe the guy would leave when the picture changed. Emiliano sat on his stool and continued reading his *Conan* comic book, trying to shut off the bad memories that had been stirred up by the laughter from within.

The red curtains moved. Emiliano hunched his shoulders as if about to be beaten. Then the curtains parted, and the man who liked movies emerged into the dingy lobby. He's leaving! Emiliano almost grinned, his gaze glued to the comic book. He's goin' out the door!

But the man who liked movies said in a soft, almost childlike voice, "I'd like a large Coke and a tub of buttered popcorn, please."

Emiliano's stomach clenched. Without letting himself look into the man's face, he got off his stool, drew the Coke into a cup from the dispenser, got the popcorn and splashed butter into it.

"More butter, please," the man who liked movies requested.

Emiliano gave the popcorn another drool of butter and slid it and the Coke across the counter. "Three bucks," he said. A five dollar bill was pushed toward him. "Keep the change," the man said, and this time his voice had a Southern accent. Startled, Emiliano looked up.

The man who liked movies stood about six four and was wearing a yellow T-shirt and green khaki trousers. Under thick black eyebrows, his eyes were hypnotically green against the amber hue of his flesh. Emiliano had already figured him to be South American as soon as he'd walked in, maybe with some Indian blood in him, too. The man's hair was black and wavy, cut close to the skull. He stared fixedly at Emiliano. "I want to see the movie again," he said quietly, and his voice carried what might've been a Brazilian accent again.

"Uh . . . *Mondo Bizarro*'s about to come on in a coupla minutes. Projection guy's prob'ly got the first reel on—"

"No," the man who liked movies said, and he smiled slightly. "I want to see *that* movie again. Right now."

"Yeah. Well, listen. I mean . . . I don't make the decisions here, right? Y'know? I just work behind the counter. I don't have any say-so about—" And then the man reached out and touched Emiliano's face with cold, butter-smeared fingers, and Emiliano's jaw seized up as if it had frozen solid.

The world seemed to spin around him for a second, and his bones were a cage of ice. Then he blinked and his whole body trembled, and he was standing behind the counter and the man who liked movies was gone. Damn! he thought. Bastard *touched* me! He grabbed a paper napkin and wiped his face where the fingers had been, but he could still feel the chill they'd left. The five dollar bill remained on the countertop. He put it in his pocket and came out from behind the counter, and he peeked through the curtains into the theater.

On the screen, in glorious and gory color, were blackened corpses being pulled from the wreckage of cars by firemen. The narrator was saying, "*Face of Death* will pull no punches. Everything you see will be real. If you are in any way squeamish, you should now be on your way out. . . ."

The man who liked movies was sitting in the front row. Emiliano could see the outline of his head against the screen. The laughter began, and as Emiliano backpedaled away from the curtains he looked dumbly at his wristwatch and realized that almost twenty minutes of his life was a black hole. He went through a door and up a flight of stairs to the projection booth, where Willy sat sprawled on a couch reading *Hustler*.

"Hey!" Emiliano said. "What's goin' on, man? How come you showin' that shit again?"

Willy stared at him for a moment over the edge of the magazine. "You lost your marbles, kid?" he inquired. "You and your friend just come up here and asked me to. Wasn't fifteen minutes ago. So I put it back on. Don't mean shit to me, one way or the other. Anyway, I don't argue with no old perverts."

"Old perverts? What're you talkin' about, man?"

"Your friend," Willy said. "Guy must be seventy years old. Beard makes him look like Rip Van Winkle. Where do these perverts *come* from?"

"You're . . . crazy," Emiliano whispered. Willy shrugged and returned to his reading.

Outside, Cecily looked up as Emiliano ran into the street. He glanced back at her, shouted, "I ain't stayin' in there! No way! I quit!" and ran away along Forty-second Street and into the gloom. Cecily crossed herself, rechecked the lock on the ticket booth's door and prayed for dawn.

In his seat in the front row, the man who liked movies dug a hand into his buttered popcorn and stuffed his mouth full. Before him were scenes of broken bodies being extracted from the rubble of a London building bombed by Irish terrorists. He cocked his head to one side, appreciating the sight of crushed bones and blood. The camera, blurred and unsteady, focused on the frantic face of a young woman as she cradled a dead child.

The man who liked movies laughed as if he were watching a comedy. In the sound of that laughter was the shriek of napalm bombs, incendiary rockets and Tomahawk missiles; it echoed through the theater, and if other people had been sitting there each one would have squirmed with the memory of a private terror.

And in the reflected light from the screen, the man's face was undergoing a transformation. No longer did he look Swedish, or Brazilian, or have a gray Rip Van Winkle beard; his facial features were running together like the slow melting of a wax mask, the bones shifting beneath the skin. The features of a hundred faces rose and fell like suppurating sores. As the screen showed an autopsy in close-up progress, the man clapped his hands together with merry glee.

Almost time! he thought. Almost time for the show to start!

He'd been waiting a long time for the curtain to rise, had worn many skins and many faces, and the moment was soon, very soon. He'd watched the lurch toward destruction through many eyes, had smelled fire and smoke and blood in the air like intoxicating perfumes. The moment was soon, and the moment would belong to him.

Oh, yes! Almost time for the show to start!

He was a creature of patience, but now he could hardly keep himself from dancing. Maybe a little Watusi up the aisle would be in order, and then he'd slamdance that cockroach behind the candy counter. It was like waiting for a birthday party, and when the candles were lit he would rear his head back and roar loud enough to stagger God.

Almost time! Almost time!

But where would it start? he wondered. Who would push the first button? No matter; he could almost hear the fuse crackling and the flame drawing near. It was the music of the Golan Heights, of Beirut and Teheran, of Dublin and Warsaw, Johannesburg and Vietnam—only this time the music would end in a final, deafening crescendo.

He stuffed popcorn into a mouth that opened greedily on his right cheek. Party down! he thought, and he giggled with a noise like grinding glass.

Last night he'd stepped off a Trailways bus from Philadelphia and, strolling down Forty-second Street, had seen that this film was playing. He took the opportunity to admire his performances in *The Face of Death, Part Four* whenever he could. Just in the background, of course, always part of the crowd, but he could always recognize himself. There was a good shot of him standing over a mass of corpses after the bombing of an Italian soccer stadium, looking suitably shocked; another brief glimpse showed him, wearing a different face, at an airport massacre in Paris.

Lately he'd been on tour, riding the bus from city to city, seeing America. There were so many terrorist groups and armed firebrands in Europe that his influence was hardly needed, though he'd enjoyed helping plant that nice potent bomb in Beirut. He'd stayed a while in Washington, but none of the theaters were showing *The Face of Death, Part Four* there. Still, Washington held so many possibilities, and when you mixed and mingled with Pentagon boys and cabinet members at some of those parties you never knew what you might stir up.

It was all coming around to him now. He sensed the nervous fingers hovering near red buttons all over the world. Jet pilots would be scrambling, submarine commanders would be listening to their sonars, and old lions would be eager to bite. And the amazing thing was that they were doing it all themselves. It almost made him feel useless—but his starring role was coming around very soon.

His only concern was that it wouldn't be finished yet, not even with all the lightning soon to strike. There might still be pockets of humanity left, and small towns struggling to survive in the dark like rats in a collapsed basement. He understood very well that the firestorms, the whirlwinds of radiation and black rain would destroy most of them, and the ones that remained would wish they were dead a thousand times over.

And in the end, he would Watusi on their graves, too.

It was almost time. Tick tock tick tock, he thought. Nothing ever stops the clock!

He was a patient creature, but it had been a long wait. A few more hours would only whet his appetite, and he was very, very hungry. For the time being, he could enjoy watching himself in this fine film.

Curtain's going up! he thought, and the mouth in the center of his forehead grinned before it disappeared into the flesh like a gray worm in damp ground.

It's *showtime!*

Seven

10:16 A.M. Eastern Daylight Time
New York City

A blue light was spinning. Cold rain came down, and a young man in a yellow rain slicker reached out his arms. "Give her to me, lady," he said, his voice as hollow as if he were speaking from the bottom of a well. "Come on. Let me have her."

"NO!" Sister Creep shouted, and the man's face fragmented into pieces like the shattering of a mirror. She thrust out her hands to push it away, but then she was sitting up and the nightmare was whirling away in pieces like silver bats. The sound of her cry echoed back and forth between the walls of rough gray brick, and she sat staring at nothing for a moment as the sputtering of nerves shook her body.

Oh, she thought when her head cleared, that was a bad one! She touched her clammy forehead and her fingers came away damp. That was close, she thought. The young demon in the yellow raincoat was there again, very near, and he almost got my . . .

She frowned. Got my *what?* The thought was gone now; whatever it had been, it had flipped over to the dark side of her memory. She often dreamed of the demon in the yellow raincoat, and he was always wanting her to give him something. In the dream, a blue light was always flashing, hurting her eyes, and rain was hitting her in the face. Sometimes the surroundings seemed terribly familiar, and sometimes she almost—*almost*—knew what it was he wanted, but she knew he was a demon—or probably the Devil himself, trying to pull her away from Jesus—because her head pounded so badly after the dream was over.

She didn't know what time it was, or whether it was day or night, but her stomach was rumbling with hunger. She had tried to sleep on a subway bench, but the noise of some shouting kids scared her, so she'd trundled off with her bag in search of a more secure place. She'd found it at the bottom of a ladder that descended in a darkened section of subway tunnel. About thirty feet beneath the main tunnel was a drainage pipe, large enough for her to move through if she stooped over. Dirty water streamed past her sneakers, and the tunnel was illuminated by an occasional blue utility lamp that showed the network of cables and pipes just overhead. The tunnel shook with the thunder of a subway train passing, and Sister Creep realized she was under the rails; but as she continued along the tunnel the noise of the trains faded to a polite, distant growl. She soon found evidence that this was a popular place for members of the Ragtag Nation—a beat-up old mattress pushed back into a cubbyhole, a couple of empty wine bottles and some dried human excrement. She didn't mind; she'd seen worse. And so she'd slept on the mattress until the nightmare of the demon in the yellow raincoat had awakened her; she was hungry, and she decided she'd climb back up to the subway station to search for scraps in the garbage cans, maybe try to find a newspaper, too, to see if Jesus had come while she was sleeping.

Sister Creep stood up, put the strap of her bag around her shoulder and left the cubbyhole. She started back along the tunnel, tinged by the dim blue glow of the utility bulbs, and hoped she'd find a hot dog today. She'd always been fond of hot dogs, with plenty of good spicy mus—

The tunnel suddenly trembled.

She heard the sound of concrete cracking. The blue lamps flickered, went dark and then brightened again. There was a noise like the howl of wind, or a runaway subway train speeding overhead. The blue lamps continued to brighten until the light was almost blinding, and Sister Creep squinted in the glare. She took three more uncertain steps forward; the utility bulbs began to explode. She put her hands up to shield her face, felt pieces of glass strike her arms, and she thought with sudden clarity: I'll sue somebody for this!

In the next instant the entire tunnel whipped violently to one side, and Sister Creep fell into the stream of dirty water. Chunks of concrete and rock dust cascaded from the ceiling. The tunnel whipped back in the other direction with a force that made Sister Creep think her insides were tearing loose, and the concrete chunks hit her head and shoulders as her nostrils filled with grit. "Lord Jesus!" she shouted, about to choke. "Oh, Lord Jesus!"

Sparks shot overhead as the cables began to rip free. She smelled the wet heat of steam and heard a pounding noise like the footsteps of a behemoth treading above her head. As the tunnel pitched and swayed Sister Creep clung to her bag, riding out the gut-twisting undulations, a scream straining behind her clenched teeth. A wave of heat passed over her, stealing her breath. God help me! she shrieked in her mind as she struggled for air. She heard something pop and tasted blood streaming from her nose. I can't breathe, oh sweet Jesus, I can't breathe! She gripped at her throat, opened her mouth and heard her own strangled scream wail away from her through the shivering tunnel. Finally her tortured lungs dragged in a breath of scorched air, and she lay curled up on her side in the darkness, her body racked with spasms and her brain shocked numb.

The violent twisting motion of the tunnel had stopped. Sister Creep drifted in and out of consciousness, and through the haze came the distant roar of that runaway subway train again.

Only now it was getting louder.

Get up! she told herself. Get up! It's Judgment Day, and the Lord has come in His chariot to take the righteous up into the Rapture!

But a calmer, clearer voice spoke, perhaps from the dark

side of her memory, and it said: Bullshit! Something *bad's* happened up there!

Rapture! Rapture! Rapture! she thought, forcing the wicked voice away. She sat up, wiped blood from her nose and drew in steamy, stifling air. The noise of the runaway train was closer. Sister Creep realized that the water she was sitting in had gotten hot. She grasped her bag and slowly rose to her feet. Everything was dark, and when Sister Creep felt the tunnel's walls her fingers found a crazy quilt of cracks and fissures.

The roaring was much louder, and the air was heating up. The concrete against her fingers felt like city pavement at noon in August, ready to fry eggs sunny side up.

Far away along the tunnel there was a flicker of orange light, like the headlamp on a speeding subway train. The tunnel had begun to tremble again. Sister Creep stared, her face tightening, as the orange light grew brighter, showing streaks of incandescent red and purple.

She realized then what it was, and she moaned like a trapped animal.

A blast of fire was roaring toward her along the tunnel, and she could already feel the rush of air being sucked into it as if into a vacuum. In less than a minute it would be upon her.

Sister Creep's trance snapped. She turned and fled, holding her bag close, her sneakers splashing through steaming water. She leaped broken pipes and pushed aside fallen cables with the frenzy of the doomed. She looked back and saw the flames shooting out red tendrils that snapped in the air like whips. The vacuum suction pulled at her, trying to draw her backward into the fire, and when she screamed the air sizzled in her nostrils and at the back of her throat.

She could smell burning hair, felt her back and arms rippling with blisters. In maybe thirty seconds she'd be joining her Lord and Master, and it astounded her that she wasn't ready and willing to go.

With a startled cry of terror, she suddenly tripped and fell headlong to the floor.

As she started to scramble up she saw she'd tripped over a grate into which the stream was draining. Beneath the grate was only darkness. She looked at the onrushing fire, and her eyebrows singed, her face broke into oozing blisters. The air was unbreathable. There was no time to get up and run; the fire was almost upon her.

She gripped the bars of the grate and wrenched upward. One of the grate's rusted screws snapped, but the second held tight.

The flames were less than forty feet away, and Sister Creep's hair caught fire.

God help me! she screamed inwardly, and she pulled upward on the grate so hard she felt her shoulders almost rip loose from their sockets.

The second screw snapped.

Sister Creep flung the grate aside, had a second to grab her bag, then lunged headfirst into the hole.

She fell about four feet into a coffin-sized space that held eight inches of water.

The flames passed overhead, sucking the air from her lungs and scorching every inch of her exposed skin. Her clothes burst into flame, and she rolled frantically in the water. For a few seconds there was nothing but the roaring and the agony, and she smelled the odor of hot dogs being boiled in a vendor's cart.

The wall of fire moved on like a comet, and in its wake returned a *whooosh* of outside air that carried the thick smell of charred flesh and molten metal.

Down in the hole that fed drainage water to a sewer pipe, Sister Creep's body hitched and contorted. Three inches of water had risen as mist and evaporated, blunting the full force of the fire. Her burned, tattered body struggled for a breath, and finally gasped and sputtered, the blistered hands tightly gripping her smoldering canvas bag.

And then she lay still.

Eight

8:31 A.M. Mountain Daylight Time
Blue Dome Mountain, Idaho

The steady buzzing of the telephone on the table beside his bed brought the man up from a dreamless sleep. Go away, he thought. Leave me alone. But the buzzing continued, and finally he slowly turned over, switched on the lamp and, squinting in the light, picked up the receiver. "Macklin," he said, his voice slurred and sleepy.

"Uh . . . Colonel, sir?" It was Sergeant Schorr. "I've got some people in orientation waiting to meet you, sir."

Colonel James "Jimbo" Macklin looked at the little green alarm clock next to the phone and saw he was more than thirty minutes late for the orientation and hand-shaking session. Damn it to Hell! he thought. I set that alarm for 0630 sharp! "All right, Sergeant. Keep them there another fifteen minutes." He hung up and then checked the back of the alarm clock; he saw that the little lever was still pressed down. Either he'd never set the alarm or he'd turned it off in his sleep. He sat on the edge of the bed, trying to summon the energy to get up, but his body felt sluggish and bloated; years ago, he mused grimly, he'd never needed an alarm clock to wake him: He could've been snapped out of sleep by the sound of a footstep in wet grass and he would've been as alert as a wolf within seconds.

Passing time, he thought. Long gone.

He willed himself to stand up. Willed himself to walk across the bedroom, its walls decorated with photographs of Phantom and Thunderchief jets in flight, and walked into the small bathroom. He switched on the light and ran water into the sink; it came out rusty. He splashed the water on his face, dried himself with a towel and stood staring bleary-eyed at the stranger in the mirror.

Macklin stood six foot two, and until five or six years ago his body had been lean and hard, his ribs covered with muscle, his shoulders strong and straight, his chest thrust out like Chobham armor on the snout of an M-1 tank. Now the definitions of his body were blurred by loose flesh, and his potbelly resisted the fifty situps he did every morning—that is, when he had time to do them. He detected a stoop in his shoulders, as if he were being bowed by an invisible weight, and the hair on his chest was sprinkled with gray. His biceps, once rock-hard, had deteriorated into flab. He'd once broken the neck of a Libyan soldier in the crook of his arm; now he didn't feel as if he had the strength to crack a walnut with a sledgehammer.

He plugged in his electric razor and guided it over the stubble on his jaw. His dark brown hair was clipped in a severe crewcut, showing flecks of gray at the temples; beneath a square slab of a forehead, his eyes were frosty blue and sunken in deep hollows of fatigue, like bits of ice floating on muddy water. As he shaved Macklin thought that his face had come to resemble any one of the hundreds of battlefield maps he'd pored over long ago: the jutting cliff of his chin leading to the rugged ravine of his mouth, up to the highlands of his chiseled cheekbones and the craggy ridge of his nose, down again into the swamps of his eyes, then an upward sweep into the brown forests of his thick eyebrows. And all the terrain marks were there, as well: the pockmark craters of the severe acne he'd had as an adolescent, the small trench of a scar zigzagging through his left eyebrow, compliments of a ricocheting bullet in Angola. Across his left shoulder blade was a deeper and longer scar carved by a knife in Iraq, and a reminder of a Viet Cong bullet puckered the skin over the right side of his rib cage. Macklin was forty-four years old, but sometimes he awakened feeling seventy, with shooting pains in his arms and legs from bones that had been broken in battles on distant shores.

He finished shaving and drew aside the shower curtain to run the water, then he stopped, because littering the bottom of the small shower stall were ceiling tiles and bits of rubble. Water was dripping from a series of holes where the shower stall ceiling had given way. As he stared at the leaking water, realizing he was running late and could not take a shower, anger suddenly rose within him like molten iron in a blast furnace; he slammed his fist against the wall once, and then again; the second time, the force of his blow left a network of minute cracks.

He leaned over the sink, waiting for the rage to pass, as it usually did. "Steady," he told himself. "Discipline and control. Discipline and control." He repeated it a few more times, like a mantra, drew a long, deep breath and straightened up. Time to go, he thought. They're waiting for me. He used his stick deodorant under his arms, then went out to the bedroom closet to choose his uniform.

He picked a pair of crisply pressed dark blue trousers, a light blue shirt and his beige poplin flight jacket with leather patches on the elbows and MACKLIN printed across the breast pocket. He reached up to the overhead shelf, where he kept a case containing his Ingram gun and ammo clips, and lovingly took his Air Force colonel's cap down; he brushed an imaginary bit of lint off the polished brim and put the cap on his head. He checked himself in the full-length mirror on the back of the closet door: buttons polished, check; trousers creased, check; shoes shining, check. He straightened his collar, and then he was ready to go.

His private electric cart was parked outside his quarters on the Command Center Level; he locked his door with one of the many keys he carried on a key chain, then got into the cart and drove along the corridor. Behind him, past his own quarters, was the sealed metal door of the weapons storage room and the emergency food and water supply. Down at the other end of the corridor, past the quarters of other Earth House technicians and employees, was the generator room and the air-filtration system controls. He passed the door of Perimeter Control, which contained the screens of the small portable battlefield surveillance radars set out to guard the entry to Earth House, and the main screen of the skyward-trained radar dish that sat atop Blue Dome Mountain. Within Perimeter Control was also the hydraulic system that sealed the air vents and the lead-lined doorway in the event of a nuclear attack, and the various radar screens were manned around the clock.

Macklin guided the cart up a ramp to the next level and headed for the Town Hall. He passed the open doors of the gymnasium, where an aerobics class was in session. A few morning joggers were running in the corridor, and Macklin nodded at them as he sped past. Then he was in the wider corridor of Earth House's Town Square, a junction of hallways with a rock garden at its center. All around were various "shops" with storefronts made to resemble those in a country town. Earth House's Town Square contained a tanning salon, a theater where videotaped movies were shown, a library, an infirmary staffed by a doctor and two nurses, a game arcade and a cafeteria. Macklin caught the aroma of bacon and eggs as he drove past the cafeteria's doors and wished he'd had time for breakfast. It was not his way to be late. Discipline and control, he thought. Those were the two things that made a man.

But he was still angry about the collapsed ceiling in his shower stall. Lately, it seemed that the walls and ceiling in several areas of Earth House were cracking and giving way. He'd called the Ausley brothers many times, but they'd told him the structural reports showed settling was to be expected. Settling, my ass! Macklin had said. We've got a water drainage problem here! Water's collecting over the ceilings and leaking through!

"Don't get yourself in a dither, Colonel," Donny Ausley had told him from San Antonio. "If *you* get nervous, them folks are gonna get nervous, right? And there ain't no sense in gettin' nervous, 'cause that mountain's been standing for a few thousand years, and it ain't goin' nowhere."

"It's not the mountain!" Macklin had said, his fist tightening around the receiver. "It's the tunnels! My cleanup crews are finding new cracks every day!"

"Settlin', that's all. Now listen, Terry and me have pumped 'bout ten million big ones into that place, and we built it to *last.* If we didn't have bidness to run, we'd be right there with you. Now, that far underground, you're gonna have some settlin' and water leaks. Ain't no way 'round it. And we're payin' you one hundred thousand dollars a year to endorse Earth House and live down there, you bein' a big war hero and all. So you fix them cracks and keep everybody happy."

"*You* listen, Mr. Ausley: If I don't get a structural engineer to look this place over within a week, I'm leaving. I don't give a damn about my contract. I'm not going to encourage people to stay down here if it's not safe!"

"I believe," Donny Ausley had said, his Texas accent getting a few degrees cooler, "you'd better calm yourself down, Colonel. Now, you don't want to walk out on a bidness deal. That ain't good manners. You just 'member how Terry and me found you and brought you along 'fore you start flyin' off the handle, okay?"

Discipline and control! Macklin had thought, his heart hammering. Discipline and control! And then he'd listened as Donny Ausley had told him he'd send an engineer up from San Antone within two weeks to go over Earth House with a fine-tooth comb. "But meantime, you're head honcho. You got a problem, you fix it. Right?"

And that had been almost a month ago. The structural engineer had never come.

Colonel Macklin stopped his cart near a pair of double doors. Above the doors was the sign TOWN HALL in ornate, old-timey lettering. Before he went in, he tightened his belt another notch, though the trousers were already squeezed around his midsection; then he drew himself up tall and straight and entered the auditorium.

About a dozen people sat in the red vinyl seats that faced the podium, where Captain Warner was answering questions and pointing out features of Earth House on the wall map displayed behind him. Sergeant Schorr, who stood ready to field the more difficult questions, saw the colonel enter and quickly stepped to the podium's microphone. "Excuse me, Captain," he said, interrupting an explanation about the plumbing and water-filtration system. "Folks, I want to introduce you to someone who certainly needs no introduction: Colonel James Barnett Macklin."

The colonel continued at a crisp pace along the center aisle as the audience applauded. He took his place behind the podium, framed by an American flag and the flag of Earth House, and looked out at the gallery. The applause went on, and a middle-aged man in a camouflage combat jacket rose to his feet, followed by his similarly dressed wife; then all of them were standing and applauding, and Macklin let it continue for another fifteen seconds before he thanked them and asked them to be seated.

Captain "Teddybear" Warner, a husky ex-Green Beret who'd lost his left eye to a grenade in the Sudan and now wore a black patch, took a seat behind the colonel, and Schorr sat beside him. Macklin paused, gathering in his mind what he was going to say; he usually gave the same welcoming speech to all the new arrivals at Earth House, told them how secure the place was and how it would be the last American fortress when the Russians invaded. Afterward, he took their questions, shook their hands and signed a few autographs. That was what the Ausley boys paid him for.

He looked into their eyes. They were used to nice, clean beds, sweet-smelling bathrooms and roast beef on Sunday afternoons. Drones, he thought. They lived to breed and eat and shit, and they thought they knew all about freedom and loyalty and courage—but they didn't know the first thing about those attributes. He cast his gaze over the faces, saw nothing but softness and weakness; these were people who *thought* they'd sacrifice their wives and husbands, infant children, homes and all their possessions as the price of keeping the Russian filth off our shores, but they would not, because their spirits were weak and their brains were corrupted by mental junk food. And here they were, like all the others, waiting for him to tell them they were true patriots.

He wanted to open his mouth and tell them to get the hell out of Earth House, that the place was structurally unsound and that they—the weak-willed losers!—ought to go home and cower in their basements. Jesus Christ! he thought. What the hell am I *doing* here?

Then a mental voice, like the sound of a cracking bullwhip, said, Discipline and control! Shape up, mister!

It was the voice of the Shadow Soldier. Macklin closed his eyes for a second. When he opened them, he was staring into the face of a bony, fragile-looking boy sitting in the second row between his father and mother. A good strong wind would knock that kid to the ground, he decided, but he paused, examining the boy's pale gray eyes. He thought he recognized something in those eyes—determination, cunning, willpower—that he remembered from pictures of himself at that age, when he was a fat, clumsy slob that his Air Force captain father had kicked in the ass at every opportunity.

Of all of them sitting before me, he thought, that skinny kid *might* have a chance. The others were dogmeat.

He braced himself and started giving the orientation speech with as much enthusiasm as if he were digging a latrine ditch.

As Colonel Macklin spoke Roland Croninger examined him with intent interest. The colonel was a lot heavier than the photographs in *Soldier of Fortune*, and he looked sleepy and bored. Roland was disappointed; he'd expected a trim and hungry war hero, not a used car salesman dressed up in military duds. It was hard to believe that this was the same man who had shot down three MiGs over the Thanh Hoa Bridge to save a buddy's crippled plane and then had ejected from a disintegrating aircraft.

Rip-off, Roland decided. Colonel Macklin was a rip-off, and he was beginning to think Earth House might be a rip-off, as well. That morning he'd awakened to find a dark water stain on his pillow; the ceiling was leaking from a crack two inches wide. There had been no hot water from the shower head, and the cold water was full of grit and rust. His mother had thrown a fit about not being able to get her hair clean, and his father had said he'd mention the problem to Sergeant Schorr.

Roland was fearful of setting up his computer because the air in his bedroom was so damp, and his first impression of Earth House as a neat-o medieval-type fortress was wearing thin. Of course, he'd brought books to read—tomes on Machiavelli and Napoleon and a study of medieval siege warfare—but he'd counted on programming some new dungeons for his King's Knight game while he was here. King's Knight was his own creation—128K of an imaginary world shattered into feudal kingdoms at war with one another. Now it looked as if he was going to have to read all the time!

He watched Colonel Macklin. Macklin's eyes were lazy, and his face was fat. He looked like an old bull that had been put out to pasture because he couldn't get it up anymore. But as Macklin's eyes met his and held for a couple of seconds before they slid away again, Roland was reminded of a picture he'd seen of Joe Louis when the boxing champion had been a Las Vegas hotel greeter. In that picture, Joe Louis looked flabby and tired, but he had one massive hand clasped around the frail white hand of a tourist, and Joe Louis' eyes were hard and dark and somewhere far away—maybe back in the ring, remembering the feel of a blow slammed against another man's midsection almost to the backbone. Roland thought that the same distant stare was in Colonel Macklin's eyes, and, just as you knew Joe Louis could've smashed the bones in that tourist's hand with one quick squeeze, Roland sensed that the warrior within Colonel Macklin was not yet dead.

As Macklin's address continued the wall telephone beside the display map buzzed. Sergeant Schorr got up and answered it; he listened for a few seconds, hung the receiver up and started back across the platform toward the colonel. Roland thought that something in Schorr's face had been altered in the time he was on the telephone; Schorr appeared older now, and his face was slightly flushed. He said, "Excuse me, Colonel," and he placed his hand over the microphone.

Macklin's head snapped around, his eyes angry at the interruption.

"Sir," Schorr said quietly, "Sergeant Lombard says you're needed in Perimeter Control."

"What is it?"

"He wouldn't say, sir. I think . . . he sounded pretty damned shaken."

Crap! Macklin thought. Lombard got "shaken" every time the radar picked up a flock of geese or an airliner passing overhead. Once they'd sealed Earth House because Lombard thought a group of hang gliders were enemy paratroopers. Still, Macklin would have to check it out. He motioned for Captain Warner to follow him, and then he told Schorr to dismiss the orientation after they'd gone. "Ladies and gentlemen," Macklin said into the microphone, "I'm going to have to leave you now to take care of a small problem, but I hope to see each of you later this afternoon at the newcomers' reception. Thank you for your attention." And then he stalked up the aisle with Captain Warner right behind him.

They drove back in the electric cart the way Macklin had come, Macklin muttering all the way about Lombard's stupidity. When they went into the Perimeter Control Room, they found Lombard peering into the screen that showed the returns from the sky radar atop Blue Dome. Near him stood Sergeant Becker and Corporal Prados, both staring at the screen as well. The room was full of electronic equipment, other radar screens and the small computer that stored the arrival and departure dates of Earth House's residents. On a shelf above a row of radar screens, a voice was blaring from a shortwave radio, almost obscured by the crackling of static. The voice was panicked, babbling so fast Macklin couldn't understand what was being said. But Macklin didn't like the sound of it, and instantly his muscles tensed and his heart began to pound.

"Move aside," he told the other men. He stood where he could get a good look at the screen.

His mouth went dry, and he heard the sizzling of circuits in his own brain at work. "God in Heaven," he whispered.

The garbled voice from the shortwave radio was saying, "New York got it . . . wiped out . . . the missiles are comin' in over the east coast . . . hit Washington . . . Boston . . . I can see flames from here. . . ." Other voices surged out of the storm of static, bits and pieces of information hurtling along the network of ham radio operators across the United States and picked up by Blue Dome Mountain's antennas. Another voice with a Southern accent broke in, shouting, "Atlanta just went dead! I think Atlanta got hit!" The voices overlapped, swelled and faded, commingled into a language of sobs and shouts, weak, faint whispers and the names of American cities repeated like a litany of the dead: Philadelphia . . . Miami . . . Newport News . . . Chicago . . . Richmond . . . Pittsburgh . . .

But Macklin's attention was fixed on what the radar screen showed. There could be no doubt about what they were. He looked up at Captain Warner and started to speak, but he couldn't find his voice for a second. Then he said, "Bring the perimeter guards in. Seal the doorway. We're under attack. *Move it!*"

Warner picked up a walkie-talkie and hustled off. "Get Schorr down here," Macklin said, and Sergeant Becker—a loyal and reliable man who had served with Macklin in Chad—instantly picked up the telephone and started pressing buttons. From the shortwave radio a frantic voice said, "This is KKTZ in St. Louis! Calling anybody! I'm lookin' at a fire in the sky! It's everywhere! God A'mighty, I've never seen such a—" A piercing squeal of static and other distant voices flooded into the empty hole left by St. Louis.

"This is it," Macklin whispered. His eyes were shining, and there was a light sheen of sweat on his face. "Ready or not, this is it."

And deep inside him, in the pit where no light had shone for a very long time, the Shadow Soldier cried out with joy.

Nine

10:46 A.M. Central Daylight Time
On Interstate 70,
Ellsworth County, Kansas

Twenty-four miles west of Salina, Josh Hutchins's battered old Pontiac gave a wheeze like an old man with phlegm in his lungs. Josh saw the temperature gauge's needle zoom toward the red line. Though all the windows were lowered, the inside of the car felt like a steam bath, and Josh's white cotton shirt and dark blue trousers were plastered to his body with sweat. Oh, Lord! he thought, watching the red needle climb. She's about to blow!

An exit was coming up on the right, and there was a weathered sign that said PawPaw's! Gas! Cold Drinks! One Mile! and had an exaggerated drawing of an old geezer sitting on a mule smoking a corncob pipe.

I hope I can make another mile, Josh thought as he guided the Pontiac onto the exit ramp. The car kept shuddering, and the needle was into the red but the radiator hadn't blown yet. Josh drove northward, following PawPaw's sign, and before him, stretching to the horizon, were immense fields of corn grown to the height of a man and withering under the terrible July heat. The two-lane county road cut straight across them, and not a puff of breeze stirred the stalks; they stood on both sides of the road like impenetrable walls and might have gone on, as far as Josh knew, for a hundred miles both east and west.

The Pontiac wheezed and gave a jolt. "Come on," Josh urged, the sweat streaming down his face. "Come on, don't give out on me now." He didn't relish the idea of walking a mile in hundred-degree sun; they'd find him melted into the concrete like an ink blot. The needle continued its climb, and red warning lights were flashing on the dashboard.

Suddenly there was a crackling noise that made Josh think of the Rice Krispies he used to like as a kid. And then, in the next instant, the windshield was covered with a crawling brown mass of *things.*

Before Josh could finish drawing a surprised breath, a brown cloud had swept through the open windows on the Pontiac's right side and he was covered with crawling, fluttering, chattering things that got down the collar of his shirt, into his mouth, up his nostrils and in his eyes. He spat them from his mouth and clawed them away from his eyes with one hand while the other clenched the steering wheel. It was the most ungodly noise of chattering he'd ever heard, a deafening roar of whirring wings. And then his eyes cleared and he could see that the windshield and the car's interior were covered with thousands of locusts, swarming all over him, flying through his car and out the windows on the left side. He switched on the windshield wipers, but the weight of the mass of locusts pinned the wipers to the glass.

In the next few seconds they began flying off the windshield, first five or six at a time and then suddenly the whole mass in a whirling brown tornado. The wipers slapped back and forth, smearing some unlucky ones who were too slow. And then steam billowed up from under the hood and the Pontiac Bonneville lurched forward. Josh looked at the temperature gauge; a locust clung to the glass, but the needle was way over the red line.

This sure isn't turning out to be my day, he thought grimly as he brushed the remaining locusts from his arms and legs.

They, too, whirred out of the car and followed the huge cloud that was moving over the sunburned corn, heading in a northwesterly direction. One of the things flew right up in his face, and its wings made a noise like a Bronx cheer before it darted out the window after the others. Only about twenty or so remained in the car, crawling lazily over the dashboard and the passenger seat.

Josh concentrated on where he was going, praying that the engine would give him just a few more yards. Through the cloud of steam he saw a small, flat-roofed cinder block structure coming up on his right. Gas pumps stood out front, under a green canvas awning. On the building's roof was a full-sized old Conestoga wagon, and printed in big red letters on the wagon's side was PAWPAW'S.

He breathed a sigh of relief and turned into the gravel driveway, but before he could reach the gas pumps and a water hose the Pontiac coughed, faltered and backfired at the same time. The engine made a noise like a hollow bucket being kicked, and then the only sound was the rude hiss of steam.

Well, Josh thought, that's that.

Bathed in sweat, he got out of the car and contemplated the rising plume of steam. When he reached out to pop the hood open, the metal burned his hand like a bite. He stepped back and, as the sun beat down from a sky almost white with heat haze, Josh thought his life had reached its lowest ebb.

A screen door slammed. "Got y'self some trouble?" a wizened voice inquired.

Josh looked up. Approaching him from the cinder block building was a little humpbacked old man wearing a sweat-stained ten-gallon hat, overalls and cowboy boots. "I sure do," Josh replied.

The little man, who stood maybe five foot one, stopped. His ten-gallon hat—complete with a snakeskin hatband and an eagle's feather sticking up—almost swallowed his head. His face was as brown as sunbaked clay, his eyes dark, sparkling dots. "*Oooooeeeee!*" he rasped. "You're a big 'un, ain't you! Lordy, I ain't seen one as big as you since the circus passed through!" He grinned, revealing tiny, nicotine-stained teeth. "How's the weather up there?"

Josh's sweaty frustration tumbled out in a laugh. He grinned widely as well. "The same as down there," he answered. "Mighty hot."

The little man shook his head in awe and walked in a circle around the Bonneville. He, too, attempted to get the hood up, but the heat stung his fingers. "Hose is busted," he decided. "Yep. Hose. Seen a lot of 'em lately."

"Do you have spares?"

The man tilted his neck to look up, still obviously impressed with Josh's size. "Nope," he said. "Not a one. I can get you one, though. Order it from Salina, should be here in . . . oh, two or three hours."

"Two or three *hours?* Salina's only about thirty miles away!"

The little man shrugged. "Hot day. City boys don't like hot days. Too used to air conditionin'. Yep, two or three hours'll do it."

"Damn! I'm on my way to Garden City!"

"Long drive," the man offered. "Well, we'd best let 'er cool off some. I got cold drinks, if you want one." He motioned for Josh to follow and started toward the building.

Josh was expecting a tumbledown mess of oil cans, old batteries and a wall full of hubcaps, but when he stepped inside he was surprised to find a neat, orderly country grocery store. A throw rug had been put down right at the doorway, and behind the counter and cash register was a little alcove where the man had been sitting in his rocking chair, watching television on a portable Sony. Now, though, the TV's screen showed only static.

"Thing went out on me just before you drove up," he said. "I was watchin' that show about the hospital and them folks always gettin' in trouble. Lord God, they'd put you *under* the jail around here for some of them shenanigans!" He cackled and took off his hat. His scalp was pale, and he had white hair that stood up in sweat-damp spikes. "All the other channels are off too, so I guess we got to *talk*, huh?"

"I guess so." Josh stood in front of a fan atop the counter, letting the deliciously cool air separate his wet shirt from his skin.

The little man opened a refrigerator unit and brought out two canned Cokes. He handed one to Josh, who snapped the tab and drank thirstily. "No charge," the man said. "You look like you've had a rough mornin'. My name's PawPaw Briggs—well, PawPaw ain't my real name. It's what my boys call me. So that's what the sign says."

"Josh Hutchins." They shook hands, and the little man grinned again and pretended to wince under the pressure of Josh's grip. "Do your boys work here with you?"

"Oh, no." PawPaw chuckled. "They got their own place, up the road four or five miles."

Josh was grateful to be out of the hot sun. He walked around the store, rolling the cold can across his face and feeling the flesh tighten. For a country store out in the middle of a cornfield, he realized after another moment, the shelves of PawPaw's place held an amazing variety of items: loaves of wheat bread, rye bread, raisin bread and cinnamon rolls; cans of green beans, beets, squash, peaches, pineapple chunks and all kinds of fruit; about thirty different canned soups; cans of beef stew, corned beef hash, Spam, and sliced roast beef; an array of utensils, including paring knives, cheese graters, can openers, flashlights and batteries; and a shelf full of canned fruit juices, Hawaiian Punch, Welch's Grape Juice and mineral water in plastic jugs. A rack on the wall held shovels, picks and hoes, a pair of garden shears and a water hose. Near the cash register was a magazine stand displaying periodicals like *Flying, American Pilot, Time* and *Newsweek, Playboy* and *Penthouse.* This place, Josh thought, was the supermarket of country stores! "Lot of people live around here?" Josh asked.

"Few." PawPaw whacked the TV with his fist, but the static remained. "Not too many."

Josh felt something crawling under his collar; he reached back and dug out a locust.

"Things are hell, ain't they?" PawPaw asked. "Get into everythin', they do. Been flyin' out of the fields by the thousands for the last two, three days. Kinda peculiar."

"Yeah." Josh held the insect between his fingers and went

to the screen door. He opened it and flicked the locust out; it whirled around his head for a couple of seconds, made a soft chirring noise and then flew toward the northwest.

A red Camaro suddenly pulled off the road, swerved around Josh's sick Bonneville and halted at the pumps. "More customers," Josh announced.

"Well, well. We got us a regular convention today, don't we?" He came around the counter to stand beside Josh, barely the height of Josh's breastbone. The doors of the Camaro opened, and a woman and a little blond-haired girl got out. "Hey!" the woman, who was squeezed into a red halter top and tight, uncomfortable-looking jeans, called toward the screen door. "Can I get some unleaded gas here?"

"Sure can!" PawPaw went outside to pump the gas for her. Josh finished his Coke, crumpled the can and dropped it into a wastebasket; when he looked through the screen door again, he saw that the child, who wore a little powder-blue jumpsuit, was standing right in the blazing sun, staring at the moving cloud of locusts. The woman, her poorly dyed blond hair tangled and wet with sweat, took the child's hand and led her toward PawPaw's place. Josh stepped aside as they entered, and the woman—who had a blackened right eye—shot Josh a distrustful glance and then stood before the fan to cool off.

The child stared up at Josh as if peering toward the highest branches of a redwood tree. She was a pretty little thing, Josh thought; her eyes were a soft, luminous shade of blue. The color reminded Josh of what the summer sky had looked like when he himself was a child, with all the tomorrows before him and no place to go in any particular hurry. The little girl's face was heart-shaped and fragile-looking, her complexion almost translucent. She said, "Are you a giant?"

"Hush, Swan!" Darleen Prescott said. "We don't talk to strangers!"

But the little girl continued to stare up at him, expecting an answer. Josh smiled. "I guess I am."

"Sue Wanda!" Darleen grabbed Swan's shoulder and turned her away from Josh.

"Hot day," Josh said. "Where are you two heading?"

Darleen was silent for a moment, letting the cool air play over her face. "Anywhere but here," she replied, her eyes closed and her head tilted upward to catch the air on her throat.

PawPaw returned, wiping the sweat from his forehead with a much-used handkerchief. "Gotcha filled up there, lady. Be fifteen dollars and seventy-five cents, please."

Darleen dug in her pocket for the money, and Swan nudged her. "I need to go right *now!*" Swan whispered. Darleen laid a twenty dollar bill on the counter. "You got a ladies' room, mister?"

"Nope," he replied, and then he looked down at Swan—who was obviously in some discomfort—and shrugged. "Well, I reckon you can use *my* bathroom. Hold on a minute." He reached down and pulled back the throw rug in front of the counter. Beneath it was a trapdoor. PawPaw threw back a bolt and lifted it. The aroma of rich, dark earth wafted from the open square, and a set of wooden steps descended into the basement. PawPaw went down a few steps, flicked on an overhanging light bulb and then came back up. "Bathroom's through the little door on the right," he told Swan. "Go ahead."

She glanced at her mother, who shrugged and motioned her down, and Swan went through the trapdoor. The basement had walls of hard-packed dirt; the ceiling was criss-crossed with thick wooden beams. The floor was made of poured concrete, and the room—which was about twenty feet long, ten feet wide and seven or eight feet high—held a cot, a record player and radio, a shelf of dog-eared Louis L'Amour and Brett Halliday paperbacks, and had a poster of Dolly Parton on one wall. Swan found the door and entered a tiny cubicle that had a sink, a mirror and a toilet.

"Do you *live* down there?" Josh asked the old man as he peered through the trapdoor.

"Sure do. Used to live in a farmhouse a couple of miles east, but I sold that after the wife passed on. My boys helped me dig the basement out. It ain't much, but it's home."

"Ugh!" Darleen wrinkled her nose. "It smells like a graveyard."

"Why don't you live with your sons?" Josh inquired.

PawPaw looked at him curiously, his brow knitting. *"Sons?* I ain't got no sons."

"I thought you said your boys helped you dig the basement out."

"My boys did, yeah. The underground boys. They said they'd made me a real good place to live in. See, they come here all the time and stock up, 'cause I'm the closest store."

Josh couldn't make sense of what the old man was talking about. He tried once more: "Come here from *where?"*

"Underground," PawPaw replied.

Josh shook his head. The old man was nuts. "Listen, could you take a look at my radiator now?"

"I reckon so. One minute, and we'll go see what she wrote." PawPaw went behind the counter, rang up Darleen's gas purchase and gave her change from the twenty. Swan started coming up the basement steps. Josh braced himself for the stunning heat and went outside, walking toward his still-steaming Bonneville.

He had almost reached it when he felt the earth shake beneath his feet.

He stopped in his tracks. What was *that?* he wondered. An earthquake? Yeah, that would just about put the capper on the day!

The sun was brutal. The cloud of locusts was gone. Across the road, the huge cornfield was as still as a painting. The only sounds were the hissing of steam and the steady *tick . . . tick . . . tick* of the Pontiac's fried engine.

Squinting in the harsh glare, Josh looked up at the sky. It was white and featureless, like a clouded mirror. His heart was beating harder. The screen door slammed behind him, and he jumped. Darleen and Swan had come out and were walking toward the Camaro. Suddenly Swan stopped, too, but Darleen walked on a few more paces before she realized the child was not beside her. "Come on! Let's get on the road, hon!"

Swan's gaze was directed at the sky. It's so quiet, she thought. So *quiet.* The heavy air almost pressed her to her knees, and she was having trouble drawing a breath. All day long she'd noted huge flocks of birds in flight, horses running skittishly around their pastures and dogs baying at the sky. She sensed something about to happen—something very bad, just as she had last night when she'd seen the fireflies. But the feeling had gotten stronger all morning, ever since they'd left the motel outside Wichita, and now it made goose bumps break out on her arms and legs. She sensed danger in the air, danger in the earth, danger everywhere.

"Swan!" Darleen's voice was both irritated and nervous. "Come on, now!"

The little girl stared into the brown cornfields that stretched to the horizon. Yes, she thought. And danger there, too. Especially there.

The blood pounded in her veins, and an urge to cry almost overcame her. "Danger," she whispered. "Danger . . . in the corn . . ."

The ground shook again beneath Josh's feet, and he thought he heard a deep grinding growl like heavy machinery coming to life. Darleen shouted, "Swan! *Come on!*"

What the *hell . . . ?* Josh thought.

And then there came a piercing, whining noise that grew louder and louder, and Josh put his hands to his ears and wondered if he was going to live to see his paycheck.

"God A'mighty!" PawPaw shouted, standing in the doorway.

A column of dirt shot up about four hundred yards into the cornfield to the northwest, and hundreds of cornstalks burst into flame. A spear of fire emerged, made a noise like bacon sizzling in a skillet as it sped upward several hundred feet, then arced dramatically to a northwesterly course and vanished in the haze. Another burning spear burst from the ground a half mile or so away, and this one followed the first. Further away, two more shot upward and climbed out of sight within two seconds; then the burning spears were coming up all over the cornfield, the nearest about three hundred yards away and the most distant fiery dots five or six miles across the fields. Geysers of dirt exploded as the things rose with incredible speed, their flaming trails leaving blue afterimages on Josh's retinas. The corn was on fire, and the hot wind of the burning spears fanned the flames toward PawPaw's place.

Waves of sickening heat washed over Josh, Darleen and Swan. Darleen was still screaming for Swan to get to the car. The child watched in horrified awe as dozens of burning spears continued to explode from the cornfield. The earth shuddered with shock waves under Josh's feet. His senses reeling, he realized that the burning spears were missiles, roaring from their hidden silos in a Kansas cornfield in the middle of nowhere.

The underground boys, Josh thought—and he suddenly knew what PawPaw Briggs had meant.

PawPaw's place stood on the edge of a camouflaged missile base, and the "underground boys" were the Air Force technicians who were now sitting in their bunkers and pressing the buttons.

"God A'mighty!" PawPaw shouted, his voice lost in the roar. "Look at 'em *fly!*"

Still the missiles were bursting from the cornfield, each one following the other into the northwest and vanishing in the rippling air. Russia, Josh thought. Oh, my God Jesus—they're heading for Russia!

All the newscasts he'd heard and stories he'd read in the past few months came back to him, and in that awful instant he knew World War III had begun.

The swirling, scorched air was full of fiery corn, raining down on the road and on the roof of PawPaw's place. The green canvas awning was smoking, and the canvas of the Conestoga wagon was already aflame. A storm of burning corn was advancing across the ravaged field, and as the shock waves collided in fifty-mile-an-hour winds the flames merged into a solid, rolling wall of fire twenty feet high.

"Come on!" Darleen shrieked, grabbing Swan up in her arms. The child's blue eyes were wide and staring, hypnotized by the spectacle of fire. Darleen started running for her car with Swan in her arms, and as a shock wave knocked her flat

the first red tendrils of flame began to reach toward the gas pumps.

Josh knew the fire was about to jump the road. The pumps were going to blow. And then he was back on the football field before a roaring Sunday afternoon crowd, and he was running for the downed woman and child like a human tank as the stadium clock ticked the seconds off. A shock wave hit him, threw him off balance, and burning corn swept over him; but then he was scooping the woman up with one thick arm around her waist. She clung to the child, whose face had frozen with terror. "Lemme go!" Darleen shrieked, but Josh whirled around and sprinted for the screen door, where PawPaw stood watching the flight of the burning spears in open-mouthed wonder.

Josh had almost reached it when there was an incandescent flash like a hundred million high-wattage bulbs going off at the same instant. Josh was looking away from the field, but he saw his shadow projected onto PawPaw Briggs—and in the space of a millisecond he saw PawPaw's eyeballs burst into blue flame. The old man screamed, clawed at his face and fell backward into the screen door, tearing it off its hinges. "Oh God, oh Jesus, oh God!" Darleen was babbling. The child was silent.

The light got brighter still, and Josh felt a wash of heat on his back—gentle at first, like the sun on a nice summer day. But then the heat increased to the level of an oven, and before Josh could reach the door he heard the skin on his back and shoulders sizzling. The light was so intense he couldn't see where he was going, and now his face was swelling so fast he feared it would explode like a beach ball. He stumbled forward, tripped over something—PawPaw's body, writhing in agony in the doorway. Josh smelled burning hair and scorched flesh, and he thought crazily, I'm one barbecued sonofabitch!

He could still see through the slits of his swollen eyes; the world was an eerie blue-white, the color of ghosts. Ahead of him, the trapdoor yawned open. Josh reached down with his free hand, grabbed the old man's arm and dragged him, along with the woman and child, toward the open square. An explosion sent shrapnel banging against the outside wall—the pumps, Josh knew—and a shard of hot metal flew past the right side of his head. Blood streamed down, but he had no time to think of anything but getting into that basement, for behind him he heard a wailing cacophony of wind like a symphony of fallen angels, and he dared not look back to see what was coming out of that cornfield. The whole building was shaking, cans and bottles jumping off the shelves. Josh flung PawPaw Briggs down the steps like a sack of grain and then leapt down himself, skinning his ass on the wood but still clinging to the woman and child. They rolled to the floor, the woman screaming in a broken, strangled voice. Josh scrambled back up to close the trapdoor.

And then he looked through the doorway and saw what was coming.

A tornado of fire.

It filled the sky, hurling off jagged spears of red and blue lightning and carrying with it tons of blackened earth gouged from the fields. He knew in that instant that the tornado of fire was advancing on PawPaw's grocery store, bringing half the dirt from the field with it, and it would hit them within seconds.

And, simply, either they would live or they would die.

Josh reached up, slammed the trapdoor in place and jumped off the steps. He landed on his side on the concrete floor.

Come on! he thought, his teeth gritted and his hands over his head. *Come on, damn it!*

An unearthly commingling of the mighty roar of whirling wind, the crackle of fire and the bellowing crash of thunder filled the basement, forcing everything from Josh Hutchins's mind but cold, stark terror.

The basement's concrete floor suddenly shook—and then it lifted three feet and cracked apart like a dinner plate. It slammed down with brutal force. Pain pounded at Josh's eardrums. He opened his mouth and knew he was screaming, but he couldn't hear it.

And then the basement's ceiling caved in, the beams

cracking like bones in hungry hands. Josh was struck across the back of the head; he had the sensation of being lifted up and whirled in an airplane spin while his nostrils were smothered with thick, wet cotton, and all he wanted to do was get out of this damned wrestling ring and go home.

Then he knew no more.

Ten
10:17 A.M. Mountain Daylight Time
Earth House

"More bogies at ten o'clock!" Lombard said as the radar swept around again and the green dots flickered across the display screen. "Twelve heading southeast at fourteen thousand feet. Jesus Christ, look at those mothers *move!*" Within thirty seconds, the blips had passed out of radar range. "Five more coming over, Colonel." Lombard's voice shook with a mixture of horror and excitement, his heavy-jowled face flushed and his eyes large behind aviator-style glasses. "Heading northwest at seventeen-oh-three. They're ours. Go for it, baby!"

Sergeant Becker whooped and smacked a fist into the palm of his open hand. "Wipe Ivan off the map!" he shouted. Behind him, Captain Warner smoked a cork-tipped cheroot and impassively watched the radar screen through his good eye. A couple of other uniformed technicians monitored the perimeter radar. Across the room, Sergeant Schorr was slumped in a chair, his eyes glassy and unbelieving, and every once in a while his tortured gaze crept toward the main radar screen and then quickly moved back to a spot on the opposite wall.

Colonel Macklin stood over Lombard's right shoulder, his

arms crossed over his chest and his attention fixed on the green blips that had been moving across the screen for the last forty minutes. It was easy to tell which were Russian missiles, because they were heading southeast, on trajectories that would take them hurtling into the midwestern air force bases and ICBM fields. The American missiles were speeding northwest, toward deadly rendezvous with Moscow, Magadan, Tomsk, Karaganda, Vladivostok, Gorky and a hundred other target cities and missile bases. Corporal Prados had his earphones on, monitoring the weak signals that were still coming in from shortwave operators across the country. "Signal from San Francisco just went off the air," he said. "Last word was from KXCA in Sausalito. Something about a fireball and blue lightning—the rest was garbled."

"Seven bogies at eleven o'clock," Lombard said. "Twelve thousand feet. Heading southeast."

Seven more, Macklin thought. My God! That brought to sixty-eight the number of "incoming mail" picked up by Blue Dome's radar—and God only knew how many hundreds, possibly thousands, had streaked over out of radar range. From the panicked reports of shortwave radio operators, American cities were being incinerated in a full-scale nuclear assault. But Macklin had counted forty-four pieces of "outgoing mail" headed for Russia, and he knew that thousands of ICBMs, Cruise missiles, B-1 bombers and submarine-based nuclear weapons were being used against the Soviet Union. It didn't matter who'd started it; all the talking was over. It only mattered now who was strong enough to withstand the atomic punches the longest.

Earth House had been ordered sealed when Macklin saw the first blips of Soviet missiles on the radar screen. The perimeter guards had been brought in, the rock doorway lowered and locked in place, the system of louver-like baffles activated in the ventilation ducts to prevent entry of radioactive dust. There was one thing that remained to be done: Tell the civilians inside Earth House that World War III had started, that their homes and relatives had possibly been vaporized already, that everything they'd known and loved might well be gone in the flash of a fireball. Macklin had rehearsed it in his mind many times before; he would call the civilians together in the Town Hall, and he would calmly explain to them what was happening. They would understand that they would have to stay here, inside Blue Dome Mountain, and they could never go home again. Then he would teach them discipline and control, mold hard shells of armor over those soft, sluggish civilian bodies, teach them to *think* like warriors. And from this impregnable fortress they would hold off the Soviet invaders to the last breath and drop of blood, because he loved the United States of America and no man would ever make him kneel and beg.

"Colonel?" One of the young technicians looked up from his perimeter radar screen. "I've got a vehicle approaching. Looks like an RV, coming up the mountain pretty damned fast."

Macklin stepped over to watch the blip approaching up the mountain road. The RV was going so fast its driver was in danger of slinging it right off Blue Dome.

It was still within Macklin's power to open the front doorway and bring the RV inside by using a code that would override the computerized locking system. He imagined a frantic family inside that vehicle, perhaps a family from Idaho Falls, or from one of the smaller communities at the base of the mountain. Human lives, Macklin thought, struggling to avoid decimation. He looked at the telephone. Punching in his ID number and speaking the code into the receiver would make the security computer abort the lock and raise the doorway. By doing so, he would save those people's lives.

He reached toward the telephone.

But something stirred within him—a heavy, dark, unseen thing shifting as if from the bottom of a primeval swamp.

Sssstop! The Shadow Soldier's whisper was like the hiss of a fuse on dynamite. Think of the food! More mouths, less food!

Macklin hesitated, his fingers inches from the phone.

More mouths, less food! Discipline and control! Shape up, mister!

"I've got to let them in," Macklin heard himself say, and the other men in the control room stared at him.

Don't backtalk me, mister! More mouths, less food! And

you know *all* about what happens when a man's hungry, don't you?

"Yes," Macklin whispered.

"Sir?" the radar technician asked.

"Discipline and control," Macklin replied, in a slurred voice.

"Colonel?" Warner gripped Macklin's shoulder.

Macklin jerked, as if startled from a nightmare. He looked around at the others, then at the telephone again, and slowly lowered his hand. For a second he'd been down in the pit again, down in the mud and shit and darkness, but now he was okay. He knew where he was now. Sure. Discipline and control did the trick. Macklin shrugged free of Captain Warner and regarded the blip on the perimeter radar screen through narrowed eyes. "No," he said. "No. They're too late. Way too late. Earth House stays sealed." And he felt damned proud of himself for making the manly decision. There were over three hundred people in Earth House, not including the officers and technicians. More mouths, less food. He was sure he'd done the right thing.

"Colonel Macklin!" Lombard called; his voice cracked. "Look at this!"

At once, Macklin stood beside him, peering into the screen. He saw a group of four bogies streaking within radar range—but one seemed slower than the others, and as it faltered the faster three vanished over Blue Dome Mountain. "What's going on?"

"That bogie's at twenty-two thousand four," Lombard said. "A few seconds ago, it was at twenty-five. I think it's *falling.*"

"It can't be falling! There aren't any military targets within a hundred miles!" Sergeant Becker snapped, pushing forward to see.

"Check again," Macklin told Lombard, in the calmest voice he could summon.

The radar arm swept around with agonizing slowness. "Twenty thousand two, sir. Could be malfunctioned. The bastard's coming down!"

"Shit! Get me an impact point!"

A plastic-coated map of the area around Blue Dome Mountain was unfolded, and Lombard went to work with his compass and protractor, figuring and refiguring angles and speeds. His hands were trembling, and he had to start over more than once. Finally, he said, "It's going to pass over Blue Dome, sir, but I don't know what the turbulence is doing up there. I've got it impacting right here," and he tapped his finger at a point roughly ten miles west of Little Lost River. He checked the screen again. "It's just coming through eighteen thousand, sir. It's falling like a broken arrow."

Captain "Teddybear" Warner grunted. "There's Ivan's technology for you," he said. "All fucked up."

"No, sir." Lombard swiveled around in his chair. "It's not Russian. It's one of ours."

There was an electric silence in the room. Colonel Macklin broke it by expelling the air in his lungs. "Lombard, what the *hell* are you saying?"

"It's a friendly," he repeated. "It was moving northwest before it went out of control. From the size and speed, I'd guess it's a Minuteman III, maybe a Mark 12 or 12A."

"Oh . . . Jesus," Ray Becker whispered, his ruddy face gone ashen.

Macklin stared at the radar screen. The runaway blip seemed to be getting larger. His insides felt bound by iron bands, and he knew what would happen if a Minuteman III Mark 12A hit anywhere within fifty miles of Blue Dome Mountain; the Mark 12As carried three 335-kiloton nuclear warheads—enough power to flatten seventy-five Hiroshimas. The Mark 12s, carrying payloads of three 170-kiloton warheads, would be almost as devastating, but suddenly Macklin was praying that it was only a Mark 12, because maybe, *maybe,* the mountain could withstand that kind of impact without shuddering itself to rubble.

"Falling through sixteen thousand, Colonel."

Five thousand feet above Blue Dome Mountain. He could feel the other men watching him, waiting to see if he was made of iron or clay. There was nothing he could do now, except pray that the missile fell far beyond Little Lost River. A bitter smile crept across his mouth. His heart was racing, but his mind was steady. Discipline and control, he thought. Those were the things that made a man.

Earth House had been constructed here because there were no nearby Soviet targets, and all the government charts showed the movement of radioactive winds would be to the south. He'd never dreamed in his wildest scenarios that Earth House would be hit by an American weapon. Not fair! he thought, and he almost giggled. Oh no, not fair at *all!*

"Thirteen thousand three," Lombard said, his voice strained. He hurriedly did another calculation on the map, but he didn't say what he found and Macklin didn't ask him. Macklin knew they were going to take one hell of a jolt, and he was thinking of the cracks in the ceilings and walls of Earth House, those cracks and weak, rotted areas that the sonofabitching Ausley brothers should have taken care of before they opened this dungeon. But now it was too late, much too late. Macklin stared at the screen through slitted eyes and hoped that the Ausley brothers had heard their skin frying before they died.

"Twelve thousand two, Colonel."

Schorr let out a panicked whimper and drew his knees up to his chest; he peered into empty air like a man seeing the time, place and circumstances of his own death in a crystal ball.

"Shit," Warner said softly. He drew once more on his cigar and crushed it out in an ashtray. "I guess we'd better get comfortable, huh? Poor bastards upstairs are gonna be thrown around like rag dolls." He squeezed himself into a corner, bracing against the floor with his hands and feet.

Corporal Prados took off his earphones and braced himself against the wall, beads of sweat glistening on his cheeks. Becker stood beside Macklin, who watched the approaching blip on Lombard's radar screen and counted the seconds to impact.

"Eleven thousand two." Lombard's shoulders hunched up. "It's cleared Blue Dome! Passing to the northwest! I think it's going to make the river! Go, you bastard, *go!*"

"Go," Becker breathed.

"Go," Prados said, and he squeezed his eyes shut. "Go. Go."

The blip had vanished from the screen. "We've lost it, Colonel! It's gone below radar range!"

Macklin nodded. But the missile was still falling toward the forest along Little Lost River, and Macklin was still counting.

All of them heard a humming like a distant, huge swarm of hornets.

Then silence.

Macklin said, "It's dow—"

And in the next second the radar screen exploded with light, the men around it crying out and shielding their eyes. Macklin was momentarily blinded by the dazzle, and he knew the sky radar atop Blue Dome had just been incinerated. The other radar screens brightened like green suns and shorted out as they picked up the flash. The noise of hornets was in the room, and blue sparks spat from the control boards as the wiring blew. "Hang on!" Macklin shouted. The floors and walls shook, a jigsaw of cracks running across the ceiling. Rock dust and pebbles fell into the room, the larger stones rattling down on the control boards like hailstones. The floor heaved violently enough to drop both Macklin and Becker to their knees. Lights flickered and went out, but within seconds the emergency lighting system had switched on and the illumination—harsher, brighter, throwing deeper shadows than before—came back.

There was one last weak tremor and another rain of dust and stones, and then the floor was still.

Macklin's hair was white with dust, his face gritty and scratched. But the air-filtration system was throbbing, already drawing the dust into the wall vents. "Everybody okay?" he shouted, trying to focus past the green dazzle that remained on his eyeballs. He heard the sound of coughing and someone —Schorr, he thought it must be—sobbing. "Is everybody *okay?*"

He got a reply back from all but Schorr and one of the technicians. "It's over!" he said. "We made it! We're okay!" He knew that there would be broken bones, concussions and cases of shock among the civilians on the upper level, and they were probably panicked right now, but the lights were on and the filtration system was pumping and Earth House hadn't blown apart like a house of cards in a high wind. It's *over!* We made it! Still blinking to see past the green haze, he struggled to his feet. A short, hollow bark of a laugh escaped between his clenched teeth—and then the laughter bubbled up from his throat, and he was laughing louder and louder because he was alive and his fortress was still standing. His blood was hot and singing again like it had been in the steamy jungles and parched plains of foreign battlefields; on those fields of fire, the enemy wore a devil's face and did not hide behind the mask of Air Force psychiatrists, bill collectors, scheming ex-wives and cheating business partners. He was Colonel Jimbo Macklin, and he walked like a tiger, lean and mean, with the Shadow Soldier at his side.

He had once again beaten death and dishonor. He grinned, his lips white with grit.

But then there was a sound like cloth being ripped between cruel hands. Colonel Macklin's laughter stopped.

He rubbed his eyes, straining through the green glare, and was able at last to see where that noise was coming from.

The wall before him had fractured into thousands of tiny interconnected cracks. But at the top of it, where the wall met the ceiling, a massive crack was moving in fits and leaps, zigzagging as it went, and rivulets of dark, evil-smelling water streamed down the wall like blood from a monstrous wound. The ripping sound doubled and tripled; he looked at his feet, made out a second huge crack crawling across the floor. A third crack snaked across the opposite wall.

He heard Becker shout something, but the voice was garbled and in slow motion, as if heard in a nightmare. Chunks of stone fell from above, ripping the ceiling tile loose, and more streams of water splattered down. Macklin smelled the sickening odor of sewage, and as the water dripped all over him he realized the truth: that somewhere in the network of pipes the sewage system had exploded—perhaps weeks ago, or months—and the backed-up sludge had collected not only above the first level, but *between* Levels One and Two as well, further eroding the unsteady, overstressed rock that held the warren of Earth House together.

The floor pitched at an angle that threw Macklin off

balance. Plates of rock rubbed together with the noise of grinding jaws, and as the zigzagging cracks connected a torrent of foul water and rock cascaded from the ceiling. Macklin fell over Becker and hit the floor; he heard Becker scream, and as he twisted around he saw Ray Becker fall through a jagged crevice that had opened in the floor. Becker's fingers grasped the edge, and then the two sides of the crevice slammed shut again and Macklin watched in horror as the man's fingers exploded like overstuffed sausages.

The entire room was in violent motion, like a chamber in a bizarre carnival funhouse. Pieces of the floor collapsed, leaving gaping craters that fell into darkness. Schorr screamed and leaped toward the door, jumping a hole that opened in his path, and as the man burst out into the corridor Macklin saw that the corridor walls were veined with deep fissures as well. Huge slabs of rock were crashing down. Schorr disappeared into whirling dust, his scream trailing behind him. The corridor shook and pitched, the floor heaving up and down as if the iron reinforcing rods had turned to rubber. And all around, through the walls and the floor and ceiling, there was a pounding like a mad blacksmith beating on an anvil, coupled with the grinding of rock and the sound of reinforcing rods snapping like off-key guitar notes. Over the cacophony, a chorus of screams swelled and ebbed in the corridor. Macklin knew the civilians on the upper level were being battered to death. He sat huddled in a corner in the midst of the noise and chaos, realizing that the shock waves from that runaway missile were hammering Earth House to pieces.

Filthy water showered down on him. A storm of dust and rubble crashed into the corridor, and with it was something that might have been a mangled human body; the debris blocked the control room's doorway. Someone—Warner, he thought—had his arm and was trying to pull him to his feet. He heard Lombard howling like a hurt dog. Discipline and control! he thought. *Discipline and control!*

The lights went out. The air vents exhaled a gasp of death. And an instant afterward, the floor beneath Macklin collapsed. He fell, and he heard himself screaming. His shoulder hit an outcrop of rock, and then he struck bottom with a force that knocked the breath out of him and stopped his scream.

In utter darkness, the corridors and rooms of Earth House were caving in, one after the other. Bodies were trapped and mangled between pincers of grinding rock. Slabs of stone fell from above, crashing through the weakened floors. Sludge streamed knee-deep in the sections of Earth House that still held together, and in the darkness people crushed each other to death fighting for a way out. The screams, shrieks and cries for God merged into a hellish voice of pandemonium, and still the shock waves continued to batter Blue Dome Mountain as it caved in on itself, destroying the impregnable fortress carved in its guts.

Eleven

1:31 P.M. Eastern Daylight Time
Aboard Airborne Command

The president of the United States, his eyes sunken into purple craters in his ashen face, looked to his right out the oval Plexiglas window and saw a turbulent sea of black clouds beneath the Boeing E-4B. Yellow and orange flashes of light shimmered thirty-five thousand feet below, and the clouds boiled up in monstrous thunderheads. The aircraft shook, was sucked downward a thousand feet and then, its four turbofan engines screaming, battled for altitude again. The sky had turned the color of mud, the sun blocked by the massive, swirling clouds. And in those clouds, tossed upward thirty thousand feet from the surface of the earth, was the debris of civilization: burning trees, entire houses, sections of buildings, pieces of bridges and highways and railroad tracks glowing incandescent red. The objects boiled up like rotting vegetation stirred from the bottom of a black pond and then were sucked downward again, to be replaced by a new wave of humanity's junk.

He couldn't stand to watch it, but he couldn't make himself stop looking. With dreadful, hypnotic fascination, he watched blue streaks of lightning lance through the clouds. The Boeing shuddered, leaned over on its port wing and strained upward again, plummeted and rose like a roller-coaster ride. Something huge and flaming streaked past the president's window, and he thought that it might've been part of a train thrown into the air by the tremendous shock waves and super-tornado-force winds shrieking across the scorched earth below.

Someone reached forward and pulled down the smoked-glass visor that shielded the president's window. "I don't think you need to look anymore, sir."

For a few seconds, the president struggled to recognize the man who sat in the black leather seat facing his own. Hans, he thought. Secretary of Defense Hannan. He looked around himself, his mind groping for equilibrium. He was in the Boeing Airborne Command Center, in his quarters at the tail of the aircraft. Hannan was seated in front of him, and across the aisle sat a man in the uniform of an Air Force Special Intelligence captain; the man was ramrod-straight and square-shouldered, and he wore a pair of sunglasses that obscured his eyes. Around his right wrist was a handcuff, and the other end of the chain was attached to a small black briefcase that sat on the Formica-topped table before him.

Beyond the door of the president's cubicle, the aircraft was a bristling nerve center of radar screens, data processing computers, and communications gear linked to Strategic Air Command, North American Air Defense, SHAPE command in Europe, and all the air force, naval and ICBM bases in the United States. The technicians who operated the equipment had been chosen by the Defense Intelligence Agency, which had also chosen and trained the man with the black briefcase. Also aboard the aircraft were DIA officers and several air force and army generals, assigned special duty on Airborne Command, whose responsibility was constructing a picture of reports coming in from the various theaters of conflict.

The jet had been circling over Virginia since 0600 hours, and at 0946 the first electrifying reports had come in from Naval Central: contact between hunter-killer task forces and a large wolf pack of Soviet nuclear submarines north of Bermuda.

According to the early reports, the Soviet submarines had

fired ballistic missiles at 0958, but the later reports indicated that an American submarine commander might have launched Cruise missiles without proper authorization in the stress of the moment. It was hard now to tell who had fired first. Now it no longer mattered. The first Soviet strike had hit Washington, D.C., three warheads plowing into the Pentagon, a fourth hitting the Capitol and a fifth striking Andrews Air Force Base. Within two minutes the missiles launched at New York had struck Wall Street and Times Square. In rapid succession the Soviet SLBMs had marched along the eastern seaboard, but by that time B-1 bombers were flying toward the heart of Russia, American submarines ringing the Soviet Union were firing their weapons, and NATO and Warsaw Pact missiles were screaming over Europe. Russian submarines lurking off the West Coast launched nuclear warheads, striking Los Angeles, San Francisco, San Diego, Seattle, Portland, Phoenix and Denver, and then the longer-range Russian multiple-warhead ICBMs—the really nasty bastards—had streaked in over Alaska and the pole, hitting air force bases and midwestern missile installations, incinerating heartland cities in a matter of minutes. Omaha had been one of the first targets, and with it Strategic Air Command headquarters. At 1209 hours the last garbled signal from NORAD had come through the technicians' earphones: "Final birds away."

And with that message, which meant that a last few Minuteman III or Cruise missiles had been fired from hidden silos somewhere in western America, NORAD went off the air.

Hannan wore a pair of earphones, through which he'd been monitoring the reports as they filtered in. The president had taken his earphones off when NORAD had gone dead. He tasted ashes in his mouth, and he couldn't bear to think about what was in that black briefcase across the aisle.

Hannan listened to the distant voices of submarine commanders and bomber pilots, still hunting targets or trying to avoid destruction in fast, furious conflicts halfway around the planet. Naval task forces on both sides had been wiped out, and now western Europe was being hammered between the ground troops. He kept his mind fixed on the faraway, ghostly voices floating through the storm of static, because to think about anything else but the job at hand might have driven him crazy. He wasn't called Iron Hans for nothing, and he knew he must not let memories and regrets weaken him.

The Airborne Command Center was hit by turbulence that lifted the aircraft violently and then dropped it again with sickening speed. The president clung to the armrests of his seat. He knew he would never see his wife and son again. Washington was a lunar landscape of burning rubble, the Declaration of Independence and the Constitution ashes in the shattered Archives building, the dreams of a million minds destroyed in the inferno of the Library of Congress. And it had happened so fast—so *fast!*

He wanted to cry and wanted to scream, but he was the president of the United States. His cuff links bore the presidential seal. He recalled, as if from a vast and terrible distance, asking Julianne how the blue checked shirt would look with his tan suit. He hadn't been able to choose a tie, because it was too much of a decision. He couldn't think anymore, couldn't figure anything out; his brain felt like a lump of saltwater taffy. Julianne had chosen the proper tie for him, had put the cuff links in his shirt. And then he'd kissed her and embraced his son, and the Secret Service men had taken them away with other staff members to the Basement.

It's all gone, he thought. Oh, Jesus . . . it's all gone. He opened his eyes and pushed up the visor again. Black clouds, glowing with red and orange centers, loomed around the aircraft. From the midst of them shot gouts of fire and lightning streaking upward a thousand feet above the plane.

Once upon a time, he thought, we had a love affair with fire.

"Sir?" Hannan said quietly. He took his earphones off. The president's face was gray, and his mouth was twitching badly. Hannan thought the man was going to be airsick. "Are you all right?"

The deadened eyes moved in the pallid face. "A-OK," he whispered, and he smiled tightly.

Hannan listened to more voices coming in. "The last of the

B-1s just went down over the Baltic. The Soviets hit Frankfurt eight minutes ago, and six minutes ago London was struck by a multiple-warhead ICBM," he relayed to the president.

The other man sat like stone. "What about casualty estimations?" he asked wearily.

"Not coming through yet. The voices are so garbled even the computers can't squelch all the static out."

"I always liked Paris," the president whispered. "Julianne and I had our honeymoon in Paris, you know. What about Paris?"

"I don't know. Nothing's coming out of France."

"And China?"

"Still silent. I think the Chinese are biding their time."

The aircraft lurched and dropped again. Engines screamed through the dirty air, fighting for altitude. A reflection of blue lightning streaked across the president's face. "All right," he said. "Here we are. Where do we go from here?"

Hannan started to reply, but he didn't know what to say. His throat had closed up. He reached out to shut the visor again, but the president said firmly, "No. Leave it up. I want to see." His head slowly turned toward Hannan. "It's over, isn't it?"

Hannan nodded.

"How many millions are already dead, Hans?"

"I don't know, sir. I wouldn't care to—"

"Don't patronize me!" the president shouted suddenly, so loud even the rigid air force captain jumped. "I asked you a question and I want an answer—a best estimate, a guess, *anything!* You've been listening to those reports! Tell me!"

"In . . . the northern hemisphere," the secretary of defense replied shakily, his iron façade beginning to crack like cheap plastic, "I'd estimate . . . between three hundred and five hundred fifty. Million."

The president's eyes closed. "And how many are going to be dead a week from now? A month? Six months?"

"Possibly . . . another two hundred million in the next month, from injuries and radiation. Beyond that . . . no one knows but God."

"God," the president repeated. A tear broke and trickled down his cheek. "God's looking at me right now, Hans. I feel Him watching me. He knows I've murdered the world. *Me.* I've murdered the world." He put his hands to his face and moaned. America is gone, he thought. Gone. "Oh . . ." he sobbed. "Oh . . . no . . ."

"I think it's time, sir." Hannan's voice was almost gentle.

The president looked up. His wet, glassy eyes moved toward the black briefcase across the aisle. He snapped his gaze away again and stared out the window. How many could possibly be still alive in that holocaust, he wondered. No. A better question was: How many would *want* to be alive? Because in his briefings and research on nuclear warfare, one thing was very clear to him: The hundreds of millions who perished in the first few hours would be the lucky ones. It was the survivors who would endure a thousand forms of damnation.

I am still the president of the United States of America, he told himself. Yes. And I still have one more decision to make.

The airplane vibrated as if over a cobblestone road. Black clouds enveloped the craft for a few seconds, and in the dark domain fire and lightning leapt at the windows. Then the plane veered to starboard and continued circling, weaving between the black plumes.

He thought of his wife and son. Gone. Thought of Washington and the White House. Gone. Thought of New York City and Boston. Gone. Thought of the forests and highways of the land beneath him, thought of the meadows and prairies and beaches. Gone, all gone.

"Take us there," he said.

Hannan flipped open one of his armrests and exposed the small control console there. He pressed a button that opened the intercom line between the cubicle and the pilot's deck, then he gave his code name and repeated coordinates for a new course. The aircraft circled and began flying inland, away from the ruins of Washington. "We'll be in range within fifteen minutes," he said.

"Will you . . . pray with me?" the president whispered, and together they bowed their heads.

When they had finished their prayer, Hannan said, "Captain? We're ready now," and he gave up his seat to the officer with the briefcase.

The man sat across from the president and held the briefcase on his knees. He unlocked the handcuff with a little laser that resembled a pocket flashlight. Then he took a sealed envelope from the inside pocket of his coat and tore it open, producing a small golden key. He inserted the key into one of two locks on the briefcase and turned it to the right. The lock disengaged with a high electronic tone. The officer turned the briefcase to face the president, who also brought out a sealed envelope from his coat pocket, tore it open and took out a silver key. He slipped it into the briefcase's second lock, clicked it to the left, and again there was a high tone, slightly different from the first.

The air force captain lifted the briefcase's lid.

Inside was a small computer keyboard, with a flat screen that popped up as the lid was raised. At the bottom of the keyboard were three small circles: green, yellow and red. The green one had begun flashing.

Beside the president's seat, fixed to the aircraft's starboard bulkhead beneath the window, was a small black box with two cords—one red and one green—coiled under it. The president uncoiled the cords, slowly and deliberately; at the ends of the cords were plugs, which he inserted into appropriate sockets on the side of the computer keyboard. The black power pack now connected the keyboard to one of the five-mile-long retractable antennae that trailed behind the Airborne Command craft.

The president hesitated only a few seconds. The decision was made.

He typed in his three-letter identification code.

HELLO, MR. PRESIDENT, the computer screen read out.

He settled back to wait, a nerve twitching at the corner of his mouth.

Hannan looked at his watch. "We're within range, sir."

Slowly, precisely, the president typed, *Here is Belladonna, the Lady of the Rocks, the lady of situations.*

The computer replied, HERE IS THE MAN WITH THREE STAVES, AND HERE THE WHEEL.

The aircraft was buffeted and tossed. Something scraped along the port side of the jet like fingernails along a blackboard.

The president typed, *And here is the one-eyed merchant, and this card—*

WHICH IS BLANK, IS SOMETHING HE CARRIES ON HIS BACK, replied the computer.

Which I am forbidden to see, the president typed.

The yellow circle illuminated.

The president took a deep breath, as if about to leap into dark, bottomless water. He typed, *I do not find The Hanged Man.*

FEAR DEATH BY WATER, came the reply.

The red circle illuminated. Immediately, the screen cleared.

Then the computer reported, TALONS ARMED, SIR. TEN SECONDS TO ABORT.

"God forgive me," the president whispered, and his finger moved toward the N key.

"Jesus!" the air force captain suddenly said. He was staring through the window, his mouth agape.

The president looked.

Through a tornado of burning houses and chunks of scorched rubble, a fiery shape streaked upward toward the Airborne Command Center like a meteor. It took the president a precious two seconds to comprehend what it was: a crushed, mangled Greyhound bus with burning wheels, and hanging from the broken windows and front windshield were charred corpses.

The destination plate above the windshield said CHARTER.

The pilot must've seen it at the same time, because the engines shrieked as they were throttled to their limit and the nose jerked up with such violence that g-forces crushed the president into his seat as if he weighed five hundred pounds. The briefcase and the computer keyboard spun off the captain's knees, the two plugs wrenching loose; the briefcase fell into the aisle and slid along it, jamming beneath another seat. The president saw the wrecked bus roll on its side, spilling bodies from the windows. They fell like burning leaves. And then the bus hit the starboard wing with a shuddering crash, and the outboard engine exploded.

Half of the wing was sheared raggedly away, the second starboard engine shooting plumes of flame like Roman candles going off. Ripped apart by the impact, pieces of the Greyhound bus fell back into the maelstrom and were sucked downward out of sight.

Crippled, the Airborne Command Center heeled over on its port wing, the two remaining functional engines vibrating, about to burst loose from their bolts under the strain. The president heard himself scream. The aircraft fell out of control for five thousand feet as the pilot battled with straining flaps and rudders. An updraft caught it and flung the jet a thousand feet higher, and then it screamed downward another ten thousand feet. The aircraft spun wing over wrecked wing and finally angled down toward the ruined earth.

The black clouds closed in its wake, and the president of the United States was gone.

THREE
Lights Out

'Round the mulberry bush / Not yet three / The holy axe / The world's champion upchucker / Come a cropper / Start with one step

Twelve

I'm in Hell! Sister Creep thought hysterically. I'm dead and in Hell and burning with the sinners!

Another wave of raw pain crashed over her. "Help me, Jesus!" she tried to scream, but she could only manage a hoarse, animalish moan. She sobbed, clenching her teeth until the pain had ebbed again. She lay in total darkness, and she thought she could hear the screams of the burning sinners from the distant depths of Hell—faint, horrible wailings and shrieks that came floating to her like the odors of brimstone, steam and scorched flesh that had brought her back to consciousness.

Dear Jesus, save me from Hell! she begged. Don't let me burn forever!

The fierce pain returned, gnawing at her. She contorted into a fetal position, and water sloshed into her face and up her nose. She half sputtered, half screamed and drew a breath of acrid, steamy air. Water, she thought. Water. I'm lying in water. And the memories began to glow in her feverish mind like hot coals at the bottom of a grill.

She sat up, her body heavy and swollen, and when she lifted a hand to her face the blisters on her cheeks and forehead broke, streaming fluids. "I'm not in Hell," she rasped. "I'm not dead . . . yet." She remembered now where she was, but she couldn't understand what had happened, or where the fire had come from. "I'm not dead," she repeated, in a louder voice. She heard it echo in the tunnel, and she shouted *"I'm not dead!"* through her cracked and blistered lips.

Still, agonizing pain continued to course through her. One second she was burning up, and the next she was freezing; she was tired, very tired, and she wanted to lie down in the water again and sleep, but she was afraid that if she did she might not wake up. She reached out in the darkness, seeking her canvas bag, and had a few seconds of panic when she couldn't find it. Then her hands touched charred and soggy canvas and she drew the bag to her, clutching it as closely as a child.

Sister Creep tried to stand. Her legs gave way almost at once, so she sat in the water enduring the pain and trying to summon up her strength. The blisters on her face were puckering again, tightening her face like a mask. Lifting her hand, she felt along her forehead and then up into her hair; her cap was gone, and her hair felt like the stubbly grass of a lawn that had gone a whole sweltering summer without a drop of rain. I'm burned baldheaded! she thought, and a half giggle, half sob came up from her throat. More blisters burst on her scalp, and she quickly took her hand away because she didn't want to know any more. She tried to stand again, and this time she made it all the way up.

She touched the edge of the tunnel floor, at a level just above her stomach's bulge. She was going to have to pull herself out by sheer strength. Her shoulders were still throbbing from the effort of tearing the grate loose, but that pain was nothing compared to the suffering of her blistered skin. Sister Creep tossed the canvas bag up; sooner or later she'd have to force herself to climb out and get it. She placed her palms on the concrete and tensed herself to push upward, but her willpower evaporated, and she stood there thinking that some maintenance man was going to come down here in a year or two and find a skeleton where a living woman had once been.

She pushed upward. The strained muscles of her shoulders shrieked with pain, and one elbow threatened to give way. But as she started to topple backward into the hole she brought a knee up and got it on the edge, then got the other knee up. Blisters burst on her arms and legs with little wet popping sounds. She scrabbled over the edge like a crab and lay on her stomach on the tunnel floor, dizzy and breathing heavily, her hands again clutching the bag.

Get up, she thought. Get moving, you slob bucket, or you're going to die here.

She stood up, holding her bag protectively in front of her, and began to stumble through the darkness; her legs were stiff as chunks of wood, and several times she fell over rubble or broken cables. But she paused only long enough to catch her breath and fight back the pain, and then she struggled to her feet and went on.

She bumped into a ladder and climbed it, but the shaft was blocked by cables, chunks of concrete and pipe; she returned to the tunnel and kept going in search of a way out. In some places the air was hot and thin, and she took little gulps of breath to keep from passing out. She felt her way along the tunnel, came to dead ends of jumbled debris and had to retrace her path, found other ladders that ascended to blocked shafts or manhole covers that refused to be budged. Her mind battered back and forth like a caged animal. One step at a time, she told herself. One step and then the next gets you where you're going.

Blisters rose and fell on her face, arms and legs. She stopped and sat down for a while to rest, her lungs wheezing in the heavy air. There were no sounds of subway trains or cars or burning sinners. Something terrible's happened up there, she thought. Not the Rapture, not the Second Coming —something *terrible.*

Sister Creep forced herself onward. One step at a time. One step and then the next.

She found another ladder and looked up. About twenty feet above, at the top of the shaft, was a half moon of murky light. She climbed up until she was near enough to touch a manhole cover, shaken two inches out of its socket by the same shock wave that had made the tunnel vibrate. She got the fingers of one hand in between the iron and the concrete and shoved the manhole cover out of the way.

The light was the color of dried blood, and as hazy as if filtered through layers of thick gauze. Still, she had to squint until her eyes were used to light again.

She was looking up at the sky, but a kind of sky she'd never seen before: dirty brown clouds were spinning over Manhattan, and flickers of blue lightning crackled out of them. A hot, bitter wind swirled into her face, the force of it almost knocking her loose from the ladder. In the distance there was the rumble of thunder, but a different kind of thunder than she'd ever heard—this sounded like a sledgehammer banging iron. The wind made a howling noise as it swept into the manhole, pushing her backward, but she pulled herself and her bag up the last two rungs of the ladder and crawled into the outside world again.

The wind blew a storm of grit into her face, and she was blinded for a few seconds. When her vision cleared again, she saw that she had come out of the tunnel into what looked like a junkyard.

Around her were the crushed hulks of cars, taxis and trucks, some of them melted together to form strange sculptures of metal. The tires on some of the vehicles were still smoking, while others had dissolved into black puddles. Gaping fissures had burst open in the pavement, some of them five and six feet wide; through many of the cracks came gouts of steam or water like gushing geysers. She looked around, dazed and uncomprehending, her eyes slitted against the gritty wind. In some places the earth had collapsed, and in others there were mountains of rubble, miniature Everests of metal, stone and glass. Between them the wind shrieked and turned, spun and rose around the fragments of buildings, many of which had been shaken apart right to their steel skeletons, which in turn were warped and bent like licorice sticks. Curtains of dense smoke from burning buildings and heaps of debris flapped before the rushing wind, and lightning streaked to earth from the black heart of roiling, immense clouds. She couldn't see the sun, couldn't even tell where it lay in the turbulent sky. She looked for the Empire State Building, but there were no more skyscrapers; all the buildings she could see had been sheared off, though she couldn't tell if the Empire State was still standing or not because of the smoke and dust. It was not Manhattan anymore, but a ravaged junkyard of rubble mountains and smoke-filled ravines.

Judgment of God, she thought. God has struck down an evil city, has swept all the sinners down to burn in Hell forever! Crazy laughter rang out inside her, and as she lifted her face toward the dirty clouds the fluids of burst blisters streamed down her cheeks.

A spear of lightning hit the exposed framework of a nearby building, and sparks danced madly in the air. Beyond the rise of a huge mountain of debris, Sister Creep could see the funnel of a tornado in the distance, and another one writhing to the right. Up in the clouds, fiery things were being tossed like red balls in the hands of a juggler. All gone, all destroyed, she thought. The end of the world. Praise God! Praise blessed Jesus! The end of the world, and all the sinners burning in—

She clasped her hands over her ears and screamed. Something inside her brain cracked like a funhouse mirror that existed only to reflect a distorted world, and as the fragments of the funhouse mirror fell apart other images were revealed behind it: herself as a younger, more attractive woman, pushing a stroller in a shopping mall; a suburban brick house with a small green yard and a station wagon in the driveway; a town with a main street and a statue in the square; faces, some of them dark and indistinct, others just on the edge of memory; and then the blue flashing lights and the rain and the demon in a yellow raincoat, reaching out and saying, "Give her to me, lady. It's okay, just give her to me now. . . ."

All gone, all destroyed! Judgment of God! Praise Jesus!

"Just give her to me now. . . ."

No, she thought. No!

All gone, all destroyed! All the sinners, burning in Hell!

No! *No! No!*

And then she opened her mouth and shrieked because

everything was gone and destroyed in fire and ruin, and in that instant she realized no God of Creation would destroy His masterpiece in one fit of flame like a petulant child. This was not Judgment Day, or Rapture, or the Second Coming—this had nothing to do with God; this was utter, evil destruction without sense or purpose or sanity.

For the first time since crawling out of the manhole Sister Creep looked at her blistered hands and arms, at the tattered rags of her clothing. Her skin was splotched with angry red burns, the blisters stretched tight with yellow fluid. Her bag was just barely held together by scraps of canvas, her belongings spilling out through burned holes. And then around her, in the pall of dust and smoke, she saw other things that at first her mind had not let her see: flattened, charred things that could only remotely be recognized as human remains. A pile of them lay almost at her feet, as if heaped there by someone sweeping out a coal scuttle. They littered the street, lay half in and half out of the crushed cars and taxis; here was one wrapped around the remnants of a bicycle, there was another with its teeth showing startlingly white against the crisped, featureless face. Hundreds of them lay around her, their bones melded into shapes of surrealistic horror.

Lightning flashed, and the wind wailed with a banshee voice of the dead around Sister Creep's ears.

She ran.

The wind whipped into her face, blinding her with smoke, dust and ashes. She ducked her head, hobbling up the side of a rubble mountain, and she realized she'd left her bag behind but she couldn't bear returning to that valley of the dead. She tripped over debris, dislodging an avalanche of junk that cascaded around her legs—shattered television sets and stereo equipment, the melted mess of home computers, ghetto blasters, radios, the burned rags of men's silk suits and women's designer dresses, broken fragments of fine furniture, charred books, antique silverware reduced to chunks of metal. And everywhere there were more smashed vehicles and bodies buried in the wreckage—hundreds of bodies and pieces of bodies, arms and legs protruding from the debris as stiffly as those of department store mannequins. She reached the top of the mountain, where the hot wind was so fierce she had to fall to her knees to keep from being thrown off. Looking in all directions, she saw the full extent of the disaster: To the north, the few remaining trees in Central Park were burning, and fires extended all along what had been Eighth Avenue, glowing like blood-red rubies behind the curtain of smoke; to the east, there was no sign of Rockefeller Center or Grand Central Station, just shattered structures rising up like rotten teeth from a diseased jaw; to the south, the Empire State Building seemed to be gone, too, and the funnel of a tornado danced near Wall Street; to the west, ridges of debris marched all the way to the Hudson River. The panorama of destruction was both a pinnacle of horror and a numbing of it, because her mind reached the limit of its ability to accept and process shock and began flipping out memories of cartoons and comedies she'd seen as a child: Jetsons, Huckleberry Hound, Mighty Mouse and Three Stooges. She crouched at the top of the mountain in the grip of a shrieking wind and stared dumbly out at the ruins while a hideous fixed smile stretched her mouth, and only one sane thought got through: Oh my Jesus, what's happened to the magic place?

And the answer was: All gone, all destroyed.

"Get up," she said to herself, though the wind swept her voice away. "Get up. You think you're gonna stay here? You can't stay here! Get up, and take one step at a time. One step and then the next gets you where you're going."

But it was a long time before she could move again, and she stumbled down the far side of the rubble mountain like an old woman, muttering to herself.

She didn't know where she was going, nor did she particularly care. The intensity of the lightning increased, and thunder shook the ground; a black, nasty-looking drizzle began to fall from the clouds, blowing like needles before the howling wind. Sister Creep stumbled from one mountain of wreckage to the next. Off in the distance she thought she heard a woman screaming, and she called out but wasn't answered. The rain fell harder, and the wind blew into her face like a slap.

And then—she didn't know how much longer it was—she came down a ridge of debris and stopped in her tracks beside the crushed remnant of a yellow cab. A street sign stood nearby, bent almost into a knot, and it said Forty-second. Of all the buildings along the street, only one was standing.

The marquee above the Empire State Theater was still blinking, advertising *Face of Death, Part Four* and *Mondo Bizarro*. On both sides of the theater building, the structures had been reduced to burned-out shells, but the theater itself wasn't even scorched. She remembered passing that theater the night before, and the brutal shove that had knocked her into the street. Smoke passed between her and the theater, and she expected the building to be gone like a mirage in the next second, but when the smoke whipped on the theater was still there, and the marquee was still blinking merrily.

Turn away, she told herself. Get the hell out of here!

But she took one step toward it, and then the next got her where she was going. She stood in front of the theater doors and smelled buttered popcorn from within. No! she thought. It's not possible!

But it was not possible, either, that the city of New York should be turned into a tornado-swept wasteland in a handful of hours. Staring at those theater doors, Sister Creep knew that the rules of this world had been suddenly and drastically changed by a force she couldn't even begin to understand. "I'm crazy," she told herself. But the theater was real, and so was the aroma of buttered popcorn. She peered into the ticket booth, but it was empty; then she braced herself, touched the crucifix and gemclip chain that hung around her neck, and went through the doors.

There was no one behind the concession counter, but Sister Creep could hear the movie going on in the auditorium behind a faded red curtain; there was the grating sound of a car crash, and then a narrator's voice intoning, "And here before your eyes is the result of a head-on collision at sixty miles an hour."

Sister Creep reached over the counter, grabbed two Hershey bars from the display, and was about to eat one when she heard the snarl of an animal.

The sound rose, reaching the register of a human laugh. But in it Sister Creep heard the squeal of tires on a rain-slick highway and a child's piercing, heartbreaking scream: *"Mommy!"*

She clapped her hands over her ears until the child's cry was gone, and she stood shivering until all memory of it had faded. The laughter was gone, too, but whoever had made it was still sitting in there, watching a movie in the middle of a destroyed city.

She crammed half a Hershey bar into her mouth, chewed and swallowed it. Behind the red curtain, the narrator was talking about rapes and murders with cool, clinical detachment. The curtain beckoned her. She ate the other half of the Hershey bar and licked her fingers. If that awful laughter swelled again, she thought, she might lose her mind, but she had to see who had made it. She walked to the curtain and slowly, slowly, drew it aside.

On the screen was the bruised, dead face of a young woman, but such a sight held no power to shock Sister Creep anymore. She could see the outline of a head—someone sitting up in the front row, face tilted upward at the screen. The rest of the seats were empty. Sister Creep stared at that head, could not see the face and didn't want to, because whoever—whatever—it was couldn't possibly be human.

The head suddenly swiveled toward her.

Sister Creep drew back. Her legs wanted to run, but she didn't let them go. The figure in the front row was just staring at her as the film continued to show close-ups of people lying on coroners' slabs. And then the figure stood up from the seat, and Sister Creep heard popcorn crunch on the floor beneath its shoes. Run! she screamed inwardly. Get out! But she stood her ground, and the figure stopped before its face was revealed by the light from the concession counter.

"You're all burned up." It was the soft and pleasant voice of a young man. He was thin and tall, about six feet four or five, dressed in a pair of dark green khaki trousers and a yellow T-shirt. On his feet were polished combat boots. "I guess it's over out there by now, isn't it?"

"All gone," she murmured. "All destroyed." She caught a dank chill, the same thing she'd experienced the previous night in front of the theater, and then it was gone. She could see the faintest impression of features on the man's face, and she thought she saw him smile, but it was a terrible smile; his mouth didn't seem to be exactly where it should. "I think . . . everyone's dead," she told him.

"Not everyone," he corrected. "*You're* not dead, are you? And I think there are others still alive out there, too. Hiding somewhere, probably. Waiting to die. It won't be long, though. Not long for *you,* either."

"I'm not dead yet," she said.

"You might as well be." His chest expanded as he drew in a deep breath. "Smell that air! Isn't it sweet?"

Sister Creep started to take a backward step. The man said, almost gently, *"No,"* and she stopped as if the most important—the *only* important—thing in the world was to obey.

"My best scene's coming up." He motioned toward the screen, where flames shot out of a building and broken bodies were lying on stretchers. "That's me! Standing by the car! Well, I didn't say it was a *long* scene." His attention drifted back to her. "Oh," he said softly. "I like your necklace." His pale hand with its long, slender fingers slid toward her throat.

She wanted to cringe away because she couldn't bear to be touched by that hand, but she was transfixed by his voice, echoing back and forth in her mind. She flinched as the cold fingers touched the crucifix. He pulled at it, but both the crucifix and the gemclip chain were sealed to her skin.

"It's burned on," the man said. "We'll fix that."

With a quick snap of his wrist he ripped the crucifix and chain off, taking Sister Creep's skin with it. Pain shot through her like an electric shock, at the same time breaking up the echo of the man's command and clearing her head. Tears burned fiery trails down her cheeks.

The man held his hand palm up, the crucifix and chain

dangling before Sister Creep's face. He began to sing in the voice of a little boy: "Here we go 'round the mulberry bush, the mulberry bush, the mulberry bush . . ."

His palm caught fire, the flames crawling up along his fingers. As the man's hand became a glove of flame the crucifix and chain began to melt and dribble to the floor.

"Here we go 'round the mulberry bush, so early in the morrrrning!"

Sister Creep looked into his face. By the light of the flaming hand she could see the shifting bones, the melting cheeks and lips, eyes of different colors surfacing where there were no sockets.

The last droplet of molten metal spattered to the floor. A mouth opened across the man's chin like a red-rimmed wound. The mouth grinned. "Lights *out!*" it whispered.

The film stopped, the frame burning away on the screen. The red curtain that Sister Creep was still holding on to burst into flames, and she screamed and jerked her hands away. A wave of sickening heat swept through the theater, the walls drooling fire.

"Tick tock tick tock!" the man's voice continued, in a merry singsong rhythm. "Nothing ever stops the clock!"

The ceiling blazed and buckled. Sister Creep shielded her head with her arms and staggered backward through the fiery curtains as he advanced on her. Streams of chocolate ran from the concession counter. She ran toward the door, and the thing behind her brayed, "Run! Run, you pig!"

She was three strides out the door before it became a sheet of fire, and then she was running madly through the ruins of Forty-second Street. When she dared to look back, she saw the entire theater bellowing flame, the building's roof imploding as if driven down by a brutal fist.

She flung herself behind a block of stone as a storm of glass and bricks hurtled around her. It was all over in a few seconds, but Sister Creep stayed huddled up, shivering with terror, until all the bricks had stopped falling. She peered out from behind her shelter.

Now the ruins of the theater were indistinguishable from

any of the other piles of ash. The theater was gone, and so—thankfully—was the thing with the flaming hand.

She touched the raw circle of flesh that ringed her throat, and her fingers came away bloody. It took another moment for her to grasp that the crucifix and chain were really gone. She couldn't remember where she'd gotten it from, but it was something she'd been proud of. She'd thought that it protected her, too, and now she felt naked and defenseless.

She knew she'd looked into the face of evil there in that cheap theater.

The black rain was falling harder. Sister Creep curled up, her hand pressed to her bleeding throat, and she closed her eyes and prayed for death.

Jesus Christ was not coming in His flying saucer after all, she realized. Judgment Day had destroyed the innocent in the same flames that killed the guilty, and the Rapture was a lunatic's dream.

A sob of anguish broke from her throat. She prayed, Please, Jesus, take me home, please, right now, this minute, please, please . . .

But when she opened her eyes the black rain was still falling.

The wind was getting stronger, and now it carried a winter's chill. She was drenched, sick to her stomach, and her teeth were chattering.

Wearily, she sat up. Jesus was not coming today. She would have to die later, she decided. There was no use lying out here like a fool in the rain.

One step, she thought. One step and then the next gets you where you're going.

Where that was, she didn't know, but from now on she'd have to be very careful, because that evil thing with no face and all faces could be lurking anywhere. *Anywhere.* The rules had changed. The Promised Land was a boneyard, and Hell itself had broken through the earth's surface.

She had no idea what had caused such destruction, but a terrible thing occurred to her: What if everywhere was like this? She let the thought go before it burned into her brain, and she struggled to her feet.

The wind staggered her. The rain was falling so heavily that she couldn't see beyond four feet in any direction. She decided to go toward what she thought was north, because there might be a tree left to rest under in Central Park.

Her back bowed against the elements, she started with one step.

Thirteen

"House fell in, Mama!" Josh Hutchins yelled as he struggled free of the dirt, rubble and pieces of snapped timbers that covered his back. "Twister's done gone!" His mother didn't answer, but he could hear her crying. "It's all right, Mama! We're gonna be . . ."

The memory of an Alabama tornado that had driven Josh, his sister and his mother into the basement of their home when he was seven years old suddenly broke and whirled apart. The cornfield, the burning spears and the tornado of fire came back to him with horrifying clarity, and he realized the crying woman was the little girl's mother.

It was dark. A weight still bore down on Josh, and as he fought against it a mound of rubble, mostly the dirt and broken wood, slid off him. He sat upright, his body throbbing with dull pain.

His face felt funny—so tight it was about to rip. He lifted his fingers to touch his forehead, and a dozen blisters broke, the fluids oozing down his face. More blisters burst on his cheeks and jaw; he touched the flesh around his eyes and found they were swollen into slits. The pain was getting sharper, and his back felt as if it had been splashed with boiling water. Burned, he thought. Burned to hell and back. He smelled the odor of fried bacon, and he almost puked but he was too intent on finding out the extent of his injuries. At his right ear there was a different kind of pain. He gently touched it. His fingers grazed a stub of flesh and crusted blood where his ear had been. He remembered the explosion of the pumps, and he figured that a hot sliver of metal had sliced most of his ear clean off.

I'm in fine shape, he thought, and he almost laughed out loud. Ready to take on the world! He knew that if he ever stepped into a wrestling ring again, he wouldn't need a Frankenstein mask to resemble a monster.

And then he did throw up, his body heaving and shuddering, the fried bacon smell thick in his nostrils. When his sickness had passed, he crawled away from the mess. Under his hands were loose dirt, timbers, broken glass, dented cans and cornstalks.

He heard a man moaning, remembered PawPaw's burning eyeballs, and figured that the man was lying somewhere to his right, though his ear on that side was clogged up. The woman's sobbing would put her a few feet in front of him; the little girl, if she was still alive, was silent. The air was still warm, but at least it was breathable. Josh's fingers closed on a wooden shaft, and he followed it to the end of a garden hoe. Digging into the dirt around him, he found a variety of objects: can after can, some of them broken open and leaking; a couple of melted things that might have once been plastic milk jugs; a hammer; some charred magazines and packs of cigarettes. The entire grocery store had caved in on top of them, spilling everything into PawPaw's fallout shelter. And that's surely what it was, Josh reasoned. The underground boys must have known he might need it someday.

Josh tried to stand, but he bumped his head before he could straighten up from a crouch. He felt a ceiling of hard-packed dirt, planks and possibly hundreds of rough cornstalks jammed together about four and a half feet off the basement floor. Oh, Jesus! Josh thought. There must be tons of earth right over our heads! He figured they had nothing more than a pocket of air down here, and when that was gone . . .

"Stop crying, lady," he said. "The old man's hurt worse than you are."

She gasped, as if she hadn't realized anyone else was alive.

"Where's the little girl? She okay?" Blisters popped on Josh's lips.

"Swan!" Darleen shouted. She searched for Sue Wanda through the dirt. "I can't find her! Where's my baby? Where's Swan?" Then her left hand touched a small arm. It was still warm. "Here she is! Oh, God, she's buried!" Darleen started digging frantically.

Josh crawled to her side and made out the child's body with his hands. But only her legs and left arm were buried; her face was free, and she was breathing. Josh got the child's legs uncovered, and Darleen embraced her daughter. "Swan, you okay? Say somethin', Swan! Come on now! Talk to Mama!" She shook the child until one of Swan's hands came up and pushed weakly at her.

"Quit." Swan's voice was a hoarse, slurred whisper. "Wanna sleep . . . till we get there."

Josh crawled toward the man's moaning. He found PawPaw curled up and half buried. Carefully, Josh dug him out. PawPaw's hand caught in the shreds of Josh's shirt, and the old man muttered something that Josh couldn't understand. He said, "What?" and bent his head closer.

"The sun," PawPaw repeated. "Oh, Lord . . . I saw the sun blow up." He started muttering again, something about his bedroom slippers. Josh knew he couldn't last much longer and went back to Darleen and Swan.

The little girl was crying—a quiet, deeply wounded sound. "Shhhh," Darleen said. "Shhhh, honey. They're gonna find us. Don't you worry. They'll get us out of here." She still didn't fully grasp what had happened; everything was hazy and jumbled past the moment when Swan had pointed to the PAWPAW's sign on the interstate and said she was going to bust if she couldn't go to the bathroom.

"I can't see, Mama," Swan said listlessly.

"We're gonna be all right, honey. They're gonna find us real . . ." She'd reached up to smooth back her daughter's hair and jerked her hand away. Her fingers had found stubble. "Oh, my God. Oh, Swan, oh, baby . . ." She was afraid to touch her own hair and face, but she felt nothing more uncomfortable than the pain of a moderate sunburn. I'm okay, she told herself. And Swan's okay, too. Just lost some hair, that's all. We're gonna be just fine!

"Where's PawPaw?" Swan asked. "Where's the giant?" She had a toothache all over her body, and she smelled breakfast cooking.

"I'm right here," Josh answered. "The old man's not too far away. We're in the basement, and the whole place caved in on—"

"We're gonna get out!" Darleen interrupted. "It won't be too long before somebody finds us!"

"Lady, that might not be for a while. We're going to have to settle down and save our air."

"Save our air?" Panic flared anew. "We're breathin' okay!"

"Right now, yeah. I don't know how much room we've got in here, but I figure the air's going to get pretty tight. We might have to stay in here for . . . for a long time," he decided to say.

"You're crazy! Don't you listen to him, honey. I'll bet they're comin' to dig us out right this minute." She began to rock Swan like an infant.

"No, lady." It was pointless to pretend. "I don't think anybody's going to dig us out anytime soon. Those were missiles that came out of that cornfield. Nuclear missiles. I don't know if one of them blew up or what, but there's only one reason those damned things would've gone off. The whole world may be shooting missiles at itself right now."

The woman laughed, the sound edging toward hysteria. "You ain't got the sense God gave a pissant! Somebody had to see all that fire! They'll send help! We gotta get to Blakeman!"

"Right," Josh said. He was tired of talking, and he was using up precious air. He crawled away a few feet and burrowed a place to fit his body into. Intense thirst taunted him, but he had to relieve himself, too. Later, he thought, too tired to move. The pain was getting bad again. His mind began to drift beyond PawPaw's basement, beyond the burned cornfield toward what might remain out there, if, indeed, World War III had started. It might be over by now. The Russians might be invading, or the Americans pushing into Russia. He thought of Rose and the boys; were they dead or alive? He might never know. "Oh, God," he whispered in the dark, and he curled his body up to stare at nothing.

"Uh . . . uh . . . uh." PawPaw was making a stuttering, choking noise. Then he said loudly, "Gopher's in the hole! Amy! Where're my bedroom slippers?"

The little girl made another hurt, sobbing sound, and Josh clenched his teeth to hold back a scream of outrage. Such a pretty child, he thought. And now dying—like all of us are dying. We're already in our graves. Already laid out and waiting.

He had the sensation of being pinned to the mat by an opponent he'd not planned to meet. He could almost hear the referee's hand slap the canvas: *One . . . two . . .*

Josh's shoulders shifted. Not yet *three*. Soon, but not yet.

And he drifted into a tortured sleep with the sound of the child's pain haunting his soul.

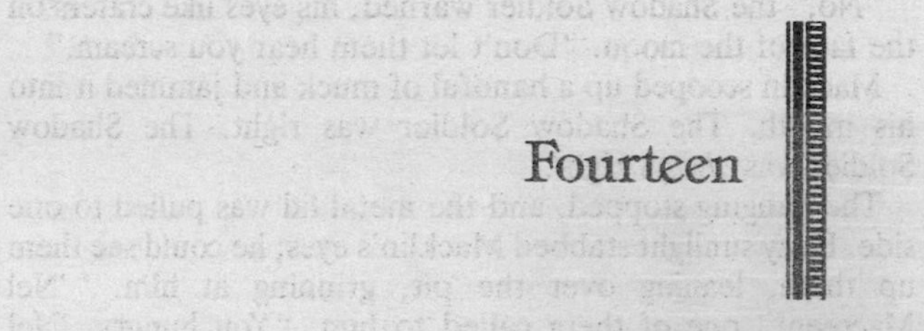

Fourteen

"Discipline and control," the Shadow Soldier said, in a voice like the crack of a belt across a little boy's legs. "That's what makes a man. Remember . . . remember . . ."

Colonel James Macklin cowered in the muddy pit. There was only a slit of light, twenty feet above him, between the ground and the edge of the corrugated metal lid that covered the pit. It was enough to let the flies in, and they buzzed in circles around his face, darting to the piles of filth that surrounded him. He didn't remember how long he'd been down here; he figured the Charlies came once a day, and if that was true then he'd been in the pit for thirty-nine days. But maybe they came twice a day, so his calculations might be wrong. Maybe they skipped a day or two. Maybe they came three times in one day and skipped the next two days. Maybe . . .

"Discipline and control, Jimbo." The Shadow Soldier was sitting cross-legged against one wall of the pit, about five feet away. The Shadow Soldier was wearing a camouflage uniform, and he had dark green and black camouflage warpaint across his sallow, floating face. "Shape up, soldier."

"Yes," Macklin said. "Shape up." He lifted a skinny hand and waved the flies away.

And then the banging started, and Macklin whimpered and drew himself up tightly against the wall. The Charlies were overhead, hitting the metal with bamboo sticks and billy clubs. The sound echoed, doubled and tripled in the pit, until Macklin put his hands to his ears; the hammering kept on, louder and louder, and Macklin felt a scream about to rip itself from his throat.

"No," the Shadow Soldier warned, his eyes like craters on the face of the moon. "Don't let them hear you scream."

Macklin scooped up a handful of muck and jammed it into his mouth. The Shadow Soldier was right. The Shadow Soldier was *always* right.

The banging stopped, and the metal lid was pulled to one side. Hazy sunlight stabbed Macklin's eyes; he could see them up there, leaning over the pit, grinning at him. "'Nel Macreen!" one of them called to him. "You hungry, 'Nel Macreen?"

His mouth full of mud and filth, Macklin nodded and sat up like a dog begging for a scrap. "Careful," the Shadow Soldier whispered. "Careful."

"You hungry, 'Nel Macreen?"

"Please," Macklin said, muck running from his mouth. He lifted his emaciated arms toward the light.

"Catch, 'Nel Macreen!" An object fell into the mud a few feet away, near the decaying corpse of an infantryman named Ragsdale. Macklin crawled over the body and picked the object up; it was a cake of oily, fried rice. He began to gnaw at it greedily, tears of joy springing to his eyes. The Charlies above him were laughing. Macklin crawled over the remains of an air force captain the other men had known as "Mississippi" because of his thick drawl; now Mississippi was a silent bundle of cloth and bones. In the far corner was a third corpse—another infantryman, an Oklahoma kid named McGee—slowly moldering in the mud. Macklin crouched by McGee and chewed on the rice, almost sobbing with pleasure.

"Hey, 'Nel Macreen! You a dirty thing! Bath time!"

Macklin whimpered and flinched, hunching his head down between his arms because he knew what was coming.

One of the Charlies overturned a bucket of human waste into the pit, and the sludge streamed down on top of Macklin, running over his back, shoulders and head. The Charlies howled with laughter, but Macklin concentrated on the rice cake. Some of the mess had splattered onto it, and he paused to wipe it off on the tatters of his air force flight jacket.

"There go!" the Charlie who'd dumped the bucket called down. "You creen boy now!"

The flies were rioting around Macklin's head. This was a good meal today, Macklin thought. This one would keep him alive a while longer, and as he chewed it the Shadow Soldier said, "That's right, Jimbo. Eat every bit of it. Every last bit."

"You stay creen, now!" the Charlie said, and the metal lid was pulled back into place, sealing off the sunlight.

"Discipline and control." The Shadow Soldier had crept closer. "That's what makes a man."

"Yes, sir," Macklin answered, and the Shadow Soldier watched him with eyes that burned like napalm in the dark.

"Colonel!"

A faraway voice was calling him. It was hard to concentrate on that voice, because pain was spreading through his bones. Something heavy lay on top of him, almost snapping his spine. A sack of potatoes, he thought. No, no. Heavier than that.

"Colonel Macklin!" the voice persisted.

Go away, Macklin wished. Please go away. He tried to lift his right hand to wave the flies from his face, but when he did a bolt of white-hot agony was driven through his arm and shoulder, and he groaned as it continued into his backbone.

"Colonel! It's Ted Warner! Can you hear me?"

Warner. Teddybear Warner. "Yes," Macklin said. Pain lanced his rib cage. He knew he hadn't spoken loudly enough, so he tried again. "Yes. I can hear you."

"Thank God! I've got a flashlight, Colonel!" A wash of light crept under Macklin's eyelids, and he allowed it to pry them open.

The flashlight's beam probed down from about ten feet

above Macklin's head. The rock dust and smoke were still thick, but Macklin could tell he was lying at the bottom of a pit. By slowly turning his head, the pain about to make him pass out again, he saw that the opening was hardly large enough to let a man crawl through; how he'd been compressed into a space like this he didn't know. Macklin's legs were drawn up tightly beneath him, his back bent by the weight, not of a potato sack, but of a human body. A dead man, but who it was Macklin couldn't tell.

Jammed into the pit on top of him was a tangle of cables and broken pipes. He tried to push against the awful weight to at least get his legs some room, but the searing pain leapt at his right hand again. He swiveled his head back around the other way, and with the aid of the light from above he saw what he considered a major problem.

His right hand had disappeared into a crack in the wall. The crack was maybe one inch in width, and rivulets of blood gleamed on the rock.

My hand, he thought numbly. The images of Becker's exploding fingers came to him. He realized his hand must've slipped into a fissure when he fell down there, and then when the rock had shifted again . . .

He felt nothing beyond the excruciating manacle at his wrist. His hand and fingers were dead meat. Have to learn to be a southpaw, he thought. And then a realization hit him with stunning force: My trigger finger's gone.

"Corporal Prados is up here with me, Colonel!" Warner called down. "He's got a broken leg, but he's conscious. The others are in worse shape—or dead."

"How about you?" Macklin asked.

"My back's wrenched all to hell." Warner sounded as if he were having trouble getting a breath. "Feel like I'd split apart if my balls weren't holding me together. Spitting up some blood, too."

"Anybody left to get a damage report?"

"Intercom's out. Smoke's coming from the vents. I can hear people screaming somewhere, so some of them made it. Jesus, Colonel! The whole mountain must've moved!"

"I've got to get out of here," Macklin said. "My arm's pinned, Teddy." Thinking about the mangled mess of his hand brought the pain up again, and he had to grit his teeth and wait it through. "Can you help me get out?"

"How? I can't reach you, and if your arm's pinned . . ."

"My hand's crushed," Macklin told him; his voice was calm, and he felt he was in a dream state, everything floating and unreal. "Get me a knife. The sharpest knife you can find."

"What? A knife? What for?"

Macklin grinned savagely. "Just do it. Then get a fire going up there and char me a piece of wood." He was oddly dissociated from what he was saying, as if what had to be done concerned the flesh of another man. "The wood has to be red hot, Teddy. Hot enough to cauterize a stump."

"A . . . *stump?*" He paused. Now he was getting the picture. "Maybe we can get you out some other—"

"There's no other way." To get out of this pit, he would have to leave his hand. Call it a pound of flesh, he thought. "Do you understand me?"

"Yes, sir," Warner replied, ever obedient.

Macklin turned his face away from the light.

Warner crawled from the edge of the hole that had opened in the control room's floor. The entire room was tilted at a thirty-degree angle, so he was crawling slightly downhill over broken equipment, fallen rocks and bodies. The flashlight beam caught Corporal Prados, sitting against one cracked and slanting wall; the man's face was disfigured, and bone gleamed wetly from his thigh. Warner continued into what was left of the corridor. Huge holes had ripped open in the ceiling and walls, water pouring from above onto the mess of rocks and pipes. He could still hear screaming in the distance. He was going to have to find someone to help him free Colonel Macklin, because without Macklin's leadership they were all finished. And there was no way his injured back would let him crawl down into the hole where the colonel was trapped. No, he was going to have to find someone else—someone small enough to fit, but tough enough to get the job done. God only knew what he would find when he crawled up to Level One.

The colonel was counting on him, and he would not let the colonel down.

Slowly and painfully, he picked his way over the rubble, crawling in the direction of the screams.

Fifteen

Roland Croninger was huddled on the crooked floor in the wreckage of what had been Earth House's cafeteria, and over the wailing and screaming he was listening to one grim inner voice that said, A King's Knight . . . A King's Knight . . . A King's Knight never cries. . . .

Everything was dark except for occasional tongues of flame that leapt up where the kitchen had been, and the fitful light illuminated fallen rock, broken tables and chairs, and crushed human bodies. Here and there someone staggered in the gloom like a sufferer in the caverns of Hell, and broken bodies jerked under the massive boulders that had crashed through the ceiling.

At first there'd been a tremor that had knocked people out of their chairs; the main lights had gone out, but then the emergency floods had switched on, and Roland was on the floor with his breakfast cereal all over the front of his shirt. His mother and father had sprawled near him, and there were maybe forty other people who'd been eating breakfast at the same time; a few of them were already hollering for help, but most were shocked silent. His mother had looked at him, orange juice dripping from her hair and face, and said, "Next year we go to the beach."

Roland had laughed, and his father was laughing, too; and then his mother began to laugh, and for a moment they were all connected by that laughter. Phil had managed to say, "Thank God I don't handle the insurance on this place! I'd have to sue my own—"

And then he was drowned out by a monstrous roar and the sound of splitting rock, and the floor had heaved and tilted crazily, with such force that Roland was thrown away from his parents and collided with other bodies. A barrage of rocks and ceiling tiles caved in, and something had struck him hard in the head. Now, as he sat with his knees drawn up to his chin, he lifted his hand to his hairline and felt sticky blood. His lower lip was gashed and bleeding, too, and his insides felt deeply bruised, as if his entire body had been stretched like a rubber band and then brutally snapped. He didn't know how long the earthquake had gone on, or how he'd come to be huddled up like a baby, or where his parents were. He wanted to cry, and there were tears in his eyes, but a King's Knight never cries, he told himself; that was in the King's Knight handbook, one of the rules he'd written for the proper conduct of a warrior: A King's Knight never cries—he just gets even.

There was something clenched in his right fist, and he opened it: his glasses, the left lens cracked and the right one completely gone. He thought he remembered taking them off, when he was lying under the table, to clean the milk off the lenses. He put them on and tried to stand, but it took a moment to coordinate his legs. When he did stand up, he bumped his head against a buckled ceiling that had been at least seven feet high before the tremors had started. Now he had to crouch to avoid dangling cables and pipes and snapped iron reinforcement rods. "Mom! Dad!" he shouted, but he heard no answer over the cries of the injured. Roland stumbled through the debris calling for his parents, and he stepped on something that gave like a wet sponge. He looked down at what might've been a huge starfish caught between two slabs of rock; the body bore no resemblance to anything remotely human, except it did wear the tatters of a bloody shirt.

Roland stepped over other bodies; he'd seen corpses only in the pictures of his father's mercenary soldier magazines, but these were different. These were battered featureless and sexless but for the rags of clothes. But none of them were his mother and father, Roland decided; no, his mom and dad were alive, somewhere. He *knew* they were, and he kept searching. In another moment he stopped just short of plunging into a jagged chasm that had split the cafeteria in two, and he peered into it but saw no bottom. "Mom! Dad!" he shouted to the other side of the room, but again there was no reply.

Roland stood on the edge of the chasm, his body trembling. One part of him was dumbstruck with terror, but another, deeper part seemed to be strengthening, surging toward the surface, shivering not with fear but with a pure, cold excitement that was beyond anything he'd ever felt before. Surrounded by death, he experienced the pounding of life in his veins with a force that made him feel lightheaded and drunk.

I'm alive, he thought. *Alive.*

And suddenly the wreckage of the Earth House cafeteria seemed to ripple and change; he was standing in the midst of a battlefield strewn with the dead, and fire licked up in the distance from the burning enemy fortress. He was carrying a dented shield and a bloody sword, and he was about to go over the edge into shock, but he was still standing and still alive after the holocaust of battle. He had led a legion of knights into war on this rubbled field, and now he stood alone because he was the last King's Knight left.

One of the battered warriors at his feet reached out and grasped his ankle. "Please," the bloody mouth rasped. "Please help me . . ."

Roland blinked, stunned. He was looking down at a middle-aged woman, the lower half of her body caught under a slab of rock. "Please help me," she begged. "My legs . . . oh . . . my legs . . ."

A woman wasn't supposed to be on the battlefield, Roland thought. Oh, no! But then he looked around himself and remembered where he was, and he pulled his ankle free and moved away from the chasm's edge.

He kept searching, but he couldn't find his father or mother. Maybe they were buried, he realized—or maybe they'd gone down into that chasm, down into the darkness below. Maybe he'd seen their bodies but couldn't recognize them. "Mom! Dad!" he yelled. "Where are you?" No reply, only the sound of someone sobbing and voices in keening agony.

A light glinted through the smoke and found his face.

"You," someone said, in a pained whisper. "What's your name?"

"Roland," he replied. What was his last name? He couldn't remember it for a few seconds. Then, "Roland Croninger."

"I need your help, Roland," the man with the flashlight said. "Are you able to walk okay?"

Roland nodded.

"Colonel Macklin's trapped down below, in the control room. What's *left* of the control room," Teddybear Warner amended. He was drawn up like a hunchback. He leaned on a piece of reinforcement rod that he was using as a walking stick. Some of the passageways had been completely blocked by rockslides, while others slanted at crazy angles or were split by gaping fissures. Screams and cries for God echoed through Earth House, and some of the walls were bloody where bodies had been battered to death by the shock waves. He had found only a half-dozen able-bodied civilians in the wreckage, and of those only two—an old man and a little girl—weren't raving mad; but the old man had a snapped wrist through which the bones protruded, and the little girl wouldn't leave the area where her father had disappeared. So Warner had continued to the cafeteria, looking for someone to help him, and also figuring that the kitchen would hold a useful assortment of knives.

Now Warner played the beam over Roland's face. The boy's forehead was gashed and his eyes were swimming with shock, but he seemed to have escaped major injury. Except for the blood, the boy's face was pallid and dusty, and his dark blue cotton shirt was ripped and showing more gashes across his sallow, skinny chest. He's not much, Warner thought, but he'll have to do.

"Where're your folks?" Warner asked, and Roland shook his head. "Okay, listen to me: We've been nuked. The whole fucking country's been nuked. I don't know how many are dead in here, but we're alive, and so is Colonel Macklin. But to *stay* alive, we've got to get things in order as much as we can, and we've got to help the colonel. Do you understand what I'm saying?"

"I think so," Roland replied. Nuked, he thought. Nuked. . . nuked . . . nuked. His senses reeled; in a few minutes, he thought, he'd wake up in bed in Arizona.

"Okay. Now I want you to stick with me, Roland. We're going back into the kitchen, and we're going to find something sharp: a butcher knife, a meat cleaver—whatever. Then we're going back to the control room." If I can find my way back, Warner thought—but he didn't dare say it.

"My mom and dad," Roland said weakly. "They're here . . . somewhere."

"They're not going anywhere. Right now Colonel Macklin needs you more than they do. Understand?"

Roland nodded. King's Knight! he thought. The King was trapped in a dungeon and needed his help! His parents were gone, swept away in the cataclysm, and the King's fortress had been nuked. But I'm alive, Roland thought. I'm alive, and I'm a King's Knight. He squinted into the flashlight beam. "Do I get to be a soldier?" he asked the man.

"Sure. Now stay close to me. We're going to find a way into the kitchen."

Warner had to move slowly, leaning all his weight on the iron rod. They picked their way into the kitchen, where pockets of fire still burned voraciously. Warner realized that what was afire was the remains of the food pantry; dozens of cans had exploded, and the burned mess clung to the walls. Everything was gone—powdered milk, eggs, bacon and ham, everything. But there was still the emergency food storeroom, Warner knew—and his guts tightened at the thought that they could've been trapped down here in the dark without food or water.

Utensils were scattered everywhere, blown out of the kitchen equipment pantry by the shock. Warner uncovered a meat cleaver with the tip of his makeshift cane. The blade was serrated. "Get that," he told the boy, and Roland picked it up.

They left the kitchen and cafeteria, and Warner led Roland to the ruins of the Town Square. Slabs of stone had crashed from above, and the entire area was off-balance and riddled with deep cracks. The video arcade was still burning, the air dense with smoke. "Here," Warner said, motioning with his light toward the infirmary. They went inside, finding most of the equipment smashed and useless, but Warner kept searching until he discovered a box of tourniquets and a plastic bottle of rubbing alcohol. He told Roland to take one of the tourniquets and the bottle, and then he picked through the shattered drug cabinet. Pills and capsules crunched underfoot like popcorn. Warner's light fell upon the dead face of one of the nurses, crushed by a piece of rock the size of an anvil. There was no sign of Dr. Lang, Earth House's resident physician. Warner's cane uncovered unbroken vials of Demerol and Percodan, and these he asked Roland to pick up for him; Warner stuffed them in his pockets to take back to the colonel.

"You still with me?" Warner asked.

"Yes, sir." I'll wake up in a few minutes, Roland thought. It'll be a Saturday morning, and I'll get out of bed and turn on the computer.

"We've got a long way to go," Warner told him. "We'll have to crawl part of the way. But stay with me, understand?"

Roland followed him out of the infirmary; he wanted to go back to search for his parents but he knew that the King needed him more. He was a King's Knight, and to be needed like this by the King was a high honor. Again, one part of him recoiled at the horror and destruction that lay around him, and shouted Wake up! Wake up! in the whining voice of an anxious schoolboy; but the other part that was getting stronger looked around at the bodies exposed in the flashlight beam and knew that the weak had to die so the strong might live.

They moved into the corridors, stepping over bodies and ignoring the cries of the wounded.

Roland didn't know how long it took them to reach the wrecked control room. He looked at his wristwatch by the light of a burning heap of rubble, but the crystal had cracked and time had stopped at ten thirty-six. Warner crawled uphill to the edge of the pit and shone his light down. "Colonel!" he called. "I've brought help! We're going to get you out!"

Ten feet below, Macklin stirred and turned his sweating face toward the light. "Hurry," he rasped, and then he closed his eyes again.

Roland crawled to the pit's rim. He saw two bodies down there, one lying on top of the other, jammed in a space the size of a coffin. The body on the bottom was breathing, and his hand disappeared into a fissure in the wall. Suddenly Roland knew what the meat cleaver was for; he looked at the weapon, could see his face reflected in the blade by the spill of light—except it was a distorted face, and not the one he remembered. His eyes were wild and shiny, and blood had crusted into a star-shaped pattern on his forehead. His entire face was mottled with bruises and swollen like a toadfrog's, and he looked even worse than the day Mike Armbruster had beaten his ass for not letting him cheat off Roland's paper during a chemistry test. "Little queer! Little four-eyed queer!" Armbruster had raged, and everyone who ringed them laughed and jeered as Roland tried to escape but was knocked to the dirt again and again. Roland had started to sob, huddled on the ground, and Armbruster had bent down and spat in his face.

"Do you know how to tie a tourniquet?" the hunchback with the eye patch asked him. Roland shook his head. "I'll guide you through it when you get down there." He shone his light around and saw several things that would make a good, hot fire—the pieces of a desk, the chairs, the clothes off the corpses. They could get the fire started with the burning rubble they'd passed in the corridor, and Warner still had his lighter in his pocket. "Do you know what's got to be done?"

"I . . . think so," Roland replied.

"Okay, now pay attention to me. I can't squeeze down into that hole after him. *You* can. You're going to draw that tourniquet tight around his arm, and then I'm going to pass down the alcohol. Splash it all over his wrist. He'll be ready when you are. His wrist is probably smashed, so it won't be too hard to get the cleaver through the bones. Now *listen* to me, Roland! I don't want you hacking down there for a fucking five minutes! Do it hard and quick and get it over with, and once you start don't you even *think* about stopping before it's done. Do you hear me?"

"Yes sir," Roland answered, and he thought, Wake up! I've got to wake up!

"If you've tied the tourniquet right, you'll have time to seal the wound before it starts bleeding. You'll have something to burn the stump with—and you make *sure* you set fire to it, hear me? If you don't, he'll bleed to death. The way he's jammed in down there, he won't fight you much, and anyway, he knows what has to be done. Look at me, Roland."

Roland looked into the light.

"If you do what you're supposed to, Colonel Macklin will live. If you fuck up, he'll die. Pure and simple. Got it?"

Roland nodded; his head was dizzy, but his heart was pounding. The King's trapped, he thought. And of all the King's Knights, I'm the only one who can set him free! But no, no—this wasn't a game! This was real life, and his mother and father were lying up there somewhere, and Earth House had been nuked, the whole country had been nuked, everything was destroyed—

He put a hand to his bloody forehead and squeezed until the bad thoughts were gone. King's Knight! Sir Roland is my name! And now he was about to go down into the deepest, darkest dungeon to save the King, armed with fire and steel.

Teddybear Warner crawled away to get a fire built, and Roland followed him like an automaton. They piled the pieces of the desk, the chairs and the clothes from the corpses into a corner and used some burning pieces of cable from the hallway to start the fire. Teddybear, moving slowly and in agony, piled on ceiling tiles and added some of the alcohol to the flames. At first there was just a lot of smoke, but then the red glow began to strengthen.

Corporal Prados still sat against the opposite wall, watching them work. His face was damp with sweat, and he kept babbling feverishly, but Warner paid him no attention. Now the pieces of the desk and the chairs were charring, the bitter smoke rising up into the holes and cracks in the ceiling.

Warner hobbled to the edge of the fire and picked up a leg of one of the broken chairs; the other end of it was burning brightly, and the wood had turned from black to ash-gray. He poked it back into the bonfire and turned toward Roland. "Okay," he said. "Let's get it done."

Though he ground his teeth with the pressure that wrenched his back, Warner grasped Roland's hand and helped lower him into the pit. Roland stepped on the dead body. Warner kept the light directed at Macklin's trapped arm and talked Roland through the application of the tourniquet to the colonel's wrist. Roland had to lie in a contorted position on the corpse to reach the injured arm, and he saw that Macklin's wrist had turned black. Macklin suddenly shifted and tried to look up, but he couldn't lift his head. "Tighter," Macklin managed to say. "Tie *knots* in the bastard!"

It took Roland four tries to get it tight enough. Warner dropped the bottle of alcohol down, and Roland splashed the blackened wrist. Macklin took the bottle with his free hand and finally twisted his head up to look at Roland. "What's your name?"

"Roland Croninger, sir."

Macklin could tell it was a boy from the weight and the voice, but he couldn't make out the face. Something glinted, and he angled his head to look at the meat cleaver the boy held. "Roland," he said, "you and I are going to get to know each other real well in the next couple of minutes. Teddy! Where's the fire?"

Warner's light vanished for a minute, and Roland was alone in the dark with the colonel. "Bad day," Macklin said. "Haven't seen any worse, have you?"

"No, sir." Roland's voice shook.

The light returned. Warner was holding the burning chair leg like a torch. "I've got it, Colonel! Roland, I'm going to drop this down to you. Ready?"

Roland caught the torch and leaned over Colonel Macklin again. The colonel, his eyes hazy with pain, saw the boy's face in the flickering light and thought he recognized him from somewhere. "Where are your parents, son?" he asked.

"I don't know. I've lost them."

Macklin watched the burning end of the chair leg and prayed that it would be hot enough to do the job. "You'll be okay," he said. "I'll make sure of that." His gaze moved from the torch and fixed on the meat cleaver's blade. The boy crouched awkwardly over him, straddling the corpse, and stared at Macklin's wrist where it joined the rock wall. "Well," Macklin said, "it's time. Okay, Roland: let's get it done before one of us turns chickenshit. I'm going to try to hang on as much as I can. You ready?"

"He's ready," Teddybear Warner said from the lip of the pit.

Macklin smiled grimly, and a bead of sweat ran down the bridge of his nose. "Make the first lick a hummer, Roland," he urged.

Roland gripped the torch in his left hand and raised his right, with the meat cleaver in it, back over his head. He knew exactly where he was going to strike—right where the blackened skin was swallowed up in the fissure. Do it! he told himself. Do it *now!* He heard Macklin draw a sharp breath. Roland's hand clenched the cleaver, and it hung at the zenith over his head. Do it *now!* He felt his arm go as rigid as an iron rod. Do it *now!*

And he sucked in his breath and brought the cleaver down with all of his strength on Colonel Macklin's wrist.

Bone crunched. Macklin jerked but made no sound. Roland thought the blade had gone all the way through, but he saw with renewed shock that it had only penetrated the man's thick wrist to the depth of an inch.

"Finish it!" Warner shouted.

Roland pulled the cleaver out.

Macklin's eyes, ringed with purple, fluttered closed and then jerked open again. "Finish it," he whispered.

Roland lifted his arm and struck down again. Still the wrist wouldn't part. Roland struck down a third time, and a fourth, harder and harder. He heard the one-eyed hunchback shouting at him to hurry, but Macklin remained silent. Roland pulled the cleaver free and struck a fifth time. There was a lot of blood now, but still the tendons hung together. Roland began to grind the cleaver back and forth; Macklin's face had turned a pasty yellow-white, his lips as gray as graveyard dirt.

It had to be finished before the blood started bursting out like a firehose. When that happened, Roland knew, the King would die. He lifted the cleaver over his head, his shoulder throbbing with the effort—and suddenly it was not a meat cleaver anymore; it was a holy axe, and he was Sir Roland of the Realm, summoned to free the trapped King from this suffocating dungeon. He was the only one in all the kingdom who could do it, and this moment was his. Righteous power pulsed within him, and as he brought the holy axe flashing down he heard himself shout in a hoarse, almost inhuman voice.

The last of the bone cracked. Sinews parted under the power of the holy axe. And then the King was writhing, and a grotesque bleeding thing with a surface like a sponge was thrust up into Roland's face. Blood sprayed over his cheeks and forehead, all but blinding him.

"Burn it!" Warner yelled.

Roland put the torch to the bleeding spongy thing; it jerked away from him, but Roland grabbed and held it while Macklin thrashed wildly. He pressed the torch to the wound where the colonel's hand had been. Roland watched the stump burn with dreadful fascination, saw the wound blacken and pucker, heard the hiss of Macklin's burning blood. Macklin's body was fighting involuntarily, the colonel's eyes rolled back in his head, but Roland hung on to the wounded arm. He smelled blood and burnt flesh, drew it deeply into his lungs like a soul-cleansing incense, and kept searing the wound, pressing fire to flesh. Finally Macklin stopped fighting, and from his mouth came a low, eerie moan, as if from the throat of a wounded beast.

"Okay!" Warner called down. "That's it!"

Roland was hypnotized by the sight of the melting flesh. The torn sleeve of Macklin's jacket was on fire, and smoke whirled around the walls of the pit.

"That's *enough!*" Warner shouted. The boy wouldn't stop! "*Roland!* That's enough, damn it!"

This time the man's voice jolted him back to reality. Roland released the colonel's arm and saw that the stump had been burned black and shiny, as if coated with tar. The flames on Macklin's jacket sleeve were gnawing themselves out. It's over, Roland realized. All over. He beat the piece of wood against the pit's wall until the fire was out, and then he dropped it.

"I'm going to try to find some rope to get you out with!" Warner called. "You okay?"

Roland didn't feel like answering. Warner's light moved away, and Roland was left in darkness. He could hear the colonel's harsh breathing, and he crawled backward over the corpse that lay jammed between them until his back was against rock; then he drew his legs up and clutched the holy axe close to his body. A grin was fixed on his blood-flecked face, but his eyes were circles of shock.

The colonel moaned and muttered something that Roland couldn't understand. Then he said it again, his voice tight with pain: "Shape up." A pause, then again, "Shape up . . . shape up, soldier. . . ." The voice was delirious, getting louder and then fading to a whisper. "Shape up . . . yes, sir . . . every bit of it . . . yes, sir . . . yes, sir . . ." Colonel Macklin's voice began to sound like a child, cringing from a whipping. "Yes, sir . . . please . . . yes, sir . . . yes, sir . . ." He ended with a sound that was half moan, half shuddering sob.

Roland had been listening carefully. That had not been the voice of a triumphant war hero; it had sounded more like a cringing supplicant, and Roland wondered what lived inside the King's mind. A king shouldn't beg, he thought. Not even in his worst nightmares. It was dangerous for a king to show weakness.

Later—how much later Roland didn't know—something prodded his knee. He groped in the dark and touched an arm. Macklin had gained consciousness.

"I owe you," Colonel Macklin said, and now he sounded like the tough war hero again.

Roland didn't reply—but it had dawned on him that he was going to need protection to survive whatever was ahead. His father and mother might be dead—probably were—and their bodies lost forever. He was going to need a shield from the dangers of the future, not only within Earth House but beyond it—that is, he told himself, if they ever saw the outside world again. But he planned on staying close to the King from now on; it might be the only way that he could get out of these dungeons alive.

And, if anything, he wanted to live to see what remained of the world beyond Earth House. One day at a time, he thought—and if he'd lived through the first day, he could make it through the second and the third. He'd always been a survivor—that was part of being a King's Knight—and now he'd do whatever it took to keep himself alive.

The old game's over, he thought. The new game's about to begin! And it might be the greatest game of King's Knight he'd ever experienced, because it was going to be *real.*

Roland cradled the holy axe and waited for the one-eyed hunchback to return, and he imagined he heard the sound of dice rattling in a cup of bleached bone.

Sixteen

"Lady, I sure as hell wouldn't drink that if I was you."

Startled by the voice, Sister Creep looked up from the puddle of black water she'd been crouching over.

Standing a few yards away was a short, rotund man wearing the tattered, burned rags of a mink coat. Beneath the rags were red silk pajamas; his birdlike legs were bare, but he had a pair of black wingtips on his feet. His round, pale moon of a face was cratered with burns, and all his hair had been scorched away except for his gray sideburns and eyebrows. His face was badly swollen, his large nose and jowls ballooned up as if he were holding his breath and the blue threads of broken blood vessels were showing. In the slits of his eye sockets, his dark brown eyes moved from Sister Creep's face to the puddle of water and back again. "That shit's poison," he said, pronouncing it *pizzen*. "Kill you right off."

Sister Creep stayed crouched over the puddle like a beast protecting a water hole. She'd found shelter from the pouring rain in the hulk of a taxi and had tried to sleep there through the long and miserable night, but her few minutes of rest had been disturbed by hallucinations of the thing with the melting face in the theater. As soon as the black sky had lightened to the color of river mud, she'd left her shelter—trying very hard not to look at the corpse in the front seat—and gone in search of food and water. The rain had slowed to an occasional drizzle of needles, but the air was getting colder; the chill felt like early November, and she was shivering in her drenched rags. The puddle of rainwater beneath her face smelled like ashes and brimstone, but she was so dried out and thirsty that she'd been about to plunge her face in and open her mouth.

"Busted water main's shootin' up a geyser back that way," the man said, and he motioned toward what Sister Creep thought was north. "Looks like Old Faithful."

She leaned back from the contaminated puddle. Thunder growled in the distance like a passing freight train, and there was no way to see the sun through the low, muddy clouds. "You find anything to eat?" she asked him through swollen lips.

"A couple of onion rolls, in what was a bakery, I guess. Couldn't keep 'em down, though. My wife says I'm the world's champion upchucker." He put a blistered hand on his belly. "Got ulcers and a nervous stomach."

Sister Creep stood up. She was about three inches taller than he. "I'm thirsty," she said. "Will you take me to the water?"

He looked up at the sky, cocking his head toward the sound of thunder, then stood dumbly regarding the ruins around them. "I'm tryin' to find a phone or a policeman," he said. "I been lookin' all night. Can't find either one when you need 'em, right?"

"Something terrible's happened," Sister Creep told him. "I don't think there *are* any phones or cops anymore."

"I *gotta* find a phone!" the man said urgently. "See, my wife's gonna wonder what happened to me! I gotta call her and let her know . . . I'm . . . okay . . ." His voice trailed off, and he stared at a pair of legs that protruded stiffly from a pile of twisted iron and concrete slabs. "Oh," he whispered, and Sister Creep saw his eyes glaze over like fog on window glass. He's crazy as hell, she thought, and she started walking north, climbing up a high ridge of rubble.

In a few minutes she heard the fat little man breathing heavily as he caught up with her. "See," he said, "I'm not from around here. I'm from Detroit. Got a shoe store at Eastland Shopping Center. I'm here for a convention, see? If my wife hears about this on the radio, she's gonna worry herself sick!"

Sister Creep grunted in reply. Her mind was on finding water.

"The name's Wisco," he told her. "Arthur Wisco. Artie for short. I *gotta* find a phone! See, I lost my wallet and my clothes and every damned thing! Me and some of the boys stayed out late the night before it happened. I was upchuckin' all over the place that mornin'. Missed my first two sales meetings and stayed in bed. I had the covers over my head, and all of a sudden there was a godawful light and a roarin', and my bed fell right through the floor! Hell, the whole hotel started shakin' to pieces, and I crashed through a hole in the lobby and ended up in the basement, still in my bed! When I dug myself out of there, the hotel was gone." He gave a crazy little giggle. "Jesus, the whole *block* was gone!"

"A lot of blocks are gone."

"Yeah. Well, my feet were cut up pretty bad. How 'bout that? Me, Artie Wisco, with no shoes on my feet! So I had to take a pair of shoes off a . . ." He trailed off again. They climbed nearer to the top of the ridge. "Bastards are way too small," he said. "But my feet are swollen up, too. I tell you, shoes are important! Where would people be without shoes? Now, take those sneakers you got on. They're cheap, and they ain't gonna last you very—"

Sister Creep turned toward him. "Will you shut *up?*" she demanded, and then she kept climbing.

He lasted about forty seconds. "My wife said I shouldn't come on this trip. Said I'd regret spendin' the money. I'm not a rich man. But I said, hell, it's once a year! Once a year in the Big Apple ain't too—"

"Everything's *gone!*" Sister Creep screamed at him. "You crazy fool! Look *around!*"

Artie stood motionless, staring at her, and when he opened his mouth again his tight, strained face looked about to rip. "Please," he whispered. "Please don't . . ."

The guy's hanging on by his fingernails, she realized. There was no need to chop his fingers off. She shook her head. The important thing was to keep from falling to pieces. Everything was gone, but she still had a choice: she could either sit down here in the rubble and wait to die, or she could find that water. "Sorry," she said. "I didn't sleep too well last night."

His expression slowly began to register life again. "It's gettin' cold," he observed. "Look! I can see my breath." He exhaled ghostly air. "Here, you need this more than I do." He started to take his mink coat off. "Listen, if my wife ever finds out I was wearin' a mink, I'll never get off the hook!" She waved the coat away when he offered it, but Artie persisted. "Hey, don't worry! There're plenty where this one came from." Finally, just to get them moving once more, Sister Creep let him put the tattered coat on her, and she ran her hand across the scorched mink.

"My wife says I can be a real gentleman when I wanna be," Artie told her. "Hey, what happened to your neck?"

Sister Creep touched her throat. "Somebody took something that belonged to me," she replied, and then she clasped the mink coat around her shoulders to ward off the chill and continued climbing. It was the first time she'd ever worn mink. When she reached the top of the ridge she had the wild urge to shout, "Hey, all you poor, dead sinners! Roll over and take a look at a lady!"

The decimated city stretched out in all directions. Sister Creep started down the other side of the ridge, with Artie Wisco following close behind. He was still jabbering about Detroit and shoes and finding a phone, but Sister Creep tuned him out. "Show me the water," she told him when they reached the bottom. He stood looking around for a minute, as if trying to decide where to grab a bus. "This way," he finally said, and they had to climb again over the rough terrain of broken masonry, smashed cars and twisted metal. So many corpses, in varying degrees of disfigurement, lay underfoot that Sister Creep stopped flinching when she stepped on one.

At the top, Artie pointed. "There it is." Down in the valley of wreckage below was a fountain of water spewing up from a fissure in the concrete. In the sky to the east, a network of red lightning streaks shot through the clouds, followed by a dull, reverberating explosion.

They descended into the valley and walked over piles of what had been civilization's treasures two days before: burned paintings still in their gilded frames; half-melted television sets and stereos; the mangled remains of sterling silver and gold punchbowls, cups, knives and forks, candelabras, music boxes, and champagne buckets; shards of what had been priceless pottery, antique vases, Art Deco statues, African sculpture and Waterford crystal.

The lightning flashed again, nearer this time, and the red glow sparked off thousands of bits of jewelry scattered in the wreckage—necklaces and bracelets, rings and pins. She found a sign sticking up from the debris—and she almost laughed, but she feared that if she started she might laugh on until her brains burst. The sign said Fifth Avenue.

"See?" Artie held up mink coats in both hands. "I told you there were more!" He was standing knee-deep in blackened finery: leopardskin cloaks, ermine robes, sealskin jackets. He chose the best coat he could find and shrugged painfully into it.

Sister Creep paused to poke through a pile of leather bags and briefcases. She found a large bag with a good, solid strap and slipped it over her shoulder. Now she no longer felt quite as naked. She looked up at the black façade of the building that the leather items had blown out of, and she could just make out the remnants of a sign: GUCCI. It was probably the best bag she'd ever had.

They were almost to the geyser of water when a flash of lightning made things on the ground glint like embers. Sister Creep stopped, leaned down and picked one of them up. It was a piece of glass the size of her fist; it had been melted into a lump, and imbedded in it was a scatter of small jewels—rubies, burning dark red in the gloom. She looked around herself and saw that the lumps of glass lay everywhere in the debris, all of them formed into strange shapes by the heat, as if fashioned by a maniacal glassblower. There was nothing left of the building that stood before her but a fragment of green marble wall. But she looked to the ruins of the structures that stood off to the left, and she squinted to see through the twilight. On an arch of battered marble were letters: TIF ANY.

Tiffany's, Sister Creep realized. And . . . if that was where Tiffany's had been . . . then she was standing right in front of . . .

"Oh, no," she whispered as tears sprang to her eyes. "Oh, no . . . oh, no . . ."

She was standing in front of what had been her magic place—the Steuben Glass shop—and all that remained of the beautiful, sculptured treasures were the misshapen lumps at her feet. The place where she'd come to dream at the displays of cool glass was gone, ripped from its foundations and scattered. The sight of this waste against the memory of what had been was as nerve-shattering as if the door of Heaven had been slammed shut in her face.

She stood motionless, except for the tears crawling over her blistered cheeks.

"Look at this!" Artie called. He picked up a deformed octagon of glass full of diamonds, rubies and sapphires. "Have you ever seen anythin' like this before? Look! They're all over the damned place!" He reached into the debris and brought up handfuls of melted glass studded with precious jewels. "Hey!" He laughed like the bray of a mule. "We're rich, lady! What're we gonna buy first?" Still laughing, he threw the pieces of glass into the air. "Anything you want, lady!" he shouted. "I'll buy you anything you want!"

The lightning flashed, streaked across the sky, and Sister Creep saw the entire remaining wall of the Steuben Glass shop explode in dazzling bursts of color: ruby red, deep emerald, midnight sapphire blue, smoky topaz and diamond white. She approached the wall, her shoes crunching on grit, reached out and touched it; the wall was full of jewels, and Sister Creep realized that the treasures of Tiffany's, Fortunoff's and Cartier's must've blown out of the buildings, whirled in a fantastic hurricane of gemstones along Fifth Avenue—and mingled with the melting glass sculptures of the magic place. The hundreds of jewels in the scorched green marble wall held the light for a few seconds, and then the glow faded like multicolored lamps going out.

Oh, the waste, she thought. Oh, the awful, awful waste . . .

She stepped back, her eyes stinging with tears, and one foot slipped on loose glass. She went down on her rear end and sat there with no more will to get up again.

"You okay?" Artie walked carefully toward her. "Did you hurt yourself, lady?"

She didn't answer. She was tired and used up, and she decided she was going to stay right there in the ruins of the magic place and maybe rest for a while.

"Aren't you gonna get up? The water's just over there."

"Leave me alone," she told him listlessly. "Go away."

"Go *away?* Lady . . . where the hell am I gonna *go?*"

"I don't care. I don't give a shit. Not a single . . . rotten . . . shit." She picked up a handful of melted glass and ashes and let the mess fall through her fingers. What was the use of taking one more step? The little man was right. There was nowhere to go. Everything was gone, burned and ruined. "No hope," she whispered, and she dug her hand deeply into the ashes beside her. "No hope."

Her fingers closed around more junk glass, and she brought it up to see what kind of garbage her dreams had been twisted into.

"What the hell is *that?*" Artie asked.

In Sister Creep's hand was a doughnut-shaped ring of glass with a hole at its center about six or seven inches around. The ring itself was about two inches thick, and maybe seven inches in diameter. Jutting up around the top of the ring at irregular intervals were five glass spikes, one ice-pick thin, a second about as wide as a knife blade, a third hooked, and the other two just plain ugly. Trapped within the glass were hundreds of various-sized dark ovals and squares. Strange, spider web lines interconnected deep within the glass.

"It's shit," she muttered, and she started to toss it back on the trash heap when the lightning flashed again.

The ring of glass suddenly exploded into fiery light, and for an instant Sister Creep thought it had burst into flame in her hand. She howled and dropped it, and Artie yelled, "Jesus!"

The light went out.

Sister Creep's hand was trembling. She looked at her palm and fingers to make sure she hadn't been burned; there'd been no heat, just that blinding flare of light. She could still see it, pulsing behind her eyeballs.

She reached toward it, then pulled her hand back again. Artie came closer and bent down a few feet away.

Sister Creep let her fingers graze the glass before she jerked her hand away once more. The glass was smooth, like cool velvet. She let her fingers linger on it, and then she gripped it in her hand and picked it up from the ashes.

The circle of glass remained dark.

Sister Creep stared at it and felt her heart pounding.

Deep within the glass circle, there was a flicker of crimson.

It began to grow like a flame, to spread to other points within the ring, pulsing, pulsing, getting stronger and brighter by the second.

A ruby the size of Sister Creep's thumbnail flared bright red; another smaller one winked with light, like a match glowing in the dark. A third ruby burned like a comet, and then a fourth and a fifth, embedded deep inside the cool glass, began to come to life. The red glow pulsed, pulsed—and Sister realized its rhythm was in time with her own heartbeat.

More rubies glinted, flared, burned like coals. A diamond suddenly glowed a clear blue-white, and a four-carat sapphire exploded into dazzling cobalt fire. As Sister Creep's heartbeat quickened, so did the bursting into light of the hundreds of jewels trapped within the circle of glass. An emerald glowed cool green, a pear-shaped diamond burned white hot and incandescent, a topaz pulsed a dark reddish brown, and now the rubies, sapphires, diamonds and emeralds by the dozen were awakening with light; the light rippled, traveling along the spider web lines that wove all through the glass. The lines were threads of precious metals—gold, silver and platinum—that had melted and been trapped as well, and as they ignited like sizzling fuses they set off still more explosions of emerald, topaz and amethyst's deep purple.

The entire ring of glass glowed like a multicolored circle of fire, yet there was no heat under Sister Creep's fingers. It was pulsating rapidly now, as was her heartbeat, and the vibrant, stunning colors grew still brighter.

She had never seen anything like this—never, not even in the display windows of any store along Fifth Avenue. Jewels of incredible color and clarity were caught within the glass, some of them upwards of five and six carats, some only tiny specks that nevertheless burned with ferocious energy. The glass circle pulsed . . . pulsed . . . pulsed. . . .

"Lady?" Artie whispered, his swollen eyes shining with light. "Can I . . . hold it?"

She was reluctant to give it up, but he stared at it with such wonder and longing that she could not refuse him.

His burned fingers closed around it, and as it left Sister Creep's grasp the glass circle's pulse changed, picking up Artie Wisco's heartbeat. The colors subtly changed as well, as more deep blues and greens swelled and the white-hot glare of diamonds and rubies faded a fraction. Artie caressed it, and its velvety surface reminded him of the way his wife's skin had felt when she was young and they were newlyweds just starting out. He thought of how much he loved his wife, and how he longed for her. He had been wrong, he realized in that instant. There *was* somewhere to go. Home, he thought. I've got to get back home.

After a few minutes he carefully gave the object back to Sister Creep. It changed again, and she sat holding it between her hands and peering into its beautiful depths.

"Home," Artie whispered, and the woman looked up. Artie's mind would not let go of the memory of his wife's soft skin. "I've got to get back home," he said, his voice getting stronger. He suddenly blinked as if he'd been slapped across the face, and Sister Creep saw tears glint in his eyes.

"There . . . ain't no more phones, are there?" he asked. "And no policemen, either."

"No," she said. "I don't think so."

"Oh." He nodded, looked at her and then back at the pulsating colors. "You . . . ought to go home, too," he said.

She smiled grimly. "I don't have anywhere to go."

"Why don't you go with *me,* then?"

She laughed. "Go with you? Mister, haven't you noticed the buses and cabs are a little off schedule today?"

"I've got shoes on my feet. So do you. My legs still work, and yours do, too." He pulled his gaze away from the ring of fiery light and peered around at the destruction as if seeing it clearly for the first time. "Dear God," he said. "Oh, dear God, *why?"*

"I don't think . . . God had much to do with this," Sister Creep said. "I remember . . . I prayed for the Rapture, and I prayed for Judgment Day—but I never prayed for anything like this. *Never."*

Artie nodded toward the glass ring. "You oughta hold onto that thing, lady. You found it, so I guess it's yours. It might be worth something someday." He shook his head in awe. "That's not junk, lady," he said. "I don't know *what* it is, but it's sure not junk." He suddenly stood up and lifted the collar of his mink coat around his neck. "Well . . . I hope you make out okay, lady." With one last longing gaze at the glass ring, he turned and started walking.

"Hey!" Sister stood up, too. "Where do you think you're going?"

"I told you," he replied without looking back, "I gotta get home."

"Are you crazy? Detroit's not just around the block!"

He didn't stop. He's nuts! she thought. Crazier'n *I* am! She put the circle of glass into her new Gucci bag, and as she took her hand away from it the pulsing ceased and the colors instantly faded, as if the thing were going to sleep again. She walked after Artie. "Hey! Wait! What are you going to do about food and water?"

"I guess I'll find it when I need it! If I can't find it, I'll do without! What choice do I have, lady?"

"Not much," she agreed.

He stopped and faced her. "Right. Hell, I don't know if I'll get there. I don't even know if I'll get out of this damned junkyard! But this ain't my home. If a person's gotta die, he oughta die tryin' to go home to somebody he loves, don't you think?" He shrugged. "Maybe I'll find some more people. Maybe I'll find a car. If you want to stay here, that's your business, but Artie Wisco's got shoes on his feet, and Artie Wisco's walkin'." He waved and started off again.

He's not crazy anymore, she thought.

A cold rain began falling, the drops black and oily. Sister Creep opened her bag again and touched the misshapen glass circle with one finger to see what would happen.

A single sapphire blazed to life, and she was reminded of the spinning blue light flashing in her face. A memory was close—very close—but before she could grasp it, it had streaked away again. It was something, she knew, that she was not yet ready to remember.

She lifted her finger, and the sapphire went dark.

One step, she told herself. One step and then the next gets you where you're going.

But what if you don't know *where* to go?

"Hey!" she shouted at Artie. "At least look for an umbrella! And try to find a bag like the one I've got, so you can put food and stuff in it!" Christ! she thought. This guy wouldn't make it a mile! She ought to go with him, she decided, if only to keep him from breaking his neck. "Wait for me!" she shouted. And then she walked a few yards to the geyser of the broken water main and stood under it, letting the water wash the dust, ashes and blood off her. She opened her mouth and drank until her stomach sloshed. Now hunger took thirst's place. Maybe she could find something to eat and maybe not, she considered. But at least she was no longer thirsty. One step, she thought. One step at a time.

Artie was waiting for her. Sister Creep's instincts caused her to gather up a few smaller chunks of glass with jewels embedded in them, and she wrapped them in a ragged blue scarf and put them into her Gucci bag. She nosed around the wreckage, a bag lady's paradise, and found a pretty jade box, but it played a tune when she lifted the lid and the sweet music in the midst of so much death saddened her. She returned the box to the broken concrete.

Then she started walking toward Artie Wisco through the chilly rain, and she left the ruins of the magic place behind.

Seventeen

"Gopher's in the hole!" PawPaw Briggs raved. "Lord God, we come a cropper!"

Josh Hutchins had no idea what time it was, or how long they'd been there; he'd been sleeping a lot and having awful dreams about Rose and the boys running before a tornado of fire. He was amazed that he could still breathe; the air was stale, but it seemed okay. Josh expected to close his eyes very soon and not awaken again. The pain of his burns was bearable as long as he stayed still. He lay listening to the old man babble on, and Josh thought that suffocating probably wouldn't be such a bad way to die; maybe it was only like getting the hiccups just before you went to sleep, and you weren't really aware that your lungs were hitching for oxygen. He felt sorriest for the little girl. So *young,* he thought. So young. Didn't even have a chance to grow up.

Well, he decided, I'm going back to sleep now. Maybe this would be the last time. He thought of those people in the wrestling arena at Concordia and wondered how many of them were dead or dying right now, this minute. Poor Johnny Lee Richwine! Busted leg one day, and *this* the next! Shit. It's not fair . . . not fair at all. . . .

Something tugged at his shirt. The movement sent little panics of pain shooting through his nerves.

"Mister?" Swan asked. She'd heard his breathing and had crawled to him through the darkness. "Can you hear me, mister?" She tugged at his shirt again for good measure.

"Yes," he answered. "I can hear you. What is it?"

"My mama's sick. Can you help her?"

Josh sat upright. "What's wrong with her?"

"She's breathing funny. Please come help her."

The child's voice was strained, but she wasn't giving in to tears. Tough little kid, Josh thought. "Okay. Take my hand and lead me to her." He held his hand out, and after a few seconds she found it in the darkness and clenched three of his fingers in her hand.

Swan led him, both of them crawling, across the basement to where her mother lay in the dirt. Swan had been asleep, curled close to her mother, when she was awakened by a noise like the rasp of a rusted hinge. Her mother's body was hot and damp, but Darleen was shivering. "Mama?" Swan whispered. "Mama, I brought the giant to help you."

"I just need to rest, honey." The voice was drowsy. "I'm okay. Don't you worry about me."

"Are you hurting anywhere?" Josh asked her.

"Shitfire, what a question. I'm hurtin' all *over*. Christ, I don't know what hit me. I was feeling' fine just a while ago—like I had a sunburn, is all. But, shit! I've had worse sunburns than *this!*" She swallowed thickly. "I sure could use a beer right now."

"There might be something down here to drink." Josh started searching, uncovering more dented cans. Without a light, though, he couldn't tell what they contained. He was thirsty and hungry, too, and he knew the child must be. PawPaw could surely use some water. He found a can of something that had burst open and was leaking out, and he tasted the liquid. Sugary peach juice. A can of peaches. "Here." He held the can to the woman's mouth so she could drink.

Darleen slurped at it, then pushed it weakly away. "What're you tryin' to do, *poison* me? I said I need a beer!"

"Sorry. This is the best I can do for now." He gave the can to Swan and told her to drink.

"When're they comin' to dig us out of this shithole?" Darleen asked.

"I don't know. Maybe . . ." He paused. "Maybe soon."

"Jesus! I feel like . . . one side of me is bein' cooked and the other's in a deep freeze. It hit me all of a sudden."

"You'll be all right," Josh said; it was ridiculous, but he didn't know what else to say. He sensed the child close to him, silent and listening. She *knows,* he thought. "Just rest, and you'll get your strength back."

"See, Swan? I told you I was gonna be fine."

Josh could do nothing else. He took the can of peaches from Swan and crawled over to where PawPaw lay raving. "Come a cropper!" PawPaw babbled. "Oh, Lord . . . did you find the key? Now how'm I gonna start a truck without a key?"

Josh put an arm under the old man's head, tilting it up and then putting the broken can to his lips. PawPaw was both shivering and burning up with fever. "Drink it," Josh said, and the old man was as obedient as an infant with a bottle.

"Mister? Are we going to get out of here?"

Josh hadn't realized the little girl was nearby. Her voice was still calm, and she was whispering so her mother couldn't hear. "Sure," he replied. The child was silent, and again Josh had the feeling that even in the dark she'd seen through his lie. "I don't know," he amended. "Maybe. Maybe not. It depends."

"Depends on what?"

Not going to let me off the hook, are you? he thought. "I guess it depends on what's left outside. Do you understand what's happened?"

"Something blew up," she answered.

"Right. But a lot of other places might have blown up, too. Whole cities. There might be . . ." He hesitated. Go ahead and say it. You might as well get it out. "There might be millions of people dead, or trapped just like we are. So there might not be anybody left to get us out."

She paused for a moment. Then she replied, "That's not what I asked. I asked: Are *we* going to get out of here?"

Josh realized she was asking if they were going to try to get themselves out, instead of waiting for someone else to come help them. "Well," he said, "if we had a bulldozer handy, I'd say yes. Otherwise, I don't think we're going anywhere anytime soon."

"My mama's real sick," Swan said, and this time her voice cracked. "I'm *afraid.*"

"So am I," Josh admitted. The little girl sobbed just once, and then she stopped as if she'd pulled herself together with tremendous willpower. Josh reached out and found her arm. Blisters broke on her skin. Josh flinched and withdrew his hand. "How about you?" he asked her. "Are you hurting?"

"My skin hurts. It feels like needles and pins. And my stomach's sick. I had to throw up a while ago, but I did it in the corner."

"Yeah, I feel kind of sick myself." He felt a pressing need to urinate as well, and he was going to have to figure out a makeshift sanitation system. They had plenty of canned food and fruit juices, and no telling what else was buried around them in the dirt. Stop it! he thought, because he'd allowed himself a flicker of hope. The air's going to be gone soon! There's no way we can survive down here!

But he knew also that they were in the only place that could have sheltered them from the blast. With all that dirt above them, the radiation might not get through. Josh was tired and his bones ached, but he no longer felt the urge to lie down and die; if he did, he thought, the little girl's fate would be sealed, too. But if he fought off the weariness and got to work organizing the cans of food, he might be able to keep them all alive for . . . how long? he wondered. One more day? Three more? A week?

"How old are you?" he asked.

"I'm nine," she answered.

"Nine," he repeated softly, and he shook his head. Rage and pity warred in his soul. A nine-year-old child ought to be playing in the summer sun. A nine-year-old child shouldn't be down in a dark basement with one foot in the grave. It wasn't fair! Damn it to Hell, it wasn't *right!*

"What's your name?"

It was a minute before he could find his voice. "Josh. And yours is Swan?"

"Sue Wanda. But my mama calls me Swan. How'd you get to be a giant?"

There were tears in his eyes, but he smiled anyway. "I guess I ate my mama's cornbread when I was about your age."

"*Cornbread* made you a giant?"

"Well, I was always big. I used to play some football—first at Auburn University, then for the New Orleans Saints."

"Do you still?"

"Nope. I'm a . . . I was a wrestler," he said. "Professional wrestling. I was the bad guy."

"Oh." Swan thought about that. She recalled that one of her many uncles, Uncle Chuck, used to like to go to the wrestling matches in Wichita and watched them on TV, too. "Did you *like* that? Being the bad guy, I mean?"

"It's kind of a game, really. I just acted bad. And I don't know if I liked it or not. It was just something I started do—"

"Gopher's in the hole!" PawPaw said. "Lordy, lookit him go!"

"Why does he keep talking about a gopher?" Swan asked.

"He's hurt. He doesn't know what he's saying." PawPaw rambled on about finding his bedroom slippers and something about the crops needing rain, then he lapsed again into silence. Heat radiated off the old man's body as if from an open oven, and Josh knew he couldn't last much longer. God only knew what looking into that blast had done inside his skull.

"Mama said we were going to Blakeman," Swan said, pulling her attention away from the old man. She knew he was dying. "She said we were going home. Where were you going?"

"Garden City. I was supposed to wrestle there."

"Is that your home?"

"No. My home's down in Alabama—a long, long way from here."

"Mama said we were going to go see my granddaddy. He lives in Blakeman. Does your family live in Alabama?"

He thought of Rose and his two sons. But they were part of someone else's life now—if indeed they were still alive. "I don't have any family," Josh replied.

"Don't you have anybody who loves you?" Swan asked.

"No," he said. "I don't think so." He heard Darleen moan, and he said, "You'd better see to your mother, huh?"

"Yes, sir." Swan started to crawl away, but then she looked back into the darkness where the black giant was. "I *knew* something terrible was going to happen," she said. "I knew it the night we left Uncle Tommy's trailer. I tried to tell my mama, but she didn't understand."

"How did you know?"

"The fireflies told me," she said. "I saw it in their lights."

"Sue Wanda?" Darleen called weakly. "Swan? Where are you?"

Swan said, "Here, Mama," and she crawled back to her mother's side.

The fireflies told her, Josh thought. Right. At least the little girl had a strong imagination. That was good; sometimes the imagination could be a useful place to hide in when the going got rough.

But he suddenly remembered the cloud of locusts that had flown through his car. "Been flyin' out of the fields by the thousands for the last two, three days," PawPaw had told him. "Kinda peculiar."

Had the locusts known something was about to happen in those cornfields? Josh wondered. Had they been able to sense disaster—maybe smell it on the wind, or in the earth itself?

He turned his mind to more important matters. First he had to find a corner to pee into before his bladder burst. He'd never had to crouch and pee at the same time before. But if the air was all right and they lasted for a while, something was going to have to be done with their waste. He didn't like the idea of crawling through his own, much less anyone else's.

The floor was of concrete, but it had cracked wide open during the tremors; he recalled he'd felt a garden hoe in the debris that might be useful in digging a latrine.

And he was going to search the basement from one end to the other on his hands and knees, gathering up all the cans and everything else he could find. They obviously had plenty of food, and the cans would contain enough water and juices to keep them for a while. It was light he wanted more than anything else, and he'd never known how much he could miss electricity.

He crawled into a far corner to relieve himself. Going to be a long time before your next bath, he thought. Won't be needing sunglasses anytime soon, either.

He winced. The urine burned like battery acid spewing out of him.

But I'm alive! he reassured himself. There might not be a whole hell of a lot to live for, but I'm alive. Tomorrow I may be dead, but today I'm alive and pissing on my knees.

And for the first time since the blast he allowed himself to dream that somehow—some way—he might live to see the outside world again.

Eighteen

The dark came with no warning. December's chill was in the July air, and a black, icy rain continued to fall on the ruins of Manhattan.

Sister Creep and Artie Wisco stood together atop a ridge of wreckage and looked west. Fires were still burning across the Hudson River, in the oil refineries of Hoboken and Jersey City—but other than the orange flames, the west was without light. Raindrops pattered on the warped, gaily colored umbrella that Artie had found in what remained of a sporting goods store. The store had also yielded up other treasures—a Day-Glo orange nylon knapsack strapped to Artie's back, and a new pair of sneakers on Sister Creep's feet. In the Gucci bag around her shoulder was a charred loaf of rye bread, two cans of anchovies with the handy keys that rolled the lids back, a package of ham slices that had cooked in the plastic, and a miraculously unbroken bottle of Canada Dry ginger ale that had survived the destruction of a deli. It had taken them several hours to cover the terrain between upper Fifth Avenue and their first destination, the Lincoln Tunnel. But the tunnel itself had collapsed, and the river had flooded right up to the toll gates along with a wave of crushed cars, concrete slabs and corpses.

They had turned away in silence. Sister Creep had led Artie southward, toward the Holland Tunnel and another route under the river. Darkness had fallen before they'd made it, and now they'd have to wait until morning to find out if the Holland had collapsed as well. The last street sign that Sister Creep had found said West 22nd, but it was lying on its side in the ashes and could've blown far from where that street had actually been.

"Well," Artie said quietly, staring across the river, "don't look like anybody's home, does it?"

"No." Sister Creep shivered and drew the mink coat tighter around her. "It's gotten colder. We're going to have to find some shelter." She looked through the darkness at the vague shapes of the few structures that hadn't been toppled. Any one of them might fall on their heads, but Sister Creep didn't like the way the temperature was dropping. "Come on," she said, and she started walking toward one of the buildings. Artie followed her without question.

During their journey they had found only four other people who hadn't been killed in the detonation, and three of those had been so mangled they were very near death. The fourth was a terribly burned man in a pin-striped business suit who had howled like a dog when they'd approached and had scuttled back into a crevice to hide. So Sister Creep and Artie had gone on, walking over so many bodies that the horror of death lost its impact; now they were shocked whenever they heard a groan in the rubble or, as had happened once, someone laughing and shrieking off in the distance. They had gone in the direction of the voice, but they'd seen no one living. The mad laughter haunted Sister Creep; it reminded her of the laughter she'd heard inside that theater, from the man with the burning hand.

"There are others still alive out there," he'd said. "Waiting to die. It won't be long. Not long for you, either."

"We'll see about that, fucker," Sister Creep said.

"What?" Artie asked.

"Oh. Nothing. I was just . . . thinking." *Thinking,* she realized. Thinking was not something she did much of. The last several years were blurred, and beyond those was a darkness broken only by the flashing blue light and the demon in the yellow raincoat. My real name's not Sister Creep! she thought suddenly. My real name is . . . but she didn't know what it was, and she didn't know who she was or where she'd come from. How did I get here? she asked herself, but she could provide no answer.

They entered the remains of a gray stone building by climbing up a rubble heap and crawling through a hole in the wall. The interior was pitch dark and the air was dank and smoky, but at least they were within a windbreak. They groped their way along a tilting floor until they found a corner. When they'd gotten settled, Sister Creep reached into her bag to bring out the loaf of bread and the bottle of ginger ale. Her fingers grazed the circle of glass, which she'd wrapped up in a scorched striped shirt she'd taken off a mannequin. The other pieces of glass, wrapped in the blue scarf, were down at the bottom of the bag.

"Here." She tore off a piece of the bread and gave it to Artie, then tore a piece for herself. There was only a burned taste, but it was better than nothing. She unscrewed the cap off the bottle of ginger ale, and the soda instantly foamed up and spewed everywhere. She quickly put it to her mouth, drank several swallows and passed the bottle to Artie.

"I hate ginger ale," Artie said after he'd finished drinking, "but this is the best damned stuff I ever drank in my life."

"Don't drink it all." She decided against opening the anchovies, because their saltiness would only make them more thirsty. The slices of ham were too precious to eat yet. She gave him another small bit of bread, took another for herself and put the loaf away.

"Know what I had for dinner the night before it happened?" Artie asked her. "A steak. A big T-bone steak at a place on East Fiftieth. Then some of the guys and me started hittin' the bars. That was a night, I'll tell you! We had a helluva time!"

"Good for you."

"Yeah. What were *you* doin' that night?"

"Nothing special," she said. "I was just around."

Artie was quiet for awhile, chewing on his bread. Then he said, "I called my wife before I left the hotel. I guess I told her a whopper, 'cause I said I was just gonna go out and have a nice dinner and come back to bed. She said for me to be careful, and she said she loved me. I told her I loved her, and that I'd see her in a couple of days." He was silent, and when he sighed Sister Creep heard his breath hitch. "Jesus," he whispered. "I'm glad I called her. I'm glad I got to hear her voice before it happened. Hey, lady—what if Detroit got hit, too?"

"Got hit? What do you mean, got *hit?*"

"A nuclear bomb," he said. "What else do you think could've done this? A nuclear bomb! Maybe more than one. The things probably fell all over the country! Probably hit all the cities, and Detroit, too!" His voice was getting hysterical, and he forced himself to wait until he was under control again. "Damned Russians bombed us, lady. Don't you read the papers?"

"No. I don't."

"What've you been doin'? Livin' on Mars? Anybody who reads the papers and watches the tube could've seen this shit comin'! The Russians bombed the hell out of us . . . and I guess we bombed the hell out of them, too."

A nuclear bomb? she thought. She hardly remembered what that was; nuclear war was something she'd worried about in another life.

"I hope—if they got Detroit—that she went fast. I mean, that's okay to hope for, isn't it? That she went fast, without pain?"

"Yes. I think that's all right."

"Is it . . . is it okay that I told her a lie? It was a white lie. I didn't want her to be worried about me. She worries that I'm gonna drink too much and make a fool of myself. I can't hold my liquor too good. Is it okay that I told her a white lie that night?"

She knew he was begging her to say it was all right. "Sure," she told him. "A lot of people did worse things that night. She went to sleep without worrying, didn't—"

Something sharp pricked Sister Creep's left cheek. "Don't move," a woman's voice warned. "Don't even breathe." The voice shook; whoever was speaking was scared to death.

"Who's there?" Artie asked, startled almost out of his skin. "Hey, lady! You okay?"

"I'm okay," Sister Creep answered. She reached up to her cheek and felt a jagged, knifelike piece of glass.

"I said don't move!" The glass jabbed her. "How many are with you?"

"Just one more."

"Artie Wisco. My name's Artie Wisco. Where are you?"

There was a long pause. Then the woman said, "You've got food?"

"Yes."

"Water." It was a man's voice this time, further to the left. "Have you got water?"

"Not water. Ginger ale."

"Let's see what they look like, Beth," the man said.

A lighter's flame popped up, so bright in the darkness that Sister Creep had to close her eyes against the glare for a few seconds. The woman held the flame closer to Sister Creep's face, then toward Artie. "I think they're all right," she told the man, who moved into the range of the light.

Sister Creep could make out the woman crouched next to her. Her face was swollen and there was a gash across the bridge of her nose, but she appeared to be young, maybe in her mid-twenties, with a few remaining ringlets of curly light brown hair dangling from her blistered scalp. Her eyebrows had been burned off, and her dark blue eyes were puffy and bloodshot; she was a slim woman, and she wore a blue striped dress that was splotched with blood. Her long, frail arms seethed with blisters. Draped around her shoulders was what looked like part of a gold-colored curtain.

The man wore the rags of a cop's uniform. He was older, possibly in his late thirties, and most of his dark, crewcut hair remained on the right side of his head; on the left, it had been burned away to raw scalp. He was a big, heavyset man, and his left arm was wrapped up and supported in a sling made of that same coarse gold material.

"My God," Artie said. "Lady, we found a cop!"

"Where'd you two come from?" Beth asked her.

"Out there. Where else?"

"What's in the bag?" The woman nodded toward it.

"Are you asking me or mugging me?"

She hesitated, glanced at the policeman and then back at Sister Creep, and lowered the piece of glass. She stuck it through a sash tied around her waist. "I'm asking you."

"Burned bread, a couple of cans of anchovies, and some ham slices." Sister Creep could almost see the young woman start salivating. She reached in and brought out the bread. "Here. Eat it in good health."

Beth tore off a chunk and handed the dwindling loaf to the policeman, who also gouged off some and stuffed it into his mouth as if it were God's manna. "Please," Beth said, and she reached for the ginger ale. Sister Creep obliged her, and by the time she and the policeman had both had a taste there were maybe three good swallows left. "All the water's contaminated," Beth told her. "One of us drank some from a puddle yesterday. He started throwing up blood last night. It took him almost six hours to die. I've got a watch that still works. See?" She proudly showed Sister Creep her Timex; the crystal was gone, but that old watch was still ticking. The time was twenty-two minutes past eight.

"One of us," she'd said. "How many more people are here?" Sister Creep asked.

"Two more. Well, really one. The Spanish woman. We lost Mr. Kaplan last night—he drank the water. The boy died yesterday, too. And Mrs. Ivers died in her sleep. There are four of us left."

"Three," the policeman said.

"Yeah. Right. Three of us left. The Spanish woman's down in the basement. We can't get her to move, and neither of us understand Spanish. Do you?"

"No. Sorry."

"I'm Beth Phelps, and he's Jack . . ." She couldn't remember his last name and shook her head.

"Jack Tomachek," he supplied.

Artie reintroduced himself, but Sister Creep said, "Why aren't you people up here instead of in the basement?"

"It's warmer down there," Jack told her. "And safer, too."

"Safer? How's that? If this old building shifts again, it'll come down on your heads."

"We *were* up here yesterday," Beth explained. "The boy—he was about fifteen, I guess—was the strongest of us. He was Ethiopian or something, and he could only speak a little English. He went out to find food, and he brought back some cans of corned beef hash, cat food, and a bottle of wine. But . . . they followed him back here. They found us."

"They?" Artie asked. "They who?"

"Three of them. Burned so bad you couldn't tell if they were men or women. They followed him back here, and they were carrying hammers and broken bottles. One of them had an axe. They wanted our food. The boy fought them, and the one with the axe . . ." She trailed off, her eyes glassy and staring at the orange flame of the lighter in her hand. "They were crazy," she said. "They . . . they weren't *human.* One of them cut me across the face. I guess I was lucky. We ran from them and they took our food. I don't know where they went. But I remember . . . they smelled like . . . like burned cheeseburgers. Isn't that funny? That's what I thought of—burned cheeseburgers. So we went down into the basement to hide. There's no telling what other kinds of . . . of *things* are out there."

You don't know the half of it, Sister Creep thought.

"I tried to fight them off," Jack said. "But I guess I'm not in fighting shape anymore." He turned around, and both Sister Creep and Artie flinched. Jack Tomachek's back from shoulders to waist was a scarlet, suppurating mass of burned tissue. He turned to face them again. "Worst fucking sunburn this old Polack ever got." He smiled bitterly.

"We heard you up here," Beth told them. "At first we

thought those things had come back. We came up to listen, and we heard you eating. Listen . . . the Spanish woman hasn't eaten, either. Can I take her some bread?"

"Take us to the basement." Sister Creep got to her feet. "I'll open up the ham."

Beth and Jack led them into a hallway. Water was streaming down from above, forming a large black pool on the floor. Through the hallway, a flight of wooden stairs without a bannister descended into the darkness. The staircase shook precariously under their feet.

It did seem warmer, if only by five or six degrees, in the basement, though exhaled breath was still visible. The stone walls were still holding together, and the ceiling was mostly intact but for a few holes that let rainwater seep through. This was an old building, Sister Creep thought, and they didn't put them up like this anymore. Stone pillars set at intervals supported the ceiling; some of those were riddled with cracks, but none of them had collapsed. *Yet,* Sister Creep told herself.

"There she is." Beth walked toward a figure huddled at the base of one of the pillars. Black water was streaming down right over the figure's head; she was sitting in a spreading pool of contaminated rain, and she was holding something in her arms. Beth's lighter went out. "Sorry," she said. "It gets too hot to hold, and I don't want to use up all the fluid. It was Mr. Kaplan's."

"What did you do with the bodies?"

"We took them away. This place is full of corridors. We took them way down to the end of one and left them. I . . . I wanted to say a prayer over them, but . . ."

"But what?"

"I forgot how to pray," she replied. "Praying . . . just didn't seem to make much sense anymore."

Sister Creep grunted and reached into her bag for the package of ham slices. Beth bent down and offered the bottle of ginger ale to the Spanish woman. Rainwater splattered her hand. "Here," she said. "It's something to drink. El drink-o."

The Spanish woman made a whimpering, crooning sound but didn't respond.

"She won't move away from there," Beth said. "The water's getting all over her, and she won't move six feet to a dry place. Do you want food?" she asked the Spanish woman. "Eat eat? Christ, how can you live in New York City without knowing English?"

Sister Creep got most of the plastic peeled away from the ham. She tore off a piece and bent on her knees beside Beth Phelps. "Use your lighter again. Maybe if she sees what we've got, we can pull her away from there."

The lighter flared. Sister Creep looked into the blistered but still pretty face of a Hispanic girl who was maybe all of twenty. Her long black hair was crisped on the ends, and there were raw holes here and there on her scalp where circles of hair had been burned away. The woman paid no attention to the light. Her large, liquid brown eyes were fixed on what she cuddled in her arms.

"Oh," Sister Creep said softly. "Oh . . . no."

The child was maybe three years old—a girl, with glossy black hair like her mother's. Sister Creep couldn't see the child's face. She didn't want to. But one small hand was rigidly curled as if reaching up for her mother, and the stiffness of the corpse in the woman's arms told Sister Creep that the child had been dead for some time.

The water was leaking down through a hole in the ceiling, running through the Spanish woman's hair and over her face like black tears. She began to croon gently, lovingly rocking the corpse.

"She's out of her mind," Beth said. "She's been like that since the child died last night. If she doesn't get out of that water, she's going to die, too."

Sister Creep heard Beth only vaguely, as if from a vast distance. She held out her arms toward the Spanish woman. "Here," she said, in what sounded like a stranger's voice. "I'll take her. Give her to me." Rainwater ran down her hands and arms in streaks of ebony.

The Spanish woman's crooning got louder.

"Give her to me. I'll take her."

The Spanish woman began to rock the corpse more furiously.

"Give her to me." Sister Creep heard her own voice echo crazily, and suddenly there was a flashing blue light in her eyes. "I'll . . . take . . . her. . . ."

The rain was falling, and thunder rumbled like the voice of God, *You! You sinner! You drunken sinner, you've killed her, and now you have to pay. . . .*

She looked down. In her arms was the corpse of a little girl. There was blood in the child's blond hair, and the little girl's eyes were open and full of rain. The blue light of the state trooper car was spinning, and the trooper in the yellow raincoat who was crouched on the road in front of her said gently, "Come on. You have to give her to me now." He looked back over his shoulder, at the other trooper who was setting out flares near the wreckage of an overturned car. "She's out of her mind. I can smell alcohol, too. You're going to have to help me."

And then they were both reaching toward her, both of the demons in yellow raincoats, trying to take her baby. She recoiled and fought them, screaming, "No! You can't have her! I won't let you have her!" But the thunder commanded, *Give her up, you sinner, give her up,* and when she cried out and put her hands over her ears to block off the voice of judgment they took her baby away from her.

And from the little girl's hand fell a globe of glass, the kind of trinket that holds a little snow scene within it, a make-believe village in a fairy-tale land.

"Mommy," she remembered the child saying excitedly, "look what I won at the party! I pinned the tail on the donkey the best!"

The child had shaken the globe, and for a moment—just a moment—her mother had looked away from the road to focus her blurred vision on the scene of snow falling amid the roofs of a distant and perfect land.

She watched the glass globe fall, in terrible slow motion, and she screamed because she knew it was about to break on the concrete, and when it broke everything would be gone and destroyed.

It hit in front of her, and as it shattered into a thousand

pieces of glittering junk her scream stopped with a strangled moan.

"Oh," she whispered. "Oh . . . no."

Sister Creep stared at the dead child in the Spanish woman's arms. My little girl is dead, she remembered. I was drunk, and I picked her up at a birthday party, and I drove right off the road into a ditch. Oh, God . . . oh, dear Jesus. A sinner. A drunken, wicked sinner. I killed her. I killed my little girl. Oh, God . . . oh, God, forgive me. . . .

Tears scorched her eyes and ran down her cheeks. In her mind whirled fragments of memory like dead leaves in a high wind: her husband wild with rage, cursing her and saying he never wanted to see her again; her own mother, looking at her with disgust and pity and telling her she was never meant to bear a child; the doctor at the sanitarium, nodding his head and checking his watch; the halls of the hospital, where grotesque, shambling, insane women chattered and shrieked and fought one another over combs; and the high fence that she had climbed over, in the dead of night and in swirling snow, to reach the woods beyond.

My little girl is dead, she thought. Dead and gone, a long time ago.

The tears almost blinded her, but she saw well enough to know that her little girl had not suffered as this one in the Spanish woman's arms had. Her little girl had been laid to rest under a shade tree atop a hill; this one would lie forever in a cold, damp basement in a city of the dead.

The Spanish woman lifted her head and looked at Sister Creep through haunted eyes. She blinked and slowly reached through the rain to touch Sister Creep's cheek; a tear balanced on the tip of her finger for a second before it dropped.

"Give her to me," Sister Creep whispered. "I'll take her."

The Spanish woman looked again, longingly, at the corpse, and then the tears ran from her eyes and mingled with the black rain on her face; she kissed the dead child's forehead, cradled it against her for a moment—and then she held the corpse toward Sister Creep.

She took the body as if she was accepting a gift and started to stand up.

But the Spanish woman reached out again and touched the crucifix-shaped wound at Sister Creep's neck. She said wonderingly, *"Bendito. Muy bendito."*

Sister Creep stood up, and the Spanish woman slowly crawled out of the water and lay on the floor, huddled and shivering.

Jack Tomachek took the corpse from Sister Creep and went off into the darkness.

Beth said, "I don't know how, but you did it." She bent down to offer the Spanish woman the bottle of ginger ale; the woman took it from Beth and finished it.

"My God," Artie Wisco said, standing behind her. "I just realized . . . I don't even know your name."

"It's . . ." What? she wondered. What's my name? Where do I come from? Where is that shade tree that shelters my little girl? None of the answers would come to her. "You can call me . . ." She hesitated. I'm a bag lady, she thought. I'm nothing but a bag lady with no name, and I don't know where I'm going—but at least I know how I got here.

"Sister," she replied. "You can call me . . . Sister."

And it came to her like a shout: *I'm not crazy anymore.*

"Sister," Artie repeated. He pronounced it "Sista." "That ain't much of a name, but I guess it'll do. Glad to know you, Sister."

She nodded, the shadowy memories still whirling. The pain of what she'd remembered was still with her and would remain, but that had happened a long time ago, to a weaker and more helpless woman.

"What are we going to do?" Beth asked her. "We can't just stay here, can we?"

"No. We can't. Tomorrow Artie and I are going through the Holland Tunnel, if it hasn't caved in. We're walking west. If you three want to go with us, you're welcome."

"Leave New York? What if . . . what if there's nothing out there? What if everything's gone?"

"It won't be easy," Sister said firmly. "It'll be damned hard and damned dangerous. I don't know what the weather's going to do, but we start with one step, and that's the only way I know to get anywhere. Right?"

"Right," Artie echoed. "You've got good shoes, Beth. Those shoes'll take you a long way."

We've got a long way to go, Sister considered. A very long way—and God only knows what we'll find out there. Or what will find *us*.

"Okay," Beth decided. "Okay. I'm with you." She put the flame of her lighter out again to save fuel.

But this time it didn't seem nearly as dark.

again, to the [illegible] but we start with one step, and that's the only way [illegible] get anywhere. Right?"

"Right," Rose agreed. "You've got good shoes, Beth. Those shoes'll take you a long way."

"We've got a long way to go," Sister considered. "A very long way—and God only knows what we'll find out there. Or what will find us."

"Okay," Beth decided. "Okay. I'm with you." She put the [illegible] of her [illegible] on again to save [illegible].

But this time it didn't seem nearly as dark.

FOUR
Land of the Dead

The biggest tomb in the world / Belly of the beast / The most wonderful light / Summer's over / Tunnel trolls / Protect the child / Dreamwalking / New turn of the game

Nineteen

The man with bloody strips of shirt bandaged around the stump of his right wrist moved cautiously along the wrecked corridor. He didn't want to fall down and start that stump bleeding again; it had been dribbling for hours before it had finally crusted over. He was weak and lightheaded, but he pushed himself onward because he had to see for himself. His heart was pounding, and the blood sang in his ears. But what his senses fixed on was an acute itching between the first and second fingers of the right hand that wasn't there anymore. The itching of that phantom hand was about to drive him crazy.

Beside him was the one-eyed hunchback, and in front of him, carrying the flashlight and negotiating a path, was the boy with the cracked eyeglasses. In his left hand the boy gripped a meat cleaver, its blade rimmed with Colonel Jimbo Macklin's dried blood.

Roland Croninger stopped, the beam of his light spearing through the haze before him.

"There it is," Teddybear said. "There it is. See? I told you, didn't I? I *told* you!"

Macklin moved forward a few paces and took the flashlight from Roland. He played it over the wall of boulders and slabs that completely blocked the corridor in front of them, looking for a chink, a weak place, an area to apply leverage, anything. There wasn't a space large enough for a rat to squeeze through. "God help us," Macklin said quietly.

"I told you! See? Didn't I tell you?" Teddybear Warner babbled. Finding this blockage had snapped the last of the willpower that was holding him together.

Beyond that wall of rock lay Earth House's emergency food supply and equipment room. They were cut off from everything—the spare flashlights and batteries, toilet paper, flares, *everything*.

"We're fucked," Teddybear giggled. "Oh, are we *fucked!*"

Dust filtered down through the flashlight beam. Macklin raised it and saw the jagged fissures that cleaved the corridor's ceiling. More of the corridor might cave in at any time. Cables and wires dangled, and the iron reinforcement beams that were supposed to have supported Earth House through a nuclear attack were entirely cut through. Teddybear's giggling was mixed with sobs, and as Macklin realized the full extent of the disaster he could no longer stand the sound of human weakness; he ground his teeth, his face contorting in rage, and he turned to strike Teddybear across the face with his itching right hand.

But he had no right hand, and as he reared his arm back there was a searing, ripping pain, and fresh blood dripped through the bandages.

Macklin cradled his injured arm against his body and squeezed his eyes tightly shut. He felt sick, about to throw up or pass out. Discipline and control, he thought. Shape up, soldier! *Shape up, damn you!*

When I open my eyes again, he told himself, that wall of rock won't be there. We'll be able to walk right on through the corridor to where the food is. We'll be okay. Please, God . . . please make everything okay.

He opened his eyes.

The wall of rock remained. "Anybody got any plastic explosive?" Macklin asked; his voice echoed in the corridor.

It was a lunatic voice, the voice of a man down in the bottom of a muddy pit with bodies sprawled all around him.

"We're going to die," Teddybear said, giggling and sobbing, his one good eye wild. "We've got the biggest tomb in the world!"

"Colonel?"

It was the boy speaking. Macklin shone the light in Roland's face. It was a dusty, blood-splattered, emotionless mask.

"We've got hands," Roland said.

"Hands. Sure. I've got one hand. You've got two. Teddybear's two aren't worth shit. Sure, we've got hands."

"Not our hands," Roland replied calmly. An idea had come to him, clear and precise. "*Their* hands. The ones who are still alive up there."

"The civilians?" Macklin shook his head. "We probably couldn't find ten men able to work! And look at that ceiling. See those cracks? The rest of it's about to fall. Who's going to work with that hanging over their heads?"

"How far is it from that wall to the food?"

"I don't know. Maybe twenty feet. Maybe thirty."

Roland nodded. "What if we tell them it's *ten* feet? And what if they don't *know* about the ceiling? Do you think they'd work, or not?"

Macklin hesitated. This is a *kid,* he thought. What does this kid know about anything?

"We three are going to die," Roland said, "if we can't get to that food. And we won't get there if we can't make someone else do the work. Maybe the ceiling will fall, maybe it won't. But if it does fall, we won't be the ones underneath it, will we?"

"They'll know the ceiling's weak. All they have to do is look up and see those goddamned cracks!"

"They can't see them," Roland said quietly, "in the dark. And you're holding the only light, aren't you?" A smile touched the corners of his mouth.

Macklin blinked slowly. There seemed to be a movement in the gloom, over Roland Croninger's shoulder. Macklin adjusted the flashlight beam a few degrees. Crouched down on his haunches was the Shadow Soldier, wearing his camouflage uniform and a helmet with green netting; beneath the black and green warpaint, his face was the color of smoke. "The boy's right, Jimbo," the Shadow Soldier whispered. He rose to his full height. "Make the civilians do the work. Make them work in the dark, and tell them it's only ten feet to the food. Shit, tell them it's *six* feet. They'll work harder. And if they break through, fine. If not . . . they're only civilians. Drones. Breeders. Right?"

"Yes, sir," Macklin answered.

"Huh?" Roland saw that the colonel seemed to be looking at something just over his right shoulder, and he was using that same fawning voice that he'd used when he was in delirium down in the pit. Roland looked around, but of course there was nothing there.

"Drones," Macklin said. "Breeders. Right." He nodded and pulled his attention away from the Shadow Soldier back to the boy. "Okay. We'll go up and sec if we can find enough to make a work detail. Maybe some of my men are still alive, too." He remembered Sergeant Schorr running wildly from the command center. "Schorr. What the hell happened to him?" Teddybear shook his head. "What about Dr. Lang? Is he still alive?"

"He wasn't in the infirmary." Teddybear made an effort not to look at that wall of rock. "I didn't check his quarters."

"We'll check them, then. We may need him and whatever painkillers he can scrounge up. I'm going to need more bandages, too. And we need bottles—plastic bottles, if we can find them. We can get water out of the toilets."

"Colonel, sir?" Roland immediately got Macklin's full attention. "One more thing: the air."

"What about the air?"

"The generator's out. The electrical system's gone. How are the fans going to pull air into the vents?"

Macklin had been building a hope, however faint, that they might survive. Instantly it crumbled. Without the fans, no air would be circulated through Earth House. The dank air that Earth House now held would be all they could expect, and when the carbon dioxide levels grew high enough they would die.

But how long that would take, he didn't know. Hours? Days? Weeks? He couldn't let himself think beyond the moment, and the most important thing right now was finding a drink of water, a bite of food, and a work detail. "We've got plenty of air," he said. "Enough for everybody, and by the time it starts getting thin we'll have found a way out of here. Right?"

Roland wanted to believe, and he nodded. Behind him, the Shadow Soldier nodded, too, and said to Macklin, "Good boy."

The colonel checked his own quarters, just up the corridor. The door had been torn off its hinges and part of the ceiling had collapsed; a hole had opened in the floor, swallowing his bed and the bedside table in its depths. The bathroom was a wreck as well, but Macklin's flashlight found a few handfuls of water remaining in the toilet bowl. He drank from it, and then Roland and Teddybear took their turns. Water had never tasted so sweet.

Macklin went to the closet. Everything had collapsed inside and lay on the floor in a heap. He got down on his knees and, holding the flashlight in the crook of his arm, began to go through the mess, looking for something he knew must be there.

It took him a while to find it. "Roland," he said. "Come here."

The boy stood behind him. "Yes, sir?"

Macklin gave him the small Ingram machine gun that had been on the closet shelf. "You're in charge of that." He stuffed bullet clips into the pockets of his flight jacket.

Roland slid the handle of the holy axe down inside his belt and held the Ingram gun in both hands. It wasn't heavy, but it felt . . . *righteous.* Yes. Righteous and important, like some vital signet of empire that a King's Knight ought to be in charge of.

"Do you know anything about guns?" Macklin asked him.

"My dad takes me . . ." Roland stopped. No, that wasn't

right. Not right at all. "I used to go shooting at a target range," he replied. "But I've never used anything like this."

"I'll teach you what you need to know. You're going to be my trigger finger when I need one." He shone the light at Teddybear, who was standing a few feet away and listening. "This boy stays near me from now on," he told Teddybear, and the other man nodded but said nothing. Macklin didn't trust Teddybear anymore; Teddybear was too close to going over the edge. But not the boy. Oh, no—the boy was strong-minded and smart, and it had taken sheer guts for him to crawl down into that pit and do what had to be done. The kid looked like a ninety-pound weakling, but if he was going to crack he would've cracked by now.

Roland put the gun's sling around his shoulder and adjusted it so it was tight and he could get to the weapon in a hurry. Now he was ready to follow the King anywhere. Faces surfaced from the muddy waters of his memory—a man and a woman—but he pushed them down again. He didn't want to remember those faces anymore. There was no use for it, and it only weakened him.

Macklin was ready. "Okay," he said. "Let's see what we can find." And the one-eyed hunchback and the boy with cracked eyeglasses followed him into the darkness.

Twenty

"Lady," Jack Tomachek said, "if you think we can get through *that,* you belong in Bellevue."

Sister didn't reply. A bitter wind was blowing in her face off the Hudson River, and she narrowed her eyes against stinging needles of ice that were whirling down from the black clouds above them, stretching from horizon to horizon like a funeral shroud. Sickly yellow rays of sunlight found holes in the clouds and moved like search lamps from a grade-B prison escape movie, then were extinguished when the holes closed. The river itself was turbid with corpses, floating trash and the hulks of burned boats and barges, all moving sluggishly southward to the Atlantic. Across the frightful river, the oil refinery fires were still blazing, and thick black smoke swirled in a maelstrom over the Jersey shore.

Behind her stood Artie, Beth Phelps and the Spanish woman, all of them wrapped up in layers of curtains and coats to ward off the wind. The Spanish woman had cried most of the night, but her eyes were dry now; all her crying was done.

Below the ridge they stood on was the entrance to the Holland Tunnel. It was jammed with vehicles whose gas tanks had exploded, but that wasn't the worst of it; the worst, Sister saw, was that the remains of those cars were about wheel-rim-deep in dirty Hudson River water. Somewhere inside that long and dark tunnel the ceiling had ruptured, and the river was streaming in—not enough, yet, to collapse it like the Lincoln Tunnel, but enough to make the passage a dangerous slog through a swamp of burned cars, bodies and God only knew what else.

"I'm not up to swimming," Jack said. "Or drowning. If that bastard fell in on our heads, we could kiss our asses good-bye."

"Okay, what's a better suggestion?"

"We go east, to the Brooklyn Bridge. Or we go across the Manhattan Bridge. Anything but in there."

Sister pondered that for a moment. She held her leather bag close to her side, and within it she could feel the outline of the glass circle. Sometime during the long night she'd had a dream of the thing with the burning hand, stalking through the smoke and ruins, its eyes searching for her. She feared that thing more than the half-flooded tunnel. "What if the bridges are gone?"

"Huh?"

"What if both those bridges are gone?" she repeated calmly. "Look around and tell me if you think those spindly bridges could survive what blew down the World Trade Center and the Empire State Building."

"They might have. We won't know unless we see."

"And that'll be another day gone. By that time, the tunnel might be completely flooded. I don't know about the rest of you, but I don't mind getting my feet wet."

"Uh-uh." Jack shook his head. "No way I'm going in there, lady! And you're nuts if *you* do. Listen, why do you want to leave Manhattan, anyway? We can find food here, and we can go back to the basement! We don't have to leave!"

"You might not," Sister agreed. "I do. There's nothing here."

"I'm going with you," Artie said. "I'm not afraid."

"Who said I was *afraid?*" Jack countered. "I'm not afraid! I'm just not fucking crazy, is all!"

"Beth?" Sister turned her attention to the young woman. "What about you? Are you going with us or not?"

She stared fearfully at the clogged tunnel entrance, and finally she replied, "Yes. I'm going with you."

Sister touched the Spanish woman's arm, pointed down at the Holland Tunnel and made a walking gesture with two fingers. The other woman was still too shocked to respond. "We'll have to stay close together," Sister told Beth and Artie. "I don't know how deep the water'll be in there. I think we should link hands and go through so nobody gets lost. Okay?"

Both of them nodded. Jack snorted. "You're crazy! All of you are out of your minds!"

Sister, Beth and Artie started down the ridge toward the tunnel entrance. The Spanish woman followed. Jack shouted, "You'll never make it through there, lady!" But the others didn't pause or look back, and after another moment Jack came down the ridge behind them.

Sister stopped in chilly water up to her ankles. "Let me have your lighter, Beth," she said. Beth gave it to her, but she didn't spark it yet. She took Beth's hand, and Beth grasped Artie's, and Artie held onto the Spanish woman's hand. Jack Tomachek completed the chain.

"Okay." She heard fear in her voice, and she knew she had to take the next step before her nerve broke. "Let's go." She started walking around the hulks of vehicles into the Holland Tunnel, and the water crept up to her knees. Dead rats bobbed in it like corks.

Less than ten feet into the tunnel, the water had risen to her thighs. She flicked the lighter, and its meager flame popped up. The light revealed a nightmarish phantasmagoria of tangled metal before them—cars, trucks and taxis torn into half-submerged, otherworldly shapes. The tunnel walls were scorched black and seemed to swallow up the light instead of reflecting it. Sister knew there must have been an ungodly inferno in here when all the gas tanks blew. In the distance, far ahead, she heard the echoing noise of a waterfall.

She pulled the human chain onward. Things floated around her that she avoided looking at. Beth gave a little gasp of terror. "Keep going," Sister told her. "Don't look around, keep going."

The water crawled up her thighs.

"I stepped on something!" Beth cried out. "Oh, Jesus . . . there's something under my foot!"

Sister squeezed her hand tightly and guided her on. The water had reached Sister's waist by the time she'd taken another half dozen steps. She looked over her shoulder at the entrance, now about sixty feet behind them, its murky light pulling at her. But she returned her attention to what lay ahead, and immediately her heart stuttered. The lighter's flame glinted off a huge, mangled knot of metal that almost completely blocked the tunnel—a pile of what used to be cars, melded together by the heat. Sister found a narrow space to slip around, her feet sliding on something slick at the bottom. Now rivulets of water were falling from above, and Sister concentrated on keeping the lighter dry. The waterfall's noise still lay ahead.

"It's about to cave in!" Jack shouted. "God . . . it's gonna fall in on us!"

"Keep going!" Sister yelled at him. "Don't stop!"

Ahead of them, except for the small glow of the flame, was total, unfathomable darkness. What if it's blocked up? she thought, and she felt the scurryings of panic. What if we can't make it? Settle down, settle down. One step at a time. One step.

The water reached her waist and continued to climb.

"Listen!" Beth said suddenly, and she stopped. Artie bumped into her and almost slipped into the foul water.

Sister could hear nothing but the increased rumble of the waterfall. She started to pull Beth on—and then there was a deep groaning noise from above them. We're in the belly of the beast, Sister thought. Like Jonah, being swallowed alive.

Something splashed into the water in front of her. Other falling objects banged loudly off the wreckage, like the noise of sledgehammers at work.

Chunks of stone, Sister realized. Dear God—the ceiling's about to collapse!

"It's *falling!*" Jack shouted, about to choke on terror. Sister heard him thrashing through the water, and she knew his nerve had given out. She looked back and could see him struggling wildly the way they'd come. He slipped into the water, came up sobbing. "I don't wanna die!" he screamed. "I don't wanna die!" And the sound of his screaming trailed away after him.

"Don't anybody move!" Sister commanded before the others fled, too. Stones were still falling all around, and she clasped Beth's hand so hard her knuckles popped. The chain trembled, but it held. Finally, the stones ceased to fall, and the groaning noise stopped, too. "Everybody okay? Beth? Artie, is the woman all right?"

"Yeah," he answered shakily. "I think I've shit in my pants, though."

"Shit I can deal with. Panic I can't. Do we go on or not?"

Beth's eyes were glassy. She's checked out, Sister thought. Maybe that was for the best. "Artie? You ready?" she asked, and all Artie could do was grunt.

They slogged onward, through water that rose toward their shoulders. Still there was no light ahead, no sign of a way out. Sister winced as a piece of stone the size of a manhole cover slammed into a wrecked truck about ten feet away. The noise of the waterfall was nearer, and over their heads the tunnel groaned with the strain of holding back the Hudson River. She heard a faint voice from behind them: "Come back! Please come back!" She wished Jack Tomachek well, and then the waterfall's roar drowned him out.

Her bag was full of water, her clothes pulling heavily at her, but she kept the lighter extended over her head. It was uncomfortably hot in her hand, though she dared not flick the flame off. Sister could see her breath pluming out into the light, the water numbing her legs and stiffening her knees. One more step, she resolved. Then the next. Keep going!

They passed another surrealistic heap of melded vehicles, and the Spanish woman cried out in pain as an edge of underwater metal gashed her leg, but she gritted her teeth and didn't falter. A little further on, Artie's feet got tangled up in something and he went down, coming up sputtering and coughing, but he was okay.

And then the tunnel curved, and Sister said, *"Stop."*

Before them, glittering in the feeble light, was a torrent of water pouring from above, stretching the width of the tunnel. They would have to pass through the downpour, and Sister knew what that meant. "I'm going to have to put the lighter out now, until we get past," she said. "Everybody hold on tight. Ready?"

She felt Beth squeeze her hand, and Artie croaked, "Ready."

Sister closed the lighter's lid. The darkness consumed all. Sister's heart was pounding, and she gripped the lighter protectively in her fist and started forward.

The water hit her so hard it knocked her under. She lost Beth's hand and heard the young woman scream. Frantically, Sister tried to get her footing, but there was something slick and oozy all over the bottom. Water was in her mouth and eyes, she couldn't draw a breath and the darkness distorted her sense of direction. Her left foot was trapped and held by an underwater object, and a shriek was very close, but she knew that if she let it go they were all lost. She flailed around with her free hand, trying to hold the lighter up with the other—and fingers gripped her shoulder. "I've got you!" Beth shouted, her own body being battered by the waterfall. She steadied Sister, who wrenched her leg free with an effort that almost tore the sneaker off her foot. Then she was loose and moving again, guiding the others away from the snag.

She didn't know how long it took them to clear the waterfall—maybe two minutes, maybe three—but suddenly they were past it, and she wasn't gasping for air anymore. Her skull and shoulders felt as bruised as if she'd been used as a punching bag. She shouted, "We made it!" and led them a distance away before her side bumped metal. Then she took the lighter in her fingers again and tried to strike it.

A spark leaped, but there was no flame.

Oh, Jesus! Sister thought. She tried it again. Another star of sparks—but no flame, and no light.

"Come on, come on!" she breathed. The third time was no charm. "Light, damn you!" But it wouldn't, not on the fourth or fifth attempts, and she prayed that the lighter hadn't gotten too wet to catch.

On the eighth try a small, weak flame appeared, wavered and almost died again. Fluid's almost gone, Sister realized. They had to get out of here before it was used up, she thought, and before that instant she'd never known how sanity could depend on a tiny, flickering flame.

Beside her, the crumpled radiator grille and hood of a Cadillac protruded from the water like an alligator's snout. In front of her, another car lay on its roof, all but submerged, the tires shredded from its wheels. They were amid a maze of wreckage, their circle of light cut to a fraction of what it had been before. Sister's teeth had begun to chatter, her legs like cold chunks of lead.

They went on, step by careful step. The tunnel groaned above them again, and more rubble tumbled down—but suddenly Sister realized that the water was back down to her waist.

"We're coming out!" she shouted. "Thank God, we're coming out!" She strained to see light ahead, but the exit wasn't yet in sight. Don't stop! You're almost there!

She stumbled over something on the bottom.

A gurgle of bubbles exploded in her face, and from the water in front of her rose a corpse, blackened and gnarled like a piece of wood, its arms frozen stiffly over its face, its mouth straining in a soundless scream.

The lighter went out.

The corpse leaned against Sister's shoulder in the dark. She stood motionlessly, her heart about to burst through her chest, and she knew she could either lose her mind in that moment or . . .

She took a shuddering breath and pushed the thing aside with her forearm. The corpse slid under again with a noise like a giggle.

"I'm going to get us out of here," she heard herself vow, and in her voice there was a dogged strength she hadn't known she possessed. "Fuck the dark! We're getting out!"

She took the next step, and the next one after that.

Slowly, the water descended to their knees. And—how much later and how many steps further Sister didn't know—she saw the Holland Tunnel's exit before them.

They had reached the Jersey shore.

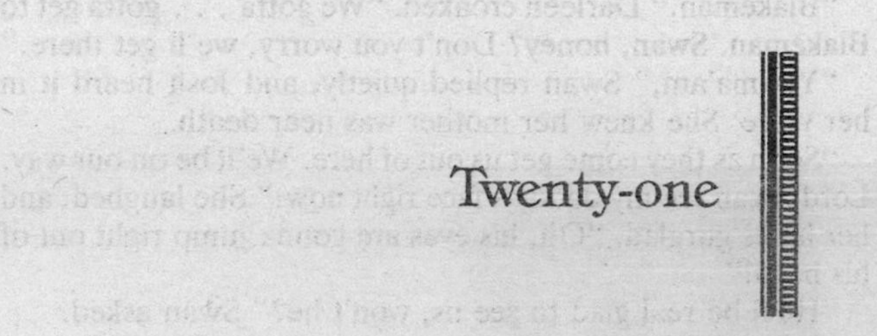

Twenty-one

"Water . . . please . . . let me have some water. . . ."

Josh opened his eyes. Darleen's voice was getting weaker. He sat up and crawled over to where he'd piled up all the cans he'd uncovered. There were dozens of them, many of them burst open and leaking, but their contents seemed okay. Their last meal had been baked beans washed down with V-8 juice, the task of can-opening made simpler by a screwdriver he'd discovered. The dirt had also yielded up a shovel with a broken blade and a pickaxe, along with other bits and pieces from the grocery's shelves. Josh had put everything in the corner, organizing the tools, large and small cans with the single-minded concentration of a packrat.

He found the V-8 and crawled to Darleen. The exertion left him sweating and tired again, and the smell of the latrine trench he'd dug over on the far side of the basement didn't help the air any, either.

He reached out in the darkness and touched Swan's arm. She was cradling her mother's head. "Here." He tipped the can to Darleen's mouth; she drank noisily for a moment and then pushed the can away.

"Water," she begged. "Please . . . some water."

"I'm sorry. There's not any."

"Shit," she muttered. "I'm burnin' up."

Josh gently laid a hand on her forehead; it was like touching a griddle, much worse than his own fever. Further away, PawPaw was still hanging on, intermittently babbling about gophers, his missing truck keys and some woman named Goldie.

"Blakeman," Darleen croaked. "We gotta . . . gotta get to Blakeman. Swan, honey? Don't you worry, we'll get there."

"Yes ma'am," Swan replied quietly, and Josh heard it in her voice: She knew her mother was near death.

"Soon as they come get us out of here. We'll be on our way. Lord, I can see my daddy's face right now!" She laughed, and her lungs gurgled. "Oh, his eyes are gonna jump right out of his head!"

"He'll be real glad to see us, won't he?" Swan asked.

"Sure will! Damn it, I wish . . . they'd come on and get us out of here! When are they *comin'?*"

"Soon, Mama."

That kid's aged ten years since the blast, Josh thought.

"I . . . had a dream about Blakeman," Darleen said. "You and me were . . . were walkin', and I could see the old house . . . right in front of us, across the field. And the sun . . . the sun was shinin' so *bright*. Oh, it was such a pretty day. And I looked over the field and saw my daddy standin' on the porch . . . and he was wavin' for me to come on across. He didn't . . . he didn't hate me anymore. And all of a sudden . . . my mama came out of the house, and she was standin' on the porch beside him . . . and they were holdin' hands. And she called 'Darleen! Darleen! We're waitin' for you, child! Come on home, now!'" She was silent, just the wet sound of her breathing. "We . . . we started 'cross the field, but Mama said, 'No, honey! Just you. Just you. Not the little girl. Just you.' But I didn't want to go across without my angel, and I was afraid. And Mama said, 'The little girl's got to go on. Got to go on a long, long way.' Oh . . . I *wanted* to cross that field . . . I wanted to . . . but . . . I couldn't." She found Swan's hand. "I want to go home, honey."

"It's all right," Swan whispered, and she smoothed back the sweat-damp remnants of her mother's hair. "I love you, Mama. I love you so much."

"Oh . . . I've messed things up." A sob caught in Darleen's throat. "I messed up . . . everything I ever touched. Oh, God . . . who's gonna watch out for my angel? I'm afraid . . . I'm so afraid. . . ." She began to sob brokenly, and Swan cradled her head and whispered, "Shhhh, Mama. I'm here. I'm right here."

Josh crawled away from them. He found his corner and curled up in it, trying to escape.

He didn't know how much time had passed—maybe hours—when he heard a noise near him. He sat up.

"Mister?" Swan's voice was weak and wounded. "I think . . . my mama's gone home."

She broke then and began to cry and moan at the same time.

Josh folded his arms around her, and she clung to his neck and cried. He could feel the child's heart beating, and he wanted to scream and rage, and if any of the prideful fools who had pushed those buttons were anywhere within reach, he could've snapped their necks like matchsticks. Thinking about how many millions might be lying dead out there warped Josh's mind, like trying to figure out how big the universe was, or how many billions of stars winked in the skies. But right now there was just this little girl, sobbing in his arms, and she could never see the world in the same way as before. No matter what happened to them she would forever be marked by this moment—and Josh knew he would as well. Because it was one thing to know that there might be millions of faceless dead out there; it was something else again to know that a woman who used to breathe and talk and whose name was Darleen was lying dead in the dirt less than ten feet away.

And he would have to bury her in that same dirt. Have to use the pickaxe and the broken shovel and dig the grave on his knees. Have to bury her deep, so they wouldn't crawl over her in the dark.

He felt the child's tears on his shoulder, and when he

reached up to touch her hair his fingers found blisters and burned stubble.

And he prayed to God in that moment that, if they were going to die, the child would pass away before him so she wouldn't be alone with the dead.

Swan cried herself out; she gave a last whimper and leaned limply against Josh's shoulder. "Swan?" he said. "I want you to sit here and not move for a while. Will you do like I say?"

She made no response—then, finally, she nodded.

Josh set her aside, got the pickaxe and shovel. He decided to dig the hole as far away as possible from the corner where Swan lay, and he started scooping away a mess of cornstalks, broken glass and splintered wood.

His right hand brushed something metal buried in the loose dirt, and at first he thought it was another can he could add to the others. But this one was different; it was a slim cylinder. He picked it up in both hands and ran his fingers over it.

Not a can, he realized. Not a can. My God—oh, Jesus!

It was a flashlight, and it held enough weight to suggest that there were batteries inside.

He found the off–on switch with his thumb. But he dared not press it yet, not until he'd closed his eyes and whispered, "Please, please. Let it still work. *Please.*"

He took a deep breath and pressed the little switch.

There was no change, no sensation of light against his closed eyelids.

Josh opened his eyes and looked at darkness. The flashlight was useless.

He thought he would burst out laughing for a second, but then his face contorted with anger and he shouted, "Damn it to Hell!" He reared his arm back to fling the flashlight to pieces against the wall.

And as the flashlight jiggled an instant before he let it fly, a weak yellow ray speared from its bulb—but to Josh it looked like the mightiest, most wonderful light in all of creation. It all but dazzled him blind, and then it flickered and went out again. He jiggled it furiously; the light played an impish game, coming on and going off again and again. And then

Josh reached two fingers through the cracked plastic lens to the tiny bulb itself. Carefully, his fingers trembling, he gave the bulb a gentle clockwise turn.

And this time the light stayed: a dim, murky light, yes—but *light*.

Josh lowered his head and wept.

Twenty-two

Night caught them on Communipaw Avenue in the ruins of Jersey City, just east of Newark Bay. They found a bonfire of debris burning within the roofless hulk of a building, and it was there that Sister decided they should rest. The building's walls deflected the freezing wind, and there was enough flammable material around to keep the fire burning until morning; they huddled close around the bonfire, because standing only six feet away was like being in a meat locker.

Beth Phelps held her palms toward the fire. "God, it's so cold! Why's it so cold? It's still July!"

"I'm no scientist," Artie ventured, sitting between her and the Spanish woman, "but I guess the blasts threw so much dust and junk into the air that it's done somethin' to the atmosphere—screwed up the sun's rays or somethin'."

"I've never . . . never been so cold before!" Her teeth chattered. "I just can't get *warm!*"

"Summer's over," Sister said as she rummaged through the contents of her bag. "I don't think it's going to be summer again for a long time." She brought out the ham slices, the last of the soggy bread, and the two cans of anchovies. Also in the water-shrunken bag were several items that Sister had found today: a small aluminum pot with a black rubber-coated handle, a little knife with a serrated blade, a jar of Folger's freeze-dried coffee, and a single thick garden glove with two fingers burned away. Stuffed into the bottom of the bag was the glass ring, which Sister had neither looked at nor disturbed since they'd come out of the tunnel. She wanted to save looking at and holding the treasure for later, like a gift she would give herself at the end of the day.

None of them had spoken again about the Holland Tunnel. It seemed more like a hideous dream, something they wanted to forget. But Sister felt stronger now. They had made it through the tunnel. They could make it through another night, and another day. "Take some bread," she told them. "Here. Go easy on the ham." She chewed on a soggy hunk of bread and watched the Spanish woman eat. "Do you have a name?" Sister asked. The Spanish woman looked at her incuriously. "A *name.*" Sister made the motion of writing in the air. "What's your name?"

The Spanish woman busied herself with tearing a slice of ham into small, bite-size pieces.

"Maybe she's crazy," Artie said. "You know, maybe losin' her kid like that made her crazy. Think that could be?"

"Maybe," Sister agreed, and she got the ashy-tasting bread down her throat.

"I guess she's Puerto Rican," Beth offered. "I almost took Spanish in college, but I wound up taking a music appreciation course instead."

"What do you . . ." Artie stopped himself. He smiled wanly, and slowly the smile faded. "What did you do for a living, Beth?"

"I'm a secretary for the Holmhauser Plumbing Supply Company, on West Eleventh. Third floor, corner office, the Broward Building. I'm Mr. Alden's secretary—he's the vice-president. I mean . . . he *was* the vice-president." She hesitated, trying to remember. "Mr. Alden had a headache. He asked me to go across the street to the drugstore to get him a bottle of Excedrin. I remember . . . I was standing on the corner of Eleventh and Fifth, waiting for the light to change. This nice-looking guy asked me if I knew where some sushi restaurant was, but I said I didn't know. The light changed, and everybody started across the street. But I wanted to keep talking to that guy, because he was really cute and . . . well, I don't really get to meet a lot of guys I'd like to go out with. We were about halfway across, and he looks at me and smiles and says, 'My name's Keith. What's yours?'" Beth smiled sadly and shook her head. "I never got to answer him. I remember a loud roaring sound. I had a feeling that a wave of heat just knocked me off my feet. Then . . . I think somebody grabbed my hand and told me to run. I did. I ran like hell, and I could hear people screaming, and I think I was screaming, too. All I remember after that is hearing somebody say, 'She's still alive.' I got mad. I thought, of *course* I'm still alive! Why *wouldn't* I still be alive? I opened my eyes, and Mr. Kaplan and Jack were bending over me." Beth's gaze focused on Sister. "We're . . . we're not the only ones who made it, are we? I mean . . . it's not just us *alone,* is it?"

"I doubt it. The ones who could make it out have probably already moved west—or north or south," Sister said. "There's sure as hell no reason to go *east.*"

"My God." Beth drew in a sharp breath. "My mom and dad. My little sister. They live in Pittsburgh. You don't think . . . Pittsburgh is like this, do you? I mean, Pittsburgh could be okay, right?" She grinned crookedly, but her eyes were wild. "What's to bomb in Pittsburgh, right?"

"Right," she agreed, and she concentrated on opening one of the anchovy cans with its little key. She knew the salty taste of the things might make them more thirsty, but food was food. "Anybody want one of these?" She scooped a fillet up on her finger and put it in her mouth; the fishy taste almost made her tongue curl, but she got the thing down, figuring fish had iodine or something that would be good for her. Both Artie and Beth took an anchovy, but the Spanish woman turned her head away.

They finished the bread. Sister put the remaining slices of ham back in her bag, then poured the oil from the anchovy can onto the ground and returned the can to the bag as well. The ham and fish might carry them a couple of days more if rationed properly. What they had to do tomorrow was find something to drink.

They sat huddled around the bonfire as the wind shrieked beyond the building's walls. Every so often an errant blast got inside the building and swept up cinders like comets before it spun itself out. There was only the noise of the wind and the fanning flames, and Sister stared into the seething orange heart of the bonfire.

"Sister?"

She looked toward Artie.

"Would you . . . would you mind if I held it?" he asked hopefully.

She knew what he meant. Neither of them had held it since that day in the ruins of the Steuben Glass shop. Sister reached down into her bag, pushed aside the other junk and put her hand around the object wrapped in a scorched striped shirt. She brought it up and peeled the still-wet shirt away.

Instantly the glass circle with its five spires and its embedded jewels burst into brilliance, absorbing the bonfire's light. The thing shone like a fireball, perhaps even brighter than before. It pulsed with her heartbeat, as if her own life force powered it, and the threads of gold, platinum and silver sizzled with light.

"Oh," Beth breathed. The gemstone lights were reflected in her eyes. "Oh . . . what *is* that? I've never . . . I've never seen anything like that . . . in my life."

"Sister found it," Artie replied; his voice was reverent, his attention riveted to the glass ring. He tentatively held out both hands. "May I . . . please?"

Sister gave it to him. When Artie had it, the pulsations of the gemstones shifted speed and rhythm, picking up Artie's heartbeat. He shook his head with wonder, his eyes full of rainbow colors. "Holding this makes me feel good," he said. "It makes me feel . . . like all the beauty in the world isn't dead yet." He ran his fingers over the glass spires and circled his forefinger over an emerald the size of a large almond. "So green," he whispered. "So green . . ."

He smelled the clean, fresh aroma of a pine woods. He was

holding a sandwich in his hands—pastrami on rye with hot spicy mustard. Just the way he liked it. Startled, he looked up and saw around himself a vision of green forest and emerald meadowland. Beside him was a cooler with a bottle of wine in it, and a paper cup full of wine sat close at hand. He was sitting on a green-striped tablecloth. A wicker picnic basket was open in front of him, displaying a bounty of food. I'm dreaming, he thought. My God—I'm dreaming with my eyes open!

But then he saw his hands—blistered and burned. He was still wearing the fur coat and his red pajamas. The sturdy black wingtips were still on his feet. But he felt no pain, and the sunshine was bright and warm, and a silken breeze stirred through the pine forest. He heard a car door slam. Parked about thirty feet away was a red T-Bird. A tall, smiling young woman with curly brown hair was walking toward him, carrying a transistor radio that was playing "Smoke Gets in Your Eyes."

"We couldn't have asked for a better day, could we?" the young woman asked, swinging the radio at her side.

"Uh . . . no," Artie replied, stunned. "I guess not." He had never smelled air so fresh and clean before. And that T-Bird! My God, he thought. The T-Bird had a foxtail hanging on the antenna! He remembered that set of wheels now! It was the finest, fastest car he'd ever owned, and—Wait a minute, he thought as the young woman approached. Hold the phone! What the *hell* is—

"Drink your wine," the woman offered. "Aren't you thirsty?"

"Uh . . . yeah. Yeah, I am thirsty." He picked up the cup and drank the wine in three swallows. His throat had been burning with thirst. He held the cup out for more and downed that one just as fast. And then Artie looked into the woman's soft blue eyes, saw the oval shape of her face and realized who she was; but she couldn't be! She was nineteen years old, and here they were back on their picnic on the afternoon he had asked her to marry him.

"You're staring, Artie," she said teasingly.

"I'm sorry. It's just . . . I mean, you're young again, and

I'm sittin' here like a French fry in red pajamas. I mean . . . it's not *right.*"

She frowned, as if she couldn't fathom what he was talking about. "You're silly," she decided. "Don't you like your sandwich?"

"Sure. Sure, I do." He bit into it, expecting it to dissolve like a mirage between his teeth, but he had a mouthful of pastrami, and if this was a dream it was the best damned dream sandwich he'd ever eaten! He poured himself a third cup of wine and guzzled it merrily. The sweet, clean scent of the pine woods filled the air, and Artie breathed deeply. He stared out at the green woods and the meadow, and he thought, My God, my God, it's *good* to be alive!

"You all right?"

"Huh?" The voice had startled him. He blinked and was looking at Sister's blistered face. The glass ring was still between his hands.

"I asked you if you're all right," she said. "You've been looking into that thing for about half a minute, just sitting there staring."

"Oh." Artie saw the bonfire, the faces of Beth and the Spanish woman, the ruined walls of the building. I don't know where I went, he thought, but I'm back now. He imagined that he could taste pastrami, spicy mustard and wine lingering in his mouth. He even felt just a bit light-headed, as if he'd drunk too much too fast. But his stomach felt full now, and he wasn't thirsty anymore. "Yeah, I'm all right." He let his fingers play along the glass ring for a moment longer, and then he handed it back to Sister. "Thank you," he said.

She took it. For an instant she thought she smelled—what was it? Liquor? But then the faint odor was gone. Artie Wisco leaned back and belched.

"Can I hold that?" Beth asked her. "I'll be careful with it." She took it from Sister as the Spanish woman admired it over her shoulder. "It reminds me of something. Something I've seen," she said. "I can't think of what, though." She peered through the glass at the sparkle of topaz and diamonds. "Oh, Lord, do you know what this must be *worth?*"

Sister shrugged. "I guess it would've been worth some money a few days ago. Now I'm not so sure. Maybe it's worth some cans of food and a can opener. Maybe a pack of matches. At the most, a jug of clean water."

Water, Beth thought. It had been over twenty-four hours since she'd had a drink of the ginger ale. Her mouth felt like a dry field. A drink of water—just a *sip*—would be so wonderful.

Her fingers suddenly submerged *into* the glass.

Except it was not glass anymore; it was a stream of water, running over multicolored stones. She pulled her hand away, and drops of water fell like diamonds from the tips of her fingers back into the flowing stream.

She sensed Sister watching her, but she also felt distanced from the other woman, distanced from the wreckage of the city around them; she felt Sister's presence, but it was as if the woman was in another room of a magic mansion to which Beth had just found the front door key. The cool stream of water made an inviting chuckling sound as it passed over the colored stones. There *can't* be water running right across my *lap,* Beth thought, and for an instant the stream wavered and started to fade, a thing of mist burned off by the stark sun of reason. No! she wished. Not yet!

The water continued flowing, right under her hands, moving from beyond to beyond.

Beth put her hand into it again. So cool, so cool. She caught some of the water in her palm and brought it to her mouth. It tasted better than any glass of Perrier she'd ever had. Again she drank from it, and then she lowered her head to the stream and drank as the water rushed around her cheek like a lingering kiss.

Sister thought Beth Phelps had gone into some kind of trance. She'd watched Beth's eyes suddenly glaze over. Like Artie, Beth hadn't moved for over thirty seconds. "Hey!" Sister said. She reached out and poked Beth. "Hey, what's wrong with you?"

Beth looked up. Her eyes cleared. "What?"

"Nothing. I think it's time we got some rest." Sister started to take the glass circle back, but the Spanish woman abruptly grabbed it and scrambled away, sinking down amid the broken stones and clasping it to her body. Both Sister and Beth stood up—and Beth thought she felt her stomach slosh.

Sister walked to the Spanish woman, who was sobbing with her head bent over. Sister knelt beside her and said gently, "Come on, let me have that back, okay?"

"Mi niña me perdona," the woman sobbed. *"Madre de Dios, mi niña me perdona."*

"What's she saying?" Beth asked, standing behind Sister.

"I don't know." Sister put her hand around the glass ring and slowly pulled it toward her. The Spanish woman held onto it, shaking her head back and forth. "Come on," Sister urged. "Let me have it—"

"My child forgives me!" the Spanish woman suddenly said. Her eyes were wide and full of tears. "Mother of God, I saw my child's face in this! And she said she forgives me! I'm free! Mother of God, I'm *free!*"

Sister was stunned. "I . . . didn't think you knew English."

Now it was the Spanish woman's turn to blink dazedly. "What?"

"What's your name? How come you haven't spoken English before this?"

"My name is Julia. Julia Castillo. English? I don't . . . know what you mean."

"Either I'm crazy or she is," Sister said. "Come on, let me have this." She pulled the ring away, and Julia Castillo let it go. "Okay. Now how come you haven't spoken English before now, Julia?"

"No comprendo," she replied. "Good morning. Good day. I am happy to see you, sir. Thank you." She shrugged and motioned vaguely southward. *"Mantanzas,"* she said. *"Cuba."*

Sister turned her head toward Beth, who had stepped back a couple of paces and had a weird expression on her face. "Who's crazy, Beth? Julia or me? Does this lady know English or *not?*"

Beth said, "She . . . was speaking in Spanish. She never said one word of English. Did you . . . understand what she said?"

"Hell yes, I understood her! Every damned word! Didn't . . ." She stopped speaking. Her hand holding the glass ring was tingling. Beyond the bonfire, Artie suddenly sat up and hiccuped. "Hey!" he said in a slightly slurred voice. "Where's the party?"

Sister held the glass circle out toward Julia Castillo again. The Spanish woman touched it hesitantly. "What did you say about Cuba?" Sister asked.

"I'm . . . from Mantanzas, in Cuba," Julia replied, in perfect English. Her eyes were large and puzzled. "My family came over in a fishing boat. My father could speak a little English, and we came north to work in a shirt factory. How do you . . . know *my* language?"

Sister looked at Beth. "What do you hear? Spanish or English?"

"Spanish. Isn't that what *you* heard?"

"No." She pulled the ring out of Julia's grasp. "Now say something. Say anything."

Julia shook her head. *"Lo siento, no comprendo."*

Sister stared at Julia for a moment, and then she slowly lifted the ring closer to her face to peer into its depths. Her hand was trembling, and what felt like little jolts of energy coursed through her forearm to her elbow. "It's this," Sister said. "This glass thing. I don't know why or how, but . . . this thing lets me understand her, and she can understand me, too. I heard her speak English, Beth . . . and I think she heard *me* speak Spanish."

"That's crazy!" Beth said, but she thought of the cool stream that had flowed across her lap, and her throat that was no longer parched. "I mean . . . it's just glass and jewels, isn't it?"

"Here." Sister offered it to her. "Find out for yourself."

Beth traced one of the spires with a finger. "The Statue of Liberty," she said.

"What?"

"The Statue of Liberty. That's what this reminds me of. Not the statue itself, but . . . the lady's *crown.*" She lifted the circle to her head, the spires jutting up. "See? It *could* be a crown, couldn't it?"

"I've never seen a lovelier princess," said a man's voice, from the darkness beyond the bonfire.

Instantly Beth had the glass circle protected in her arms and was backing away from the direction of the voice. Sister tensed. "Who's there?" She sensed movement: Someone was walking slowly across the ruins, approaching the firelight's edge.

He stepped into the light. His gaze lingered on each of them in turn. "Good evening," he said politely, addressing Sister.

He was a tall, broad-shouldered man with a regal bearing, dressed in a dusty black suit. A brown blanket was wrapped around his shoulders and throat like a peasant's serape, and across his pallid, sharp-chinned face were the scarlet streaks of deep burns, like welts inflicted by a whip. A blood-crusted gash zigzagged across his high forehead, cut through his left eyebrow and ended at his cheekbone. Most of his reddish-gray hair remained, though there were bare spots the size of silver dollars on his scalp. The breath curled from his nose and mouth. "Is it all right if I come nearer?" he asked, his voice pained and halting.

Sister didn't answer. The man waited. "I won't bite," he said.

He was shivering, and she could not deny him the fire. "Come ahead," she said cautiously, and she stepped back as he did.

He winced as he hobbled forward, and Sister saw what was hurting him: a jagged splinter of metal had pierced his right leg just above the knee and stuck out about three inches on the other side. He passed between Sister and Beth and went straight to the fire, where he warmed his outstretched hands. "Ah, that feels good! It must be thirty degrees out there!"

Sister had felt the cold as well, and she returned to the fire. Behind her, Julia and Beth, who was still protectively clinging to the glass ring, followed.

"Who the hell are *you?*" Artie stared bleary-eyed across the bonfire.

"My name is Doyle Halland," the man answered. "Why didn't you people leave with the rest of them?"

"The rest of who?" Sister asked, still watching him warily.

"The ones who got out. Yesterday, I guess it was. Hundreds of them, leaving"—he smiled wanly and waved his hand around—"leaving the Garden State. Maybe there are shelters further west. I don't know. Anyway, I didn't expect anyone was left."

"We came from Manhattan," Beth told him. "We made it through the Holland Tunnel."

"I didn't think anybody could've lived through what hit Manhattan. They say it was at least two bombs. Jersey City burned fast. And the winds . . . my God, the *winds.*" He closed his fists before the flames. "It was a tornado. More than one, I think. The winds just . . . tore buildings off their foundations. I was lucky, I suppose. I got into a basement, but the building blew apart over my head. The wind did this." He gingerly touched the metal splinter. "I've heard of tornadoes putting straws unbroken through telephone poles. I guess this is about the same principle, huh?" He looked at Sister. "I realize I'm not at my best, but why are you staring at me like that?"

"Where'd you come from, Mr. Halland?"

"Not far. I saw your fire. If you don't want me to stay, just say so."

Sister was ashamed of what she'd been thinking. He winced again, and she saw that fresh blood had begun to ooze around the splinter. "I don't own this place. You can stay wherever you please."

"Thank you. It's not a pleasant night to be walking." His gaze moved to the sparkle of the glass circle Beth was holding. "That thing shines, doesn't it? What *is* it?"

"It's . . ." She couldn't find the right word. "It's *magic,*" she blurted out. "You won't believe what just happened! You see that woman over there? She can't speak English, and this thing—"

"It's junk," Sister interrupted, taking it from Beth. She didn't trust this stranger yet, and she didn't want him knowing any more about their treasure. "It's just shiny junk, that's all." She put it into the bottom of her bag, and the glow of the gems faded and went out.

"You want shiny junk?" the man inquired. "I'll show you some." He looked around, then hobbled away a few yards and painfully bent down. He picked up something and brought it back to the fire. "See? It shines just like yours," he said, showing them what he held.

It was a piece of stained-glass window, a swirl of deep blue and purple.

"You're standing in what used to be my church," he said, and he pulled the blanket away from his throat to reveal the soiled white collar of a priest. Smiling bitterly, he tossed the colored glass into the fire.

Twenty-three

In the darkness, sixteen civilians—men, women and children—and three badly injured members of Colonel Macklin's army struggled to work the tightly jammed puzzle of rocks loose from the lower-level corridor. It's only six feet to the food, Macklin had told them, six feet. It won't take you long to break through, once you get a hole opened. The first one to reach that food gets a triple ration.

They had been laboring in total darkness for almost seven hours when the rest of the ceiling caved in on their heads with no warning.

Roland Croninger, on his knees in the cafeteria's kitchen, felt the floor shake. Screams drifted up through an air vent—and then silence.

"Damn!" he said, because he knew what had happened. Who was going to clear that corridor now? But then, on the other side of the coin, the dead didn't use up air. He went back to his task of scooping up bits of food from the floor and putting them into a plastic garbage bag.

He'd suggested that Colonel Macklin set up headquarters in the gymnasium. They'd found a treasure: a mop bucket, in which they could store the toilet bowl water. When Roland, his stomach gnawing with hunger, had left them to forage in the kitchen, both Macklin and Captain Warner had been asleep; Roland had the Ingram gun on a strap around his shoulder, and the handle of the holy axe was secured by his waistband. Near him, the flashlight lay on the floor, illuminating clumps of food that had exploded from cans in the pantry. The kitchen garbage pails had yielded some finds, too: banana peels, bits of tomato, cans with not all their contents quite scraped out, and a few breakfast biscuits. Anything and everything edible went into Roland's bag, except for the biscuits, which were his first meal since the disaster.

He picked up a black piece of something and started to shove it into the bag but hesitated. The black thing reminded him of what he'd done to Mike Armbruster's pet hamsters the day Armbruster had brought them to biology class. The hamsters had been left at the back of the room after school, while Armbruster went to football practice. Roland had gotten the cage of hamsters, without being seen by the cleaning women, and had sneaked stealthily to the school's automotive workshop. In one corner stood a metal vat that held a greenish-brown liquid, and over the vat was a red sign that said Wear Your Gloves!

Roland had put on a pair of heavy asbestos gloves and made cooing noises to the two little hamsters, and he'd thought about Mike Armbruster laughing and spitting on him while he was down in the dust.

Then he'd picked up the cage by its handle and lowered it into the vat of acid, which was used to make rusted radiators shine like new.

He'd let the hamsters stay under until the bubbles stopped. When he brought the cage up, he noted that the acid had attacked the metal and chewed it down to a polished gleam. Then he took his gloves off and carried the cage back to the biology room on the end of a broom.

He'd often wondered what Mike Armbruster's face had looked like when he saw the two black things where the hamsters used to be. Armbruster hadn't realized, Roland often mused later, the many ways a King's Knight can get even.

Roland tossed whatever it was into the bag. He turned up a box of oatmeal and—wonder of wonders!—a single green apple. Both of those went into the bag. He continued crawling, lifting the smaller rocks and avoiding the fissures in the floor.

He was getting too far from the flashlight, and he stood up. The garbage bag had some weight to it now. The King was going to be well pleased. He started toward the light, stepping nimbly over the dead.

There was a noise behind him. Not a loud noise, just a *whirrrr* of disturbed air, and he knew he was no longer alone.

Before he could turn, a hand clamped across his mouth. "Get the bag!" a man said. "Hurry!"

It was torn from his grip. "Little fucker's got an Ingram gun!" That, too, was ripped off his shoulder. The hand moved from his mouth, replaced by an arm at his throat. "Where's Macklin? Where's the sonofabitch hiding?"

"I can't . . . I can't breathe," Roland croaked.

The man cursed and flung him to the floor. Roland's glasses flew off, and a boot pressed down on his spine. "Who you gonna kill with that gun, kid? You gonna make sure you get all the food for yourself and the colonel?"

One of the others retrieved the flashlight and aimed it in Roland's face. He thought there were three of them from the voices and movements, but he couldn't be positive. He flinched as he heard the Ingram gun's safety click off. "Kill him, Schorr!" one of the men urged. "Blow his fucking brains out!"

Schorr. Roland knew that name. Hospitality Sergeant Schorr.

"I know he's alive, kid." Schorr was standing over him, his foot planted on Roland's back. "I went down to the command center, and I found those people working in the dark. I found Corporal Prados, too. He told me a kid got Macklin out of a hole, and that the colonel was hurt. He just left Prados down there to die, didn't he?"

"The corporal . . . couldn't move. He couldn't stand up, because of his leg. We had to leave him."

"Who else is with Macklin?"

"Captain Warner," Roland gasped. "That's all."

"And he sent you here to find food? Did he give you the Ingram gun and tell you to kill everybody else?"

"No, sir." The wheels of Roland's brain were spinning, trying to find a way to squirm out of this.

"Where's he hiding? How many weapons does he have?"

Roland was silent. Schorr bent down beside him and put the gun's barrel to Roland's temple. "There are nine other people not too far from here who need food and water, too," Schorr said tersely. "*My* people. I thought I was going to die, and I've seen things . . ." He stopped, shaken, couldn't go on for a moment. "Things nobody ought to see and live to remember. Macklin's to blame for all this. He knew this place was falling apart—he *must've* known it!" The barrel bruised Roland's skull. "High and mighty Macklin with his tin soldiers and his worn-out medals! Just marching the suckers in and out of here! He *knew* what was going to happen! Isn't that right?"

"Yes, sir." Roland felt the holy axe pressed against his stomach. Slowly, he began to work his hand under his body.

"He knows there's no way in Hell to get to the emergency food, doesn't he? So he sent you here to get the scraps before anybody else could! You little bastard!" Schorr grabbed his collar and shook him, which helped Roland slide his hand closer to the holy axe.

"The colonel wants to stockpile everything," Roland said. Buy time! he thought. "He wants to get everybody together and ration out the food and wa—"

"You're a *liar!* He wants it all for himself!"

"No! We can still get through to the emergency food."

"Bullshit!" the man roared, and insanity leapt in his voice. "I heard the rest of Level One fall in! I know they're all dead! He wants to kill all of us so he can have the food!"

"Finish him, Schorr," the other man said. "Shoot his balls off."

"Not yet, not yet. I want to know where Macklin is! Where's he hiding, and how many weapons does he have?"

Roland's fingers were almost touching the blade. Closer . . . closer. "He's got . . . he's got a lot of guns. Got a pistol. And another machine gun." Closer, and closer still. "He's got a whole arsenal in there."

"In *there?* In where?"

"In . . . one of the rooms. It's way down the corridor." Almost got it!

"What room, you little shit?" Schorr grabbed him again, shook him angrily, and Roland took advantage of the movement; he slid the holy axe out of his waistband and lay on top of it, getting a good, strong grip around the handle. When he decided to strike, it would have to be fast, and if the other two men had guns, he was finished.

Cry! he told himself. He forced a sob. "Please . . . please don't hurt me! I can't see without my glasses!" He blubbered and shook. "Don't hurt me!" He made a retching noise—and he felt the Ingram gun's barrel move away from his skull.

"Little shitter. Little candy-ass shitter! Come on! Stand up like a man!" He grasped Roland's arm and started to haul him to his feet.

Now, Roland thought—very calmly, very deliberately. A King's Knight was not afraid of death.

He let the man's strength pull him up, and then he uncoiled like a spring, twisting around and slashing out with the holy axe that still bore some of the King's dried blood on its blade.

The flashlight's beam glinted off the cleaver; the blade sliced into Schorr's left cheek like it was carving off a piece of Thanksgiving turkey. He was too shocked to react for a second, but then the blood burst out of the wound and his finger jerked involuntarily on the trigger, sending a rattle of bullets whining past Roland's head. Schorr staggered backward, half his face peeled open to the bone. Roland rushed him, hacking wildly before the man could aim that gun again.

One of the others grabbed Roland's shoulder, but Roland broke away, tearing the rest of his shirt almost off. He swung again at Schorr and caught the meaty part of his gun arm. Schorr stumbled over a dead body, the Ingram gun clattering to the stones at Roland's feet.

Roland scooped it up. His face contorted into a savage rictus and he whirled upon the man holding the flashlight. He braced his legs in the firing position the colonel had taught him, aimed and squeezed the trigger.

The gun hummed like a sewing machine, but its recoil knocked him back over the rubble and set him on his ass. As he fell he saw the flashlight explode in the man's hand, and there was a grunt followed by a shrill cry of pain. Someone whimpered and scrabbled away across the floor. Roland fired into the dark, the red trajectories of tracer bullets ricocheting off the walls. There was another scream that broke into gurgling fragments and grew distant, and Roland thought that one of the men must've stepped into a hole in the floor and fallen through. He sprayed the cafeteria with bullets, and then he stopped firing because he knew he was alone again.

He listened; his heart was racing. The sweet aroma of a fired weapon hung in the air. "Come on!" he shouted. "You want some more? *Come on!*"

But there was only silence. Whether he'd killed them all or not, he didn't know. He was sure he'd hit at least one. "Bastards," Roland breathed. "You bastards, next time I'll kill you."

He laughed. It startled him, because it didn't sound like the laughter of anyone he knew. He wished the men would come back. He wanted another chance at killing them.

Roland searched for his glasses. He found the garbage bag, but his glasses were lost. Everything would be blurred from now on, but that was okay; there was no more light, anyway. His hands found warm blood and a body to go with it. He spent a minute or two kicking the dead man's skull in.

Roland picked up the garbage bag and, keeping the Ingram gun ready, carefully moved across the cafeteria toward where he knew the exit to be; his toes probed for holes in the floor, but he made it safely into the corridor.

He still trembled with excitement. Everything was black and silent but for the slow dripping of water somewhere. He felt his way toward the gymnasium with his bag of booty, eager to tell the King that he'd fought off three tunnel trolls, and that one of them was named Schorr. But there would be more trolls! They wouldn't give up so easily, and besides, he wasn't sure if he'd killed the hospitality sergeant or not.

Roland grinned into the darkness, his face and hair damp with cold sweat. He was very, very proud of himself for protecting the King, though he regretted losing the flashlight. In the corridor he stepped on bodies that were swelling like gasbags.

This was turning out to be the greatest game he'd ever played. This beat the computer version by a light-year!

He'd never shot anybody before. And he'd never felt so powerful before, either.

Surrounded by darkness and death and carrying a bagful of scraps and a warm Ingram gun, Roland Croninger knew true ecstasy.

Twenty-four

A squeaking sound coming from a corner of the basement made Josh reach to his side for the flashlight and switch it on. The weak bulb threw a dim yellow spear of light, but Josh guided it toward that corner to find out what was over there.

"What is it?" Swan asked, sitting up a few feet beside him.

"I think we've got a rat." He played the light around, saw only a tangle of timbers, cornstalks and the mound of dirt where Darleen Prescott lay buried. Josh quickly moved the light away from the grave. The child was just now getting her senses back. "Yeah, I think it's a rat," Josh decided. "Probably had a nest hidden down here somewhere. Hey, Mr. Rat!" he called. "Mind if we share your basement for a while?"

"He sounds like he's hurt."

"He probably thinks we sound pretty bad, too." He kept the flashlight's beam away from the little girl; he'd already seen her once in the meager light, and that was enough. Almost all of her beautiful blond hair was burned away, her face a mass of red, watery blisters. Her eyes, which he remembered as being so stunningly blue, were deep-sunken and a cloudy gray. He was aware that the blast hadn't spared his looks, either; the backwash of the light revealed splotched gray burns that covered his hands and arms. More than that, he didn't care to know. He was going to wind up looking like a zebra. But at least they were both still alive, and though he had no way of calculating how much time had passed since the explosion, he thought they'd been down here for maybe four or five days. Food was no longer a problem, and they had plenty of canned juices. Air must be entering from somewhere, though the basement remained stuffy. The worst concern Josh had was the latrine's smell, but that couldn't be helped right now. Maybe later he'd figure out a neater sanitation system, perhaps using the empty cans and burying those in the dirt.

Something moved in the light's beam.

"Look!" Swan said. "Over there!"

A small, burned little animal perched on a tiny hillock of dirt. Its head tilted toward Swan and Josh, and then the animal squeaked again and disappeared into the debris.

Josh said, "That's not a rat! It's a—"

"It's a *gopher!*" Swan finished for him. "I've seen lots of them before, digging out near the trailer park."

"A gopher," Josh repeated. He remembered PawPaw's voice, saying *Gopher's in the hole!*

Swan was pleased to see something else alive down here with them. She could hear it sniffing in the dirt, over beyond the light and the mound where . . . She let the thought go, because she couldn't stand it. But her mama wasn't hurting anymore, and that was a good thing. Swan listened to the gopher snuffling around; she was very familiar with the things, because of all the holes they dug in her garden. . . .

All the holes they dug, she thought.

"Josh?" Swan said.

"Yeah?"

"Gophers dig holes," she said.

Josh smiled faintly at what he took to be just a childlike statement—but then his smile froze as what she was getting at struck him. If a gopher had a nest down here, then there might indeed be a *hole*, leading out! Maybe that was where the air was coming from! Josh's heart leaped. Maybe PawPaw knew there was a gopher hole somewhere in the basement, and that was the message he'd been trying to relay. A gopher hole could be enlarged to make a tunnel. We've got a pickaxe and shovel, he thought. Maybe we can dig ourselves out!

Josh crawled to where the old man lay. "Hey," Josh said. "Can you hear me?" He touched PawPaw's arm.

"Oh Lord," Josh whispered.

The old man's body was cool. It lay stiffly, the arms rigid by the sides. Josh shone the light into the corpse's face, saw the mottled scarlet burns like a strange birthmark across the cheeks and nose. The eye sockets were dark brown, gaping holes. PawPaw had been dead for several hours, at least. Josh started to close PawPaw's eyelids, but there were none; those, too, had been incinerated and vaporized.

The gopher squeaked. Josh turned away from the corpse and crawled toward the noise. Probing into the debris with his light, he found the gopher licking at its burned hind legs. It abruptly darted under a piece of wood wedged into the corner. Josh reached after it, but the wood was stuck tight. As patiently as he could, he began to work it free.

The gopher chattered angrily at the invasion. Slowly, Josh got the splintered piece of timber loose and pulled it away. The light revealed a small round hole in the dirt wall, about three inches off the floor.

"Found it!" Josh exclaimed. He got down on his belly and shone the light up into the hole. About two or three feet out of the basement, it crooked to the left and continued on beyond the range of the light. "This thing's got to lead to the surface!" He was as excited as a kid on Christmas morning, and he was able to get his fist up into the hole. The ground was hard-packed and unyielding, burned even at this depth to the solidity of asphalt. Digging through it was going to be an absolute bitch, but following the hole would make the work easier.

One question nagged at him: did they *want* to get out of the basement anytime soon? The radiation might kill them outright. God only knew what the surface world would be like. Did they dare find out?

Josh heard a noise behind him. It was a hoarse rattling sound, like congested lungs struggling for air.

"Josh?" Swan had heard the noise too, and it made the remaining hairs on the back of her neck stand up; she had sensed something moving in the darkness just a few seconds before.

He turned and shone the light at her. Swan's blistered face was turned to the right. Again, there came that hideous rattling noise. Josh shifted the light—and what he saw made him feel as if a freezing hand had clenched his throat.

PawPaw's corpse was shivering, and that awful noise was emanating from it. He's still alive, Josh thought incredulously; but then: No, no! He was dead when I touched him! He was *dead!*

The corpse lurched. Slowly, arms still stiff at its sides, the dead man began to sit up. Its head started turning inch by inch, like a clockwork automaton, toward Josh Hutchins, its raw eye sockets seeking the light. The burned face rippled, the mouth straining to open—and Josh thought that if those dead lips parted he would lose whatever marbles he had left right then and there.

With a hiss and rattle of air, the mouth opened.

And from it came a voice like the rush of wind through dried-up reeds. It was at first an unintelligible sound, thin and distant, but it was getting stronger, and it said: *"Pro . . . tect . . ."*

The eye sockets faced the beam of light as if there were still eyeballs in them. *"Protect,"* the awful voice repeated. The mouth with its gray lips seemed to be straining to form words. Josh shrank backward, and the corpse racheted out, *"Protect . . . the . . . child."*

There was a quiet *whoosh* of air. The corpse's eye sockets caught fire. Josh was mesmerized, and he heard Swan give a soft, stunned *"Oh."* The corpse's head burst into a fireball, and the fire spread and enveloped the entire body in a writhing, reddish-blue cocoon. An intense wave of heat licked at Josh's face, and he put up his hand to shield his eyes; when he lowered it again, he saw the corpse dissolving at the center of its fiery shroud. The body remained sitting upright, motionless now, every inch of it ablaze.

The burning went on for maybe thirty seconds longer; then the fire began to flicker out, and the last to burn were the soles of PawPaw's shoes.

But what lingered was white ash, in the shape of a man sitting upright.

The fire went out. The ashen shape crumbled; it was ash through and through, even the bones. It collapsed in a heap on the floor, and what remained of PawPaw Briggs was ready for a shovel.

Josh stared. Ash drifted lazily through the light. I'm going off my bird! he thought. All those body slams've caught up with me!

Behind him, Swan bit her lower lip and fought off frightened tears. I won't cry, she told herself. Not anymore. The urge to sob passed, and she let her shocked eyes drift toward the black giant.

Protect the child. Josh had heard it. But PawPaw Briggs had been dead, he reasoned. *Protect the child*. Sue Wanda. Swan. Whatever had spoken through the dead man's lips was gone now; it was just Josh and Swan, alone.

He believed in miracles, but of the biblical version—the parting of the Red Sea, the turning of water to wine, the feeding of the multitude from a basket of bread and fish; up until this moment, he'd thought the age of miracles was long past. But maybe it was a small miracle that they'd both found this grocery store, he realized. It was certainly a miracle that they were still alive, and a corpse that could sit up and speak was not something you saw every day.

Behind him, the gopher scrabbled in the dirt. He smells the food leaking from the cans, Josh figured. Maybe that gopher hole was a small miracle, too. He could not stop staring at the pile of white ashes, and he would hear that reedy voice for the rest of his life—however long that might be.

"You all right?" he asked Swan.

"Yes," she replied, barely audible.

Josh nodded. If something beyond his ken wanted him to protect the child, he thought, then he was damned well going to protect the child. After a while, when he got his bones thawed out again, he crawled to get the shovel, and then he switched off the light to let it rest. In the darkness, he covered the ashes of PawPaw Briggs with cornfield dirt.

Twenty-five

"Cigarette?"

A pack of Winstons was offered. Sister took one of the cigarettes. Doyle Halland flicked a gold butane lighter with the initials RBR on its side. When the cigarette was lit, Sister drew the smoke deeply into her lungs—no use to fret about cancer now!—and let it trickle through her nostrils.

A fire crackled in the hearth of the small, wood-framed suburban house in which they'd decided to shelter for the night. All the windows were broken out, but they'd been able to trap some heat in the front room due to a fortunate discovery of blankets and a hammer and nails. They'd nailed the blankets up over the largest windows and huddled around the fireplace. The refrigerator yielded up a can of chocolate sauce, some lemonade in a plastic pitcher, and a head of brown lettuce. The pantry held only a half-full box of raisin bran and a few other cans and jars of left-behinds. Still, all of it was edible, and Sister put the cans and jars in her bag, which was beginning to bulge with things she'd scavenged. It was soon going to be time to find a second bag.

During the day they had walked a little more than five miles through the silent sprawl of the east Jersey suburbs, heading west along Interstate 280 and crossing the Garden State Parkway. The bitter cold gnawed at their bones, and the sun was no more than an area of gray in a low, muddy brown sky streaked with red. But Sister noted that the further away they got from Manhattan, the more buildings were still intact, though almost every one of them had blasted-out windows, and they leaned as if they'd been knocked off their foundations. Then they reached an area of two-story, close-cramped houses—thousands of them, brooding and broken like little gothic manors—on postage-stamp-sized lawns burned the color of dead leaves. Sister noted that none of the trees or bushes she saw had a scrap of vegetation. Nothing was green anymore; everything was colored in the dun, gray and black of death.

They did see their first cars that weren't twisted into junk. Abandoned vehicles, their paint blistered off and windshields smashed, stood here and there on the streets, but only one of them had a key, and that one was broken off and wedged in the ignition. They went on, shivering in the cold, as the gray circle of the sun moved across the sky.

A laughing woman wearing a flimsy blue robe, her face swollen and lacerated, sat on a front porch and jeered at them as they passed. "You're too late!" she shouted. "Everybody's gone! You're too late!" She was holding a pistol in her lap, and so they kept going. On another corner, a dead man with a purple face, his head hideously misshapen, leaned against a bus stop sign and grinned up at the sky, his hands locked around a business briefcase. It was in the coat pocket of this corpse that Doyle Halland had found the pack of Winstons and the butane lighter.

Everyone was, indeed, gone. A few corpses lay in front lawns or on curbs or draped over steps, but those who were still living and still halfway sane had fled from the radius of the holocaust. Sitting in front of the fire and smoking a dead man's cigarette, Sister envisioned an exodus of suburbanites, frantically packing pillowcases and paper bags with food and everything they could carry as Manhattan melted beyond the Palisades. They had taken their children and abandoned their pets, fleeing westward before the black rain like an army of tramps and bag ladies. But they had left their blankets behind, because it was the middle of July. Nobody expected it to get cold. They just wanted to get away from the fire. Where were they going to run to, and where were they going to hide? The cold was going to catch them, and many of them would already be deep asleep in its embrace.

Behind her, the others were curled up on the floor, sleeping on sofa cushions and covered by rugs. Sister drew on the cigarette again and then looked at Doyle Halland's craggy profile. He stared into the fire, a Winston between his lips, one long-fingered hand tentatively massaging his leg where the splinter was driven through. The man was damned tough, Sister thought; he'd never once asked to stop and rest his leg today, though the pain of walking had bled his face chalky.

"So what were you planning on doing?" Sister asked him. "Staying around that church forever?"

He hesitated a moment before he answered. "No," he said. "Not forever. Just until . . . I don't know, just until someone came along who was going somewhere."

"Why didn't you leave with the other people?"

"I stayed to give the last rites to as many as I could. Within six hours of the blast, I'd done so many that I lost my voice. I couldn't speak, and there were so many more dying people. They were begging me to save their souls. Begging me to get them into Heaven." He glanced quickly at her and then away. He had gray eyes flecked with green. "Begging me," he repeated softly. "And I couldn't even speak, so I gave them the Sign of the Cross, and I . . . I *kissed* them. I kissed them to sleep, and they all trusted me." He drew on the cigarette, exhaled the smoke and watched it drift toward the fireplace. "St. Matthew's has been my church for over twelve years. I kept coming back to it and walking through the ruins, trying to figure out what had happened. We had some lovely statues and stained-glass windows. Twelve years." He slowly shook his head.

"I'm sorry," Sister offered.

"Why should you be? You didn't have anything to do with this. It's just . . . something that got out of control. Maybe nobody could've stopped it." He glanced at her again, and this time his gaze lingered at the crusted wound in the hollow of her throat. "What's that?" he asked her. "It looks almost like a crucifix."

She touched it. "I used to wear a chain with a cross on it."

"What happened?"

"Someone—" She stopped. How could she describe it? Even now her mind skittered away from the memory; it was not a safe thing to think about. "Someone took it from me," she continued.

He nodded thoughtfully and leaked smoke from the corner of his mouth. Through the blue haze, his eyes searched hers. "Do you believe in God?"

"Yes, I do."

"Why?" he asked quietly.

"I believe in God because someday Jesus is going to come and take everyone worthy up in the Rap—" *No,* she told herself. *No.* That was Sister Creep babbling about things she'd heard other bag ladies say. She paused, getting her thoughts in order, and then she said, "I believe in God because I'm alive, and I don't think I could've made it this far by myself. I believe in God because I believe I will live to see another day."

"You believe because you believe," he said. "That doesn't say much for logic, does it?"

"Are you saying you *don't* believe?"

Doyle Halland smiled vacantly. The smile slowly slipped off his face. "Do you really think that God has His eye on *you,* lady? Do you think He really cares whether you live one more day or not? What singles *you* out from all those corpses we passed today? Didn't God care about them?" He held the lighter with its initials in the palm of his hand. "What about Mr. RBR? Didn't he go to church enough? Wasn't he a good boy?"

"I don't know if God has an eye on me or not," Sister replied. "But I hope He does. I hope I'm important enough—that we're *all* important enough. As for the dead . . . maybe they were the lucky ones. I don't know."

"Maybe they were," he agreed. He returned the lighter to

his pocket. "I just don't know what there is to live for anymore. Where are we going? Why are we going *anywhere?* I mean . . . one place is as good as another to die in, isn't it?"

"I'm not planning on dying anytime soon. I think Artie wants to get back to Detroit. I'll go there with him."

"And after that? If you make it as far as Detroit?"

She shrugged. "Like I say, I'm not planning on dying. I'll keep going as long as I can walk."

"No one plans on dying," he said. "I used to be an optimist, a long time ago. I used to believe in miracles. But do you know what happened? I got *older.* And the world got meaner. I used to serve and believe in God with all my heart, with every ounce of faith in my body." His eyes narrowed slightly, as if he were looking at something far beyond the fire. "As I say, that was a long time ago. I used to be an optimist . . . now I suppose I'm an opportunist. I'm very good at judging which way the wind blows—and I'd have to say that now I judge God, or the power that we know as God, to be very, very weak. A dying candle, if you like, surrounded by darkness. And the darkness is closing in." He sat without moving, just watching the fire burn.

"You don't sound much like a priest."

"I don't feel much like one, either. I just feel . . . like a worn-out man in a black suit with a stupid, dirty white collar. Does that shock you?"

"No. I don't think I can be shocked anymore."

"Good. Then that means you're becoming less of an optimist too, doesn't it?" He grunted. "I'm sorry. I guess I don't sound like Spencer Tracy in *Boys Town,* do I? But those last rites I gave . . . they fell out of my mouth like ashes, and I can't get that damned taste out of my mouth." His gaze slipped down to the bag at Sister's side. "What's that thing I saw you with last night? That glass thing?"

"It's something I found on Fifth Avenue."

"Oh. May I see it?"

Sister brought it out of her bag. The jewels trapped within the glass circle burst into blazing rainbow colors. The reflections danced on the walls of the room and striped both Sister's and Doyle Halland's faces. He drew in his breath, because it was the first time he'd really gotten a good look at it. His eyes widened, the colors sparkling in his pupils. He reached out to touch it but drew his hand back at the last second. "What *is* it?"

"Just glass and jewels, melted together. But . . . last night, just before you came, this thing . . . did something wonderful, something I still can't explain." She told him about Julia Castillo and being able to understand each other's language when they were linked by the glass circle. He sat listening intently. "Beth said this thing's *magic.* I don't know about that, but I do know it's pretty strange. Look at it pick up my heartbeat. And the way the thing *glows*—I don't know what this is, but I'm sure as hell not going to throw it away."

"A crown," he said softly. "I heard Beth say it could be a crown. It looks like a tiara, doesn't it?"

"I guess it does. Not quite like the tiaras in the Tiffany windows, though. I mean . . . it's all crooked and weird-looking. I remember I wanted to give up. I wanted to die. And then I found this, and it made me think that . . . I don't know, it's stupid, I guess."

"Go on," he urged.

"It made me think about *sand,"* Sister told him. "That sand is about the most worthless stuff in the world, yet look what sand can become in the right hands." She ran her fingers over the velvet surface of the glass. "Even the most worthless thing in the world can be beautiful," she said. "It just takes the right touch. But seeing this beautiful thing, and holding it in my hands, made me think I wasn't so worthless, either. It made me want to get up off my ass and *live.* I used to be crazy, but after I found this thing . . . I wasn't so crazy anymore. Maybe part of me's still crazy, I don't know; but I *want* to believe that all the beauty in the world isn't dead yet. I want to believe that beauty can be saved."

"I haven't seen very much beauty in the last few days," he replied. "Except for that. You're right. It is a very, very beautiful piece of junk." He smiled faintly. "Or crown. Or whatever it is you choose to believe."

Sister nodded and peered into the depths of the glass circle. Beneath the glass, the threads of precious metals flared like sparklers. The pulsing of a large, deep brown topaz caught her attention; she could sense Doyle Halland watching her, could hear the crackle of the fire and the sweep of the wind outside, but the brown topaz and its hypnotic rhythm—so soft, so steady—filled up her vision. Oh, she thought, what *are* you? What *are* you? What—

She blinked.

She was no longer holding the circle of glass.

And she was no longer sitting before the fire in the New Jersey house.

Wind swept around her, and she smelled dry, scorched earth and . . . something else. What was it?

Yes. Now she knew. It was the odor of burned corn.

She was standing on a vast, flat plain, and the sky above her was a whirling mass of dirty gray clouds through which electric-blue streaks of lightning plunged. Charred cornstalks lay about her by the thousands—and the only feature on that awful wasteland was a large dome that looked like a grave about a hundred yards away.

I'm dreaming, she thought. I'm really sitting in New Jersey. This is a dreamscape—a picture in my mind, that's all. I can wake up anytime I want to, and I'll be back in New Jersey again.

She looked at the strange dome and wondered how far she could push the limits of this dream. If I take a step, she thought, will the whole thing fall to pieces like a movie set? She decided to find out, and she took a single step. The dreamscape remained intact. If this is a dream, she told herself, then, by God, I'm dreamwalking somewhere a long way from New Jersey, because I can *feel* that wind in my face!

She walked over the dry earth and cornstalks toward the dome; no dust plumed beneath her feet, and she had the sensation of *drifting* over the landscape like a ghost instead of actually walking, though she knew her legs were moving. As she neared the dome she saw it was a mass of dirt, thousands of burned cornstalks, pieces of wood and cinder blocks all jammed together. Nearby was a twisted thing of metal that might once have been a car, and another one lay ten or fifteen yards beyond the first. Other pieces of metal, wood and debris lay scattered around her: here was what appeared to be the nozzle from a gas pump, there was the burned lid of a suitcase. The rags of clothes—small clothes—were lying about. Sister walked—*dreamwalked,* she thought—past part of a wagon wheel half buried in the dirt, and there was the remnant of a sign that still held barely decipherable letters: P . . . A . . . W.

She stopped about twenty yards from the gravelike dome. This is a funny thing to be dreaming about, she thought. I could be dreaming about a thick steak and an ice cream sundae.

Sister looked in all directions, saw nothing but desolation.

But no. Something on the ground caught her eye—a little figure of some kind—and she dreamwalked toward it.

A doll, she realized as she got nearer. A doll with a bit of blue fur still clinging to its body, and two plastic eyes with little black pupils that Sister knew would jiggle around if it was picked up. She stood over the doll. The thing was somehow familiar, and she thought of her own dead daughter perched in front of the TV set. Reruns of an old show for kids called "Sesame Street" had been one of her favorite programs.

And Sister remembered the child pointing gleefully at the screen and shouting: "Cooookies!"

The Cookie Monster. Yes. That's who that was, lying there at her feet.

Something about that doll there on the desolate plain struck a note of terrible sadness in Sister's heart. Where was the child to whom this doll belonged? Blown away with the wind? Or buried and lying dead under the earth?

She bent down to pick up the Cookie Monster doll.

And her hands went right through it—as if either the scene or she were made of smoke.

This is a *dream,* Sister thought. This is not real! This is a mirage inside my head, and I'm dreamwalking through it!

She stepped back from the doll. It was for the best that it remain there, in case the child who had lost it someday came back this way.

Sister squeezed her eyes shut. I want to go back now, she

thought. I want to go back where I was, back far away from here. Far away. Far a—

". . . for your thoughts."

Sister was startled by the voice, which seemed to be whispered right into her ear. She looked to her side. Doyle Halland's face hovered above her, caught between the fire-light and the reflection of the jewels. "What?"

"I said, a penny for your thoughts. Where'd you go?"

Where indeed, Sister wondered. "Far away from here," she said. Everything was as it had been before. The vision was gone, but Sister imagined she could still smell burned corn and feel that wind on her face.

The cigarette was burning down between her fingers. She took one last draw from it and then thumped it into the fireplace. She put the glass ring down into her bag again and held the bag close to her body. Behind her eyes, she could still clearly see the dome of dirt, the wagon wheel, the mangled remains of cars and the blue-furred Cookie Monster.

Where was I? she asked herself—and she had no answer.

"Where do we go in the morning?" Halland inquired.

"West," she answered. "We keep going west. Maybe we'll find a car with a key in the ignition tomorrow. Maybe we'll find some other people. I don't think we'll have to worry much about food for a while. We can scavenge enough to eat as we go. I was never very fussy about my meals, anyway." Water was still going to be a problem, though. The kitchen and bathroom faucets in this house were dry, and Sister figured that the shock waves had shattered water mains all over the metro area.

"Do you really think it's going to be better anywhere else?" He lifted his burned eyebrows. "The wind's going to throw radiation all over this country. If the blast and the fires and the radiation don't finish people off, it's going to be hunger, thirst and the cold. I'd say there's nowhere to go after all, is there?"

Sister stared into the fire. "Like I say," she said finally, "nobody has to go with me who doesn't want to. I'm getting some sleep now. Good night." She crawled over to where the others were huddled under the rugs, and she lay down between Artie and Beth and tried to find sleep while the wind shrieked beyond the walls.

Doyle Halland carefully touched the metal splinter in his leg. He sat slightly slumped forward, and his gaze ticked toward Sister and the bag she held so protectively. He grunted thoughtfully, smoked his cigarette down to the filter and tossed it into the fireplace. Then he positioned himself in a corner, facing Sister and the others, and he stared at them for perhaps a full five minutes, his eyes glittering in the gloom, before he leaned his head back and went to sleep sitting up.

Twenty-six

It began with a mangled voice calling from beyond the gymnasium's barricaded door: "Colonel? Colonel Macklin?"

Macklin, on his knees in the dark, did not answer. Not far away, Roland Croninger clicked the safety off the Ingram gun, and he could hear Warner's harsh breathing over to his right.

"We know you're in the gym," the voice continued. "We searched everywhere else. Got yourself a nice little fortress, don't you?"

As soon as Roland had reported the incident at the cafeteria, they'd gone to work blocking the gym's doorway with stones, cables and parts of broken-up Nautilus machines. The boy had had the good idea to scatter shards of glass out in the corridor, to cut the marauders up when they came creeping through the dark on their hands and knees. A moment before the voice, Macklin had heard curses and pained mutterings, and he knew the glass had done its job. In his left hand he held a makeshift weapon that had been part of a Nautilus Super Pullover machine—a curved metal bar about two feet long, with twelve inches of chain and a dangling, macelike sprocket at its business end.

"Is the boy in there?" the voice inquired. "I'm looking for you, boy. You really did a job on me, you little fucker." And now Roland knew Schorr had escaped, but from the way he sounded the hospitality sergeant had lost half his mouth.

Teddybear Warner's nerve shattered. "Go away! Leave us alone!"

Oh, shit, Macklin thought. Now they know they've got us!

There was a long silence. Then, "I've got some hungry people to feed, Colonel, sir. We know you've got a bagful of food in there. It's not right for you to have it all, is it?" When Macklin didn't reply, Schorr's distorted voice roared, "Give us the food, you sonofabitch!"

Something gripped Macklin's shoulder; it felt like a cold, hard claw digging into his skin. "More mouths, less food," the Shadow Soldier whispered. "You know what it's like to be hungry, don't you? Remember the pit, back in Nam? Remember what you did to get that rice, mister?"

Macklin nodded. He did remember. Oh, yes, he did. He remembered knowing that he was going to die if he didn't get more than one fourth of a small rice cake every time the Cong guards dropped one down, and he'd known the others—McGee, Ragsdale and Mississippi—could read their own tombstones, too. A man had a certain look in his eyes when he was pushed against the wall and stripped of his humanity; his entire face changed, as if it was a mask cracking open to show the face of the real beast within.

And when Macklin had decided what it was he had to do, the Shadow Soldier had told him how to do it.

Ragsdale had been the weakest. It had been a simple thing to press his face into the mud while the others were sleeping.

But one third of the rice wasn't enough, the Shadow Soldier said. Macklin had strangled McGee, and then there were two.

Mississippi had been the toughest to kill. He was still strong, and he'd fought Macklin off again and again. But Macklin had kept at him, attacking him when he tried to sleep, and finally Mississippi had lost his mind and crouched in the corner, calling for Jesus like a hysterical child. It had been an easy thing, then, to grasp Mississippi's chin and wrench his head violently backward.

Then all the rice was his, and the Shadow Soldier said he'd done very, very well.

"Can you hear me, Colonel, sir?" Schorr sneered beyond the barricade. "Just give us the food and we'll go!"

"Bullshit," Macklin answered. There was no more use in hiding. "We've got weapons in here, Schorr." He desperately wanted the man to believe they had more than just one Ingram gun, a couple of metal clubs, a metal cleaver and some sharp rocks. "Back off!"

"We've brought along some toys of our own. I don't think you want to find out what they are."

"You're bluffing."

"Am I? Well, sir, let me tell you this: I found a way to get to the garage. There's not much left. Most everything's smashed to hell, and you can't get to the drawbridge crank. But I found what I needed, Colonel, sir, and I don't give a damn how many guns you've got in there. Now: Does the food come out, or do we take it?"

"Roland," Macklin said urgently, "get ready to fire."

The boy aimed the Ingram gun in the direction of Schorr's voice.

"What we've got stays here," Macklin told him. "You find your own food, just like we found ours."

"There *is* no more!" Schorr raged. "You sonofabitch, you're not going to kill us like you killed everybody else in this damn—"

"Fire," Macklin ordered.

Roland squeezed the trigger with no hesitation.

The gun jumped in his hands as the tracers streaked across the gym like scarlet comets. They hit the barricade and the wall around the door, popping and whining madly as they ricocheted. In the brief, jerky light, a man—not Schorr—could be seen trying to climb through the space between the pile of rubble and the top of the door. He started to pull back when the firing began, but he suddenly screamed, caught in the glass and metal cables that Roland had arranged. Bullets hit him and he writhed, getting more tangled up. His screaming stopped. Arms came up, grabbed the body and heaved it backward into the corridor.

Roland released the trigger. His pockets were full of ammo clips, and the colonel had drilled him in changing the clips quickly. The noise of the machine gun faded. The marauders were silent.

"They're gone!" Warner shouted. "We ran 'em off!"

"Shut up!" Macklin warned him. He saw a flicker of light from the corridor—what might've been a match being struck. In the next instant, something afire came flying over the barricade. It hit with the sound of shattering glass, and Macklin had a second to smell gasoline before the Molotov cocktail blew, a sheet of fire leaping across the gym. He jerked his head down behind his rock pile hiding place as glass whined like yellowjackets around his ears. The flames shot past him, and when the explosion was over he looked up and saw a puddle of gas burning about fifteen feet away.

Roland had ducked as well, but small fragments of glass had nicked his cheek and shoulder. He lifted his head and fired again at the doorway; the bullets hit the top of the barricade and ricocheted harmlessly.

"You like that, Macklin?" Schorr taunted. "We found us a little gasoline in some of the car tanks. Found us some rags and a few beer bottles, too. We've got more where that one came from. You like it?"

Firelight flickered off the walls of the wrecked gym. Macklin hadn't counted on this; Schorr and the others could stand behind the barricade and toss those bastards over the top. He heard a metal tool of some kind scrape against the debris that blocked the door, and some of the rocks slid away.

A second gasoline-filled bottle, a flaming rag jammed down into it, sailed into the gym and exploded near Captain Warner, who cowered behind a mound of stones, bent metal and Nautilus weights. The gas spattered like grease from a skillet, and the captain cried out as he was hit by flying glass. Roland fired the Ingram gun at the doorway as a third bomb landed between him and Colonel Macklin, and he had to leap aside as burning gas splashed at his legs. Shards of glass tugged at Macklin's jacket, and one caught him over the right eyebrow and snapped his head back like a punch.

The gym's rubble—mats, towels, ceiling tiles, ripped-up carpeting and wood paneling—was catching fire. Smoke and gasoline fumes swirled through the air.

When Roland looked up again, he could see blurred figures furiously digging their way over the barricade. He gave them another burst of bullets, and they scattered back into the corridor like roaches down a hole. A gas-filled Dr Pepper bottle exploded in reply, the whoosh of flames searing Roland's face and sucking the breath from his lungs. He felt a stinging pain and looked at his left hand; it was covered in flame, and silver-dollar-sized circles of fire burned all over his arm. He shouted with terror and scrambled toward the mop bucket full of toilet water.

The flames were growing, merging and advancing across the gym. More of the barricade crumbled, and Macklin saw the marauders coming in; Schorr was leading them, armed with a broom handle sharpened into a spear, a bloodstained rag wrapped around his swollen, wild-eyed face. Behind him were three men and a woman, all carrying primitive weapons: jagged-edged stones and clubs made from broken furniture. As Roland frantically washed off the burning gasoline Teddy-bear Warner hobbled out from his shelter and fell down on his knees in front of Schorr, his hands upraised for mercy. "Don't kill me!" he begged. "I'm with you! I swear to God, I'm with—"

Schorr drove the sharpened broomstick into Warner's throat. The others swarmed over him as well, beating and kicking the captain as he flopped on the end of the spear. The flames threw their shadows on the walls like dancers in Hell. Then Schorr jerked the spear from Warner's throat and whirled toward Colonel Macklin.

Roland picked up the Ingram gun at his side. A hand suddenly clamped around the back of his neck, jerking him to his feet. He saw the blurred image of a man in tattered clothes standing over him, about to smash a rock into his skull.

Schorr charged Macklin. The colonel staggered to his feet to defend himself with the high-tech mace.

The man gripping Roland's neck made a choking sound. He was wearing eyeglasses with cracked lenses held together at the bridge of his nose with a Band-Aid.

Schorr feinted with the spear. Macklin lost his balance and fell, twisting away as the spear grazed his side. "Roland, help me!" he screamed.

"Oh . . . my God," the man with the cracked eyeglasses breathed. "Roland . . . you're alive. . . ."

Roland thought the man's voice was familiar, but he wasn't sure. Nothing was certain anymore but the fact that he was a King's Knight. All that had gone before this moment were shadows, flimsy and insubstantial, and this was real life.

"Roland!" the man said. "Don't you know your own—"

Roland brought the Ingram gun up and blew most of the man's head away. The stranger staggered back, broken teeth chattering in a mask of blood, and fell into the fire.

The other people threw themselves upon the garbage bag and tore wildly at it, splitting it open and fighting one another for the scraps. Roland turned toward Schorr and Colonel Macklin; Schorr was jabbing at the colonel with his spear while Macklin used his metal club to parry the thrusts. Macklin was being steadily forced into a corner, where the leaping firelight revealed a large airshaft set in the cracked wall, its wire mesh grille hanging by one screw.

Roland started to shoot, but smoke swirled around the figures and he feared hitting the King. His finger twitched on the trigger—and then something struck him in the small of the back and knocked him onto his face on the floor, where he lay struggling for breath. The machine gun fell from his hand, and the woman with insane, red-rimmed eyes who'd thrown the rock scrabbled on her hands and knees to get it.

Macklin swung the mace at Schorr's head. Schorr ducked, stumbling over the rocks and burning debris. "Come on!" Macklin yelled. "Come and get me!"

The crazy woman crawled over Roland and picked up the Ingram gun. Roland was stunned, but he knew both he and the King were dead if she was able to use the weapon; he grabbed her wrist, and she shrieked and fought, her teeth gnashing at his face. She got her other hand up and went for his eyes with her fingers, but he twisted his head away to keep from being blinded. The woman wrenched her wrist loose and, still shrieking, aimed the machine gun.

She fired it, the tracers streaking across the gym.

But she was not aiming at Colonel Macklin. The two men who were fighting over the garbage can were caught by the bullets and made to dance as if their shoes were aflame. They went down, and the crazy woman scrambled toward the scraps with the gun clutched against her breasts.

The chatter of the Ingram gun had made Schorr's head swivel around—and Macklin lunged forward, striking at the other man's side with the mace. He heard Schorr's ribs break like sticks trodden underfoot. Schorr cried out, tried to backpedal, tripped and fell to his knees. Macklin lifted the mace high and smashed it down on the center of Schorr's forehead, and the man's skull dented in the shape of a Nautilus cam. Then Macklin was standing over the body, striking the skull again and again. Schorr's head started to change shape.

Roland was on his feet. A short distance away, the crazy woman was stuffing her mouth with the burned food. The flames were growing higher and hotter, and dense smoke whirled past Macklin as, finally, the strength of his left arm gave out. He dropped the mace and gave Schorr's corpse one last kick to the ribs.

The smoke got his attention. He watched it sliding into the shaft, which was about three feet high and three feet wide—large enough to crawl through, he realized. It took him a minute to clear the fatigue out of his mind. The smoke was being drawn into the airshaft. *Drawn* in. Where was it going? To the surface of Blue Dome Mountain? To the outside world?

He didn't care about the garbage bag anymore, didn't care about Schorr or the crazy woman or the Ingram gun. There had to be a way out up there somewhere! He wrenched the grille off and crawled into the shaft. It led upward at a forty degree angle, and Macklin's feet found the heads of bolts in the aluminum surface to push himself against. There was no light ahead, and the smoke was almost choking, but Macklin knew that this might be their only chance to get out. Roland followed him, inching upward after the King in this new turn of the game.

Behind them, in the burning gym, they heard the crazy woman's voice float up into the tunnel: "Where'd everybody go? It's hot in here . . . so hot. God knows I didn't come all this way to cook in a mine shaft!"

Something about that voice clutched at Roland's heart. He remembered a voice like that, a long time ago. He kept moving, but when the crazy woman screamed and the smell of burning meat came up into the tunnel he had to stop and clasp his hands over his ears, because the sound made the world spin too fast and he feared being flung off. The screaming stopped after a while, and all Roland could hear was the steady sliding of the King's body further along the shaft. Coughing, his eyes watering, Roland pushed himself onward.

They came to a place where the shaft had been crushed closed. Macklin's hand found another shaft branching off from the one they'd been following: this one was a tighter fit, and it clamped around the colonel's shoulders as he squeezed into it. The smoke was still bad, and his lungs were burning. It was like creeping up a chimney with a fire blazing below, and Roland wondered if this was what Santa Claus felt like.

Further along, Macklin's questing fingers touched Fiberglas. It was part of the system of air filters and baffles that purified what Earth House residents breathed in case of nuclear attack. Sure helped a whole hell of a lot, didn't it? he thought grimly. He ripped away the filter and kept crawling. The shaft curved gradually to the left, and Macklin had to tear through more filters and louverlike baffles made of rubber and nylon. He was straining hard to breathe, and he heard Roland gasping behind him. The kid was damned tough, he thought. Anybody who had a will to live like that kid did was a person to reckon with, even if he looked like a ninety-pound weakling.

Macklin stopped. He'd touched metal ahead of him, blades radiating from a central hub. One of the fans that drew air in from the outside. "We must be close to the surface!" he said.

Smoke was still moving past him in the dark. "We've got to be close!"

He put his hand against the fan's hub and pushed until the muscles in his shoulder cracked. The fan was bolted securely in place and wasn't going to move. Damn you! he seethed. Damn you to Hell! He pushed again, as hard as he could, but all he did was exhaust himself. The fan wasn't going to let them out.

Macklin laid his cheek against cool aluminum and tried to think, tried to picture the blueprints of Earth House in his mind. How were the intake fans serviced? Think! But he was unable to see the blueprints correctly; they kept shivering and falling to pieces.

"Listen!" Roland cried out.

Macklin did. He couldn't hear anything but his own heartbeat and his raw lungs heaving.

"I hear wind!" Roland said. "I hear wind moving up there!" He reached up, felt the movement of air. The faint sound of shrilling wind came from directly above. He ran his hands over the crumpled wall to his right, then to his left—and he discovered iron rungs. "There's a way up! There's another shaft right over our heads!" Grasping the bottom rung, Roland drew himself up, rung by rung, to a standing position. "I'm climbing up," he told Macklin, and he began to ascend.

The windscream was louder, but there was still no light. He had climbed maybe twenty feet when his hand touched a metal flywheel over his head. Exploring, his fingers glided over a cracked concrete surface. Roland thought it must be the lid of a hatch, like a submarine's conning tower hatch that could be opened and closed by the flywheel. But he could feel the strong suction of air there, and he figured the blast must have sprung the hatch, because it was no longer securely sealed.

He grasped the flywheel, tried to turn it. The thing wouldn't budge. Roland waited a minute, building up his strength and determination; if ever he needed the power of a King's Knight, it was at this moment. He attacked the flywheel again; this time he thought it might have moved a half inch, but he wasn't sure.

"Roland!" Colonel Macklin called from below. He'd finally put the blueprints together in his mind. The vertical shaft was used by workmen to change the air filters and baffles in this particular sector. "There should be a concrete lid up there! It opens to the surface!"

"I've found it! I'm trying to get it open!" He braced himself with one arm through the nearest rung, grasped the flywheel and tried to turn it with every ounce of muscle left in his body. He shook with the effort, his eyes closed and beads of sweat popped up on his face. Come on! he urged Fate, or God, or the Devil, or whoever worked these things. Come on!

He kept straining against it, unwilling to give up.

The flywheel moved. An inch. Then two inches. Then four. Roland shouted, "I've got it!" and he started cranking the flywheel with a sore and throbbing arm. A chain clattered through the teeth of gears, and now the wind was shrieking. He knew the hatch was lifting, but he saw no light.

Roland had given the wheel four more revolutions when there was a piercing wail of wind, and the air, full of stinging grit, thrashed madly around the shaft. It almost sucked him right out, and he hung onto a rung with both hands as the wind tore at him. He was weak from his battle with the flywheel, but he knew that if he let go the storm might lift him up into the dark like a kite and never set him down again. He shouted for help, couldn't even hear his own voice.

An arm without a hand locked around his waist. Macklin had him, and they slowly descended the rungs together. They retreated into the shaft.

"We made it!" Macklin shouted over the howling. "That's the way out!"

"But we can't survive in that! It's a tornado!"

"It won't last much longer! It'll blow itself out! We made it!" He started to cry, but he remembered that discipline and control made the man. He had no conception of time, no idea how long it had been since he'd first seen those bogies on the radar scope. It must be night, but the night of which day he didn't know.

His mind drifted toward the people who were still down in Earth House, either dead or insane or lost in the dark. He thought of all the men who'd followed him into this job, who'd had faith in him and respected him. His mouth twitched into a crooked grin. It's crazy! he thought. All those experienced soldiers and loyal officers lost, and just this skinny kid with bad eyes left to go on at his side. What a joke! All that remained of Macklin's army was one puny-looking high school geek!

But he recalled how Roland had rationalized putting the civilians to work, how he'd calmly done the job down in that awful pit where Macklin's hand remained. The kid had guts. More than guts; something about Roland Croninger made Macklin a little uneasy, like knowing a deadly little thing was hiding beneath a flat rock you had to step over. It had been in the kid's eyes when Roland had told him about Schorr waylaying him in the cafeteria, and in his voice when Roland had said, "We've got hands." Macklin knew one thing for sure: He'd rather have the kid at his side than at his back.

"We'll get out when the storm's over!" Macklin shouted. "We're going to *live!*" And then tears did come to his eyes, but he laughed so the kid wouldn't know it.

A cold hand touched his shoulder. Macklin's laughter stopped.

The Shadow Soldier's voice was very close to his ear. "Right, Jimbo. We're going to live."

Roland shivered. The wind was cold, and he pushed his body against the King's for warmth. The King hesitated—and then laid his handless arm across Roland's shoulder.

Sooner or later the storm would stop, Roland knew. The world would wait. But it would be a different world. A different *game*. He knew it would be nothing like the one that had just ended. In the new game, the possibilities for a King's Knight might be endless.

He didn't know where they would go, or what they would do; he didn't know how much remained of the old world—but even if all the cities had been nuked, there must be packs of survivors, roaming the wastelands or huddled in basements, waiting. Waiting for a new leader. Waiting for someone strong enough to bend them to his will and make them dance in the new game that had already begun.

Yes. It would be the greatest game of King's Knight ever. The game board would stretch across ruined cities, ghost towns, blackened forests and deserts where meadows used to be. Roland would learn the rules as he went along, just like everybody else. But he was already one step ahead, because he recognized that there was great power to be grabbed up by the smartest and strongest. Grabbed up and used like a holy axe, poised over the heads of the weak.

And maybe—just maybe—his would be the hand that held it. Alongside the King, of course.

He listened to the roar of the wind and imagined that it spoke his name in a mighty voice and carried that name over the devastated land like a promise of power yet to be.

He smiled in the dark, his face splattered with the blood of the man he'd shot, and waited for the future.

FIVE
Wheel of Fortune Turning

Black circle / The hurting sound / Strange new flower / Tupperware bowls / Big fist a-knockin' / Citizen of the world / Paper and paints

Twenty-seven

Sheets of freezing rain the color of nicotine swirled over the ruins of East Hanover, New Jersey, driven before sixty-mile-an-hour winds. The storm hung filthy icicles from sagging roofs and crumbling walls, broke leafless trees and glazed all surfaces with contaminated ice.

The house that sheltered Sister, Artie Wisco, Beth Phelps, Julia Castillo and Doyle Halland trembled on its foundations. For the third day since the storm had hit they huddled before the fire, which boomed and leapt as wind shot down the chimney. Almost all the furniture was gone, broken up and fed to the flames in return for life-sustaining heat. Every so often they heard the walls pop and crack over the incessant shriek of the wind, and Sister flinched, thinking that at any minute the entire flimsy house would go up like cardboard—but the little bastard was tough and hung together. They heard noises like trees toppling, and Sister realized it must be the sound of other houses blowing apart around them and scattering before the storm. Sister asked Doyle Halland to lead them in prayer, but he looked at her through bitter eyes and crawled into a corner to smoke the last cigarette and stare grimly at the fire.

They were out of food and had nothing more to drink. Beth Phelps had begun to cough up blood, fever glistening in her eyes. As the fire ebbed Beth's body grew hotter—and, admit it or not, the others sat closer around her to absorb the warmth.

Beth leaned her head against Sister's shoulder. "Sister?" she asked, in a soft, exhausted voice. "Can I . . . can I hold it? Please?"

Sister knew what she meant. The glass thing. She took it from her bag, and the jewels glowed in the low orange firelight. Sister looked into its depths for a few seconds, remembering her experience of dreamwalking across a barren field strewn with burned cornstalks. It had seemed so *real!* What *is* this thing? she wondered. And why do *I* have it? She put the glass ring into Beth's hands. The others were watching, the reflection of the jewels scattered across their faces like the rainbow lamps of a faraway paradise.

Beth clutched it to her. She stared into the ring and whispered, "I'm thirsty. I'm so very, very thirsty." Then she was silent, just holding the glass and staring, with the colors slowly pulsating.

"There's nothing left to drink," Sister replied. "I'm sorry."

Beth didn't answer. The storm made the house shake for a few seconds. Sister felt someone staring a hole through her, and she looked up at Doyle Halland. He was sitting a few feet away, his legs outstretched toward the fire and the sliver through his thigh catching a glint of light.

"That's going to have to come out sooner or later," Sister told him. "Ever heard of gangrene?"

"It'll keep," he said, and his attention drifted to the circle of glass.

"Oh," Beth whispered dreamily. Her body shivered, and then she said, "Did you see it? It was there. Did you see it?"

"See *what?*" Artie asked.

"The stream. Flowing between my fingers. I was thirsty, and I drank. Didn't anybody else see it?"

The fever's got her, Sister thought. Or maybe . . . maybe *she* had gone dreamwalking, too.

"I put my hands in," Beth continued, "and it was so cool. So cool. Oh, there's a wonderful place inside that glass. . . ."

"My God!" Artie said suddenly. "Listen, I . . . I didn't say anything before, because I thought I was going nuts. But . . ." He looked around at all of them, finally stopped at Sister. "I want to tell you about something *I* saw, when I looked into that thing." He told them about the picnic with his wife. "It was weird! I mean, it was so real I could taste what I'd eaten after I came back. My stomach was full, and I wasn't hungry anymore!"

Sister nodded, listening intently. "Well," she said, "let me tell you where *I* went when I looked into it." When she was finished, the others remained silent. Julia Castillo was watching Sister, her head cocked to one side; she couldn't understand a word that was being said, but she saw them all looking at the glass thing, and she knew what they were discussing.

"My experience was pretty real, too," Sister went on. "I don't know what it means. Most likely it doesn't mean anything. Maybe it's a picture that just floated out of my head, I don't know."

"The stream is real," Beth said. "I know it is. I can feel it, and I can taste it."

"That food filled my belly," Artie told them. "It kept me from being hungry for a while. And what about being able to talk to *her*"—he motioned toward Julia—"with that thing? I mean, that's damned strange, isn't it?"

"This is something very special. I know it is. It gives you what you want when you need it. Maybe it's . . ." Beth straightened up and peered into Sister's eyes. Sister felt the fever rolling off her in waves. "Maybe it *is* magic. A kind of magic that's never been before. Maybe . . . maybe the blast made it magic. Something with the radiation, or s—"

Doyle Halland laughed. They all jumped, startled by the harshness of that laugh, and looked at him. He grinned in the firelight. "This is about the craziest thing I've ever heard in my life, folks! Magic! Maybe the blast made it magic!" He shook his head. "Come *on!* It's just a piece of glass with some jewels stuck in it. Yes, it's pretty. Okay. Maybe it's sensitive, like a tuning fork or something. But I say it hypnotizes you. I say the colors do something to your mind; maybe they trigger the pictures in your mind, and you think you're eating a picnic lunch, or drinking from a stream, or walking on a burned-up field."

"What about my being able to understand Spanish, and her understanding English?" Sister asked him. "That's a hell of a hypnosis, isn't it?"

"Ever heard of *mass* hypnosis?" he asked pointedly. "This thing comes under the same heading as bleeding statues, visions and faith-healing. Everybody wants to believe, so it comes true. Listen, I *know*. I've seen a wooden door that a hundred people swear holds a picture of Jesus in the grain. I've seen a window glass that a whole block sees as an image of the Virgin Mary—and do you know what it was? A mistake. An imperfection in the glass, that's all. There's nothing magic about a mistake. People see what they want to see, and they hear what they want to hear."

"You don't want to believe," Artie countered defiantly. "Why? Are you *afraid?*"

"No, I'm just a realist. I think, instead of jabbering about a piece of junk, we ought to be finding some more wood for that fire before it goes out."

Sister glanced at it. The flames were gnawing away the last of a broken chair. She gently took the glass ring back from Beth; it was hot from the other woman's palms. Maybe the colors and pulsations did trigger pictures in the mind, she thought. She was suddenly reminded of an object from a distant childhood: a glass ball filled with black ink, made to look like a pool-table eight-ball. You were supposed to make a wish, think about it real hard, and then turn it upside down. At the bottom of the eight-ball a little white polyhedron surfaced with different things written on each side, such as *Your Wish Will Be Granted, It's a Certainty, It Appears Doubtful,* and the aggravating *Ask Again Later*. They were all-purpose answers to the questions of a child who desperately wanted to believe in magic; you could make whatever you wanted to out of those answers. And maybe this was what the glass thing was, too: a cryptic eight-ball that made you see what you wanted to see. Still, she thought, she'd had no desire to go dreamwalking across a burned prairie. The image had just appeared and carried her along. So what was this thing—cryptic eight-ball or doorway to dreams?

Dream food and dream water might be good enough to soothe desire for such things, Sister knew, but they needed the real stuff. Plus wood for that fire. And the only place to get any of that was outside, in one of the other houses. She put the glass thing back into her bag. "I've got to go out," she said. "Maybe I can find us some food and something to drink in the next house. Artie, will you go with me? You can help me break up a chair or whatever for some more wood. Okay?"

He nodded. "Okay. I'm not afraid of a little wind and rain."

Sister looked at Doyle Halland. His gaze skittered up from the Gucci bag. "How about you? Will you go with us?"

Halland shrugged. "Why not? But if you and he go in one direction, I ought to go in another. I can look through the house to the right, if you go to the one on the left."

"Right. Good idea." She stood up. "We need to find some sheets that we can wrap wood and stuff up in to carry it. I think we'd be safer crawling than walking. If we stay close to the ground, maybe the wind won't be so bad."

Artie and Halland found sheets and clutched them under their arms to keep them from opening like parachutes in the wind. Sister made Beth comfortable and motioned for Julia to stay with her.

"Be careful," Beth said. "It doesn't sound too nice out there."

"We'll be back," Sister promised, and she went across the room to the front door—which was about the only wooden thing that hadn't gone into the fire. She pushed against the door, and immediately the room was full of cold, spinning wind and icy rain. Sister dropped to her knees and crawled out onto the slick porch, holding her leather bag. The light was the color of graveyard dirt, and the wind-blasted houses around them were as crooked as neglected tombstones. Followed closely by Artie, Sister began to crawl slowly down the front steps to the frosted-over lawn. She looked back, squinting against the stinging whipstrike of ice, and saw Doyle Halland inching toward the house on the right, drawing his injured leg carefully after him.

It took them almost ten freezing minutes to reach the next house. The roof had been torn almost off, and ice coated everything. Artie went to work, finding a crevice in which to tie the sheet into a bag and then gathering up the shards of timbers that lay everywhere. In the remains of the kitchen, Sister slipped on ice and fell hard on her rear end. But she found some cans of vegetables in the pantry, some frozen apples, onions and potatoes, and in the refrigerator some rock-hard TV dinners. All that could be stuffed into her bag went in, and by that time her hands were stiff claws. Lugging her bundle of booty, she found Artie with a bulging sheet-bagful of bits and pieces of wood. "You ready?" she shouted against the wind, and he nodded that he was.

The trip back was more treacherous, because they were holding their treasures so tightly. The wind thrust against them, even though they crawled on their bellies, and Sister thought that if she didn't get to a fire soon her hands and face would fall off.

Slowly they covered the territory between houses. There was no sign of Doyle Halland, and Sister knew that if he'd fallen and hurt himself he could freeze to death; if he didn't return in five minutes, she'd have to go looking for him. They crawled up the ice-coated steps to the front porch and through the door into the blessed warmth.

When Artie was in, Sister pushed the door shut and latched it. The wind beat and howled outside like something monstrous deprived of playthings. A skin of ice had begun to melt from Sister's face, and little icicles dangled from Artie's earlobes.

"We made it!" Artie's jaws were stiff with cold. "We got some—"

He stopped speaking. He was staring past Sister, and his eyes with their icy lashes were widening in horror.

Sister whirled around.

She went cold. Colder than she'd been in the storm.

Beth Phelps was lying on her back before the guttering fire. Her eyes were open, and a pool of blood was spreading around her head. There was a hideous wound in her temple, as if a knife had been driven right through her brain. One hand was upraised, frozen in the air.

"Oh . . . Jesus." Artie's hand pressed to his mouth.

In a corner of the room Julia Castillo lay curled up and contorted. Between her sightless eyes there was a similar wound, and blood had sprayed like a Chinese fan over the wall behind her.

Sister clenched her teeth to trap a scream.

And then a figure stirred, in a corner beyond the fire's faint glow.

"Come in," Doyle Halland said. "Excuse the mess."

He stood to his full height, his eyes catching a glint of orange light like the reflecting pupils of a cat. "Got your goodies, didn't you?" His voice was lazy, the voice of a man who'd stuffed himself at dinner but couldn't refuse dessert. "I got *mine*, too."

"My God . . . my God, what's happened here?" Artie held onto Sister's arm for support.

Doyle Halland lifted a finger into the air and slowly aimed it at Sister. "I remembered you," he said softly. "You were the woman who came into the theater. The woman with the necklace. See, I met a friend of yours back in the city. He was a policeman. I ran into him while I was wandering." Sister saw his teeth gleam as he grinned, and her knees almost buckled. "We had a nice chat."

Jack Tomachek. Jack Tomachek couldn't go through the Holland Tunnel. He'd turned back, and somewhere in the ruins he'd come face to face with—

"He told me some others had gotten out," Doyle Halland continued. "He said one of them was a woman, and do you know what he remembered most about her? That she had a wound on her neck, in the shape of . . . well, you know. He told me she was leading a group of people west." His hand with the extended finger jiggled back and forth. "Naughty, naughty. No fair sneaking when my back's turned."

"You killed them." Her voice quavered.

"I *freed* them. One of them was dying, and the other was half dead. What did they have to hope for? I mean, *really?*"

"You . . . followed *me?* Why?"

"You got out. You were leading others out. That's not very fair, either. You ought to let the dead lie where they fall. But I'm glad I followed you . . . because you have something that interests me very much." His finger pointed to the floor. "You can put it at my feet now."

"What?"

"You know what. It. The glass thing. Come on, don't make a scene."

He waited. Sister realized she hadn't sensed his cold spoor, as she had on Forty-second Street and in the theater, because *everything* was cold. And now here he was, and he wanted the only thing of beauty that remained. "How did you find me?" she asked him, trying desperately to think of a way out. Beyond the latched door at her back, the wind keened and shrieked.

"I knew if you got through the Holland Tunnel, you'd have to cross Jersey City. I followed the path of least resistance, and I saw your fire. I stood listening to you, and watching. And then I found a piece of stained glass, and I realized what the place had been. I found a body, too, and I took the clothes off it. I can make any size fit. See?" His shoulders suddenly rippled with muscle, his spine lengthening. The priest's jacket split along the seams. Now he stood about two inches taller than he had a second before.

Artie moaned, shaking his head from side to side. "I don't . . . I don't understand."

"You don't have to, cupcakes. This is between the lady and me."

"What . . . *are* you?" She resisted the urge to retreat before him, because she feared that one backward step would bring him on her like a dark whirlwind.

"I'm the winner," he said. "And you know what? I didn't even have to work up a sweat. I just laid back and it all came to me." His grin turned savage. "It's party time, lady! And my party's going to go on for a long, long time."

Sister did step back. The Doyle Halland-thing glided forward. "That glass circle *is* pretty. Do you know what it is?"

She shook her head.

"I don't either—but I know I don't like it."

"Why? What's it to you?"

He stopped, his eyes narrowing. "It's dangerous. For you, I mean. It gives you false hope. I listened to all that bullshit about beauty and hope and sand a few nights ago. I had to bite my tongue or I would've laughed in your face. Now . . . tell me you don't really believe in that crap and make my day, won't you?"

"Yes," Sister said firmly. Her voice only trembled a little bit. "I do believe."

"I was afraid of that." Still grinning, he reached down to the metal splinter in his leg. Its point was smeared with gore. He began to draw it out, and Sister knew what had made those wounds. He pulled the dagger free and straightened up. His leg did not bleed.

"Bring it to me," he said, in a voice as smooth as black velvet.

Sister's body jerked. The willpower seemed to drain out of her as if her soul had become a sieve. Dazed and floating, she wanted to go to him, wanted to reach into the bag and draw out the circle of glass, wanted to place it in his hand and offer her throat to the dagger. That would be the easy thing to do, and all resistance seemed incredibly, insufferably difficult.

Shivering, her eyes round and wet, she winnowed her hand into the bag, past the cans and the hard-frozen TV dinners, and touched the circle.

Diamond-white light flared under her fingers. Its brilliance startled her to her senses, the willpower flooding back into her mind. She stiffened her legs as if rooting them to the floor.

"Come to papa," he said—but there was a tense, rough edge in his voice. He wasn't used to being disobeyed, and he could feel her resisting him. She was tougher by far than the kid in the theater, who had resisted about as much as a marshmallow pie against a buzz saw. He could peer behind her eyes, and he saw leaping, shadowy images: a spinning blue light, a rainy highway, the figures of women drifting through dim corridors, the feel of harsh concrete and brutal blows. This woman, he reasoned, had learned to make suffering her companion.

"I *said* . . . bring it to me. Now."

And he won, after a few more seconds of struggle. He won, as he knew he must.

Sister tried to prevent her legs from moving forward, but they continued on as if they might snap off at the knees and keep going without her torso. His voice licked at her senses, drew her steadily onward: "That's right. Come on, bring it here."

"Good girl," he said when she got within a few feet. Behind her, Artie Wisco still cringed near the door.

The Doyle Halland-thing reached slowly out to take the glowing glass circle. His hand paused, inches from touching it. The jewels pulsed rapidly. He cocked his head to one side. Such a thing should not be. He would feel much better about it when it was ground to bits under his shoe.

He snatched it from her fingers.

"Thank you," he whispered.

The ring of glass changed.

It happened in an instant: The rainbow lights faded, became murky and ugly, turning swamp-mud brown, pus-gray, coal-mine black. The glass circle did not pulse; it lay dead in his grip.

"Shit," he said, amazed and confounded, and one of his gray eyes bleached pale blue.

Sister blinked, felt cold chills running down her spine. The blood tingled in her legs again. Her heart labored like an engine straining to kick over after a night in the cold.

His attention was directed to the black circle, and she knew she only had a second or two to save her life.

She braced her legs and swung the leather bag right at the side of his skull. His head jerked up, his lips twisting into a grimace; he started to juke aside, but the Gucci bag full of cans and frozen dinners hit him with every ounce of strength Sister could summon. She expected him to take it like a stone wall and scream like hellfire, so she was astounded when he grunted and staggered back against the wall as if his bones were made of papier-mâché.

Sister's free hand shot out and grabbed the ring, and they held it between them. Something akin to an electric shock rippled through her arm, and she had the mental vision of a face studded with a hundred noses and mouths and blinking eyes of all shapes and colors; she thought it must be his true face, a face of masks and changes, tricks and chameleonic evil.

Her half of the circle erupted into light, even brighter than before. The other half, in his grasp, remained black and cold.

Sister ripped it away from him, and the rest of the ring blossomed into incandescent fire. She saw the Doyle Halland-thing squint in its glare and throw a hand over his face to avoid the light. Her heartbeat was making the ring pulse wildly, and the creature before her recoiled from that fiery light as if he was stunned by both its strength and her own. She saw what might have been fear in his eyes.

But it was only there for an instant—because suddenly his eyes were sucked down into hoods of flesh, his entire face shifting. The nose collapsed, the mouth slithered away; a black eye opened at the center of his forehead, and a green eye blinked on his cheek. A sharklike mouth yawned over the point of the chin, and exposed within the cavity were small yellow fangs.

"Let's parrrrrty, bitch!" the mouth howled, and the metal splinter flashed with light as he lifted it over his head to strike.

The dagger came down like vengeance.

But Sister's bag was there like a shield, and the dagger punched through but couldn't penetrate a frozen turkey dinner. He reached for her throat with his other hand, and what she did next she did from street fighting, down-and-dirty ball-kicking experience: She swung the glass circle at his face and buried one of the spikes in the black eye at the center of his forehead.

A scream like a cat being skinned came from that gaping mouth, and the Doyle Halland-thing's head thrashed so quickly that the glass spike broke off, still full of light and imbedded in the eye like Ulysses's spear in the orb of the Cyclops. He flailed wildly with his dagger, the other eye rolling in its socket and percolating through the flesh. Sister shouted, "Run!" to Artie Wisco and then turned and fled herself.

He fumbled with the latch and almost took the door with him as he ran from the house; the wind caught him, knocked his legs out from under him. He slid on his belly, still gripping the bagful of wood shards, down the steps to the icy curb.

Sister followed him, also lost her balance on the steps and went down. She shoved the glass ring deep into her bag and crawled along the ice, skimming away from the house on her belly like a human sled. Artie scrabbled after her.

And from behind them, tattered by the wind's scream, came his maddened roar: "I'll find you! I'll find you, bitch! You can't get away!" She looked back, saw him through the storm; he was trying to pull the black spike out of his eye, and suddenly his feet went out from under him and he fell on the front porch. "I'll find you!" he promised, struggling to get up. "You can't get a—" The noise of the storm took his voice, and Sister realized she was sliding faster, going downhill over the tea-colored ice.

An ice-covered car loomed in front of her. There was no way to avoid it. She scrunched herself down and went under it, something snagging and ripping her fur coat as she shot beneath the car and continued down the incline, out of control. She looked back and saw Artie spinning like a saucer, but his course took him around the car and out of danger.

They sped down the hill, two human toboggans passing along a street lined with dead and crumpled houses, the wind thrusting them onward and sleet stinging their faces.

They would find shelter somewhere, Sister thought. Maybe another house. And they had plenty of food. Wood to start a fire. No matches or lighter, but surely the looters and fleeing survivors hadn't carried off everything that would throw a spark.

She still had the glass ring. The Doyle Halland-thing had been right. It was hope, and she would never let it go. Never.

But it was something else, too. Something special. Something, as Beth Phelps had said, *magic*. But what the purpose of that magic was, she couldn't yet fathom.

They were going to live, and they were skidding further and further away from the monster who wore a priest's suit. I'll find you! she heard it bellowing in her mind. I'll find you!

And she feared that someday—somehow—it just might.

They skidded down to the end of the hill, past more abandoned cars, and continued along the thoroughfare about forty more yards before they bumped the curb.

Their ride was over, but their journey had just begun.

Twenty-eight

Time passed.

Josh judged its passage by the number of empty cans that were piling up in what he thought of as the city dump—that foul area over in the far corner where they both used the bathroom and tossed the empties. They went through one can of vegetables every other day, and one can of a meat product like Spam or corned beef on alternating days. The way Josh calculated the passage of a day was by his bowel movements. He'd always been as regular as clockwork. So the trips to the city dump and the pile of empties gave him a reasonable estimation of time, and he figured now that they'd been in the basement between nineteen and twenty-three days. Which would make it anywhere between the fifth and thirteenth of August. Of course, there was no telling how long they'd been there before they'd gotten semi-organized, either, so Josh thought it was probably closer to the seventeenth—and that would mean one month had passed.

He'd found a packet of flashlight batteries in the dirt, so they were okay on that account. The light showed him that they'd passed the halfway point of their food supply. It was time to start digging. As he gathered up the shovel and pickaxe, he heard their gopher scrambling happily amid the city dump's cans. The little beast thrived on their leftovers—which didn't amount to much—and licked the cans so clean you could see your face reflected on the bottom. Which was something Josh definitely avoided doing.

Swan was asleep, breathing quietly in the darkness. She slept a lot, and Josh figured that was good. She was saving her energy, hibernating like a little animal. Yet when Josh woke her she came up instantly, focused and alert. He slept a few feet away from her, and it amazed him how attuned he'd become to the sound of her breathing; usually it was deep and slow, the sound of oblivion, but sometimes it was fast and ragged, the gasp of memories, bad dreams, the sinking in of realities. It was that sound that awakened Josh from his own uneasy sleep, and often he heard Swan call for her mother or make a garbled utterance of terror, as if something was stalking her across the wasteland of nightmares.

They'd had plenty of time to talk. She'd told him about her mother and "uncles," and how much she enjoyed planting her gardens. Josh had asked her about her father; she'd said he was a rock musician but hadn't offered anything else.

She'd asked him what it felt like to be a giant, and he'd told her he'd be a rich man if he had a quarter for every time he'd bumped his head at the top of a doorway. Also, it was tough finding clothes big enough—though he didn't tell her that he'd already noticed his waistband was loosening—and that his shoes were specially made. So I guess it's expensive to be a giant, he'd said. Otherwise, I guess I'm about the same as everybody else.

In telling her about Rose and the boys, he'd tried very hard not to let his voice break. He could have been talking about strangers, people he knew only as pictures in somebody else's wallet. He told Swan about his football days, how he'd been Most Valuable Player in three games. Wrestling wasn't so bad, he'd told her; it was honest money, and a man as big as he couldn't do much else that was legal. The world was too small for giants; it built doorways too low, furniture too flimsy, and there wasn't a mattress made that didn't pop and squall when he lay down to rest.

During the times they talked, Josh kept the flashlight off. He didn't want to see the child's blistered face and stubble of hair and remember how pretty she'd been—and also, he wanted to spare her the sight of his own repellent mug.

PawPaw Briggs's ashes were buried. They did not talk about that at all, but the command *Protect the child* remained in Josh's mind like the tolling of an iron bell.

He switched on the flashlight. Swan was curled up in her usual place, sleeping soundly. The dried fluids of burst blisters glistened on her face. Flaps of skin were dangling from her forehead and cheeks like thin layers of flaking paint, and underneath them the raw, scarlet flesh was growing fresh blisters. He gently prodded her shoulder, and her eyes immediately opened. They were bloodshot, the lashes gummy and yellow, her pupils shrinking to pinpoints. He moved the light away from her. "Time to wake up. We're going to start digging."

She nodded and sat up.

"If we both work, it'll be faster," he said. "I'm going to start with the pickaxe, then I'd like for you to shovel away the loose dirt. Okay?"

"Okay," she replied, and she got on her hands and knees to follow him.

Josh was about to crawl over to the gopher hole when he noticed something in the spill of light that he'd not seen before. He shifted the beam back to where she'd been sleeping. "Swan? What is *that?*"

"Where?" Her gaze moved along the light.

Josh put aside the shovel and pickaxe and reached down.

Where Swan customarily slept were hundreds of tiny, emerald-green blades of grass. They formed a perfect image of a child's curled-up body.

He touched the grass. Not exactly grass, he realized. Shoots of some kind. Tiny shoots of . . . were they new cornstalks?

He shone the light around. The soft, downlike vegetation was growing in no other place but where Swan slept. He plucked up a bit of it, to examine the roots, and he noted that Swan flinched. "What's wrong?"

"I don't like that sound."

"*Sound?* What sound?"

"A hurting sound," she answered.

Josh didn't know what she was talking about, and he shook his head. The roots trailed down about two inches, delicate filaments of life. They'd obviously been growing there for some time, but Josh couldn't understand how the shoots had rooted in tainted dirt without a drop of water. It was the only bit of green life he'd seen since they'd been trapped here. But there had to be a simple explanation; he figured that the whirlwind had carried seeds in, and somehow they'd rooted and popped up. That's all.

Right, he thought. Rooted without water and popped up without an iota of sunlight. That made about as much sense as PawPaw deciding to emulate a Roman candle.

He let the green shoots drift down again. At once, Swan picked up a handful of loose dirt, worked it between her fingers for a few seconds with single-minded interest, and covered the shoots over.

Josh leaned back, his knees up against his chest. "It's only growing where you lie down to sleep. It's kind of peculiar, don't you think?"

She shrugged. She could feel him watching her carefully.

"You said you heard a sound," he continued. "What kind of sound was it?"

Again, a shrug. She didn't know how to talk about it. Nobody had ever asked her such things before.

"I didn't hear anything," Josh said, and he reached toward the shoots again.

She grasped his hand before he got there. "Like I said . . . a hurting sound. I don't know exactly."

"When I plucked them up?"

"Yes."

Lord, Josh thought, I'm just about ready for a rubber room! He'd been thinking, as he looked at the pattern of green in the dirt, that they were growing there because her body made them grow. Her chemistry or something, reacting with the earth. It was a crazy idea, but there they were. "What's it like? A voice?"

"No. Not like that."

"I'd like to hear about it."

"Really?"

"Yes," Josh said. "Really."

"My mama said it was 'magination."

"Is it?"

She hesitated, and then she said firmly, "No." Her fingers touched the new shoots tenderly, barely grazing them. "One time my mama took me to a club to hear the band. Uncle Warren was playing the drums. I heard a noise like the hurting sound, and I asked her what made it. She said it was a steel guitar, the kind you put on your lap and play. But there are other things in the hurting sound, too." Her eyes found his. "Like the wind. Or a train's whistle, way far off. Or thunder, long before you see the lightning. A lot of things."

"How long have you been able to hear it?"

"Since I was a little girl."

Josh couldn't help but smile. Swan misread it. "Are you making fun of me?"

"No. Maybe . . . I wish I could hear a sound like that. Do you know what it is?"

"Yes," Swan answered. "It's death."

His smile faltered and went away.

Swan picked up some dirt and slowly worked it, feeling its dry, brittle texture. "In the summer it's the worst. That's when people bring their lawn mowers out."

"But . . . it's just *grass,*" Josh said.

"In the fall the hurting sound's different," she continued, as if she hadn't heard him. "It's like a great big sigh, and then the leaves come down. Then in winter, the hurting sound stops, and everything sleeps." She shook nuggets of dirt from her palm, mixed them with the rest. "When it starts getting warm again, the sun makes things think about waking up."

"*Think* about waking up?"

"Everything can think and feel, in its own way," she replied, and she looked up at him. The eyes in her young face were very old, Josh thought. "Bugs, birds, even grass—everything has its own way of speaking and knowing. Just depends on whether you can understand it or not."

Josh grunted. *Bugs,* she'd said. He was remembering the swarm of locusts that had whirled through his Pontiac the day of the blast. He'd never thought before about the things she was saying, but he realized there was truth to it. Birds knew to migrate when the clock of seasons changed, ants built anthills in a frenzy of communication, flowers bloomed and withered but their pollen lived on, all according to a great, mysterious schedule that he'd always taken for granted. It was as simple as grass growing and as complex as a firefly's light.

"How do you know these things?" he asked. "Who taught you?"

"Nobody. I just figured it out." She recalled her first garden, growing from a sandbox at a nursery school playground. It had been years before she found out that holding earth didn't make everybody's hands tingle with a pins-and-needles sensation, or that everybody couldn't tell from its buzz whether a wasp wanted to sting or just investigate your ear. She'd always known, and that was that.

"Oh," he said. He watched her rubbing the dirt in her hands. Swan's palms were tingling, her hands warm and moist. He looked at the green shoots again. "I'm just a wrestler," he said, very quietly. "That's all. I mean . . . *damn,* I'm just a nobody!" *Protect the child,* he thought. Protect her from what? From whom? And why? "What the hell," he whispered, "have I got myself into?"

"Huh?" she asked.

"Nothing," he said. Her eyes were those of a little girl again, and she mixed the rest of the warm dirt into the ground around the shoots. "We'd better start digging now. Are you up to it?"

"Yes." She grasped the shovel he'd laid aside. The tingling, glowing sensation was slowly ebbing away.

But he wasn't ready, not just yet. "Swan, listen to me for a minute. I want to be truthful with you, because I think you can handle it. We're going to try to get out of here, but that's not saying we can. We'll have to dig a pretty wide tunnel to squeeze my blubber through. It's going to take us some time, and it sure as hell won't be easy work. If it caves in, we'll have to start all over again. What I'm saying, I guess, is that I'm not sure we can get out. I'm not sure at all. Do you understand?"

She nodded, said nothing.

"And one more thing," he added. "If—when—we get out . . . we might not like what we find. Everything might be changed. It might be like . . . waking up after the worst nightmare you can think of, and finding that the nightmare followed you into daylight. Understand?"

Again, Swan nodded. She'd already thought about what he was saying, because no one had ever come to get them out like her mama had said. She put on her most grown-up face and waited for him to make the next move.

"Okay," Josh said. "Let's start digging."

Twenty-nine

Josh Hutchins stared, squinted and blinked. "Light," he said, the walls of the tunnel pressing against his shoulders and back. "I see light!"

Behind him, about thirty feet away in the basement, Swan called, "How far is it?" She was utterly filthy, and there seemed to be so much dirt up her nostrils that they might sprout gardens, too. The thought had made her giggle a few times, a sound she'd never believed she'd make again.

"Maybe ten or twelve feet," he answered, and he continued digging with his hands and pushing the dirt behind him, then pushing it further back with his feet. The pickaxe and shovel approach had been a valiant effort, but after three days of working they'd realized the best tools were their hands. Now, as he squeezed his shoulders forward to grab more dirt, Josh looked at the weak red glimmer way up at the gopher hole's entrance and thought it was the most beautiful light he'd ever seen. Swan entered the tunnel behind him and scooped the loose dirt up in a large can, carrying it back to the basement to empty over the slit trench. Her hands, arms, face, nostrils and knees—everything that was covered with dirt—tingled all the way down to her bones. She felt like she had a flame burning in her backbone. Across the basement, the young green shoots were four inches tall.

Josh's face was plastered with dirt; even his teeth were gritty with it. The soil was heavy, with a thick, gummy consistency, and he had to stop to rest.

"Josh? You all right?" Swan asked.

"Yeah. Just need a minute to get my wind." His shoulders and forearms ached mercilessly, and the last time he'd been so weary was after a ten-man battle royal in Chattanooga. The light seemed further away than he'd first reckoned, as if the tunnel—which they'd both come to love and hate—was elongating, playing a cruel trick of perception. He felt as if he'd crawled into one of those Chinese tubes that lock your fingers, one stuck into each end, except his whole body was jammed tight as a monk's jockstrap.

He started again, bringing a double handful of the heavy earth back and underneath him as if he were swimming through dirt. My mama raised herself a gopher, he thought, and he had to grin despite his weariness. His mouth tasted like he'd been dining on mud pies.

Six more inches dug away. One more foot. Was the light closer, or further away? He pushed himself onward, thinking about how his mama used to scold him for not scrubbing behind his ears. Another foot, and another. Behind him, Swan crawled in and carried the loose dirt out again and again, like clockwork. The light was getting closer now; he was sure of it. But now it wasn't so beautiful. Now it was sickly, not like sunlight at all. Diseased, Josh thought. And maybe deadly, too. But he kept going, one double handful after the next, inching slowly toward the outside world.

Dirt suddenly plopped down on the back of his neck. He lay still, expecting a cave-in, but the tunnel held. For God's sake, don't stop now! he told himself, and he reached out for the next handful.

"I'm almost there!" he shouted, but the earth muffled his voice. He didn't know if Swan had heard or not. "Just a few more feet!"

But just short of the opening, which was not quite as large as Josh's fist, he had to stop and rest again. Josh lay staring longingly at the light, the hole about three feet away. He could smell the outside now, the bitter aromas of burned earth, scorched cornstalks and alkali. Rousing himself, he pushed onward. The earth was tougher near the surface, full of glazed stones and metallic lumps. The fire had burned the dirt into something resembling pavement. Still he strained upward, his shoulders throbbing, his gaze fixed on the hole of ugly light. And then he was close enough to thrust his hand through it, but before he tried he said, "I'm there, Swan! I'm at the top!" He clawed away dirt, and his hand reached the hole. But the underside of the surface around it felt like pebbled asphalt, and he couldn't get his fingers through. He balled up his fist, the flesh mottled gray and white, and pushed. Harder. Harder still. Come on, come on, he thought. Push, damn it!

There was a dry, stubborn cracking sound. At first Josh thought it was his arm breaking, but he felt no pain, and he kept pushing as if trying to punch the sky.

The earth cracked again. The hole began to crumble and widen. His fist started going through, and he envisioned what it might look like to someone standing on the surface: the blossoming of a zebra-blotched fist like a strange new flower through the dead earth, the fist opening and fingers stretching petallike under the weak red light.

Josh shoved his arm through almost to the elbow. Cold wind snapped at his fingertips. That movement of air exhilarated him, jarred him as if from a long somnolence. "We're out!" he shouted, about to sob with joy. "Swan! We're out!"

She was behind him, crouched in the tunnel. "Can you see anything?"

"I'm going to put my head through," he told her. "Here goes."

He pushed upward, his shoulder following his arm, breaking the hole wider. Then his entire arm was out, and the top of his head was ready to press through. As he pushed he thought of watching his sons being born, their heads straining to enter the world. He felt as giddy and afraid as any infant could possibly be. Behind him, Swan was pushing at him, too, giving him support as he stretched to break free.

The earth parted with a sound like baked clay snapping apart. With a surge of effort, Josh thrust his head through the opening and into a biting, turbulent wind.

"Are you there yet?" Swan asked. "What can you see?"

Josh narrowed his eyes, his hand up to ward off flying grit.

He saw a desolate, grayish-brown landscape, featureless except for what appeared to be the mangled remnants of the Bonneville and Darleen's Camaro. Overhead was a low sky plated with thick gray clouds. From dead horizon to dead horizon, the clouds were slowly, ponderously rotating, and here and there were quicksilver glints of harsher scarlet. Josh looked over his shoulder. About fifteen feet behind him and to his left was a large dome of dirt, mashed-down cornstalks, pieces of wood and metal from the gas pumps and cars. He realized it was the grave they'd been buried in, and at the same time he knew that if the tons of cornfield dirt hadn't sealed them in they would have been burned to death. Other than that, and a few drifts of cornstalks and debris, the land was scraped clean.

The wind was blowing into his face. He crawled up out of the hole and sat on his haunches, looking around at the destruction, while Swan emerged from the tunnel. The cold sliced to her bones, and her bloodshot eyes moved incredulously over what had become a desert. "Oh," she whispered, but the wind stole her voice. "Everything's . . . gone. . . ."

Josh hadn't heard her. He couldn't get any sense of direction. He knew the nearest town—or what was left of it—was Salina. But which direction was east, and which west? Where was the sun? Flying grit and dust obscured everything beyond twenty yards or so. Where was the highway? "There's nothing left," Josh said, mostly to himself. "There's not a damned thing left!"

Swan saw a familiar object lying nearby. She stood up and walked with an effort against the wind to the small figure. Most of the blue fur had been burned off of it, but its plastic eyes with the little black rolling pupils were intact. Swan reached down and picked it up. The cord with its pull ring dangled from the doll's back; she yanked it and heard the Cookie Monster ask for more cookies in a slow, distorted voice.

Josh rose to his feet. Well, he thought, now we're out. Now what the hell do we do? Where do we go? He shook his head in disgust. Maybe there was nowhere to go. Maybe everything, everywhere, was just like this. What was the point of leaving their basement? He looked grimly at the hole they'd just crawled from, and he thought for a moment of shimmying back down there like a big gopher and spending the rest of his days licking out cans and shitting in a slit trench.

Careful, he warned himself. Because that hole back to the basement—back to the grave—was suddenly too appealing. Much, much too appealing. He stepped away from the hole a few paces and tried to think coherently.

His gaze slid toward the child. She was covered with tunnel dirt, her ragged clothes flapping around her. She stared into the distance, her eyes narrowed against the wind, with that dumb doll cradled in her arms. Josh looked at her for a long time.

I could do it, he told himself. Sure. I could make myself do it, because it would be the right thing. *Might* be the right thing. Wouldn't it? If everything is like this, what's the damned point of living, right? Josh opened his hands, closed them again. I could make it quick, he thought. She'd never feel a thing. And then I could just mosey over to that junk pile and find a nice piece of metal with a sharp edge and finish the job on myself, too.

That would be the right thing to do. Wouldn't it?

Protect the child, he thought—and a deep, terrible shame stabbed him. Some protection! he thought. But Jesus Christ, everything's gone! Everything's been blown to Hell!

Swan turned her head, and her eyes sought his. She said something, but he couldn't understand her. She walked closer to him, shivering and bowed against the wind, and she shouted, "What are we going to do?"

"I don't know!" he shouted back.

"It's not like this everywhere, is it?" she asked him. "There must be other people somewhere! There must be towns and people!"

"Maybe. Maybe not. Damn, it's cold!" He trembled; he'd been dressed for a hot July day, and now he hardly had a shirt on.

"We can't just *stand* here!" Swan said. "We've got to go *somewhere!*"

"Right. Well, take your choice of directions, little lady. They all look the same to me."

Swan stared at him for a few seconds more, and again Josh felt shamed. Then she turned in all directions as if trying to choose one. Suddenly her eyes filled with tears, and they stung so much she almost screamed; but she bit her lower lip, bit it until it almost bled. She had wished for a moment that her mama was at her side, to help her and tell her what to do. She needed her mama to guide her, now more than ever. It wasn't fair that her mama was gone! It wasn't kind, and it wasn't right!

But that was thinking like a little girl, she decided. Her mama had gone home, to a peaceful place far from this—and Swan had to make some decisions for herself. Starting right now.

Swan lifted her hand and pointed away from the source of the wind. "That way," she decided.

"Any particular reason?"

"Yes." She turned and gave him a look that made him feel like the stupidest clown on earth. "Because the wind'll be at our backs. It'll push us, and walking won't be as hard."

"Oh," Josh said meekly. In the distance she'd pointed out was nothing—just swirling dust and utter desolation. He couldn't see the reason in making his legs move.

Swan sensed he was ready to sit down, and when he did that there was no way she could pry his giant butt up again. "We worked hard to get out of there, didn't we?" she shouted to him over the wind. He nodded. "We proved we could do something if we really wanted to, didn't we? You and me? Kind of like a team? We worked hard, and we shouldn't ought to stop working hard now."

He nodded dully.

"We've got to *try!*" Swan shouted.

Josh looked down at the hole again. At least it was warm down there. At least they'd had food. What was so wrong with stay—

He sensed movement from the corner of his eye.

The little girl, Cookie Monster doll in arms, had begun to walk off in the direction she'd chosen, the wind pushing her along.

"Hey!" Josh yelled. Swan didn't stop or slow down. *"Hey!"* She kept going.

Josh took the first step after her. The wind hit him behind his knees—a clip! Fifteen yards penalty! he thought—and then caught him in the small of the back, staggering him forward. He took a second step, then a third and a fourth. And then he was following her, but the wind was so strong at his back that it seemed more like flying than walking. He caught up with her, walking a few yards off to the side, and again Josh felt a pang of shame at his weakness, because she didn't even grace him with a glance. She was walking with her chin uplifted, as if in defiance of the bleakness that faced them; Josh thought that she looked like the little queen of a realm that had been stolen from her, a tragic and determined figure.

There's nothing out there, Swan thought. A deep, terrible sadness wrenched at her, and if the wind hadn't been pushing so hard she might've crumpled to her knees. It's all gone. All gone.

Two tears ran through the crusted dirt and blisters on her face. Everything *can't* be gone, she told herself. There have to be towns and people left somewhere! Maybe a mile ahead. Maybe two. Just through the dust and over the horizon.

She kept going, step after step, and Josh Hutchins walked at her side.

Behind them, the gopher popped his head out of the crater and looked in all directions. Then he made a little chattering sound and disappeared again into the safety of the earth.

Thirty

Two figures trudged slowly along Interstate 80, with the snow-covered Poconó Mountains of eastern Pennsylvania at their backs. The fallen snow was dirty gray, and from it protruded rough rocks like warts growing in leprous flesh. New gray snow was tumbling from the sullen, sickly green and sunless sky, and it hissed softly amid the thousands of leafless black hickories, elms and oaks. The evergreens had turned brown and were losing their needles. From horizon to horizon, as far as Sister and Artie could see, there was no green vegetation, not a green vine or leaf.

The wind whipped past them, blowing the ashy snow into their faces. Both of them were bundled up with layers of clothes they'd been able to scavenge in the twenty-one days since they'd escaped from the monster that called itself Doyle Halland. They'd found a looted Sears department store on the outskirts of Paterson, New Jersey, but almost everything had been carried out of it except for some merchandise at the back, under a big sign with painted icicles that read WINTER IN JULY SALE! SAVE THE SEARS WAY!

The racks and tables had been untouched, and they yielded up heavy herringbone overcoats, plaid mufflers, wool caps and gloves lined with rabbit fur. There was even thermal underwear and a supply of boots, which Artie praised as being high-quality merchandise. Now, after more than one hundred miles, the boots were supple but their feet were bloody, wrapped in rags and newspapers after their socks had fallen apart.

Both of them carried knapsacks on their backs, laden with other scavenged objects: cans of food, a can opener, a couple of sharp all-purpose knives, some kitchen matches, a flashlight and extra batteries, and the lucky find of a six-pack of Olympia beer. Around her shoulder, as well, Sister supported a dark green duffel bag from the Paterson Army-Navy surplus store, which had taken the place of the smaller Gucci bag and held a thermal blanket, some bottles of Perrier and a few items of packaged cold cuts found in an almost-empty grocery store. At the bottom of the duffel bag was the glass circle, placed so Sister could feel it through the canvas whenever she wanted to.

A red plaid muffler and an electric green woolen cap protected Sister's face and head from the wind, and she was wrapped in a woolen coat over two sweaters. Baggy brown corduroy pants and leather gloves completed her wardrobe, and she moved slowly through the snow with the weight that pressed on her, but at least she was warm. Artie, too, was burdened with a heavy coat, a blue muffler and two caps, one over the other. Only the area around their eyes was exposed to the blowing snow, the flesh raw and windburned. The gray, ugly snow swirled about them; the interstate pavement was covered to a depth of about four inches, and higher drifts grew amid the denuded forest and deep ravines on either side.

Walking a few yards in front of Artie, Sister lifted her hand and pointed to the right. She trudged over to four dark clumps lying in the snow, and she peered down at the frozen corpses of a man, a woman and two children. All were wearing summer clothes: short-sleeved shirts and light pants. The man and woman had died holding hands. Except the third finger of the woman's left hand had been chopped off. Her wedding ring, Sister thought. Somebody had cut the whole finger off to get it. The man's shoes were gone, and his feet were black. His sunken eyes glistened with gray ice. Sister turned away.

Since crossing over into Pennsylvania, passing a big green sign that said WELCOME TO PENNSYLVANIA, THE KEYSTONE STATE about thirty miles and seven days ago, they had found almost three hundred frozen bodies on Interstate 80. They'd sheltered for a while in a town called Stroudsburg, which had been decimated by a tornado. The houses and buildings lay scattered under the filthy snow like the broken toys of a mad giant, and there'd been plenty of corpses, too. Sister and Artie had found a pickup truck—the tank drained of gas—on the town's main thoroughfare and had slept in the cab. Then it was back onto the interstate again, heading west in their supple, blood-filled boots, passing more carnage, wrecked cars and overturned trailers that must have been caught in a crush of traffic fleeing westward.

The going was rough. They could make, at the most, five miles a day before they had to find shelter—the remnants of a house, a barn, a wrecked car—anything to hold back the wind. In twenty-one days of traveling they'd seen only three other living people; two of those were raving mad, and the third had fled wildly into the woods when he'd seen them coming. Both Sister and Artie had been sick for a while, had coughed and thrown up blood and suffered splitting headaches. Sister had thought she was going to die, and they'd slept huddled together, each of them breathing like a bellows; but the worst of the sickness and weak, feverish dizziness had gone, and though they both sometimes still coughed uncontrollably and vomited up a little blood, their strength had returned, and they had no more headaches.

They left the four corpses behind and soon came to the wreckage of an exploded Airstream trailer. A scorched Cadillac had smashed into it, and a Subaru had rear-ended the Caddy. Nearby, two other vehicles had locked and burned. Further on, another group of people lay where they'd frozen to death, their bodies curled around one another in a vain search for warmth. Sister passed them without pausing;

the face of death was no stranger to her now, but she couldn't stand to look too closely.

. About fifty yards further, Sister stopped abruptly. Just ahead of her, through the tumbling snow, an animal was gnawing at one of two corpses that lay against the right-hand guardrail. The thing looked up and tensed. It was a large dog, Sister saw—maybe a wolf, come down from the mountains to feed. The beast was about the size of a German shepherd, with a long snout and a reddish-gray hide. It had chewed a leg down to the bone, and now it crouched over its prize and stared menacingly at Sister.

If that bastard wants fresh meat, we're dead, she thought. She stared back at the thing, and they challenged each other for about thirty seconds. Then the animal gave a short, muttering growl and returned to its gnawing. Sister and Artie gave it a wide berth, and they kept looking back until they'd rounded a curve and the thing was out of sight.

Sister shuddered under her weight of clothes. The beast's eyes had reminded her of Doyle Halland's.

Her fear of Doyle Halland was worst when darkness fell—and there seemed to be no regularity to the coming of darkness, no twilight or sense of the sun going away. The darkness might fall after two or three hours of gloom, or it might hold off for what seemed like twenty-four hours—but when it did fall, it was absolute. In the dark, every noise was enough to make Sister sit up and listen, her heart pounding and cold sweat popping up on her face. She had something the Doyle Halland-thing wanted, something he didn't understand—as she certainly did not—but that he'd vowed to follow her to get. And what would he do with the glass ring if he got it? Smash it to pieces? Probably so. She kept looking over her shoulder as she walked, fearful of seeing a dark figure coming up behind her, its face malformed, with jagged teeth showing in a sharklike grin.

"I'll find you," he'd promised. *"I'll find you, bitch."*

The day before, they'd sheltered in a broken-down barn and had made a small fire in the hay. Sister had taken the glass ring from her duffel bag. She'd thought of her future-predicting glass eight-ball, and she'd mentally asked: What's ahead for us?

Of course, there was no little white polyhedron surfacing with all-purpose answers. But the colors of the jewels and their pulsing, steady rhythm had soothed her; she'd felt herself drifting, entranced by the glow of the ring, and then it seemed as if all her attention, all her *being,* was drawn deeper and deeper into the glass, deeper and deeper, as if into the very heart of fire. . . .

And then she'd gone dreamwalking again, across that barren landscape where the dome of dirt was, and the Cookie Monster doll lay waiting for a lost child. But this time it was different; this time, she'd been dreamwalking toward the dome—with the sensation of her feet not quite touching the earth—when she suddenly stopped and listened.

She thought she'd heard something over the noise of the wind—a muffled sound that might have been a human voice. She listened, strained to hear it again, but could not.

And then she saw a small hole in the baked ground, almost at her feet. As she watched, she imagined that she saw the hole begin to widen, and the earth crack and strain around it. In the next moment . . . yes, yes, the earth *was* cracking, and the hole was getting larger, as if something was burrowing underneath it. She stared, both fearful and fascinated, as the sides of the hole crumbled, and she thought, I am not alone.

From the hole came a human hand.

It was splotched with gray and white—a large hand, the hand of a giant—and the thick fingers had clawed upward like those of a dead man digging himself out of a grave.

The sight had startled her so much that she'd jerked backward from the widening hole. She was afraid to see what kind of monster was emerging, and as she ran across the empty plain she'd wished frantically, Take me back, please, I want to go back where I was. . . .

And she was sitting before the small fire in the broken-down barn. Artie was looking at her quizzically, the raw flesh around his eyes like the Lone Ranger's mask.

She'd told him what she'd seen, and he asked her what she thought it meant. Of course, she couldn't say; of course, it was probably just something plucked from her mind, perhaps a response to seeing all the corpses on the highway. Sister had put the glass ring back in her duffel bag, but the image of that hand stretching upward from the earth was burned into her brain. She could not shake it.

Now, as she trudged through the snow, she touched the ring's outline in the canvas bag. Just knowing it was there reassured her, and right now that was all the magic she needed.

Her knees locked.

Another wolf or wild dog or whatever it was stood in the road before her, about fifteen feet away. This one was skinny, with raw red sores on its hide. Its eyes bored into hers, and the lips slowly pulled away from the fangs in a snarl.

Oh, shit! was her first reaction. This one looker hungrier and more desperate than the other. And behind it in the gray snow were two or three more, loping to the right and left.

She looked over her shoulder, past Artie. Two more wolf shapes were behind them, half hidden by the snow but near enough that Sister could see their outlines.

Her second reaction was, *Our butts are hambur—*

Something leapt from the left—a blur of motion—and slammed into Artie's side. He yelled in pain as he fell, and the beast—which Sister thought might have been the reddish-gray animal they'd seen feasting on a corpse—grabbed part of Artie's knapsack between its teeth and violently shook its head back and forth, trying to rip the pack off. Sister reached down to grasp Artie's outstretched hand, but the beast dragged Artie about ten feet through the snow before it let go and darted off just to the edge of visibility. It continued to circle and lick its chops.

She heard a guttural growl and turned just as the skinny animal with the red sores leapt for her. It struck her shoulder and knocked her sprawling, the jaws snapping shut inches from her face with a noise like a bear trap cracking together. She smelled rotted meat on its breath, and then the animal had the right sleeve of her coat and was tearing at it. Another beast feinted in from the left, and a third darted boldly forward and grabbed her right foot, trying to drag her. She thrashed and yelled; the skinny one spooked and ran, but the other one pulled her on her side through the snow. She grasped the duffel bag in both arms and kicked with her left boot, hitting the beast three times in the skull before it yelped and released her.

Behind her, Artie was attacked by two at once, from opposite sides. One caught his wrist, the teeth almost meeting flesh through his heavy coat and sweater, the second snapping at his left shoulder and worrying him with a frenzied surge of strength. "Get off! Get off!" he was screaming as they strained at each other to pull him in different directions.

Sister tried to stand. She slipped in the snow, fell heavily again. Panic hit her like a punch to the gut. She saw Artie being dragged by an animal that held his wrist, and she realized the beasts were trying to separate them, much like they might separate a herd of deer or cattle. As she was struggling up one of the things lunged in and grabbed her ankle, dragging her another few yards from Artie. Now he was just a struggling form, surrounded by the shapes of the circling animals in the swirling gray murk.

"Get away, you bastard!" she shouted. The animal jerked her so hard she thought her leg had popped from its socket. With a scream of rage, Sister swung the duffel bag at it, clipping its snout, and the thing turned tail. But a second later another one was straddling her, its fangs snapping for her throat; she threw her arm up, and the jaws clamped onto it with brutal force. The wolf-dog started shredding the cloth of her coat. She swung her left fist at it, caught it in the ribs and heard it grunt, but it kept tearing through the coat, now reaching the first layer of sweater. Sister knew this sonofa-bitch wasn't stopping until he tasted meat. She hit it again and tried to wrench free, but now something had her ankle again and was pulling her in another direction. She had the crazy mental image of saltwater taffy being stretched until it snapped.

She heard a sharp *crack!* and thought that this time her leg had broken. But the beast that was worrying her shoulder yelped and jumped, running madly off through the snow. There was a second *crack!* followed closely by a third. The wolf-dog that had her ankle shuddered and shrieked, and Sister saw blood spewing from a hole in its side. The animal let her go and began to spin in a circle, snapping at its tail. A fourth shot rang out—Sister realized the beast had been pierced by a bullet—and she heard an agonized howling over where Artie Wisco lay. Then the others were fleeing, slipping and sliding and crashing into one another in their haste to escape. They were gone from sight within five seconds.

The wounded animal fell on its side a few feet away from Sister, its legs kicking frantically. She sat up, stunned and dumbfounded, and saw Artie struggling to rise, too. His feet went out from under him, and he flopped down again.

A figure wearing a dark green ski mask, a beat-up brown leather jacket and blue jeans glided past Sister. He had on snowshoes laced around battered boots, and slung around his neck was a cord that pierced the necks of three empty plastic jugs, knotted at the ends to keep them from sliding off. On his back was a dark green hiker's pack, a bit smaller than the ones Sister and Artie carried.

He stood over Sister. "You okay?" His voice sounded like steel wool scrubbing a cast-iron skillet.

"Yeah, I think so." She had bruises on bruises, but nothing was broken.

He planted the rifle he was carrying butt first in the snow, then unwrapped the cord that held the plastic jugs from around his shoulder. He set these down, too, near the still-kicking animal. His pack was shrugged off, and then he unzipped it with gloved fingers and took out an assortment of various-sized Tupperware bowls with sealed plastic lids. He set them in an orderly row in the snow before him.

Artie came trudging toward them, holding his wrist. The man with the ski mask looked up quickly and then continued his work, taking off his gloves and untying one of the knots in the cord so he could slide the jugs off. "Sonofabitch get you?" he asked Artie.

"Yeah. Gashed my hand. I'm okay, though. Where'd *you* come from?"

"That way." He jerked his head toward the woods, then began to uncap the plastic jugs with rapidly reddening fingers.

The animal was still kicking violently. The man stood up, pulled his rifle out of the snow and began to smash the animal's skull in with the weapon's butt. It took a minute to finish, but then the beast made a muffled, moaning sound, trembled and lay still. "I didn't think anybody else would be coming this way," the man said. "Thought everybody was long gone by now." He knelt again next to the body, took a knife with a long, curved blade from a pouch at his belt and cut a slit in the gray underbelly. The blood gouted. He reached for one of the plastic jugs and held it beneath the stream; the blood pattered merrily in, rapidly filling up the jug. He capped it, put it aside and reached for another as Sister and Artie watched with sickened fascination. "Thought everybody else must be dead by now," he continued, paying close attention to his work. "Where are you two from?"

"Uh . . . Detroit," Artie managed to say.

"We came from Manhattan," Sister told him. "We're on our way to Detroit."

"You run out of gas? Have a blowout?"

"No. We're walking."

He grunted, glanced at her and then went back to his task. The stream of blood was weakening. "Long way to walk," he said. "Hell of a long way, especially for nothing."

"What do you mean?"

"I mean that there's no Detroit anymore. It was blown away. Just like there's no Pittsburgh or Indianapolis or Chicago or Philadelphia anymore. I'd be surprised if any city's left. By now, I guess the radiation's done a number on the little towns, too." The flow of blood had almost stopped. He capped the second jug, which was about half full, and then he carved a longer slit in the dead animal's belly. He thrust his naked hands into the steaming wound up to his wrists.

"You don't know that!" Artie said. "You can't know that!"

"I know," the man replied, but he offered nothing more. "Lady," he said, "start opening those Tupperware bowls for me, will you?"

She did as he asked, and he started pulling out handfuls of bloody, steaming intestines. He chopped them up and began filling the bowls. "Did I get that other bastard?" he asked Artie.

"What?"

"The other one I shot at. I think you'll remember that it was chewing on your arm."

"Oh. Right. Yeah." Artie watched the guts being stuffed into brightly colored Tupperware bowls. "No. I mean . . . I think you hit him, but he let me go and ran off."

"They can be tough motherfuckers," he said, and then he began to carve the animal's head from its neck. "Open that big bowl, lady," he told her.

He reached up into the severed head, and the brains plopped into the big bowl.

"You can put the lids on now," he said.

Sister did, about to choke on the coppery smell of blood. He wiped his hands on the beast's hide and then slid the two jugs back on the cord and retied the knot; he put his gloves back on, returned the knife to its pouch and the filled Tupperware containers to his pack, and then rose to a standing position. "You two got any guns?"

"No," Sister said.

"How about food?"

"We've . . . we've got some canned vegetables and fruit juice. And some cold cuts, too."

"Cold cuts," he repeated disdainfully. "Lady, you can't go very far in this weather on cold cuts. You say you've got some vegetables? I hope it's not broccoli. I *hate* broccoli."

"No . . . we've got some corn, and green beans, and boiled potatoes."

"Sounds like the makings of a stew to me. My cabin's about two miles north of here, as the crow flies. If you want to go back with me, you'll be welcome. If not, I'll say have a good trip to Detroit."

"What's the nearest town?" Sister asked.

"St. Johns, I guess. Hazleton's the nearest town of any size, and that's about ten miles south of St. Johns. There may be a few people left, but after that flood of refugees washed in from the east I'd be surprised if you'd find much in any town along I-80. St. Johns is about four or five miles west." The man looked at Artie, who was dripping blood onto the snow. "Friend, that's going to attract every scavenger within smelling distance—and believe me, some of those bastards can sniff blood a long, long way."

"We ought to go with him," Artie said to Sister. "I might bleed to death!"

"I doubt it," the man countered. "Not from a scratch like that. It'll freeze up pretty soon, but you'll have a blood smell on your clothes. Like I say, they'll come out of the mountains with knives and forks between their teeth. But you do what you want to do; I'm hitting the trail." He shrugged into his pack, wrapped the cord around his shoulder and picked up his rifle. "Take care," he said, and he started gliding across the snowy highway toward the woods.

It took Sister about two more seconds to make up her mind. "Wait a minute!" He stopped. "Okay. We'll come with you, Mr.—"

But he was already moving again, heading into the edge of the dense forest.

They had no choice but to hurry after him. Artie looked over his shoulder, terrified of more lurking predators coming up behind him. His ribs ached where the beast had hit him, and his legs felt like short pieces of soft rubber. He and Sister entered the woods after the shuffling figure of the man in the ski mask and left the highway of death behind.

Thirty-one

The outlines of small, blocky one-story buildings and red brick houses began to appear from the deepening scarlet gloom. A town, Josh realized. Thank God!

The wind was still shoving mightily at his back, but after what seemed like eight hours of walking yesterday and at least five today, he was about to topple to the ground. He carried the exhausted child in his arms, as he had for the past two hours, and walked stiff-legged, the soles of his feet oozing with blisters and blood in shoes that were coming apart at the seams. He thought he must look like a zombie, or like the Frankenstein monster carrying the fainted heroine in his arms.

They had spent last night in the windbreak of an overturned pick-up truck; bound-up bales of hay had been scattered around, and Josh had lugged them over to build a makeshift shelter that would contain their body heat. Still, they'd been out in the middle of nowhere, surrounded by wasteland and dead fields, and both of them had dreaded first light because they knew they had to start walking again.

The dark town—just a scatter of wind-ravaged buildings and a few widely spaced houses on dusty lots—beckoned him onward. He saw no cars, no hint of light or life. There was a Texaco station with one pump and a garage whose roof had collapsed. A sign flapping back and forth on its hinges advertised TUCKER'S HARDWARE AND FEEDS, but the store's front window was shattered and the place looked bare as Mother Hubbard's cupboard. A small café had also collapsed, except for the sign that read GOOD EATS! Every step an exercise in agony, Josh walked past the crumbled buildings. He saw that dozens of paperback books lay in the dust around him, their pages flipping wildly in the restless hand of the wind, and to the left were the remains of a little clapboard structure with a hand-painted SULLIVAN PUBLIC LIBRARY sign.

Sullivan, Josh thought. Whatever Sullivan had once been, it was dead now.

Something moved at the corner of his vision. He looked to the side, and something small—a jackrabbit? he wondered—darted out of sight behind the ruins of the café.

Josh was stiff with cold, and he knew Swan must be freezing, too. She held onto that Cookie Monster doll like life itself and occasionally flinched in her tormented sleep. He approached one of the houses but stopped when he saw a body curled up like a question mark on the front porch steps. He headed for the next house, further along and across the road.

The mailbox, supported on a crooked pedestal, was painted white and had what appeared to be an eye, with upper and lower lids, painted on it in black. The hand-lettered name was *Davy and Leona Skelton*. Josh walked across the dirt lot and up the porch steps to the screen door. "Swan?" he said. "Wake up, now." She mumbled, and he set her down; then he tried the door but found it latched from the inside. He lifted his foot and kicked at its center, knocking it off its hinges, and they crossed the porch to the front door.

Josh had just put his hand on the knob when the door flew open and the barrel of a pistol looked him in the eyes.

"You broke my screen door," a woman's voice said in the gloom. The pistol did not waver.

"Uh . . . I'm sorry, ma'am. I didn't think anybody was here."

"Why'd you think the door was *locked,* then? This is private property!"

"I'm sorry," Josh repeated. He saw the woman's gnarled finger on the trigger. "I don't have any money," he said. "I'd pay you for the door if I did."

"Money?" She hawked and spat past him. "Money ain't worth nothin' no more! Hell, a screen door is worth a bagful of gold, fella! I'd blow your damn head off if I wouldn't have to clean up the mess!"

"If you don't mind, we'll just go on our way."

The woman was silent. Josh could see the outline of her head, but not her face; her head angled toward Swan. "A little girl," she said softly. "Oh, my Lord . . . a little girl . . ."

"Leona!" a weak voice called from inside the house. "Leo—" And then it was interrupted by a strangling, terrible spasm of coughing.

"It's all right, Davy!" she called back. "I'll be there directly!" She turned her attention to Josh again, the pistol still stuck in his face. "Where'd you two come from? Where're you goin'?"

"We came from . . . out there." He motioned toward one end of the town. "And I guess we're going that way." He motioned to the other end.

"Not much of a travel plan."

"I don't guess it is," he agreed, uneasily watching the black eye of that pistol.

She paused, looked down at the little girl again and then sighed deeply. "Well," she finally said, "since you're halfway broke in already, you might as well come on in the rest of the way." She motioned with the gun and retreated through the doorway.

Josh took Swan's hand, and they entered the house.

"Shut the door," the woman said. "Thanks to you, we'll be up to our ears in dust pretty soon."

Josh did as she asked. A small fire was burning in the fireplace, and the woman's squat figure was outlined in red as she moved about the room. She lit a hurricane lantern on the mantel, then a second and third lantern placed strategically around the room to give the most light. The pistol was uncocked, but she kept it at her side.

She finished with the lanterns and turned around to get a good look at Josh and Swan.

Leona Skelton was short and wide, wearing a thick pink sweater atop ragged overalls and furry pink slippers on her feet. Her square face appeared to have been carved from an apple, then dried under the sun; there wasn't a smooth place on it for all the winding cracks and ravines. Her large, expressive blue eyes were surrounded by webs of wrinkles, and the deep lines in her broad forehead looked like a clay etching of ocean waves. Josh figured she was in her mid- to late sixties, though her curly, swept-back hair was dyed garish red. Now, as her gaze wandered between Josh and Swan, her lips slowly parted, and Josh saw that several of her front teeth were silver.

"God A'mighty," she said quietly. "You two got burnt, didn't you? Oh, Jesus . . . I'm sorry, I don't mean to stare, but . . ." She looked at Swan, and her face seemed to compress with pain. There was a glimmer of tears in her eyes. "Oh, Lord," Leona whispered. "Oh, my Lord, you two have been . . . hurt so bad."

"We're alive," Josh said. "That's what counts."

"Yes," she agreed, nodding. Her eyes found the hardwood floor. "Forgive my rudeness. I was brought up better'n that."

"Leona!" the man rasped, and again he was savaged by a fit of coughing.

"I'd best see to my husband," she said, leaving the room through a hallway. While she was gone, Josh looked around the room; it was sparsely furnished, with unpainted pine furniture and a threadbare green throw rug in front of the fireplace. He avoided peering into a mirror on one wall and walked toward a glass-fronted cabinet nearby. On the cabinet's shelves were dozens of crystal spheres of varying sizes, the smallest about pebble-sized and the largest as big as both of Josh's fists clenched together—about half as big as a bowling ball. Most of them were the size of baseballs and perfectly clear, though others held tints of blue, green and yellow. Added to the collection were different kinds of feathers, some dried-out corncobs with multicolored kernels, and a couple of fragile-looking, almost transparent snakeskins.

"Where are we?" Swan asked him, still hugging her Cookie Monster. Beneath her eyes were dark purple hollows of fatigue, and thirst burned the back of her throat.

"A little town called Sullivan. There's not much here. It looks like everybody's already gone, except these people." He approached the mantel to examine some framed Polaroids displayed there; in one of the pictures, Leona Skelton was sitting in a porch swing with a smiling, stout, middle-aged man who had more belly than hair, but his eyes were young and a bit mischievous behind wire-rimmed spectacles. He had his arm around Leona, and one hand appeared to be creeping toward her lap. She was laughing, her mouth full of silver flash, and her hair wasn't quite as red; in any event, she appeared to be at least fifteen years younger.

In another picture, Leona was rocking a white cat in her arms like a baby, the cat's feet stuck up contentedly in the air. A third picture showed the pot-bellied man with a younger fellow, both of them carrying fishing rods and displaying bite-sized fish.

"That's my family," Leona said, coming into the room. She had left the gun behind. "My husband's name is Davy, our son's named Joe and the cat's called Cleopatra. *Was* called Cleopatra, I mean. I buried her about two weeks ago, out back. Put her deep, so nothin' could get at her. Have you two got names, or were you hatched?"

"I'm Josh Hutchins. This is Sue Wanda, but she's called Swan."

"Swan," Leona repeated. "That's a pretty name. I'm pleased to meet the both of you."

"Thank you," Swan said, not forgetting her manners.

"Oh, Lordy!" Leona bent and picked up some farming and *House Beautiful* magazines that had tumbled off the coffee table, and then she took a broom from the corner and started sweeping dust toward the fireplace. "House is a godawful wreck!" she apologized as she worked. "Used to be able to keep it as neat as a needle, but lately time slips away. I ain't had no visitors for quite a number of days!" She swept up the last of the dust and stood staring out a window at the red gloom and the wind-lashed remains of Sullivan. "Used to be a fine town," she said listlessly. "Had more'n three hundred people livin' right around here. Fine people, too. Ben McCormick used to say he was fat enough to make three more folks. Drew and Sissy Stimmons lived in that house, over there." She pointed. "Oh, Sissy loved her hats! Had about thirty of 'em, wore a different hat every Sunday for thirty Sundays and then started over again. Kyle Doss owned the café. Geneva Dewberry ran the public library, and oh, Lordy, could she talk about books!" Her voice was getting quieter and quieter, drifting away. "Geneva said she was gonna sit down and write herself a romance someday. I always believed she would." She motioned in another direction. "Norm Barkley lived down there at the end of the road. You can't see the house from here, though. I almost married Norman, when I was a young thing. But Davy stole me away with a rose and a kiss on a Saturday night. Yes, sir." She nodded, and then she seemed to remember where she was. Her spine stiffened, and she returned the broom to its corner as if she were giving up a dance partner. "Well," she said, "that was our town."

"Where'd they all go?" Josh asked.

"Heaven," she replied. "Or Hell. Whichever claimed them first, I reckon. Oh, some of 'em packed up and lit out." She shrugged. "Where to, I can't say. But most of us stayed here, in our homes and on our land. Then the sickness started hitting folks . . . and Death moved in. It's like a big fist a-knockin' at your door—boom boom, boom boom, like that. And you know you can't keep it from comin' in, but you got to *try*." She moistened her lips with her tongue, her eyes glazed and distant. "Sure is some kinda crazy weather for August, ain't it? Cold enough to freeze a witch's tit."

"You . . . do know what's happened, don't you?"

She nodded. "Oh, yes," she said. "Lee Procter had the radio goin' full blast at the hardware store when I was there buyin' nails and wire to hang a picture. I don't know what station he was tuned to, but all of a sudden there was a godawful squallin', and this man's voice came on talkin' real fast about a state of emergency and bombs and all. Then there was a sizzlin' noise like grease in a hot skillet and the radio went dead. Couldn't raise a whisper on it. Wilma James come runnin' in, yellin' for everybody to look up at the sky. We went out and looked, and we seen the airplanes or bombs or whatever they were passin' overhead, some of 'em near about to collide with each other. And Grange Tucker said, 'It's happenin'!' Armageddon is happenin'!' And he just plopped down on the curb in front of his store and watched those things fly past.

"Then the wind came, and the dust, and the cold," she said, still staring out the window. "The sun went blood-red. Twisters passed through, and one of 'em hit the McCormick farm and just took it away, didn't leave nothin' but foundation stones. Not a trace of Ben, Ginny or the kids. 'Course, everybody in town started comin' to me, wantin' to know what lay in the future and all." She shrugged. "I couldn't tell 'em I saw skulls where their faces used to be. How can you tell your friends somethin' like that? Well, Mr. Laney—the postman from Russell County—didn't show up, and the phone lines were down and there was no 'lectricity. We knew whatever had happened had been a whomper. Kyle Doss and Eddie Meachum volunteered to drive the twenty miles to Matheson and find out what was goin' on. They never come back. I saw skulls where their faces were, too, but what could I say? You know, sometimes there just ain't no sense in tellin' somebody their time's about up."

Josh wasn't following the old woman's ramblings. "What do you mean, you saw skulls where their faces were?"

"Oh. Sorry. I forget that everybody beyond Sullivan don't know about me." Leona Skelton turned from the window, a faint smile on her dried-apple face. She picked up one of the lamps, walked across the room to a bookcase and withdrew a leather-bound scrapbook; she took it to Josh and opened it. "There you go," she said. "That's me." She pointed to a yellowed picture and article, carefully scissored from a pulp magazine.

The headline read, KANSAS SEER FORETOLD KENNEDY DEATH

6 MONTHS BEFORE DIXON! And below that, a smaller line proclaimed, *Leona Skelton sees riches, new prosperity for America!* The photograph showed a much younger Leona Skelton surrounded by cats and crystal balls.

"That's from *Fate* magazine, back in 1964. See, I wrote a letter to President Kennedy warning him to stay out of Dallas, because he was giving a speech on television and I saw a skull where his face was, and then I used the tarot cards and the Ouija board and found out that Kennedy had a powerful enemy in Dallas, Texas. I even got part of the name, but it came out as Osbald. Anyway, I wrote this letter, and I even made a copy of it." She flipped the page, showing him a battered, almost illegible handwritten letter dated April 19, 1963. "Two FBI men came to the house and wanted to have a long talk with me. I was pretty calm, but they like to have scared poor Davy out of his clodhoppers! Oh, they were silky-talkin' fellas, but they could look a hole right through you! I saw they thought I was a crazy lunatic, and they told me not to write any more letters and then they left."

She turned another page. The headline on this article read TOUCHED BY AN ANGEL AT BIRTH, KANSAS 'JEANNE DIXON' VOWS. "That's from the *National Tattler,* about 1965. I just happened to mention to that writer lady that my mama always told me she had a vision of an angel in white robes kissin' my forehead when I was a baby. Anyway, this one came out right after I found a little boy who'd been missin' from his folks in Kansas City. He just got mad and ran away from home, and he was hidin' in an old house about two blocks away." She flipped more pages, proudly pointing to different articles from the *Star,* the *Enquirer,* and *Fate* magazine. The last article, in a small Kansas newspaper, was printed in 1987. "I haven't been doin' so well lately," she said. "Sinus trouble and arthritis. Kinda clouded me up, I guess. Anyway, that's who I am."

Josh grunted. He'd never believed in extrasensory perception, but from what he'd witnessed lately, anything was possible. "I noticed your crystal balls over there."

"That's my most favorite collection! Those are from all over the world, you know!"

"They're real pretty," Swan added.

"Thank you kindly, little lady." She smiled down at Swan, then returned her gaze to Josh. "You know, I didn't see this thing happenin'. Maybe I'm gettin' too old to see much anymore. But I had a bad, deep-down gut feelin' about that astro-nut president. I thought he was the kind to let too many cooks stir the pot. Davy and me, neither one of us voted for him, no sir!"

The coughing rattled from the back room again. Leona cocked her head, listening intently, but the coughing faded, and Leona visibly relaxed once more. "I don't have much to offer in the way of food," she explained. "Got some old corn muffins as hard as cinder blocks and a pot of vegetable soup. I can still do my cookin' over the fireplace, but I've gotten used to eatin' food that's as cold as a virgin's bed. Got a well in the back yard that still pumps up clean water. So you're welcome to whatever you'll have."

"Thank you," Josh said. "I think some soup and corn muffins would be pretty fine, cold or not. Is there any way I can get some of this dirt off me?"

"You mean you want to take a bath?" She thought for a minute. "Well, I reckon we can do it the old-fashioned way: heat buckets of water in the fire and fill the tub up like that. Little lady, I expect you ought to scrub up, too. 'Course, my drains might clog with all the dirt, and I don't believe the plumber makes housecalls anymore. What've you two been doin'? Rollin' in the ground?"

"Sort of," Swan said. She thought a bath—warm water or cold—was a fine idea. She knew she smelled like a pigsty; still, she was afraid of what her skin might look like under all the dirt. She knew it wasn't going to be very pretty.

"I'll fetch you a couple of buckets, then, and you can pump your own water. Which one wants to go first?"

Josh shrugged and motioned to Swan.

"All righty. I'd help you pump, but I've got to be close to Davy in case he has a spell. You bring the buckets in, and we'll warm 'em up in the fireplace. I've got a nice claw-footed bathtub that hasn't nestled a body since this damned mess started."

Swan nodded and said thank you, and Leona Skelton waddled off to get the buckets from the kitchen. In the back bedroom, Davy Skelton coughed violently a few times, then the noise subsided.

Josh was tempted to step back there and take a look at the man, but didn't. That coughing sounded bad; it reminded him of Darleen's coughing just before she'd died. He figured it must be radiation poisoning. "The sickness started hitting folks," Leona had said. Radiation poisoning must have wiped out almost the whole town. But it had occurred to Josh that some people might be able to resist the radiation better than others; maybe it poleaxed some right off and slowly crept up on the rest. He was tired and weak from walking, but otherwise he felt okay; Swan, too, was in pretty good shape except for her burns, and Leona Skelton seemed healthy enough. Back in the basement, Darleen had been fit and boisterous one day, laid low and scalding with fever the next. Maybe some people could go for weeks or months without feeling the full effects of it. He hoped.

But right now the idea of a warm bath and a meal eaten from a bowl with a real spoon made him delirious. "You okay?" he asked Swan, who stared into space.

"I'm better," she replied, but her mind had drifted back to her mama, lying dead under the dirt, and to what PawPaw—or whatever had taken hold of PawPaw—had said. What did it mean? What was the giant supposed to protect her from? And why *her?*

She thought of the green seedlings growing from the dirt in the shape of her body. Nothing like that had ever happened to her before. She really hadn't even had to *do* anything, not even knead the dirt between her hands. Of course, she was used to the tingling sensation, to feeling sometimes like a fountain of energy was coming up from the earth and through her backbone . . . but this was different.

Something had changed, she thought. I could always make flowers grow. Bringing them up from wet earth when the sun shone down was easy. But she'd made grass grow in the dark, without water, and she hadn't even *tried*. Something had changed.

And it came to her, just like that: I'm stronger than I was before.

Josh crossed to the window and peered out at the dead town, leaving Swan alone with her thoughts. A figure caught his attention out there—a small animal of some kind, standing in the wind. Its head lifted, watching Josh. A dog, he realized. A little terrier. They stared at each other for a few seconds—and then the dog darted away.

Good luck to you, he thought, and then he turned away, because he knew the animal was bound to die, and he had a sickened gutful of death. Davy coughed twice and called weakly for Leona. She brought the buckets in from the kitchen for Swan's bathwater, and then she hurried back to see about her husband.

Thirty-two

Sister and Artie had found a little piece of Heaven.

They walked into a small log cabin, hidden in a grove of naked evergreens on the shore of an ice-skimmed lake, and into the wonderful warmth of a kerosene space heater. Tears almost burst from Sister's eyes as she stumbled across the threshold, and Artie gasped with pleasure.

"This is the place," the man in the ski mask said.

Four other people were already in the cabin: a man and woman, both dressed in ragged summer clothing, who appeared to be young, maybe in their early twenties—but it was hard to tell, because both of them had severe, brown-crusted burns in weird geometric shapes on their faces and arms and under the torn places of their clothing. The young man's dark hair hung almost to his shoulders, but the crown of his scalp was burned bald and splotched with the brown marks. The woman might have been pretty, with large blue eyes and the fine bones of a fashion model, but her curly auburn hair was almost all scorched away, and the brown crusted marks lay diagonally, like precise penstrokes, across her face. She was wearing cutoff blue jeans and sandals, and her bare legs were also splotched with burns. Her feet were swathed in rags, and she was curled up next to the heater.

The other two were a thin older man, maybe in his mid-fifties, with bright blue burns disfiguring his face, and a teen-aged boy, sixteen or so, wearing jeans and a T-shirt with BLACK FLAG LIVES! in untidy, scrawled letters on the front. Two small studs were pinned in the boy's left earlobe, and he had all of his rooster-cut orange hair, but gray burn marks streamed down his strong-jawed face as if someone had lit a candle over his forehead and let the wax drip. His deep-socketed green eyes watched Sister and Artie with a hint of amusement.

"Meet my other guests," the man in the ski mask said, laying his pack on a bloodstained porcelain counter next to the sink after he'd shut the door and latched it. "Kevin and Mona Ramsey"—he motioned toward the young couple—"Steve Buchanan"—toward the teenage boy—"and the most I can get out of the old man is that he's from Union City. I didn't get your names."

"Artie Wisco."

"You can call me Sister," she said. "What's yours?"

He peeled off the ski mask and hung it on the hook of a coatrack. "Paul Thorson," he told her. "Citizen of the world." He took off the jugs of blood and lifted the Tupperware bowls with their grisly contents from his pack.

Sister was shocked. Paul Thorson's face was unmarked by burns, and it had been a long time since Sister had seen a normal human face. He had long black hair flecked with gray, and gray swirled back from the corners of his mouth in his full black beard. His flesh was white from lack of sunshine, but it was weathered and wrinkled, and he had a high, deeply creased forehead and the rough-hewn look of an outdoorsman. Sister thought he resembled a mountain man, somebody who might have lived alone in a shack and come down to the valley only to trap beavers or something. Beneath black eyebrows, his eyes were a frosty gray-blue surrounded by dark circles of weariness. He shrugged off his parka—which had made him appear a lot heftier than he actually was—and hung that up as well, then started dumping the contents of the bowls into the sink. "Sister," he said, "let's have some of those vegetables you're carrying around. We're going to have asshole stew tonight, folks."

"Asshole stew?" Sister asked, and frowned. "Uh . . . what the hell is *that?*"

"It means you're a stupid asshole if you don't eat it, because that's all we've got. Come on, let's have the cans."

"We're going to eat . . . that?" Artie recoiled from the bloody mess. His ribs were hurting, and he had his hand pressed on the pain under his coat.

"It's not too bad, man," the teenager with orange hair said, in a flat Brooklyn accent. "You get used to it. Hell, one of those fuckers tried to eat *me*. Serves 'em right to be eaten by us, huh?"

"Absolutely," Paul agreed, going to work with his knife.

Sister took off her pack, opened the duffel bag and gave him some of the canned vegetables. Paul opened them with a can opener and dumped them into a big iron pot.

Sister shuddered, but the man obviously knew what he was doing. The cabin seemed to be only two large rooms. In this front room, along with the space heater, was a small fireplace of rough stones, a fire burning cheerfully within it and throwing off more warmth and light. A few candles melded to saucers and a kerosene lamp were set around the room, which contained two unrolled sleeping bags, a cot, and a nest of newspapers tucked away in a corner. A cast-iron stove and a good-sized pile of split logs stood on the other side of the room, and when Paul said, "Steve, you can get the stove going now," the boy got up off the floor, took a shovel from beside the fireplace and put burning pieces of wood into the stove. Sister felt a new rush of joy. They were going to have a hot meal!

"It's time now," the old man spoke up, looking at Paul. "It's time, isn't it?"

Paul glanced at his wristwatch. "Nope. Not quite yet." He continued chopping up the intestines and brains, and Sister noted that his fingers were long and slender. He had artistic hands, she thought—particularly unsuited to the task they were now performing.

"This your place?" she asked.

He nodded. "Been living here . . . oh, about four years now. During the summer, I'm the caretaker for the Big Pines Ski Area, about six or seven miles that way." He motioned in the direction of the lake behind the cabin. "In the winter, I cozy on in and live off the land." He glanced up and smiled grimly. "Winter came early this year."

"What were you doing on the highway?"

"The wolves go up there to chow down. I go up there to hunt wolves. That's how I found all these other poor souls, wandering around on I-80. I've found quite a few more, too. Their graves are out back. I'll show you, if you like."

She shook her head.

"See, the wolves have always lived in the mountains. They've never had reason to come down before. They eat rabbits, deer, and whatever other animals they can find. But now the small animals are dying in their holes, and the wolves can smell new food. So they're coming down in droves to Supermarket I-80 for the freshest meat. These people made it here before the snow started falling—if you can call that radioactive shit snow." He grunted with disgust. "Anyway, the food chain's been knocked off kilter. No small animals for the big ones to eat. Just people. And the wolves are getting real desperate—and real brave." He plopped the hunks of innards into the pot, then uncapped one of the blood jugs and poured the stuff in. The smell of blood permeated the room. "More wood in there, Steve. We want this shit to *boil.*"

"Right."

"I know it's time!" the old man whined. "It's got to be!"

"No, it's not," Kevin Ramsey told him. "Not until after we've had our food."

Paul added the other jug of blood to the pot and began to stir it with a wooden spoon. "You people might as well take off your coats and stay for dinner, unless you want to head for the next restaurant down the road."

Sister and Artie looked at each other, both of them queasy

from the smell of the stew. Sister was the first to take off her gloves, coat and woolen cap, and then Artie reluctantly did the same.

"Okay." Paul lifted the pot and put it on one of the stove's burners. "Stoke that baby's engine and let's get the fire up." As Steve Buchanan worked on the fire, Paul turned to a cupboard and produced a bottle that still had a little red wine left in it. "This is the last soldier," he told them. "Everybody gets one good jolt."

"Wait." Sister unzipped her knapsack again and brought out the six-pack of Olympia beer. "This might go better with the stew."

Their eyes lit up like penny candles.

"My God!" Paul said. "Lady, you just bought my soul." He gingerly touched the six-pack as if afraid it might evaporate, and when it didn't, he worked one can from its plastic ring. He shook it carefully, was pleased to find it hadn't frozen. Then he popped the tab and tilted it to his mouth, drinking long and deep with his eyes closed in rapture.

Sister handed beers to everyone but Artie and shared the bottle of Perrier with him. It wasn't as satisfying as the beer, but it tasted fine anyway.

The asshole stew made the cabin reek like a slaughterhouse. From outside came a low, distant howling.

"They smell it," Paul said, glancing out a window. "Oh, those bastards are going to be all around this place in a few minutes!"

The howling continued and grew as more wolf voices added dissonant notes and vibrato.

"It's got to be time!" the old man insisted after he'd finished his beer. "Isn't it?"

"It's almost time." Mona Ramsey had a gentle, lovely voice. "But not yet. Not yet."

Steve was stirring the pot. "It's boiling. I think the shit's as ready as it's gonna be."

"Great." Artie's stomach was about to curdle.

Paul ladled the stew out in brown clay bowls. It was thicker than Sister had thought it would be, and the smell was heavy, but not quite as bad as some of the things she'd scavenged from garbage bags back in Manhattan. The stuff was dark red, and if you didn't look too closely you might have thought it was just a bowl of hearty beef stew.

Outside, the wolves howled in unison, much closer to the cabin than before, as if they knew that one of their kin was about to go down human gullets.

"Down the hatch," Paul Thorson said, and he took the first sip.

Sister tilted the bowl to her mouth. The soup was bitter and gritty, but the meat wasn't too bad. The saliva suddenly flooded into her mouth, and she gulped the hot food down like an animal herself. After two swallows, Artie had begun to go pale.

"Hey," Paul said to him, "if you're gonna puke, do it *outside*. One speck on my clean floor and you sleep with the wolves."

Artie shut his eyes and kept eating. The others attacked their bowls, scraping them clean with their fingers and holding them out for more like orphans from *Oliver Twist*.

The wolves howled and clamored just outside the cabin. Something slammed against the wall, and Sister jumped so hard she spilled asshole stew on her sweater.

"They're just curious," Steve told her. "Don't sweat it, lady. It's cool."

Sister had a second bowl. Artie looked at her in horror and crawled away, his hand pressed against a throbbing pain at his ribs. Paul noticed, but he said nothing.

No sooner had the pot been cleaned out than the old man said irritably, "It's time! Right *now!*"

Paul put aside his empty bowl and checked his wristwatch again. "It hasn't been a whole day yet."

"Please." The old man's eyes were like those of a lost puppy's. "Please . . . all right?"

"You know the rules. Once a day. No more, no less."

"Please. Just this once . . . can't we do it early?"

"Aw, shit!" Steve said. "Let's go ahead and get it over with!"

Mona Ramsey shook her head violently. "No, it isn't time! It hasn't been a whole day yet! You know the rules!"

The wolves were still growling outside, as if they had their muzzles right up to the cracks in the door. Two or more of them started a gnashing, howling fight. Sister had no idea what everyone in the room was talking about, but whatever it was must be vital, she thought. The old man was near tears.

"Just this once . . . just this once," he moaned.

"Don't do it!" Mona told Paul, her eyes defiant. "We've got to have rules!"

"Oh, fuck the rules!" Steve Buchanan banged his bowl down on the counter. "I say we do it and get it over with!"

"What's going on here?" Sister asked, puzzled.

The others stopped arguing and looked at her. Paul Thorson glanced at his wristwatch, then sighed heavily. "Okay," he said. "Just this once, we do it early." He held up a hand to ward off the young woman's objections. "We're only going to be about an hour and twenty minutes early. That's not enough to hurt."

"Yes it is!" Mona was almost shouting. Her husband put his hands on her shoulders, as if to restrain her. "It could ruin *everything!*"

"Let's vote on it, then," Paul offered. "We're still a democracy, right? Everybody say 'aye' who wants to do it early." Immediately the old man shouted, *"Aye!"* Steve Buchanan stuck his thumb up in the air. The Ramseys were silent. Paul paused, listening to the call of the wolves, and Sister could see him thinking. Then he quietly said, "Aye. The ayes have it."

"What about *them?*" Mona pointed at Sister and Artie. "Don't they get votes?"

"Hell, no!" Steve said. "They're *new!* They don't get votes yet!"

"The ayes have it," Paul repeated firmly, staring at Mona. "One hour and twenty minutes early won't make a big difference."

"It will!" she replied, and then her voice cracked. She started sobbing, while her husband held her shoulders and tried to soothe her. "It'll ruin everything! I know it will!"

"You two come with me," Paul told Sister and Artie, and he motioned them into the cabin's other room.

In the room there was a regular bed with a quilted cover, a few shelves of paperback and hardbound books, and a desk and chair. On the desk was a battered old Royal typewriter and a thin sheaf of typing paper. Balls of paper were scattered around an overflowing wicker trash can. An ashtray was full of matches, and tobacco ash had spilled from the bowl of a black briar pipe. A couple of candles were set in saucers on a little table beside the bed, and a window looked out toward the tainted lake.

But that was not all the window revealed.

Parked behind the cabin was an old Ford pickup truck, the battleship-gray paint flaking off its sides and hood and red creepers of rust starting to eat through the metal.

"You've got a truck!" Sister said excitedly. "My God! We can get out of here!"

Paul glanced at the truck, scowled and shrugged. "Forget it, lady."

"What? What do you mean, *forget* it? You've got a truck! We can get to civilization!"

He picked up his pipe and jammed a finger into the bowl, digging at a carbon deposit. "Yeah? And where might that be?"

"Out there! Along I-80!"

"How far, do you think? Two miles? Five? Ten? What about fifty?" He put the pipe aside and glared at her, then he drew a green curtain shut between this room and the other. "Forget it," he repeated. "That truck's got about a teacupful of gas in it, the brakes are shot, and I doubt if it'll even crank. The battery was fucked up even on the best of days."

"But . . ." She looked out at the vehicle again, then at Artie and finally back to Paul Thorson. "You've got a *truck,*" she said, and she heard herself whine.

"The wolves have got *teeth,*" he replied. "Sharp ones. Do you want those poor souls out there to find out how sharp? You want to pile them in a pickup truck and go for a nice excursion through the Pennsylvania countryside with a teacupful of gas in the tank? Sure. No problem to call a tow truck when we break down. Take us right to the gas pumps, and we'll pull out our trusty credit cards and be on our way."

He was silent for a moment, and then he shook his head. "Please don't torture yourself. Forget it. We're here to *stay*."

Sister heard the wolves howling, the sound floating through the woods and over the frozen lake, and she feared that he might be right.

"Talking about that bum truck's not why I asked you in here." He bent down and pulled an old wooden footlocker out from beneath the bed. "You two still seem to have most of your marbles," he said. "I don't know what you've been through, but those people out there are hanging on by their fingernails."

The footlocker was sealed by a fist-sized padlock. He fished a key from his jeans pocket and opened the lock. "We play a little game around here. It might not be a very nice game, but I figure it keeps them from letting go. It's kind of like walking to the mailbox every day because you're expecting a love letter or a check." He lifted the footlocker's lid.

Inside, cushioned with newspapers and rags, were three bottles of Johnny Walker Red Label Scotch, a .357 Magnum revolver and a box or two of ammunition, some moldy-looking manuscripts bound with rubber bands, and another object wrapped in heavy plastic. He began to unfold the plastic. "It's funny as shit, it really is," he said. "I came out here to nowhere to get *away* from people. Can't stand the breed. Never could. I'm sure as hell no Good Samaritan. And then all of a sudden the highway's covered with cars and corpses, and people are running like hell and I'm up to my *ears* in the human race. I say screw it! We deserved everything we got!" He unfolded the last layer of plastic to reveal a radio with an intricate set of dials and knobs. He lifted it from the footlocker, opened the desk drawer and got out eight batteries. "Shortwave," he told them as he began to put the batteries in the back of the radio. "I used to like to listen to concerts from Switzerland in the middle of the night." He closed the footlocker and snapped the padlock on again.

"I don't understand," Sister said.

"You will. Just don't get too bent out of shape, no matter what happens out there in the next few minutes. Like I say, it's all a game, but they're pretty jumpy today. I just wanted to prepare you." He motioned for them to follow, and they returned to the front room.

"It's my turn today!" the old man cried out, sitting up on his knees, his eyes shining.

"You did it yesterday," Paul told him calmly. "It's Kevin's turn today." He offered the radio to the young man. Kevin hesitated, then took it as if accepting a child in swaddling clothes.

The others gathered around him, except for Mona Ramsey, who crawled petulantly away. But even she watched her husband excitedly. Kevin grasped the tip of the radio's recessed antenna and drew it all the way out; it jutted up about two feet, the metal shining like a promise.

"Okay," Paul said. "Switch it on."

"Not yet," the young man balked. "Please. Not just yet."

"Go ahead, man!" Steve Buchanan's voice shook. "Do it!"

Kevin slowly turned one of the knobs, and the red needle moved all the way to one end of the frequency dial. Then he laid his finger against a red button and let it rest there as if he couldn't bear to press it. He drew a sudden, sharp breath—and his finger punched the ON button.

Sister winced, and everyone else breathed or flinched or shifted, too.

No sound came from the radio.

"Crank the volume up, man!"

"It's already set high," Kevin told him, and slowly—delicately—he began to move the needle along the frequency dial.

A quarter inch more, and still dead air. The red needle continued to move, almost imperceptibly. Sister's palms were sweating. Slowly, slowly: another fraction of an inch further.

A high burst of static suddenly wailed from the speaker, and Sister and everyone else in the room jumped. Kevin looked up at Paul, who said, "Atmosphere's supercharged." The red needle moved on, through the thickets of little numbers and decimal points, searching for a human voice.

Different tones of static faded in and out, weird cacophonies of atmospheric violence. Sister heard the howl of the wolves outside mingling with the static noise—a lonely sound, almost heartbreaking in its loneliness. Spaces of dead air alternated with the grating, terrible static—and Sister knew she was hearing ghosts from the black craters where cities had been.

"You're going too fast!" Mona objected and he slowed the needle's progress to a speed that might tempt a spider to spin a web between his fingers. Sister's heart pounded at every infinitesimal change in the pitch or volume of static pouring from the speaker.

Finally, Kevin came to the end of the dial. His eyes were luminous with tears.

"Try AM," Paul told him.

"Yeah! Try AM!" Steve said, pressing over Kevin's shoulder. "There's gotta be somethin' on AM!"

Kevin turned another small dial to change from shortwave to AM, and he began to lead the red searching needle back over the numbers again. This time, except for abrupt pops and clicks and a faint, distant humming noise like honeybees at work, the band was almost completely dead. Sister didn't know how long it took Kevin to reach the other end of the dial; it could have been ten minutes, or fifteen, or twenty. But he stretched it out to the very last faint sizzle—and then he sat holding the radio between his hands, staring at it as a pulse beat steadily at his temple.

"Nothing," he whispered, and he pressed the red button.

Silence.

The old man put his hands to his face.

Sister heard Artie, who was standing beside her, give a helpless, despairing sigh. "Not even Detroit," he said listlessly. "Dear God . . . not even Detroit."

"You turned it way too fast, man!" Steve told Kevin Ramsey. "Shit, you *spun* through it! I thought I heard something—it sounded like a voice!—and you went right through it!"

"No!" Mona shouted. "There was no voice! We did it too early, and that's why there was no voice! If we'd done it on

time, by the rules, we would've heard somebody this time! I *know* it!"

"It was my turn." The old man's pleading eyes turned toward Sister. "Everybody always steals my turn."

Mona began to sob. "We didn't go by the rules! We missed the voice because we didn't go by the rules!"

"Fuck it!" Steve snapped. "I heard a voice! I swear to God I did! It was right . . ." He started to take the radio, but Paul Thorson snatched it out of Kevin's hands before he could. Paul lowered the antenna and turned away, going back through the curtain into the other room. Sister couldn't believe what she'd just witnessed; anger stirred within her, and pity for the poor, hopeless souls. She strode purposefully into the room where Paul Thorson was wrapping the radio back up in its protective plastic.

He looked up at her, and she lifted her right hand and gave him a slap across the face with all the fury of judgment behind it. The blow knocked him sprawling and left a red handprint on his cheek. Still, as he fell, he grasped the radio protectively to his chest and took the fall on his shoulder. He lay blinking up at her.

"I've never seen anything so cruel in all my life!" Sister raged. "Do you think that's *funny?* Do you get pleasure out of that? Get up, you sonofabitch! I'll knock your ass right through that wall!" She advanced on him, but he held up a hand to ward her off, and she hesitated.

"Wait," he croaked. "Hold on. You don't get it yet, do you?"

"You're gonna get it, shitass!"

"Back off. Just wait, and watch. Then you can kick butt if you still want to." He pulled himself up, continued wrapping the radio and replaced it in the footlocker; then he snapped the padlock shut and pushed the footlocker underneath the bed again. "After you," he said, motioning her into the front room.

Mona Ramsey was bent over in the corner, sobbing as her husband tried to comfort her. The old man had curled up against one wall, staring into space, and Steve was kicking and hammering at the wall with his fist, shouting obscenities. In the center of the room, Artie stood very still as the red-haired teenager rampaged around him.

"Mona?" Paul said, with Sister standing just behind him and to the side.

The young woman raised her eyes to his. The old man looked at him, and so did Kevin, and Steve stopped hammering at the walls.

"You're right, Mona," Paul went on. "We didn't go by the rules. That's why we didn't hear a voice. Now, I'm not saying we *will* hear one if we go by the rules tomorrow. But tomorrow is another day, right? That's what Scarlett O'Hara said. Tomorrow we'll turn the radio on and try again. And if we don't hear anything tomorrow, we'll try the day after that. You know, it would take some time to repair a radio station and kick the juice back on. It would take quite a while. But tomorrow we'll try again. Right?"

"Sure!" Steve said. "Hell, it would take a while to get the juice back on!" He grinned, looking at all of them in turn. "I bet they're trying to get the stations back on the air right now! God, that'd be a job, wouldn't it?"

"I used to listen to the radio all the time!" the old man spoke up. He was smiling, too, as if he'd stepped into a dream. "I used to listen to the Mets on the radio in the summertime! Tomorrow we'll hear somebody, I'll bet you!"

Mona clutched at her husband's shoulder. "We didn't go by the rules, did we? See? I told you—it's important to have rules!" But her crying was over, and just as suddenly she started to laugh. "God'll let us hear somebody if we follow the rules! Tomorrow! Yes, I think it might be tomorrow!"

"Right!" Kevin agreed, hugging her close. "Tomorrow!"

"Yeah." Paul looked around the room; he was keeping a smile on his face, but his eyes were pain-ridden and haunted. "I kind of think it might be tomorrow, too." His gaze met Sister's. "Don't you?"

She hesitated, and then she understood. These people had nothing to live for but that radio in the footlocker. Without it, without being able to look forward to a very special time once a day, they might very well kill themselves. Keeping it on all the time would waste batteries and blunt the hope, and she saw that Paul Thorson knew they might never hear a human voice on that radio again. But, in his own way, he *was* being a Good Samaritan. He was keeping these people alive in more ways than by just feeding them.

"Yes," she finally said. "I think it might be."

"Good." His smile deepened, and so did the networks of lines around his eyes. "I hope you two are poker players. I've got a hot deck of cards and plenty of matches. You weren't going anywhere in a hurry, were you?"

Sister glanced at Artie. He was standing stoop-shouldered, his eyes vacant, and she knew he was thinking of the hole where Detroit had been. She watched him for a moment, and finally he straightened up and answered in a weak but courageous voice, "No. I'm not hurrying anywhere. Not anymore."

"We play five-card draw around here. If I win, I get to read my poetry to you, and you have to smile and enjoy it. Either that or you can dump the crap buckets—your choice."

"I'll make up my mind when I come to it," Sister replied, and she decided that she liked Paul Thorson very much.

"You sound like a real gambler, lady!" He clapped his hands together with mock glee. "Welcome to the club!"

Thirty-three

Swan had avoided it as long as she possibly could. But now, as she stepped out of the bathtub's wonderfully warm water—leaving it murky brown with shed skin and grime—and reached for the large towel that Leona Skelton had set out for her, she had to do it. She *had* to.

She looked in the mirror.

The light came from a single lamp, its wick turned low, but it was enough. Swan stared into the oval glass over the basin, and she thought she might be seeing someone in a grotesque, hairless Halloween mask. One hand fluttered up to her lips; the awful image did the same.

Shreds of skin were hanging from her face, peeling off like tree bark. Brown, crusty streaks lay across her forehead and the bridge of her nose, and her eyebrows—once so blond and thick—had been burned clean away. Her lips were cracked like dry earth, and her eyes seemed to be sunken down into dark holes in her skull. On her right cheek were two small black warts, and on her lips were three more of them. She'd seen those same wartlike things on Josh's forehead, had seen the brown burns on his face and the mottled gray-white of his skin, but she'd gotten used to what Josh looked like. Seeing herself with a stubble where her hair had been and the dead white skin dangling from her face jarred loose tears of shock and horror.

She was startled by a polite knock at the bathroom door. "Swan? You all right, child?" Leona Skelton asked.

"Yes, ma'am," she answered, but her voice was unsteady, and she knew the woman had heard.

After a pause, Leona said, "Well, I've got some grub for you when you're ready."

Swan thanked her and said she'd be out in a few minutes, and Leona went away. The Halloween-mask monster peered at her from the mirror.

She had left her grimy clothes with Leona, who'd said she'd try to wash them in a pot and dry them before the fire, and so she wrapped herself up in the floppy plaid boy's-size robe and thick white socks that Leona had left for her. The robe was part of a trunkful of clothes that had belonged to Leona's son, Joe—who now, the woman had said proudly, lived in Kansas City with a family of his own and was the manager of a supermarket. Been meanin' to throw that trunk out, Leona had told Swan and Josh, but somehow I just never got around to the job.

Swan's body was clean. The soap she'd used had smelled like lilacs, and she thought wistfully of her gardens bright with color beneath the sun. She hobbled out of the bathroom, leaving the lantern burning for Josh to see by when he took his bath. The house was chilly, and she went directly to the fireplace to warm herself again. Josh was asleep on the floor under a red blanket with his head on a pillow. Near his head was a TV tray with an empty bowl and cup on it and a couple of corn muffin crumbs. The blanket had pulled off his shoulder, and Swan bent down and tucked it up underneath his chin.

"He told me how you two got together," Leona said, quietly so as not to disturb Josh; he was sleeping so soundly, though, that she doubted he'd wake if a truck came through the wall. She continued into the room from the kitchen, bringing Swan a TV tray with a bowl of lukewarm vegetable soup, a cup of well water and three corn muffins. Swan took the tray and sat down in front of the fireplace. The house was quiet. Davy Skelton was asleep, and except for the occasional rush of wind around the roof there was no sound but the crackling of embers and the ticking of a windup clock on the mantel that said it was forty minutes after eight.

Leona eased herself into a chair covered with a garish flower-patterned fabric. Her knees popped. She winced and rubbed them with a gnarled, age-spotted hand. "Old bones like to talk," she said. She nodded toward the sleeping giant. "He says you're a mighty brave little girl. Says once you set your mind, you don't give up. That true?"

Swan didn't know what to say. She shrugged, chewing on a rock-hard corn muffin.

"Well, that's what he told me. And it's good to have a tough mind. Especially in times like these." Her gaze moved past Swan and to the window. "Everything's changed now. All that was is gone. I know it." Her eyes narrowed. "I can hear a dark voice in that wind," she said. "It's sayin', 'All mine . . . all mine.' I don't figure a whole lot of people are gonna be left out there, I'm sorry to say. Maybe the whole world's just like Sullivan: blowin' away, changin', turnin' into somethin' different than what it was before."

"Like what?" Swan asked.

"Who knows?" Leona shrugged. "Oh, the world's not gonna end. That's what I thought first off. But the world has got a tough mind, too." She lifted a crooked finger for emphasis. "Even if all the people in all the big cities and little towns die, and all the trees and the crops turn black, and the clouds never let the sun through again, the world'll keep turnin'. Oh, God gave this world a mighty spin, He did! And He put mighty tough minds and souls in a lot of people, too—people like *you,* maybe. And like your friend over there."

Swan thought she heard a dog barking. It was an uncertain sound, there for a few seconds and then masked by the wind. She stood up, looked out one window and then another, but couldn't see much of anything. "Did you hear a dog bark?"

"Huh? No, but you probably did, all right. Strays pass

through town all the time, lookin' for food. Sometimes I leave a few crumbs and a bowl of water on the porch steps." She busied herself getting the new wood situated in the fireplace so it would catch amid the embers.

Swan took another swallow from her cup of water and decided her teeth couldn't take the battle with the corn muffins. She picked up a muffin and said, "Would it be okay if I took this water and the muffin out there?"

"Sure, go ahead. Guess strays need to eat, too. Watch out the wind don't grab you 'way, though."

Swan took the muffin and cup of water out to the porch steps. The wind was stronger than it had been during daylight, carrying waves of dust before it. Her robe flapping around her, Swan put the food and water on one of the lower steps and looked in all directions, shielding her eyes from the dust. There was no sign of a dog. She went back up to where the screen door had been and stood there for a moment, and she was about to go back inside when she thought she detected a furtive movement off to the right. She waited, beginning to shiver.

At last a small gray shape came nearer. The little terrier stopped about ten feet from the porch and sniffed the ground with his furry snout. He smelled the air next, trying to find Swan's scent. The wind ruffled through his short, dusty coat, and then the terrier looked up at Swan and trembled.

She felt a deep pang of pity for the creature. There was no telling where the dog had come from; it was frightened and wouldn't approach the food, though Swan was standing up at the top of the steps. The terrier abruptly turned and bolted into the darkness. Swan understood; it didn't trust human beings anymore. She left the food and water and went back into the house.

The fire was burning cheerfully. Leona stood before it, warming her hands. Under his blanket, Josh kicked and snored more loudly, then quieted down again. "Did you see the dog?" Leona asked.

"Yes, ma'am. It wouldn't take the food while I was standing there, though."

"'Spect not. Probably got his pride, don't you think?" She turned toward Swan, a round figure outlined in orange light, and Swan had to ask a question that had occurred to her while she was basking in the tub: "I don't mean this to sound bad, but . . . are you a witch?"

Leona laughed huskily. "Ha! You say what you think, don't you, child? Well, that's fine! That's too rare of a thing in this day and age!"

Swan paused, waiting for more. When it didn't come, Swan said, "I'd still like to know. Are you? My mama used to say that anybody who had second sight or could tell the future had to be evil, because those things come from Satan."

"Did she say that? Well, I don't know if I'd call myself a witch or not. Maybe I am, at that. And I'll be the first to tell you that not everything I see comes true. In fact, I've got a pretty low score for a seer. I figure life is like one of those big jigsaw puzzles you have to put together, and you can't figure it out—you just have to go at it piece by piece, and you try to jam wrong pieces in where they don't fit, and you get so weary you just want to hang your head and cry." She shrugged. "I'm not sayin' the puzzle is already put together, but maybe I have the gift of seein' which piece fits next. Not *all* the time, mind you. Just sometimes, when that next piece is real important. I figure Satan would want to scatter those pieces, burn 'em up and destroy 'em. I don't figure Old Scratch would like to see the puzzle neat and clean and pretty, do you?"

"No," Swan agreed. "I don't guess so."

"Child, I'd like to show you something—if that's all right with you."

Swan nodded.

Leona took one of the lamps and motioned for Swan to follow. They went along the hallway, past the closed door where Davy slept, and to another door at the end of the hall. Leona opened it and led Swan into a small pine-paneled room full of bookshelves and books, with a square card table and four chairs at the room's center. A Ouija board sat atop the table, and underneath the table was a multicolored five-pointed star, painted on the wooden floor.

"What's *that?*" Swan asked, pointing to the design as the lamplight revealed it.

"It's called a pentacle. It's a magic sign, and that one's supposed to draw in good, helpful spirits."

"Spirits? You mean *ghosts?*"

"No, just good feelings and emotions and stuff. I'm not exactly sure; I ordered the pattern from an ad in *Fate* magazine, and it didn't come with much background information." She put the lamp on the table. "Anyway, this is my seein' room. I bring . . . *used* to bring my customers in here, to read the crystal ball and the Ouija board for 'em. So I guess this is kinda my office, too."

"You mean you make money off this?"

"Sure! Why not? It's a decent way to make a livin'. Besides, everybody wants to know about their favorite subject—themselves!" She laughed, and her teeth sparkled silver in the lamplight. "Looky here!" She reached down beside one of the bookshelves and brought up a crooked length of wood that looked like a skinny tree branch, about three feet long, with two smaller branches jutting off at opposite angles on one end. "This is Crybaby," Leona said. "My *real* moneymaker."

To Swan it just looked like a weird old stick. "That thing? How?"

"Ever heard of a dowsing rod? This is the best dowsing rod you could wish for, child! Old Crybaby here'll bend down and weep over a puddle of water a hundred feet under solid rock. I found it in a garage sale in 1968, and Crybaby's sprung fifty wells all over this county. Sprung my own well, out back. Brought up the cleanest water you could ever hope to curl your tongue around. Oh, I love this here booger!" She gave it a smacking kiss and returned it to its resting place. Then her sparkling, impish gaze slid back to Swan. "How'd you like to have your future told?"

"I don't know," she said uneasily.

"But wouldn't you *like* to? Maybe just a little bit? Oh, I mean for fun . . . nothin' more."

Swan shrugged, still unconvinced.

"You interest me, child," Leona told her. "After what Josh

said about you, and what the both of you went through . . . I'd like to take a peek at that big ol' jigsaw puzzle. Wouldn't you?"

Swan wondered if Josh had told her about PawPaw's commandment, and about the grass growing where she'd been sleeping. Surely not, she thought. They didn't know Leona Skelton well enough to be revealing secret things! Or, Swan wondered, if the woman *was* a witch—good or bad—maybe she somehow already knew, or at least guessed that something was strange from Josh's story. "How would you do it?" Swan asked. "With one of those crystal balls? Or that board over there on the table?"

"No, I don't think so. Those things have their uses, but . . . I'd do it with *these.*" And she took a carved wooden box from a place on one of the shelves and stepped over toward the table where the light was stronger. She put the Ouija board aside, set the box down and opened it; the inside was lined with purple velvet, and from it Leona Skelton withdrew a deck of cards. She turned the deck face up and with one hand skimmed the cards out so Swan could see—and Swan caught her breath.

On the cards were strange and wonderful pictures—swords, sticks, goblets and pentacles like the one painted on the floor, the objects in assorted numbers on each card and presented against enigmatic drawings that Swan couldn't fathom—three swords piercing a heart, or eight sticks flying through a blue sky. But on some of the other cards were drawings of people: an old man in gray robes, his head bowed and a staff in one hand, in the other a six-pointed glowing star in a lantern; two naked figures, a man and woman, curled around each other to form a single person; a knight with red, flaming armor on a horse that breathed fire, the hooves striking sparks as it surged forward. And more and more magical figures—but what set them to life were the colors impressed into the cards: emerald green, the red of a thousand fires, glittering gold and gleaming silver, royal blue and midnight black, pearly white and the yellow of a midsummer sun. Bathed in those colors, the figures seemed to move and breathe, to perform whatever range of action they were involved in. Swan had never seen such cards before, and her eyes couldn't get enough of them.

"They're called tarot cards," Leona said. "This deck dates from the 1920s, and each color was daubed in by somebody's hand. Ain't they somethin'?"

"Yes," Swan breathed. "Oh . . . *yes.*"

"Sit down right there, child"—Leona touched one of the chairs—"and let's see what we can see. All right?"

Swan wavered, still uncertain, but she was entranced by the beautiful, mysterious figures on those magic cards. She looked up into Leona Skelton's face, and then she slid into the chair as if it had been made for her.

Leona took the chair across from her and moved the lamp toward her right. "We're going to do something called the Grand Cross. That's a fancy way to arrange the cards so they'll tell a story. It might not be a clear story; it might not be an easy story, but the cards'll lock together, one upon the next, kinda like that jigsaw puzzle we were talkin' about. You ready?"

Swan nodded, her heart beginning to thump. The wind hooted and wailed outside, and for an instant Swan thought she did hear a dark voice in it.

Leona smiled and rummaged through the cards, looking for a particular one. She found it and held it up for Swan to see. "This one'll stand for you, and the other cards'll build a story around it." She placed the card down on the table in front of Swan; it was trimmed in gold and red and bore the picture of a youth in a long gold cape and a cap with a red feather, holding a stick before him with green vines curled around it. "That's the Page of Rods—a child, with a long way yet to go." She pushed the rest of the deck toward Swan. "Can you shuffle those?"

Swan didn't know how to shuffle cards, and she shook her head.

"Well, just scramble 'em, then. Scramble 'em real good, around and around, and while you're doin' that you think real hard about where you've been, and who you are, and where you're wantin' to go."

Swan did as she asked, and the cards slipped around in all

directions, their faces pressed to the table and just their golden backs showing. She concentrated on the things that Leona had mentioned, thought as hard as she could, though the noise of the wind kept trying to distract her, and finally Leona said, "That's good, child. Now put 'em together into a deck again, face down, in any order you please. Then cut the deck into three piles and put 'em on your left."

When that was done, Leona reached out, her hand graceful in the muted orange light, and picked up each pile to form a deck once more. "Now we start the story," she said.

She placed the first card face up, directly over the Page of Rods. "This covers you," she said. It was a large golden wheel, with figures of men and women as the spokes in it, some with joyous expressions at the top of the wheel and others, on the wheel's bottom, holding their hands to their faces in despair. "The Wheel of Fortune—ever turnin', bringin' change and unfoldin' Fate. That's the atmosphere you're in, maybe things movin' and turnin' around you that you don't even know about yet."

The next card was laid across the Wheel of Fortune. "This crosses you," Leona said, "and stands for the forces that oppose you." Her eyes narrowed. "Oh, Lordy." The card, trimmed in ebony and silver, showed a figure shrouded almost entirely in a black cloak and cowl except for a white, masklike and grinning face; its eyes were silver—but there was a third eye of scarlet in its forehead. At the top of the card was scrolled, intricate lettering that read—

"The Devil," Leona said. "Destruction unleashed. Inhumanity. You have to be on guard and watch yourself, child."

Before Swan could ask about that card, which gave her a shiver, Leona dealt the next one out, above the other two. "This crowns you, and says what you yearn for. The Ace of Cups—peace, beauty, a yearning for understanding."

"Aw, that's not *me!*" Swan said, embarrassed.

"Maybe not yet. But maybe someday." The next card was laid below the hateful-looking Devil. "This is beneath you, and tells a story about what you've been through to get where you are." The card showed the brilliant yellow sun, but it was turned upside down. "The Sun like that stands for loneliness, uncertainty . . . the loss of someone. Maybe the loss of part of yourself, too. The death of innocence." Leona glanced up quickly and then back to the cards. The next card, the fifth that Leona had dealt from the scrambled pack, was placed to the left of the Devil card. "This is behind you, an influence passin' away." It was the old man carrying a star in a lantern, but this one was upside down, too. "The Hermit. Turned upside down, it means withdrawal, hidin', forgettin' your responsibilities. All those things are passin' away. You're goin' out into the world—for better or worse."

The sixth card went to the right of the Devil. "This is before you, and says what will come."

Leona examined the card with interest. This one showed a youth in crimson armor, holding an upraised sword while a castle blazed in the background. "The Page of Swords," Leona explained. "A young girl or boy who craves power. Who lives for it, needs it like food and water. The Devil's lookin' in that direction, too. Could be there's some kinda link between 'em. Anyway, that's somebody you might run up against—somebody real crafty—and maybe dangerous, too."

Before she could turn the next card over, a voice drifted through the hallways: "Leona! *Leona!*" Davy began coughing violently, almost choking, and instantly she put the cards aside and rushed out of the room.

Swan stood up. The Devil card—a man with a scarlet eye, she thought—seemed to be staring right at her, and she felt goose bumps come up on her arms. The deck that Leona had put aside was only a few inches away, its top card beckoning her to take a peek.

Her hand drifted toward it. Stopped.

Just a peek. A small, itty-bitty peek.

She picked up the top card and looked.

It showed a beautiful woman in violet robes, the sun shining above her, and around her a sheaf of wheat, a waterfall and flowers. At her feet lay a lion and a lamb. But her hair was afire, and her eyes were fiery too, determined and set on some distant obstacle. She carried a silver shield with a design of fire at its center, and on her head was a crown that burned with colors like trapped stars. Ornate lettering at the top of the card said THE EMPRESS.

Swan allowed herself to linger over it until all the details were impressed in her mind. She put it down, and the deck's next card pulled at her. No! she warned herself. You've gone far enough! She could almost feel the Devil's baleful scarlet eye, mocking her to lift one more card.

She picked up the following card. Turned it over.

She went cold.

A skeleton in armor sat astride a rearing horse of bones, and in the skeleton's arms was a blood-smeared scythe. The thing was reaping a wheat field, but the sheaves of wheat were made up of human bodies lashed together, nude and writhing in agony as they were slashed by the flailing scythe. The sky was the color of blood, and in it black crows circled over the human field of misery. It was the most terrible picture Swan had ever seen, and she did not have to read the lettering at the top of this card to recognize what it was.

"What are you up to in here?"

The voice almost made her jump three feet in the air. She whirled around, and there was Josh standing in the doorway. His face, splotched with gray and white pigment and brown crusted burns, was grotesque, but Swan realized in that instant that she loved it—and him. He looked around the room, frowning. "What's all this?"

"It's . . . Leona's seeing room. She was reading my future in the cards."

Josh walked in and took a look at the cards laid out on the table. "Those are real pretty," he said. "All except *that* one." He tapped the Devil card. "That reminds me of a nightmare I had after I ate a salami sandwich and a whole box of chocolate doughnuts."

Still unnerved, Swan showed him the last card she'd picked up.

He took it between his fingers and held it nearer the light. He'd seen tarot cards before, in the French Quarter in New Orleans. The lettering spelled out DEATH.

Death reaping the human race, he thought. It was one of

the grimmest things he'd ever seen, and in the tricky light the silver scythe seemed to slash back and forth through the human sheaves, the skeletal horse rearing while its rider labored under the blood-red sky. He flipped it back onto the table, and it slid halfway across the card with the demonic, scarlet-eyed figure on it. "Just cards," he said. "Paper and paints. They don't mean anything."

"Leona said they tell a story."

Josh gathered the cards into a deck again, getting the Devil and Death out of Swan's sight. "Paper and paints," he repeated. "That's all."

They couldn't help but hear Davy Skelton's gasping, tormented coughing. Seeing those cards, especially the one with the grim reaper, had given Josh a creepy feeling. Davy sounded as if he were strangling, and they heard Leona crooning to him, trying to calm him down. Death's near, Josh knew suddenly. It's very, very near. He walked out of the seeing room and down the hall. The door to Davy's room was ajar. Josh figured he might be able to help, and he started into the sickroom.

He saw first that the sheets were splotched with blood. A man's agonized face was illuminated by yellow lamplight, eyes dazed with sickness and horror, and from his mouth as he coughed came gouts of thick, dark gore.

Josh stopped in the doorway.

Leona was leaning over her husband, a porcelain bowl in her lap and a blood-damp rag in her hand. She sensed Josh's presence, turned her head and said with as much dignity as she could muster, "Please. Go out and close the door."

Josh hesitated, stunned and sick.

"*Please,*" Leona implored, as her husband coughed his life out in her lap.

He backed out of the room and pulled the door shut.

Somehow he found himself sitting before the fireplace again. He smelled himself. He stank, and he needed to get some buckets of water from the well, heat them in the fire and immerse himself in that bath he'd been looking forward to. But the yellow, strained face of the dying man in the other room was in his mind and would not let him move; he remembered Darleen, dying in the dirt. Remembered the corpse that lay out there on somebody's porch steps in the moaning dark. The image of that skeletal rider running riot through the wheat field of humanity was leeched in his brain.

Oh God, he thought as the tears started to come. Oh, God, help us all.

And then he bowed his head and sobbed—not just for his memories of Rose and the boys, but for Davy Skelton and Darleen Prescott and the dead person out in the dark and all the dead and dying human beings who'd once felt the sun on their faces and thought they'd live forever. He sobbed, the tears rolling down his face and dropping from his chin, and he could not stop.

Someone put an arm around his neck.

The child.

Swan.

Josh pulled her to him, and this time she clung to him while *he* cried.

She held tight. She loved Josh, and she couldn't bear to hear his hurting sound.

The wind shrieked, changed direction, attacked the ruins of Sullivan from another angle.

And in that wind she thought she heard a dark voice whispering, "*All mine . . . all mine.*"

SIX
Hell Freezes

Dirtwarts / The waiting Magnum / Zulu warrior / The elemental fist / Dealing with the Fat Man / Paradise / The sound of somebody being reborn

Thirty-four

Torches whipped in the cold wind on the desert flatland thirty miles northwest of Salt Lake City's crater. Some three hundred ragged, half-starved people huddled on the shore of the Great Salt Lake, in a makeshift city of cardboard boxes, broken-down automobiles, tents and trailers. The torchlight carried for miles over the flat terrain and drew scattered bands of survivors who were struggling eastward from the ruined cities and towns of California and Nevada. Every day and night groups of people, their belongings strapped to their backs, carried in their arms, lugged in suitcases or pushed in wheelbarrows and grocery carts, came into the encampment and found a space of hard, bare earth to crouch on. The more fortunate ones came with tents and knapsacks of canned food and bottled water and had guns to protect their supplies; the weakest ones curled up and expired when their food and water was either used up or stolen—and the bodies of suicides floated in the Great Salt Lake like grim, bobbing logs. But the smell of the salt water in the wind drew bands of wanderers as well; those without fresh water tried to drink it, and those suffering from festered wounds and burns sought its cleansing, agonizing embrace with the single-minded desire of religious flagellants.

At the western edge of the encampment, on rough and rock-stubbled ground, over a hundred corpses lay where they'd collapsed. The bodies had been stripped naked by scavengers, who lived in pits in the dirt and were contemptuously called "dirtwarts" by the people who lived closest to the lake shore. Strewn out almost to the western horizon was a junkyard of cars, RVs, campers, Jeeps and motorcycles that had run out of gas or whose engines had locked for want of oil. The scavengers scrambled out, tore the seats out of cars, took the tires off, ripped the doors and hoods and trunks away to make their own bizarre dwellings. Gas tanks were drained by parties of armed men from the main encampment, the gas set aside to fuel the torches—because light had become strength, an almost mystic protection against the horrors of the dark.

Two figures, both laden with backpacks, trudged across the desert toward the light of the torches, about a half mile ahead. It was the night of August twenty-third, one month and six days after the bombs. The two figures walked through the junkyard of vehicles, not hesitating as they stepped on the occasional nude corpse. Over the odors of corruption they could smell the salt lake. Their own car, a BMW stolen from a lot in the ghost town of Carson City, Nevada, had run out of gas about twelve miles back, and they'd been walking all night, following the glow of the lights reflected off low-lying clouds.

Something rattled off to the side, behind the scavenged wreck of a Dodge Charger. The figure in the lead stopped and drew a .45 automatic from a shoulder holster under a blue goosedown parka. The sound did not repeat itself, and after a silent moment the two figures began to walk toward the encampment again, their pace faster.

The lead figure had taken about five more steps when a hand burst from the loose dirt and sand at his feet and grabbed his left ankle, jerking him off balance. His shout of alarm and the .45 went off together, but the gun fired toward the sky. He hit hard on his left side, the air whooshing from his lungs with the shock, and a human shape scrabbled like a crab from a pit that had opened in the earth. The crab-thing fell upon the man with the knapsack, planted a knee in his throat and began to batter his face with a left-hand fist.

The second figure screamed—a woman's scream—then turned and started running through the junkyard. She heard footsteps behind her, sensing something gaining on her, and as she turned her head to look back she tripped over one of the naked corpses and went down on her face. She tried to scramble up, but suddenly a sneakered foot pressed on the back of her head, forcing her nostrils and mouth into the dirt. Her body thrashing, she began to suffocate.

A few yards away, the crab-thing shifted, using the left knee to pin the young man's gun hand to the ground, the right knee pressed into his chest. The young man was gasping for air, his eyes wide and stunned over a dirty blond beard. And then the crab-thing drew with its left hand a hunting knife from a leather sheath under a long, dusty black overcoat; the hunting knife slashed fast and deep across the young man's throat—once, again, a third time. The young man stopped struggling and his lips pulled back from his teeth in a grimace.

The woman fought for life; she got her head turned, her cheek mashed into the ground, and she begged, "Please . . . don't kill me! I'll give you . . . give you what you want! Please don't . . ."

The sneakered foot suddenly drew back. The point of what felt like an ice pick pricked her cheek just below her right eye.

"No tricks." It was a boy's voice, high and reedy. "Understand?" The ice pick jabbed for emphasis.

"Yes," she answered. The boy grabbed a handful of her long, raven-black hair and pulled her up to a sitting position. She was able to make out his face in the dim wash of the distant lights. He was just a kid, maybe thirteen or fourteen years old, wearing an oversized, filthy brown sweater and gray trousers with holes where the knees had been; he was skinny to the point of emaciation, his high-cheekboned face pale and cadaverous. His dark hair was plastered to his skull with grime and sweat, and he wore a pair of goggles—the kind of goggles, trimmed in battered leather, that she figured

World War II fighter pilots might have worn. The lens magnified his eyes as if through fishbowls. "Don't hurt me, okay? I swear I won't scream."

Roland Croninger laughed. That was about the stupidest fucking thing he'd ever heard. "You can scream if you want to. Nobody gives a shit whether you scream or not. Take the pack off."

"You got him?" Colonel Macklin called, from where he crouched atop the other body.

"Yes, sir," Roland answered. "It's a woman."

"Bring her over here!"

Roland picked up the pack and stepped backward. "Start moving." She started to rise, but he shoved her down again. "No. Not on your feet. Crawl."

She started crawling through the dirt, over the festering bodies. A scream was locked behind her teeth, but she didn't let it get loose. "Rudy?" she called weakly. "Rudy? You okay?"

And then she saw the figure in the black coat ripping open Rudy's backpack, and she saw all the blood, and she knew they'd stepped into deep shit.

Roland tossed the other pack over to Colonel Macklin, then put his ice pick away in the elastic waistband of the trousers he'd stripped from the corpse of a boy about his age and size. He pried the automatic out of Rudy's dead fingers as the woman sat nearby, numbly watching.

"Good gun," he told the King. "We can use it."

"Got to have more clips," Macklin answered, digging through the pack with one hand. He pulled out socks, underwear, toothpaste, an army surplus mess kit—and a canteen that sloshed when he shook it. "Water!" he said. "Oh, Jesus—it's fresh water!" He got the canteen between his thighs and unscrewed the cap, then took several swigs of sweet, delicious water; it ran down through the gray-swirled stubble of his new beard and dripped to the ground.

"You got a canteen, too?" Roland asked her.

She nodded, pulling the canteen strap from her shoulder under the ermine coat she'd taken from a Carson City boutique. She was wearing leopard-spotted designer jeans and expensive boots, and around her neck were ropes of pearls and diamond chains.

"Give it here."

She looked into his face and drew her back up straight. He was just a punk, and she knew how to handle punks. "Fuck you," she told him, and she uncapped it and started drinking, her hard blue eyes challenging him over the canteen's rim.

"Hey!" someone called from the darkness; the voice was hoarse, scabrous-sounding. "You catch a woman over there?"

Roland didn't answer. He watched the woman's silken throat working as she drank.

"I've got a bottle of whiskey!" the voice continued. "I'll trade you!"

She stopped drinking. The Perrier suddenly tasted foul.

"A bottle of whiskey for thirty minutes!" the voice said. "I'll give her back to you when I'm through! Deal?"

"I've got a carton of cigarettes!" another man called, from off to the left beyond an overturned Jeep. "Fifteen minutes for a carton of cigarettes!"

She hurriedly capped the canteen and threw it at the kid's sneakered feet. "Here," she said, keeping her eyes fixed on his. "You can have it all."

"Ammo clips!" Macklin exclaimed, pulling three of them out of Rudy's pack. "We've got ourselves some *firepower!*"

Roland opened the canteen, took a few swallows of water, recapped it and slid the strap over his shoulder. From all around them drifted the voices of other dirtwarts, offering caches of liquor, cigarettes, matches, candy bars and other valuables for time with the newly snared woman. Roland remained quiet, listening to the rising bids with the pleasure of an auctioneer who knows he has a prize of real worth. He studied the woman through the eyeglass-goggles he'd made for himself, gluing the appropriate-strength lenses—found in the wreckage of a Pocatello optometry shop—into army surplus tank commander goggles. She was unmarked except for several small, healing gashes on her cheeks and forehead —and that alone made her a very special prize. Most of the women in the encampment had lost their hair and eyebrows and were marked with keloid scars of various colors, from dark brown to scarlet. This woman's black hair cascaded around her shoulders; it was dirty, but there were no bald patches in it—the first signs of radiation poisoning. She had a strong, square-chinned face; a haughty face, Roland thought. The face of roughneck royalty. Her electric-blue eyes moved slowly from the gun to Rudy's corpse and back to Roland's face, as if she were figuring the precise points of a triangle. Roland thought she might be in her late twenties or early thirties, and his eyes slid down to the mounds of her breasts, swelling a red T-shirt with RICH BITCH stenciled across it in rhinestones underneath the ermine coat. He thought he detected her nipples sticking out, as if the danger and death had revved her sexual engine.

He felt a pressure in his stomach, and he quickly lifted his gaze from her nipples. He had suddenly wondered what one of them might feel like between his teeth.

Her full-lipped mouth parted. "Do you like what you see?"

"A flashlight!" one of the dirtwarts offered. "I'll give you a flashlight for her!"

Roland didn't respond. This woman made him think of the pictures in the magazines he'd found in the bottom drawer of his father's dresser, back in his other, long-ago life. His belly was tightening, and there was a pounding in his nuts as if they were being squeezed by a brutal fist. "What's your name?"

"Sheila," she answered. "Sheila Fontana. What's yours?" She had determined, with the cold logic of a born survivor, that her chances were better here, with this punk kid and the man with one hand, than out in the dark with those other things. The one-handed man cursed and dumped the rest of Rudy's pack on the ground.

"Roland Croninger."

"Roland," she repeated, making it sound like she was licking a lollipop. "You're not going to give me to *them*, are you, Roland?"

"Was he your husband?" Roland prodded Rudy's body with his foot.

"No. We traveled together, that's all." Actually, they had lived together for almost a year, and he'd done some pimping for her back in Oakland, but there was no need to confuse the kid. She looked at Rudy's bloody throat and then quickly away; she felt a pang of regret, because he had been a good business manager, a fantastic lover, and he'd kept them supplied with plenty of blow. But he was just dead meat now, and that was how the world turned. As Rudy himself would've said, you cover your own ass, at all and any cost.

Something moved on the ground behind Sheila, and she turned to look. A vaguely human shape was crawling toward her. It stopped about seven or eight feet away, and a hand covered with open, running sores lifted a paper bag. "Candy barsssss?" a mangled voice offered.

Roland fired the automatic, and the noise of the shot made Sheila jump. The thing on the ground grunted and then made a sound like a yelping dog; it scrambled to its knees and scurried away amid the junked vehicles.

Sheila knew the kid wasn't going to turn her over to them, after all. Hoarse, garbled laughter came from other, hidden pits in the dirt. Sheila had seen plenty of Hell since she and Rudy had left a coke dealer's cabin in the Sierras, where they'd been hiding from the San Francisco cops when the bombs had hit, but this was by far the worst. She looked down into the kid's goggled eyes, because her height approached six feet; she was as big-boned as an Amazon warrior, but all curves and compliance when it met her needs, and she knew he was hooked through the cock.

"What the *hell* is this shit?" Macklin said, leaning over the items he'd pulled out of Sheila's backpack.

Sheila knew what the one-handed man had found. She approached him, disregarding the kid's .45, and saw what he was holding: a plastic bag full of snow-white, extra-fine Colombian sugar. Scattered around him were three more plastic bags of high-grade cocaine, and about a dozen plastic bottles of poppers, Black Beauties, Yellowjackets, Bombers, Red Ladies, PCP and LSD tabs. "That's my medicine bag, friend," she told him. "If you're looking for food, I've got a couple of old Whoppers and some fries in there, too. You're welcome to it, but I want my stash back."

"Drugs," Macklin realized. "What is this? Cocaine?" He

dropped the bag and picked up one of the bottles, lifting his filthy, blood-splattered face toward her. His crewcut was growing out, the dark brown hair peppered with gray. His eyes were deep holes carved in a rocklike face. "Pills, too? What are you, an addict?"

"I'm a *gourmet,*" she replied calmly. She figured the kid wasn't going to let this crazy one-handed fucker hurt her, but her muscles were tensed for fight or flight. "What are *you?*"

"His name is Colonel James Macklin," Roland told her. "He's a war hero."

"Looks to me like the war's over. And we lost . . . hero," she said, staring directly into Macklin's eyes. "Take what you want, but I need my stash back."

Macklin sized the young woman up, and he decided he might not be able to throw her to the ground and rape her, as he had intended until this instant. She might be too much to take with one hand, unless he wrestled her down and got the knife to her throat. He didn't want to try and fail in front of Roland, though his penis had begun to pound. He grunted and dug for the hamburgers. When he found them, he flung the pack to Sheila, and she started gathering up the packets of coke and the pill bottles.

Macklin crawled over and pulled the shoes off Rudy's feet; he worked a gold Rolex wristwatch from the corpse's left wrist and put it on his own.

"How come you're out here?" Sheila asked Roland, who was watching her pack the cocaine and pills away. "How come you're not over there, closer to the light?"

"They don't want dirtwarts," Macklin replied. "That's what they call us. Dirtwarts." He nodded toward the rectangular hole a few feet away; it had been covered with a tarpaulin, impossible to detect in the darkness, and looked to Sheila to be about five feet deep. The corners of the tarp were held down with stones. "They don't think we *smell* good enough to be any closer." Macklin's grin held madness. "How do *you* think I smell, lady?"

She thought he smelled like a hog in heat, but she shrugged and motioned toward a can of Right Guard deodorant that had fallen out of Rudy's pack.

Macklin laughed. He was unbuckling Rudy's belt in preparation to pull the trousers off. "See, we live out here on what we can get and what we can *take*. We wait for new ones to pass through on their way to the light." He motioned with a nod of his head toward the lake shore. "Those people have the power: guns, plenty of canned food and bottled water, gas for their torches. Some of them even have tents. They roll around in that salt water, and we listen to them scream. They won't let us near it. Oh, no! They think we'd pollute it or something." He got Rudy's trousers off and flung them into the pit. "See, the hell of all this is that the boy and I should be living in the light right now. We should be wearing clean clothes, and taking warm showers, and having all the food and water we want. Because we were *prepared* . . . we were *ready!* We knew the bombs were going to fall. Everybody in Earth House knew it!"

"Earth House? What's that?"

"It's where we came from," Macklin said, crouching on the ground. "Up in the Idaho mountains. We walked a long way, and we saw a lot of death, and Roland figured that if we could get to the Great Salt Lake we could wash ourselves in it, clean all the radiation off, and the salt would heal us. That's right, you know. Salt heals. Especially this." He held up his bandaged stump; the blood-caked bandages were hanging down, and some of them had turned green. Sheila caught the reek of infected flesh. "I need to bathe it in that salt water, but they won't let us any closer. They say that we live off the dead. So they shoot at us when we try to cross open ground. But now—*now*—we've got our own firepower!" He nodded toward the automatic Roland held.

"It's a big lake," Sheila said. "You don't have to go through that encampment to get there. You could go *around* it."

"No. Two reasons: somebody would move into our pit while we were gone and take everything we have; and second, nobody keeps Jimbo Macklin from what he wants." He grinned at her, and she thought his face resembled a skull. "They don't know who I am, or what I am. But I'm going to show them—oh, yes! I'm going to show all of them!" He turned his head toward the encampment, sat staring at the distant torches for a moment, then looked back at her. "You wouldn't want to fuck, would you?"

She laughed. He was about the dirtiest, most repulsive thing she'd ever seen. But even as she laughed, she knew it was a mistake; she stopped her laugh in mid-note.

"Roland," Macklin said quietly, "bring me the gun."

Roland hesitated; he knew what was about to happen. Still, the King had delivered a command, and he was a King's Knight and could not disobey. He took a step forward, hesitated again.

"Roland," the King said.

This time Roland walked to him and delivered the pistol to his outstretched left hand. Macklin awkwardly gripped it and pointed it at Sheila's head. Sheila lifted her chin defiantly, hooked the pack's strap over her shoulder and stood up. "I'm going to start walking toward the camp," she said. "Maybe you can shoot a woman in the back, war hero. I don't think you can. So long, guys; it's been fun." She made herself step over Rudy's corpse, then started walking purposefully through the junkyard, her heart pounding and her teeth gritted as she waited for the bullet.

Something moved off to her left. A figure in rags ducked down behind the wreckage of a Chevy station wagon. Something else scrambled across the dirt about twenty feet in front of her, and she realized she'd never make the camp alive.

"They're waiting for you," Roland called. "They'll never let you get there."

Sheila stopped. The torches seemed so far away, so terribly far. And even if she reached them without being raped—or worse—there was no certainty she wouldn't be raped in the camp. She knew that without Rudy she was walking meat, drawing flies.

"Better come back," Roland urged. "You'll be safer with us."

Safer, Sheila thought sarcastically. Sure. The last time she'd been safe was when she was in kindergarten. She'd run away from home at seventeen with the drummer in a rock band, had landed in Hollyweird and gone through phases of being a waitress, a topless dancer, a masseuse in a Sunset Strip parlor, had done a couple of porno flicks and then had latched up with Rudy. The world had become a crazy pinwheel of coke, poppers and faceless johns, but the deep truth was that she enjoyed it. For her there was no whining of might-have-beens, no crawling on her knees for forgiveness; she liked danger, liked the dark side of the rock where the night things hid. Safety was boredom, and she'd always figured she could only live once, so why not blow it out?

Still, she didn't think running the gauntlet of those crawling shapes would be too much fun.

Someone giggled, off in the darkness. It was a giggle of insane anticipation, and the sound of it put the lid on Sheila's decision.

She turned around and walked back to where the kid and the one-handed war hero waited, and she was already figuring out how to get that pistol and blow both their heads off. The pistol would help her get to the torches at the edge of the lake.

"Get on your hands and knees," Macklin commanded, his eyes glittering above his dirty beard.

Sheila smiled faintly and shrugged her pack off to the ground. What the hell? It would be no worse than some of the other johns off the Strip. But she didn't want to let him win so easily. "Be a sport, war hero," she said, her hands on her hips. "Why don't you let the kid go first?"

Macklin glanced at the boy, whose eyes behind the goggles looked like they were about to burst from his head. Sheila unbuckled her belt and started to peel the leopard-spotted pants off her hips, then her thighs, then over the cowboy boots. She wore no underwear. She got down on her hands and knees, opened the pack and took out a bottle of Black Beauties; she popped a pill down her throat and said, "Come on, honey! It's *cold* out there!"

Macklin suddenly laughed. He thought the woman had courage, and though he didn't know what was to be done with her after they'd finished, he knew she was of his own kind. "Go ahead!" he told Roland. "Be a man!"

Roland was scared shitless. The woman was waiting, and

the King wanted him to do it. He figured this was an important rite of manhood for a King's Knight to pass through. His testicles were about to explode, and the dark mystery between the woman's thighs drew him toward her like a hypnotic amulet.

Dirtwarts crawled closer to get a view of the festivities. Macklin sat watching, his eyes hooded and intense, and he stroked the automatic's barrel back and forth beneath his chin.

He heard hollow laughter just over his left shoulder, and he knew the Shadow Soldier was enjoying this, too. The Shadow Soldier had come down from Blue Dome Mountain with them, had walked behind them and off to the side, but always there. The Shadow Soldier liked the boy; the Shadow Soldier thought the boy had a killer instinct that bore developing. Because the Shadow Soldier had told Macklin, in the silence of the dark, that his days of making war were not over yet. This new land was going to need warriors and warlords. Men like Macklin were going to be in demand again—as if they had ever gone out of demand. All this the Shadow Soldier told him, and Macklin believed.

He started laughing then, too, at the sight in front of him, and his laughter and that of the Shadow Soldier intertwined, merged, and became as one.

Thirty-five

Over two thousand miles away, Sister sat next to the hearth. Everyone else was asleep on the floor around the room, and it was Sister's night to watch over the fire, to keep it banked and the embers glowing so they wouldn't have to waste matches. The space heater had been turned low to save their dwindling supply of kerosene, and cold had begun to sneak through chinks in the walls.

Mona Ramsey muttered in her sleep, and her husband shifted his position and put his arm around her. The old man was dead to the world, Artie lay on a bed of newspapers, and every so often Steve Buchanan snored like a chainsaw. But Sister was disturbed by the wheeze of Artie's breathing. She'd noticed him holding his ribs, but he'd said he was okay, that he was sometimes short of breath but otherwise feeling, as he put it, "as smooth as pickles and cream."

She hoped so, because if Artie was hurt somewhere inside—maybe when that damned wolf had slammed into him on the highway about ten days ago—there was no medicine to stave off infection.

The duffel bag was beside her. She loosened the drawstring

and reached inside, found the glass ring and drew it out into the emberglow.

Its brilliance filled the room. The last time she'd peered into the glass circle, during her firewatch duty four nights before, she'd gone dreamwalking again. One second she was sitting right there, holding the circle just as she was doing now, and the next she'd found herself standing over a table—a square table, with what appeared to be cards arranged on its surface.

The cards were decorated with pictures, and they were unlike any cards Sister had ever seen before. One of them in particular caught her attention: the figure of a skeleton on a rearing skeletal horse, swinging a scythe through what seemed to be a grotesque field of human bodies. She thought there were shadows in the room, other presences, the muffled voices of people speaking. And she thought, as well, that she heard someone coughing, but the sound was distorted, as if heard through a long, echoing tunnel—and when she came back to the cabin she realized it was Artie coughing and holding his ribs.

She'd thought often of that card with the scythe-swinging skeleton. She could still see it, lodged behind her eyes. She thought also of the shadows that had seemed to be in the room with her—insubstantial things, but maybe that was because all her attention had been focused on the cards. Maybe, if she'd concentrated on giving form to the shadows, she might have seen who was standing there.

Right, she thought. You're acting like you really *go* somewhere when you see pictures in the glass circle! And that's only what they were, of course. Pictures. Fantasy. Imagination. Whatever. There was nothing real about them at all!

But she did know that dreamwalking, and coming back from dreamwalking, was getting easier. Not every time she peered into the glass was a dreamwalk, though; most often it was just an object of fiery light, no dream pictures at all. Still, the glass ring held an unknown power; of that she was certain. If it wasn't something with a powerful purpose, why had the Doyle Halland-thing wanted it?

Whatever it was, she had to protect it. She was responsible for its safety, and she could not—she *dared* not—lose it.

"Jesus in suspenders! What's that?"

Startled, Sister looked up. Paul Thorson, his eyes swollen from sleep, had come through the green curtain. He pushed back his unruly hair and stood, open-mouthed, as the ring pulsed in rhythm with Sister's heartbeat.

She almost shoved it back into the duffel bag, but it was too late.

"That thing's . . . on fire!" he managed to say. "What is it?"

"I'm not sure yet. I found it in Manhattan."

"My God! The colors . . ." He knelt down beside her, obviously overwhelmed. A flaming circle of light was about the last thing he'd expected to find when he'd stumbled in to warm himself by the embers. "What makes it pulse like that?"

"It's picking up my heartbeat. It does that when you hold it."

"What is it, some kind of Japanese thing? Does it run on batteries?"

Sister smiled wryly. "I don't think so."

Paul reached out and poked it with a finger. He blinked. "It's *glass!*"

"That's right."

"Wow," he whispered. Then: "Would it be okay if I held it? Just for a second?"

She was about to answer yes, but Doyle Halland's promise stopped her. That monster could make itself look like anyone; any of the people in this room could be the Doyle Halland-thing, even Paul himself. But no; they'd left the monster behind them, hadn't they? How did such a creature travel? "I followed the line of least resistance," she recalled him saying. If he wore human skin, then he traveled as a human, too. She shuddered, imagining him walking after them in a pair of dead man's shoes, walking day and night without a rest until the shoes flayed right off his feet, and then he stopped to yank another pair off a corpse because he could make any size fit. . . .

"Can I?" Paul urged.

Where was Doyle Halland? Sister wondered. Out there in the dark right now, passing by on I-80? Up ahead a mile or two, running down another pair of shoes? Could he fly in the wind, with black cats on his shoulders and his eyes filled with flame, or was he a tattered highway hiker who looked for campfires burning in the night?

He was behind them. Wasn't he?

Sister took a deep breath and offered the glass ring to Paul. He slid his hand around it.

The light remained constant. The half that Paul held took on a new, quickened rhythm. He drew it to himself with both hands, and Sister let her breath out.

"Tell me about this," he said. "I want to know."

Sister saw the gems reflected in his eyes. On his face was a childlike amazement, as if the years were peeling rapidly away. In another few seconds he appeared a decade younger than his forty-three years. She decided then to tell him all of it.

He was quiet for a long time when she'd finished. The ring's pulsing had speeded up and slowed down all through the telling. "Tarot cards," Paul said, still admiring the ring. "The skeleton with the scythe stands for Death." With an effort, he looked up at her. "You know all that sounds crazy as hell, don't you?"

"Yes, I do. Here's the scar where the crucifix was torn off. Artie saw the thing's face change, too, though I doubt he'll admit it to you. He hasn't mentioned it since it happened, and I guess that's for the best. And here's the glass circle, missing one spike."

"Uh-huh. You haven't been slipping into my Johnny Walker, have you?"

"You know better. *I* know I see things when I look into the glass. Not every time, but enough to tell me I've either got a hummer of an imagination or—"

"Or what?"

"Or," Sister continued, "there's a reason for me to have it. Why should I see a Cookie Monster doll lying in the middle of a desert? Or a hand coming out of a hole? Why should I see a table with tarot cards on it? Hell, I don't even know what the damned things are!"

"They're used to tell the future by gypsies. Or witches." He summoned a half smile that made him almost handsome. It faded when she didn't return it. "Listen, I don't know anything about demons with roaming eyeballs or dream-walking, but I do know this is one hell of a piece of glass. A couple of months ago, this thing would've been worth—" He shook his head. "Wow," he said again. "The only reason you've got it is that you were in the right place at the right time. That's magic enough, isn't it?"

"But you don't believe what I've told you, right?"

"I want to say the radiation's unscrewed your bolts. Or maybe the nukes blew the lid right off Hell itself, and who can say what slithered out?" He returned the ring to her, and she put it back in the bag. "You take care of that. It may be the only beautiful thing left."

Across the room, Artie winced and sucked in his breath when he changed position, then lay still again.

"He's hurt inside," Paul told her. "I've seen blood in his crap bucket. I figure he's got a splintered rib or two, probably cutting something." He worked his fingers, feeling the warmth of the glass circle in them. "I don't think he looks too good."

"I know. I'm afraid whatever's wrong may be infected."

"It's possible. Shit, with these living conditions you could die from biting your fingernails."

"And there's no medicine?"

"Sorry. I popped the last Tylenol about three days before the bombs hit. A poem I was writing fell to pieces."

"So what are we going to do when the kerosene runs out?"

Paul grunted. He'd been expecting that question, and he'd known no one would ask it but her. "We've got another week's supply. Maybe. I'm more worried about the batteries for the radio. When they're dead, these folks are going to freak. I guess then we'll get out the scotch and have a party." His eyes were old again. "Just play spin the bottle, and whoever gets lucky can check out first."

"Check out? What's that supposed to mean?"

"I've got a .357 Magnum in that footlocker, lady," he reminded her. "And a box of bullets. I've come close to using it on myself twice: once when my second wife left me for a kid half my age, took all my money and said my cock wasn't worth two cents in a depression, and the other time when the poems I'd been working on for six years burned up along with the rest of my apartment. That was just after I got kicked off the staff at Millersville State College for sleeping with a student who wanted an A on her English Lit final." He continued working his knuckles, avoiding Sister's stare. "I'm not what you'd call a real good-luck type of guy. As a matter of fact, just about everything I've ever tried to do turned into a shitcake. So that Magnum's been waiting for me for a long time. I'm overdue."

Sister was shocked by Paul's matter-of-factness; he talked about suicide like the next step in a natural progression. "My friend," she said firmly, "if you think I've come all this way to blow my brains out in a shack, you're as crazy as I used to—" She bit her tongue. Now he was watching her with heightened interest.

"So what are you going to do, then? Where are you going to go? Down to the supermarket for a few steaks and a six-pack? How about a hospital to keep Artie from bleeding to death inside? In case you haven't noticed, there's not much left out there."

"Well, I never would've taken you for a coward. I thought you had guts, but it must've been just sawdust stuffing."

"Couldn't have said it better myself."

"What if *they* want to live?" Sister motioned toward the sleeping figures. "They look up to you. They'll do what you tell them. So you're going to tell them to check out?"

"They can decide for themselves. But like I say, where are they going to go?"

"Out there," she said, and she nodded at the door. "Into the world—what's left of it, at least. You don't know what's five or ten miles down the highway. There might be a Civil Defense shelter, or a whole community of people. The only way to find out is to get in your pick-up truck and drive west on I-80."

"I didn't like the world as it used to be. I sure as hell don't like it now."

"Who asked you to like it? Listen, don't jive me. You need people more than you want to believe."

"Sure," he said sarcastically. "Love 'em, every one."

"If you don't need people," Sister challenged, "why'd you go up to the highway? Not to kill wolves. You can do that from the front door. You went up to the highway looking for people, didn't you?"

"Maybe I wanted a captive audience for my poetry readings."

"Uh-huh. Well, when the kerosene's gone, I'm heading west. Artie's going with me."

"The wolves'll like that, lady. They'll be happy to escort you."

"I'm also taking your rifle," she said. "And the rifle bullets."

"Thanks for asking my permission."

She shrugged. "All you need is the Magnum. I doubt if you'll have to worry much about the wolves after you're dead. I'd like to take the pick-up truck, too."

Paul laughed without mirth. "In case you've forgotten, I told you it doesn't have much gas, and the brakes are screwed up. The radiator's probably frozen solid by now, and I doubt if there's a gasp in the battery."

Sister had never met anybody so full of reasons to sit on his ass and rot. "Have you tried the truck lately? Even if the radiator's frozen, we can light a fire under the damned thing!"

"You've got it all figured out, huh? Going to make it to the highway in a broken-down old truck and right around the bend will be a shining city full of Civil Defense people, doctors and policemen doing their best to put this fine country back together again. Bet you'll find all the king's horses and all the king's men there, too! Lady, I *know* what's around the bend! More fucking highway, that's what!" He was working his knuckles harder, a bitter smile flickering at the edges of his mouth. "I wish you luck, lady. I really do."

"I don't want to wish you luck," she told him. "I want you to come with me."

He was silent. His knuckles cracked. "If there's anything left out there," he said, "it's going to be worse than Dodge City, Dante's Inferno, the Dark Ages and No Man's Land all rolled up in one. You're going to see things that'll make your demon with the roaming eyeballs look like one of the Seven Dwarves."

"You like to play poker, but you're not much of a gambler, are you?"

"Not when the odds have teeth."

"I'm going west," Sister said, giving it one last shot. "I'm taking your truck, and I'm going to find some help for Artie. Anybody who wants to can go with me. How about it?"

Paul stood up. He looked at the sleeping figures on the floor. They trust me, he thought. They'll do what I say. But we're warm here, and we're safe, and—

And the kerosene would last only a week longer.

"I'll sleep on it," he said huskily, and he went through the curtain to his own quarters.

Sister sat listening to the shriek of the wind. Artie made another gasp of pain in his sleep, his fingers pressed to his side. From off in the distance came the thin, high howling of a wolf, the sound quavering like a violin note. Sister touched the glass circle through the duffel bag's canvas and turned her thoughts toward tomorrow.

Behind the green curtain, Paul Thorson opened the foot-locker and picked up the .357 Magnum. It was a heavy gun, blue-black, with a rough dark brown grip. The gun felt as if it had been made for his hand. He turned the barrel toward his face and peered into its black, dispassionate eye. One squeeze, he thought, and it would all be over. So simple, really. The end of a fucked-up journey, and the beginning of . . . what?

He drew a deep breath, released it and put the gun down. His hand came up with a bottle of scotch, and he took it to bed with him.

Thirty-six

Josh dug the grave with a shovel from Leona Skelton's basement, and they buried Davy in the back yard.

While Leona bowed her head and said a prayer that the wind took and tore apart, Swan looked up and saw the little terrier sitting about twenty yards away, its head cocked to one side and its ears standing straight up. For the last week, she'd been leaving scraps of food for it on the porch steps; the dog had taken the food, but he never got close enough for Swan to touch. She thought that the terrier was resigned to living off scraps, but it wasn't enough of a beggar yet to fawn and wag its tail for handouts.

Josh had finally taken his bath. He could've sewn a suit from the dead skin that peeled away, and the water looked like he'd dumped a shovelful of dirt into it. He had washed the crusted blood and dirt away from the nub where his right ear had been; the blood had gotten down deep into the canal, and it took him a while to swab it all out. Afterward he realized he'd only been hearing through one ear; sounds were startlingly sharp and clear again. His eyebrows were still gone, and his face, chest, arms, hands and back were striped and splotched with the loss of black pigment, as if he'd been caught by a bucketful of beige paint. He consoled himself with the idea that he resembled a Zulu warrior chieftain in battle regalia or something. His beard was growing out, and it, too, was streaked with white.

Blisters and sores were healing on his face, but on his forehead were seven small black nodules that looked like warts. Two of them had connected with each other. Josh tried to scrape them off with his finger, but they were too tough, and the pain made his entire skull ache. Skin cancer, he thought. But the warts were just on his forehead, nowhere else. I'm a zebra toadfrog, he thought—but those nodules for some reason disturbed him more than any of his other injuries and scars.

He had to put his own clothes back on because nothing in the house would fit him. Leona washed them and went over the holes with a needle and thread, but they were in pretty sorry shape. She did supply him with a new pair of socks, but even those were much too tight. Still, his own socks were bags of holes held together with dried blood, totally useless.

After the body was buried, Josh and Swan left Leona alone beside her husband's grave. She gathered a threadbare brown corduroy coat around her shoulders and turned her face from the wind.

Josh went to the basement and began to prepare for the journey they'd agreed on. He brought a wheelbarrow upstairs and filled it with supplies—canned food, some dried fruit, petrified corn muffins, six tightly sealed Mason jars full of well water, blankets and various kitchen utensils—and covered the whole thing with a sheet, which he lashed down with heavy twine. Leona, her eyes puffy from crying but her spine rigid and strong, finally came in and started packing a suitcase; the first items to go in were the framed photographs of her family that had adorned the mantel, and those were followed by sweaters, socks and the like. She packed a smaller bag full of Joe's old clothes for Swan, and as the wind whipped around the house Leona walked from room to room and sat for a while in each one, as if drawing from them the aromas and memories of the life that had inhabited them.

They were going to head for Matheson at first light. Leona

had said she'd take them there, and on their way they'd pass across a farm that belonged to a man named Homer Jaspin and his wife Maggie. The Jaspin farm, Leona told Josh, lay about midway between Sullivan and Matheson, and there they would be able to spend the night.

Leona packed away several of her best crystal balls, and from a box on a closet shelf she took out a few yellowed envelopes and birthday cards—"courting letters" from Davy, she told Swan, and cards Joe had sent her. Two jars of salve for her rheumatic knees went into her suitcase, and though Leona had never said so, Josh knew that walking that distance—at least ten miles to the Jaspin farm—was going to be sheer torture for her. But there were no available vehicles, and they had no choice.

The deck of tarot cards went into Leona's suitcase as well, and then she picked up another object and took it out to the front room.

"Here," she told Swan. "I want you to carry this."

Swan accepted the dowsing rod that Leona offered her.

"We can't leave Crybaby here all alone, can we?" Leona asked. "Oh, my, no. Crybaby's work isn't done yet—not by a far sight!"

The night passed, and Josh and Swan slept soundly in beds they were going to regret leaving.

He awakened with gloomy gray light staining the window. The wind's force had died down, but the window glass was bitterly cold to the touch. He went into Joe's room and woke Swan up, and then he walked out into the front room and found Leona sitting before the cold hearth, dressed in overalls, clodhoppers, a couple of sweaters, the corduroy coat and gloves. Bags sat on either side of her chair.

Josh had slept in his clothes, and now he shrugged into a long overcoat that had belonged to Davy. During the night, Leona had ripped and resewn the shoulders and arms so he could get it on, but he still felt like an overstuffed sausage.

"I guess we're ready to go," Josh said when Swan emerged, carrying the dowsing rod and clad in a pair of Joe's blue jeans, a thick, dark blue sweater, a fleece-lined jacket and red mittens.

"Just a minute more." Leona's hands were clamped together in her lap. The windup clock on the mantel was no longer ticking. "Oh, Lordy," she said. "This is the best house I've ever lived in."

"We'll find you another house," Josh promised.

A wisp of a smile surfaced. "Not like this one. This one's got my life in its bricks. Oh, Lordy . . . oh, Lordy . . ." Her head sank down into her hands. Her shoulders shook, but she made no sound. Josh went to a window, and Swan started to put her hand on Leona's arm, but at the last second she did not. The woman was hurting, Swan knew, but Leona was preparing herself, too, getting ready for what was to come.

After a few minutes, Leona rose from her chair and went to the rear of the house. She returned with her pistol and a box of bullets, and she tucked both of those under the sheet that covered the wheelbarrow. "We might need those," she said. "Never can tell." She looked at Swan, then lifted her eyes to Josh. "I think I'm ready now." She picked up the suitcase, and Swan took the smaller bag.

Josh lifted the wheelbarrow's handles. They weren't so heavy now, but the day was fresh. Suddenly Leona's suitcase thumped to the floor again. "Wait!" she said, and she hurried into the kitchen; she came back with a broom, which she used to sweep ashes and dead embers from the floor into the hearth.

"All right." She put the broom aside. "I'm ready now."

They left the house and started in a northwesterly direction, through the remains of Sullivan.

The little gray-haired terrier followed them at a distance of about thirty yards, his stubby tail straight up to balance against the wind.

Thirty-seven

Darkness found them short of the Jaspin farm. Josh tied the bull's-eye lantern to the front of the wheelbarrow with twine. Leona had to stop every half hour or so, and while she laid her head in Swan's lap, Josh gently massaged her legs; the tears Leona was weeping from the pain in her rheumatic knees crisscrossed the dust that covered her cheeks. Still, she made no sound, no complaint. After she'd rested for a few minutes she would struggle up again, and they'd continue on across rolling grassland burned black and oily by radiation.

The lantern's beam fell upon a rail fence about four feet tall and half blown down by the wind. "I think we're near the house!" Leona offered.

Josh manhandled the wheelbarrow over the fence, then lifted Swan over and helped Leona across. Facing them was a black cornfield, the diseased stalks standing as high as Josh and whipping back and forth like strange seaweed at the bottom of a slimy pool. It took them about ten minutes to reach the far edge of the field, and the lantern's beam hit the side of a farmhouse that had once been painted white, now splotched brown and yellow like lizard's skin.

"That's Homer and Maggie's place!" Leona shouted against the wind.

The house was dark, not a candle or lantern showing. There was no sign of a car or truck anywhere around, either. But something was making a loud, irregular banging noise off to the right, beyond the light's range. Josh untied the lantern and walked toward the sound. About fifty feet behind the house was a sturdy-looking red barn, one of its doors open and the wind banging it against the wall. Josh returned to the house and aimed the light at the front door; it was wide open, the screen door unlatched and thumping back and forth in the wind as well. He told Swan and Leona to wait where they were, and he entered the dark Jaspin farmhouse.

Once inside, he started to ask if anyone was home, but there was no need. He smelled the rank odor of decomposing flesh and almost gagged on it. He had to wait for a moment, bent over a decorative brass spittoon with a dead bunch of daisies in it, before he was sure he wouldn't throw up. Then he began to move through the house, sweeping the light slowly back and forth, looking for the bodies.

Outside, Swan heard a dog barking furiously in the black cornfield they'd just come through. She knew that the terrier had shadowed them all day, never coming closer than twenty feet, darting away when Swan bent down to summon it nearer. The dog's found something out there, Swan thought. Or . . . something's found *it*.

The barking was urgent—a "come see what I've got!" kind of bark.

Swan set her bag down and leaned Crybaby against the wheelbarrow. She took a couple of steps toward the black, swaying cornfield. Leona said, "Child! Josh said to stay right here!"

"It's all right," she answered. And she took three more steps.

"Swan!" Leona warned when she realized where the little girl was heading; she started to go after her, but immobilizing pain shot through her knees. "You'd best not go in there!"

The terrier's barking summoned Swan, and she stepped

into the cornfield. The black stalks closed at her back. Leona shouted, *"Swan!"*

In the farmhouse, Josh followed the beam of light into a small dining area. A cupboard had been flung open, and the floor was littered with chips and pieces of shattered crockery. Chairs had been smashed against the wall, a dining table hacked apart. The smell of decay was stronger. The light picked out something scrawled on the wall: ALL SHALL PRAISE LORD ALVIN.

Written in brown paint, Josh thought. But no, no. The blood had run down the wall and gathered in a crusty little patch on the floor.

A doorway beckoned him. He took a deep breath, straining the horrid smell through his clenched teeth, and walked through the doorway.

He was in a kitchen with yellow-painted cupboards and a dark rug.

And there he found them.

What was left of them.

They had been tied to chairs with barbed wire. The woman's face, framed with blood-streaked gray hair, resembled a bloated pincushion punctured by an assortment of knives, forks, and the little two-pronged handles that stick into the ends of corn on the cob. On the man's bared chest someone had drawn a target in blood and gone to work with a small-caliber pistol or rifle. The head was missing.

"Oh . . . my *God,"* Josh croaked, and this time he couldn't hold back the sickness. He stumbled across the kitchen to the sink and leaned over it.

But the lantern's light, swinging in his hand, showed him that the sink's basin was already occupied. As Josh shouted in terror and revulsion the hundreds of roaches that covered Homer Jaspin's severed head broke apart and scurried madly over the sink and countertop.

Josh staggered backward, the bile burning in his throat, and his feet slipped out from under him. He fell to the floor, where the dark rug lay, and felt crawling things on his arms and legs.

The floor, he realized. The . . . floor . . .

The floor around the bodies was an inch deep in surging, scrambling roaches.

As the roaches swarmed over his body Josh had a sudden ridiculous thought: You can't kill those things! Not even a nuclear disaster can kill 'em!

He leaped up from the floor, sliding on roaches, and started running from that awful kitchen, swatting at the things as he ran, swiping them off his clothes and skin. He fell to the carpet in the front room and rolled wildly on it, then he got up again and barreled for the screen door.

Leona heard the noise of splintering wood and ripping screen, and she turned toward the house in time to see Josh bring the whole door with him like a charging bull. There goes another screen door, she thought, and then she saw Josh fling himself to the ground and start rolling, swatting and squirming as if he'd run into a nest of hornets.

"What is it?" she called, hobbling toward him. "What the hell's wrong with you?"

Josh got up on his knees. He was still holding the lantern, while the other hand flopped and flipped here and there all over his body. Leona stopped in her tracks, because she'd never seen such terror in human eyes in her life. "What . . . is it?"

"Don't go in there! Don't you go in there!" he babbled, squirming and shaking. A roach ran over his cheek, and he grabbed it and flung it away with a shiver. "You stay out of that damned house!"

"I will," she promised, and she peered at the dark square where the door had been. A bad odor reached her; she'd smelled that reek before, back in Sullivan, and she knew what it was.

Josh heard a dog barking. "Where's Swan?" He stood up, still dancing and jerking. "Where'd she go?"

"In there!" Leona pointed toward the black cornfield. "I told her not to!"

"Damn!" Josh said, because he'd realized that whoever had done such a job on Homer and Maggie Jaspin might still be in the area—maybe was even in that barn, watching and waiting. Maybe was out in that field with the child.

He dug the pistol and the box of bullets out of the wheelbarrow and hurriedly slid three shells into their cylinders. "You stay right *here!*" he told Leona. "And don't you go in that house!" Then, lantern in one hand and pistol in the other, he sprinted into the cornfield.

Swan was following the terrier's barking. The sound ebbed and swelled with the wind, and around her the long-dead cornstalks rustled and swayed, grabbing at her clothes with leathery tendrils. She felt as if she were walking through a cemetery where all the corpses were standing upright, but the dog's frantic summons pulled her onward. There was something important in the field, something the dog wanted known, and she was determined to find out what it was. She thought the barking was off to the left, and she began to move in that direction. Behind her, she heard Josh shout, "Swan!" and she replied, "Over here!" but the wind turned. She kept going, her hands up to shield her face from the whipping stalks.

The barking was closer. No, Swan thought, now it was moving to the right again. She continued on, thought she heard Josh calling her again. "I'm here!" she shouted, but she heard no reply. The barking moved again, and Swan knew the terrier was following something—or someone. The barking said, "Hurry! Hurry, come see what I've found!"

Swan had taken six more steps when she heard something crashing toward her through the field. The terrier's voice got louder, more urgent. Swan stood still, watching and listening. Her heart had begun to pound, and she knew that whatever was out there was coming in her direction and getting closer. "Who's there?" she shouted. The crashing noise was coming right at her. "Who's there?" The wind flung her voice away.

She saw something coming toward her through the corn—something not human, something *huge*. She couldn't make out its shape, or what it was, but she heard a rumbling noise and backed away, her heart about to hammer through her chest. The huge, misshapen thing was coming right at her, faster and faster now, cleaving right through the dead, swaying stalks, and in another few seconds it would be upon her. She wanted to run, but her feet had rooted to the ground, and there was no time, because the thing was crashing at her and the terrier was barking an urgent warning.

The monster tore through the cornstalks and towered over her, and Swan cried out, got her feet uprooted and stumbled back, back, was falling, hit the ground on her rear and sat there while the monster's legs pounded toward her.

"Swan!" Josh shouted, bursting through the stalks behind her and aiming his light at what was about to trample her.

Dazzled by the light's beam, the monster stopped in its tracks and reared up on its hind legs, blowing steam through its widened nostrils.

And both Swan and Josh saw what it was.

A horse.

A piebald, black-and-white blotched horse with frightened eyes and oversized, shaggy hooves. The terrier was yapping tenaciously at its heels, and the piebald horse whinnied with fear, dancing on its hind legs for a few seconds before it came down again inches from where Swan sat in the dirt. Josh hooked Swan's arm and yanked her out of harm's way as the horse pranced and spun, the terrier darting around its legs with undaunted courage.

Swan was still shaking, but she knew in an instant that the horse was more terrified. It turned this way and that, confused and dazed, looking for a way of escape. The dog's barking was scaring it further, and suddenly Swan pulled free from Josh and took two steps forward, almost under the horse's nose; she lifted her hands and clapped her palms together right in front of the horse's muzzle.

The horse flinched but ceased jittering around; its fear-filled eyes were fixed on the little girl, steam curling from its nostrils, its lungs rumbling. Its legs trembled as if they might give way or take flight.

The terrier kept yapping, and Swan pointed a finger at it. *"Hush!"* she said. The dog scrambled away a few feet but caught back the next bark; then, as if deciding it had come too close to the humans and compromised its independence, darted away into the cornfield. It stood its distance and continued to bark intermittently.

Swan's attention was aimed at the horse, and she kept its eyes locked with her own. Its large, less-than-lovely head trembled, wanting to pull away from her, but it either would not or could not. "Is it a boy or a girl?" Swan asked Josh.

"Huh?" He still thought he felt roaches running up and down his backbone, but he shifted the lantern's beam. "A boy," he said. And a whopper of a boy, he thought.

"He hasn't seen people for a long time, I bet. Look at him; he doesn't know whether to be glad to see us or to run away."

"He must've belonged to the Jaspins," Josh said.

"Did you find them in the house?" She kept watching the horse's eyes.

"Yes. I mean . . . no, I didn't. I found signs of them. They must've packed up and gone." There was no way he was letting Swan into that house.

The horse rumbled nervously, its legs moving from side to side for a few steps.

Swan slowly lifted her hand toward the horse's muzzle.

"Be careful," Josh warned. "He'll snap your fingers right off!"

Swan continued to reach upward, slowly and surely. The horse backed away, its nostrils wide and its ears flicking back and forth. It lowered its head, sniffing the ground, then pretended to be looking off in another direction, but Swan saw the animal appraising her, trying to make up his mind about them. "We're not going to hurt you," Swan said quietly, her voice soothing. She stepped toward the horse, and he snorted a nervous warning.

"Watch out! He might charge you or something!" Josh knew absolutely nothing about horses, and they'd always scared him. This one was big and ugly and ungainly, with shaggy hooves and a floppy tail and a swayed back that looked like he'd been saddled with an anvil.

"He's not too sure about us," Swan told Josh. "He's still making up his mind whether to run or not, but I think he's kind of glad to see people again."

"What are you, an expert on horses?"

"No. I can just tell, from the set of his ears and the way his tail is swishing back and forth. Look at how he's smelling us—he doesn't want to seem too friendly. Horses have got a lot of pride. I think this one likes people, and he's been lonely."

Josh shrugged. "I sure can't tell any of that."

"My mama and I lived in a motel one time, next to a pasture where somebody's horses grazed. I used to climb over the fence and walk around with them, and I guess I learned how to talk to them, too."

"*Talk* to them? Come on!"

"Well, not human talk," she amended. "A horse talks with his ears and tail, and how he holds his head and his body. He's talking right now," she said as the horse snorted and gave a nervous whinny.

"What's he saying?"

"He's saying . . . that he wants to know what *we're* talking about." Swan continued to lift her hand toward the animal's muzzle.

"Watch your fingers!"

The horse retreated a pace. Swan's hand continued to rise—slowly, slowly. "No one's going to hurt you," Swan said, in a voice that sounded to Josh like the music of a lute, or a lyre, or some instrument that people had forgotten how to play. Its soothing quality almost made him forget the horrors tied to chairs back in the Jaspin farmhouse.

"Come on," Swan urged. "We won't hurt you." Her fingers were inches away from the muzzle, and Josh started to reach out and pull her back before she lost them to crunching teeth.

The horse's ears twitched and slanted forward. He snorted again, pawed at the ground and lowered his head to accept Swan's touch.

"That's right," Swan said. "That's right, boy." She scratched his muzzle, and he pushed inquisitively at her arm with his nose.

Josh wouldn't have believed it if he hadn't seen it. Still, Swan was probably right; the horse simply missed people. "I think you've made a friend. Doesn't look like much of a horse, though. Looks like a swayback mule in a clown suit."

"I think he's kind of pretty." Swan rubbed between the horse's eyes, and the animal obediently lowered his head so she wouldn't have to stretch up so far. The horse's eyes were still frightened, and Swan knew if she made a sudden move he'd bolt into the cornfield and probably not return, so she kept all her movements slow and precise. She thought that the horse was likely old, because there was a weary patience in the droop of his head and flanks, as if he was resigned to a life of pulling a plow across the very field in which they stood. His dappled skin jittered and jumped, but he allowed Swan to rub his head and made a low noise in his throat that sounded like a sigh of relief.

"I left Leona over by the house," Josh said. "We'd better get back."

Swan nodded and turned away from the horse, following Josh through the field. She'd taken about a half-dozen steps when she sensed rather than heard the heavy footfalls in the dirt behind her; she looked over her shoulder. The horse stopped, freezing like a statue. Swan continued after Josh, and the horse followed at a respectful distance, at its own ambling pace. The terrier darted out and yapped a couple of times just for the sake of being nettlesome, and the piebald horse kicked its hind hooves backward in disdain and showered the dog with dirt.

Leona was sitting on the ground, massaging her knees. Josh's light was coming, and when they reappeared from the field she saw Swan and the horse in the beam's backwash. "Lord A'mighty! What'd you find?"

"This thing was running wild out there," Josh told her, helping her to her feet. "Swan charmed the horseshoes right off him, got him settled down."

"Oh?" Leona's eyes found the little girl's, and she smiled knowingly. "Did she?" Leona hobbled forward to look at the horse. "Must've belonged to Homer. He had three or four horses out here. Well, he's not the handsomest animal I've ever seen, but he's got four strong legs, don't he?"

"Looks like a mule to me," Josh said. "Those hooves are as big as skillets." He caught a whiff of decay from the Jaspin farmhouse. The horse's head jerked, and he whinnied as if he'd smelled death as well. "We'd better get out of this wind." Josh motioned toward the barn with his lantern. He put the pistol and the lantern back in the wheelbarrow and went on ahead to make sure whoever had killed Homer and Maggie Jaspin wasn't hiding in there, waiting for them. He wondered who Lord Alvin was—but he was surely in no hurry to find out. Behind him, Swan picked up her bag and Crybaby, and Leona followed with her suitcase. Trailing them at a distance was the horse, and the terrier yapped at their backs and began to roam around the farmyard like a soldier on patrol.

Josh checked the barn out thoroughly and found no one else there. Plenty of hay was strewn about, and the horse came inside with them and made himself at home. Josh unpacked the blankets from the wheelbarrow, hung the lantern from a wall and opened a can of beef stew for their dinner. The horse sniffed around them for a while, more interested in hay than in canned stew; he returned when Josh opened a Mason jar of well water, and Josh poured a bit out for him in an empty bucket. The horse licked it up and came back for more. Josh obliged him, and the animal pawed the ground like a newborn colt. "Get out of here, mule!" Josh said when the horse's tongue tried to slip into the Mason jar.

After most of the stew was gone and just the juice remained, Swan took the can outside and left it for the terrier, as well as the rest of the water from the Mason jar. The dog came to within ten feet, then waited for Swan to go back into the barn before coming any closer.

Swan slept under one of the blankets. The horse, which Josh had christened Mule, ambled back and forth, chomping on hay and peering out through the cracked door at the dark farmhouse. The terrier continued to patrol the area for a while longer; then it found a place to shelter against one of the outside walls and lay down to rest.

"Both of them were dead," Leona said as Josh sat against a post with a blanket draped over his shouders.

"Yeah."

"Do you want to talk about it?"

"No. And neither do you. We've got another long, hard day tomorrow."

She waited for a few minutes to see if he would tell her or not, but she really didn't want to know. She pulled her blanket over her and went to sleep.

Josh was afraid to close his eyes, because he knew what was waiting for him behind the lids. Across the barn, Mule rumbled quietly; it was an oddly reassuring sound, like the noise of heat coming through a vent into a cold room, or a town crier signaling that all was well. Josh knew he had to get some sleep, and he was about to close his eyes when he detected a small movement just to his right. He stared and saw a little roach crawling slowly over the scattered bits of hay. Josh balled up his fist and started to slam it down on the insect, but his hand paused in mid-air.

Everything alive's got its own way of speaking and knowing, Swan had said. Everything alive.

He stayed the killing blow, watching the insect struggle tenaciously onward, getting caught in pieces of hay and working itself loose, plowing forward with stubborn, admirable determination.

Josh opened his fist and drew his arm back. The insect kept going, out of the light's range and into the darkness on its purposeful journey. Who am I to kill such a thing? he asked himself. Who am I to deliver death to even the lowest form of life?

He listened to the keening of the wind whistling through holes in the walls, and he pondered the thought that there might be something out there in the dark—God or Devil or something more elemental than either—that looked at humankind as Josh had viewed the roach—less than intelligent, certainly nasty, but struggling onward on its journey, never giving up, fighting through obstacles or going around them, doing whatever it had to do to survive.

And he hoped that if the time ever came for that elemental fist to come crashing down, its wielder might take a moment of pause as well.

Josh drew the blanket around himself and lay down in the straw to sleep.

Thirty-eight

"This is our power!" Colonel Macklin said, holding up the .45 automatic he'd taken off the dead young man from California.

"No," Roland Croninger replied. "*This* is our power." And he held up one of the bottles of pills from Sheila Fontana's drug cache.

"Hey!" Sheila grabbed at it, but Roland held it out of her reach. "That's my stash! You can't—"

"Sit down," Macklin told her. She hesitated, and he rested the pistol on his knee. "Sit *down,"* he repeated.

She cursed quietly and sat down in the filthy pit while the kid continued to tell the one-handed war hero how the pills and cocaine were stronger than any gun could ever be.

Dawn came with a cancerous, yellow sky and needles of rain. A black-haired woman, a man with one hand in a dirty overcoat, and a boy wearing goggles trudged across the landscape of rotting corpses and wrecked vehicles. Sheila Fontana was holding up a pair of white panties as a flag of truce, and close behind her Macklin kept the .45 aimed at the small of her back. Roland Croninger, bringing up the rear, carried Sheila's knapsack. He remembered how the woman's hair had felt in his hands, how her body had moved like a roller-coaster ride; he wanted to have sex again, and he would hate it if she made a wrong move now and had to be executed. Because after all, they'd shown her the highest chivalry last night; they'd saved her from the rabble, and they'd given her some food—dog biscuits they'd been living on from the wreck of a camper, the dog's carcass having been consumed long ago—and a place to rest after they were done with her.

They reached the edge of the dirtwart land and started across open territory. Ahead of them lay the tents, cars and cardboard shelters of the privileged people who lived on the lake shore. They were about halfway across, heading for a battered, dented Airstream trailer at the center of the encampment, when they heard the warning shout: "Dirtwarts coming in! Wake up! Dirtwarts coming in!"

"Keep going," Macklin told Sheila when she faltered. "Keep waving those panties, too."

People started coming out of their shelters. In truth, they were every bit as ragged and dirty as the dirtwarts, but they had guns and supplies of canned food and bottled water, and most of them had escaped serious burns. The majority of dirtwarts, on the other hand, were severely burned, had contagious illnesses or were insane. Macklin understood the balance of power. It was centered within the Airstream trailer, a shining mansion amid the other hovels.

"Turn back, fuckers!" a man hollered from a tent's entrance; he aimed a high-velocity rifle at them. "Go back!" a woman shouted, and someone threw an empty can that hit the ground a few feet in front of Sheila. She stopped, and Macklin pushed her on with a shove of the automatic.

"Keep moving. And *smile.*"

"Go back, you filth!" a second man, wearing the remnants of an Air Force uniform and a coat stained with dried blood, shouted; he had a revolver, and he came within twenty feet of them. "You graverobbers!" he shouted. "You dirty, lice-ridden . . . *heathen!*"

Macklin didn't worry about him; he was a young man, maybe in his mid-twenties, and his eyes kept sneaking toward Sheila Fontana. He wasn't going to do anything. Other people approached them, shouting and jeering, brandishing guns and rifles, knives and even a bayonet. Rocks, bottles and cans were thrown, and though they came dangerously close, none of them connected. "Don't you bring your diseases in here!" a middle-aged man in a brown raincoat and woolen cap hollered. He was holding an axe. "I'll kill you if you take another goddamned step!"

Macklin wasn't worried about him, either. The men were puzzled by Sheila Fontana's presence, but he recognized the lust on their faces as they surged around, hollering threats. He saw a thin young woman with stringy brown hair, her body engulfed in a yellow raincoat and her sunken eyes fixed on Sheila with deadly intent. She was carrying a butcher knife, fingering the blade. Macklin *did* feel a pang of worry about her, and he guided Sheila away from the young woman. An empty can hit him in the side of the head and glanced off. Someone came close enough to spit on Roland. "Keep going, keep going," Macklin said quietly, his eyes narrowed and ticking back and forth.

Roland heard shouts and taunting laughter behind them, and he glanced over his shoulder. Back in the dirtwart land, about thirty or forty dirtwarts had crawled from their holes and were jumping up and down, screaming like animals in expectation of a slaughter.

Macklin smelled salt water. Before him, through the misting rain and beyond the encampment, the Great Salt Lake stretched to the far horizon; it smelled antiseptic, like the halls of a hospital. The stump of Macklin's wrist burned and seethed with infection, and he longed to plunge it into the healing water, to baptize himself in cleansing agony.

A burly, bearded red-haired man in a leather jacket and dungarees, a bandage plastered to his forehead, stepped in front of Sheila. He aimed a double-barreled shotgun at Macklin's head. "That's as far as you go."

Sheila stopped, her eyes wide. She waved the pair of panties in front of his face. "Hey, don't shoot! We don't want any trouble!"

"He won't shoot," Macklin said easily, smiling at the bearded man. "See, my friend, I've got a gun pointed at the young lady's back. If you blow my head off—and if *any* of you dumb fucks shoot either me or the boy—my finger's going to twitch on this trigger and sever her spine. Look at her, fellas! Just look! Not a burn on her! Not a burn *anywhere!* Oh, yeah, fill your eyes full, but don't touch! Isn't she something?"

Sheila had the impulse to pull her T-shirt up and give the gawkers a tit show; if the war hero had ever decided to give pimping a try, he'd have racked up. But this whole experience was so unreal, it was almost like flying on a tab of LSD, and she found herself grinning, about to laugh. The filthy men who stood around her with their guns and knives just stared, and further behind them was a collection of skinny, dirty women who watched her with absolute hatred.

Macklin saw they were about fifty feet from the Airstream trailer. "We want to see the Fat Man," he told the guy with the beard.

"Sure!" The other man hadn't lowered his shotgun yet. His mouth curled sarcastically. "He sees dirtwarts all the time! Serves 'em champagne and caviar!" He snorted. "Who the *fuck* do you think you are, mister?"

"My name is Colonel James B. Macklin. I served in Vietnam as a pilot, and I was shot down and spent one year in a hole that makes this place look like the Ritz-Carlton. I'm a *military* man, you dumb bastard!" Macklin's face was reddening. Discipline and control, he told himself. Discipline and control makes the man. He took a couple of deep breaths; around him several people jeered at him, and someone's spit landed on his right cheek. "We want to see the Fat Man. He's the leader here, isn't he? He's the one with the most food and guns?"

"Run 'em out!" a stocky, curly-haired woman shouted, brandishing a long barbecue fork. "We don't want their damned diseases!"

Roland heard a pistol being cocked, and he knew someone was holding a gun just behind his head. He flinched, but then he turned slowly around, grinning rigidly. A blond-haired boy about his age, wearing a bulky plaid jacket, was aiming a .38 right between his eyes. "You stink," the blond-haired kid said, his dead brown eyes challenging Roland to make a move. Roland stood very still, his heart going like a jackhammer.

"I said we want to see the Fat Man," Macklin repeated. "Do you take us, or what?"

The bearded man laughed harshly. "You've got a lot of guts for a dirtwart!" His eyes flickered toward Sheila Fontana, lingered on her body and breasts, then went back to the pistol Macklin held.

Roland slowly lifted his hand in front of the blond kid's face, then just as slowly brought his hand down and reached into the pocket of his trousers. The blond boy's finger was on the trigger. Roland's hand found what he was after, and he began to draw it out.

"You can leave the woman and we won't kill you," the bearded man told Macklin. "Just walk out and go back to your hole. We'll forget that you even—"

A little plastic bottle hit the ground in front of his left boot.

"Go ahead," Roland told him. "Pick it up. Take a sniff."

The man hesitated, glanced around at the others who were still shouting and jeering and eating Sheila Fontana alive with their eyes. Then he knelt down, picked up the bottle Roland had tossed over, uncapped it and sniffed. "What the *hell—!*"

"Want me to kill him, Mr. Lawry?" the blond kid asked hopefully.

"No! Put that damned gun down!" Lawry sniffed the contents of the bottle again, and his wide blue eyes began to water. "Put the gun *down!*" he snapped, and the boy obeyed reluctantly.

"You going to take us to the Fat Man?" Macklin asked. "I think he'd like to get a sniff, don't you?"

"Where'd you get this shit?"

"The Fat Man. *Now.*"

Lawry capped the vial. He looked around at the others, looked back at the Airstream trailer and paused, trying to make up his mind. He blinked, and Roland could tell the man didn't exactly have a mainframe computer between his ears. "Okay." He motioned with the shotgun. "Move ass."

"Kill 'em!" the stocky woman shrieked. "Don't let 'em contaminate us!"

"Now listen, all of you!" Lawry held the shotgun at his side and kept the plastic vial gripped tightly in his other hand. "They're not burned or anything! I mean . . . they're just dirty! They're not like the other dirtwarts! I'll take responsibility for them!"

"Don't let them in!" another woman shouted. "They don't *belong!*"

"Move," Lawry told Macklin. "You try anything funny, and I swear to God you'll be one headless motherfucker. Got it?"

Macklin didn't answer. He pushed Sheila forward, and Roland followed him toward the large silver trailer. A pack of people stalked at their heels, including the trigger-happy kid with the .38 revolver.

Lawry ordered them to stop when they'd gotten ten feet from the trailer. He walked up a few bricks that had been set up as steps to the trailer's door and knocked on it with the butt of his shotgun. A high, thin voice from inside asked, "Who is it?"

"Lawry, Mr. Kempka. I've got something you need to see."

There was no reply for a moment or so. Then the whole trailer seemed to tremble, to creak over a few degrees as Kempka—the Fat Man who, Macklin had learned from another dirtwart, was the leader of the lake shore encampment—approached the door. A couple of bolts snapped back. The door opened, but Macklin was unable to see who had opened it. Lawry told Macklin to wait where he was, then he entered the trailer. The door shut. As soon as he was gone, the curses and jeers got louder, and again bottles and cans were flung.

"You're crazy, war hero," Sheila said. "You'll never get out of here alive."

"If we go, so do you."

She turned on him, disregarding the pistol, and her eyes flashed with anger. "So kill me, war hero. As soon as you pull that trigger, these horny bastards'll take you apart piece by piece. And who said you could use my stash, huh? That's high-grade Colombian sugar you're throwing around, man!"

Macklin smiled thinly. "You like to take chances, don't you?" He didn't wait for the answer, because he already knew it. "You want food and water? You want to sleep with a roof over your head and not expect somebody to kill you in the night? You want to be able to wash and not squat in your own shit? I want those things, too, and so does Roland. We don't belong out there with the dirtwarts; we belong here, and this is a chance we've got to take."

She shook her head, and though she was infuriated at losing her stash, she knew he was right. The kid had shown real smarts in suggesting it. "You're crazy."

"We'll see."

The trailer's door opened. Lawry stuck his head out. "Okay. Come on up. But you give me the gun first."

"No deal. The gun stays with me."

"You heard what I said, mister!"

"I heard. The gun stays with me."

Lawry looked over his shoulder at the man inside the trailer. Then: "Okay. Come on—and be quick about it!"

They went up the steps into the trailer, and Lawry closed the door behind Roland, sealing off the shouts of the mob. Lawry swung his shotgun up at Macklin's head.

A blob wearing a food-stained T-shirt and overalls was sitting at a table on the other side of the trailer. His hair was dyed orange and stood up in inch-high spikes on his scalp, and he had a beard streaked with red and green food coloring. His head looked too small for his chest and massive belly, and he had four chins. His eyes were beady black holes in a pallid, flabby face. Scattered around the trailer were cases of canned food, bottled Cokes and Pepsis, bottled water and about a hundred six-packs of Budweiser stacked up against one wall. Behind him was a storehouse of weapons: a rack of seven rifles, one with a sniperscope, an old Thompson submachine gun, a bazooka, and a variety of pistols hanging on hooks. Before him on the table, he had sifted a small mound of cocaine from the plastic vial and was rubbing some of it between his fleshy fingers. Within reach of his right hand was a Luger, its muzzle pointed in the direction of his visitors. He lifted some of the cocaine to his nostrils and sniffed delicately, as if testing French perfume. "Do you have names?" he asked, in a voice that was almost girlish.

"My name is Macklin. Colonel James B. Macklin, ex-United States Air Force. This is Roland Croninger and Sheila Fontana."

Kempka picked up another bit of cocaine and let it drift back down. "Where did this come from, Colonel Macklin?"

"My stash," Sheila said. She thought she'd seen all the repulsive things in the world, but even in the low yellow light of the two lamps that illuminated the trailer, she could hardly bear the Fat Man. He looked like a circus freak, and from each of his long, fat earlobes hung diamond-studded earrings.

"And this is the extent of that 'stash'?"

"No," Macklin replied. "Not nearly all. There's plenty more cocaine, and all kinds of pills, too."

"Pills," Kempka repeated. His black eyes aimed at Macklin. "What kind of pills?"

"All kinds. LSD. PCP. Painkillers. Tranquilizers. Uppers and downers."

Sheila snorted. "War hero, you don't know *shit* about goodies, do you?" She took a step toward Kempka, and the Fat Man's hand rested on the Luger's butt. "Black Beauties, Yellowjackets, Blue Angels, bennies, poppers, and Red Stingers. All high-quality floats."

"Is that so? Were you in the business, young lady?"

"Yeah, I guess so." She looked around at the messy, cluttered trailer. "What kind of business were you in? Pig farming?"

Kempka stared at her. Then, slowly, his belly began to wobble, followed by his chins. His entire face shook like a plateful of Jell-O, and a high, feminine laugh squeaked between his lips. "Hee hee!" he said, his cheeks reddening. "Hee hee! Pig farming. Hee hee!" He waved a fat hand at Lawry, who forced a nervous laugh as well. When he'd stopped laughing, Kempka said, "No, dear one, it was not pig farming. I owned a gun shop in Rancho Cordova, just east of Sacramento. Fortunately, I had time to pack up some of my stock and get out when the bombs hit the Bay Area. I also had the presence of mind to visit a little grocery store on the way east. Mr. Lawry was a clerk at my store, and we found a place to hide for a while in the Eldorado National Forest. The road brought us here, and other people started arriving. Soon we had a little community. Most of the people came to soak themselves in the lake. There's a belief that bathing in the salt water washes off the radiation and makes you immune." He shrugged his fleshy shoulders. "Maybe it does, maybe it doesn't. In any case, I kind of enjoy playing King of the Hill and the Godfather. If someone doesn't do as I say, I simply banish them to the dirtwart land . . . or I kill them." He giggled again, his black eyes sparkling merrily. "You see, I make the laws here. Me, Freddie Kempka, lately of Kempka's Shootist Supermarket, Incorporated. Oh, I'm having a real ball!"

"Good for you," Sheila muttered.

"Yes. Good for me." He rubbed cocaine between his fingers and sniffed a bit up each nostril. "My, my! That is a potent dust, isn't it?" He licked his fingers clean, and then he looked at Roland Croninger. "What are you supposed to be, a space cadet?"

Roland didn't answer. I'll zap your big fat ass, he thought.

Kempka giggled. "How come you to be out in the dirtwart land, Colonel?"

Macklin told him the whole story, how Earth House had collapsed and how he and the boy had gotten out. Macklin made no mention of the Shadow Soldier, because he knew the Shadow Soldier didn't like to be talked about to strangers.

"I see," Kempka said when he'd finished. "Well, like they say: The best-laid plans often go shitty, don't they? Now, I suppose you came here and brought this potent dust for a purpose. What is it?"

"We want to move into the encampment. We want a tent, and we want a supply of food."

"The only tents that are here were brought on people's backs. They're all filled up. No room in the inn, Colonel."

"Make room. We get a tent and some food and you get a weekly ration of cocaine and pills. Call it rent."

"What would I do with drugs, sir?"

Roland laughed, and Kempka regarded him through

hooded eyes. "Come on, mister!" Roland stepped forward. "You know you can sell those drugs for whatever you want! You can buy people's *minds* with that stuff, because everybody'll pay to forget. They'll pay anything you ask: food, guns, gasoline—anything."

"I already have those things."

"Maybe you do," Roland agreed. "But are you sure you've got *enough* of them? What if somebody in a bigger trailer comes into the encampment tomorrow? What if they've got more guns than you do? What if they're stronger and meaner? Those people out there"—he nodded toward the door—"are just waiting for somebody strong to tell them what to do. They *want* to be commanded. They don't want to have to think for themselves. Here's a way to put their minds in your pocket." He motioned to the snowy mound.

Kempka and Roland stared at each other for a silent moment, and Roland had the sensation of looking at a giant slug. Kempka's black eyes bored into Roland's, and finally a little smile flickered across his wet mouth. "Would these drugs," he said, "buy me a sweet young space cadet?"

Roland didn't know what to say. He was stunned, and it must've shown on his face because Kempka snorted and laughed. When his laughter was spent, the Fat Man said to Macklin, "What's to keep me from killing you right now and taking your precious drugs, Colonel?"

"One simple thing: the drugs are buried out in the dirtwart land. Roland's the only one who knows where they are. He'll go out and bring you a ration once a week, but if anybody follows him or tries to interfere, they get their brains blown out."

Kempka tapped his fingers on the tabletop, looking from the mound of cocaine to Macklin and Roland—contemptuously dismissing the girl—and then back to the Colombian sugar.

"We could use that stuff, Mr. Kempka," Lawry offered. "Fella came in yesterday with a gas heater that sure would warm this trailer up. Another guy's got some whiskey he lugged along in a tow sack. We're gonna need tires for the truck, too. I would've already taken that heater and the bottles of Jack Daniel's, but both of those new arrivals are armed to the teeth. Might be a good idea to trade the drugs for their guns, too."

"I'll decide what's a good idea and what's not." Kempka's face folded up as he frowned thoughtfully. He drew a long breath and exhaled it like a bellows. "Find them a tent. Close to the trailer. And spread the word that if anybody touches them, they answer to Freddie Kempka." He smiled broadly at Macklin. "Colonel, I believe you and your friends are going to be very interesting additions to our little family. I guess we could call you pharmacists, couldn't we?"

"I guess so." Macklin waited until Lawry had lowered his shotgun, and then he in turn lowered the automatic.

"There. Now we're all happy, aren't we?" And his black, ravenous eyes found Roland Croninger.

Lawry took them to a small tent staked down about thirty yards from the Airstream trailer. It was occupied by a young man and a woman who held an infant with bandaged legs. Lawry stuck the shotgun in the young man's face and said, "Get out."

The man, drawn and gaunt, hollow-eyed with fatigue, scrabbled under his sleeping bag. His hand came up with a hunting knife, but Lawry stepped forward and caught the man's thin wrist beneath his boot. Lawry put all his weight down, and Roland watched his eyes as he broke the man's bones: they were empty, registering no emotion even when the snapping noise began. Lawry was simply doing what he'd been told. The infant started crying, and the woman was screaming, but the man just hugged his broken wrist and stared numbly up at Lawry.

"Out." Lawry put the shotgun's barrel to the young man's skull. "Are you deaf, you dumb bastard?"

The man and woman wearily got to their feet. He paused to gather up their sleeping bags and a knapsack with his uninjured hand, but Lawry grabbed him by the scruff of the neck and hauled him out, throwing him to the ground. The woman sobbed and cringed at her husband's side. A crowd was gathering to watch, and the woman shrieked, "You animals! You dirty animals! That's our tent! It belongs to *us!*"

"Not anymore." Lawry motioned with the shotgun toward the dirtwart land. "Start walking."

"It's not fair! Not fair!" the woman sobbed. She looked around imploringly at the people who were gathering. Roland, Macklin and Sheila did, too, and they all saw the same thing in those faces: an impassive, uninvolved curiosity, as if they were watching television violence. Though there were faint expressions of disgust and pity here and there, the majority of the onlookers had already been shocked devoid of all emotion.

"Help us!" the woman begged. "Please . . . somebody help us!"

Several of the people had guns, but none of them intervened. Macklin understood why: It was the survival of the fittest. Freddie Kempka was the emperor here, and Lawry was his lieutenant—probably one of many lieutenants Kempka used as his eyes and ears.

"Get out," Lawry told the couple. The woman kept shrieking and crying, but finally the man stood up and, his eyes dead and defeated, began to trudge slowly toward the grim land of car hulks and decaying corpses. Her expression turned to hatred; she stood up with the wailing infant in her arms and shouted to the crowd, "It'll happen to you! You'll see! They'll take everything you have! They'll come and drag you out of—"

Lawry struck out with the stock of the shotgun. It crunched into the infant's skull, the force of the blow knocking the young woman to the ground.

The infant's crying abruptly stopped.

She looked down into her child's face and made a weak choking sound.

Sheila Fontana couldn't believe what she'd just witnessed; she wanted to turn away, but the scene had a dark hold on her. Her stomach churned with revulsion, and she could still hear the infant's cry, echoing over and over in her mind. She put her hand over her mouth and pressed.

The young man, a corpse in clothes, was walking on across the plain, not even bothering to look back.

Finally, with a shuddering gasp, the woman rose to her

feet, the silent infant clasped to her chest. Her hideous, hollowed-out eyes met Sheila's and lingered. Sheila felt as if her soul had been burned to a cinder. If . . . only the baby had stopped crying, Sheila thought. If only . . .

The young mother turned and began to follow her husband into the mist.

The onlookers drifted away. Lawry wiped the stock of his shotgun on the ground and motioned toward the tent. "Looks like we just got a vacancy, Colonel."

"Did you . . . have to do that?" Sheila asked. Inside she was trembling and sick, but her face showed no sign of it, her eyes cold and flinty.

"Every once in a while they forget who makes the rules. Well? Do you want the tent or not?"

"We do," Macklin said.

"There you go, then. Even got a couple of sleeping bags and some food in there. Cozy as home, huh?"

Macklin and Roland entered the tent. "Where am *I* supposed to live?" Sheila asked Lawry.

He smiled, examined her up and down. "Well, I've got an extra sleeping bag over in the trailer. See, I bunk with Mr. Kempka, but I'm not funny. He likes young boys, couldn't give a shit about women. What do you say?"

She smelled his body odor and couldn't decide whose was worse, his or the war hero's. "Forget it," she said. "I'll stay here."

"Suit yourself. I'll get you, sooner or later."

"When Hell freezes."

He licked a finger and held it up to catch the wind. "It's getting pretty frosty, darlin'." Then he laughed and sauntered off toward the trailer.

Sheila watched him go. She looked in the direction of the dirtwart land, and she saw the vague outlines of the young couple heading into the mist, into the unknown that lay beyond it. Those two wouldn't have spit's chance out there, she thought. But maybe they already knew that. The baby would've died anyway, she told herself. Sure. The kid was half dead already.

But that incident had knocked her off her tracks more than

anything ever had before, and she couldn't help thinking that a few minutes before there was a living person where a ghost was now. And it had happened because of her drugs, because she'd come in there with the war hero and the punk playing big shots.

The young couple disappeared into the gray rain.

As Rudy said, you cover your own ass. And in this day and time, those were words to live by.

Sheila turned her back on the dirtwart land and slipped into the tent.

Thirty-nine

"Light!" Josh shouted, pointing into the distance. "Look at that! There's light ahead!"

They'd been following a highway over gently rolling country, and now they saw the light that Josh pointed toward: a bluish-white illumination reflecting off low-lying, turbulent clouds.

"That's Matheson," Leona said, from her bareback perch atop Mule. "Lord A'mighty! They've got the 'lectricity on in Matheson!"

"How many people live there?" Josh asked her, speaking loudly over the rush and pull of the wind.

"Thirteen, fourteen thousand. It's a regular *city!*"

"Thank God! They must've fixed their power lines! We're going to have hot meals tonight! Thank God!" He started shoving the wheelbarrow with new-found energy, as if his heels had sprouted wings. Swan followed him, carrying the dowsing rod and her small bag, and Leona kicked her heels into Mule's sides to urge the horse onward. Mule obeyed without hesitation, glad to be of use again. Behind them, the little terrier sniffed the air and growled quietly but followed nevertheless.

Flickers of lightning shot through the cloud cover over Matheson, and the wind brought the rumble of thunder. They'd left the Jaspin farm early that morning, had walked all day along the narrow highway. Josh had tried to put a saddle and bridle on Mule, but though the horse stood docilely, Josh couldn't get the damned things on right. The saddle kept slipping, and he couldn't figure out how to get the bridle on at all. Every time Mule had even grumbled, Josh had jumped back out of the way, expecting the animal to buck and rear, and finally he gave the job up as a lost cause. Still, the horse accepted Leona's weight without complaint; he had also borne Swan for a few miles. The horse seemed content to follow Swan, almost like a puppy. And off in the darkness, the terrier yapped every once in a while to let them know he was still around.

Josh's heart was hammering. That was one of the most beautiful lights he'd ever seen, next to the glorious flashlight beam that had speared through the basement. Oh, Lord! he thought. A hot meal, a warm place to sleep, and—glory of glories!—maybe even a real toilet again! He smelled ozone in the air. A thunderstorm was approaching, but he didn't care. They were going to rest in the lap of luxury tonight!

Josh turned his face toward Swan and Leona. "Lord God, we made it back to civilization!" He let out a loud whoop that put the wind to shame and even made Mule jump.

But the smile froze on Leona's face. Slowly, it began to slide off. Her fingers curled through Mule's coarse black mane.

She wasn't sure what she'd seen, wasn't sure at all. It had been a trick of the light, she told herself. A trick of the light. Yes. That's all.

Leona thought she'd seen a skull where Josh Hutchins's face had been.

But it had been so fast—there and then gone in an eye-blink.

She stared at the back of Swan's head. Oh, God, Leona thought, what'll I do if the child's face is like that, too?

It took her a while to gather her courage, and then she said, "Swan?" in a thin, scared voice.

Swan glanced back. "Ma'am?"

Leona was holding her breath.

"Ma'am?" Swan repeated.

Leona found a smile. "Oh . . . nothin'," she said, and she shrugged. The vision of a skull beneath the skin was not there. "I . . . just wanted to see your face," Leona told her.

"My *face?* Why?"

"Oh, I was just thinkin' . . . how pretty you must've been." She stammered at her own error. "I mean, how pretty you're gonna be again, once your skin heals up. And it will, too. Skin's a real tough thing, y'know. Sure is! It'll heal up pretty as a picture!"

Swan didn't answer; she remembered the horror that had stared back at her from the bathroom mirror. "I don't think my face'll ever heal up," she said matter-of-factly. A sudden awful thought struck her. "You don't think . . ." She paused, unable to spit it out. Then: "You don't think . . . I'll *scare* people in Matheson, do you?"

"Of course not! And don't you even think such a thing!" In truth, Leona hadn't considered that before, but now she could envision residents of Matheson cringing away from Josh and Swan. "Your skin'll heal up soon enough," Leona assured her. "Besides, that's just your outside face."

"My *outside* face?"

"Yep. Everybody's got two faces, child—the outside face and the inside face. The outside face is how the world sees you, but the *inside* face is what you really look like. It's your true face, and if it was flipped to the outside you'd show the world what kind of person you are."

"Flipped to the outside? How?"

Leona smiled. "Well, God hasn't figured a way to do that yet. But He will. Sometimes you can see a person's inside face—but only for a second or two—if you look close and hard enough. The eyes give away the inside face, and likely as not it's a whole lot different than the mask that's stuck on the outside." She nodded, looking toward the lights of Matheson. "Oh, I've met some mighty handsome people who had monstrous ugly faces on the inside. And I've met some homely folks with buck teeth and big noses and the light of

Heaven in their eyes, and you know that if you saw their inside faces the beauty would knock you right to your knees. I kind of figure it might be like that for *your* inside face, child. And Josh's as well. So what does it matter about your outside face?"

Swan pondered for a moment. "I'd like to believe that."

"Then take it as true," Leona said, and Swan was quiet.

The light beckoned them onward. The highway climbed over one more hill, then began to curve gently down toward the town. Lightning jumped across the horizon. Beneath Leona, Mule snorted and whinnied.

Swan heard a nervous note in the horse's whinny. Mule's excited because we're going to find more people, she thought. But no, no—that hadn't been a sound of excitement; Swan had heard it as distrust, edginess. She began to pick up the horse's nervousness, to feel a little wary herself, like the time she'd been strolling across a wide golden field and a farmer in a red cap had yelled, "Hey, little girl! Watch out for rattlers in them weeds!"

Not that she was afraid of snakes—far from it. Once, when she was five years old, she'd picked up a colorful snake right out of the grass, run her fingers across the beautiful diamonds on its back and the bony-looking ridges on its tail. Then she'd set the snake down and watched as it crawled unhurriedly away. It was only later, when she'd told her mama and gotten a rear-blistering whipping in return, that Swan had realized she was supposed to be afraid.

Mule made a whickering sound and tossed his head. The road flattened out as it approached the outskirts of town, where a green sign proclaimed, *Welcome to Matheson, Kansas! We're Strong, Proud and Growing!*

Josh stopped, and Swan almost bumped into him.

"What is it?" Leona asked him.

"Look." Josh motioned toward the town.

The houses and buildings were dark; no light came from their windows or front porches. There were no streetlights, no headlights of cars, no traffic lights. The glow that reflected up off the low clouds was coming from deeper within the town, beyond the dead, dark structures that were scattered on both sides of the main highway. There was no sound but the shrill whine of the wind. "I think that light's coming from the center of town," he told Swan and Leona. "But if the electricity's back on, why aren't there lights in the house windows, too?"

"Maybe everybody's in one place," Leona offered. "Like at the auditorium, or City Hall or somewhere."

Josh nodded. "There ought to be cars," he decided. "Ought to be traffic lights working. I don't see any."

"Maybe they're savin' the 'lectricity. Maybe the wires aren't too strong yet."

"Maybe," Josh replied, but there was something spooky about Matheson; why were there no lights in the windows, yet something at the center of Matheson ablaze with light? And everything was so still, so very still. He had the feeling that they should turn back, but the wind was cold and they had come so far; there *had* to be people here! Sure! They're all in one place, like Leona had suggested. Maybe they're having a town meeting or something! In any case, there was no turning back. He started pushing the wheelbarrow again. Swan followed him, and the horse that bore Leona followed Swan, and off to the left the terrier kept to the tall weeds and ran ahead.

Another roadside sign advertised the Matheson Motel—Swimming Pool! Cable TV!—and a third sign said the best coffee and steaks in town could be found at the Hightower Restaurant on Caviner Street. They followed the road between plowed fields and passed a dark softball diamond and a public pool where the lounge chairs and umbrellas were blown into a chain-link fence. A final roadside sign announced the July Firecracker Sale at the K-Mart on Billups Street, and then they entered Matheson.

It had been a pretty town, Josh thought as they walked along the center line. The buildings were either made of stones or logs, meant to resemble a frontier town. The houses were made of brick, most of them one story, nothing fancy, but nice enough. A statue of somebody on his knees, one hand covering what might've been a Bible and the other extended toward the sky, stood atop a pedestal in a district of small shops and stores that reminded Josh of that Mayberry show with Andy Griffith. A canopy flapped over a store with a barber pole in front of it, and the windows of the Matheson First Citizen's Bank were broken out. Furniture had been dragged out of a furniture store, piled in a heap in the street and set afire. Nearby was an overturned police car, also burned to a hulk. Josh did not look inside. Thunder growled overhead, and lightning danced across the sky.

Further on, they found a used car lot. Trade at Uncle Roy's! the sign urged. Under rows of flapping multicolored banners were six dusty cars. Josh began to check them all, one by one, as Swan and Leona waited behind and Mule grumbled uneasily. Two of them were sitting on flat tires, and a third's windshield and windows were shattered. The other three—an Impala, a Ford Fairlane and a red pickup truck—seemed in pretty good shape. Josh walked to the small office building, found the door wide open, and with the light of the bull's-eye lantern located the keys to all three vehicles on a pegboard. He took the keys out to the lot and methodically tried them. The Impala wouldn't make a sound, the pickup truck was dead, and the Fairlane's engine popped and stuttered, made a noise like a chain being dragged along gravel and then went silent. Josh opened the Fairlane's hood and found that the engine had been attacked with what might've been an axe, the wiring, belts and cables hacked apart. "Damn it!" Josh swore, and then his lantern revealed something written in dried grease on the inside of the hood: ALL SHALL PRAISE LORD ALVIN.

He stared at the scrawled writing, remembering that he'd seen the same thing—though written in a different hand and in a different substance—at the Jaspin farmhouse the night before. He walked back to Swan and Leona, and he said, "Those cars are shot. I think somebody wrecked them on purpose." He looked toward the light, which was much closer now. "Well," he said finally, "I guess we go find out what that is, right?"

Leona glanced at him, then quickly away; she wasn't sure that she hadn't seen the skull again, but in this strange light she couldn't tell. Her heart had begun to pump harder, and she didn't know what to do or say.

Josh pushed the wheelbarrow forward. Off in the distance, they heard the terrier bark a few times, then silence. They continued along the main street, passing more stores with broken windows, more overturned and burned vehicles. The light pulled them onward, and though they all had their private concerns they were drawn to that light like moths to a candle.

On a corner was a small sign that pointed to the right and said *Pathway Institute, 2 mi.* Josh looked in that direction and saw nothing but darkness.

"That's the asylum," Leona said.

"The *asylum?*" The word lanced him. "What asylum?"

"The crazy house. You know, where they put folks who go off their rockers. That one's famous all over the state. Full of people too crazy to go to prison."

"You mean . . . the criminally insane?"

"Yeah, that's right."

"Great," Josh said. The sooner they were out of this town, the better! He didn't like being even two miles from an asylum full of lunatic murderers. He peered off into the darkness where the Pathway Institute was, and he felt the flesh ripple all up and down his backbone.

And then they went through another area of silent houses, passing the dark Matheson Motel and the Hightower Restaurant, and they entered a huge paved parking lot.

Before them, every light illuminated and blazing, was a K-Mart and, next to it, a similarly lit Food Giant supermarket.

"God Almighty!" Josh breathed. "A shopping center!"

Swan and Leona just stared, as if they'd never seen such light or huge stores before. Dark-sensitive photon lamps cast a yellow glow over the parking lot, which held perhaps fifty or sixty cars, campers, and pickup trucks, all covered with Kansas dust. Josh was completely stunned and had to catch his balance before the wind knocked him over. It was running through his head that if the electricity was on, then the freezers in the supermarket would be operating, too, and inside would be steaks, ice cream, cold beer, eggs, bacon, ham, and God only knew what else. He looked at the brilliantly lit K-Mart, his brain reeling. What sort of treasures would be in there? Radios and batteries, flashlights and lanterns, guns, gloves, kerosene heaters, raincoats! He didn't know whether to laugh or sob with joy, but he pushed the wheelbarrow aside and started walking toward the K-Mart as if in a delirious daze.

"Wait!" Leona called. She got down off Mule and hobbled after Josh. "Hold up a minute!"

Swan set her bag down but kept hold of Crybaby and followed Leona. Behind her, Mule plodded along. The terrier barked a couple of times, then slipped under an abandoned Volkswagen and stayed there, watching the humans moving across the parking lot.

"Wait!" Leona called again, but she couldn't keep pace with him, and he was heading for the K-Mart like a steam engine. Swan said, "Josh! Wait for us!" and she hurried to catch him.

Some of the windows were broken out of the K-Mart, but Josh figured the wind had done that. He had no idea why the lights were on there and nowhere else. The K-Mart and the supermarket next to it were akin to waterholes in a burning desert. His heart was about to blast through his chest. Candy bars! he thought wildly. Cookies! Glazed doughnuts! He feared his legs would collapse before he reached the K-Mart, or that the entire vision would tremble and dissolve as he went through one of the front doors. But it didn't, and he did, and there he stood inside the huge store with the treasures of the world on racks and displays before him, the magic phrases *Snacks and Candy* and *Sporting Goods* and *Automotives* and *Housewares* on wooden arrows pointing to various sections of the store.

"My God," Josh said, half drunk with ecstasy. "Oh, my God!"

Swan came in, then Leona. As the door was swinging shut a blurred form darted in, and the terrier shot past Josh and vanished along the center aisle. Then the door shut, and they stood together in the glare while Mule whinnied and pawed the concrete outside.

Josh strode past a display of outdoor grills and bags of charcoal to a counter full of candy bars, his desire for chocolate fanned to a fever. He sucked three Milky Ways right out of their wrappers and started on a half-pound bag of M&Ms. Leona went to a table piled with thick athletic socks. Swan wandered amid the counters, dazzled by the amount of merchandise and the brightness of the lights. His mouth crammed with gooey chocolate, Josh turned to a display of cigarettes, cigars and pipe tobacco; he chose a pack of Hav-A-Tampa Jewels, found some matches nearby, stuck one of the cigars between his teeth and lit it, inhaling deeply. He felt as if he'd stepped into paradise, and the pleasures of the supermarket were yet to be experienced. From far back in the store, the terrier yapped several times in rapid succession. Swan looked back along the aisle but couldn't see the dog. She didn't like the sound of that barking, though; it carried a warning, and as the terrier began to bark again she heard it yip as if it had been kicked. A barrage of barking followed.

"Josh?" Swan called. A cocoon of cigar smoke obscured his head.

He puffed on the stogie and chewed more candy bars. His mouth was so full he couldn't even answer Swan; he just waved to her.

Swan walked slowly toward the back of the store as the terrier continued to bark. She came to three mannequins, all wearing suits. The one in the middle had on a blue baseball cap, and Swan thought it didn't go at all with the suit, but it might be made to fit her own head. She reached up and plucked it off.

The entire waxen-fleshed head toppled from the mannequin's shoulders, right out of the stiff white shirt collar, and fell to the floor at Swan's feet with a sound like a hammer whacking a watermelon.

Swan stared, wide-eyed, the baseball cap in one hand and Crybaby in the other. The head had thinning gray hair and dark-socketed eyes that had rolled upward, and on its cheeks and chin was a stubble of gray whiskers. Now she could see the dried red matter and the yellow nub of bone where it had been hacked off the human neck.

She blinked and looked up at the other two mannequins. One of them had the head of a teenage boy, his mouth slack and tongue lolling, both eyeballs turned to the ceiling and a crust of blood at the nostrils. The third one's head was that of an elderly man, his face heavily lined and the color of chalk.

Swan stepped back across the aisle—and hit a fourth and fifth mannequin, dressed in women's clothes. The severed heads of a middle-aged woman and a little girl with red hair fell out of the collars and thumped to the floor on either side of her; the little girl's face was directed up at Swan, the awful blood-drained mouth open in a soundless cry of terror.

Swan screamed. Screamed long and loud and couldn't stop screaming. She backpedaled away from the human heads, still screaming, and as she spun around she saw another mannequin nearby, and another and another, some of the heads beaten and battered and the others painted and prettied with makeup to give them false and obscene smiles. She thought that if she couldn't stop screaming her lungs would burst, and as she ran for Josh and Leona the scream died because all her air was gone. She pulled in breath and raced away from the grisly heads, and over Josh's shouts she heard the terrier give a yipe-yipe-yipe of pain from the rear of the K-Mart.

"Swan!" Josh yelled, spitting out half-chewed candy. He saw her coming toward him, her face as yellow as the Kansas dust and tears streaming down her cheeks. "What is—"

"Blue Light Special!" a merry voice sang over the K-Mart's intercom system. "Attention, shoppers! Blue Light Special! Three new arrivals at the front! Hurry for the best bargains!"

They heard the rough roar of a motorcycle's engine firing. Josh scooped Swan up as a motorcycle hurtled at them along the center aisle, its driver dressed like a traffic cop except for his Indian headdress.

"Look out!" Leona shouted, and Josh leaped across a counter full of ice cube trays with Swan in his arms, the motorcycle skidding past them into a display of transistor radios. More figures were running toward them along the other aisles, and there was an ungodly whooping and hollering that drowned out the "Blue Light Special!" being repeated over the intercom.

Here came a mountainous, black-bearded man pushing a gnarled dwarf in a shopping cart, followed by other men of all ages and descriptions, wearing all kinds of clothing from suits to bathrobes, some of them with streaks of warpaint on their faces, others daubed white with powder. Josh realized—sickeningly—that most of them were carrying weapons: axes, picks, hoes, garden shears, pistols and rifles, knives and chains. The aisles were acrawl with them, and they jumped over the counters grinning and yelling. Josh, Swan and Leona were driven together and ringed by a shouting mob of forty or more men.

Protect the child! Josh thought, and as one of the men darted in to grab Swan's arm Josh delivered a kick to his ribs that snapped bones and sent him flying back into the rabble. The move brought more gleeful cheers. The gnarled dwarf in the shopping cart, whose wrinkled face was decorated with orange lightning bolts, crowed, "Fresh meat! Fresh meat!"

The others took up the shout. An emaciated man plucked at Leona's hair, and someone else grabbed her arm to pull her into the crowd. She became a wildcat, kicking and biting, driving her tormentors back. A heavy body landed on Josh's shoulders, raking at his eyes, but he twisted and flung the man off into the sea of leering faces. Swan struck out with Crybaby, hit one of those ugly faces in the nose and saw it pop open.

"Fresh meat!" the dwarf yelled. "Come get your fresh meat!" The black-bearded man began to clap his hands and dance.

Josh hit someone square in the mouth, and two teeth flew like dice in a crap game. "Get away!" he roared. "Get away from us!" But they were closing in now, and there were just too many. Three men were pulling Leona into the throng, and Josh caught a glimpse of her terrified face; a fist rose and fell, and Leona's legs buckled. Damn it! Josh raged, kicking the nearest maniac in the kneecap. Protect the child! I've got to protect the—

A fist struck him in the kidneys. His legs were kicked out from under him, and he lost his grip on Swan as he fell. Fingers gouged at his eyes, a fist crashed into his jaw, shoes and boots pummeled his sides and back and the whole world seemed to be in violent motion. "Swan!" he shouted, trying to get up. Men clung to him like rats.

He looked up through a red haze of pain and saw a man with bulging, fishlike eyes standing over him, lifting an axe. He flung his arm up in an ineffectual gesture to ward it off, but he knew the axe was about to fall, and that would be the end of it. Oh, damn! he thought as blood trickled from his mouth. What a way to go! He braced for the blow, hoping that he could stand up with his last strength and knock the bastard's brains out.

The axe reached its zenith, poised to fall.

And a booming voice shouted over the tumult: "*Cease!*"

The effect was like a bullwhip being cracked over the heads of wild animals. Almost to a man, they flinched and drew back. The fish-eyed man lowered the axe, and the others released Josh. He sat up, saw Swan a few feet away and drew her to him; she was still holding onto Crybaby, her eyes swimming with shock. Leona was on her knees nearby, blood oozing from a cut above her left eye and a purple swelling coming up on her cheekbone.

The mob backed away, opened to make passage for someone. A heavyset, fleshy, bald-headed man in overalls and cowboy boots, his chest bare and his muscular arms decorated with weird multicolored designs, walked into the circle. He was carrying an electric bullhorn, and he looked down at Josh with dark eyes beneath a protruding Neanderthal brow.

Oh, shit! Josh thought. The guy was at least as big as some of the heavyweight wrestlers he'd grappled. But then behind the bald-headed Neanderthal came two other men with painted faces, supporting a toilet between them, hoisted up on their shoulders. And on that toilet sat a man draped in a deep purple robe, his hair a blond, shoulder-length mane of loose curls. He had a downy beard of fine blond hair covering a gaunt, narrow face, and under thick blond brows his eyes were murky olive-green. The color reminded Josh of the water of a swimming hole near his childhood home where two young boys had drowned on a summer morning. It was said, he recalled, that monsters lay coiled in wait at the bottom of that cloudy green water.

The young man, who might have been anywhere from twenty to twenty-five, wore white gloves, blue jeans, Adidas sneakers and a red plaid shirt. On his forehead was a green dollar sign; on his left cheekbone was a red crucifix, and on his right was a black devil's pitchfork.

The Neanderthal lifted the bullhorn to his mouth and roared, "All shall praise Lord Alvin!"

Forty

Macklin had heard the siren song of screaming in the night, and now he knew it was time.

He eased out of his sleeping bag, careful not to jostle Roland or Sheila; he didn't want either of them to go with him. He was afraid of the pain, and he didn't want them to see him weak.

Macklin walked out of the tent into the cold, sweeping wind. He began to head in the direction of the lake. Torches and campfires flickered all around him, and the wind tugged at the greenish-black bandages that trailed off the stump of Macklin's right wrist. He could smell the sickly odor of his own infection, and for days the wound had been oozing gray fluid. He put his left palm over the handle of the knife in the waistband of his trousers. He was going to have to open the wound again and expose the flesh to the healing agony of the Great Salt Lake.

Behind him, Roland Croninger had sat up as soon as Macklin left the tent. The .45 was gripped in his hand. He always slept with it, even kept hold of it when Sheila Fontana let him do the dirty thing to her. He liked to watch, also, when Sheila took the King on. In turn, they fed Sheila and protected her from the other men. They were becoming a very close trio. But now he knew where the King was going, and why. The King's wound had been smelling very bad lately. Soon there would be another scream in the night, like the others they heard when the encampment got quiet. He was a King's Knight, and he thought he should be at the King's side to help him, but this was something the King wanted to do alone. Roland lay back down, the pistol resting on his chest. Sheila muttered something and flinched in her sleep. Roland listened for the cry of the King's rebirth.

Macklin passed other tents, cardboard box shelters and cars that housed whole families. The smell of the salt lake stung his nostrils, promised a pain and a cleansing beyond anything Macklin had ever experienced. The land began to slope slightly downward toward the water's edge, and lying on the ground around him were blood-caked clothes, rags, crutches and bandages torn off and discarded by other supplicants before him.

He remembered the screams he'd heard in the night, and his nerve faltered. He stopped less than twenty feet from where the lake rippled up over the rocky shore. His phantom hand was itching, and the stump throbbed painfully with his heartbeat. I can't take it, he thought. Oh, dear God, I *can't!*

"Discipline and control, mister," a voice said, off to his right. The Shadow Soldier was standing there, white, bony hands on hips, the moonlike face streaked with commando greasepaint under the helmet's rim. "You lose those, and what have you got?"

Macklin didn't answer. The lapping of the water on the shore was both seductive and terrifying.

"Your nerve going bye-bye, Jimmy boy?" the Shadow Soldier asked, and Macklin thought that the voice was similar to his father's. It carried the same note of taunting disgust. "Well, I'm not surprised," the Shadow Soldier continued. "You sure pulled a royal fuckup at Earth House, didn't you? Oh, you really did a fine job!"

"No!" Macklin shook his head. "It wasn't my fault!"

The Shadow Soldier laughed quietly. "You *knew,* Jimmy boy. You knew something was wrong in Earth House, and you kept packing the suckers in because you smelled the green of the Ausley cash, didn't you? Man, you *killed* all those poor chumps! You buried 'em under a few hundred tons of rock and saved your own ass, didn't you?"

Now Macklin thought it really was his father's voice, and he thought that the Shadow Soldier's face was beginning to resemble the fleshy, hawk-nosed face of his long-dead father as well. "I had to save myself," Macklin replied, his voice weak. "What was I supposed to do, lie down and die?"

"Shit, that kid's got more sense and guts than you do, Jimmy boy! He's the one who got you out! He kept you moving, and he found food to keep your ass alive! If it wasn't for that kid, you wouldn't be standing here right now shaking in your shoes because you're afraid of a little pain! That kid knows the meaning of discipline and control, Jimmy boy! You're just a tired old cripple who ought to go out in that lake, duck your head under and take a quick snort like they did." The Shadow Soldier nodded toward the lake, where the bloated bodies of suicides floated in the brine. "You used to think being head honcho at Earth House was the bottom of the barrel. But *this* is the bottom, Jimmy boy. Right here. You're not worth a shit, and you've lost your nerve."

"No I haven't!" Macklin said. "I . . . haven't."

A hand gestured toward the Great Salt Lake. "Prove it."

Roland sensed someone outside the tent. He sat up, clicking the safety off the automatic. Sometimes the men came around at night, sniffing for Sheila, and they had to be scared off.

A flashlight shone in his face, and he aimed the pistol at the figure who held it.

"Hold it," the man said. "I don't want any trouble."

Sheila cried out and sat bolt upright, her eyes wild. She drew herself away from the man with the light. She'd been having that nightmare again, of Rudy shambling to the tent, his face bleached of blood and the wound at his throat gaping like a hideous mouth, and from between his purple lips came a rattling voice that asked, "Killed any babies lately, Sheila darlin'?"

"You'll get trouble if you don't back off." Roland's eyes were fierce behind the goggles. He held the pistol steady, his finger poised on the trigger.

"It's me. Judd Lawry." He shone the flashlight on his own face. "See?"

"What do you want?"

Lawry pointed the light at Macklin's empty sleeping bag. "Where'd the Colonel go?"

"Out. What do you want?"

"Mr. Kempka wants to talk to you."

"What about? I delivered the ration last night."

"He wants to talk," Lawry said. "He says he's got a deal for you."

"A deal? What kind of deal?"

"A business proposal. I don't know the details. You'll have to see him."

"I don't *have* to do anything," Roland told him. "And whatever it is can wait until daylight."

"Mr. Kempka," Lawry said firmly, "wants to do business right *now*. It's not important that Macklin be there. Mr. Kempka wants to deal with *you*. He thinks you've got a good head on your shoulders. So are you coming or not?"

"Not."

Lawry shrugged. "Okay, then, I guess I'll tell him you're not interested." He started to back out of the tent, then stopped. "Oh, yeah: He wanted me to give you this." And he dropped a boxful of Hershey bars on the ground in front of Roland. "He's got plenty of stuff like that over in the trailer."

"Jesus!" Sheila's hand darted into the box and plucked out some of the chocolate bars. "Man, it's been a long time since I've had one of these!"

"I'll tell him what you said," Lawry told Roland, and again he started to leave the tent.

"Wait a minute!" Roland blurted out. "What kind of deal does he want to talk about?"

"Like I say, you'll have to see him to find out."

Roland hesitated, but he figured whatever it was couldn't hurt. "I don't go anywhere without the gun," he said.

"Sure, why not?"

Roland got out of his sleeping bag and stood up. Sheila, already finishing one of the chocolate bars, said, "Hey, hold on! What about me?"

"Mr. Kempka just wants the boy."

"Kiss my ass! I'm not staying out here alone!"

Lawry shrugged the strap of his shotgun off his shoulder and handed it to her. "Here. And don't blow your head off by accident."

She took it, realizing too late that it was the same weapon he'd used to kill the infant. Still, she wouldn't dare be left out there alone without a gun. Then she turned her attention to the box of Hershey bars, and Roland followed Judd Lawry to the Airstream trailer, where yellow lantern light crept through the slats of the drawn window blinds.

On the edge of the lake, Macklin took off his black overcoat and the filthy, bloodstained T-shirt he wore. Then he began to unwrap the bandages from the stump of his wrist as the Shadow Soldier watched in silence. When he was done, he let the bandages fall. The wound was not pretty to look at, and the Shadow Soldier whistled at the sight.

"Discipline and control, mister," the Shadow Soldier said. "That's what makes a man."

Those were the exact words of Macklin's father. He had grown up hearing them pounded into his head, had fashioned them into a motto to live by. Now, though, to make himself walk into that salty water and do what had to be done was going to take every ounce of discipline and control he could summon.

The Shadow Soldier said in a singsong voice, "Hup two three four, hup two three four! Get it in gear, mister!"

Oh, Jesus, Macklin breathed. He stood with his eyes tightly shut for a few seconds. His entire body shook with the cold wind and his own dread. Then he took the knife from his waistband and walked down toward the chuckling water.

"Sit down, Roland," the Fat Man said as Lawry escorted Roland into the trailer. A chair had been pulled up in front of the table that Kempka sat behind. "Shut the door."

Lawry obeyed him, and Roland sat down. He kept his hand on the pistol, and the pistol in his lap.

Kempka's face folded into a smile. "Would you like something to drink? Pepsi? Coke? Seven-Up? How about something stronger?" He laughed in his high, shrill voice, and his many chins wobbled. "You *are* of legal age, aren't you?"

"I'll take a Pepsi."

"Ah. Good. Judd, would you get us two Pepsis, please?"

Lawry got up and went to another room, which Roland figured must be a kitchen.

"What'd you want to see me about?" Roland asked.

"A business deal. A proposition." Kempka leaned back, and his chair popped and creaked like fireworks going off. He wore an open-collared sport shirt that showed wiry brown hair on his flabby chest, and his belly flopped over the belt line of his lime-green polyester trousers. Kempka's hair had been freshly pomaded and combed, and the interior of the trailer smelled like cheap, sweet cologne. "You strike me as a very intelligent young boy, Roland. Young *man*, I should say." He grinned. "I could tell right off that you had intelligence. And fire, too. Oh, yes! I like young men with fire." He glanced at the pistol Roland held. "You can put that aside, you know. I want to be your friend."

"That's nice." Roland kept the pistol aimed in Freddie Kempka's direction. On the wall behind the Fat Man, the many rifles and handguns on their hooks caught the baleful yellow lamplight.

"Well," Kempka shrugged, "we can talk anyway. Tell me about yourself. Where are you from? What happened to your parents?"

My parents, Roland thought. What had happened to them? He remembered them all going into Earth House together, remembered the earthquake in the cafeteria, but everything else was still crazy and disjointed. He couldn't even recall exactly what his mother and father had looked like. They had died in the cafeteria, he thought. Yes. Both of them had been buried under rock. He was a King's Knight now, and there was no turning back. "That's not important," he decided to say. "Is *that* what you wanted to talk about?"

"No, it's not. I wanted to—ah, here are our refreshments!"

Lawry came in with Pepsis in two plastic glasses; he set one glass in front of Kempka and handed Roland the other. Lawry started to walk behind Roland, but the boy said sharply, "Stay in front of me while I'm in here," and Lawry stopped. The man smiled, lifted his hands in a gesture of peace and sat on a pile of boxes against the wall.

"As I say, I like young men with fire." Kempka sipped at his drink. It had been a long time since Roland had tasted a soft drink, and he chugged almost half the glassful down without stopping. The drink had lost most of its fizz, but it was still about the best stuff he'd ever tasted.

"So what is it?" Roland asked. "Something about the drugs?"

"No, nothing about that." He smiled again, a fleeting smile. "I want to know about Colonel Macklin." He leaned forward, and the chair squalled; he rested his forearms on the table and laced his thick fingers together. "I want to know . . . what Macklin offers you that *I* can't."

"What?"

"Look around," Kempka said. "Look what I've got here: food, drink, candy, guns, bullets—and *power,* Roland. What does Macklin have? A wretched little tent. And do you know what? That's all he'll ever have. I *run* this community, Roland. I guess you could say I'm the law, the mayor, the judge and the jury all rolled up into one! Right?" He glanced quickly at Lawry, and the other man said, "Right," with the conviction of a ventriloquist's dummy.

"So what does Macklin do for you, Roland?" Kempka lifted his eyebrows. "Or should I ask what *you* do for him?"

Roland almost told the Fat Man that Macklin was the King—shorn of his crown and kingdom now, but destined to return to power someday—and that he had pledged himself as a King's Knight, but he figured Kempka was about as smart as a bug and wouldn't understand the grand purpose of the game. So Roland said, "We travel together."

"And where are you going? To the same garbage dump Macklin is headed toward? No, I think you're smarter than that."

"What do you mean?"

"I mean . . . that I have a large and comfortable trailer, Roland. I have a *real* bed." He nodded toward a closed door. "It's right through there. Would you like to see it?"

It suddenly dawned on Roland what Freddie Kempka had been getting at. "No," he said, his gut tightening. "I wouldn't."

"Your friend can't offer you what I can, Roland," Kempka said in a silken voice. "He has no power. I have it all. Do you think I let you in here just because of the drugs? No. I want *you*, Roland. I want you here, with me."

Roland shook his head. Dark motes seemed to spin before his eyes, and his head felt heavy, as if he couldn't balance it any longer on his neck.

"You're going to find that power rules this world." Kempka's voice sounded to Roland like a record played too fast. "It's the only thing that's worth a damn anymore. Not beauty, not love—nothing but power. And the man who has it can take anything he wants."

"Not me," Roland said. The words felt like marbles rolling off his tongue. He thought he was about to puke, and there was a needles-and-pins sensation in his legs. The lamplight was hurting his eyes, and when he blinked it took an effort to lift his lids again. He looked down into the plastic glass he held, and he could see grainy things floating at the bottom. He tried to stand up, but his legs gave way and he fell to his knees on the floor. Someone was bending over him, and he felt the .45 being taken from his nerveless fingers. Too late, he tried to grasp it back, but Lawry was grinning and stepping out of reach.

"I found a use for some of those drugs you brought me." Now Kempka's voice was slow and murky, an underwater slur. "I mashed up a few of those pills and made a nice little mixture. I hope you enjoy your trip." And the Fat Man began to rise ponderously from his chair and stalk across the room toward Roland Croninger while Lawry went outside to smoke a cigarette.

Roland shivered, though sweat was bursting out on his face, and scurried away from the man on his hands and knees. His brain was doing flip-flops, everything was lurching, speeding up and then slowing to a crawl. The whole trailer wobbled as Kempka went to the door and threw the latches. Roland squeezed himself into a corner like a trapped animal, and when he tried to shout for the King to help him his voice almost blew his eardrums out.

"Now," Kempka said, "we'll get to know each other better, won't we?"

Macklin stood in cold water up to the middle of his thighs, the wind whipping into his face and wailing off beyond the encampment. His groin crawled, and his hand gripped the knife so hard his knuckles had gone bone-white. He looked at the infected wound, saw the dark swelling that he needed to probe with the knife's gleaming tip. Oh, God, he thought; dear God, help me. . . .

"Discipline and control." The Shadow Soldier was standing behind him. "That's what makes a man, Jimmy boy."

My father's voice, Macklin thought. God bless dear old Dad, and I hope the worms have riddled his bones.

"Do it!" the Shadow Soldier commanded.

Macklin lifted the knife, took aim, drew in a breath of frigid air and brought the point of the blade down, down, down into the festered swelling.

The pain was so fierce, so white-hot, so all-consuming that it was almost pleasure.

Macklin threw back his head and screamed, and as he screamed he dug the blade deeper into the infection, deeper still, and the tears were running down his face and he was on fire between pain and pleasure. He felt his right arm becoming lighter as the infection drained out of it. And as his scream went up into the night where the other screams had gone before his, Macklin threw himself forward into the salt water and immersed the wound.

"Ah!" The Fat Man stopped a few feet from Roland and cocked his head toward the door. Kempka's face was flushed, his eyes shining. The scream was just drifting away. "Listen to that music!" he said. "That's the sound of somebody being reborn." He began to unbuckle his belt and draw it through the many loops of his huge waistband.

The images tumbling through Roland's brain were a mixture of funhouse and haunted house. In his mind he was hacking at the wrist of the King's right arm, and as the blade severed the hand a spray of blood-red flowers shot from the wound; a chorus line of mangled corpses in top hats and tuxedos kicked their way down the wrecked corridor of Earth House; he and the King were walking on a superhighway under a sullen scarlet sky, and the trees were made of bones and the lakes were steaming blood, and half-rotted remnants of human beings sped past in battered cars and tractor-trailer trucks; he was standing on a mountaintop as the gray clouds boiled above him. Below, armies fought with knives, rocks and broken bottles. A cold hand touched his shoulder and a voice whispered, "It can all be yours, Sir Roland."

He was afraid to turn his head and look at the thing that stood behind him, but he knew he must. The power of hideous hallucination forced his head around, and he stared into a pair of eyes that wore Army surplus goggles. The flesh of that face was mottled with brown, leprous growths, the lips all but eaten away to reveal misshapen, fanged teeth. The nose was flat, the nostrils wide and ravaged. The face was his own, but distorted, ugly, reeking evil and bloodlust. And from that face his own voice whispered, "It can all be yours, Sir Roland—and mine, too."

Towering over the boy, Freddie Kempka tossed his belt to the floor and began to shimmy out of his polyester trousers. His breathing sounded like the rumbling of a furnace.

Roland blinked, squinted up at the Fat Man. The hallucinatory visions were tumbling madly away, but he could still hear the thing's whisper. He was shaking, couldn't stop. Another vision whirled up from his mind, and he was on the ground, trembling as Mike Armbruster towered over him, about to beat him to a bloody pulp as the other high school kids and football jocks shouted and jeered. He saw Mike Armbruster's crooked grin, and Roland felt a surge of maniacal hatred more powerful than anything he'd ever known. Mike Armbruster had already beaten him once, had already kicked him and spat on him as he was sobbing in the dust—and now he wanted to do it all over again.

But Roland knew he was far different—far stronger, far more cunning—than the little pansy-assed wimp who'd let himself be beaten until he'd peed in his pants. He was a King's Knight now, and he'd seen the underside of Hell. He was about to show Mike Armbruster how a King's Knight gets even.

Kempka had one leg out of his pants. He was wearing red silk boxer shorts. The boy was staring up at him, eyes slitted behind those damned goggles, and now the boy began to make a deep, animalish sound down in his throat, a cross between a growl and an unearthly moan.

"Stop that," Kempka told him. That noise gave him the creeps. The boy didn't stop, and the awful sound was getting louder. "Stop it, you little bastard!" He saw the boy's face changing, tightening into a mask of utter, brutal hatred, and the sight of it scared the shit out of Freddie Kempka. He realized that the mind-altering drugs were doing something to Roland Croninger that he hadn't counted on. "Stop it!" he shouted, and he lifted his hand to slap Roland across the face.

Roland leaped forward, and like a battering ram his head plowed into Kempka's bulging stomach. The Fat Man cried out and fell backward, his arms windmilling. The trailer rocked back and forth, and before Kempka could recover, Roland plowed into him again with a force that sent Kempka crashing to the floor. Then the boy was all over him, punching and kicking and biting. Kempka shouted, "Lawry! Help me!" but even as he said it he remembered that he had double-bolted the door to keep the boy from escaping. Two fingers jabbed into his left eye and almost ripped it from the socket; a fist crunched into his nose, and Roland's head came forward in a vicious butting blow that hit Kempka full in the mouth, split his lips and knocked two of his front teeth into his throat. *"Help me!"* he shrieked, his mouth full of blood. He hit Roland with a flailing forearm and swiped him off, then flopped over on his stomach and began to crawl toward that locked door. *"Help me, Lawry!"* he yelled through his cracked lips.

Something went around Kempka's throat and tightened, catching the blood in the Fat Man's head and reddening his face like an overripe tomato. He realized, panic-stricken, that the lunatic boy was strangling him with his own belt.

Roland rode on Kempka's back like Ahab on the white whale. Kempka gagged, fighting to pry the belt loose. The blood pulsed in his head with a force that he feared would blow his eyeballs out. There was a hammering at the door, and Lawry's voice shouted, "Mr. Kempka! What is it?"

The Fat Man reared up, twisted his shuddering body and slammed Roland against the wall, but still the boy held on. Kempka's lungs strained for air, and again he threw his body to the side. This time he heard the boy's cry of pain, and the belt loosened. Kempka squalled like a hurt pig, scrabbling wildly toward the door. He reached up to release one of the latches—and a chair smashed him across the back, splintering and shooting agony up his spine. Then the boy was beating at him with a chair leg, hitting him in the head and face, and Kempka screamed, "He's gone crazy! He's gone crazy!"

Lawry pounded at the door. "Let me in!"

Kempka took a dazing blow to the forehead, felt blood running down his face, and he struck out blindly at Roland. His left fist connected, and he heard the breath whoosh out of the boy. Roland collapsed to his knees.

Kempka wiped blood out of his eyes, reached up and tried to slide the first bolt back. There was blood on his fingers, and he couldn't get a good grip. Lawry was pounding on the door, trying to force it open. "He's crazy!" Kempka wailed. "He's trying to kill me!"

"Hey, you dumb fuck!" the boy snarled behind him.

Kempka looked back and whined with terror.

Roland had picked up one of the kerosene lamps that illuminated the trailer. He was grinning madly, his goggles streaked with blood. "Here you go, Mike!" he yelled, and he flung the lamp.

It hit the Fat Man's skull and shattered, dousing his face and chest with kerosene that rippled into flame, setting his beard, hair and the front of his sport shirt on fire. "Burnin' me! Burnin' me!" Kempka squalled, rolling and thrashing.

The door shuddered as Lawry kicked it, but the Airstream trailer people had built it to be strong.

As Kempka jitterbugged horizontally and Lawry kicked at the door, Roland turned his attention to the rack of rifles and the handguns on their hooks. He had not finished showing Mike Armbruster how a King's Knight gets even. Oh, no . . . not yet.

He walked around the table and chose a beautiful .38 Special with a mother-of-pearl handle. He opened the cylinder and found three bullets inside. He smiled.

On the floor, the Fat Man had beaten the fire out. His face was a mass of scorched flesh, burned hair and blisters, his eyes so swollen he could hardly see. But he could see the boy well enough, approaching him with the gun in his hand. The boy was smiling, and Kempka opened his mouth to scream, but a croak came out.

Roland knelt in front of him. The boy's face was covered with sweat, and a pulse beat at his temple. He cocked the .38 and held the barrel about three inches from Kempka's skull.

"Please," Kempka begged. "Please . . . Roland . . . don't . . ."

Roland's smile was rigid, his eyes huge behind the goggles. He said, "*Sir* Roland. And don't you forget it."

Lawry heard a shot. Then, about ten seconds later, there was a second shot. He gripped the boy's automatic in his right hand and threw his shoulder against the door. It still wouldn't give. He kicked at it again, but the damned thing was stubborn. He was about to start shooting through the door when he heard the bolts being thrown back.

The door opened.

The boy was standing there, a .38 dangling in his hand,

gore splattered across his face and in his hair. He was grinning, and he said in a fast, excited, drugged voice, "It's over I did it I did it I showed him how a King's Knight gets even I did it!"

Lawry lifted the automatic to blow the boy away.

But the twin barrels of a shotgun probed the back of his neck.

"Uh-uh," Sheila Fontana said. She'd heard the commotion and had come over to see what was happening, and other people were coming through the dark as well, carrying lanterns and flashlights. "Drop it or you get dropped."

The automatic hit the ground.

"Don't kill me," Lawry whimpered. "Okay? I just worked for Mr. Kempka. That's all. I just did what he said. Okay?"

"Want me to kill him?" Sheila asked Roland. The boy just stared and grinned. He's shitfaced, she thought. He's either drunk or stoned!

"Listen, I don't care what the kid did to Kempka." Lawry's voice cracked. "He wasn't anything to me. I just drove for him. Just followed his orders. Listen, I can do the same for you, if you want. You, the kid and Colonel Macklin. I can take care of things for you—keep everybody around here in line. I'll do whatever you say to do. You say jump, I'll ask how high."

"I showed him I sure did," Roland rattled on, beginning to weave on his feet. "I *showed* him!"

"Listen, you and the kid and Colonel Macklin are the head honchos around here, as far as I can see," Lawry told Sheila. "I mean . . . if Kempka's dead."

"Let's go take a look, then." Sheila poked his neck with the shotgun, and Lawry eased past Roland into the trailer.

They found the Fat Man crumpled in a bloody heap against one wall. There was the smell of burnt skin in the air. Kempka had been shot through the skull and through the heart at close range.

"All the guns, the food and everything are yours now," Lawry said. "I just do what I'm told. You just tell me what to do, I'll do it. I swear to God."

"Drag that fat carcass out of our trailer, then."

Startled, Sheila looked toward the door.

Macklin stood there, leaning against the doorframe, shirtless and dripping. The black overcoat was draped over his shoulders, the stump of his right arm hidden in its folds. His face was pale, his eyes sunken in violet hollows. Roland stood beside him, weaving and swaying, about to collapse. "I don't know . . . what the hell happened here," Macklin said, speaking with an effort, "but if everything belongs to us now . . . we're moving into the trailer. Get that *thing* out of here."

Lawry looked stricken. "By *myself?* I mean . . . he's gonna be damned heavy!"

"Either drag him or join him."

Lawry went to work.

"And clean up this mess when you get through," Macklin told him, going over to the rack of rifles and handguns. God, what an arsenal! he thought. He had no idea what had transpired here, but Kempka was dead and somehow they were in control. The trailer was theirs, the food, the water, the arsenal, the whole encampment was theirs! He was stunned, still exhausted by the pain he'd endured—but he felt somehow stronger, too, somehow . . . *cleaner*. He felt like a man again instead of a sniveling, scared dog. Colonel James B. Macklin had been reborn.

Lawry had almost manhandled the corpse to the door. "I can't make it!" he protested, trying to catch his breath. "He's too heavy!"

Macklin whirled around and walked toward Lawry, stopping only when their faces were about four inches apart. Macklin's eyes were bloodshot, and they bored into the other man's with furious intensity. "You listen to me, slime," Macklin said menacingly. Lawry listened. "I'm in charge here now. *Me*. What I say goes, without question. I'm going to teach you about discipline and control, mister. I'm going to teach *everybody* about discipline and control. There will be *no* questions, no hesitations when I give an order, or there *will* be . . . executions. Public executions. You care to be the first?"

"No," Lawry said in a small, scared voice.

"No . . . *what?*"

"No . . . sir," was the reply.

"Good. But you spread the word around, Lawry. I'm going to get these people organized and off their asses. If they don't like my way of doing things, they can get out."

"Organized? Organized for *what?*"

"You think there won't come a time when we'll have to *fight* to keep what we've got? Mister, there are going to be plenty of times we'll have to fight—if not to keep what we have, then . . . to take what we want."

"We're not any fucking army!" Lawry said.

"You will be," Macklin promised, and he motioned toward the arsenal. "You're going to learn to be, mister. And so is everybody else. Now get that piece of shit out of here . . . *Corporal.*"

"Huh?"

"Corporal Lawry. That's your new rank. And you'll be living in the tent out there. This trailer is for headquarters staff."

Oh, Christ! Lawry thought. This guy's gone wacko! But he kind of liked the idea of being a corporal. That sounded important. He turned away from the colonel and started hauling Kempka's body again. A funny thought hit him, and he almost giggled, but he held it back. The king is dead! he thought. Long live the king! He hauled the corpse down the steps, and the trailer door shut. He saw several men standing around, attracted by all the ruckus, and he began barking orders at them to pick up Freddie Kempka's corpse and carry it out to the edge of the dirtwart land. They obeyed him like automatons, and Judd Lawry figured he might grow to enjoy playing soldiers.

"Not a thing."

"No . . . sir," was the reply.

"Good. But you spread the word around, Lawry. I'm going to get these people organized and off their asses. If they don't like my way of doing things, they can get out."

"Organize? Organized for what?"

"You think there won't come a time when we'll have to *fight* to keep what we've got? Mister, there are going to be plenty of times we'll have to fight—if not to keep what we have, then . . . to take what we want."

"We're not any fucking army!" Lawry said.

"You will be," Macklin promised, and he motioned toward the arsenal. "You're going to learn to be, mister. And so is everybody else. Now get that piece of shit out of here, Corporal."

"Huh?"

"Corporal Lawry. That's your new rank. And you'll be living in the tent out there. This trailer is for headquarters staff."

Oh, Christ! Lawry thought. This guy's gone wacko! But he kind of liked the idea of being a corporal. That sounded important. He turned away from the colonel and started hauling Kempka's body again. A funny thought hit him, and he almost giggled, but he held it back. The king is dead! he thought. Long live the king! He hauled the corpse down the steps, and the trailer door shut. He saw several men standing around, attracted by all the ruckus, and he began barking orders at them to pick up Freddie Kempka's corpse and carry it out to the edge of the [illegible] land. They obeyed him like automatons, and Lawry figured he might grow to enjoy playing soldiers.

SEVEN
Thinking About Tomorrow

Heads will roll / The straitjacket game / Suicide mission / My people / A smoky old glass / Christian in a Cadillac / Green froth

Forty-one

"My name is Alvin Mangrim. I'm Lord Alvin now. Welcome to my kingdom." The young blond madman, sitting on his toilet-throne, motioned with a slender hand. "Do you like it?"

Josh was sickened by the smell of death and decay. He, Swan and Leona were sitting together on the floor of the K-Mart's pet department at the rear of the store. In the small cages around them were dozens of dead canaries and parakeets, and dead fish lay moldering in their tanks. Beyond a glassed-in display area, a few kittens and puppies were drawing flies.

He longed to bash that grinning, blond-bearded face, but his wrists and ankles were chained and padlocked. Both Swan and Leona were bound by ropes. Around them stood the bald-headed Neanderthal, the man with bulging fish-eyes, and about six or seven others. The black-bearded man and the dwarf in the shopping cart lurked nearby, the dwarf clutching Swan's dowsing rod in his stubby fingers.

"I fixed the juice," Lord Alvin offered, reclining on his throne and eating grapes. "That's why the lights are on." His murky green eyes shifted from Josh to Swan and back again. Leona was still bleeding from the gash in her head, and her eyes fluttered as she fought off shock. "I hooked a couple of portable generators up to the electrical system. I've always been good with electricity. And I'm a very good carpenter, too. Jesus was a carpenter, you know." He spat out seeds. "Do you believe in Jesus?"

"Yes," Josh managed to croak.

"I do, too. I had a dog named Jesus once. I crucified him, but he didn't come back to life. Before he died, he told me what to do to the people in the brick house. Off went their heads."

Josh sat very still, looking up into those green, bottomless eyes.

Lord Alvin smiled, and for a moment he resembled a choirboy, all draped in purple and ready to sing. "I fixed the lights here so we'd attract plenty of fresh meat—like you folks. Plenty of play toys. See, everybody left us at Pathway. All the lights went out, and the doctors went home. But we found some of them, like Dr. Baylor. And then I baptized my disciples in the blood of Dr. Baylor and sent them out into the world, and the rest of us stayed here." He cocked his head to one side, and his smile faded. "It's dark outside," he said. "It's always dark, even in the daytime. What's your name, friend?"

Josh told him. He could smell his own scared sweat over the odor of dead animals.

"Josh," Lord Alvin repeated. He ate a grape. "Mighty Joshua. Blew those old walls of Jericho right fucking down, didn't you?" He smiled again and motioned at a young man with slicked-back black hair and red paint circling his eyes and mouth. The young man came forward, holding a jar of something.

Swan heard some of the men giggle with excitement. Her heart was still pounding, but the tears were gone now, and so was the molasses that had been jamming up her brain gears. She knew these crazy men had escaped from the Pathway place, and she knew that death was before her, sitting on a toilet. She wondered what had happened to Mule, and since she'd bumped into the mannequins—she shoved that memory quickly aside—there'd been no sight or sound of the terrier.

The young man with red paint on his face knelt in front of Josh, unscrewed the lid of the jar and revealed white greasepaint. He got a dab of the stuff on his forefinger and reached toward Josh's face; Josh jerked his head back, but the Neanderthal gripped Josh's skull and held it steady as the greasepaint was applied.

"You're going to look pretty, Josh," Lord Alvin told him. "You're going to enjoy this."

Through the waves of pain in her legs and the numbing frost of shock, Leona watched the greasepaint going on. She realized the young man was painting Josh's face to resemble a skull.

"I know a game," Lord Alvin said. "A game called Straitjacket. I made it up. Know why? Dr. Baylor said, 'Come on, Alvin! Come get your pill like a good boy,' and I had to walk down that long, stinking corridor every day." He held up two fingers. "*Twice* a day. I'm a very good carpenter, though." He paused, blinking slowly as if trying to get his thoughts back in whack. "I used to build dog houses. Not just ordinary dog houses. I built mansions and castles for dogs. I built a replica of the Tower of London for Jesus. That's where they chopped the heads of witches off." The corner of his left eye began ticking. He was silent, staring into space as the finishing touches were put to the greasepaint skull that covered Josh's face.

When the job was done, the Neanderthal released Josh's head. Lord Alvin finished his grapes and licked his fingers. "In the Straitjacket game," he said between licks, "you get taken to the front of the store. The lady and the kid stay here. Now, you get a choice—what do you want freed, your arms or your legs?"

"What's the point of this shit?"

Lord Alvin waggled an admonishing finger. "Arms or legs, Josh?"

I need my legs free, Josh reasoned. Then: no, I can always hop or hobble. I've got to have my arms free. No, my legs! It was impossible to decide without knowing what was going to happen. He hesitated, trying to think clearly. He felt Swan watching him; he looked at her, but she shook her head, could offer no help. "My legs," Josh finally said.

"Good. That didn't hurt, did it?" Again, there was a giggle and rustle of excitement from the onlookers. "Okay, you get taken up to the front and your legs are freed. Then you get five minutes to make it all the way through the store back here." He pulled up the right sleeve of his purple robe. On his arm were six wristwatches. "See, I can keep the time to the exact second. Five minutes from when I say go—and not one second more, Josh."

Josh released a sigh of relief. Thank God he'd chosen his legs to be freed! He could see himself crawling and hobbling through the K-Mart in this ridiculous farce!

"Oh, yes," Lord Alvin continued. "My subjects are going to try their best to kill you between the front of the store and here." He smiled cheerfully. "They'll be using knives, hammers, axes—everything except guns. See, guns wouldn't be fair. Now, don't worry too much: You can use the same things, if you find them—and if you can get your hands on them. Or you can use anything else to protect yourself with, but you won't find any guns out there. Not even a pellet rifle. Isn't that a fun game?"

Josh's mouth tasted like sawdust. He was afraid to ask, but he had to: "What . . . if I don't get back here . . . in five minutes?"

The dwarf jumped up and down in the shopping cart and pointed the dowsing rod at him like a jester's scepter. "Death! Death! Death!" he yelled.

"Thank you, Imp," Lord Alvin said. "Josh, you've seen my mannequins, haven't you? Aren't they pretty? So lifelike, too! Want to know how we make them?" He glanced up at someone behind Josh and nodded.

Immediately there was a guttural growl that ascended into a high-pitched whining. Josh smelled gasoline. He already knew what the sound was, and his gut clenched. He looked over his shoulder and saw the Neanderthal standing there holding a whirring chainsaw that was streaked and clumped with dried gore.

"If you don't beat the clock, friend Josh," Lord Alvin said, leaning forward, "the lady and the child will join my mannequin collection. Their heads will, I mean." He lifted a finger, and the chainsaw rattled to a halt.

"Heads will roll!" Imp jumped and grinned. "Heads will roll!"

"Of course," the madman in the purple robe added, "if they kill you out there, it won't matter very much, will it? We'd have to find a big body to go along with your head, wouldn't we? Well? Are we ready?"

"Ready!" Imp shouted.

"Ready!" the black-bearded brute said.

"Ready!" the others hollered, dancing and capering. "*Reaaaady!*"

Lord Alvin reached over and took the dowsing rod from Imp. He tossed it to the floor about three feet away. "Cross that line, friend Josh, and you shall know wonders."

He'll kill us anyway, Josh knew. But he had no choice; his eyes met Swan's. She stared at him calmly and resolutely, and she tried to send the thought "I believe in you" to him. He gritted his teeth. Protect the child. Yeah! I've done a damned fine job, haven't I?

The black-bearded man and another of the lunatics hauled Josh to his feet.

"Kick ass," Leona whispered, the pain in her skull all but blinding her.

Josh was half carried, half dragged out of the pet department, through the housewares, the sporting goods, and then out along the center aisle to the row of cash registers at the front. A third man was waiting, armed with a double-barreled shotgun and a ring of keys dangling from his belt. Josh was thrown to the floor, the breath whistling between his teeth, "Legs," he heard the bearded man say, and the one with the keys bent down to unsnap the padlocks.

Josh was aware of a steady roaring noise, and he looked at the windows. A torrential rain was falling, some of it sweeping in through the broken glass. There was no sign of the horse, and Josh hoped it would find a dry place to die in. God help us all! he thought. Though he hadn't seen any of the other maniacs when he was being brought to the front, he knew they were out there in the store—hiding, waiting, getting ready for the game to begin.

Protect the child. The rasping voice that had come from PawPaw's throat was fresh in his mind. *Protect the child.* He had to get across that line in five minutes, no matter what the crazy shitters threw at him. He would have to use all the moves he remembered from his football days, have to make those rusty knees young again. Oh, Lord, he prayed, if You ever smiled on a dumb fool, show those pearly whites right *now!*

The last padlock was unsnapped, and the chains were removed from Josh's legs. He was pulled to his feet, his wrists still shackled tightly together, the chain curled around his forearms and hands as well. He could open and close his left hand, but the right was balled shut and immobile. He looked toward the rear of the K-Mart, and his heart lurched; the damned place seemed as long as ten football fields.

In the pet department, Swan had laid her head on Leona's shoulder. The woman was breathing erratically, fighting to keep her eyes open. Swan knew Josh was going to do all he could to reach them, but she knew also that he might fail. Lord Alvin was smiling at her beatifically, like a saint's smile on a stained-glass window. He regarded the watches on his wrist, then pointed the electric bullhorn toward the front and blared, "Let the Straitjacket game start . . . *now!* Five minutes, friend Josh!"

Swan flinched and waited for what would be.

Forty-two

Josh jumped at the sound of the bullhorn. Before he could take one stride forward, an arm clamped around his neck from behind and started squeezing. It was old Blackbeard, he realized. Bastard's trying to nail me right off!

Instinctively, Josh threw his head backward in what was known as a "Reverse Coconut Butt" in the ring—but this time he let it go full-throttle. His skull smacked into Blackbeard's forehead, and suddenly the restraining arm was gone. Josh spun around to finish the job and found Blackbeard sitting on his ass, his eyes glazed and his forehead already purpling. The other lunatic swung the shotgun up. "Go," he ordered, and he grinned with green teeth.

Josh had no time to waste; he turned and started running full-bore along the center aisle.

He'd taken six long strides when a baseball bat swung out along the floor and clipped his right ankle. He fell, hit the floor on his belly and slid another eight feet across the linoleum. Instantly he twisted to face his attacker, who'd been hiding behind a counter of socks and underwear. The man, who wore a red football helmet, rose up and rushed Josh, swinging the bat for a game-ending home run.

Josh drew his knees to his chest, kicked out and up and caught the maniac right in the stomach with both feet, lifting him about four feet in the air. The man came down on his tailbone, and Josh scrambled up to kick him in the groin as if he were making a fifty-yard field goal. As the man contorted into a shivering ball, Josh got his left hand around the bat and snatched it up; he worked his grip down to the handle, and though he had no real leverage, at least he had a weapon. He turned to continue along the aisle—and faced a skinny dude with an axe and another bastard with a blue-painted face who was carrying a sledgehammer.

No *way!* Josh thought, and he darted along one of the other aisles, intending to swing toward the pet department from a different angle. He skidded into a female mannequin, and the brown-haired head tumbled off the shoulders to the floor.

"Four minutes, friend Josh!" Lord Alvin's voice announced.

A figure with an upraised butcher knife burst from amid a rack of dresses in Josh's path. Can't stop! Josh knew, unable to lock his knees in time. Instead, he plowed forward, threw himself off his feet in a body block that slammed into the knife wielder and drove him into the dress rack, which collapsed around them. The man struck with the knife, missed, struck again and snagged the blade in fabric. Josh got astride his chest and brought the bat's shaft down on the man's skull—once, twice and a third time. The body quivered as if plugged into an electric socket.

A stabbing pain hit Josh in the neck. He looked around and saw a dungareed, leering maniac holding a fishing rod. The line was taut between them, and Josh knew there was a hook in his skin. The lunatic fisherman wrenched on the rod as if he were landing a prize marlin, and the hook ripped out of Josh's neck. The rod was snapped again, the hook flashing toward Josh's face, but he ducked it and scrabbled out of the dresses, regaining his feet and running for the pet department again.

"Three minutes left, friend Josh!"

No! Josh thought. *No!* The bastard was cheating! Another minute couldn't have passed yet!

He sprinted past a well-dressed mannequin in the men's department—but suddenly the mannequin came to life and leapt on his back, fingers clawing at his eyes. He kept running as the man held on, the jagged fingernails carving Josh's cheeks, and ahead of him stood a lean, bare-chested black man with a screwdriver in one hand and a garbage can lid in the other.

Josh ran full steam at the waiting assassin, then abruptly stopped, sliding across the floor. He hunched over and spun his shoulders. The man on his back lost his grip and hurtled through the air, but Josh's aim was off. Instead of crashing into the black man, as Josh had hoped, the well-dressed lunatic sailed over a counter full of summer shirts and hit the floor.

The black man attacked, moving like a panther. Josh swung the bat, but the garbage can lid was there to deflect it. The screwdriver drove in at Josh's stomach; he twisted away, and the weapon grazed his ribs. They fought at close quarters, Josh desperately avoiding the thrusts of the screwdriver and trying vainly to get a good strike with his bat. As they grappled, Josh caught movement on both sides—more of them, coming in for the kill. He knew he was finished if he couldn't get away from this crazy bro, because a husky man with garden shears was almost upon him. The black man's teeth snapped at Josh's cheek; Josh saw his opening and dropped to his knees, scooting between the man's legs like a greased pig. When the bro whirled around, he was met by a blow that crumpled his face and knocked teeth through the air. He took two wobbly steps and fell like a tree.

Josh kept going, the breath wheezing in his lungs.

"Two minutes!" Lord Alvin crowed.

Faster! Josh urged himself. Faster, damn it! The pet department was still so far away, and the sonofabitch was rushing time! Protect the child! Got to protec—

A maniac with a white-powdered face rose up from behind a counter and slammed a tire iron across Josh's left shoulder. Josh cried out in pain and tumbled into a display of Quaker State oil cans, agony shooting from his shoulder to his fingertips. He'd lost the baseball bat; it was rolling across the aisle, way out of reach. The white-faced madman attacked him, flailing wildly with the tire iron while Josh fought in a frenzy. The tire iron smashed down beside Josh's head and burst one of the cans open, and then they were fighting like two animals, kill or be killed.

Josh caught the man in the ribs with a knee and drove him back, but he leapt in again. They rolled in motor oil across the floor, Josh's opponent squirming like an eel. And then the man was up on his feet; he charged Josh, the tire iron upraised for a blow to the skull.

But his shoes slipped out from under him in the oil, and he crashed to the floor on his back. At once Josh got astride him, one knee trapping the tire iron and the other knee pressed to the man's throat. He lifted both hands and heard himself bellow with fury as he brought the chain down, at the same time putting all his weight on the throat. He felt his knee break through something soft, and the scarlet imprint of the chain was left on the distorted face like a tattoo.

Josh struggled to his feet, his lungs heaving. His shoulder pounded with excruciating pain, but he couldn't give in to it. Keep going! he told himself. Move, you fool! A hammer sailed past him, clattering into a display of hubcabs. He slipped, fell to his knees. Blood was in his mouth and crawling down his face, and the seconds were ticking. He thought of the roach on the barn floor, the survivor of insecticides and stomping boots and a nuclear holocaust. If such a thing as that had the will to live, then he damned well did, too.

Josh stood up. He ran along the aisle, saw three more figures coming toward him; he jumped over a counter into another aisle. A left turn, and a clear aisle lined with housewares, pots and pans stretched before him.

And way down at the end of it sat Lord Alvin, watching from his throne. On the wall behind him was the sign *Pets*. Josh could see the dwarf jumping up and down in the shopping cart, and Swan's face was turned toward him. Crybaby lay so close, but so far away.

"One minute!" Lord Alvin announced through the bull-horn.

I've made it! Josh realized. Dear God, I'm almost there! It can't be more than forty feet to the dowsing rod!

He started forward.

But he heard the low growl and the rising whine, and the Neanderthal with the chainsaw stepped into the aisle to block his way.

Josh stopped with a jolt. The Neanderthal, his bald head shining under the lights, smiled faintly and waited for him, the chainsaw's teeth a blur of deadly metal.

Josh looked around for some other way to go. The housewares aisle was an unbroken sweep of kitchen items, glasses and crockery except for an aisle that turned to the right about ten feet away—and three maniacs guarded that portal, all armed with knives and garden tools. He turned to retrace his path, and about five yards away stood the madman with the fishing rod and the green-toothed lunatic with the shotgun. He saw more of them coming, taking positions to watch the finale of the Straitjacket game.

The ass is *grass*, Josh knew. But not just his—Swan and Leona were dead if he didn't reach the finish line. There was no way except through the Neanderthal.

"Forty seconds, friend Josh!"

The Neanderthal swiped at the air with the chainsaw, daring Josh to come on.

Josh was almost used up. The Neanderthal handled that chainsaw with childish ease. Had they come all this way to die in a damned K-Mart full of escaped fruitcakes? Josh didn't know whether to laugh or cry, so he just said, "Shit!" Well, he decided, if they were going to die, he was going to do his best to take the Neanderthal with him—and Josh stood to his full height, swelled out his chest and let loose a roaring laugh.

The Neanderthal grinned too.

"Thirty seconds," Lord Alvin said.

Josh threw his head back, released a war whoop at the top of his lungs, and then he charged like a runaway Mack truck.

The Neanderthal stood his ground, braced his legs and swung the chainsaw.

But Josh suddenly juked back out of range, the chainsaw's breeze brushing his face as it swept past. The other man's rib cage was an open target, and before the Neanderthal could bring the chainsaw back around, Josh kicked those ribs like he was aiming at next week.

The man's face scrunched up with pain, and he went back a few feet but did not go down. Then he was balanced again, and now he was rushing forward and the chainsaw was coming at Josh's head.

Josh had no time to think, just to act. He flung his arms up in front of his face. The saw's teeth hit the chains around his wrists, shooting sparks. The vibration sent Josh and the Neanderthal reeling in opposite directions, but still neither one fell.

"Twenty seconds!" the bullhorn blared.

Josh's heart was hammering, but he was strangely calm. It was reach the finish line or not, and that was it. He crouched and warily advanced, hoping to trip the other man up somehow. And then the Neanderthal sprang forward, faster than Josh had expected the big man to move, and the chainsaw slashed at Josh's skull; Josh started to leap back, but the chainsaw strike was a feint. The Neanderthal's booted right foot came up and caught Josh in the stomach, knocking him along the aisle. He crashed into the counter of pots, pans and kitchen tools, clattering around him in a shower of metal. *Roll!* Josh screamed mentally, and as he whipped aside the Neanderthal brought the chainsaw down where he'd been lying, carving a foot-long trench across the floor.

Quickly, Josh twisted back to the other side and kicked upward, hitting his opponent just under the jawbone. The Neanderthal was lifted off his feet, and then he, too, crashed into the housewares display—but he kept tight hold of the saw and started getting to his feet as blood dribbled from both corners of his mouth.

The audience hooted and clapped.

"Ten seconds!"

Josh was on his knees before he realized what was scattered around him: not only pots and pans, but an array of carving knives. One with a blade about eight inches long lay right in front of him. He put his left hand around its grip and forced the fingers shut with sheer willpower, and the knife was his.

The Neanderthal, his eyes clouded with pain, spat out teeth and what might have been part of his tongue.

Josh was on his feet. "Come on!" he shouted, feinting with the knife. "Come on, you crazy asshole!"

The other man obliged him; he began stalking down the aisle toward Josh, sweeping the chainsaw back and forth in a deadly arc.

Josh kept moving backward. He glanced quickly over his shoulder, saw the mad fisherman and the shotgun wielder about five feet behind him. In a fraction of a second, he realized that Green Teeth was holding his shotgun in a loose, casual grip. The ring of keys dangled at the man's belt.

The Neanderthal was advancing steadily, and when he grinned blood drooled out.

"You're going the wrong way, friend Josh!" Lord Alvin said. "It doesn't matter, anyway. Time's up! Come on and take your pill!"

"Kiss my ass!" Josh shouted—and then he whirled around in a blur of motion and drove the blade up to the hilt in Green Teeth's chest, just above the heart. As the madman's mouth opened in a shriek, Josh clamped his left hand around the shotgun's trigger guard, wrenching the weapon loose. The man fell to the floor in a spray of arterial blood.

The Neanderthal charged.

Josh turned in what seemed like nightmarish slow motion. He fought to hold the shotgun steady, trying to get his finger on the trigger. The Neanderthal was almost on him, and the saw was coming up for a vicious, sideswiping slash. Josh braced the butt of the shotgun against his chest, felt the awful breeze of the chainsaw. His finger found the trigger, and he squeezed.

The Neanderthal was within three feet, the chainsaw about to bite flesh.

But in the next instant a fist-sized hole opened in his stomach and half his back blew out. The force of the blast shook Josh and almost knocked the Neanderthal out of his boots. The chainsaw flashed past Josh's face, its weight spinning the dead man like a top along the bloody-floored aisle.

"No fair!" Lord Alvin shouted, jumping up from his throne. "You didn't play right!"

The corpse hit the floor, still gripping the chainsaw, and the metal teeth chewed a circle in the linoleum.

Josh saw Lord Alvin throw aside the bullhorn and reach into his robes; the madman's hand emerged with an extra gleaming finger—a crescent-bladed hunting knife, like a miniature scythe. Lord Alvin turned upon Swan and Leona.

With the shotgun's blast, the other psychos had fled for cover. Josh had one shell left, and he couldn't afford to waste it. He sprinted forward, leaped over the jittering body, and barreled for the pet department, where Lord Alvin—his face contorted with a mixture of rage and what might have been pity—knelt before Swan and grasped the back of her neck with his free hand.

"Death! Death!" Imp shrieked.

Swan looked up into Lord Alvin's face and knew she was about to die. Tears burned her eyes, but she lifted her chin defiantly.

"Time to go to sleep," Lord Alvin whispered. He lifted the crescent blade.

Josh slipped on the bloody floor and went down, skidding into a counter six feet short of the dowsing rod. He scrambled to get up, but he knew that he'd never make it.

Lord Alvin smiled, two tears rolling from his murky green eyes. The crescent blade was poised, about to fall. *"Sleep,"* he said.

But a small gray form had already streaked out from behind sacks of dog food and kitty litter and, growling like a hound from Hell, it leaped toward Lord Alvin's face.

The terrier snapped his teeth around Alvin Mangrim's thin and delicate nose, crunched through flesh and cartilage and snapped the man's head back. Lord Alvin fell on his side, writhing and screaming, frantically trying to push the animal away, but the terrier kept hold.

Josh jumped over Crybaby, saw Swan and Leona still alive, saw the terrier gnawing on Lord Alvin's nose and the madman flailing with his hunting knife. Josh aimed the shotgun at Lord Alvin's skull, but he didn't want to hit the dog and he knew he'd need that shell. The terrier suddenly freed Lord Alvin and scrambled back with bloody flesh between his teeth, then planted his paws and let out a fusillade of barks.

Lord Alvin sat up, what remained of his nose hanging from his face and his eyes wide with shock. Shrieking "Blasphemy! Blasphemy!" he bolted to his feet and ran, still screaming, out of the pet department. Nearby, Imp was the last of Lord Alvin's subjects left in the vicinity; the dwarf was hissing curses at Josh, who lunged over to the shopping cart, spun it around and sent it flying down the aisle. Imp bailed out a few seconds before it crashed into fish tanks and upended.

Alvin Mangrim had left his knife behind, and Josh spent a couple of anxious minutes cutting the ropes loose from Swan and Leona. When Swan's hands were freed, she put her arms around Josh's neck and held tight, her body shaking like a tough sapling in a tornado. The terrier came close enough for Josh to touch and sat back on its haunches, its muzzle scarlet with Lord Alvin's blood. For the first time, Josh saw that the dog was wearing a flea collar, and on it was a little metal name tag that said "Killer."

Josh knelt over Leona and shook her. The woman's eyelids fluttered, her face slack, a terrible purple swelling around the gash over her left eye. Concussion, Josh realized. Or worse. She lifted a hand to touch the smeared greasepaint on Josh's face, and then her eyes opened. She smiled weakly. "You done good," she said.

He helped her up. They had to get out fast. Josh braced the shotgun against his belly and started along the aisle where the Neanderthal lay. Swan retrieved the dowsing rod, grasped Leona's hand and pulled her forward like a sleepwalker. Still barking, Killer darted ahead.

Josh came to Green Teeth's body and took the ring of keys. He'd worry later about which key unlocked his wrist chains. Right now they had to get out of this asylum before Lord Alvin rallied the maniacs.

They sensed furtive movements on both sides of the aisle as they continued through the K-Mart, but Lord Alvin's subjects had no initiative of their own. Someone threw a shoe, and a red rubber ball came bouncing at them, but otherwise they made the front doors without incident.

Cold rain was still pouring down, and within seconds they were drenched. The parking lot lamps cast harsh yellow halos over the abandoned cars. Josh felt the weight of exhaustion creeping up on him. They found their wheelbarrow overturned, their supplies either stolen or scattered. Their bags and belongings were gone, including Swan's Cookie Monster doll. Swan looked down and saw a few of Leona's tarot cards lying on the wet pavement, along with broken shards of her crystal ball collection. Lord Alvin's subjects had left them nothing but the soaked clothes sticking to their bodies.

Swan glanced back toward the K-Mart and felt horror like a cold hand placed to a burn.

They were coming out the doors. Ten or eleven figures, led by one in a purple robe that blew around his shoulders. Some of them were carrying rifles.

"Josh!" she shouted.

He kept walking, about ten feet ahead. He hadn't heard her for the storm.

"Josh!" she shouted again, and then she sprinted the distance between them and whacked him across the back with Crybaby.

He spun around, eyes stricken—and then he saw them coming, too. They were thirty yards away, zigzagging between the cars. There was a flash of gunfire, and the rear windshield of a Toyota van behind Josh exploded. "Get down!" he yelled, shoving Swan to the pavement. He grabbed Leona as more pinpoints of fire sparked. Another car's windshield blew out, but by then Josh, Swan and Leona were huddled in the shelter of a blue Buick with two flat tires.

Bullets ricocheted, and glass showered around them. Josh crouched, waiting for the bastards to come closer before he reared up and fired the last shell.

A hand grasped the shotgun's barrel.

Leona's face was drawn and weary, but the heat of life shone in her eyes. She gripped the shotgun firmly, trying to pull it away from him. He resisted, shaking his head. Then he saw the blood that trickled from a corner of Leona's mouth.

He looked down. The bullet wound was just below her heart.

Leona smiled wanly, and Josh could just make out what she said from the movement of her lips: *"Go."* She nodded toward the far expanse of the rainswept parking lot. *"Now,"* she told him.

He'd already seen how much blood she was losing. She knew, too; it was in her face. She wouldn't let go of the shotgun, and she spoke again. Josh couldn't hear her, but he thought it might have been: "Protect the child."

The rain was streaming down Josh's face. There was so much to say, so *much,* but neither of them could hear the other over the voice of the storm, and words were flimsy. Josh glanced at Swan, saw that she'd seen the wound, too. Swan lifted her gaze to Leona's, then to Josh's, and she knew what had been decided.

"No!" she shouted. "I won't let you!" She grabbed Leona's arm.

A gunshot blasted the side window of a pickup truck nearby. More bullets hit the truck's door, blew out the front tire and whined off the wheel.

Josh looked into the woman's eyes. He released the shotgun. She pulled it to her and put her finger on the trigger, then motioned for them to go. Swan clung to her. Leona grasped Crybaby and pushed the dowsing rod firmly against Swan's chest, then deliberately pulled her arm free from Swan's fingers. The decision was made. Now Leona's eyes were clouding, the flow of blood fast and fatal.

Josh kissed her cheek, hugged her tight to him for a few seconds. And then he mouthed the words "Follow me" to Swan and started off in a half crawl, half crouch between the cars. He couldn't bear to look at Leona again, but he would remember every line in her face until the day he died.

Leona ran the fingers of one hand over Swan's cheek and smiled, as if she'd seen the child's inside face and held it like a cameo in her heart. Then Swan saw the woman's eyes go hard, preparing for what was ahead. There was nothing more. Swan lingered as long as she dared before she followed Josh into the maze of vehicles.

Leona rose to a crouch. The pain below her heart was an irritating sting compared to her rheumatic knees. She waited, the rain pounding down on her, and she was not afraid. It was time to fly from this body now, time to see clearly what she'd only beheld through a dark glass.

She waited a moment longer, and then she stood up and stepped out from behind the Buick, facing the K-Mart like a gunfighter at the O.K. Corral.

Four of them were standing about six feet away, and behind them were two others. She didn't have time to make sure the one in the purple robe was there; she aimed the shotgun in their midst and pulled the trigger even as two of the madmen fired their guns at her.

Josh and Swan broke from the cover of the cars and ran across the open lot. Swan almost looked back, *almost,* but did not. Josh staggered, the exhaustion about to drive him down. Off to the side, the terrier kept pace with them, looking like a drowned rat.

Swan wiped rain from her eyes. There was motion ahead. Something was coming through the storm. Josh had seen it, too, couldn't tell what it was—but if the lunatics had circled around them, they were finished.

The piebald horse broke from a sweeping curtain of rain, charging toward them—but it didn't appear to be the same animal. This horse looked stronger, somehow more valiant, with a straighter back and courage in its forward-thrust neck. Josh and Swan both could have sworn they saw Mule's hooves striking showers of sparks off the pavement.

The horse careened to a stop in front of them, reared and pawed at the air. When the animal came down again, Josh grabbed Swan's arm by his free hand and flung her up onto Mule. He wasn't sure which he was more scared of, riding the horse or facing the madmen; but when he dared to look around, he saw figures running through the rain, and he made up his mind right quick.

He swung up behind Swan and kicked Mule's ribs with both heels. The horse reared again, and Josh saw the pursuing figures abruptly stop. The one in the lead wore purple, had long, wet blond hair and a mangled nose. Josh had a second to lock stares with Lord Alvin, the hatred flaming through his bones, and he thought, Someday, you sonofabitch. Someday you'll pay.

Gunfire leapt. Mule whirled around and raced out of the parking lot as if he were going for the roses in the Kentucky Derby. Killer followed behind, plowing through the storm.

Swan gripped hold of Mule's mane to guide him, but the horse was deciding their direction. They sped away from the K-Mart, away from the dead town of Matheson, through the rain along a highway that stretched into darkness.

But in the last of the light from the lunatic K-Mart, they saw a roadside sign that read Welcome to Nebraska, the Cornhusker State. They passed it in a blur, and Swan wasn't sure what it had said. The wind blew into her face, and she held Crybaby in one hand and Mule's mane with the other, and they seemed to be cleaving a fiery path through the dark and leaving a sea of sparks in their wake.

"I don't think we're in Kansas anymore!" Swan shouted.

"Damn straight!" Josh answered.

They raced into the storm, heading toward a new horizon.

And a couple of minutes after they'd passed, the terrier came bounding after them.

Forty-three

A wolf with yellow eyes darted in front of the pickup truck.

Paul Thorson instinctively hit the brake, and the truck slewed violently to the right, narrowly missing the burned wreckage of a tractor-trailer rig and a Mercedes-Benz in the middle of I-80's westbound lanes before the worn tires gripped pavement again. The truck's engine racketed and snorted like an old man having a bad dream.

In the passenger seat, Steve Buchanan stuck the Magnum's barrel through the slit of his rolled-down window and took aim, but before he could fire the animal had vanished into the woods again. "Jesus H. Christ," Steve said. "Those fuckers are comin' out of the woodwork now. This is a suicide mission, man!"

Another wolf ran in front of the truck, taunting them. Paul could've sworn the bastard smiled. His own face was set like stone as he concentrated on weaving a path through the wreckage, but inside he was lanced by icy fear of a kind he'd never known. There would not be enough bullets to hold off the wolves when the time came. The people in the truck would look to him for help, but he would fail them. I'm afraid. Oh, dear God, I'm afraid. He picked up the bottle of

Johnny Walker Red that sat between himself and the teenager, uncapped it with his teeth and took a swig that made his eyes water. He handed it to Steve, who drank some courage of his own.

For perhaps the hundredth time in the last five minutes, Paul glanced at the gas gauge. The needle was about three hairs shy of the big red E. They'd passed two gas stations in the last fifteen miles, and Paul's worst nightmares were coming true; one of the stations had been razed to the ground, and the other had a sign that said NO GAS NO GUNS NO MONEY NO NOTHING.

The pickup labored west under a leaden sky. The highway was a junkyard of wrecked hulks and frozen, wolf-gnawed corpses. Paul had seen a dozen or so wolves trailing them. *Waiting for us to start walking,* he knew. *They can smell that tank drying up. Damn it to Hell, why did we leave the cabin? We were safe! We could've stayed there—*

Forever? he wondered.

A gust of wind hit the pickup broadside, and the vehicle shuddered right down to its slick treads. Paul's knuckles turned white as he fought the wheel. The kerosene had run out a day earlier, and the day before that Artie Wisco had begun coughing up blood. The cabin was twenty miles behind them now. They'd passed a point of no return, everything around them desolate and as gray as undertakers' fingers. *I should never have listened to that crazy woman!* he thought, taking the bottle from Steve. *She'll get us all killed yet!*

"Suicide mission, man," Steve repeated, a crooked grin carved across his burn-scarred face.

Sister sat beside Artie in the rear of the truck, both of them protected from the wind by a blanket. She was holding onto Paul's rifle; he'd taught her how to load and fire it, and had told her to blow hell out of any wolves that got too close. The fifteen or so that were following slipped back and forth between the wreckage, and Sister decided not to waste bullets.

Nearby, also covered by a blanket, were the Ramseys and the old man who'd forgotten his name. The old man clutched the shortwave radio, though the batteries had died days ago.

Over the engine's racket, Sister could hear Artie's agonized breathing. He held his side, blood flecking his lips, his face contorted with pain. The only chance for him was to find medical help of some kind, and Sister had come too far with him to let him die without a struggle.

Sister had one arm around the duffel bag. The previous night she'd looked into the shining jewels of the glass circle and seen another strange image: what appeared to be a roadside sign at night, dimly illuminated by a distant glow, that read *Welcome to Matheson, Kansas! We're Strong, Proud and Growing!*

She'd had the impression of dreamwalking along a highway that led toward a light, reflected off the bellies of low clouds; there were figures around her, but she couldn't quite make out who they were. Then, abruptly, she'd lost her grip on the vision, and she was back in the cabin, sitting in front of a dying fire.

She'd never heard of Matheson, Kansas, before—if there was really such a place. Looking into the depths of the glass ring caused the imagination to boil like soup in a stockpot, and why should what bubbled out of it have any connection with reality?

But what if there *was* a Matheson, Kansas? she'd asked herself. Would that mean her visions of a desert where a Cookie Monster doll lay and of a table where fortune-telling cards were arranged were also real places? No! Of course not! I used to be crazy, but I'm not crazy anymore, she'd thought. It was all imagination, all wisps of fantasy that the colors of the glass circle created in the mind.

"I want it," the thing in its Doyle Halland disguise had said, back in that bloody room in New Jersey. "I want it."

And I have it, Sister thought. Me, of all possible people. Why *me?*

She answered her own question: Because when I want to hold onto something, even the Devil himself can't pry it loose, that's why.

"Goin' to Detroit!" Artie said. He was smiling, his eyes bright with fever. " 'Bout time I got home, don't you think?"

"You're going to be all right." She took his hand. The flesh was wet and hot. "We're going to find some medicine for you."

"Oh, she's gonna be *sooooo* mad at me!" he continued. "I was supposed to call her that night. I went out with the boys. Supposed to call her. Let her down."

"No, you didn't. It's all right. You just be quiet and—"

Mona Ramsey screamed.

Sister looked up. A yellow-eyed wolf the size of a Doberman had scrambled up on the rear bumper and was trying to hitch itself over the tailgate. The animal's jaws snapped wantonly at the air. Sister had no time to aim or fire; she just clubbed the beast's skull with the rifle barrel, and the wolf yelped and dropped back to the highway. It was gone into the woods before Sister could get her finger on the trigger. Four others who'd been shadowing the truck scattered for cover.

Mona Ramsey was babbling hysterically. "Hush!" Sister demanded. The young woman stopped her jabbering and gaped at her. "You're making me nervous, dear," Sister said. "I get very cranky when I'm nervous."

The pickup swerved over ice, its right side scraping along the wreckage of a six-car pileup before Paul could regain control. He threaded a passageway between wrecks, but the highway ahead was an auto graveyard. More animals skulked at the edges of the road, watching the pickup rumble past.

The gas gauge's needle touched E. "We're running on fumes," Paul said, and he wondered how far they could get on the Johnny Walker Red.

"Hey! Look there!" Steve Buchanan pointed. To the right, over the leafless trees, was a tall Shell gas station sign. They rounded a curve, and they both saw the Shell station—abandoned, with REPENT! HELL IS ON EARTH! painted in white across the windows. Which was just as well, Paul reasoned, because the off-ramp was blocked by the mangled hulk of a bus and two other crashed vehicles.

"Good shoes!" Artie said in the rear of the truck. Sister dragged her gaze away from the message—or warning—on the Shell station's windows. "Nothin' beats a pair of good, comfortable walkin' shoes!" He lost his breath and began coughing, and Sister cleaned his mouth with an edge of the blanket.

The pickup truck stuttered.

Paul felt the blood drain from his face. "Come on, come on!" They'd just started up a hill; its top was about a quarter mile away, and if they could make it they could coast down the other side. Paul leaned forward against the steering wheel, as if to shove the truck the rest of the way. The engine rattled and wheezed, and Paul knew it was about to give up the ghost. The tires kept turning, though, and the truck was still climbing the hill.

"Come *on!*" he shouted as the engine caught, sputtered—and then died.

The tires rolled on about twenty yards, getting slower and slower, before the truck stopped. Then the tires began to roll backward.

Paul plunged his foot on the brake, pulled up the parking brake and put the gears into first. The truck halted about a hundred yards from the hilltop.

Silence fell.

"That's that," Paul said. Steve Buchanan was sitting with one hand on the Magnum and the other strangling the scotch bottle's neck.

"What now, man?"

"Three choices: We sit here for the rest of our lives, we go back to the cabin or we start walking ahead." He took the bottle, got out into the cold wind, and walked around to the tailgate. "Tour's over, friends. We're out of gas." He snapped a sharp glance at Sister. "You satisfied, lady?"

"We've still got legs."

"Yeah. So do they." He nodded toward the two wolves that were standing at the edge of the forest, watching intently. "I think they'd beat us in a footrace, don't you?"

"How far is it back to the cabin?" Kevin Ramsey asked, his arms around his shivering wife. "Can we make it before dark?"

"No." He regarded Sister again. "Lady, I'm one damned

fool for letting you talk me into this. I *knew* the gas stations were going to be shut down!"

"Then why'd you come?"

"Because . . . because I wanted to believe. Even though I knew you were wrong." He sensed motion to his left, saw three more wolves coming through the wrecks on the eastbound lanes. "We were safe in the cabin. I knew there wasn't anything left!"

"All the people who passed this way had to be going *somewhere,*" she insisted. "You would've sat in that cabin until your ass grew roots."

"We should've stayed!" Mona Ramsey wailed. "Oh, Jesus, we're going to die out here!"

"Can you stand up?" Sister asked Artie. He nodded. "Do you think you can walk?"

"Got good shoes," he rasped. He sat up, pain stitched across his face. "Yeah, I think I can."

She helped him to his feet, then lowered the tailgate and just about lifted Artie to the pavement. He clutched at his side and leaned against the truck. Sister slung the rifle's strap around her shoulder, hefted the duffel bag carefully to the ground and stepped down from the truck bed. She looked Paul Thorson in the face. "We're going that way." She motioned toward the hilltop. "Are you coming with us or staying here?"

Her eyes were the color of steel against her sallow, burn-blotched face. Paul realized that she was either the craziest or toughest mutha he'd ever met. "There's nothing over there but more nothing."

"There's nothing where we came from." Sister picked up the duffel bag and, with Artie leaning on her shoulder, started walking up the hill.

"Give me the rifle," Paul told her. She stopped. "The rifle," he repeated. "That won't do you a damned bit of good. By the time you get it unslung you'll be hash. Here." He offered her the bottle. "Take a long swig. Everybody gets a drink before we start. And for God's sake, keep those blankets around you. Protect your faces as much as you can.

Steve, bring the blanket from the front seat. Come on, hurry it up!"

Sister drank from the bottle, gave Artie a swallow and then returned it and the rifle to Paul. "We keep together," he told all of them. "We stay in a tight group—just like the wagons when the Indians attacked. Right?" He watched the converging wolves for a moment, lifted the rifle, aimed and shot one through the side. It fell, snapping, and the others leapt upon it, tearing it to pieces. "Okay," Paul said. "Let's get on down this damned road."

They began walking, the wind whipping around them in vicious crosscurrents. Paul took the lead and Steve Buchanan brought up the rear. They'd gone no more than twenty feet when a wolf lunged out from behind an overturned car and shot across their path. Paul raised his rifle, but the animal had already found cover beyond another hulk. "Watch our backs!" he shouted to Steve.

The animals were coming in from all sides. Steve counted eight scurrying up from the rear. He eased back the Magnum's hammer, his heart whacking like a Black Flag drumbeat.

Another wolf ran in from the left, a streak of motion headed for Kevin Ramsey. Paul whirled and fired; the bullet sang off the pavement, but the animal turned away. Instantly, two more darted in from the right. "Look out!" Sister shouted, and Paul turned in time to shatter a wolf's leg with one slug. The animal danced crazily across the highway before four others dragged it down. He pumped shots at them and hit two, but the rest fled. "Bullets!" he called, and Sister dug a handful out of the box he'd given her to carry in her duffel bag. He hastily reloaded, but he'd given his gloves to Mona Ramsey, and his sweaty skin was sticking to the rifle's cold metal. The rest of the bullets went into his coat pocket.

They were seventy yards from the top of the hill.

Artie leaned heavily on Sister. He coughed blood and staggered, his legs about to fold. "You can make it," she said. "Come on, keep moving."

"Tired," he said. He was as hot as a furnace, and he spread

warmth to the others gathered around him. "Oh . . . I'm . . . so . . ."

A wolf's head lunged from the open window of a burned Oldsmobile at their side, the jaws snapping at Artie's face. Sister jerked him aside and the teeth came together with a *crack!* that was almost as loud as Paul's rifle shot a second later. The wolf's head spewed blood and brains and the beast slithered down into the car.

". . . tired," Artie finished.

Steve watched two wolves racing in from behind. He lifted the Magnum with both hands, his palms slick on the butt though he was freezing. One of the animals shot off to the side, but the other kept coming. He was just about to fire when it closed within ten feet, snarled and ran behind a wrecked Chevy. He could've sworn the snarl had spoken his name.

There was motion on his left. He started to turn, but he knew he was too late.

He screamed as a wolf shape hit him, knocking his legs out from under him. The Magnum went off, jumping out of his hands and sliding away across the ice. A large silver-gray wolf had Steve's right ankle and started dragging him toward the woods. "Help me!" he shouted. *"Help me!"*

The old man acted faster than Paul; he took three running steps, lifted the shortwave radio between his hands and smashed it down on the wolf's skull. The radio burst apart in a confetti spray of wires and transistors, and the wolf released Steve's ankle. Paul shot it through the ribs, and it, too, was jumped by three more. Steve limped over to get the Magnum, the old man staring horrified at the metallic mess in his hands; then Steve guided him back to the group, and the old man let the last of the radio fall.

Upwards of fifteen wolves were swirling around them, stopping to ravage the dying or wounded. More were coming from the forest. Holy Jesus! Paul thought as the army of wolves circled them. He took aim at the nearest.

A form squirmed out from beneath a car hulk on the side away from his rifle. "Paul!" Sister shrieked—and she saw the wolf leap for him before she could do or say anything else.

He twisted violently around, but he was hit and knocked down under a clawing, snarling weight. The beast's jaws strained for his throat—and clamped shut on the rifle that Paul had thrown up to guard his face. Sister had to let go of Artie to rush the wolf, and she kicked the thing in the side with all her strength. The wolf released Paul's rifle, snapped at her foot and tensed to spring at her. She saw its eyes—maddened, defiant, like the eyes of Doyle Halland.

The wolf leaped.

There were two cannonlike explosions, and the bullets from Steve's Magnum almost tore the wolf in half. Sister dodged aside as the wolf sailed past her, its teeth still snapping and its guts trailing behind it.

She drew a breath, turned toward Artie and saw two wolves hit him at once.

"No!" she shouted as Artie fell. She bashed one of the animals with her duffel bag and knocked it about eight feet across the pavement. The second chewed on his leg and started dragging him.

Mona Ramsey screamed and bolted from the group, running past Steve in the direction they'd come. Steve tried to grab her but missed, and Kevin went after her, caught her around the waist and lifted her off her feet just as a wolf sprang from beneath a wreck and trapped her left foot between its teeth. Kevin and the beast pulled Mona in a deadly tug-of-war as the woman screamed and thrashed and more wolves ran out of the woods. Steve tried to fire, but he feared hitting the man or woman. He hesitated, cold sweat freezing to his face, and he was still in a trance when a seventy-pound wolf hit him in the shoulder like a diesel train. He heard the sound of his shoulder breaking, and he lay writhing in pain as the wolf doubled back and began gnawing at his gun hand.

The things were everywhere now, darting in and leaping. Paul fired, missed, had to duck a shape that came flying at his head. Sister swung her duffel bag at the wolf that had Artie's leg, struck its skull and drove it back. Kevin Ramsey had lost the tug-of-war; the wolf wrenched Mona out of his grasp and was attacked by another that wanted the same prize. They fought as Mona frantically tried to crawl away.

Paul fired and hit a wolf that was about to jump Sister from behind, and then claws were on his shoulders and he was slammed face first into the pavement. The rifle spun away.

Three wolves converged on Sister and Artie. The old man was kicking wildly at the animal that was attacking Steve's hand and arm. Sister saw Paul down, his face bleeding and the beast on top of him trying to claw through his leather jacket. She realized they were less than ten yards from the top of the hill, and this was where they were going to die.

She hauled Artie up like a sack of laundry. The three wolves came in slowly, biding their time. Sister braced herself, ready to swing the duffel bag and kick for all she was worth.

Over the snarls and shouts, she heard a deep bass growling noise. She glanced toward the hilltop. The sound was coming from the other side. It must be a horde of wolves racing for their share, she realized—or the monster of all wolves awakened from its lair. "Well, come on!" she shouted at the three who were creeping up on her. They hesitated, perhaps puzzled by her defiance, and she felt craziness pulling at her mind again. "Come on, you motherfu—"

Its engine growling, a yellow snowplow came over the hilltop, its treads crunching over debris. Clinging to the outside of the glass-enclosed cab was a man in a hooded green parka, and he was carrying a rifle with a sniperscope. Following behind the plow was a white Jeep like the kind used by postmen. Its driver zipped the vehicle around the wrecks, and another man with a rifle leaned out the Jeep's passenger side, shouting and firing into the air. The man riding shotgun on the snowplow carefully aimed and squeezed off a shot. The middle of the three wolves dropped, and the other two turned tail.

The animal on Paul's back looked up, saw the oncoming vehicles and fled. Another rifle shot sang off the pavement near the two fighting over Mona Ramsey, and they ran for the forest as well. Mona reached her husband and flung her arms around him. The wolf that had made a bloody mess of Steve's arm gave it one last shake and ran as a bullet zipped past its skull. Steve sat up, shouting, "Fuckers! You fuckers!" in a high, hysterical voice.

The white Jeep skidded to a halt in front of Paul, who was still struggling to get the air back in his lungs. He got to his knees, his jaw and forehead scraped raw and his nose broken, gushing blood. The driver and the man with the rifle stepped out of the postman's Jeep. On the snowplow, the sharpshooter was still popping off bullets at the wolves heading into the woods, and he hit three of them before the highway was cleared of living animals.

The Jeep's driver was a tall, ruddy-cheeked man who wore dungarees under a fleece-lined coat. On his head was a cap that advertised Stroh's beer. His dark brown eyes shifted back and forth over the tattered group of survivors. He looked at all the dead and dying wolves, and he grunted. Then he reached work-weathered fingers into a pocket of his dungarees, withdrew something and offered it to Paul Thorson. "Gum?" he asked. Paul looked at the pack of Wrigley's Spearmint and had to laugh.

Sister was stunned. She walked past the white Jeep, still bearing Artie's weight on her shoulder. Artie's shoes scraped on the pavement. She walked past the snow plow and reached the top of the hill.

Off to the right, through dead trees, smoke was rising from the chimneys of wood-framed houses on the streets of a small village. She saw the steeple of a church, saw United States Army trucks parked on a softball field, saw a Red Cross banner hanging from the side of a building, saw tents and cars and campers by the thousands, scattered in the village streets and through the hills around it. A roadside sign just over the hilltop announced *Homewood Next Exit.*

Artie's body began to slide to the ground. "No," she said, very firmly, and she held him standing with all her strength.

She was still holding him up when they came to help her to the white Jeep.

Forty-four

By the light of an oil lamp, Colonel Macklin admired himself in the mirror of the Airstream trailer's bathroom.

The gray-green Nazi uniform was a bit tight around the chest and midsection, but the sleeves and trouser legs were long enough. At his waist was a black leather holster and a loaded Luger. On his feet were Nazi hobnailed boots—again, just a bit too small, but Macklin was determined to make them do. Medals and ribbons adorned the uniform's jacket, and though Macklin didn't know what any of them were for, he thought they looked very impressive.

The closet in the pigsty of the late Freddie Kempka's bedroom had been full of Nazi uniforms, flak jackets, boots, holsters and the like. A Nazi flag was fixed to the wall over the bed, and a bookcase held volumes such as *The Rise and Fall of the Third Reich, Military Strategy and Maneuver, Medieval Warfare,* and *A History of Torture.* Roland had gotten hold of the books and had been devouring them with pure passion. Sheila Fontana slept in the other bedroom, staying mostly to herself except when Macklin needed her; she seemed content to do her duty, though she lay cold and unmoving, and several times Macklin had heard her cry out in the night, as if waking up from a dark dream.

During the few days they'd occupied the trailer, Macklin had made a thorough inventory of what Freddie Kempka had collected: There was enough junk food and soft drinks to feed an army, plenty of bottled water and canned food as well—but Macklin and Roland were most interested in the weapons. Kempka's bedroom was an arsenal of machine guns, rifles, pistols, a crate of flares, smoke grenades and fragmentation grenades, and boxes and bags and clips of ammunition scattered around like gold in a royal treasure house. The Shadow Soldier didn't have to tell Macklin that he had found paradise.

Macklin regarded his face in the mirror. His beard was growing out, but it was so gray it made him look old. Kempka had left a straight razor behind, and Macklin decided he would give himself a shave. Also, his hair was too long and scraggly; he preferred the close-cropped military look. Kempka had also left a pair of scissors that would do the job very well.

He leaned forward, staring into his own eyes. They were still deep-sunken and bore the memory of the pain that had ripped through his wound in the Great Salt Lake—a pain so soul-shattering that it had sloughed away the old dead skin that had confined him for so long. He felt new, reborn and alive again—and in his icy blue eyes he saw the Jimbo Macklin that used to be, back in the days when he was young and fast. He knew the Shadow Soldier was proud of him, because he was a whole man again.

He did miss his right hand, but he was going to learn how to use a machine gun or rifle just as effectively with the left. After all, he had all the time in the world. The wound was bound up with strips of bedsheet, and it was still draining, but the heaviness was gone. Macklin knew the salt water had burned the infection out.

He thought he looked very handsome, very—yes—*kingly* in the Nazi uniform. Maybe it had been a German colonel's uniform, he mused. It was in fine shape, just a few moth holes in the silk lining; Kempka obviously had taken great care of his collection. There seemed to be more lines in his face, but something about that face was wolfish and dangerous. He figured he'd lost twenty-five pounds or more since the disaster at Earth House. Still, there was just one small thing about his face that bothered him. . . .

He lifted his hand and touched what seemed to be a brown scab about the size of a quarter, just under his left eye. He tried to peel it off, but it was melded tightly to the skin. On his forehead were four dime-sized scabs that he had at first taken for warts, but those couldn't be peeled off either. Maybe it's skin cancer, he thought. Maybe the radiation caused it. But he'd noticed a similar scablike growth, also the size of a dime, on Roland's chin. Skin cancer, he thought. Well, he would take the straight razor and slice them off when he shaved, and that would be the end of it. His hide was too tough for skin cancer.

But it was strange, he thought, that the little round scabs were only on his face. Not his hand, or his arms, or anywhere else. Just his face.

He heard a knock on the trailer door, and he left the bathroom to answer it.

Roland and Lawry, both carrying rifles, had returned from the recon mission they'd been on with three other able-bodied soldiers. Last night, one of the perimeter sentries had seen the flicker of lights to the south, three or four miles across the desert.

"Two trailers," Lawry reported, trying not to stare too hard at the Nazi uniform the colonel wore. Kempka had always been too fat to squirm into it. "Pulled by a Chevy van and a Pontiac. All the vehicles look in pretty good shape."

"How many people?" Macklin asked, opening one of the jugs of bottled water and offering it to Lawry.

"We saw sixteen people," Roland told him. "Six women, eight men and two children. They seemed to have plenty of gas, food and water, but all of them are burn-scarred. Two of the men can hardly walk."

"They have guns?"

"Yes, sir." Roland took the jug of water from Lawry and drank. He thought the uniform looked wonderful on the

King, and he wished there'd been one his size to wear. He couldn't remember much of what had happened that night with Freddie Kempka, but he recalled having a vivid dream in which he killed Mike Armbruster. "One of the men had a rifle."

"Just one rifle? Why do you think they haven't come here? You know they've seen our lights."

"They might be afraid," Roland said. "They might think we'll take what they have."

Macklin took the jug back, recapped it and set it aside. A door opened and closed, and Sheila Fontana walked through the corridor into the room. She stopped short when she saw the uniform. "We could use the trailers and the vehicles," Macklin decided. "But we don't need anybody with burn marks. I don't want anybody with burn marks in our camp."

"Colonel . . . there are already about thirty or more people here who were burned in . . . you know," Lawry said. "I mean . . . what does it matter?"

"I've thought a lot about this, Corporal Lawry," he replied—and though he had not, it sounded impressive. "I think people with burn marks—*keloids,*" he said, remembering the technical name of atomic-induced burns, "are detrimental to the morale of our camp. We don't need to be reminded of ugliness, do we? And people with burn marks are not going to keep themselves as clean as the rest of us, because they're ashamed of the way they appear and they're already demoralized." He found himself staring at the scab on Roland's chin. It was the size of a quarter. Hadn't it been smaller just a few days ago? His gaze shifted. There were three other small scabs at Roland's hairline. "People with burns are going to be disease spreaders," he told Corporal Lawry. He looked over Lawry's face but saw none of the scabs. "We're going to have enough trouble as it is keeping disease out of our camp. So . . . in the morning I want you to round up the ones with the burn scars and take them out of the camp. I don't want them returning. Understand?"

Lawry started to smile, because he thought the Colonel

was kidding, but Macklin's blue eyes bored into him. "Sir . . . you don't mean . . . kill all of them, do you?"

"Yes, that's what I mean."

"But . . . why not just banish them? I mean . . . tell them to go somewhere else?"

"Because," Roland Croninger, who saw to the heart of the matter, said, "they *won't* go anywhere else. At night they'll slip back into camp and try to steal food and water. They might help the dirtwarts attack us."

"Right," Macklin agreed. "So that's the new law of this camp: No one is admitted who has burn marks. And you *will* take those others out in the morning, and they will *not* come back. Roland'll go with you."

"I can do it myself!"

"Roland will go with you," Macklin said, quietly but firmly, and Judd Lawry looked at the floor. "Now, another thing: I want you to organize a work detail in the morning and distribute some of this to my people." He nodded toward the cartons of soft drinks, potato chip bags, cookies and cakes. *My* people, he realized he'd said. "I want them to be happy. Do that after you've finished the first duty."

"What about those people with the trailers out there?"

Macklin deliberated. Oh, he thought, the Shadow Soldier was going to be so proud of him! "How many soldiers do you need to go out and take those vehicles?" he asked.

"I don't know. Maybe four or five, I guess."

"Good. Then go out and bring them back—but not the people. We don't need people who aren't healthy."

"What do we need the trailers for?" Sheila asked. "We're okay as we are!" She couldn't bear to look at Judd Lawry's face, because he haunted her nightmares along with an infant that kept crying. A decayed corpse named Rudy crawled through the dust in her dreams, right up into her bed, and she thought she was going crazy.

"Because," Macklin said, turning toward her, "we're not going to stay here *forever*. As soon as we get organized and healthy, as soon as we get our morale high, we're moving out."

"Moving out?" She laughed. "Moving to *where,* war hero? The fucking moon?"

"No. Across the country. Maybe east. We can forage as we go."

"You mean . . . *everybody* moving east? What the hell for? Where is there to go?"

"The cities," Macklin answered. "Or what's left of them. The towns. The villages. We can build our own cities, if we please. We can start to put things back together again, like they should've been in the first place, before this shit happened."

"You've cracked, friend," Sheila said. "It's over. Can't you dig it?"

"It's not over. It's just beginning. We can build things back, but better than they were. We can have law and order, and we can enforce the laws—"

"What laws? Yours? The kid's? Who's going to make the laws?"

"The man with the most guns," Roland said.

Colonel Macklin turned his attention back to Judd Lawry. "You're dismissed," he said. "Have the trailers here within two hours."

Lawry left the trailer. Outside, he grinned at the night sky and shook his head. The soldier shit had gone to the Colonel's brain—but maybe he was right about getting rid of everybody who had burn scars. Lawry didn't like looking at those burns and being reminded of the holocaust, anyway. The burn marks were ugly. Keep America Beautiful, he thought, Kill a Scarface Today.

He walked on into the camp to select four men for the mission, but he knew it would be a piece of cake. He'd never felt so important in his life; before the disaster, he'd just been a clerk in a gun store, and now he was a corporal in Colonel Macklin's army! This was like waking up in a new skin. "It's not over," Colonel Macklin had said. "It's just beginning." Lawry liked the ring of that.

In the Airstream trailer, Sheila Fontana approached Macklin and looked him up and down. She saw the Nazi swastika on several of the badges he was wearing. "What are we going to start calling you? Adolf?"

Macklin's hand came out and caught her chin. His eyes flared angrily, and she realized she'd gone too far. The strength in that hand felt like it was about to crack her jaw. "If you don't like something here," he told her quietly, "you know where the door is. And if you don't watch your mouth, I'll throw you to the dirtwarts. Oh, I'm sure they'd love to have company. Aren't you, Roland?"

Roland shrugged. He could see that the King was hurting Sheila, and that bothered him.

Macklin released her. "You're a fool," he said. "You don't see what could *be,* do you?"

Sheila rubbed her jaw. "Man, the game is *done!* You're talking rebuilding and all that crap—we're lucky to have a pot to piss in!"

"You'll see." His gaze searched her face for the small scabs. "I've got plans. Important plans. You'll see." He found no evidence of the cancers on Sheila's face.

She'd noted his roving eyes. "What's wrong? I washed my hair yesterday."

"Wash it again," he said. "It stinks." He looked at Roland. A sudden inspiration struck him. "The Army of Excellence," he said. "How does that sound?"

"Fine." Roland liked it. There was a sweeping, grand, Napoleonic sound to it. "It's good."

"The Army of Excellence," Macklin repeated. "We've got a long way to go. We're going to have to find more able-bodied men—and women. We'll need more vehicles, and we'll have to carry our food and water with us. We can do it if we put our minds and our muscle to the job!" His voice rose with excitement. "We can build things back, but better than they ever were!"

Sheila thought he was off his bird. The Army of Excellence, my ass! But she held her tongue, figuring it was best to just let Macklin blow off steam.

"People will follow me," he continued. "As long as I give them food and protection, they'll follow me, and they'll do whatever I say. They don't have to love me—they don't even have to *like* me. But they'll follow me all the same, because they'll respect me. Isn't that right?" he asked Roland.

"Yes, sir," the boy answered. "People want to be told what to do. They don't want to make the decisions." Behind his goggles, Roland's eyes had begun to glint with excitement as well. He could see the vast picture the King was painting—a massive Army of Excellence moving across the land on foot, in cars and in trailers, overrunning and absorbing other encampments and communities, swelling stronger—but only with healthy, unmarked men and women who were willing to rebuild America. He grinned; oh, what a game of King's Knight this had turned out to be!

"People will follow me," Colonel Macklin said, nodding. "I'll *make* them follow me. I'll teach them all about discipline and control, and they'll do anything I say. Right?" His eyes blazed at Sheila.

She hesitated. Both the war hero and the kid were watching her. She thought of her warm bed, all the food and the guns that were here, and then she thought of the cold dirtwart land and the things that slithered in the dark. "Right," she said. "Anything you say."

Within two hours, Lawry and his raiding party returned with the Chevy van, the Pontiac and the two trailers. The small camp was taken by surprise, and there had been no wounds or casualties to Macklin's Army of Excellence. Lawry delivered several knapsacks full of canned goods and more bottled water, plus three cans of gasoline and a carton of engine oil. He emptied his pockets of wristwatches, diamond rings and a money clip full of twenties and fifties. Macklin let him keep one of the watches and told him to distribute extra rations to the rest of the raiding party. The largest of the diamond rings he offered to Sheila Fontana, who stared at it for a moment as it glittered on Macklin's palm and then took it from him. It was inscribed *From Daniel to Lisa—Love Forever*. Only after she'd put it on and was admiring it by lamplight did she realize that grains of dried blood were stuck down in the setting, giving the diamonds a dirty cast.

Roland found a road map of Utah on the rear floorboard of

the Buick, and from the glove compartment he retrieved several Flair pens and a compass. He gave all the booty to the King, and Macklin rewarded him with one of the medals adorned with a swastika.

Roland immediately pinned it on his shirt.

In the lamplight, Colonel Macklin spread the road map out on the table in his command headquarters and sat down to study it. After a few moments of silent deliberation, he picked up a red Flair pen and began to draw a jagged arrow pointing east.

"My main man," the Shadow Soldier said, leaning over Macklin's shoulder.

And in the morning, under thick gray clouds scudding slowly eastward, Roland and Lawry and ten handpicked soldiers escorted thirty-six burn-scarred men, women and children out to the edge of the dirtwart land. After the shooting was over, the dirtwarts emerged from their holes and scuttled forward to claim the corpses.

Forty-five

Swan and Josh had been following the railroad tracks through a Nebraska dust storm for three days when they found the wrecked train.

They didn't see the train until they were almost upon it. And then there it was, railroad cars scattered everywhere, some of them riding piggyback. Most of the cars were broken to pieces except for a caboose and a couple of freight cars. Swan slid down off Mule, following Josh as he walked carefully over the debris. "Watch out for nails!" he warned her, and she nodded. Killer had been turned the color of chalk by all the dust, and he advanced before Josh, sniffing warily at the splintered planks under his paws.

Josh stopped, shielding his eyes from the dust with one hand, and he looked up at the side of a freight car. The storm had almost scoured all the paint off, but he could still make out a faded panorama of clowns, lions and three rings under a big top. Scrolled red letters spelled out RYDELL CIRCUS, INC.

"It's a circus train!" he told Swan. "Probably going somewhere to set up when it got knocked off the tracks." He motioned toward the caboose. "Let's see what we can find."

For the past three nights they'd slept in barns and deserted farmhouses, and once the railroad tracks had taken them to the outskirts of a moderate-sized town—but the wind brought such a smell of decay from the town that they dared not enter it. They'd circled the town, picking up the tracks on the other side and continuing across the open plains.

The caboose's door was unlocked. It was gloomy within, but at least it was shelter. Josh figured both the horse and terrier could fend for themselves, and he stepped in. Swan followed, closing the door behind her.

Josh bumped into a small desk, making little bottles and jars clink. The air was warmer the further he went, and he made out the shape of a cot to his right. His groping fingers touched warm metal—a cast-iron, freestanding stove. "Somebody's been here," he said. "Hasn't been gone very long, either." He found the grate and opened it; inside a few coals had burned down to ashes, and an ember glowed like a tiger's eye.

He continued to feel his way around the caboose, almost tripping over a bundle of blankets lying in a corner, and made his way back to the desk. His eyes were getting used to the dim yellow murk that came through the caboose's filmy windows, and he discovered a half-burned candle stuck with wax to a saucer. Near it was a box of kitchen matches. He struck one and lit the candle's wick, and the light spread.

Swan saw what appeared to be crayons and lipsticks atop the desk. A curly red wig sat on a wigstand. In front of the desk's folding metal chair was a wooden box, about the size of a shoebox, decorated with little intricately carved lizards. Their tiny eyes were formed of multifaceted glass, and they sparkled in the candlelight.

Next to the cot Josh found an open bag of Gravy Train dog food and a plastic jug that sloshed when he nudged it with his foot.

Swan stepped closer to the stove. On a wall rack were gaudy suits with spangles, oversized buttons and floppy lapels. There was a pile of newspapers, shards of timber and coals ready for the fire. She looked toward the far corner, where the bundle of blankets lay. Except there was something else over there, too . . . something only half covered by the blankets. "Josh?" She pointed. "What's *that?*"

He brought the candle over. The light fell on the rigid smile of a clown's face.

At first Josh was startled, but then he realized what it was. "A dummy! It's a life-sized dummy!" The thing was sitting up, with white greasepaint on its face and bright red lips; a green wig was perched on its scalp, and its eyelids were closed. Josh leaned forward and poked the dummy's shoulder.

His heart kicked.

He gingerly touched the thing's cheek and smeared off some of the greasepaint. Under it was sallow flesh.

The corpse was cold and stiff and had been dead at least two or three days.

Behind them, the caboose door suddenly swung open, letting in a whirlwind of dust.

Josh spun around, stepping in front of Swan to shield her from whoever—or whatever—was coming in. He saw a figure standing there, but dust in his eyes blinded him.

The figure hesitated. In one hand was a shovel. There was a long, tense silence, and then the man in the doorway said, "Howdy," in a thick western drawl. "You folks been here long?" He closed the door, shutting off the storm. Josh watched him warily as the man walked across the caboose, his cowboy boots clomping on the planked floor, and leaned the shovel against a wall. Then the man untied a bandanna from around his nose and mouth. "Well? Can you two speak English, or am I gonna have to do all the talkin'?" He paused a few seconds, then answered himself in a high, mocking voice, "Yessir, we surely do speak English, but our eyeballs are 'bout to bug out of our heads, and if we flap our tongues they'll go flyin' out like fried eggs." He pronounced it *aigs.*

"We can speak," Josh replied. "It's just . . . you surprised us."

"Reckon I did. But the last time I walked out that door, Leroy was alone, so I'm a mite surprised myself." He took off his cowboy hat and swatted it against one denim-covered thigh. Dust welled into the air. "That's Leroy." He motioned toward the clown in the corner. "Leroy Satterwaite. He died coupla nights ago, and he was the last of 'em. I been out diggin' a hole for him."

"The last of them?" Josh prompted.

"Yep. Last of the circus people. One of the best clowns you ever laid your eyes on. Man, he could've made a stone crack a grin." He sighed and shrugged. "Well, it's over now. He was the last of 'em—except me, I mean."

Josh stepped toward the man and held the candle and saucer out to illuminate his face.

The man was thin and lanky, his scraggly, grizzled face as long and narrow as if it had been pressed in a vise. He had curly light brown hair spilling over his high forehead almost to his bushy brown eyebrows; beneath them, his eyes were large and liquid, a shade between hazel and topaz. His nose was long and thin, in keeping with the rest of him, but it was the mouth that was the centerpiece of his face: the lips were thick, rubbery folds of flesh designed to pull miraculous mugs and grins. Josh hadn't seen such a pair of lips since he'd been served a bigmouth bass in a restaurant in Georgia. The man wore a dusty denim jacket, obviously much used and abused, a dark blue flannel shirt and jeans. His lively, expressive eyes moved from Josh to Swan, lingered a few seconds, then returned to Josh. "Name's Rusty Weathers," he said. "Now who in blazes are you, and how'd you get out here?"

"My name is Josh Hutchins, and this is Swan Prescott. We haven't had any food or water in three days. Can you help us?"

Rusty Weathers nodded toward the plastic jug. "Help yourselves. That's water from a creek a coupla hundred yards from the tracks. Can't say how clean it is, but I've been drinkin' it for about—" He frowned, walked over to the wall and felt for the notches he'd carved there with his penknife. He ran a finger along them. "Forty-one days, give or take."

Josh opened the jug, sniffed at it and took a tentative swallow. The water tasted oily, but otherwise okay. He drank again and gave the jug to Swan.

"Only food I've got left is Gravy Train," Rusty said. "Fella and his wife had a dog act. Jumped French poodles through hoops and all." He plopped the cowboy hat on top of the red wig, pulled the folding chair to him, turned it around and sat down with his arms crossed on the backrest. "Been a time, I'll tell ya. Train was movin' pretty as you please one minute; the next minute the sky looked like the inside of a mine shaft, and the wind started whippin' cars right off the tracks. We get twisters back in Oklahoma, but damned if this wasn't the granddaddy of 'em all!" He shook his head, rattling loose the memories. "You got any cigarettes?"

"No. Sorry."

"Damn! Man, I could just about *eat* a carton of smokes right now!" He narrowed his eyes, examining both Josh and Swan in silence. "You two look like you been stomped by a few dozen Brahma bulls. You hurtin'?"

"Not anymore," Josh said.

"What's goin' on out there? There ain't been another train along this track in forty-one days. The dust just keeps on blowin'. What's happenin'?"

"Nuclear war. I think the bombs fell just about everywhere. Probably hit the cities first. From what we've seen so far, I don't think there's much left."

"Yeah." Rusty nodded, his eyes vacant. "I kinda figured it must be that. A few days after the wreck, me and some of the others started walkin', tryin' to find help. Well, the dust was a lot thicker and the wind stronger back then, and we made it about fifty feet before we had to come back. So we sat down to wait. But the storm didn't stop, and nobody came." He stared at a window. "Nicky Rinaldi—the lion tamer—and Stan Tembrello decided to follow the tracks. That was a month ago. Leroy was busted up inside, so I stayed here with him and Roger—all of us were clowns, see. The Three Musketeers. Oh, we put on a good show! We really made 'em laugh!" His eyes teared up suddenly, and it was a moment before he could speak again.

"Well," he said finally, "me and the others who were left started diggin' graves. The wreck killed a lot of folks outright, and there were dead animals all over the place. Dead elephant's lyin' up the tracks a ways, but he's all dried up now. Man, you couldn't believe what that smelled like! But who in hell has got the strength to dig a grave for an *elephant?* We got a regular circus cemetery not too far from here." He nodded vaguely off to the right. "Dirt's softer, once you get away from the tracks. I'd managed to find some of my gear, and I moved in here with Leroy, Roger and a few of the others. Found my make-up case." He touched the wooden box with its carved, creeping lizards. "Found my magic jacket, too." A finger hooked toward the rack where the clothes hung. "I wasn't hurt too bad. Just bruises on bruises and this." He lifted that big upper lip to display the space where a front tooth had been knocked out. "But I was okay. Then . . . everybody started dyin'."

He sat looking at the candle. "It was the damnedest thing," he said. "People who were fine one day were dead the next. One night . . ." His eyes glazed over like pond ice, and the memories had him again. "One night we were all sleepin', and I woke up cold. The stove was goin', and the caboose was warm—but I was shiverin'. And I swear to God . . . I knew the shadow of Death was here, movin' from person to person, figurin' out who to take next. I think whatever it was passed near enough to me to freeze my bones—and then it moved on. And when daylight came, Roger was dead with his eyes open, and he'd been tellin' jokes the day before. You know what that crazy Leroy says? He says, 'Rusty, let's you and me put a happy face on that sumbitch before we send him off!" So we painted him up—but it wasn't a disrespectful thing, oh, no!" Rusty shook his head. "We loved that old scudder. We just gave him the face he was most comfortable wearin'. Then me and Eddie Roscoe carried him out and buried him. Seems like I helped dig a hundred graves in a week's time, until it was just me and Leroy." He smiled faintly, looking past Swan and Josh into the corner. "Lookin' good, old buddy! Hell, I thought I'da been the one long gone before now!"

"There's no one else here but you?" Swan asked.

"Just me. I'm the last of the Rydell Circus." He looked at Josh. "Who won?"

"Who won what?"

"The war. Who won the war? Us or the Russians?"

"I don't know. If Russia looks anything like what Swan and I've seen . . . God help those people, too."

"Well, you gotta fight fire with fire," Rusty said. "That's somethin' my mama used to tell me. Fight fire with fire. So maybe there's one good thing about this: Maybe everybody shot all their bombs and missiles off, and there ain't any more. The fires just fought it out—and the old world's still here, ain't it?"

"Yes," Josh agreed. "The world's still here. And so are we."

"I reckon the world's gonna be a mite changed, though. I mean, if everywhere is like here, I believe the luxuries of life are gonna be sufferin' some."

"Forget luxuries," Josh told him. "This caboose and that stove are luxuries, friend."

Rusty grinned, showing the hole where his tooth had been. "Yep, I got a real palace here, don't I?" He gazed at Swan for a few seconds, then got up, went to the rack and took from its hanger a black velvet suit jacket. He winked at her, shrugged out of his denim jacket and put on the one made of black velvet. In the breast pocket was a white handkerchief. "I'll tell you what's still here, too—somethin' that'll never change, little lady. *Magic*. You believe in magic, hon?"

"Yes," she said.

"Good!" He whipped the white handkerchief out and suddenly there was a bouquet of brightly colored paper flowers in his hand. He offered them to Swan. "You look like a lady who might appreciate some pretty flowers. 'Course, we'd better water 'em, too! If flowers don't get their water, they might just swoon away!" He thrust his other hand forward, snapped his wrist in the air, and he was holding a small red plastic pitcher. He tipped it over the flowers, but instead of water, a trickle of yellow dust came out and floated to the floor. "Aw," Rusty said, feigning disappointment. Then his eyes brightened. "Well, maybe that's magic dust, little lady! Sure! Magic dust'll keep flowers alive just as good as water will! What do you think?"

Even though the corpse in the corner gave her the creeps, Swan had to smile. "Sure," she said. "I bet it will, too."

Rusty waved his slim hand in the air before Swan's face. She suddenly saw a red ball appear between the first and second fingers, and then another ball seemingly grew between his thumb and forefinger. He took one ball in each hand and began tossing them up in the air from hand to hand.

"Think we're missin' somethin', don't you?" he asked her, and when the balls were in mid-air he reached with his right hand toward Swan's ear. She heard a soft *pop* and his hand withdrew with a third red ball. He juggled the three of them back and forth. "There you go. Knew I'd find that thing somewhere!"

She felt her ear. "How'd you do that?"

"Magic," he explained. He plopped one ball in his mouth, then the second and third. His empty hand caressed the air, and Swan saw Rusty's throat gulp as he swallowed the balls. "Mighty tasty," he said. "Want to try 'em?" He offered his palm to her; in it were the three red balls.

"I saw you eat them!" Swan exclaimed.

"Yep, I did. These are three more. That's what I've been livin' on, see. Gravy Train and magic balls." His smile faltered, began to fade. His eyes flickered over toward the corpse, and he put the three balls in his pocket. "Well," he said, "I reckon that's enough magic for one day."

"You're pretty good," Josh said. "So you're a clown, a magician and a juggler. What else do you do?"

"Oh, I used to ride broncos in the rodeos." He took off the velvet jacket and hung it up like putting an old friend to bed. "Used to be a rodeo clown. Used to short-order cook in a carnival. Worked on a cattle ranch once. Jack of all trades and master of none, I reckon. But I've always loved magic. Hungarian magician name of Fabrioso took me under his wing when I was sixteen and taught me the craft, back when I was shillin' with the carny. Said I had hands that could either pick pockets or pull dreams out of the air." Rusty's eyes danced with light. "That Fabrioso was somethin' else, I'll tell ya! He talked to the spirits—and they sure 'nuff answered him and did what he said, too!"

"Is this magic, too?" Swan touched the wooden box covered with lizards.

"That was Fabrioso's box of tricks. I keep my makeup and stuff in it now. Fabrioso got it from a magician in Istanbul. Know where that is? Turkey. And that magician got it from one in China, so I reckon it kinda has a history."

"Like Crybaby does," Swan said, and she held up the dowsing rod.

"Crybaby? That's what you call that dowser?"

"A woman—" Josh hesitated. The loss of Leona Skelton was still too raw. "A very special woman gave that to Swan."

"Did Fabrioso give you the magic jacket?" Swan asked.

"Naw. I bought that in a magic store in Oklahoma City. But he gave me the box, and one other thing." He unlatched and opened the carved box. Inside were jars, crayons and rags smeared with a thousand colors. He dug down toward the bottom. "Fabrioso said this came with the box in a set, so it was right that it went where the box did. Here it is." He withdrew his hand.

In it was a simple oval mirror, framed in black with a scuffed black handle. There was only one ornamentation: Where the handle was attached to the mirror were two small black masklike faces peering in opposite directions. The glass was a smoky color, streaked and stained.

"Fabrioso used this to put on his stage makeup." There was a note of awe in Rusty's voice. "He said it showed a truer picture than any mirror he'd ever looked into. I don't use it, though—the glass has gone too dull." He held it out to Swan, and she took it by the handle. The thing was as light as a buttermilk biscuit.

"Fabrioso was ninety when he died, and he told me he got the mirror when he was seventeen. I'll bet it's two hundred years old if it's a day."

"Wow!" Something that old was beyond Swan's comprehension. She peered into the glass but could see her face there only dimly, as if through a curtain of mist. Even so, the burn marks still jarred her, and there was so much dust on her face she thought she resembled a clown herself. She was never going to get used to not having hair, either. She looked closer. On her forehead were two more of those strange dark wartlike things she'd noticed at Leona's; had those always been there, or had they just come up?

"I guess Fabrioso was kinda vain," Rusty admitted. "I used to catch him lookin' in that mirror all the time—except he was usually holdin' it at arm's length, like this." He stuck his own hand in front of his face as if his palm were a looking glass.

Swan thrust her arm out. The mirror was aimed at the left side of her face and her left shoulder. Now her head was only an outline in the glass. "I can't see myself like—"

There was a movement in the glass. A quick movement. And not her own.

A face with an eye in the center of its head, a gaping mouth where the nose should've been, and skin as yellow as dried-up parchment paper rose behind her left shoulder like a leprous moon.

Swan dropped the mirror. It clinked to the floor, and she spun around to her left.

There was no one there. Of course.

"Swan?" Rusty had gotten to his feet. "What is it?"

Josh put the candle and saucer aside and laid his hand on Swan's shoulder. She pressed into his side, and he could feel her racing heartbeat. Something had scared the stew out of her. He leaned over and picked up the mirror, expecting it to be shattered to pieces, but it was still whole. Looking into the glass, he was repelled by his own face, but he lingered long enough to see that there were four new warts on his chin. He handed the mirror back to Rusty. "Good thing it didn't break. I guess that would've been seven years bad luck."

"I saw Fabrioso drop it a hundred times. Once he flung it down as hard as he could on a concrete floor. It didn't even crack. See, he used to tell me this mirror was magic, too—only he didn't really understand it, so he never told me *why* he thought it was magic." Rusty shrugged. "I just think it looks like a smoky old glass, but since it went with the box I decided to hold onto it." He turned his attention to Swan, who still stared uneasily at the mirror. "Don't fret. Like I say, the thing won't break. Hell, it's stronger'n *plastic!*" He laid the mirror down on the tabletop.

"You okay?" Josh asked.

She nodded; whatever monster she'd seen behind her in that mirror, she did not care to lay eyes on it again. Whose face had that been, down in the depths of the glass? "Yes," she replied, and she made her voice sound like she meant it.

Rusty built a fire in the stove, and then Josh helped him carry the corpse out to the circus cemetery. Killer yapped along at their heels.

And while they were gone, Swan approached the mirror again. It called her, just like the tarot cards had at Leona's.

She slowly picked it up and, holding it at arm's length, angled it toward her left shoulder as she had before.

But there was no monster face. There was nothing.

Swan turned the mirror toward her right. Again, nothing.

She missed Leona deeply, and she thought of the Devil card in the tarot deck. That face, with the awful eye in the center of its head and a mouth that looked like a hallway to Hell, had reminded her of the figure on that card.

"Oh, Leona," Swan whispered, "why'd you have to leave us?"

There was a quick red glint in the mirror, just a flash and then gone.

Swan looked over her shoulder. The stove was behind her, and red flames were crackling in the grate.

She peered into the mirror again. It was dark, and she realized it was not angled toward the stove after all.

A pinpoint of ruby-red light flickered and began to grow.

Other colors flashed like distant lightning: emerald green, pure white, deep midnight blue. The colors strengthened, merging into a small, pulsating ring of light that Swan at first thought was floating in the air. But in the next moment she thought she could make out a hazy, indistinct figure holding that ring of light, but she couldn't tell if it was a man or a woman. She almost turned around, but did not, because she knew there was nothing behind her but a wall. No, this sight was only in the magic mirror—but what did it mean?

The figure seemed to be walking, wearily but with determination, if as whoever it was knew he or she had a long journey to finish. Swan sensed that the figure was a long way off—maybe not even in the same state. But for a second she might have been able to make out the facial features, and it might have been the hard-edged face of a woman; then it went all hazy again, and Swan couldn't tell. The figure seemed to be searching, bearing a ring brighter than firefly lights, and behind her there might have been other searching figures, too, but again Swan couldn't quite separate them from the mist.

The first figure and the glowing circle of many colors began to fade away, and Swan watched until it had dwindled to a point of light like the burning spear of a candle; then it winked out like a falling star and was gone.

"Come back," she whispered. "Please come back."

But the vision did not. Swan aimed the mirror to her left.

And behind that shoulder reared a skeletal horse, and on that horse was a rider made of bones and dripping gore, and in his skeleton arms was a scythe that he lifted for a slashing, killing blow. . . .

Swan turned.

She was alone. All alone.

She was trembling, and she set the mirror glass side down on the desk. She'd had enough magic to last her a while.

"Everything's changed now," she remembered Leona saying. *"All that was is gone. Maybe the whole world's just like Sullivan: blowin' away, changin', turnin' into somethin' different than it was before."*

She needed Leona to help her figure out these new pieces of the jigsaw puzzle, but Leona was gone. Now it was her and Josh—and Rusty Weathers, too, if he decided to go with them to wherever they were headed.

But what did the visions in the magic mirror mean? she wondered. Were they things that *were* going to happen, or things that *might?*

She decided to keep the visions to herself until she'd thought about them some more. She didn't know Rusty Weathers well enough yet, though he seemed okay.

When Josh and Rusty returned, Josh asked the other man if they could stay for a few days, share the water and Gravy Train—and Swan wrinkled her nose, but her belly growled.

"Where do you two figure to be goin'?" Rusty inquired.

"I don't know yet. We've got a strong-backed horse and the gutsiest damned mutt you ever saw, and I guess we'll keep going until we find a place to stop."

"That could be a long time. You don't know what's out there."

"I know what's behind us. What's ahead can't be much worse."

"You *hope,*" Rusty said.

"Yeah." He glanced at Swan. Protect the child, he thought. He was going to do his damnedest, not only because he was obeying that commandment, but because he loved the child and would do all in his power to make sure she survived whatever was ahead. And that, he realized, might be like a walk through Hell itself.

"I reckon I'll tag along, if you don't mind," Rusty decided. "All I've got are the clothes on my back, my magic jacket, the box and the mirror. I don't think there's much of a future here, do you?"

"Not much," Josh said.

Rusty looked through a filmy window. "Lord, I hope I just live long enough to see the sun come out again, and then I'm gonna kill myself with cigarettes."

Josh had to laugh, and Rusty cackled, too.

Swan smiled, but her smile faded fast.

She felt a long way from the little girl who'd walked with her mother into PawPaw Briggs's grocery store. She would be ten on the third of November, but right now she felt real old—like at least thirty. And she didn't know anything about anything! she thought. Before the bad day, her world had been confined to motels and trailers and little cinder block houses. What had the rest of the world been like? she wondered. And now that the bad day had come and gone, what was left?

"The world'll keep turnin'," Leona had said. "Oh, God gave this world a mighty spin, He did! And He put mighty tough minds and souls in a lot of people, too—people like you, *maybe."*

She thought of PawPaw Briggs sitting up and speaking.

That was something she hadn't wanted to think about too much, but now she wanted to know what that had meant. She didn't feel special in any way; she just felt tired and beat-up and dusty, and when she let her thoughts drift toward her mama all she wanted to do was break down and cry. But she did not.

Swan wanted to know more about everything—to learn to read better, if books could be found; to ask questions and learn to listen; to learn to think and reason things out. But she never wanted to grow up all the way, because she feared the grownup world; it was a bully with a fat stomach and a mean mouth who stomped on gardens before they had a chance to grow.

No, Swan decided. I want to be who I am, and nobody's going to stomp me down—and if they try, they might just get themselves a footful of stickers.

Rusty had been watching the child as he mixed their dinner of dog food; he saw she was deep in concentration. "Penny for your thoughts," he said, and he snapped the fingers of his right hand, bringing up between his thumb and forefinger the coin he'd already palmed. He tossed it to her, and Swan caught it.

She saw it wasn't a penny. It was a brass token, about the size of a quarter, and it had *Rydell Circus* written on it above the smiling face of a clown.

Swan hesitated, looked at Josh and then back to Rusty. She decided to say, "I'm thinking about . . . tomorrow."

And Josh sat with his back against the wall, listening to the shrill whine of the wind and hoping that somehow they would survive the forbidding corridor of tomorrows that stretched ahead of them.

Forty-six

The Homewood High School gymnasium had become a hospital, and Red Cross and army personnel had rigged up generators that kept the electricity going. A haggard Red Cross doctor named Eichelbaum led Sister and Paul Thorson through the maze of people lying on cots and mattresses on the floor. Sister kept the duffel bag at her side; she had not gone more than five feet from it in the three days since their gunshots had been heard by a group of sentries. A hot meal of corn, rice and steaming coffee had tasted to Sister like gourmet delicacies.

She'd gone into a cubicle in a building marked INCOMING and had submitted to being stripped by a nurse in a white suit and mask who had run a Geiger counter over her body. The nurse had jumped back three feet when the counter's needle almost went off the scale. Sister had been scrubbed with some kind of white, grainy powder, but still the counter cackled like a hen in heat. A half-dozen more scrubbings brought the reading down to an acceptable level, but when the nurse had said, "We'll have to dispose of this," and reached for the duffel bag, Sister had grabbed her by the back of the neck and asked her if she still liked living.

Two Red Cross doctors and a couple of army officers who looked like boy scouts except for the livid burns across their faces couldn't pry the bag away from Sister, and finally Dr. Eichelbaum had thrown up his arms and shouted, "Just scrub the shit out of the damned thing, then!"

The duffel bag had been scrubbed several times, and the powder had been sprayed liberally over its contents. "You just keep that damned bag *closed,* lady!" Eichelbaum fumed. One side of his face was covered with blue burns, and he had lost the sight in one eye. "If I see you open it *once,* it goes in the incinerator!"

Both Sister and Paul Thorson had been given baggy white coveralls. Most of the others wore them, and rubber boots as well, but Eichelbaum informed them that all the "antiradiation footgear" had been given out several days before.

Dr. Eichelbaum had put a Vaseline-like substance over the burn marks on her face, and he had examined closely a thickened patch of skin just underneath her chin that looked like a scab surrounded by four small, wartlike bumps. He'd found another two warts at the jawline under her left ear, and a seventh right at the fold of her left eye. He'd told her that about sixty-five percent of the survivors bore similar marks—most probably skin cancer, but there was nothing he could do about them. Slicing them off with a scalpel, he'd told her, only made them grow back larger—and he showed her the angry black scablike mark that was creeping up from the point of his own chin. The most peculiar thing about the marks, he'd said, was that they appeared only on or near the facial area; he hadn't seen any that were below the neck, or on a survivor's arms, legs or any other area of skin exposed to the blasts.

The makeshift hospital was full of burn victims, people who had radiation sickness and people in shock and depression. The worst cases were kept in the school auditorium, Eichelbaum had told her, and their mortality rate was about ninety-nine percent. Suicide was also a major problem, and as the days passed and people seemed to understand more about the disaster's scope, Dr. Eichelbaum said, the number of people found hanging from trees increased.

The day before, Sister had gone to the Homewood Public Library and found the building deserted, most of the books gone, used as fuel in the fires that kept people alive. The shelves had been ripped out, the tables and chairs carried off to be burned. Sister turned down one of the few aisles where shelves of books remained and found herself staring at the antiradiation footgear of a woman who had climbed up a stepladder and hanged herself from a light fixture.

But she'd found what she was looking for, amid a pile of encyclopedias, American history books, *Farmer's Almanacs* and other items that had been spared burning. And in it she'd seen for herself.

"Here he is," Dr. Eichelbaum said, weaving through a few last cots to the one where Artie Wisco lay. Artie was sitting up against a pillow, a tray-table between his cot and the one to his left, and he was engrossed in playing poker with a young black man whose face was covered with white, triangular burns so precise they looked like they'd been stamped on the skin.

"Hiya!" Artie said, grinning at Sister and Paul as they approached. "Full house!" He turned his cards over, and the black man said, "Sheeeyat! You cheatin', man!" But he forked over some toothpicks from a pile on his side of the tray.

"Look at this!" Artie pushed the sheet back and showed them the heavy tape that crisscrossed his ribs. "Robot here wants to play tic-tac-toe on my belly!"

"Robot?" Sister asked, and the black youth raised a finger to tip an imaginary hat.

"How're you doing today?" the doctor asked Artie. "Did the nurse take your urine sample?"

"Sure did!" Robot said, and he hooted. "Little fool's got a cock that'd hang from here to Philly!"

"There's not much privacy here," Artie explained to Sister, trying to keep his dignity. "They have to take the samples in front of God and everybody."

"Some o' these women 'round here see what *you* got, fool, they gon' be prayin' on their knees, I be tellin' you!"

"Oh, Jeez!" Artie squirmed with embarrassment. "Will you shut up?"

"You look a lot better," Sister offered. His flesh was no longer gray and sickly, and though his face was a mass of bandages and livid scarlet burn marks—keloids, Dr. Eichelbaum called them—she even thought he had healthy color in his cheeks.

"Oh, yeah, I'm gettin' handsomer all the time! Gonna look in the mirror one of these days and see Cary Grant starin' back!"

"Ain't no mirrors around here, fool," Robot reminded him. "All the mirrors done broke."

"Artie's been responding pretty well to the penicillin we've been pumping into him. Thank God we've got the stuff, or most of these people here would be dead from infections," Dr. Eichelbaum said. "He's still got a way to go yet before he's out of the woods, but I think he'll be okay."

"How about the Buchanan kid? And Mona Ramsey?" Paul asked.

"I'll have to check the list, but I don't think either one of them is critical." He looked around the gymnasium and shook his head. "There are so many, I can't keep up with them." His gaze returned to Paul. "If we had the vaccine, I'd put every one of you into rabies shots—but we don't, so I can't. You'd just better hope none of the wolves out there were rabid, folks."

"Hey, Doc?" Artie asked. "When do you think I can get out of here?"

"Four or five days at the minimum. Why? You planning on going somewhere?"

"Yeah," Artie replied without hesitation. "Detroit."

The doctor cocked his head so the one good eye was fixed firmly on Artie Wisco. "Detroit," he repeated. "I've heard Detroit was one of the first cities hit. I'm sorry, but I don't think there *is* a Detroit anymore."

"Maybe not. But that's where I'm going. That's where my home is, and my wife. Jeez, I grew up in Detroit! Whether it was hit or not, I've gotta go back there and find out what's left."

"Prob'ly the same as Philly," Robot said quietly. "Man, there ain't a *cinder* left in Philly."

"I have to go home," Artie said, his voice resolute. "That's where my wife is." He looked up at Sister. "I saw her, you know. I saw her in the glass ring, and she looked just like she did when she was a teenager. Maybe that meant something—like I had to have the faith to keep going to Detroit, to keep looking for her. Maybe I'll find her . . . and maybe I won't, but I have to go. You're gonna go with me, aren't you?"

Sister paused. Then she smiled faintly and said, "No, Artie. I can't. I've got to go somewhere else."

He frowned. "Where?"

"I've seen something in the glass ring, too, and I've got to go find out what it means. I *have* to, just like you have to go to Detroit."

"I don't know what the hell you're talking about," Dr. Eichelbaum said, "but where do you think you're going?"

"Kansas." Sister saw the doctor's single eye blink. "A town called Matheson. It's on the Rand McNally road atlas." She had disobeyed the doctor's orders and opened her bag long enough to stuff the road atlas down into it, next to the powder-covered circle of glass.

"Do you know how *far* it is to Kansas? How are you going to get there? Walk?"

"That's right."

"You don't seem to understand this situation," the doctor said calmly; Sister recognized the tone of voice as the way the attendants had addressed the crazy women in the asylum. "The first wave of nuclear missiles hit every major city in this country," he explained. "The second wave hit air force and naval bases. The third wave hit the smaller cities and rural industries. Then the fourth wave hit every other damned thing that wasn't already burning. From what I've heard, there's a wasteland east and west of about a fifty-mile radius of this point. There's nothing but ruins, dead people and people who're wishing they were dead. And you want to walk to Kansas? Sure. The radiation would kill you before you made a hundred miles."

"I lived through the blast in Manhattan. So did Artie. How come the radiation hasn't already killed us?"

"Some people seem to be more resistant than others. It's a fluke. But that doesn't mean you can keep absorbing radiation and shrug it off."

"Doctor, if I was going to die from radiation, I'd be bones by now. And the air's full of the shit anyway—you know it as well as I do! The stuff's everywhere!"

"The wind's carried it, yes," he admitted. "But you're wanting to walk right back into a supercontaminated area! Now, I don't know your reasons for wanting to go to—"

"No, you don't," she said. "And you can't. So save your breath; I'm going to rest here for a while, and then I'm leaving."

Dr. Eichelbaum started to protest again; then he saw the determination in the woman's stare, and he knew there was nothing more to be said. Still, it was in his nature to have the last word: "You're crazy." Then he turned and stalked away, figuring he had better things to do than trying to keep another fruitcake from committing suicide.

"Kansas," Artie Wisco said softly. "That's a long way from here."

"Yeah. I'm going to need a good pair of shoes."

Suddenly Artie's eyes glistened with tears. He reached out and grasped Sister's hand, pressing it against his cheek. "God bless you," he said. "Oh . . . God bless you."

Sister leaned down and hugged him, and he kissed her cheek. She felt the wetness of a tear, and her own heart ached for him.

"You're the finest lady I've ever known," he told her. "Next to my wife, I mean."

She kissed him, and then she straightened up again. Her eyes were wet, and she knew that in the years ahead she would think of him many times, and in her heart she would say a prayer for him. "You go to Detroit," she said. "You find her. You hear?"

"Yeah. I hear." He nodded, his eyes as bright as new pennies.

Sister turned away, and Paul Thorson followed her. Behind her, she heard Robot say, "Man, I had an uncle in Detroit. I was kinda thinkin' about . . ."

Sister wound her way through the hospital and out the doors. She stood staring at the football field, which was covered with tents, cars and trucks. The sky was dull gray, heavy with clouds. Off to the right, in front of the high school and under a long red canopy, was a large bulletin board where people stuck messages and questions. The board was always jammed, and Sister had walked along it the day before, looking at the pleas scribbled on scratch paper: "Searching for daughter, Becky Rollins, age fourteen. Lost in Shenandoah area July 17 . . ."; "Anybody with information about the DiBattista family from Scranton please leave . . ."; "Looking for Reverend Bowden, First Presbyterian Church of Hazleton, services urgently needed . . ."

Sister walked to the fence that surrounded the football field, set the duffel bag on the ground beside her and wound her fingers tightly through the mesh. Behind her came the sound of a woman wailing at the bulletin board, and Sister flinched. Oh, God, Sister thought, what have we done?

"Kansas, huh? What the hell do you want to go way out there for?"

Paul Thorson was beside her, leaning against the fence. There was a splint along the bridge of his broken nose. "Kansas," he prompted. "What's out there?"

"A town called Matheson. I saw it in the glass ring, and I found it in the road atlas. That's where I'm going."

"Yeah, but *why?"* He pulled up the collar of his battered leather jacket against the cold; he'd fought to keep the jacket as hard as Sister had fought for her duffel bag, and he wore it over the clean white coveralls.

"Because . . ." She paused, and then she decided to tell him what she'd been thinking since she'd found the road atlas. "Because I feel like I'm being led toward something—or someone. I think the things I've been seeing in that glass are real. My dreamwalking has been to real places. I don't know why or how. Maybe the glass ring is like . . . I don't know, like an antenna or something. Or like radar, or a key to a door I never even knew existed. I think I'm being led for some reason, and I've got to go."

"Now you're talking like the lady who saw a monster with roaming eyeballs."

"I don't expect you to understand. I don't expect you to give a shit, and I didn't ask you. What are you doing hanging around me, anyway? Didn't they assign you a tent?"

"Yeah, they did. I'm in with three other men. One of them cries all the time, and another one can't stop talking about baseball. I *hate* baseball."

"What *don't* you hate, Mr. Thorson?"

He shrugged and looked around, watching an elderly man and woman, both of their faces streaked with keloids, supporting each other as they staggered away from the bulletin board. "I don't hate being alone," he said finally. "I don't hate depending on myself. And I don't hate myself—though sometimes I don't like myself too much. I don't hate drinking. That's about it."

"Good for you. Well, I want to thank you for saving my life, and Artie's, too. You took good care of us, and I appreciate that. So—" She stuck out her hand.

But he didn't shake it. "What have you got that's worth a damn?" he asked her.

"Huh?"

"Something valuable. Do you have anything worth trading?"

"Trading for what?"

He nodded toward the vehicles parked on the field. She saw he was looking at a dented old Army Jeep with a patched convertible top painted with camouflage colors. "You got anything in that bag you could trade for a Jeep?"

"No. I don't—" And then she remembered that deep down in her duffel bag were the chunks of jewel-encrusted glass she'd picked up, along with the ring, in the ruins of Steuben Glass and Tiffany's. She'd transferred them from the Gucci bag and forgotten them.

"You're going to need transportation," he said. "You can't *walk* from here to Kansas. And what are you going to do about gasoline, food and water? You'll need a gun, matches, a good flashlight and warm clothes. Like I say, lady, what's out there is going to be like Dodge City and Dante's Inferno rolled into one."

"Maybe it will be. But why should you care?"

"I don't. I'm just trying to warn you, that's all."

"I can take care of myself."

"Yeah, I'll bet you can. I'll bet you were the bitch of the ball."

"Hey!" somebody called. "Hey, I've been lookin' for you, lady!"

Approaching them was the tall man in the fleece-lined coat and Stroh's beer cap who had been on sentry duty and heard the gunshots. "Been lookin' for you," he said as he chewed a couple of sticks of gum. "Eichelbaum said you were around."

"You found me. What is it?"

"Well," he said, "I kinda thought you was familiar the first time I seen you. He said you'd be carryin' a big leather bag, though, so I guess that's what threw me."

"What are you talking about?"

"It was two, three days before you folks got here. Fella just come ridin' along I-80 like he was out on a Sunday afternoon; he was on one of them French racin' bicycles with the handlebars slung low. Oh, I remember him, 'cause ol' Bobby Coates and me was up in the church tower on lookout, and Bobby punches me in the arm and says, 'Cleve, look at *that* shit!' Well, I looked and I seen it, but I still didn't believe it!"

"Speak *English*, friend!" Paul snapped. "What was it?"

"Oh, it was a man. Pedalin' that bike along I-80. But what was real weird was that he about had thirty or forty wolves followin' him, almost at his heels. Just paradin' along. And just before he gets to the top of the hill, this fella gets off his bike and turns around—and them wolves cower and slink like they was face-to-face with God. Then they broke and ran, and this fella walks his bike to the top of the hill." Cleve shrugged, puzzlement scrawled across his bovine face. "Well, we went out to get him. Big fella. Husky. Hard to tell how old he was, though. He had white hair, but his face was young. Anyway, he was wearin' a suit and tie and a gray raincoat. Didn't seem to be hurt or anything. He had on two-tone shoes. I remember that real well. Two-tone shoes." Cleve grunted, shook his head and directed his gaze at Sister. "He asked about *you*, lady. Asked if we'd seen a lady with a big leather bag. Said you was a relative, and that he had to find you. He seemed real eager and interested to find you, too. But me and Bobby didn't know nothin' about you, o' course, and this fella asked the other sentries, but they didn't know you, either. Said we'd take him into Homewood, give him a meal and shelter and let the Red Cross folks look him over."

Sister's heart had begun pounding, and she felt very cold. "What . . . happened to him?"

"Oh, he went on. Thanked us kindly and said he had miles to go yet. Then he wished us well and pedaled on out of sight, headin' west."

"How'd you know this guy was looking for *her?*" Paul asked. "He could've been searching for some other woman carrying a leather bag!"

"Oh no," Cleve answered, and smiled. "He described this lady here so well I could see her face right in my head. Just like a picture. That's why I thought you looked familiar at first, but I just this mornin' put it together. See, you didn't have a leather bag, and that's what threw me." He looked at Sister. "Did you know him, ma'am?"

"Yes," she replied. "Oh, yes, I know him. Did he . . . give you his name?"

"Hallmark. Darryl, Dal, Dave . . . somethin' like that. Well, he's gone west. Don't know what he'll find out there. Too bad you two missed each other so near."

"Yes." Sister felt as if her ribs had been laced with steel bands. "Too bad."

Cleve tipped his cap and went on about his business. Sister felt as if she were about to faint, and she had to lean against the fence for support.

"Who was he?" Paul asked—but the tone of his voice said that he was afraid to know.

"I've got to go to Kansas," Sister said firmly. "I've got to follow what I've seen in the glass ring. He's not going to give up looking for me, because he wants the glass ring, too. He wants to destroy it, and I can't let him get his hands on it—or

I'll never know what I'm supposed to find. Or *who* I'm looking for."

"You're going to need a gun." Paul was spooked by both Cleve's story and the terror in Sister's eyes. Nobody human could've gotten through those wolves without a scratch, he thought. And on a French racing bicycle? Was it possible that everything she'd told him was *true?* "A real big gun," he added.

"There's not one big enough." She picked up her duffel bag and started walking away from the high school, up the hill toward the tent she'd been assigned to.

Paul stood watching her go. Shit! he thought. What's going on here? That lady's got a ton of guts, but she's going to get herself slaughtered out there on old I-80! He thought she had about as much chance to get to Kansas alone as a Christian in a Cadillac had of getting to Heaven. He looked around at the hundreds of tents in the wooded hills, at the little campfires and burning lanterns that surrounded Homewood, and he shuddered.

This damned town's got too many people in it, he thought. He couldn't stand having to live in a tent with three other men. Everywhere he turned, there were people. They were all over the place, and he knew that pretty soon he'd have to hit the road or go crazy. So why not go to Kansas? *Why not?*

Because, he answered himself, we'll never get there.

So? Were you planning on living forever?

I can't let her go alone, he decided. Jesus Christ, I just *can't!*

"Hey!" he called after her, but she kept going, didn't even look back. "Hey, maybe I'll help you get a Jeep! But that's all! Don't expect me to do anything else!"

Sister kept walking, burdened with thought.

"Okay, I'll help you get some food and water, too!" Paul told her. "But you're on your own with the gun and gasoline!"

One step at a time, she was thinking. One step at a time gets you where you're going. And oh, Lord, I've got such a long way to go. . . .

"Okay, damn it! I'll help you!"

Sister finally heard him. She turned toward Paul. "What'd you say?"

"I said I'd help you!" He shrugged and started walking toward her. "I might as well add another layer to the shitcake, huh?"

"Yes," she said, and a smile played at the corners of her mouth. "You might as well."

Darkness came, and an icy rain fell on Homewood. In the woods the wolves howled, and the wind blew radiation across the land, and the world turned toward a new day.

Forty-seven

The bicycle's tires made a singing sound in the dark. Every so often they thumped over a corpse or veered around a wrecked car, but the legs that powered them had places to go.

Two-toned shoes on the pedals, the man leaned forward and pumped along Interstate 80, about twelve miles east of the Ohio line. The ashes of Pittsburgh flecked his suit. He'd spent two days amid the ruins, had found a group of survivors there and looked into their minds for the face of the woman with the circle of glass. But it wasn't in any of their heads, and before he'd left he'd convinced them all that eating the burned meat of dead bodies was a cure for radiation poisoning. He'd even helped them start on the first one.

Bon appétit, he thought. Below him, his legs pumped like pistons.

Where are you? he wondered. You can't have come this far! Not yet! Unless you're running day and night because you know I'm on your ass.

When the wolves had come out to first snap and then fawn at his heels, he'd thought they had gotten her, way back in eastern Pennsylvania. But if that were so, where was the leather bag? Her face hadn't been in the minds of the sentries back at Homewood, either, and if she'd been there, they would be the ones to know. So where was she? And—most importantly—where was the glass thing?

He didn't like the idea of its being out there somewhere. Didn't know what it was, or why it had come to be, but whatever it was, he wanted to smash it beneath his shoes. Wanted to break it into tiny fragments and grind those pieces into the woman's face.

Sister, he thought, and he sneered.

His fingers clenched the handlebars. The glass circle had to be found. Had to be. This was his party now, and such things were not allowed. He didn't like the way the woman had looked at it—and he didn't like the way she'd fought for it, either. It gave her false hope. So it was a humane thing, really, to find the glass circle and smash it and make her eat the shards. There was no telling how many others she could infect if she wasn't stopped.

Maybe she was already dead. Maybe one of her own kind had killed her and stolen her bag. Maybe, maybe, maybe . . .

There were too many maybes. But no matter who had it, or where it was, he had to find the glass circle, because such a thing as that should not be, and when it had gone dark and cold in his grip he'd known it was reading his soul.

"This is *my* party!" he shouted, and he drove over a dead man lying in his path.

But there were so many places to search, so many highways to follow. She must have turned off I-80 before she'd reached Homewood. But why would she? He remembered her saying, *"We keep going west."* And she would follow the line of least resistance, wouldn't she? Could she have taken shelter in one of the small hamlets between Jersey City and Homewood? If so, that would mean she was behind him, not ahead.

But everything and everyone was dead east of Homewood and that damned Red Cross station, right?

He slowed down, passing a crumpled sign that said NEW CASTLE NEXT LEFT. He was going to have to pull off and find a map somewhere, maybe retrace his route along another highway. Maybe she'd gone south and missed Homewood entirely. Maybe she was on a rural road somewhere right now, crouched by a fire and playing with that damned glass thing. Maybe, maybe, maybe . . .

It was a big country. But he had time, he reasoned as he swung off I-80 at the New Castle exit. He had tomorrow, and the next day, and the day after that. It was his party now, and he made the rules.

He'd find her. Oh, yes! Find her and shove that glass ring right up her . . .

He realized the wind had died down. It wasn't blowing as hard as it had been even a few hours before. That was why he hadn't been able to search properly yet. He had trouble searching when the wind was so rough—but the wind was his friend, too, because it spread the party dust.

He licked a finger with a cat-rough tongue and held it up. Yes, the wind had definitely weakened, though errant gusts still blew in his face and brought the smell of burned meat. It was time—past time—to get started.

His mouth opened. Stretched, and began to stretch wider still, while his black eyes stared from a handsome face.

A fly crawled out onto his lower lip. It was a shiny, ugly green, the kind of fly that might explode from the nostrils of a bloated corpse. It waited there, its iridescent wings twitching.

Another fly crawled from his mouth. Then a third, a fourth and a fifth. Six more scrabbled out and clung to his lower lip. A dozen others seeped out like a green tide. In another few seconds there were fifty or more flies around his mouth, a green froth that hummed and twitched with eager anticipation.

"Away," he whispered, and the movement of his lips sent the first group of them into the air, their wings vibrating against the wind until they found their balance. Others took off, nine or ten at a time, and their formations flew to all points of the compass. They were part of him, and they lived down in the damp cellar of his soul where such things grew, and after they made their slow radius of two or three miles they'd return to him as if he were the center of the universe. And when they came back, he'd see what they'd seen—a fire burning, sparking off a ring of glass; or her face, asleep in a room where she thought she was safe. If they didn't find her

tonight, there was always tomorrow. And the next day. Sooner or later, they would find a chink in a wall that brought him down on her, and this time he'd Watusi on her bones.

His face was rigid, his eyes black holes in a face that would scare the moon. The last two things that resembled flies but were extensions of his ears and eyes pushed from between his lips and lifted off, turning toward the southeast.

And still his two-toned shoes pumped the pedals, and the bike's tires sang, and the dead were ground under where they lay.

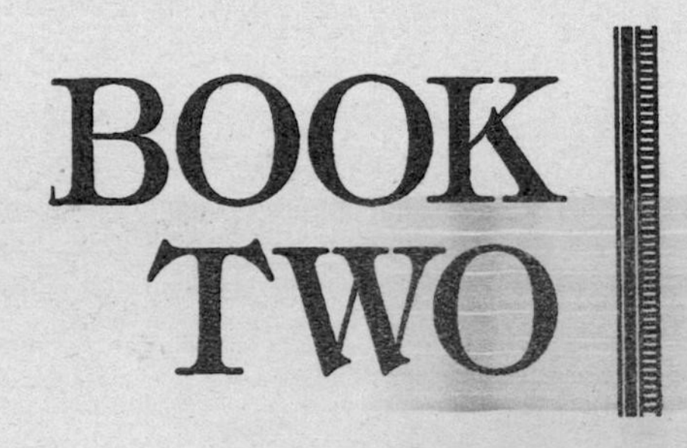

BOOK TWO

EIGHT

Toadfrog with Golden Wings

The last apple tree / Flee the mark of Cain / The good deed done / Job's Mask / Solitary journeyer / A new right hand / White blossoms

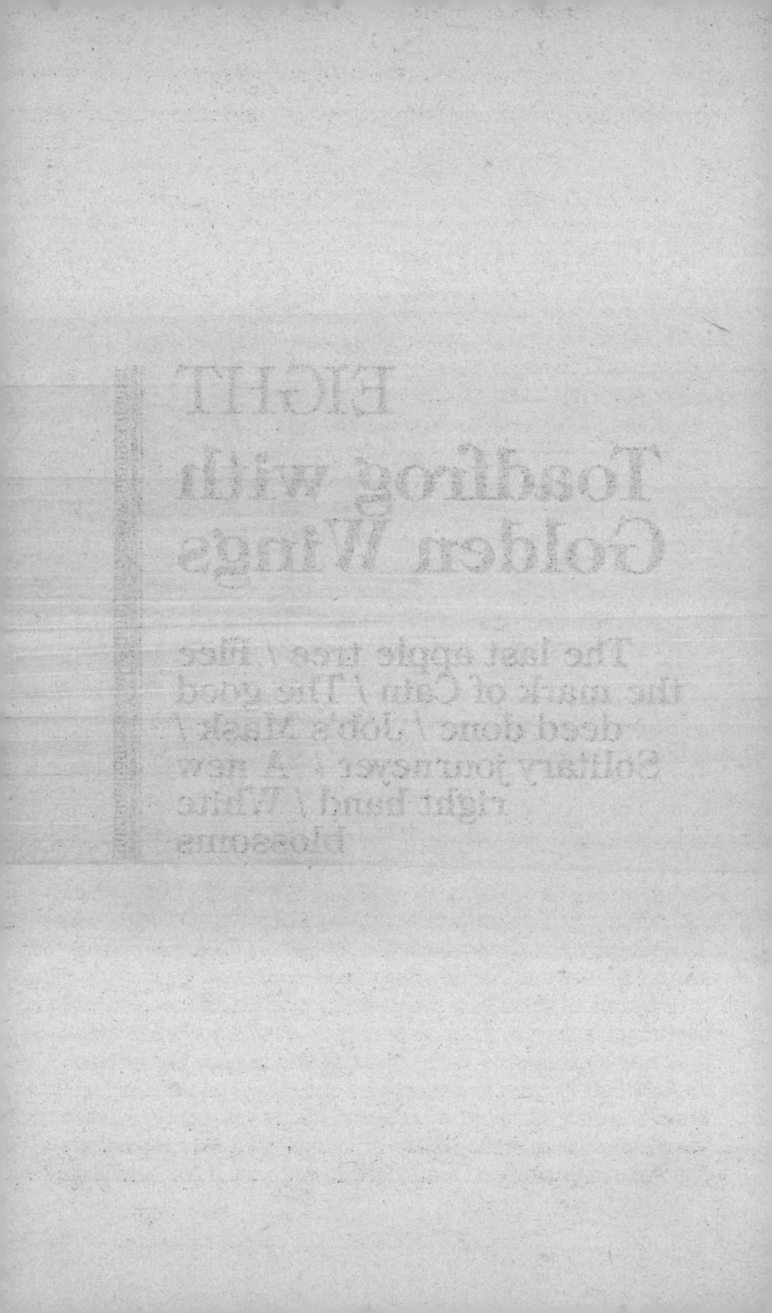

Forty-eight

Snow tumbled from the sullen sky, sweeping across a narrow country road in what had been, seven years before, the state of Missouri.

A piebald horse—old and swaybacked, but still strong-hearted and willing to work—pulled a small, crudely-built wagon, covered with a patched dark green canvas dome, that was a strange amalgam of Conestoga and U-Haul trailer. The wagon's frame was made of wood, but it had iron axles and rubber tires. The canvas dome was a two-man all-weather tent that had been stretched over curved wooden ribs. On each side of the canvas, painted in white, was the legend *Travelin' Show;* and, beneath that, smaller letters proclaimed *Magic! Music!* and *Beat the Masked Mephisto!*

A couple of thick boards served as a seat and footrest for the wagon's driver, who sat draped in a heavy woolen coat that was beginning to come apart at the seams. He wore a cowboy hat, its brim heavy with ice and snow, and on his feet were battered old cowboy boots. The gloves on his hands were essential to ward off the stinging wind, and a woolen plaid scarf was wrapped around the lower part of his face; just his eyes—a shade between hazel and topaz—and a slice of rough, wrinkled skin were exposed to the elements.

The wagon moved slowly across a snow-covered landscape, past black, dense forests stripped bare of leaves. On each side of the road, an occasional barn or farmhouse had collapsed under the weight of seven years of winter, and the only signs of life were black crows that pecked fitfully at the frozen earth.

A few yards behind the wagon, a large figure in a long, billowing gray overcoat trudged along, booted feet crunching on snow. He kept his hands thrust into the pockets of his brown corduroy trousers, and his entire head was covered with a black ski mask, the eyes and mouth ringed with red. His shoulders were bent under the whiplash of wind, and his legs ached with the cold. About ten feet behind him, a terrier followed, its coat white with snow.

I smell smoke, Rusty Weathers thought, and he narrowed his eyes to peer through the white curtain before him. Then the wind shifted direction, gnawing at him from another angle, and the smell of woodsmoke—if it had really been there at all—was gone. But in another few minutes he thought they must be getting near civilization; on the right, scrawled in red paint on the broad trunk of a leafless oak tree, was BURN YOUR DEAD.

Signs like that were commonplace, usually announcing that they were coming into a settled area. There could be either a village ahead or a ghost town full of skeletons, depending on what the radiation had done.

The wind shifted again, and Rusty caught that aroma of smoke. They were going up a gentle grade, Mule laboring as best he could but in no hurry. Rusty didn't push him. What was the use? If they could find shelter for the night, fine; if not, they'd make do somehow. Over the course of seven long years, they had learned how to improvise and use what they could find to the best advantage. The choice was simple; it was either survive or die, and many times Rusty Weathers had felt like giving up and lying down, but either Josh or Swan had kept him going with jokes or taunts—just as he had kept both of them alive over the years. They were a team that included Mule and Killer as well, and on the coldest nights when they'd had to sleep with minimal shelter, the warmth of the two animals had kept Rusty, Josh and Swan from freezing to death.

After all, Rusty thought with a faint, grim smile beneath the plaid scarf, the show must go on!

As they reached the top of the grade and started down on the winding road Rusty caught a yellow glint through the falling snow off to the right. The light was obscured by dead trees for a minute—but then there it was again, and Rusty felt sure it was the glint of a lantern or a fire. He knew calling to Josh was useless, both because of the wind and because Josh's hearing wasn't too good. He reined Mule in and pressed down with his boot a wooden lever that locked the front axle. Then he climbed down off the seat and went back to show Josh the light and tell him he was going to follow it.

Josh nodded. Only one eye showed through the black ski mask. The other was obscured by a gray, scablike growth of flesh.

Rusty climbed back onto the wagon's seat, released the brake and gave a gentle flick to the reins. Mule started off without hesitation, and Rusty figured he'd smelled the smoke and knew shelter might be near. Another road, narrower yet and unpaved, curved to the right over snow-covered fields. The glint of light got stronger, and soon Rusty could make out a farmhouse ahead, light glowing through a window. Other outbuildings were set off beside the house, including a small barn. Rusty noted that the woods had been cut away from around the house in all directions, and hundreds of stumps stuck up through the snow. There was just one dead tree remaining, small and skinny, standing about thirty yards in front of the house. He smelled the aroma of burning wood and figured that the forest was being consumed in somebody's fireplace. But burning wood didn't smell the same as it had before the seventeenth of July, and radiation had seeped into the forests; the smoke had a chemical odor, like burning plastic. Rusty remembered the sweet aroma of clean logs in a fireplace, and he figured that particular scent was lost forever, just like the taste of clean water. Now all the water tasted skunky and left a film on the inside of the mouth; drinking water from melted snow—which was about all the remaining supply—brought on headaches, stomach pains and blurred vision if consumed in too large a dose. Fresh water, like from a well or a bottled supply, was as valuable now as any fine French wine in the world that used to be.

Rusty pulled Mule up in front of the house and braked the wagon. His heart was beating harder. Here comes the tricky part, he thought. Plenty of times they'd been fired on when they stopped to ask for shelter, and Rusty carried the scar of a bullet crease across his left cheek.

There was no movement from the house. Rusty reached back and partially unzipped the tent's flap. Within, distributed around the wagon so as to keep its weight balanced, was their meager total of supplies: a few plastic jugs of water, some cans of beans, a bag of charcoal briquettes, extra clothes and blankets, their sleeping bags and the old Martin acoustic guitar Rusty was teaching himself to play. Music always drew people, gave them something to break the monotony; in one town, a grateful woman had given them a chicken when Rusty had painstakingly picked out the chords of "Moon River" for her. He'd found the guitar and a pile of songbooks in the dead town of Sterling, Colorado.

"Where are we?" the girl asked from the tent's interior. She'd been curled up in her sleeping bag, listening to the restless whine of the wind. Her speech was garbled, but when she spoke slowly and carefully Rusty could understand it.

"We're at a house. Maybe we can use their barn for the night." He glanced over to the red blanket that was wrapped around three rifles. A .38 pistol and boxes of bullets lay in a shoe box within easy reach of his right hand. Like my old mama always told me, he thought, you've gotta fight fire with fire. He wanted to be ready for trouble, and he started to pick up the .38 to hide under his coat when he approached the door.

Swan interrupted his thoughts by saying, "You're more likely to get shot if you take the gun."

He hesitated, recalling that he'd been carrying a rifle when that bullet had streaked across his cheek. "Yeah, I reckon so," he agreed. "Wish me luck." He zipped the flap again and got down off the wagon, took a deep breath of wintry air and approached the house. Josh stood by the wagon, watching, and Killer relieved himself next to a stump.

Rusty started to knock on the door, but as he raised his fist a slit opened in the door's center and the barrel of a rifle slid smoothly out to stare him in the face. Oh, shit, he thought, but his legs had locked and he stood helplessly.

"Who are you and what do you want?" a man's voice asked.

Rusty lifted his hands. "Name's Rusty Weathers. Me and my two friends out there need a place to shelter before it gets too dark. I saw your light from the road, and I see you've got a barn, so I was wonderin' if—"

"Where'd you come from?"

"West of here. We passed through Howes Mill and Bixby."

"Ain't nothin' left of them towns."

"I know. Please, mister, all we want is a place to sleep. We've got a horse that sure could use a roof over his head."

"Take off that kerchief and lemme see your face. Who you tryin' to look like? Jesse James?"

Rusty did as the man told him. There was silence for a moment. "It's awful cold out here, mister," Rusty said. The silence stretched longer. Rusty could hear the man talking to someone else, but he couldn't make out what was being said. Then the rifle barrel was suddenly withdrawn into the house, and Rusty let his breath out in a white plume. The door was unbolted—several bolts were thrown back—and then it opened.

A gaunt, hard-looking man—about sixty or so, with curly white hair and the untrimmed white beard of a hermit—stood before him, the rifle held at his side but still ready. The man's face was so tough and wrinkled it resembled carved stone, and his dark brown eyes moved from Rusty to the wagon. "What's that say on the side there? *Travelin' Show?* What in the name of Judas is *that?*"

"Just what it says. We're . . . we're entertainers."

An elderly, white-haired woman in blue slacks and a heavy white sweater peered warily over the man's shoulder. "Entertainers," the man repeated, and he frowned as if he'd smelled something bad. His gaze came back to Rusty. "You entertainers got any food?"

"We've got some canned food. Beans and stuff."

"We've got a pot of coffee and a little bit of salt pork. Put your wagon in the barn and bring your beans." Then he closed the door in Rusty's face.

When Rusty had driven the wagon into the barn, he and Josh untied Mule's traces so the horse could get to a small pile of straw and some dried corncobs. Josh poured water into a pail for Mule and found a discarded Mason jar for Killer to drink water from. The barn was well constructed and kept the wind out, so neither animal would be in danger of freezing when the light went out and the real cold descended.

"What do you think?" Josh asked Rusty quietly. "Can she go in?"

"I don't know. They seem okay, but a mite jittery."

"She can use the heat, if they've got a fire going." Josh blew into his hands and bent over to massage his aching knees. "We can make them understand it's not contagious."

"We don't know it's not."

"*You* haven't caught it, have you? If it was contagious, you'd have caught it long before now, don't you think?"

Rusty nodded. "Yeah. But how are we gonna make *them* believe that?"

The rear flap of the wagon's canvas dome was suddenly unzipped from the inside. Swan's mangled voice said from within, "I'll stay here. There's no need for me to scare anybody."

"They've got a fire in there," Josh told her, walking toward the rear of the wagon. Swan was standing up, crouched over and silhouetted by the dim lamplight. "I think it's all right if you go in."

"No, it's not. You can bring my food to me out here. It's better that way."

Josh looked up at her. She had a blanket around her shoulders and shrouding her head. In seven years, she had shot up to about five feet nine, gangly and long-limbed. It broke his heart that he knew she was right. If the people in that house were jittery, it was for the best that she stay here. "Okay," he said in a strangled voice. "I'll bring you out some food." Then he turned away from the wagon before he had to scream.

"Pass me down a few cans of those beans, will you?" Rusty asked her. She picked up Crybaby and tapped the cans with it, then moved over to pick up a couple. She put them into Rusty's hands.

"Rusty, if they can spare some books, I sure would be grateful," she said. "Anything'll do."

He nodded, amazed that she could still read.

"We won't be long," Josh promised, and he followed Rusty out of the barn.

When they had gone, Swan lowered the wooden tailgate and put a little stepladder down to the ground. Probing with the dowsing rod, she descended the ladder and walked to the barn door, her head and face still shrouded by the blanket. Killer walked along at her booted feet, tail wagging furiously, and barked for attention. His bark was not as sprightly as it had been seven years earlier, and age had taken the bounce out of the terrier's step.

Swan paused, laid Crybaby aside and picked Killer up. Then she cracked the barn door open and cocked her head way over to the left, peering out through the falling snow. The farmhouse looked so warm, so inviting—but she knew it was best that she stay where she was. In the silence, her breathing sounded like an asthmatic rasp.

Through the snow, she could make out that single remaining tree by the spill of light from the front window. Why just one tree? she wondered. Why did he cut the rest of them down and leave that one standing alone?

Killer strained up and licked into the darkness where her face was. She stood looking at that single tree for a minute longer, and then she closed the barn door, picked up Crybaby and probed her way over to Mule to rub his shoulders.

In the farmhouse, a fire blazed in a stone hearth. Over the flames, a cast-iron pot of salt pork was bubbling in a vegetable broth. Both the stern-faced elderly man and his more timid wife flinched noticeably when Josh Hutchins followed Rusty through the front door. It was his size more than the mask that startled them, for, though he'd lost a lot of flabby weight in the last few years, he'd gained muscle and was still a formidable sight. Josh's hands were streaked with white pigment, and the elderly man stared uncomfortably at them until Josh stuck them in his pockets.

"Here're the beans," Rusty said nervously, offering them to the man. He'd noted that the rifle leaned against the hearth, well within reach if the old man decided to go for it.

The cans of beans were accepted, and the old gent gave them to the woman. She glanced nervously at Josh and then went back to the rear of the house.

Rusty peeled off his gloves and coat, laid them over a chair and took his hat off. His hair had turned almost completely gray, and there were streaks of white at his temples, though he was only forty years old. His beard was ribboned with gray, the bullet scar a pale slash across his cheek. Around his eyes were webs of deep cracks and wrinkles. He stood in front of the hearth, basking in its wonderful warmth. "Good fire you got here," he said. "Sure takes the chill off."

The old man was still staring at Josh. "You can take that coat and mask off, if you like."

Josh shrugged out of his coat. Underneath he wore two thick sweaters, one on top of the other. He made no move to take off the black ski mask.

The old man walked closer to Josh, then abruptly stopped when he saw the gray growth obscuring the giant's right eye.

"Josh is a wrestler," Rusty said quickly. "The Masked Mephisto—that's him! I'm a magician. See, we're a travelin' show. We go from town to town, and we perform for whatever people can spare to give us. Josh wrestles anybody who wants to take him on, and if the other fella gets Josh off his feet, the whole town gets a free show."

The old man nodded absently, his gaze riveted on Josh. The woman came in with the cans she'd opened and dumped their contents into the pot, then stirred the concoction with a wooden spoon. Finally, the old gent said, "Looks like somebody beat the ever-lovin' shit outta you, mister. Guess that town got a free show, huh?" He grunted and gave a high, cackling laugh. Rusty's nerves untensed somewhat; he didn't think there would be any gunplay today. "I'll fetch us a pot of coffee," the old man said, and he left the room.

Josh went over to warm himself at the fire, and the woman scurried away from him as if he carried the plague. Not wanting to frighten her, he crossed the room and stood at the window, looking out at the sea of stumps and the single standing tree.

"Name's Sylvester Moody," the old man said when he returned with a tray bearing some brown clay mugs. "Folks used to call me Sly, after that fella who made all them fightin' movies." He set the tray down on a little pine wood table, then went to the mantel and picked up a thick asbestos glove; he put it on and reached into the fireplace, unhooking a scorched metal coffee pot from a nail driven into the rear wall. "Good and hot," he said, and he started to pour the black liquid into the cups. "Don't have no milk or sugar, so don't ask." He nodded toward the woman. "This is my wife, Carla. She's kinda nervous around strangers."

Rusty took one of the hot cups and downed the coffee with pure pleasure, though the liquid was so strong it could've whipped Josh in a wrestling match.

"Why one tree, Mr. Moody?" Josh asked.

"Huh?"

Josh was still standing at the window. "Why'd you leave that one? Why not cut it down with the others?"

Sly Moody picked up a cup of coffee and took it over to the masked giant. He tried very hard not to stare at the white-splotched hand that accepted the cup. "I've lived in this house for near 'bout thirty-five years," he answered. "That's a long time to live in one house, on one piece of land, ain't it? Oh, I used to have a fine cornfield back that way." He motioned toward the rear of the house. "Used to grow a little tobacco and some pole beans, and every year me and Jeanette would go out in the garden and . . ." He trailed off, blinked and glanced over at Carla, who was looking at him with wide, shocked eyes. "I'm sorry, darlin'," he said. "I mean, me and *Carla* would go out in the garden and bring back baskets of good vegetables."

The woman, seemingly satisfied, stopped stirring the pot and left the room.

"Jeanette was my first wife," Sly explained in a hushed voice. "She passed on about two months after it happened. Then one day I was walkin' up the road to Ray Featherstone's place—about a mile from here, I guess—and I came across a car that had gone off the road and was half buried in a snowdrift. Well, there was a dead man with a blue face at the wheel, and next to him was a woman who was near 'bout dead. There was a gutted carcass of a French poodle in her lap, and she had a nail file gripped in her hand—and I don't want to tell you what she did to keep herself from freezin'. Anyway, she was so crazy she didn't know anything, not even her own name or where she was from. I called her Carla, after the first girl I ever kissed. She just stayed, and now she thinks she's been livin' on this farm with me for thirty-five years." He shook his head, his eyes dark and haunted. "Funny thing, too—that car was a Lincoln Continental, and when I found her she was decked out in diamonds and pearls. I put all that junk away in a shoe box and traded it for sacks of flour and bacon. I figure she didn't need to ever see 'em again. People came along and salvaged parts off the car, and by and by there was nothin' left. Better that way."

Carla returned with some bowls and began to spoon the stew into them.

"Bad days," Sly Moody said softly, staring at the tree. Then his eyes began to clear, and he smiled faintly. "That there's my apple tree! Yessir! See, I used to have an apple orchard clear across that field. Used to bring in apples by the bushel—but after it happened and the trees died, I started cuttin' 'em down for firewood. You don't want to go too far into the forest for firewood, uh-uh! Ray Featherstone froze to death about a hundred yards from his own front door." He paused for a moment and then sighed heavily. "I planted them apple trees with my own hands. Watched 'em grow, watched 'em burst with fruit. You know what today is?"

"No," Josh said.

"I keep a calendar. One mark for every day. Worn out a lot of pencils, too. Today is the twenty-sixth day of April.

Springtime." He smiled bitterly. "I've cut 'em all down but the one and thrown 'em in the fire piece by piece. But damned if I can put an axe to that last one. Damned if I can."

"Food's almost ready," Carla announced. She had a northern accent, decidedly different from Sly's languid Missouri drawl. "Come and get it."

"Hold on." Sly looked at Rusty. "I thought you said you were with *two* friends."

"I did. There's a girl travelin' with us. She's . . ." He glanced quickly at Josh, then back to Sly. "She's out in the barn."

"A *girl?* Well, Christ A'mighty, fella! Bring her in here and let her get some hot food!"

"Uh . . . I don't think—"

"Go on and get her!" he insisted. "Barn ain't no place for a girl!"

"Rusty?" Josh was peering out the window. Night was fast descending, but he could still see the last apple tree and the figure that stood beneath it. "Come here for a minute."

Outside, Swan held the blanket around her head and shoulders like a cape and looked up at the branches of the spindly apple tree; Killer ran a couple of rings around the tree and then barked halfheartedly, wanting to get back to the barn. Above Swan's head, the branches moved like skinny, searching arms.

She walked forward, her boots sinking through five inches of snow, and placed her bare hand against the tree's trunk.

It was cold beneath her fingers. Cold and long dead.

Just like everything else, she thought. All the trees, the grass, the flowers—everything scorched lifeless by radiation many years ago.

But it was a pretty tree, she decided. It was dignified, like a monument, and it did not deserve to be surrounded by the ugly stumps of what had been. She knew that the hurting sound in this place must have been a long wail of agony.

Her hand moved lightly across the wood. Even in death, there was something proud about the tree, something defiant and elemental—a wild spirit, like the heart of a flame that could never be totally extinguished.

Killer yapped at her feet, urging her to hurry whatever she was doing. Swan said, "All right, I'm rea—"

She stopped speaking. The wind whirled around her, tugging at her clothes.

Could it be? she wondered. I'm not dreaming this . . . am I?

Her fingers were tingling. Just barely enough to register through the cold.

She placed her palm against the wood. A prickling, pins-and-needles sensation coursed through her hand—still faint, but growing, getting stronger.

Her heart leaped. *Life,* she realized. There was life there yet, deep in the tree. It had been so long—so very long—since she'd felt the stirring of life beneath her fingers. The feeling was almost new to her again, and she realized how much she'd missed it. Now what felt like a mild electric current seemed to be rising up from the earth through the soles of her boots, moving up her backbone, along her arm and out her hand into the wood. When she drew her hand away, the tingling ceased. She pressed her fingers to the tree again, her heart pounding, and there was a shock so powerful it felt as if fire had shot up her spine.

Her body trembled. The sensation was steadily getting stronger, almost painful now, her bones aching with the pulse of energy passing through her and into the tree. When she could stand it no longer, she pulled her hand back. Her fingers continued to prickle.

But she wasn't finished yet. On an impulse, she extended her index finger and traced letters across the tree trunk: S . . . W . . . A . . . N.

"Swan!" The voice came from the house, startling her. She turned toward the sound, and as she did the wind ripped at her makeshift cape and flung it back from her shoulders and head.

Sly Moody was standing between Josh and Rusty, holding a lantern. By its yellow light, he saw that the figure under the apple tree had no face.

Her head was covered by gray growths that had begun as small black warts, had thickened and spread over the passage of years, had connected with gray tendrils like groping, intertwining vines. The growths had covered her skull like a knotty helmet, had enclosed her facial features and sealed them up except for a small slit at her left eye and a ragged hole over her mouth through which she breathed and ate.

Behind Sly, Carla screamed. Sly whispered, "Oh . . . my Jesus . . ."

The faceless figure grabbed the blanket and shrouded her head, and Josh heard her heartbreaking cry as she raced to the barn.

Forty-nine

Darkness fell over the snow-covered buildings and houses of what had been Broken Bow, Nebraska. Barbed wire surrounded the town, and here and there bits of timber and rags burned in empty oil cans, the wind sending orange sparks spiraling into the sky. On the curving northwest arc of Highway 2, dozens of corpses lay frozen where they'd fallen, and the hulks of charred vehicles still spat flame.

In the fortress that Broken Bow had been for the last two days, three hundred and seventeen sick and injured men, women and children were trying desperately to keep warm around a huge central bonfire. The houses of Broken Bow were being torn apart and fed to the flames. Another two hundred and sixty-four men and women armed with rifles, pistols, axes, hammers and knives crouched in trenches hastily hacked in the earth along the barbed wire at the western rim of town. Their faces were turned westward, into the shrilling subzero wind that had killed so many. They shivered in their ragged coats, and tonight they dreaded a different kind of death.

"There!" a man with an ice-crusted bandage around his

head shouted. He pointed into the distance. "There! They're coming!"

A chorus of shouts and warnings moved along the trench. Rifles and pistols were quickly checked. The trench vibrated with nervous motion, and the breath of human beings whirled through the air like diamond dust.

They saw the headlights weaving slowly through the carnage on the highway. Then the music drifted to them on the stinging wind. It was carnival music, and as the headlights grew nearer a skinny, hollow-eyed man in a heavy sheepskin coat stood up at the center of the trench and trained a pair of binoculars at the oncoming vehicle. His face was streaked with dark brown keloids.

He put the binoculars down before the cold could seal the eyecups to his face. "Hold your fire!" he shouted to the left. "Pass it down!" The message began to go down the line. He looked to the right and shouted the same order, and then he waited, one gloved hand on the Ingram machine gun under his coat.

The vehicle passed a burning car, and the red glare revealed it to be a truck with the remnants of paint on its sides advertising different flavors of ice cream. Two loudspeakers were mounted atop the truck's cab, and the windshield had been replaced with a metal plate that had two narrow slits cut for the driver and passengers to see through. The front fender and radiator grille were shielded with metal, and from the armor protruded jagged metal spikes about two feet long. The glass of both headlights was reinforced with heavy tape and covered with wire mesh. On both sides of the truck were gunslits, and atop the truck was a crude sheet-metal turret and the snout of a heavy machine gun.

The armored Good Humor truck, its modified engine snorting, rolled with chain-covered tires over the carcass of a horse and stopped about fifty yards from the barbed wire. The merry, tape-recorded calliope music continued for perhaps another two minutes—and then there was silence.

The silence stretched. A man's voice came through the loudspeakers: "Franklin Hayes! Are you listening, Franklin Hayes?"

The skinny, weary man in the sheepskin coat narrowed his eyes but said nothing.

"Franklin Hayes!" the voice continued, with a mocking, lilting note. "You've given us a good fight, Franklin Hayes! The Army of Excellence salutes you!"

"Fuck you," a middle-aged, shivering woman said softly in the trench beside Hayes. She had a knife at her belt and a pistol in her hand, and a green keloid covered most of her face in the shape of a lily pad.

"You're a fine commander, Franklin Hayes! We didn't think you had the strength to get away from us at Dunning. We thought you'd die on the highway. How many of you are left, Franklin Hayes? Four hundred? Five hundred? And how many are able to keep fighting? Maybe half that number? The Army of Excellence has over four thousand healthy soldiers, Franklin Hayes! Some of those used to suffer for you, but they decided to save their lives and cross over to *our* side!"

Someone in the trench to the left fired a rifle, and several other shots followed. Hayes shouted, "Don't waste your bullets, damn it!" The firing dwindled, then ceased.

"Your soldiers are nervous, Franklin Hayes!" the voice taunted. "They know they're about to die."

"We're not soldiers," Hayes whispered to himself. "You crazy fucker, we're *not* soldiers!" How his community of survivors—once numbering over a thousand people trying to rebuild the town of Scottsbluff—had gotten embroiled in this insane "war" he didn't know. A van driven by a husky red-bearded man had come into Scottsbluff, and out had stepped another, frail-figured man with bandages wrapping his face—all except his eyes, which were covered with goggles. The bandaged man had spoken in a high, young voice, had said that he'd been badly burned a long time ago; he'd asked for water and a place to spend the night, but he wouldn't let Dr. Gardner even touch his bandages. Hayes himself, as mayor of Scottsbluff, had taken the young man on a walking tour of the structures they were rebuilding. Sometime during the night the two men had driven away, and three days later Scottsbluff was attacked and burned to the ground. The screams of his wife and son still reverberated in Hayes's mind. Then Hayes had started leading the survivors east to escape the maniacs that pursued them—but the "Army of Excellence" had more trucks, cars, horses, trailers and gasoline, more weapons and bullets and "soldiers," and the group that followed Hayes had left hundreds of corpses in its wake.

This was an insane nightmare with no end, Hayes realized. Once he'd been an eminent professor of economics at the University of Wyoming, and now he felt like a trapped rat.

The headlights of the armored Good Humor truck burned like two malevolent eyes. "The Army of Excellence invites all able-bodied men, women and children who don't want to suffer anymore to join us," the amplified voice said. "Just cross the wire and keep walking west, and you'll be well taken care of—hot food, a warm bed, shelter and protection. Bring your weapons and ammunition with you, but keep the barrels of your guns pointed to the ground. If you are healthy and sound of mind, and if you are unblemished by the mark of Cain, we invite you with love and open arms. You have five minutes to decide."

The mark of Cain, Hayes thought grimly. He'd heard that phrase through those damned speakers before, and he knew they meant either the keloids or the growths that covered the faces of many people. They only wanted those "unblemished" and "sound of mind." But he wondered about the young man with the eye goggles and the bandaged face. Why had he been wearing those bandages, if he himself had not been "blemished" by the "mark of Cain"?

Whoever was guiding that mob of ravagers and rapists was beyond all humanity. Somehow he—or she—had drilled bloodlust into the brains of over four thousand followers, and now they were killing, looting and burning struggling communities for the sheer thrill of it.

There was a shout to the right. Two men were struggling over the barbed wire; they got across, snagging their coats and trousers but pulling free, and started running west with their rifles pointed to the ground. "Cowards!" someone shouted. "You dirty cowards!" But the two men did not look back.

A woman went across, followed by another man. Then a man, a woman and a young boy escaped the trench and fled to the west, all carrying guns and ammunition. Angry shouts and curses were flung at their backs, but Hayes didn't blame them. None of them bore keloids; why should they stay and be slaughtered?

"Come home," the voice intoned over the loudspeakers, like the silken drone of a revival preacher. "Come home to love and open arms. Flee the mark of Cain, and come home . . . come home . . . come home."

More people were going over the wire. They vanished westward into the darkness.

"Don't suffer with the unclean! Come home, flee the mark of Cain!"

A gunshot rang out, and one of the truck's headlights shattered, but the mesh deflected the slug and the light continued to burn. Still, people climbed over the fence and scurried west.

"I ain't goin' nowhere," the woman with the lily pad keloid told Hayes. "I'm set and stayin'."

The last to go was a teen-age boy with a shotgun, his overcoat pockets stuffed with shells.

"It's time, Franklin Hayes!" the voice called.

He took out the Ingram gun and pushed the safety off.

"It's *time!*" the voice roared—and the roar was joined by other roars, rising together, mixing and mingling like a single, inhuman battle cry. But they were the roars of engines firing, popping and sputtering, blasting to full-throated life. And then the headlights came on—dozens of headlights, *hundreds* of headlights that curved in an arc on both sides of Highway 2, facing the trench. Hayes realized with numb terror that the other armored trucks, tractor-trailer rigs, and monster machines had been silently pushed almost to the barbed-wire barrier while the Good Humor truck had kept their attention. The headlights speared into the faces of those in the trenches as engines were gunned and chained tires crunched forward across snow and frozen bodies.

Hayes stood up to yell "Fire!" but the shooting had already started. Sparks of gunfire rippled up and down the trench;

bullets whined off metal tire guards, radiator shields and iron turrets. Still the battle wagons came on, almost leisurely, and the Army of Excellence held their fire. Then Hayes screamed, "Use the bombs!" but he was not heard over the tumult. The trench fighters didn't have to be told to crouch down, pick up one of the three gasoline-filled bottles they'd all been supplied with, touch the rag wicks to the flames from oil barrels and throw the homemade bombs.

The bottles exploded, sending flaming gasoline shooting across the snow, but in the leaping red light the monsters came on, unscathed, and now some of them were rolling over the barbed wire less than twenty feet from the trench. One bottle scored a direct hit on the viewslit of a Pinto's armored windshield; it shattered and sprayed fiery gas. The driver tumbled out screaming, his face aflame. He staggered toward the wire, and Franklin Hayes shot him dead with the Ingram gun. The Pinto kept going, tore through the barricade and crushed four people before they could scramble from the trench.

The vehicles tore the barbed-wire barricade to shreds, and suddenly their crude turrets and gunports erupted with rifle, pistol and machine-gun fire that swept across the trench as Hayes's followers tried to run. Dozens slithered back in or lay motionless in the dirty, blood-streaked snow. One of the burning oil cans went over, touching off unused bombs that began exploding in the trench. Everywhere was fire and streaking bullets, writhing bodies, screams and a blur of confusion. "Move back!" Franklin Hayes yelled. The defenders fled toward the second barrier about fifty yards behind—a five-foot-high wall of bricks, timbers and frozen bodies of their friends and families stacked up like cordwood.

Franklin Hayes saw soldiers on foot, fast approaching behind the first wave of vehicles. The trench was wide enough to catch any car or truck that tried to pass, but the Army of Excellence's infantry would soon swarm across—and through the smoke and blowing snow there seemed to be *thousands*. He heard their war cry—a low, animalish moan that almost shook the earth.

Then the armored radiator of a truck was staring him in the

face, and he scrambled out of the trench as the vehicle stopped two feet short. A bullet whined past his head, and he stumbled over the body of the woman with the lily pad keloid. Then he was up and running, and bullets thunked into the snow all around him, and he clambered up over the wall of bricks and bodies and turned again to face the attackers.

Explosions started blasting the wall apart, metal shrapnel flying. Hayes realized they were using hand grenades—something they'd saved until now—and he kept firing at running figures until the Ingram gun blistered his hands.

"They've broken through on the right!" somebody shouted. "They're comin' in!"

Swarms of men were running in all directions. Hayes fumbled in his pocket, found another clip and reloaded. One of the enemy soldiers leapt over the wall, and Hayes had time to see that his face was daubed with what looked like Indian warpaint before the man spun and drove a knife into the side of a woman fighting a few feet away. Hayes shot him through the head, kept shooting as the soldier jerked and fell.

"Run! Get back!" somebody yelled. Other voices, other screams pierced the wail of noise: "We can't hold 'em! They're breakin' through!"

A man with blood streaming down his face grasped Hayes's arm. "Mr. Hayes!" he shouted. "They're breaking through! We can't hold them back any—"

He was interrupted by the blade of an axe sinking into his skull.

Hayes staggered back. The Ingram gun dropped from his hands, and he sank down to his knees.

The axe was pulled loose, and the corpse fell to the snow.

"Franklin Hayes?" a soft, almost gentle voice asked.

He saw a long-haired figure standing over him, couldn't make out the face. He was tired, all used up. "Yes," he replied.

"Time to go to sleep," the man said, and he lifted his axe.

When it fell, a dwarf who had crouched atop the broken wall jumped up and clapped his hands.

Fifty

A battered Jeep with one good headlight emerged from the snow on Missouri Highway 63 and entered what had once been a town. Lanterns glowed within a few of the clapboard houses, but otherwise darkness ruled the streets.

"Stop there." Sister motioned toward a brick structure on the right. The building's windows were boarded up, but crowded around it in the gravel parking lot were several old cars and pickup trucks. As Paul Thorson guided the Jeep into the lot the single headlight washed over a sign painted in red on one of the boarded windows: Bucket of Blood Tavern.

"Uh . . . you sure you want to stop at this particular place?" Paul inquired.

She nodded, her head cowled by the hood of a dark blue parka. "Where there're cars, somebody ought to know where to find gas." She glanced at the fuel gauge. The needle hovered near Empty. "Maybe we can find out where the hell we are, too."

Paul turned off the heater, then the single headlight and the engine. He was wearing his old reliable leather jacket over a red woolen sweater, with a scarf around his neck and a brown woolen cap pulled over his skull. His beard was ashen-gray, as was much of his hair, but his eyes were still a powerful, undimmed electric blue against the heavily lined, windburned skin of his face. He glanced uneasily at the sign on the boards and climbed out of the Jeep. Sister reached into the rear compartment, where an assortment of canvas bags, cardboard boxes and crates were secured with a chain and padlock. Right behind her seat was a beat-up brown leather satchel, which she picked up with one gloved hand and took with her.

From beyond the door came the noise of off-key piano music and a burst of raucous male laughter. Paul braced himself and pushed it open, walking in with Sister at his heels. The door, fixed to the wall with tight springs, snapped shut behind them.

Instantly, the music and laughter ceased. Suspicious eyes glared at the new arrivals.

At the room's center, next to a free-standing cast-iron stove, six men had been playing cards around a table. A haze of yellow smoke from hand-rolled cigarettes hung in the air, diffusing the light of several lanterns that dangled from wall hooks. Other tables were occupied by two or three men and some rough-looking women. A bartender in a fringed leather jacket stood behind a long bar that Paul noted was pocked with bullet holes. Blazing logs popped red sparks from a fireplace in the rear wall, and at the piano sat a chunky young woman with long black hair and a violet keloid that covered the lower half of her face and exposed throat.

Both Sister and Paul had seen that most of the men wore guns in holsters at their waists and had rifles propped against their chairs.

The floor was an inch deep in sawdust, and the tavern smelled of unwashed bodies. There was a sharp *ping!* as one of the men at the center table spat tobacco juice into a pail.

"We're lost," Paul said. "What town is this?"

A man laughed. He had greasy black hair and was wearing what looked like a dogskin coat. He blew smoke into the air from a brown cigarette. "What town you tryin' to get to, fella?"

"We're just traveling. Is this place on the map?"

The men exchanged amused glances, and now the laughter spread. "What map do you mean?" the one with greasy hair asked. "Drawn up before the seventeenth of July, or after?"

"Before."

"The before maps ain't no fuckin' good," another man said. He had a bony face and was shaved almost bald. Four fishhooks dangled from his left earlobe, and he wore a leather vest over a red-checked shirt. At his skinny waist were a holster and pistol. "Everything's changed. Towns are graveyards. Rivers flooded over, changed course and froze. Lakes dried up. What was woods is desert. So the before maps ain't no fuckin' good."

Paul was aware of all that. After seven years of traveling a zigzag path across a dozen states, there was very little that shocked him or Sister anymore. "Did this town ever have a name?"

"Moberly," the bartender offered. "Moberly, Missouri. Used to be about fifteen thousand people here. Now I guess we're down to three or four hundred."

"Yeah, but it ain't the nukes that killed 'em!" a wizened woman with red hair and red lips spoke up from another table. "It's the rotgut shit you serve in *here,* Derwin!" She cackled and raised a mug of oily-looking liquid to her lips while the others laughed and hooted.

"Aw, fuck you, Lizzie!" Derwin shot back. "Your gut's been pickled since you was ten years old!"

Sister walked to an empty table and set her satchel atop it. Beneath the hood of her parka, most of her face was covered by a dark gray scarf. Unsnapping the satchel, she removed the tattered, folded and refolded Rand McNally road atlas, which she smoothed out and opened to the map of Missouri. In the dim light, she found the thin red line of Highway 63 and followed it to a dot named Moberly, about seventy-five miles north of what had been Jefferson City. "Here we are," she told Paul, who came over to look.

"Great," he said grimly. "So what does that tell us? What direction do we go from—"

The satchel was suddenly snatched off the table, and Sister looked up, stunned.

The bony-faced man in the leather vest had it and was backing away with a grin on his thin-lipped mouth. "Looky what I got *me,* boys!" he shouted. "Got me a nice new bag, didn't I?"

Sister stood very still. "Give that back to me," she said, quietly but firmly.

"Got me somethin' to shit in when it's too cold in the woods!" the man responded, and the others around the table laughed. His small black eyes darted toward Paul, daring him to move.

"Quit fuckin' around, Earl!" Derwin said. "What do you need a *bag* for?"

"'Cause I do, that's why! Let's see what we got in here!" Earl dug a hand into it and started pulling out pairs of socks, scarves and gloves. And then he reached way down and his hand came up with a ring of glass.

It flared with bloody color in his grip, and he stared at it in open-mouthed wonder.

The tavern was silent but for the popping of fireplace logs.

The red-haired hag slowly rose from her chair. "Sweet Mother of Jaysus," she whispered.

The men around the card table gawked, and the black-haired girl left her piano stool to limp closer.

Earl held the glass ring before his face, watching the colors ebb and swell like blood rushing through arteries. But his grip on the ring produced brutal hues: muddy brown, oily yellow and ebony.

"That belongs to me." Sister's voice was muffled behind the scarf. "Please give it back."

Paul took a forward step. Earl's hand went to the butt of his pistol with a gunfighter's reflexes, and Paul stopped. "Found me a play-pretty, didn't I?" Earl asked. The ring was pulsing faster, turning darker and uglier by the second. All but two of the spikes had been broken off over the years. "Jewels!" Earl had just realized where the colors were coming from. "This thing must be worth a goddamned fortune!"

"I've asked you to give it back," Sister said.

"Got me a fuckin' *fortune!*" Earl shouted, his eyes glazed and greedy. "Break this damned glass open and dig them jewels out, I got me a fortune!" He grinned crazily, lifted the ring over his head and began to prance for his friends at the table. "Looky here! I got me a halo, boys!"

Paul took another step, and instantly Earl spun to face him. The pistol was already leaving his holster.

But Sister was ready. The short-barreled shotgun she'd drawn from beneath her parka boomed like a shout from God.

Earl was lifted off the floor and propelled through the air, his body crashing over tables and his own gunshot blasting a chunk from a wooden beam above Sister's head. He landed in a crumpled heap, one hand still gripping the ring. The murky colors pulsed wildly.

The man in the dogskin coat started to rise. Sister pumped another round into the smoking chamber, whirled and pressed the barrel to his throat. "You want some of it?" He shook his head and sank down into his chair again. "Guns on the table," she ordered—and eight pistols were pushed over the grimy cards and coins to the table's center.

Paul had his .357 Magnum cocked and waiting. He caught a movement from the bartender and aimed it at the man's head. Derwin raised his hands. "No trouble, friend," Derwin said nervously. "I want to live, okay?"

The pulsing of the glass ring was beginning to stutter and slow. Paul edged toward the dying man as Sister held her sawed-off riot gun on the others. She'd found the weapon three years earlier in a deserted highway patrol station outside the ruins of Wichita, and it packed enough punch to knock an elephant down. She'd only had to use it a few times, with the same result as now.

Paul tried to avoid all the blood. A fly buzzed past his face and hovered over the ring. It was large and green, an ugly thing, and Paul was taken aback for a few seconds because it had been years since he'd seen a fly; he'd thought they were all dead. A second fly joined the first, and they swirled in the air around the twitching body and the glass circle.

Paul bent down. The ring flared bright red for an instant—and then went black. He worked it from the corpse's grip, and in his hand the rainbow colors returned. Then he shoved it down into the satchel again and covered it over with the socks, scarves and gloves. A fly landed on his cheek, and he jerked his head because the little bastard felt like a freezing nail pressed to his skin.

He returned the road atlas to the satchel. All eyes were on the woman with the shotgun. She took the satchel and retreated slowly toward the door, keeping the weapon aimed at the center of the card table. She told herself she'd had no choice but to kill the man, and that was the end of it; she'd come too far with the glass circle to let some fool break it to pieces.

"Hey," the man in the dogskin coat said. "You ain't gonna go without us buyin' you a drink, are you?"

"What?"

"Earl wasn't worth a damn," another man volunteered, and he leaned over to spit tobacco into his pail. "Trigger-happy idjit was always killin' people."

"He shot Jimmy Ridgeway dead right here, coupla months ago," Derwin said. "Bastard was too good with that pistol."

"Till now," the other man said. The card players were already dividing the dead man's coins.

"Here y'go." Derwin picked up two glasses and drew oily amber liquid from a keg. "Homemade brew. Tastes kinda funky, but it'll sure get your mind off your troubles." He offered the glasses to Paul and Sister. "On the house."

It had been months since Paul's last sip of alcohol. The strong, woody smell of the stuff drifted to him like a siren's perfume. His insides were quaking; he'd never used the Magnum on a human being before, and he prayed that he'd never have to. Paul accepted the glass and thought the fumes might sear off his eyebrows, but he took a drink anyway.

It was like gargling molten metal. Tears popped from his eyes. He coughed, sputtered and gasped as the moonshine—fermented out of God only knew what—slashed down his throat. The red-haired hag cackled like a crow, and some of the men in the back guffawed as well.

As Paul tried to regain his breath Sister set the satchel aside—not too far—and raised the second glass. The bartender said, "Yeah, you did ol' Earl Hocutt a good deed. He's been wantin' somebody to kill him ever since his wife and little girl died of the fever last year."

"Is that so?" she asked as she pulled the scarf away from her face. She lifted the glass to her deformed lips and drank without a flinch.

Derwin's eyes widened, and he backed away so fast he knocked a shelf of glasses and mugs to the floor.

Fifty-one

Sister was prepared for the reaction. She'd seen it many times before. She sipped the moonshine again, found it no better or worse than many bottles she'd drunk from on the streets of Manhattan, and sensed everyone in the bar watching her. Want a good look? she thought. Want a *real* good look? She put the glass down and turned to let them all see.

The red-haired hag stopped cackling as abruptly as if she'd been kicked in the throat.

"Good God A'mighty," the tobacco chewer managed to say, after he'd swallowed his chaw.

The lower half of Sister's face was a mass of gray growths, knotty tendrils twisted and intertwined over her chin, jaw and cheeks. The hard growths had pulled Sister's mouth slightly to the left, giving her a sardonic smile. Under the hood of her parka, her skull was a scabby crust; the growths had completely enclosed her scalp and were now beginning to send out tough gray tendrils across her forehead and over both ears.

"A leper!" One of the card players scrambled to his feet. "She's got leprosy!"

The mention of that dreaded disease made the others leap up, forgetting guns, cards and coins, and back across the tavern. "Get outta here!" another one yelled. "Don't give that shit to us!"

"Leper! Leper!" the red-haired hag shrieked, picking up a mug to throw at Sister. There were other shouts and threats, but Sister was unperturbed. This was a common scene wherever she was forced to expose her face.

Over the cacophony of voices there came a sharp, insistent *crack! . . . crack! . . . crack!*

Silhouetted by light from the fireplace, a thin figure stood against the far wall, methodically beating a wooden staff over one of the tabletops. The noise gradually won out, until an uneasy silence remained.

"Gentlemen . . . and ladies," the man with the wooden staff said in a ravaged voice, "I can assure you that our friend's affliction is *not* leprosy. As a matter of fact, I don't think it's the least bit contagious—so you don't have to ruin your underdrawers."

"What the hell do you know, scumbag?" the man in the dogskin coat challenged.

The other figure paused, then positioned the staff under his left armpit. He began to shuffle forward, his left trouser leg pinned up just above the knee. He wore a ragged dark brown coat over a dirty beige cardigan sweater, and on his hands were gloves so well worn the fingers were poking through.

Lamplight touched his face. Silver hair cascaded around his shoulders, though the crown of his scalp was bald and mottled with brown keloids. He had a short, grizzled gray beard and finely chiseled facial features, his nose thin and elegant. Sister thought he might have been handsome but for the bright crimson keloid that covered one side of his face like a port-wine stain. He stopped, standing between Sister, Paul and the others. "My name is not scumbag," he said, with an air of ruined royalty. His deep-set, tormented gray eyes shifted toward the man in the dogskin coat. "I used to be Hugh Ryan. *Doctor* Hugh Ryan, surgeon in residence at Amarillo Medical Center in Amarillo, Texas."

"*You* a doctor?" the other man countered. "Bullshit!"

"My current living standards make these gentlemen think I was born terminally thirsty," he told Sister, and he lifted one palsied hand. "Of course, I'm not suited for a scalpel anymore. But then again, who is?" He approached Sister and touched her face. The odor of his unwashed body almost knocked her down, but she'd smelled worse. "This is not leprosy," he repeated. "This is a mass of fibrous tissue originating from a subcutaneous source. How deep the fibroid layer penetrates, I don't know—but I've seen this condition many times before, and in my opinion it's not contagious."

"We've seen other people with it, too," Paul said. He was used to the way Sister looked because it had happened so gradually, beginning with the black warts on her face. He'd examined his own head and face for them, but so far he was unaffected. "What causes it?"

Hugh Ryan shrugged, still pressing at the growths. "Possibly the skin's reaction to radiation, pollutants, lack of sunshine for so long—who knows? Oh, I've seen maybe a hundred or more people with it, in many different stages. Fortunately, there seems to remain a small breathing and eating space no matter how severe the condition becomes."

"It's leprosy, *I* say!" the red-haired hag contended, but the men were settling down again, returning to their table. A few of them left the tavern, and the others continued to stare at Sister with a sickened fascination.

"It itches like hell, and sometimes my head aches like it's about to split open," Sister admitted. "How do I get rid of it?"

"That, unfortunately, I can't say. I've never seen Job's Mask regress—but then, I only saw most of the cases in passing."

"Job's Mask? Is that what it's called?"

"Well, that's what *I* call it. Seems appropriate, doesn't it?"

Sister grunted. She and Paul had seen dozens of people with "Job's Mask" scattered across the nine states they'd traveled through. In Kansas, they'd come upon a colony of forty afflicted people who'd been forced out of a nearby settlement by their own families; in Iowa, Sister had seen a man whose head was so encrusted he was unable to hold it upright. Job's Mask afflicted men and women with equal savagery, and Sister had even seen a few teenagers with it, but children younger than seven or eight seemed to be immune—or at least, Sister had never seen any babies or young children with it, though both parents might be horribly deformed. "Will I have this for the rest of my life?"

Hugh shrugged again, unable to help any further. His eyes locked with hungry need on Sister's glass of moonshine, still atop the bar. She said, "Be my guest," and he drank it down as if it were iced tea on a hot August afternoon.

"Thank you very much." He wiped his mouth on his sleeve and glanced at the dead man lying in the bloody sawdust. The chunky black-haired girl was eagerly going through the pockets. "There is no right and wrong in this world anymore," he said. "There's only a faster gun and a higher level of violence." He nodded toward the table he'd been occupying, over by the fireplace. "If you please?" he asked Sister, with a note of pleading. "It's been so long since I've been able to talk to someone of obvious breeding and intellect."

Sister and Paul were in no hurry. She picked up her satchel, sliding her shotgun into the leather sheath that hung along her hip beneath the parka. Paul returned his Magnum to its holster, and they followed Hugh Ryan.

Derwin finally steeled himself to emerge from behind the bar, and the man in the dogskin coat helped him carry Earl's body out the back door.

As Hugh got his remaining leg propped up on a chair Sister couldn't help but notice the stuffed trophies that adorned the wall around the Bucket of Blood's fireplace: an albino squirrel, a deer's head with three eyes, a boar with a single eye at the center of its forehead, and a two-headed woodchuck. "Derwin's a hunter," Hugh explained. "You can find all sorts of things in the woods around here. Amazing what the radiation's done, isn't it?" He admired the trophies for a moment. "You don't want to sleep too far from the light," he said, turning his attention back to Paul and Sister. "You really don't." He reached for the half glass of moonshine he'd been drinking before they'd come in. Two green flies buzzed around his head, and Paul watched them circling.

Hugh motioned toward the satchel. "I couldn't help but notice that glass trinket. May I ask what it is?"

"Just something I picked up."

"Where? A museum?"

"No, I found it in a pile of rubble."

"It's a beautiful thing," he said. "I'd be careful with it, if I were you. I've met people who'd behead you for a piece of bread."

Sister nodded. "That's why I carry the shotgun—and that's why I learned to use it, too."

"Indeed." He swilled down the rest of the moonshine and smacked his lips. "Ah! Nectar of the gods!"

"I wouldn't go *that* far." Paul's throat still felt as if it had been scraped with razors.

"Well, taste is relative, isn't it?" Hugh spent a moment licking the inside of the glass to get the last drops before he put it aside. "I used to be a connoisseur of French brandies. I used to have a wife, three children, and a Spanish villa with a hot tub and a swimming pool." He touched his stump. "I used to have another leg, too. But that's the past, isn't it? And beware of dwelling on the past if you want to keep your sanity." He stared into the fire, then looked across the table at Sister. "So. Where have you been, and where are you going?"

"Everywhere," she replied. "And nowhere in particular."

For the past seven years, Sister and Paul Thorson had been following a dreamwalk path—a blindman's buff of pictures Sister had seen in the depths of the glass circle. They'd traveled from Pennsylvania to Kansas, had found the town of Matheson—but Matheson had been burned to the ground, the ruins covered with snow. They'd searched Matheson, found only skeletons and destruction, and then they'd reached the parking lot of a burned-out building that might have been a department store or supermarket.

And on that snow-swept parking lot, in the midst of desolation, Sister had heard the whisper of God.

It was a small thing, at first: The toe of Paul's boot had uncovered a card.

"Hey!" Paul had called out. "Look at this!" He'd wiped the dirt and snow from it and handed it to her. The colors were bleached out, but it showed a beautiful woman in violet robes, the sun shining overhead and a lion and lamb at her feet; she held a silver shield with what might have been a flaming phoenix at its center, and she wore a blazing crown. The woman's hair was afire, and she stared courageously into the distance. At the top of the card were the faded letters THE EMPRESS.

"It's a tarot card," Paul had said, and Sister's knees had almost buckled.

More cards, bits of glass, clothes and other debris had been buried under the snow. Sister saw a spot of color, picked it up—and found she was holding an image she recognized: a card with a figure shrouded in black, its face white and masklike. Its eyes were silver and hateful, and in the center of its forehead was a third, scarlet eye. She'd torn that card to pieces rather than add it to her bag along with The Empress.

And then Sister had stepped on something soft, and as she bent down to brush the snow away and saw what it was, tears had filled her eyes.

It was a scorched, blue-furred doll. As she lifted it in her arms she saw the little plastic ring hanging down, and she pulled it. In the cold and snowy silence, a labored voice moaned *"Coookieees,"* and the sound drifted over the lot where skeletons lay dreaming.

The Cookie Monster doll had gone into Sister's bag—and then it had been time to leave Matheson, because there was no child's skeleton in that parking lot, and Sister knew now more than ever that she was searching for a child.

They'd roamed Kansas for more than two years, living in various struggling settlements; they had turned north into Nebraska, east into Iowa, and now south to Missouri. A land of suffering and brutality had unfolded itself to them like a continuing, unescapable hallucination. On many occasions, Sister had peered into the glass circle and caught sight of a hazy human face looking back, as if through a badly discolored mirror. That particular image had remained constant over seven years, and though Sister couldn't tell very much about the face, she thought that it had begun as a young face—that of a child, though whether male or female she couldn't tell—and over the years the face had changed. The last time she'd seen it was four months ago, and Sister had had the impression that the facial features were all but wiped clean. Since then the hazy image had not reappeared.

Sometimes Sister felt sure the next day would bring an answer—but the days had passed, becoming weeks, months and years, and still she continued searching. The roads kept carrying her and Paul across devastated countryside, through deserted towns and around the perimeter of jagged ruins where cities had stood. Many times she'd been discouraged, had thought of giving it up and staying in one of the settlements they'd passed through, but that was before her Job's Mask had gotten so bad. Now she was beginning to think the only place she might be welcome was in a colony of Job's Mask sufferers.

But the truth was that she feared staying in one place too long. She kept looking over her shoulder, afraid that a dark figure with a shifting face had finally found her and was coming up from behind. In her nightmares of Doyle Halland, or Dal Hallmark, or whatever he called himself now, he had a single scarlet eye in his forehead like the grim figure on the tarot card, and it was relentlessly probing for her.

Often, in the years past, Sister had felt her skin prickle as if he was somewhere very near, about to close in on her. At those times, she and Paul had hit the road again, and Sister dreaded crossroads because she knew the wrong turn could lead them to his waiting hands.

She pushed the memories out of her mind. "How about you? Have you been here long?"

"Eight months. After the seventeenth of July, I went north from Amarillo with my family. We lived in a settlement on the Purgatoire River, south of Las Animas, Colorado, for three years. A lot of Indians live around there; some of them were Vietnam vets, and they taught us stupid city folks how to build mud huts and stay alive." He smiled painfully. "It's a shock to be living in a million-dollar mansion one month and the next find yourself under a roof of mud and cow dung. Anyway, two of our children died the first year—radiation poisoning—but we were warm when the snow started falling, and we felt damned lucky."

"Why didn't you stay there?" Paul asked.

Hugh stared into the fire. It was a long time before he answered. "We . . . had a community of about two hundred people. We had a supply of corn, some flour and salted beef, and a lot of canned food. The river water wasn't exactly clean, but it was keeping us alive." He rubbed the stump of his leg. "Then they came."

"They? Who?"

"First it was three men and two women. They came in a Jeep and a Buick with an armored windshield. They stopped in Purgatoire Flats—that's what we called our town—and they wanted to buy half our food. Of course, we couldn't sell it, not for any price. We'd starve if we did. Then they threatened us. They said we'd regret not giving them what they wanted. I remember that Curtis Redfeather—he was our mayor, a big Pawnee who'd served in Vietnam—went to his hut and came back with an automatic rifle. He told them to go, and they left." Hugh paused; he slowly clenched his fists atop the table.

"They came back," he said softly. "That night. Oh, yes, they came back—with three hundred armed soldiers and trucks that they'd made into tanks. They started smashing Purgatoire Flats to the ground . . . and killing everybody. *Everybody.*" His voice cracked, and he couldn't go on for a minute. "People were running, trying to get away," he said. "But the soldiers had machine guns. I ran, with my wife and daughter. I saw Curtis Redfeather shot down and run over by a Jeep. He didn't . . . he didn't even look like a human being anymore."

Hugh closed his eyes, but there was such torment etched into his face that Sister could not look at him. She watched the fire. "My wife was shot in the back," he continued. "I stopped to help her, and I told my daughter to run for the river. I never saw her again. But . . . I was picking up my wife when the bullets hit me. Two or three, I think. In the leg. Somebody hit me in the head, and I fell. I remember . . . I woke up, and the barrel of a rifle was pointed in my face. And someone—a man's voice—said, 'Tell them the Army of Excellence passed this way.' The Army of Excellence," he repeated bitterly, and he opened his eyes. They were shocked and bloodshot. "Four or five people were left, and they made a stretcher for me. They carried me more than thirty miles to the north, to another settlement—but that one was ashes, too, by the time we got there. My leg was shattered. It had to come off. I told them how to do it. And I hung on, and we kept going, and that was four years ago." He looked at Sister and leaned slightly forward in his chair. "For God's sake," he said urgently, "don't go west. That's where the Battlelands are."

"The Battlelands?" Paul asked. "What do you mean?"

"I mean they're having war out there—in Kansas, Oklahoma, Nebraska—the Dakotas, too. Oh, I've met plenty of refugees from the west. They call it the Battlelands because so many armies are fighting out there: the American Allegiance, Nolan's Raiders, the Army of Excellence, Troop Hydra and maybe five or six others."

"The war's done." Sister frowned. "What the hell are they fighting over?"

"Land. Settlements. Food, guns, gasoline—whatever's left. They're out of their minds; they want to kill somebody, and if it can't be the Russians, they've got to invent enemies. I've heard the Army of Excellence is on a rampage against survivors with keloids." He touched the scarlet, upraised scar that covered half his face. "Supposed to be the mark of Satan."

Paul shifted uneasily in his chair. In their travels, he and Sister had heard about settlements being attacked and burned by bands of marauders, but this was the first they'd heard of organized forces. "How big are these armies? Who's leading them?"

"Maniacs, so-called patriots, military men, you name it," Hugh said. "Last week a man and woman who'd seen the

American Allegiance passed through here. They said it numbered about four or five thousand, and a crazy preacher from California is leading it. He calls himself the Savior and wants to kill everybody who won't follow him. I've heard Troop Hydra's executing blacks, Hispanics, Orientals, Jews and everybody else they consider foreign. The Army of Excellence is supposedly led by an ex-military man—a Vietnam war hero. They're the bastards with the tanks. God help us if those maniacs start moving east."

"All we want is enough gasoline to get to the next town," Paul said. "We're heading south to the Gulf of Mexico." He swatted at a fly that landed on his hand; again, there was a feeling of being pricked by a freezing nail.

Hugh smiled wistfully. "The Gulf of Mexico. My God, I haven't seen the Gulf for a long, long time."

"What's the nearest town from here?" Sister asked.

"I suppose that would be Mary's Rest, south of what used to be Jefferson City. The road's not too good, though. They used to have a big pond at Mary's Rest. Anyway, it's not far—about fifty miles."

"How do we get there on an empty tank?"

Hugh glanced over at the bloody sawdust. "Well, Earl Hocutt's truck is parked out front. I doubt he'll need the gasoline anymore, don't you?"

Paul nodded. They had a length of garden hose in the Jeep, and Paul had become very proficient at stealing gas.

A fly landed on the table in front of Hugh. He suddenly upended his moonshine glass over it and trapped the insect. It buzzed angrily around and around, and Hugh watched it circling. "You don't see flies too often," he said. "A few of them stay in here because of the warmth, I guess. And the blood. That one's mad as the Devil, isn't he?"

Sister heard the low hum of another fly as it passed her head. It made a slow circle above the table and shot toward a chink in the wall. "Is there a place we could spend the night here?" she asked Hugh.

"I can find one for you. It won't be much more than a hole in the ground with a lid over it, but you won't freeze to death and you won't get your throats slit." He tapped the glass, and the large green fly tried to attack his finger. "But if I find you a safe place to sleep," he said, "I'd like something in return."

"What's that?"

Hugh smiled. "I'd like to see the Gulf of Mexico."

"Forget it!" Paul told him. "We don't have the room."

"Oh, you'd be surprised what a one-legged old man can squeeze himself into."

"More weight means using more gasoline, not to mention food and water. No. Sorry."

"I weigh about as much as a wet feather," Hugh persisted. "And I can carry along my own food and water. If you want payment for taking me with you, perhaps I can interest you in two jugs of moonshine I've kept hidden for an emergency."

Paul was about to say no again, but his lips locked. The moonshine was about the nastiest stuff he'd ever tasted, but it sure had quickened his pulse and kicked on his furnace.

"How about it?" Hugh asked Sister. "Some of the bridges are broken down between here and Mary's Rest. I can do a lot better for you than that antique map you're carrying."

Her first impulse was to agree with Paul, but she saw the suffering in Hugh Ryan's gray eyes; he wore the expression of a once-loyal dog that had been beaten and abandoned by a trusted master.

"Please?" he said. "There's nothing for me here. I'd like to see if the waves still roll in like they used to."

Sister thought about it. No doubt the man could scrunch himself up in the back of the Jeep, and they might well need a guide to get to the next town. He was waiting for an answer. "You find us a safe place to spend the night," she said, "and we'll talk about it in the morning. That's the best I can do for now. Deal?"

Hugh hesitated, searching Sister's face. Hers was a strong face, he decided, and her eyes weren't dead like those of so many others he'd seen. It was unfortunate that most likely the Job's Mask would eventually seal them shut. "Deal," he said, and they shook on it.

They left the Bucket of Blood to get the gas from the dead man's truck. Behind them, the red-haired hag scuttled over to the table they'd left and watched the fly buzzing around in the upturned glass. She suddenly picked it up and snatched the fly as it tried to escape, and before it could get loose from her hand she shoved the fly into her mouth and crunched her teeth down on it.

Her face contorted. She opened her mouth and spat a small glob of grayish-green into the fire, where it sizzled like acid.

"Nasty!" she said, and she wiped her tongue with sawdust.

Fifty-two

He was waiting in the dark for them to come home.

The wind was strong. It sang sweetly to his soul of millions dead and the dying not yet done, but when the wind was so strong he couldn't search very far. He sat in the dark, in his new face and his new skin, with the wind shrilling around the shed like a party noisemaker, and thought that maybe—just *maybe*—it would be tonight.

But he understood the twists and turns of time, and so if it was not tonight, there was always tomorrow. He could be very patient, if he had to be.

Seven years had passed quickly for him; he had traveled the roads, a solitary journeyer, through Ohio, Indiana, Kentucky, Tennessee and Arkansas. He had sometimes lodged in struggling settlements, sometimes lived by himself in caves and abandoned cars as the mood struck him. Wherever he passed was darkened by his presence, the settlements sucked dry of hope and compassion and left to blow away as the inhabitants killed one another or themselves. He had the knack of showing them how futile life was, and what the tragedy of false hope could bring about. If your child is hungry, kill it, he urged starving mothers; think of suicide as the noble thing, he told men who asked his advice. He was a fountain of information and wisdom that he was eager to share: All dogs spread cancer and must be killed; people with brown keloids have developed a taste for the flesh of children; there's a new city being built in the wilds of Canada, and that's where you should go; you could get a lot of protein by eating your own fingers—after all, how many do you need?

He was continually astonished by how easy it was to make them believe.

It was a great party. But for one thing, and that one thing gnawed at him day and night.

Where was the ring of glass?

The woman—Sister—was surely dead by now. He didn't care about her, anyway. Where was the glass thing, and who had it? Many times he'd sensed he was close to it, that the next crossroads would take him right to it, but the instincts had always faded, and he was left deciding to try a new direction. He'd searched the mind of everyone he met, but the woman was not in there, and neither was the ring of glass. So he went on. But with the passage of years his traveling had slowed somewhat, because there were so many opportunities in the settlements, and because even if the glass ring was still out there somewhere, it didn't seem to be of any consequence. It wasn't doing anything, was it? It was still his party, and nothing had changed. The threat he'd felt from it, back in the house in New Jersey, still remained with him, but whatever else the glass ring was, it was surely not making a difference in his existence or in the things he saw around him.

No problemo, he thought—but where was it? Who had it? And why had it come to be?

Often he recalled the day he'd turned off Interstate 80 on his French racing bicycle and headed south. He'd sometimes wondered what would have happened if he'd gone back east along I-80. Would he have found the woman and the glass ring? Why hadn't the sentries at that Red Cross station seen her by then, if indeed she was still alive?

But he couldn't see everything, or know everything; he

could only see and know what his counterfeit eyes told him, or what he picked from the human mind, or what the searchers brought him back from the dark.

They were coming to him right now. He sensed the mass of them gathering together from all points of the compass and approaching against the wind. He pushed himself toward the door, and the wheels beneath him squeaked.

The first one touched his cheek and was sucked through the flesh as if into an opening vortex.

His eyes rolled back in his head, and he looked inward. Saw dark forest, heard wind shrieking, and nothing more.

Another thing that resembled a fly squeezed through a hole in the wall and landed on his forehead, instantly being drawn into the rippling flesh. Two more joined it and were pulled down.

He saw more dark woods, an icy puddle, a small animal of some kind lying dead in the brush. A crow swept in, snapped and spun away.

More flies penetrated his face. More images whirled through him: a woman scrubbing clothes in a lamplit room, two men fighting with knives in an alley, a two-headed boar snuffling in garbage, its four eyes glinting wetly.

The flies crawled over his face, being sucked through the flesh one after the other.

He saw dark houses, heard someone playing a harmonica—badly—and someone else clapping in time; faces around a bonfire, a conversation of what baseball games used to be like on summer nights; a skinny man and woman, entwined on a mattress; hands at work, cleaning a rifle; an explosion of light and a voice saying, "Found me a play-pretty, didn't—"

Stop.

The image of light and the voice froze behind his eyes like a frame of a movie.

He trembled.

Flies were still on his face, but he concentrated on the image of the light. It was just a red flare, and he couldn't tell much about it yet. His hands clenched into fists, his long and dirty nails carving half moons into the skin but drawing no blood.

Forward, he thought, and the film of memory began to unreel.

". . . I?" the voice—a man's voice—said. And then an awestruck whisper: "Jewels!"

Stop.

He was looking down from above, and there in the man's hand was . . .

Forward.

. . . the circle of glass, glowing with dark red and brown. A room with sawdust on the floor. Glasses. Cards on a table.

He knew that place. He'd been there before, and he'd sent his searchers there because it was a place where travelers stopped. The Bucket of Blood was about a mile away, just over the next hill.

His inner eye watched it unfold, from the perspective of a fly. The blast of a gun, a hot shock wave, a body spewing blood and tumbling over tables.

A woman's voice said, "You want some of it?" Then an order: "Guns on the table."

I've found you, he thought.

He caught a glimpse of her face. Turned out to be a beauty, didn't you? he mused. Was that her? Yes, yes! It had to be her! The glass ring went into a satchel. It had to be her!

The scene continued. Another face: a man with sharp blue eyes and a gray beard. "Leper! Leper!" someone shouted. And then a silver-haired man was there, and he knew that face as belonging to the one everybody called Scumbag. More voices: "Be my guest . . . Derwin's a hunter . . . used to have another leg, too . . . For God's sake, don't go west . . . supposed to be the mark of Satan . . ."

He smiled.

". . . We're heading south . . . that would be Mary's Rest . . . doubt he'll need the gasoline anymore, don't you?"

The voices grew hazy, the light changed, and there were dark woods and houses below.

He played the memory-movie over again. It was her, all right. ". . . We're heading south . . . that would be Mary's Rest . . ."

Mary's Rest, he thought. Fifty miles to the south. I've found you! Going south to Mary's Rest!

But what was the point of waiting? Sister and the circle of glass might still be over at the Bucket of Blood, only a mile away. There was still time to get over there and—

"Lester? I've brought you a bowl of—"

There was a crash of breaking pottery and a gasp of horror.

He let his eyes resurface again. At the shed's door stood the woman who'd taken him in three weeks ago as a handyman; she was still very pretty, and it was too bad that a wild animal had chewed up her little girl in the woods one evening two weeks ago, because the child had looked just like her. The woman had dropped his bowl of soup. She was a clumsy bitch, he thought. Anybody with two fingers on each hand was bound to be clumsy.

The claw of her left hand held a lantern, and by its light she'd seen the rippling, fly-swarmed face of Lester the handyman.

"Howdy, Miz Sperry," he whispered, and the fly-things whirled around his head.

The woman took a backward step toward the open door. Her face was frozen into a horrified rictus, and he wondered why he'd ever thought she was pretty.

"You're not afraid, are you, Miz Sperry?" he asked her; he reached out his arms, dug his fingers into the dirt floor and drew himself forward. The wheels squeaked, badly in need of oil.

"I . . . I . . ." She tried to speak, but she couldn't. Her legs had seized up, too, and he knew that she knew there was nowhere to run except the woods.

"Surely you're not afraid of *me,*" he said softly. "I'm not much of a man, am I? I do 'preciate you havin' pity on a poor man like me, I surely do." The wheels squeaked, squeaked.

"Stay . . . away from me . . ."

"This is ol' Lester you're talkin' to, Miz Sperry. Just ol' Lester, that's all. You can tell me *anything.*"

She almost broke away then, almost ran, but he said, "Ol' Lester makes the pain go away, don't he?" and she settled back into his grip like warm putty. "Why don't you put that lamp down, Miz Sperry? Let's have us a nice talk. I can fix thangs."

The lantern was slowly put on the floor.

So *easy*, he thought. This one particularly, because she was already walking dead.

He was bored with her. "I believe I need to fix that there gun," he said, and he nodded silkily toward the rifle in the corner. "Will you fetch it for me?"

She picked it up.

"Miz Sperry?" he said. "I want you to put the barrel in your mouth and your finger on the trigger. Yes'm, go ahead. Just like that. Oh, doin' just fine!"

Her eyes were bright and shining, and there were tears rolling down her cheeks.

"Now . . . I need you to test that there gun for me. I want you to pull the trigger and tell me if it works. Okay?"

She resisted him, just a second of the will to live that she probably didn't even know she had anymore.

"Lester's gon' fix thangs," he said. "Little tiny pull, now."

The rifle went off.

He pulled himself forward, and the wheels squeaked over her body. The Bucket of Blood! he thought. Got to get over there!

But then—no, no. Wait. Just wait.

He knew Sister was on her way to Mary's Rest. It wouldn't take him as long to walk cross-country as it would take her to drive over what was left of the road. He could beat her there and be waiting. There were a lot of people in Mary's Rest, a lot of opportunities; he'd been thinking of traveling down that way in the next few days, anyway. She might already have left the tavern and be on the road right now. This time I won't lose you, he vowed. I'll get to Mary's Rest before you. Ol' Lester's gon' fix thangs for you, too, bitch!

This was a good disguise, he decided. Some modifications were needed if he was going to walk the distance, but it would do. And by the time the bitch got to Mary's Rest, he'd be set up and ready to Watusi on her bones until she was dust for the pot.

The rest of the flies were sucked into his face, but they

brought information that was of no use to him. He stretched his torso, and after a minute or two he was able to stand.

Then he rolled down the legs of his trousers, picked up his little red wagon and began walking, his feet bare, through the snow toward the forest. He began to sing, very quietly: "Here we go 'round the mulberry bush, the mulberry bush, the mulberry bush . . ."

The darkness took him.

Fifty-three

A tall figure in a long black overcoat with polished silver buttons stalked through the burning ruins of Broken Bow, Nebraska. Corpses lay scattered across what had been Broken Bow's main street, and the tanklike trucks of the Army of Excellence ran over those that were in the way. Other soldiers were loading trucks with salvaged sacks of corn, flour, beans and drums of oil and gasoline. A pile of rifles and pistols awaited pickup by the Weapons Brigade. Bodies were being stripped by the Clothing Brigade, and members of the Shelter Brigade were gathering together tents that the dead would no longer need. The Mechanics Brigade was going over a wealth of cars, trailers and trucks that had fallen to the victors; those that could be made to run would become recon and transport vehicles, and the others would be stripped of tires, engines and everything else that could possibly be used.

But the man in the black overcoat, his polished ebony boots crunching over scorched earth, was only intent on one thing. He stopped before a pile of corpses that were being stripped, their coats and clothes thrown into cardboard boxes, and examined their faces by the light of a nearby bonfire. The soldiers around him stopped their work to salute; he quickly returned the salute and continued his examination, then went on to the next scatter of bodies.

"Colonel Macklin!" a voice called over the rumble of passing trucks, and the man in the black overcoat turned around. Firelight fell on the black leather mask that covered James B. Macklin's face; the right eyehole had been crudely stitched up, but through the other Macklin's cold blue eye peered at the approaching figure. Under his coat, Macklin wore a gray-green uniform and a pearl-handled .45 in a holster at his waist. Over his breast pocket was a black circular patch with the letters AOE sewn into it in silver thread. A dark green woolen cap was pulled over the colonel's head.

Judd Lawry, wearing a similar uniform under a fleece-lined coat, emerged from the smoke. An M-16 was slung over his shoulder, and bandoliers of ammunition crisscrossed his chest. Judd Lawry's gray-streaked red beard was closely cropped, and his hair had been clipped almost to the scalp. Across his forehead was a deep scar that ran diagonally from his left temple up through his hair. In seven years of following Macklin, Lawry had lost twenty-five pounds of fat and flab, and now his body was hard and muscular; his face had taken on cruel angles, and his eyes had retreated into their sockets.

"Any word, Lieutenant Lawry?" Macklin's voice was distorted, the words slurred, as if something was not right with his mouth.

"No, sir. Nobody's found him. I checked with Sergeant McCowan over on the northern perimeter, but he can't produce a body either. Sergeant Ulrich took a detail through the southern segment of their defensive trench, but no luck."

"What about the reports from the pursuit parties?"

"Corporal Winslow's group found six of them about a mile to the east. They tried to fight it out. Sergeant Oldfield's group found four to the north, but they'd already killed themselves. I haven't gotten word yet from the southern patrol."

"He can't have gotten away, Lawry," Macklin said forcefully. "We've got to find the sonofabitch—or his corpse. I want him—dead or alive—in my tent within two hours. Do you understand that?"

"Yes, sir. I'll do my best."

"Do more than your best. Find Captain Pogue and tell him he's in charge of bringing me the corpse of Franklin Hayes; he's a good tracker, he'll get the job done. And I want to see the casualty counts and captured weapons list by dawn. I don't want the same kind of fuckup that happened last time. Got it?"

"Yes, sir."

"Good. I'll be in my tent." Macklin started to move off, then turned back. "Where's Roland?"

"I don't know. I saw him about an hour ago, over on the south edge of town."

"If you see him, have him report to me. Carry on." Macklin stalked away toward his headquarters tent.

Judd Lawry watched him go, and he couldn't suppress a shudder. It had been more than two years since he'd last seen Colonel Macklin's face; the colonel had started wearing that leather mask to protect his skin against "radiation and pollution"—but it seemed to Lawry that Macklin's face was actually changing shape, from the way the mask buckled and strained against the bones. Lawry knew what it was: that damned disease that a lot of others in the Army of Excellence had gotten as well—the growths that got on your face and grew together, covering everything but a hole at your mouth. Everyone knew Macklin had it, and Captain Croninger was afflicted with it, too, and that was why the boy wore bandages on his face. The worst cases were rounded up and executed, and to Lawry it was a whole hell of a lot worse than the most sickening keloid he'd ever seen. Thank God, he thought, that he'd never gotten it, because he liked his face just the way it was. But if Colonel Macklin's condition was getting worse, then he wasn't going to be able to lead the AOE very much longer. Which led to a lot of interesting possibilities . . .

Lawry grunted, got his mind back on his duties and went off through the ruins.

On the other side of Broken Bow, Colonel Macklin saluted the two armed sentries who stood in front of his large headquarters tent and went in through the flap. It was dark inside, and Macklin thought he remembered leaving a lantern lit on his desk. But there was so much in his mind, so much to remember, that he couldn't be sure. He walked to the desk, reached out with his single hand and found the lantern. The glass was still warm. It blew out somehow, he thought, and he took the glass chimney off, took a lighter from his overcoat pocket and flicked the flame on. Then he lit the lamp, let the flame grow and returned the glass chimney. Dim light began to spread through the tent—and it was only then that Colonel Macklin realized he was not alone.

Behind Macklin's desk sat a slim man with curly, unkempt, shoulder-length blond hair and a blond beard. His muddy boots were propped up on the various maps, charts and reports that covered the desktop. He'd been cleaning his long fingernails with a knife in the dark, and at the sight of the weapon Macklin instantly drew the .45 from his holster and aimed the gun at the intruder's head.

"Hi," the blond-haired man said, and he smiled. He had a pale, cadaverous face—and at the center of it, where his nose had been, was a hole rimmed with scar tissue. "I've been waiting for you."

"Put the knife down. *Now.*"

The knife's blade thunked through a map of Nebraska and stood upright, quivering. "No sweat," the man said. He lifted his hands to show they were empty.

Macklin saw that the intruder wore a blood-spattered AOE uniform, but he didn't appear to have any fresh injuries. That grisly wound at the center of his face—through which Macklin could see the sinus passages and gray cartilage—had healed as much as it ever would. "Who are you and how did you get past the sentries?"

"I came in through the servants' entrance." He motioned toward the rear of the tent, and Macklin saw where the fabric had been slashed enough for the man to crawl through. "My name's Alvin." His muddy green eyes fixed on Colonel Macklin, and his teeth showed when he grinned. "Alvin Mangrim. You ought to have better security, Colonel. Somebody crazy could get in here and kill you if they wanted to."

"Like you, maybe?"

"Naw, not me." He laughed, and air made a shrill whistling sound through the hole where his nose had been. "I've brought you a couple of presents."

"I could have you executed for breaking into my headquarters."

Alvin Mangrim's grin didn't waver. "I didn't break in, man. I *cut* in. See, I'm real good with knives. Oh, yes—knives know my name. They speak to me, and I do what they say to do."

Macklin was about a half ounce of trigger pressure away from blowing the man's head off, but he didn't want to get blood and brains all over his papers.

"Well? Don't you want to see your presents?"

"No. I want you to stand up, very carefully, and start walking—" But suddenly Alvin Mangrim leaned over beside the chair to pick up something from the floor. "Easy!" Macklin warned him, and he was about to call for the sentries when Alvin Mangrim straightened up and set the severed head of Franklin Hayes on the desktop.

The face had turned blue, and the eyes had rolled back to show the whites. "There you go," Mangrim said. "Ain't he pretty?" He leaned forward and rapped his knuckles on the skull. "Knock, knock!" He laughed, the air whistling through the crater at the center of his face. "Uh-oh, nobody's home!"

"Where'd you get that?" Macklin asked him.

"Off the fucker's *neck*, Colonel! Where'd you think I got it from? I came across that wall and there was old Franklin himself, standing right in front of me—and me with my axe, too. That's what I call Fate. So I just chopped his head off and brought it here to you. I would've been here sooner, but I wanted him to finish bleeding so he wouldn't mess up your tent. You've got a real nice, neat place here."

Colonel Macklin approached the head, reached out and touched it with the .45's barrel. "You killed him?"

"Naw. I *tickled* him to death. Colonel Macklin, for such a smart man you sure are slow to figure things out."

Macklin lifted the upper lip with the gun barrel. The teeth were white and even.

"You want to knock those out?" Mangrim asked. "They'd make a nice necklace for that black-haired woman I've seen you with."

He let the lip fall back into place. "Who the hell are you? How come I haven't seen you before?"

"I've been around. Been following the AOE for about two months, I guess. Me and some friends of mine have our own camp. I got this uniform off a dead soldier. Fits me pretty good, don't you think?"

Macklin sensed motion to his left and turned to see Roland Croninger coming into the tent. The young man was wearing a long gray coat with a hood pulled up over his head; at barely twenty years of age, Captain Roland Croninger, at six foot one, stood an inch shorter than Macklin, and he was scarecrow-thin, his AOE uniform and coat hanging off his bony frame. His wrists jutted from the sleeves, his hands like white spiders. He'd been in charge of the attack that had crushed Broken Bow's defenses, and it had been his suggestion to pursue Franklin Hayes to the death. Now he stopped abruptly, and beneath the hood he squinted through his thick-lensed goggles at the head that adorned Colonel Macklin's desk.

"You're Captain Croninger, aren't you?" Mangrim asked. "I've seen you around, too."

"What's going on here?" Roland's voice was still high-pitched. He looked at Macklin, the lamplight glinting off his goggles.

"This man brought me a present. He killed Franklin Hayes, or so he says."

"Sure I did. Whack! Whack!" Mangrim pounded the table with the edge of his hand. "Off went his head!"

"This tent is off limits," Roland said coldly. "You could be shot for coming in here."

"I wanted to surprise the colonel."

Macklin lowered his pistol. Alvin Mangrim hadn't come to do him harm, he decided. The man had violated one of the strictest rules of the AOE, but the severed head was indeed a good present. Now that the mission was accomplished—Hayes was dead, the AOE had captured a bounty of vehicles, weapons and gasoline and had taken about a hundred more soldiers into the ranks—Macklin felt a letdown, just as he did after every battle. It was like wanting a woman so bad your balls ached for release, and once you'd taken her and could do with her what you pleased, she was tiresome. It was not *having* the woman that counted; it was the *taking*—of women, land or life—that stirred Macklin's blood to a boil.

"I can't breathe," he said suddenly. "I can't get my breath." He drew in air, couldn't seem to get enough of it. He thought he saw the Shadow Soldier standing just behind Alvin Mangrim, but then he blinked and the ghostly image was gone. "I can't breathe," he repeated, and he took off his cap.

He had no hair; his scalp was a ravaged dome of growths, like barnacles clinging to rotten pilings. He reached behind his head and found the mask's zipper. The mask fell away, and Macklin inhaled through what was left of his nose.

His face was a misshapen mass of thick, scablike growths that completely enclosed his features except for the single staring blue eye, a nostril hole and a slit over his mouth. Beneath the growths, Macklin's face burned and itched fiercely, and the bones ached as if they were being bent into new shapes. He couldn't bear to look at himself in the mirror anymore, and when he rutted with Sheila Fontana, she—like any number of other women who followed the AOE—squeezed her eyes shut and turned her head away. But Sheila Fontana was out of her mind anyway, Macklin knew; all she was good for was screwing, and she was always screaming in the night about somebody named Rudy crawling into her bed with a dead baby in his arms.

Alvin Mangrim was silent for a moment. Then he said, "Well, whatever it is, you've got a bad dose of it."

"You've brought your present," Macklin told him. "Now get the hell out of my tent."

"I said I brought you *two* presents. Don't you want the other one?"

"Colonel Macklin said he wants you to leave." Roland

didn't like this blond-haired sonofabitch, and he wouldn't mind killing him. He was still high on killing, the smell of blood in his nostrils like a delicious perfume. Over the past seven years, Roland Croninger had become a scholar of killing, mutilation and torture; when the King wanted information from a prisoner, he knew to summon Sir Roland, who had a black-painted trailer where many songs had been sung to the accompaniment of chains, grindstones, hammers and saws.

Alvin Mangrim leaned down to the floor again. Macklin aimed his .45—but the blond-haired man brought up a small box, tied with a bright blue ribbon. "Here," Mangrim said, offering the box. "Take it. It's just for you."

The colonel paused, glanced quickly at Roland and then laid the pistol down within reach and took the box. With his nimble left hand, he tore the ribbon off and lifted the lid.

"I made it for you. How do you like it?"

Macklin reached into the box—and brought out a right hand, covered with a black leather glove. Piercing the hand and glove were fifteen or twenty nails, driven through the back of the hand so their sharp points emerged from the palm.

"I carved it," Mangrim said. "I'm a good carpenter. Did you know that Jesus was a carpenter?"

Colonel Macklin stared in disbelief at the lifelike wooden hand. "Is this supposed to be a *joke?*"

Mangrim looked wounded. "Man, it took me three days to get that just right! See, it weighs about as much as a real hand does, and it's balanced so well you'd never know it's made out of wood. I don't know what happened to your real hand, but I kinda figured you'd appreciate this one."

The colonel hesitated; he'd never seen anything quite like this before. The wooden hand, securely tucked into a tight glove, bristled with nails like the hide of a porcupine. "What's it supposed to be? A paperweight?"

"Naw. You're supposed to *wear* it," Mangrim explained. "On your wrist. Just like a real hand. See, somebody takes a look at that hand with those nails sticking right through it, and they say, 'Whoa, that motherfucker just don't even know what pain *is!*' You wear that and somebody gives you backtalk, you give them a whack across the face and they won't have lips anymore." Mangrim grinned merrily. "I made it just for you."

"You're crazy," Macklin said. "You're out of your goddamned mind! Why the hell would I want to wear—"

"Colonel?" Roland interrupted. "He may be crazy, but I think he's got a good idea."

"What?"

Roland pushed his hood back. His face and head were covered with dirty gauze bandages secured with adhesive strips. Where the windings didn't exactly meet, there were gray growths as hard as armor plate. The bandages were thickly plastered over his forehead, chin and cheeks and came right up to the edges of his goggles. He pulled loose one of the adhesive strips, unwound about twelve inches of gauze and tore it off. He offered it to Macklin. "Here," he said. "Put it on your wrist with this."

Macklin stared at him as if he thought Roland had lost his mind as well, then he took the gauze and the strip of adhesive and worked at taping the counterfeit hand to the stump of his right wrist. He finally got it in place, so the nail-studded palm was turned inward. "It feels funny," he said. "Feels like it weighs ten pounds." But other than the weird sensation of suddenly having a new right hand, he realized that it looked very real; to someone who didn't know the truth, his gloved hand with its palmful of nails might well be attached by flesh to the wrist. He held his arm out and slowly swung it through the air. Of course, the hand's attachment to the wrist was still fragile; if he was going to wear it, he'd have to bind it tightly to the stump with a thick wrapping of strong adhesive. He liked the look of it, and he suddenly knew why: It was a perfect symbol of discipline and control. If a man could endure such pain—even symbolically—then he had supreme discipline over his own body; he was a man to be feared, a man to be followed.

"You should wear that all the time," Roland suggested.

"Especially when we have to negotiate for supplies. I don't think the leader of any settlement would hold out very long after he saw that."

Macklin was spellbound by the sight of his new hand. It would be a devastating psychological weapon, and a damned dangerous close-quarters weapon as well. He'd just have to be real careful when he scratched what was left of his nose.

"I knew you'd like it," Mangrim said, satisfied by the colonel's response. "Looks like you were born with it."

"That still doesn't excuse you from being in this tent, mister," Roland told him. "You're asking to be shot."

"No, I'm not, Captain. I'm asking to be made a sergeant on the Mechanical Brigade." His green eyes slid from Roland back to Colonel Macklin. "I'm real good with machines, too. I can fix just about anything. You give me the parts, I can put it together. And I can build things, too. Yes, sir, you make me a Mechanical Brigade sergeant and I'll show you what I can do for the Army of Excellence."

Macklin paused, his eye examining Alvin Mangrim's noseless face. This was the kind of man the AOE needed, Macklin thought; this man had courage, and he wasn't afraid to take risks to get what he wanted. "I'll make you a corporal," he replied. "If you do your work well and show leadership, I'll make you a sergeant in the Mechanical Brigade one month from today. Do you agree to that?"

The other man shrugged and stood up. "I guess so. Corporal's better than private, isn't it? I can tell the privates what to do now, can't I?"

"And a captain can put your ass before a firing squad." Roland stepped in front of him. They stared at each other face to face like two hostile animals. A thin smile crept across Alvin Mangrim's mouth. Roland's bandaged, grotesque face remained impassive. Finally, he said, "You step in this tent without permission again, and I'll personally shoot you—or maybe you'd like a guided tour of the interrogation trailer?"

"Some other time. Sir."

"Report to Sergeant Draeger at the MB tent. Move it!"

Mangrim plucked his knife from the desktop. He walked to the slit he'd cut in the tent, then bent down; but before he crawled through, he looked back at Roland. "Captain?" he said in a soft voice. "I'd be careful walking around in the dark, if I were you. Lots of broken glass out there. You could fall down and maybe cut your head right off. Know what I mean?" Before Roland could respond, he'd crawled through the slit and was gone.

"Bastard!" Roland seethed. "He'll end up in front of the firing squad!"

Macklin laughed. He enjoyed seeing Roland, who was usually as controlled and emotionless as a machine, caught off balance for once. It made Macklin feel more in control. "He'll make lieutenant in six months," Macklin said. "He's got the kind of imagination the AOE thrives on." He walked to the desk and stood looking down at the head of Franklin Hayes; with a finger of his left hand, he traced one of the brown keloids that marred the cold blue flesh. "Damned by the mark of Cain," he said. "The sooner we get rid of that filth, the sooner we can build things back like they were. No. *Better* than they were." He reached out with his new hand and brought it down on the map of Nebraska, impaling it with the nails; he dragged it across the desk to him.

"Send recon patrols out to the east and southeast at first light," he told Roland. "Tell them to search until dark before they start back."

"How long are we staying here?"

"Until the AOE's rested and up to full strength. I want all the vehicles serviced and ready to move." The main body of trucks, cars and trailers—including Macklin's own Airstream command trailer—was eight miles west of Broken Bow, and it would be moved to connect with the advance war battalion at daylight. Starting with Freddie Kempka's encampment, Macklin had built a traveling army where everyone had a duty to perform, including footsoldiers, officers, mechanics, cooks, blacksmiths, tailors, two doctors and even camp prostitutes like Sheila Fontana. All of them were linked by Macklin's leadership, the need for food, water and shelter—and a belief that those survivors who bore the mark of Cain had to be exterminated. It was common knowledge that those with the mark of Cain were infecting the human race with radiation-poisoned genes, and if America was ever going to be strong enough to strike back at the Russians, the mark of Cain had to be erased.

Macklin studied the Nebraska map. His eye moved eastward, along the red line of Highway 2, through Grand Island and Aurora and Lincoln, to the blue line of the Missouri River. From Nebraska City, the AOE could march into either Iowa or Missouri—virgin land, with new settlements and supply centers to take. And then there would be the broad expanse of the Mississippi River, and the entire eastern part of the country would lie ahead of the AOE, to be taken and cleansed just as they had cleansed large sections of Utah, Colorado, Wyoming and Nebraska. But there was always the next settlement, and the next, and Macklin was restless. He'd heard reports of Troop Hydra, Nolan's Raiders and the so-called American Allegiance. He looked forward to meeting those "armies." The AOE would crush them, just as they'd destroyed the People's Freedom Party during months of warfare in the Rocky Mountains.

"We're heading east," he told Roland. "Across the Missouri River." His eye in the growth-stricken face gleamed with the excitement of the hunt. He lifted his right arm and swung the gloved hand through the air. Then faster. And faster still.

The nails made a high, eerie whistling sound, like the noise of human screams.

Fifty-four

"*Hey!* Hey, come look at this!"

The barn door flew open, and Sly Moody tumbled in with the morning wind at his heels. Instantly, Killer jumped up from underneath the wagon and began rapid-fire barking.

"Come look at this!" Moody shouted, his face ruddy with excitement, flakes of snow melting in his hair and beard. He had dressed hurriedly, throwing on a brown coat over his long johns, and he still wore slippers on his feet. "You gotta come look!"

"What the *hell* are you jabberin' about, mister?" Rusty had sat up from the pile of hay in which he'd slept, and now he rubbed his bloodshot eyes. He could only make out the faintest light coming through the barn doorway. "Christ A'mighty! It's not even dawn yet!"

Josh was on his feet, arranging the mask he'd just pulled over his head so he could see through the eyehole. He'd slept next to the wagon, and over the years he'd learned that waking up alert was a good way to stay alive. "What is it?" he asked Moody.

"Out there!" The old man pointed through the doorway with a shaking finger. "You gotta come see! Where's the girl?

Is she awake?" He looked toward the closed folds of the wagon's tent.

"What's this all about?" Josh asked. Last night, Sly Moody had told Josh and Rusty to keep Swan in the barn; they'd taken their bowls of stew and beans and eaten in the barn with her, and she'd been nervous and silent as a sphinx. Now it made no sense to Josh that Sly Moody was *wanting* to see Swan.

"Just get her!" Moody said. "Bring her and come see!" And then he sprinted through the doorway, out into the cold wind with Killer yapping right behind him.

"Who pulled that fella's string?" Rusty muttered to himself as he shrugged into his coat and pulled his boots on.

"Swan?" Josh called. "Swan, are you a—"

And then the tent opened and Swan stood there, tall and slim and disfigured, her face and head like a gnarled helmet. She wore blue jeans, a heavy yellow sweater and a corduroy coat, and on her feet were hiker's boots. She held Crybaby in one hand, but today she'd made no effort to hide her face. Feeling her way with the dowsing rod, Swan came down the stepladder and angled her head so she could see Josh through the narrow slit of her vision. Her head was getting heavier, harder to control. Sometimes she was afraid her neck was about to snap, and whatever was beneath the growths burned so savagely that she often couldn't hold back a scream. Once she'd taken a knife to the ugly, deformed *thing* that her head had become, and she'd started slashing away in a frenzy. But the growths were too tough to cut, as unyielding as armor plate.

She'd stopped looking into the magic mirror several months before. She just couldn't stand it anymore, though the figure carrying the glowing circle had seemed to be getting nearer—but then again, the hideous moonlike face with its drifting, monstrous features had looked to be drawing closer as well.

"Come on!" Sly Moody was urging from the front of the house. "Hurry!"

"What does he want us to see?" Swan asked Josh in her mangled voice.

"I don't know. Why don't we go find out?"

Rusty put on his cowboy hat and followed Josh and Swan out of the barn. Swan walked slowly, her shoulders stooped by the weight of her head.

And then, abruptly, Josh stopped. "My God," he said softly, wonderingly.

"You see it?" Sly Moody crowed. "Look at it! Just *look!*"

Swan angled her head in a different direction so she could see in front of her. She wasn't sure what she was seeing at first, because of the blowing snow, but her heart had begun pounding as she walked toward Sly Moody. Behind her, Rusty had stopped as well; he couldn't believe what he was looking at, thought he must surely still be asleep and dreaming. His mouth opened to release a small, awed whisper.

"I told you, didn't I?" Moody shouted, and he began laughing. Carla stood near him, bundled up in a coat and white woolen cap, her expression stunned. "I *told* you!" And then Moody started dancing a jig, kicking up whorls of snow as he cavorted amid the stumps where apple trees had been.

The single remaining apple tree was no longer bare. Hundreds of white blossoms had burst open on the scraggly limbs, and as the wind carried them spinning away like tiny ivory umbrellas small, bright green leaves were exposed underneath.

"It's alive!" Sly Moody shouted joyously, kicking his heels, stumbling and falling and getting up again with snow all over his face. "My tree's come back to life!"

"Oh," Swan whispered. Apple blossoms blew past her. She could smell their fragrance in the wind—the sweet perfume of life. She tilted her head forward, looking at the trunk of the apple tree. And there, as if burned into the wood, were the marks of her palm, and the finger-drawn letters S . . . W . . . A . . . N.

A hand touched her shoulder. It was Carla, and the woman stepped back when Swan finally got her deformed face and head turned. Through the narrow field of her vision, Swan saw the horror in Carla's eyes—but there were tears in them, too, and Carla was trying to speak but was unable to summon the words. Carla's fingers clutched at Swan's shoulders, and at last the woman said, "*You* did this. *You* put life back into that tree, didn't you?"

"I don't know," Swan said. "I think I just . . . woke it up."

"It's blossomed overnight!" Sly Moody danced around the tree as if it were a maypole festooned with bright streamers. He stopped, reached up and grabbed a lower limb, pulling it down for all to see. "It's got buds on it already! Lord God, we're gonna have a bucket full of apples by the first of May! I never seen a tree go so wild before!" He shook the limb and laughed like a child as the white blossoms whirled off. And then his gaze fell upon Swan, and his grin faded. He released the limb and stared at her for a silent moment as the snowflakes and apple blossoms blew between them and the air was filled with the fragrant promise of fruit and cider.

"If I hadn't seen this with my own eyes," Sly Moody said, his voice choked with emotion, "I never would've believed it. There ain't no *natural* way a tree can be bare one day and covered with blossoms the next. Hell, that tree's got new *leaves* on it! It's growing like it used to, back when April was a warm month and you could hear summer knockin' at the door!" His voice cracked, and he had to wait before he spoke again. "I know that's your name on that tree. I don't know how it got there, or why this tree's blossomed all of a sudden—but if this is a dream, I don't want to wake up. Smell the air! Just *smell* it!" And suddenly he walked forward and took Swan's hand, pressing it against his cheek. He gave a muffled sob and sank down to his knees in the snow. "Thank you," he said. "Thank you, thank you so much."

Josh recalled the green shoots that had been growing through the dirt in the shape of Swan's body, back in the basement of PawPaw's grocery. He remembered what she'd told him about the hurting sound, about the earth being alive and everything alive having its own language and way of understanding. Swan had spoken often of the flowers and plants she'd once grown in trailer lots and behind motel rooms, and both Josh and Rusty knew that she couldn't stand looking at dead trees where a forest used to stand. But nothing had prepared them for this. Josh walked to the tree and ran his fingers over the letters of Swan's name; they were burned into the wood as if by a blowtorch. Whatever power or energy or force Swan had summoned last night, here was the physical evidence of it. "How did you do this?" he asked her, not knowing any other way to put it.

"I just touched it," she answered. "I felt like it wasn't dead, and I touched it because I wanted it to keep living." She was embarrassed that the old man was down on his knees beside her, and she wished he'd get up and stop crying. His wife was looking at Swan with a mixture of revulsion and wonder, as one might regard a toadfrog with golden wings. All this attention was making Swan more nervous than when she'd frightened the old man and woman last night. "Please," she said, tugging at his coat. "Please get up, mister."

"It's a miracle," Carla murmured, watching the blossoms blow. Nearby, Killer ran through the snow trying to catch them between his teeth. "She's made a miracle happen!" Two tears crept down her cheeks, freezing like diamonds before they reached her jawline.

Swan was jittery and cold, afraid that her misshapen head might tilt over too far to one side and break her neck. She could endure the stinging wind no longer, and she pulled away from Sly Moody's grip; she turned and walked toward the barn, probing in the snow before her with Crybaby as the old man and the others watched her go. Killer ran circles around her with an apple blossom in his mouth.

It was Rusty who got his tongue unstuck first. "What's the nearest town from here?" he asked Sly Moody, who was still on his knees. "We're heading north."

The old man blinked heavily and wiped his eyes with the back of his hand. "Richland," he said. Then he shook his head. "No, no; Richland's dead. Everybody either left Richland or died from the typhoid fever last year." He struggled to his feet. "Mary's Rest," he said finally. "That would be the next settlement of any size. It's about sixty miles north of here, across I-44. I've never been there, but I hear Mary's Rest is a real *city.*"

"I guess it's Mary's Rest, then," Josh said to Rusty. "Sounds like as good a place as any."

Moody suddenly snapped out of his daze. "You don't have

to leave *here!* You can stay with us! We've got plenty of food, and we'll find room in the house for you! Lord, I wouldn't have that girl sleepin' in the barn another night for anything!"

"Thank you," Josh said, "but we've got to go on. You need your food for yourself. And like Rusty said, we're entertainers. That's how we get by."

Sly Moody gripped Josh's arm. "Listen, you don't know what you've got, mister! That girl's a miracle worker! Look at that tree! It was dead yesterday, and now you can smell the blossoms! Mister, that girl's *special.* You don't know what she could do, if she was to set her mind to it!"

"What could she do?" Rusty was puzzled by the whole thing and feeling definitely out of his depth, the same as he had whenever he'd picked up Fabrioso's mirror and seen nothing but murk in the glass.

"Look at that tree and think of an orchard!" Sly Moody said excitedly. "Think of a cornfield, or a field of beans or squash or anything else! I don't know what's inside that girl, but she's got the power of *life!* Don't you see that? She touched that tree and brought it back! Mister, that Swan could wake the whole land up again!"

"It's just one tree," Josh reminded him. "How do you know she could do the same thing to a whole orchard?"

"You dumb fool, what's an orchard but *one* tree after another?" he growled. "I don't know how she did it or anything about her, but if she can start apples growin' again, she can start orchards and crop fields, too! You're crazy to take somebody with a God's gift like that out on the road! The country out there's full of killers, highwaymen, lunatics and only the Devil knows what all! If you stay here, she can start workin' on the fields, doin' whatever she has to do to wake 'em up again!"

Josh glanced at Rusty, who shook his head, then gently pulled free of Sly Moody. "We've got to go on."

"Why? Where to? What are you lookin' for that's worth findin'?"

"I don't know," Josh admitted. In seven years of wandering from settlement to settlement, the point of life had become wandering instead of settling. Still, Josh hoped that someday they'd find a place that would be suitable to live in for more than a few months at a time—and possibly he might someday make his way south to Mobile in search of Rose and his sons. "We'll know it when we find it, I guess."

Moody started to protest again, but his wife said, "Sylvester? It's getting very cold out here. I think they've made up their minds, and I think they should do what they feel is best."

The old man hesitated, then looked at his tree again and finally nodded. "All right," he muttered. "You have to go your own way, I reckon." He fixed a hard gaze on Josh, who stood at least four inches taller than himself. "Now you listen to me, mister," he warned. "You protect that girl, you hear me? Maybe someday she'll see her way clear to do what I've said she *can* do. You protect her, hear?"

"Yes," Josh said. "I hear."

"Then go on," Sly Moody said. Josh and Rusty started walking toward the barn, and Moody said, "God go with you!" He picked up a handful of blossoms from the snow, held them to his nose and inhaled.

An hour or so after the Travelin' Show wagon had rumbled off northward along the road, Sly Moody put his heaviest coat and boots on and told Carla that he couldn't stand to sit still a minute longer. He was going to walk through the woods to Bill McHenry's place and tell him the story of the girl who could put life back into a tree with her touch, he said. Bill McHenry had a pickup truck and some gasoline, and Sly Moody said that he was going to tell everybody within shouting distance about that girl, because he had witnessed a miracle and all hope was not yet dead in the world. He was going to find a hilltop to stand on and shout that girl's name, and when those apples came he was going to cook an apple stew and invite everybody who lived on the desolate farms for miles around to come partake of a miracle.

And then he put his arms around the woman he had taken as his wife and kissed her, and her eyes sparkled like stars.

ney from settlement to settlement; the point, or the lack of one, was wandering instead of settling. Still, Josh hoped that someday they'd find a place that would be suitable to live in for more than a few months at a time—and possibly he might someday make his way south to Mobile in search of Rose and his sons. "We'll know it when we find it, I guess."

Moody started to protest again, but his wife said, "Sylvester, it's getting very cold out here. I think they've made up their minds, and I think they should do what they feel is best."

The old man hesitated, then looked at his tree again and finally nodded. "All right," he muttered. "You have to go your own way, I reckon." He fixed a hard gaze on Josh, who stood at least four inches taller than himself. "Now you listen to me, mister," he warned. "You protect that girl, you hear me? Maybe someday she'll see her way clear to do what I've said she can do. You protect her. Hear?"

"Yes," Josh said. "I hear."

"Then go on," Sly Moody said. Josh and Rusty started walking toward the barn, and Moody said, "God go with you!" He picked up a handful of blossoms from the snow, held them to his nose and inhaled.

An hour or so after the [illegible] wagon had rumbled off northward along the road, Sly Moody put on his heaviest coat and boots on and told Carra that he couldn't stand to sit still a minute longer. He was going to walk through the woods to Bill McHenry's place and tell him the story of the girl who could put life back into a tree with her touch, he said. McHenry had a pickup truck and some gasoline, and Sly Moody said that he was going to tell everybody [illegible] about that girl, because he had witnessed a miracle and all hope wasn't dead in the world. He was going to [illegible] and where [illegible] apple [illegible]

And then he put his arms around the woman he had [illegible]

NINE

The Fountain and the Fire

Signs and symbols / The surgeon's task / Bones of a thousand candles / The seamstress

Fifty-five

The Jeep rumbled over a rutted, snow-covered road, passing wrecks and derelict vehicles that had been pulled to both sides. Here and there a frozen corpse lay in a gray snowdrift, and Sister saw one whose arms were lifted as if in a final appeal for mercy.

They came to an unmarked crossroads, and Paul slowed down. He looked over his shoulder at Hugh Ryan, who had jammed himself into the rear compartment with the luggage. Hugh was gripping his crutch with both hands and snoring. "Hey!" Paul said, and he nudged the sleeping man. "Wake up!"

Hugh snorted, finally opened his heavy-lidded eyes. "What is it? Are we there yet?"

"Hell, no! I think we must've taken the wrong road about five miles back! There's not a sign of life out here!" He glanced up through the windshield and saw the threat of new snow in the clouds. The light was just beginning to fade, and Paul didn't want to look at the gas gauge because he knew they were traveling on fumes. "I thought you knew the way!"

"I do," Hugh assured him. "But it's been a while since I've

ventured very far from Moberly." He gazed around at the bleak landscape. "We're at a crossroads," he announced.

"We know that. Now which road do we take?"

"There should be a sign. Maybe the wind's blown it down." He shifted position, trying to find a familiar landmark. The truth—which he had not told Paul and Sister—was that he'd never been this way before, but he'd wanted to get out of Moberly because he feared he'd be murdered in the night for his cache of blankets. "Let's see, now: I think I remember a big grove of old oak trees that we turned right at."

Paul rolled his eyes. On both sides of the narrow road stood thick forests. "Look," he said. "Read my lips: We're out in the middle of nowhere, and we're running out of gasoline—and this time there are no fuel tanks around for me to siphon. It's going to be dark soon, and I think we're on the wrong road. Now tell me why I shouldn't wring your damned skinny neck!"

Hugh looked wounded. "Because," he said with great dignity, "you're a decent human being." He glanced quickly at Sister, who had turned to deliver a scathing gaze. "I do know the way. I really do. I got us around that broken bridge, didn't I?"

"Which way?" Sister asked pointedly. "Left or right?"

"Left," Hugh said—and immediately wished that he'd said "right," but now it was too late and he didn't want to appear a fool.

"Mary's Rest better be around the next bend," Paul told them grimly, "or we're going to be walking real soon." He put the Jeep into gear and turned left. The road wound through a corridor of dead trees with branches that interlocked and closed off the sky.

Hugh settled back to await judgment, and Sister reached down to the floorboard for her satchel. She unzipped it, felt inside for the glass ring and drew it out. Then she held it in her lap as the trapped jewels sparkled, and she stared into its shimmering depths.

"What do you see?" Paul asked. "Anything?"

Sister shook her head. The colors pulsed, but they had not yet formed pictures. How the glass ring worked, and exactly what it was, had remained a puzzle. Paul had said that he thought the radiation had melded the glass, jewels and precious metals into some kind of supersensitive antenna, but what it was tuned to neither of them could say. But they had come to the agreement that the glass circle was leading them to someone, and that to follow it meant giving up that part of yourself that refused to believe in miracles. Using the glass ring was like a leap in the dark, a surrendering of doubt, fear and all other impurities that clouded the mind; using it was the ultimate act of faith.

Are we closer to the answer, or further away? Sister asked mentally as she peered into the ring. *Who are we searching for, and why?* Her questions, she knew, would be answered with symbols and pictures, sights and shadows and sounds that might have been distant human voices, the creaking of wheels, or the barking of a dog.

A diamond flared like a meteor, and light sizzled along threads of silver and platinum. More diamonds burst with light, like a chain reaction. Sister felt the power of the glass circle reaching for her, drawing her inward, deeper, deeper still, and all her being was fixed on the bursts of light as they flared in a hypnotic rhythm.

She was no longer in the Jeep with Paul Thorson and the one-legged doctor from Amarillo. She was standing in what looked to be a snow-covered field stubbled with the stumps of trees. But there was one tree remaining, and that one was covered with diamond-white blossoms blowing before the wind. On the tree's trunk were palm prints, as if seared into the wood—slim long fingers, the hands of a young person.

And across the trunk were letters, as if fingerpainted in fire: S . . . W . . . A . . . N.

Sister tried to turn her head, to see more of where she was standing, but the dreamwalk scene began to fade; she was aware of shadowy figures, distant voices, a moment perhaps trapped in time and somehow transmitted to Sister like a photograph through spectral wires. And then, abruptly, the dreamwalk was over, and she was back in the Jeep again with the glass ring between her hands.

She released the breath she'd been holding. "It was there

again," she told Paul. "I saw it again—the single tree in a field of stumps, the palm prints and the word 'swan' burned on the trunk. But it was clearer than last night, and this time . . . I think I could smell *apples.*" They'd traveled all day yesterday, heading for Mary's Rest, and had spent last night in the ruins of a farmhouse; it was there that Sister had looked into the glass ring and first seen that tree with the blowing blossoms. The vision was clearer than it had been; she'd been able to see every detail of the tree, every scraggly branch and even the tiny green buds that peeked out from under the blossoms. "I think we're getting closer," she said, and her heart was racing. "The image was stronger. We *must* be getting closer!"

"But all the trees are dead," Paul reminded her. "Just look around. Nothing's in bloom—and nothing's *going* to be. Why should that thing show you the image of a tree in bloom?"

"I don't know. If I did, I'd tell you." She concentrated on the glass ring again; it pulsated with her quickened heartbeat but did not invite her to go dreamwalking. The message had been delivered and, at least for now, would not be repeated.

"Swan." Paul shook his head. "That doesn't make a damned bit of sense."

"Yes, it does. Somehow it does. We've just got to put the pieces together."

Paul's hands gripped the steering wheel. "Sister," he said, with a trace of pity, "you've been saying the same thing for a long time. You've been looking into that glass ring like you were a gypsy trying to read tea leaves. And here we are, going back and forth, following signs and symbols that might not mean a damned thing." He glanced sharply at her. "Have you ever thought about that possibility?"

"We found Matheson, didn't we? We found the tarot cards and the doll." She kept her voice firm, but there had been many days and nights when she'd let herself fear the same thing—but only for a moment or two, and then her resolve returned. "I believe this is leading us to someone—someone very important."

"You mean you *want* to believe it."

"I mean I *do* believe it!" she snapped. "How could I go on if I didn't?"

Paul sighed deeply; he was tired, his beard itched and he knew he smelled like a cage of monkeys in a zoo. How long had it been, he wondered, since he'd had a bath? The best he'd been able to do in the last few weeks was scrub himself halfheartedly with ashes and snow. For the past two years, they had danced around the subject of the glass ring's fallibility like a couple of wary boxers. Paul himself could see nothing in the ring but colors, and he'd asked himself many times if the woman he was traveling with—indeed, had come to love and respect—wasn't making the signs up, interpreting them as she saw fit in order to keep them on this lunatic quest.

"I believe," she told him, "that this is a *gift.* I believe I found it for a reason. I believe it's leading us for a reason. And everything it shows us is a clue to where we need to go. Don't you under—"

"Bullshit!" Paul said, and he almost stomped on the brake, but he was afraid the Jeep would skid right off the road. Sister looked at him, her face with its hideous growths mirroring shock, anger and disillusion. "You saw a fucking clown's face in that damned thing, remember that? You saw a beat-up old Conestoga wagon or something; and you saw a thousand other things that just don't make any sense! You said go east because you thought the visions or dreamwalk pictures or whatever the shit they are were getting stronger; and then you said go back west again, because the visions started fading and you were trying to focus in on the direction. After that you said go north, and then south—and then north and south again. Sister, you're seeing what you *want* to see in that damned thing! So we found Matheson, Kansas! So what? Maybe you heard something about that town when you were a kid! Have you ever considered that?"

She was silent, clasping the glass circle closer to her, and finally she said what she'd wanted to say for a long, long time. "I believe," she told him, "that this is a gift from God."

"Right." He smiled bitterly. "Well, look around. Just look. Have you ever considered the possibility that God might be insane?"

Tears burned her eyes, and she looked away from him because she'd be damned if she'd let him see her cry.

"This whole thing is *you,* don't you see that?" he continued. "It's what *you* see. It's what *you* feel, and what *you* decide. If the damned thing is leading you somewhere—or to *somebody*—why doesn't it show you right out where you're supposed to go? Why's it playing tricks with your mind? Why does it give you these 'clues' in bits and pieces?"

"Because," Sister answered, with just a slight waver in her voice, "just getting a gift doesn't mean you know how to use it. The fault's not with the glass ring—it's with me, because there's a limit to what I can understand. I'm doing the best I can, and maybe . . . maybe the person I'm looking for isn't ready to be found yet, either."

"*What?* Come on!"

"Maybe the circumstances aren't right yet. Maybe the picture's not complete, and that's why—"

"Oh, Jesus!" Paul said wearily. "You're raving, do you know that? You're making up things that aren't true, because you want them so much to be true. You don't want to admit that we've wasted seven years of our lives searching for ghosts."

Sister watched the road unfolding before them, leading the Jeep into a dark, dead forest. "If you feel that way," she finally asked, "then why have you been traveling with me all this time?"

"I don't know. Maybe because I wanted to believe as much as you do. I wanted to think there was some method to this madness—but there's not, and there never was."

"I remember a shortwave radio," Sister said.

"What?"

"A shortwave radio," she repeated. "The one you used to keep those people in your cabin from killing themselves. You kept them going and gave them hope. Remember?"

"Okay. So what?"

"Didn't you yourself at least *hope* there'd be a human voice on that radio? Didn't you tell yourself that maybe the next day, or the next, there'd be a signal from some other survivors? You didn't go through all that just to keep a handful of strangers alive. You did it to keep yourself alive, too. And you hoped that maybe one day there'd be something more than static on that radio. Well, this is *my* shortwave radio." She ran her hands over the smooth glass. "And I believe it's tuned to a force that I can't even begin to understand—but I'm not going to doubt it. No. I'm going to keep on going, one step at a time. With you or without—"

"What the *hell . . . ?*" Paul interrupted as they came around a curve. Standing in the middle of the road, beneath the overhanging trees, were three large snowmen, all wearing caps and mufflers, with stones for their eyes and noses. One of them appeared to be smoking a corncob pipe. Instantly Paul realized that he could not stop in time, and though he put his foot on the brake the wheels skidded through the snow and the Jeep's front fender banged into one of the snowmen.

The jolt almost threw Paul and Sister through the windshield, and Hugh made a croaking sound in the back as the collision rattled his teeth. The Jeep's engine stuttered and died. Sister and Paul saw that where the snowman had been was now a pile of snow around a disguised roadblock of scrap metal, pieces of wood and stones.

"Shit!" Paul said when he could find his voice. "Some fool's put a damned—"

A pair of legs and scuffed brown boots slammed down on the Jeep's hood from above.

Sister looked up and saw a hooded figure in a long, tattered brown coat with one hand wrapped around a rope that was tied in tree branches over the road. In the figure's other hand was a .38 pistol, aimed through the windshield at Paul Thorson.

More figures, scurrying from the woods on all sides, were converging on the Jeep. "Bandits!" Hugh bleated, his eyes wide with terror. "They'll rob us and cut our throats!"

"Like hell they will," Sister said calmly, and she put her hand on the butt of the shotgun that was wedged beside her seat. She pulled it up, aiming it at the figure on the hood, and was about to fire when both of the Jeep's doors were wrenched open.

A dozen pistols, three rifles and seven sharpened wooden

spears thrust into the Jeep at Sister, and an equal number of weapons threatened Paul. "Don't kill us!" Hugh shouted. "Please don't kill us! We'll give you anything you want!"

Fine for *you* to say, since you don't own a damned thing! Sister thought as she stared into the bristling wall of firearms and spears. She calculated how long it would take her to turn the shotgun and fire at the bandits—and she knew she'd be history as soon as she made a sudden movement. She froze, one hand on the shotgun and the other trying to protect the glass ring.

"Out of the Jeep," the figure on the hood commanded. It was a young voice—the voice of a boy. The pistol shifted toward Sister. "Get your finger off that trigger if you want to keep it."

She hesitated, peering up at the boy's face, though she couldn't make out any features because of the coat's cowl. The pistol was aimed as steadily as if the boy's arm was stone, and the tone of his voice was all deadly business.

She blinked and removed her finger from the trigger.

Paul knew they had no choice. He muttered a curse, longing to get his hands around Hugh Ryan's neck, and got out.

"Some guide you are," Sister told Hugh. She took a deep breath, exhaled and stepped out.

She towered over her captors.

They were children.

All of them were thin and dirty, the youngest about nine or ten and the oldest maybe sixteen—and all of them stared as one at the pulsing glass ring.

Fifty-six

Herded before a yelling, rowdy gang of twenty-seven boy bandits, Paul, Sister and Hugh were prodded with the barrels of rifles and sharp spear tips through the snowy woods. About a hundred yards from the road, they were commanded to stop, and they waited while a few of the boys cleared brush and branches from the mouth of a small cave. A rifle barrel pushed Sister inside, and the others followed.

Beyond the opening, the cave widened into a large, high-ceilinged chamber. It was damp within, but dozens of candles were set about and burning, and at the center of the cavern a small fire glowed, the smoke curling up through a hole in the ceiling. Eight other boys, all of them skinny and sickly-looking, were waiting for their compatriots to return, and when the bags were flung open the boys shouted and laughed as Sister's and Paul's extra clothes were scattered. The bandits grabbed up ill-fitting coats and sweaters, draped themselves with woolen scarves and caps and danced around the fire like Apaches. One of them uncorked a jug of the moonshine that Hugh had brought along, and the shouts grew louder, the dancing wilder. Adding to the raucous clamor was the noise of wood blocks clapped together, rattling gourds and sticks beating a rhythm on a cardboard box.

Hugh balanced himself precariously on his crutch and single leg as the boys whirled around him, stabbing at him with their spears. He'd heard stories of the forest bandits before, and he didn't like the idea of being scalped and skinned. "Don't kill us!" he shouted over the tumult. "Please don't—" And then he went down on his rump as a tough-looking ten-year-old with shaggy black hair kicked his crutch out from under him. A gale of laughter followed him down, and more spears and guns poked at Paul and Sister. She looked across the cave and saw through the haze of smoke a small, thin boy with red hair and a chalky complexion. He was holding the glass ring between his hands, staring at it intently —and then a second boy grabbed it away from him and ran with it. A third boy attacked that one, trying to get his hands on the treasure. Sister saw a throng of raggedly dressed boys jostling and fighting in the exhilaration of the hunt, and she lost sight of the glass ring. Another boy shoved her own shotgun in her face and grinned at her as if daring her to make a move. Then he whirled away, grabbed the jug of moonshine and joined the victory dance.

Paul helped Hugh up. A spear jabbed Paul in the ribs, and he turned angrily toward his tormentor, but Sister grasped his arm to hold him back. A boy with the bones of small animals tied in his tangled blond hair thrust a spear at Sister's face and drew it back just short of impaling an eyeball. She stared at him impassively, and he giggled like a hyena and capered away.

The boy who'd taken Paul's Magnum danced past, hardly able to hold the heavy weapon in a two-handed grip. The jug of moonshine was being passed around, inflaming them to further frenzy. Sister was afraid they were going to start firing their guns at random, and in a confined place like this the ricochets would be deadly. She saw the glimmer of the glass ring as one boy grabbed it from another; then two boys were fighting for it, and Sister was sick at the thought of the glass ring lying shattered. She took a step forward, but the darting of a half-dozen spears kept her back.

And then the horrible thing happened: one of the boys, already dizzy with moonshine, lifted the glass ring over his head—and he was tackled from behind by another boy trying to grab it. The ring flew from his hands and spun through the air, and Sister felt a scream welling up. She saw it falling, as if in terrible slow motion, toward the stone floor, and she heard herself shout *"No!"* but there was nothing she could do. The circle of glass was falling . . . falling . . . falling.

A hand grasped it before it hit the floor, and the ring glittered with fiery colors as if meteors were exploding within it.

It had been caught by the figure in the cowled coat who'd landed on the Jeep's hood. He was taller than the others by at least a foot, and as he approached Sister the boys around him parted to give him room. His face was still obscured by the cowl. The shouting and noise of clapping wood blocks and drumbeats faltered and began to fade as the tallest boy walked unhurriedly through the others. The glass circle flared with a strong, slow pulse. And then the boy stood in front of Sister.

"What is this?" he asked, holding the ring before him. The others had stopped dancing and shouting, and they began to crowd around to watch.

"It belongs to me," Sister answered.

"No. It *used* to belong to you. I asked you what it is."

"It's—" She paused, trying to decide what to say. "It's magic," she told him. "It's a miracle, if you know how to use it. Please—" She heard the unaccustomed sound of pleading in her voice. "Please don't break it."

"What if I did? What if I was to let it fall and break? Would the magic spill out?"

She was silent, knowing the boy was taunting her.

He pulled the cowl back to reveal his face. "I don't believe in magic," he said. "That's just for fools and kids."

He was older than the others—maybe seventeen or eighteen. He was almost as tall as she was, and the size of his shoulders said that he was going to be a large man when he grew up and filled out. His face was lean and pallid, with sharp cheekbones and eyes the color of ashes; in his shoulder-length dark brown hair were braided small bones and feathers, and he looked as dour and serious as an Indian chief. The fine, light brown hairs of a beard covered the lower part of his face, but Sister could see that he had a strong, square jawline. Thick, dark eyebrows added to his stern countenance, and the bridge of his nose was flattened and crooked like a boxer's. He was a handsome young man, but certainly dangerous. And, Sister realized, he was neither a kid nor a fool.

He regarded the glass ring in silence. Then: "Where were you going?"

"Mary's Rest," Hugh spoke up nervously. "We're just poor travelers. We don't mean any—"

"Shut up," the boy ordered, and Hugh's mouth snapped closed. He locked stares with Paul for a few seconds, then grunted and dismissed him. "Mary's Rest," the boy repeated. "You're about fifteen miles east of Mary's Rest. Why were you going there?"

"We were going to pass through it on our way south," Sister said. "We figured we'd get some food and water."

"Is that so? Well, you're out of luck, then. The food's almost gone in Mary's Rest. They're starving over there, and their pond went dry about five months ago. They're melting snow to drink, just like everybody else."

"There's radiation in the snow," Hugh said. "Drinking melted snow will kill you."

"What are you? An expert?"

"No, but I'm—I *was*—a doctor, and I know what I'm talking about."

"A doctor? What kind of doctor?"

"I was a surgeon," Hugh said, pride creeping back into his voice. "I used to be the best surgeon in Amarillo."

"A surgeon? You mean you operated on sick people?"

"That's right. And I never lost a patient, either."

Sister decided to take a step forward. Instantly the boy's hand went to a pistol at his belt under the coat. "Listen," Sister said, "let's cut this screwing around. You've already got everything we own. We'll walk the rest of the way—but I want that glass ring back. I want it *now*. If you're going to kill me, you'd better do it, because either you give me the ring or I'm taking it from you."

The boy remained motionless, his hawklike stare challenging her.

Here goes! she thought, her heart hammering. She started to reach toward him, but suddenly he laughed and stepped back. He held the ring up, as if he might drop it to the cavern's floor.

Sister stopped. "Don't," she said. "Please don't."

His hand lingered in the air. Sister tensed, ready to go for it if the fingers opened.

"Robin?" a weak voice called from the back of the cave. "Robin?"

The boy looked into Sister's face for a few seconds longer, his eyes hard and shrewd; then he blinked, lowered his arm and offered the ring to her. "Here. It's not worth a shit, anyway."

She took it, relief coursing through her bones.

"None of you are going anywhere," the boy said. "Especially not *you,* Doc."

"Huh?" Terror lanced him.

"Walk to the back of the cave," the boy commanded. "All of you." They hesitated. "Now," he said, in a voice that was used to being obeyed.

They did as he said, and in another moment Sister saw several more figures at the rear of the chamber. Three of them were boys with Job's Mask in varying stages of severity, one of them hardly able to keep his misshapen head upright. On the floor in a corner, lying on a bed of straw and leaves, was a thin brown-haired boy of about ten or eleven, his face shining with the sweat of fever. A dressing of greasy-looking leaves had been plastered on his white chest, just under the heart, and blood had leaked out around it. The wounded boy tried to lift his head when he saw them, but he didn't have enough strength. "Robin?" he whispered. "You there?"

"I'm here, Bucky." Robin bent beside him and brushed the wet hair from the other boy's forehead.

"I'm hurting . . . so bad." Bucky coughed, and foamy

blood appeared at his lips. Robin quickly wiped it away with a leaf. "You won't let me go out where it's dark, will you?"

"No," Robin said quietly. "I won't let you go out where it's dark." He looked up at Sister with eyes that were a hundred years old. "Bucky got shot three days ago." With gentle fingers, he carefully peeled the plaster of leaves away. The wound was an ugly scarlet hole with puffy gray edges of infection. Robin's gaze moved to Hugh, then to the glass ring. "I don't believe in magic or miracles," he said. "But maybe it's kind of a miracle that we found *you* today, Doc. You're going to take the bullet out."

"Me?" Hugh almost choked. "Oh, no. I can't. Not me."

"You said you used to operate on sick people. You said you never lost a patient."

"That was a *lifetime* ago!" Hugh wailed. "Look at that wound! It's too close to the heart!" He held up a palsied hand. "I couldn't cut lettuce with a hand like this!"

Robin stood up and approached Hugh until they were almost nose to nose. "You're a doctor," he said. "You're going to take the bullet out and make him well, or you can start digging graves for you and your friends."

"I can't! There are no instruments here, no light, no disinfectants, no sedatives! I haven't operated in seven years, and I wasn't a heart surgeon, anyway! No. I'm sorry. That boy doesn't have a—"

Robin's pistol was cocked and pressed against Hugh's throat. "A doctor who can't help anybody shouldn't be living. You're just using up air, aren't you?"

"Please . . . please . . ." Hugh gasped, his eyes bulging.

"Wait a minute," Sister said. "Hugh, the hole's already there. All you have to do is bring the bullet out."

"Oh, sure! Sure! Just bring the bullet out!" Hugh giggled, on the edge of hysteria. "Sister, the bullet could be anywhere! What am I supposed to stop the blood with? How am I supposed to dig the damned thing out—with my fingers?"

"We've got knives," Robin told him. "We can heat them in the fire. That makes them clean, doesn't it?"

"There's no such thing as 'clean' in conditions like these! My God, you don't know what you're asking me to do!"

"Not asking. *Telling*. Do it, Doc."

Hugh looked to Paul and Sister for help, but there was nothing they could do. "I can't," he whispered hoarsely. "Please . . . I'll kill him if I try to take the bullet out."

"He'll die for sure if you don't. I'm the leader here. When I give my word, I keep it. Bucky got shot because I sent him out with some others to stop a truck passing through. But he wasn't ready to kill anybody yet, and he wasn't fast enough to dodge a bullet, either." He jabbed the pistol into Hugh's throat. "I *am* ready to kill. I've done it before. Now, I promised Bucky I'd do whatever I could for him. So—do you take the bullet out, or do I kill all of you?"

Hugh swallowed, his eyes watering with fear. "There's . . . there's so much I've forgotten."

"Remember it. Real quick."

Hugh was shaking. He closed his eyes, opened them again. The boy was still there. His whole body was a heartbeat. What do I remember? he asked himself. Think, damn it! Nothing would come together; it was all a hazy jumble. The boy was waiting, his finger on the trigger. Hugh realized he would have to go on instinct, and God help them all if he screwed up. "Somebody's . . . going to have to support me," he managed to say. "My balance isn't so good. And light. I've got to have light, as much as I can get. I need—" Think! "—three or four sharp knives with narrow blades. Rub them with ashes and put them in the fire. I need rags, and . . . oh, Jesus, I need clamps and forceps and probes and *I cannot kill this boy, damn you!*" His eyes blazed at Robin.

"I'll get you what you need. None of that medical shit, though. But I'll get you the other stuff."

"And moonshine," Hugh said. "The jug. For both the boy and myself. I want some ashes to clean my hands with, and I may need a bucket to puke into." He reached up with a trembling hand and pushed the pistol away from his throat. "What's your name, young man?"

"Robin Oakes."

"All right, then, Mr. Oakes. When I start, you're not to lay a finger on me. No matter what I do, no matter what you think I *ought* to be doing. I'll be scared enough for both of us." Hugh looked down at the wound and winced; it was very, very nasty. "What kind of gun was he shot with?"

"I don't know. A pistol, I guess."

"That doesn't tell me anything about the size of the bullet. Oh, Jesus, this is crazy! I can't remove a bullet from a wound that close to—" The pistol swung back up again. Hugh saw the boy's finger ready on the trigger, and something about being so close to death clicked on the façade of arrogance he had worn back in Amarillo. "Get that gun out of my face, you little swine," he said, and he saw Robin blink. "I'll do what I can—but I'm not promising a miracle, do you understand? Well? What are you standing there for? Get me what I need!"

Robin lowered the pistol. He went off to get the moonshine, the knives and the ashes.

It took about twenty minutes to get Bucky as drunk as Hugh wanted him. Under Robin's direction, the other boys brought candles and set them in a circle around Bucky. Hugh scrubbed his hands in ashes and waited for the blades to cook.

"He called you Sister," Robin said. "Are you a nun?"

"No. That's just my name."

"Oh."

He sounded disappointed, and Sister decided to ask, "Why?"

Robin shrugged. "We used to have nuns where we were, in the big building. I used to call them blackbirds, because they always flew at you when they thought you'd done something wrong. But some of them were okay. Sister Margaret said she was sure things would work out for me. Like getting a family and a home and everything." He glanced around the cavern. "Some home, huh?"

It dawned on Sister what Robin was talking about. "You lived in an orphanage?"

"Yeah. Everybody did. A lot of us got sick and died after it turned cold. Especially the really young ones." His eyes darkened. "Father Thomas died, and we buried him behind the big building. Sister Lynn died, and then so did Sister May and Sister Margaret. Father Cummings left in the night. I don't blame him—who wants to take care of a bunch of ratty punks? Some of the others left, too. The last to die was Father Clinton, and then it was just us."

"Weren't there any older boys with you?"

"Oh, yeah. A few of them stayed, but most took off on their own. Somehow, I guess I got to be the oldest. I figured that if I left, who was going to take care of the punks?"

"So you found this cave and started robbing people?"

"Sure. Why not? I mean, the world's gone crazy, hasn't it? Why shouldn't we rob people if it's the only way to stay alive?"

"Because it's wrong," Sister answered. The boy laughed. She let his laugh die, and then she said, "How many people have you killed?"

All traces of a smile left his face. He stared at his hands; they were a man's hands, rough and callused. "Four. But all of them would've killed me, too." He shrugged uneasily. "No big deal."

"The knives are ready," Paul said, returning from the fire. Standing on his crutch over the wounded boy, Hugh took a deep breath and lowered his head.

He stayed that way for a minute. "All right." His voice was low and resigned. "Bring the knives over. Sister, will you kneel down beside me and keep me steady, please? I'll need several boys to hold Bucky securely, too. We don't want him thrashing around."

"Can we just knock him out or something?" Robin asked.

"No. There's a risk of brain damage in that, and the first impulse a person has after being knocked unconscious is to throw up. We don't want that, do we? Paul, would you hold Bucky's legs? I hope seeing a little blood doesn't make you sick."

"It doesn't," Paul said, and Sister recalled the day on I-80 when he'd sliced open a wolf's belly.

The hot knives were brought in a metal pot. Sister knelt beside Hugh and let him lean his feeble weight against her. She laid the glass ring beside her on the ground. Bucky was drunk and delirious, and he was talking about hearing birds singing. Sister listened; she could only hear the keening of wind past the mouth of the cave.

"Dear God, please guide my hand," Hugh whispered. He picked up a knife. The blade was too wide, and he chose another. Even the narrowest of the available knives would be as clumsy as a broken thumb. He knew that one slip could cut into the boy's left ventricle, and then nothing could stop the geyser of blood.

"Go on," Robin urged.

"I'll start when I'm ready! Not one damned second before! Now move away from me, boy!"

Robin retreated but stayed close enough to watch.

Some of the others were holding Bucky's arms, head and body to the ground, and most of them—even the Job's Mask victims—had crowded around. Hugh looked at the knife in his hand; it was shaking, and there was no stopping it. Before his nerve broke entirely, he leaned forward and pressed the hot blade against an edge of the wound.

Infectious fluids spattered. Bucky's body jackknifed, and the boy howled with agony. "Hold him down!" Hugh shouted. "Hold him, damn it!" The boys struggled to control him, and even Paul had trouble with the kicking legs. Hugh's knife dug deeper, Bucky's cry reverberating off the walls.

Robin shouted, "You're killing him!" but Hugh paid no heed. He picked up the moonshine jug and splashed alcohol in and around the oozing wound. Now the boys could barely hold Bucky down. Hugh began to probe again, his own heart pounding as if about to burst through his breast.

"I can't see the bullet!" Hugh said. "It's gone too deep!" Blood was welling up, thick and dark red. He plucked away bone chips from a nicked rib. The red, spongy mass of the lung hitched and bubbled beneath the blade. "Hold him down, for God's sake!" he shouted. The blade was too wide; it was not a surgical instrument, it was a butchering tool. "I can't do it! I *can't!*" he wailed, and he flung the knife away.

Robin pressed the pistol's barrel to his skull. "Get it out of him!"

"I don't have the proper instruments! I can't work without—"

"Fuck the instruments!" Robin shouted. "Use your fingers, if you have to! Just get the bullet out!"

Bucky was moaning, his eyelids fluttering wildly, and his body kept wanting to curl into a fetal position. It took all the strength of the others to restrain him. Hugh was distraught; the metal pot held no blades narrow enough for the work. Robin's pistol pushed at his head. He looked to one side and saw the circle of glass on the ground.

He saw the two thin spikes, and noted where three more had been broken away.

"Sister, I need one of those spikes as a probe," he said. "Could you break one off for me?"

She hesitated only a second or two, and then the spike was in his palm and aflame with color.

Spreading the wound's edges with his other hand, he slid the spike into the scarlet hole.

Hugh had to go deep, his spine crawling at the thought of what the probe might be grazing. "Hold him!" he warned, angling the piece of glass a centimeter to the left. The heart was laboring, the body passing another threshold of shock. Hurry! Hurry! Hugh thought. Find the bastard and get out! Deeper slid the probe, and still no bullet.

He imagined suddenly that the glass was getting warm in his hand—very warm. Almost hot.

Another two seconds, and he was certain: The probe was heating up. Bucky shuddered, his eyes rolled back in his head and he mercifully passed out.

A wisp of steam came from the wound like an exhaled breath. Hugh thought he smelled scorching tissue. "Sister? I don't . . . know what's happening, but I think—"

The probe touched a solid object deep in the spongy folds of tissue, less than a half inch below the left coronary artery. "Found it!" Hugh croaked as he concentrated on determining its size with the end of the probe. Blood was everywhere, but it wasn't the bright red of an artery, and its movement was sluggish. The glass was hot in his grip, the smell of scorching flesh stronger. Hugh realized that his remaining leg and the lower half of his body were freezing cold, but steam was rising from the wound; it occurred to him that the piece of glass was somehow channeling his body heat, drawing it up and intensifying it down in the depths of the hole. Hugh felt power in his hand—a calm, magnificent power. It seemed to crackle up his arm like a bolt of lightning, clearing his brain of fear and burning away the moonshine cobwebs. Suddenly his thirty years of medical knowledge flooded back into him, and he felt young and strong and unafraid.

He didn't know what that power was—the surge of life itself, or something that people used to call salvation in the churches—but he could see again. He could bring that bullet out. Yes. He *could*.

His hands were no longer shaking.

He realized he would have to dig down beneath the bullet and lever it up with the probe until he could get two fingers around it. The left coronary artery and the left ventricle were close, very close. He began to work with movements as precise as geometry.

"Careful," Sister cautioned, but she knew she didn't have to warn him. His face was bent over the wound, and suddenly he shouted, "More light!" and Robin brought a candle closer.

The bullet came loose from the surrounding tissue. Hugh heard a sizzling noise, smelled burning flesh and blood. What the *hell . . . ?* he thought, but he had no time to let his concentration wander. The glass spike was almost too hot to hold now, though he dared not release it. He felt as if he were sitting in a deep freeze up to his chest.

"I see it!" Hugh said. "Small bullet, thank God!" He pushed two fingers into the wound and caught the bit of lead between them. He brought them out again, clenching what resembled a broken filling for a tooth, and tossed it to Robin.

Then he started withdrawing the probe, and all of them could hear the sizzling of flesh and blood. Hugh couldn't believe what he was witnessing; down in the wound, torn tissue was being cauterized and sealed up as the spike emerged.

It came out like a wand of white-hot fire. As it left the wound there was a quick hissing and the blood congealed, the infected edges rippling with blue fire that burned for four of

Sister's rapid heartbeats and went out. Where a hole had been a few seconds before was now a brown, charred circle.

Hugh held the piece of glass before his face, his features washed with pure white light. He could feel the heat, yet the hottest of the healing fire was concentrated right at the tip. He realized it had cauterized the tiny vessels and ripped flesh like a surgical laser.

The probe's inner flame began to weaken and go out. As the light steadily waned Sister saw that the jewels within it had turned to small ebony pebbles, and the interconnecting threads of precious metals had become lines of ash. The light continued to weaken until finally there was just a spark of white fire at the tip; it pulsed with the beat of Hugh's heart—once, twice and a third time—and winked out like a dead star.

Bucky was still breathing.

Hugh, his face streaked with sweat and a bloody mist, looked up at Robin. He started to speak, couldn't find his voice. His lower body was warming up again. "I guess this means," he finally said, "that you won't be killing us today?"

Fifty-seven

Josh nudged Swan. "You doing okay?"

"Yes." She lifted her misshapen head from the folds of her coat. "I'm not dead yet."

"Just checking. You've been pretty quiet all day."

"I've been thinking."

"Oh." He watched as Killer ran ahead along the road, then stopped and barked for them to catch up. Mule was walking as fast as he was going to go, and Josh held the reins loosely. Rusty trudged alongside the wagon, all but buried in his cowboy hat and heavy coat.

The Travelin' Show wagon creaked on, the road bordered by dense forest. The clouds seemed to be hanging right in the treetops, and the wind had all but stopped—a merciful and rare occurrence. Josh knew the weather was unpredictable—there could be a blizzard and a thunderstorm the same day, and the next day calm winds could whirl into tornadoes.

For the past two days, they'd seen nothing living. They'd come upon a broken-down bridge and had to detour several miles to get back to the main road; a little further on, that road was blocked by a fallen tree, so another detour had to be found. But today they'd passed a tree about three miles back with TO MARY'S REST painted on its trunk, and Josh had breathed easier. At least they were headed in the right direction, and Mary's Rest couldn't be much further.

"Mind if I ask what you're thinking about?" Josh prodded.

She shrugged her thin shoulders beneath the coat and didn't reply. "The tree," he said. "It's that, isn't it?"

"Yes." The apple blossoms blowing in the snow and stumps continued to haunt her—life amid death. "I've been thinking about it a lot."

"I don't know how you did it, but . . ." He shook his head. The rules of the world have changed, he thought. Now the mysteries hold sway. He listened to the creaking axles and the crunch of snow under Mule's hooves for a moment, and then he had to ask it: "What did . . . what did it *feel* like?"

"I don't know." Another shrug.

"Yes, you do. You don't have to be shy about it. You did a wonderful thing, and I'd like to know what it felt like."

She was silent. Up ahead about fifteen yards, Killer barked a few times. Swan heard the barking as a call that the way was clear. "It felt . . . like I was a fountain," she replied. "And the tree was drinking. It felt like I was fire, too, and for a minute"—she lifted her deformed face toward the heavy sky—"I thought I could look up and remember what it was like to see the stars, way up in the dark . . . like promises. That's what it felt like."

Josh knew that what Swan had experienced was far beyond his senses; but he could fathom what she meant about the stars. He hadn't seen them for seven years. At night there was just a vast darkness, as if even the lamps of Heaven had burned out.

"Was Mr. Moody right?" Swan asked.

"Right about what?"

"He said that if I could wake up one tree, I could start orchards and crop fields growing again. He said . . . I've got the power of *life* inside me. Was he right?"

Josh didn't answer. He recalled something else Sly Moody had said: *"Mister, that Swan could wake the whole land up again!"*

"I was always good at growing plants and flowers," Swan

continued. "When I wanted a sick plant to get better, I worked the dirt with my hands, and more often than not the brown leaves fell off and grew back green. But I've never tried to heal a tree before. I mean . . . it was one thing to grow a garden, but trees take care of themselves." She angled her head so she could see Josh. "What if I *could* grow the orchards and crops back again? What if Mr. Moody was right, and there's something in me that could wake things up and start them growing?"

"I don't know," Josh said. "I guess that would make you a pretty popular lady. But like I say, one tree isn't an orchard." He shifted uncomfortably on the hard board beneath him. Talking about this made him jittery. *Protect the child,* he thought. If Swan could indeed spark life from the dead earth, then could that awesome power be the reason for PawPaw's commandment?

In the distance, Killer barked again. Swan tensed; the sound was different, faster and higher pitched. There was a warning in that bark. "Stop the wagon," she said.

"Huh?"

"Stop the wagon."

The strength of her voice made Josh pull Mule's reins.

Rusty stopped, too, the lower half of his face shielded with a woolen muffler under the cowboy hat. "Hey! What're we stoppin' for?"

Swan listened to Killer's barking, the noise floating around a bend in the road ahead. Mule shifted in his traces, lifted his head to sniff the air and made a deep grumbling sound. Another warning, Swan thought; Mule was smelling the same danger Killer had already sensed. She tilted her head to see the road. Everything looked okay, but the vision blurred in and out in her remaining eye and she knew its sight was rapidly failing.

"What is it?" Josh asked.

"I don't know. Whatever it is, Killer doesn't like it."

"Could be the town's just around the bend!" Rusty said. "I'll mosey ahead and find out!" His hands thrust into his coat pockets, he started walking toward the bend in the road. Killer was still barking frantically.

"Rusty! Wait!" Swan called, but her voice was so garbled he didn't understand her and kept going at a brisk pace.

Josh realized that Rusty wasn't carrying a gun, and no telling what was around that bend. "Rusty!" he shouted, but the other man was already taking the curve. "Oh, shit!" Josh unzipped the wagon's flap, then opened the shoe box with the .38 in it and hastily loaded it. He could hear Killer's yap-yap-yapping echoing through the woods, and he knew that Rusty would find out what Killer had seen in just a matter of seconds.

Around the bend, Rusty was faced with nothing but more road and woods. Killer was standing in the center of the road about thirty feet away, barking wildly at something off to the right. The terrier's coat was bristling.

"What the hell's bit *your* butt?" Rusty asked, and Killer ran between his legs, almost tripping him. "Crazy fool dog!" He reached down to pick the terrier up—and that was when he smelled it.

A sharp, rank odor.

He recognized it. The heady spoor of a wild animal.

There was a nerve-shattering shriek, almost in his ear, and a gray form shot from the forest's edge. He didn't see what it was, but he flung an arm up over his face to protect his eyes. The animal slammed into his shoulder, and for an instant Rusty felt entangled by live wires and thorns. He staggered back, trying to cry out, but the breath had been knocked from his lungs. His hat spun away, spattered with blood, and he sank to his knees.

Dazed, he saw what had hit him.

Crouched about six feet away, its spine arched, was a bobcat almost the size of a calf. The thing's extended claws looked like hooked daggers, but what shocked Rusty almost senseless was the sight of the monster's two heads.

While one green-eyed face shrieked with a noise like razor blades on glass, the second bared its fangs and hissed like a radiator about to blow.

Rusty tried to crawl away. His body refused. Something was wrong with his right arm, and blood was streaming down the right side of his face. Bleedin'! he thought. I'm bleedin' *bad!* Oh, Jesus, I'm—

The bobcat came at him like a spring unwinding, its claws and double set of fangs ready to rip him to pieces.

But it was hit in mid-air by another form, and Killer almost took one of the monster's ears off. They landed in a clawing, shrieking fury, hair and blood flying. But the battle was over in another instant as the massive bobcat twisted Killer on his back and one of the fanged mouths tore the terrier's throat open.

Rusty tried to get to his feet, staggered and fell again. The bobcat turned toward him. One set of fangs snapped at him while the other head sniffed the air. Rusty got a booted foot up in the air to kick at the monster when it attacked. The bobcat crouched back on its hind legs. Come on! Rusty thought. Get it over with, you two-headed bas—

He heard the *crack!* of a pistol, and snow jumped about six feet behind the bobcat. The monster whirled around, and Rusty saw Josh running toward him. Josh stopped, took aim again and fired. The bullet went wild again, and now the bobcat began to turn one way and then the other, as if its two brains couldn't agree on which way to run. The heads snapped at each other, straining at the neck.

Josh planted his feet, aimed with his single eye and squeezed the trigger.

A hole plowed through the bobcat's side, and one head made a shrill wailing while the second growled at Josh in defiance. He fired again and missed, but he hit with his next two shots. The monster trembled, loped toward the woods, turned and streaked again toward Rusty. The eyes of one head had rolled back to show the whites, but the other was still alive, and its fangs were bared to plunge into Rusty's throat.

He heard himself screaming as the monster advanced, but less than three feet from him the bobcat shuddered and its legs gave way. It fell to the road, its living head snapping at the air.

Rusty scrambled away from the thing, and then a terrible wave of weakness crashed over him. He lay where he was as Josh ran toward him.

Kneeling beside Rusty, Josh saw that the right side of his face had been clawed open from hairline to jaw, and in the torn sleeve of his right shoulder was mangled tissue.

"Bought the farm, Josh." Rusty summoned a weak smile. "Sure did, didn't I?"

"Hang on." Josh tucked the pistol under one arm and lifted Rusty off the ground, slinging him over his back in a fireman's carry. Swan was approaching, trying to run but being thrown off balance by the weight of her head. A few feet away, the mutant bobcat's fangs came together like the crack of a steel trap; the body shook, and then its eyes rolled back like ghastly green marbles. Josh walked past the bobcat to Killer and the terrier's pink tongue emerged from its bloody mouth to lick Josh's boot.

"What happened?" Swan called frantically. "What is it?"

Killer made an effort to rise to all fours when he heard Swan's voice, but his body was beyond control. His head was hanging limply, and as Killer toppled back on his side Josh could see that the dog's eyes were already glazing over.

"Josh?" Swan called. Her hands were up in front of her, because she could hardly see where she was going. "Talk to me, damn it!"

Killer gave one quick gasp, and then he was gone.

Josh stepped between Swan and the dog. "Rusty's been hurt," he said. "It was a bobcat. We've got to get him to town in a hurry!" He grasped her arm and pulled her with him before she could see the dead terrier.

Josh gently laid Rusty in the back of the wagon and covered him with the red blanket. Rusty was shivering and only half conscious. Josh told Swan to stay with him, and then he went forward and took Mule's reins. "Giddap!" he shouted. The old horse, whether surprised by the command or by the unaccustomed urgency of the reins, snorted steam through his nostrils and bounded forward, pulling with new-found strength.

Swan drew the tent's flap open. "What about Killer? We can't just leave him!"

He couldn't yet bring himself to tell her that the terrier was dead. "Don't you worry," he said. "He'll find his way." He snapped the reins against Mule's haunches. "Giddap now, Mule! Go, boy!"

The wagon rounded the bend, its wheels passing on either side of Killer, and Mule's hooves threw up a spray of snow as the horse raced toward Mary's Rest.

Fifty-eight

The road spooled out another mile before the woods gave way to bleak, rolling land that might have once been plowed hillsides. Now it was a snow-covered waste, interrupted by black trees twisted into shapes both agonized and surrealistic. But there was a town, of sorts: Clustered along both sides of the road were maybe three hundred weather-beaten clapboard shacks. Josh thought that seven years ago a sight like this would've meant he was entering a ghetto, but now he was overjoyed to the point of tears. Muddy alleys cut between the shacks, and smoke curled into the bitter air from stovepipe chimneys. Lanterns glowed behind windows insulated with yellowed newspapers and magazine pages. Skinny dogs howled and barked around Mule's legs as Josh drew the wagon up amid the shacks. Across the road and up a ways was a charred pile of timbers where one of the buildings of Mary's Rest had burned to the ground; the fire had been some time ago, because new snow had collected in the ruins.

"Hey!" Josh shouted. "Somebody help us!"

A few thin children in ragged coats came out from the alleys to see what was going on. "Is there a doctor around here?" Josh asked them, but they scattered back into the alleys. The door of a nearby shack opened, and a black-bearded face peered cautiously out. "We need a doctor!" Josh demanded. The bearded man shook his head and shut the door.

Josh urged Mule deeper into the shantytown. He kept shouting for a doctor, and a few people opened their doors and watched him pass, but none offered assistance. Further on, a pack of dogs that had been tearing at the remains of an animal in the mud snarled and snapped at Mule, but the old horse kept his nerve and held steady. From a doorway lurched an emaciated old man in rags, his face blotched with red keloids. "No room here! No food! We don't want no strangers here!" he raved, striking the wagon's side with a gnarled stick. He was still babbling as they drew away.

Josh had seen a lot of wretched places before, but this was the worst. It occurred to him that this was a town of strangers where nobody gave a shit about who lived or died in the next hovel. There was a brooding sense of defeat and fatal depression here, and even the air smelled of rank decay. If Rusty hadn't been so badly hurt, Josh would have kept the wagon going right through the ulcer of Mary's Rest and out where the air smelled halfway decent again.

A figure with a malformed head stumbled along the roadside, and Josh recognized the same disease that both he and Swan had. He called to the person, but whoever it was—male or female—turned and ran down an alley out of sight. Lying on the ground a few yards away was a dead man, stripped naked, his ribs showing and his teeth bared in what might have been a grin of escape. A few dogs were sniffing around him, but they had not yet begun feasting.

And then Mule stopped as if he'd run into a brick wall, neighed shrilly and almost reared. "Whoa! Settle down, now!" Josh shouted, having to fight the horse for control.

He saw that someone was in the road in front of them. The figure was wearing a faded denim jacket and a green cap and was sitting in a child's red wagon. The figure had no legs, the trousers rolled up and empty below the thighs. "Hey!" Josh called. "Is there a doctor in this town?"

The face turned slowly toward him. It was a man with a scraggly light brown beard and vague, tormented eyes. "We need a doctor!" Josh said. "Can you help us?"

Josh thought the man might've smiled, but he wasn't sure. The man said, "Welcome!"

"A doctor! Can't you understand me?"

"Welcome!" the man repeated, and he laughed, and Josh realized he was out of his mind.

The man reached out, plunged his hands into the mud and began to pull himself and the wagon across the road. "Welcome!" he shouted as he rolled away into an alley.

Josh shivered, and not just from the cold. That man's eyes . . . they were the most awful eyes Josh had ever looked into. He got Mule settled down and moving forward again.

He continued to shout for help. An occasional face looked out from a doorway and then drew quickly back. Rusty's going to die, Josh feared. He's going to bleed to death, and not a single bastard in this hellhole will raise a finger to save him!

Yellow smoke drifted across the road, the wagon's tires moving through puddles of human waste. "Somebody help us!" Josh's voice was giving out. "Please . . . for God's sake . . . somebody *help* us!"

"Lawd! What's all the yellin' about?"

Startled, Josh looked toward the voice. Standing in the doorway of a decrepit shack was a black woman with long, iron-gray hair. She wore a coat that had been stitched from a hundred different scraps of cloth.

"I need to find a doctor! Can you help me?"

"What's wrong with you?" Her eyes, the color of copper pennies, narrowed. "Typhoid? The dysentery?"

"No. My friend's been hurt. He's in the back."

"Ain't no doctor in Mary's Rest. Doctor died of typhoid. Ain't nobody can help you."

"He's bleeding bad! Isn't there someplace I can take him?"

"You can take him to the Pit," she suggested. She had a sharp-featured, regal face. "'Bout a mile or so down the road. It's where all the bodies go." The dark face of a boy about seven or eight years old peeked through the doorway at her side, and she rested a hand on his shoulder. "Ain't noplace to take him but there."

"Rusty's not dead, lady!" Josh snapped. "But he's sure going to be if I don't find some help for him!" He flicked Mule's reins.

The black woman let him get a few yards further down the road, and then she said, "Hold on!"

Josh reined Mule in.

The woman walked down the cinder block steps in front of her shack and approached the rear of the wagon while the little boy nervously watched. "Open this thing up!" she said—and suddenly the rear flap was unzipped, and she was face to face with Swan. The woman stepped back a pace, then took a deep breath, summoned her courage again and looked into the wagon at the bloody white man lying under a red blanket. The white man wasn't moving. "He still alive?" she asked the faceless figure.

"Yes, ma'am," Swan replied. "But he's not breathing very good."

She could make out the "yes," but nothing more. "What happened?"

"Bobcat got him," Josh said, coming around to the back of the wagon. He was shaking so much he could hardly stand. The woman took a long, hard look at him with her piercing copper-colored eyes. "Damned thing had two heads."

"Yeah. Lots of 'em out in the woods like that. Kill you for sure." She glanced toward the house, then back at Rusty. He made a soft moaning noise, and she could see the terrible wound on the side of his face. She let the breath leak out between her clenched teeth. "Well, bring him on inside, then."

"Can you help him?"

"We'll find out." She started walking toward the shack and turned back to say, "I'm a seamstress. Pretty good with a needle and catgut. Bring him on."

The shack was as grim inside as it was out, but the woman had two lanterns lit, and on the walls were hung bright pieces of cloth. At the center of the front room stood a makeshift stove constructed from parts of a washing machine, a refrigerator and various pieces of what might have been a truck or car. A few scraps of wood burned behind a grate that was once a car's radiator grille, and the stove only provided heat within a two- or three-foot radius. Smoke leaked through the funnel that went up into the roof, giving the shack's interior a yellow haze. The woman's furniture—a table and two chairs—were crudely sawn from worm-eaten pinewood. Old newspapers covered the windows, and the wind piped through cracks in the walls. On the pinewood table were snippets of cloth, scissors, needles and the like, and a basket held more pieces of cloth in a variety of colors and patterns.

"It ain't much," she said with a shrug, "but it's better than some has. Bring him in here." She motioned Josh into a second, smaller room, where there was an iron-framed cot and a mattress stuffed with newspapers and rags. On the floor next to the cot was a little arrangement of rags, a small patchwork pillow and a thin blanket in which, Josh presumed, the little boy slept. In the room there were no windows, but a lantern burned with a shiny piece of tin behind it to reflect the light. An oil painting of a black Jesus on a hillside surrounded by sheep hung on a wall.

"Lay him down," the woman said. "Not on *my* bed, fool. On the floor."

Josh put Rusty down with his head cradled by the patchwork pillow.

"Get that jacket and sweater off him so I can see if he's still got any meat left on that arm."

Josh did as she said while Swan stood in the doorway with her head tilted way to one side so she could see. The little boy stood on the other side of the room, staring at Swan.

The woman picked up the lantern and put it on the floor next to Rusty. She whistled softly. "'Bout scraped him to the bone. Aaron, you go bring the other lamps in here. Then you fetch me the long bone needle, the ball of catgut and a sharp pair of scissors. Hurry on, now!"

"Yes, Mama," Aaron said, and he darted past Swan.

"What's your friend's name?"

"Rusty."

"He's in a bad way. Don't know if I can stitch him up, but I'll do my best. Ain't got nothin' but snow water to clean those wounds with, and you sure as hell don't want that filthy shit in an open—" She stopped, looking at Josh's mottled hands as he took off his gloves. "You black or white?" she asked.

"Does it matter anymore?"

"Naw. Don't reckon it does." Aaron brought the two lanterns, and she arranged them near Rusty's head while he went out again to get the other things she needed. "You got a name?"

"Josh Hutchins. The girl's name is Swan."

She nodded. Her long, delicate fingers probed the ragged edges of the wound at Rusty's shoulder. "I'm Glory Bowen. Make my livin' by stitchin' clothes for people, but I ain't no doctor. The closest I ever come to doctorin' was helpin' a few women have their babies—but I know about sewin' cloth, dogskin and cowhide, and maybe a person's skin ain't too much different."

Rusty's body suddenly went rigid; he opened his eyes and tried to sit up, but Josh and Glory Bowen held him down. He struggled for a minute, then seemed to realize where he was and relaxed again. "Josh?" he asked.

"Yeah. I'm here."

"Bastard got me, didn't he? Old two-headed bastard of a bobcat. Knocked me right on my ass." He blinked, looked up at Glory. "Who're *you?*"

"I'm the woman you're gonna de-*spise* in about three minutes," she answered calmly. Aaron came in with a thin, sharpened splinter of bone that must have been three inches long, and he laid it in his mother's palm along with a small, waxy-looking ball of catgut thread and a pair of scissors. Then he retreated to the other side of the room, his eyes moving back and forth between Swan and the others.

"What're you gonna do to me?" Rusty made out the bone needle as Glory put the end of the thread through the needle's eye and tied a tiny knot. "What's that for?"

"You'll find out soon enough." She picked up a rag and

wiped the sweat and blood from Rusty's face. "Gonna have to do a little sewin' on you. Gonna put you together just like a fine new shirt. That suit you?"

"Oh . . . Lord" was all Rusty could manage to say.

"We gonna have to tie you down, or are you gonna be a man about this? Don't have nothin' to kill the pain."

"Just . . . talk to me," Rusty told her. "Okay?"

"Sure. Whatcha wanna talk about?" She positioned the needle near the ripped flesh at Rusty's shoulder. "How 'bout *food?* Fried chicken. A big bucketful of Colonel Sanders with them hot spices. That sound good to you?" She angled the needle in the precise direction she wanted, and then she went to work. "Can't you just *smell* that Kentucky Fried heaven?"

Rusty closed his eyes. "Yeah," he whispered thickly. "Oh, yeah . . . I sure can."

Swan couldn't bear to watch Rusty in pain. She went to the front room, where she warmed herself by the makeshift stove. Aaron peeked around the corner at her, then jerked his head out of sight. She heard Rusty catch his breath, and she went to the door, opened it and stepped outside.

She climbed into the back of the wagon to get Crybaby, and then she stood rubbing Mule's neck. She was worried about Killer. How was he going to find them? And if a bobcat had hurt Rusty that badly, what might one do to Killer? "Don't you worry," Josh had said. "He'll find his way."

"You got a haid inside there?" a small, curious voice asked beside her.

Swan made out Aaron standing a few feet away.

"You can talk, cain't you? I heard you say somethin' to my mama."

"I can speak," she answered. "I have to talk slowly, though, or you won't be able to understand me."

"Oh. Your haid looks kinda like a big ol' gourd."

Swan smiled, her facial flesh pulling so tight it felt about to tear. She knew the youngster was being honest, not cruel. "I guess it does. And yes, I have a head inside here. It's just covered up."

"I seen some people looked like you. Mama says it's a real

bad sickness. Says you get that thing and you got it your whole life. Is that so?"

"I don't know."

"She says it ain't catchin', though. Says if it was, everybody in town would have it by now. What kinda stick is that?"

"It's a dowsing rod."

"What's that?"

She explained how a dowsing rod was supposed to find water if you held the forked ends of it just right, but she'd never found any water with it. She recalled Leona Skelton's gentle voice, as if drifting through time to whisper: "Crybaby's work isn't done yet—not by a far sight!"

"Maybe you ain't holding it right, then," Aaron said.

"I just use it like a walking stick. I don't see too well."

"I reckon not. You ain't got no eyeballs!"

Swan laughed and felt muscles in her face unfreeze. The wind brought a new whiff of a sickening odor of decay that Swan had noticed as soon as they'd entered Mary's Rest. "Aaron?" she asked. "What's that smell?"

"What smell?"

He was used to it, she realized. Human waste and garbage lay everywhere, but this was a fouler odor. "It comes and goes," she said. "The wind's carrying it."

"Oh, I reckon that's the pond. What's left of it, I mean. It ain't too far. Want to see?"

No, Swan thought. She didn't want to get near anything so awful. But Aaron sounded eager to please, and she was curious. "All right, but we'll have to walk real slow. And don't run off and leave me, okay?"

"Okay," he answered, and he promptly ran about thirty feet up a muddy alley before he turned and waited for her to catch up.

Swan followed him through the narrow, filthy alleys. Many of the shacks had been burned down, people still digging shelters in the ruins. She probed ahead with Crybaby and was frightened by a skinny yellow dog that lunged out of an intersecting alley; Aaron kicked at it and ran it off. Behind a closed door, an infant wailed with hunger. Further on, Swan almost stumbled over a man lying curled up in the mud. She started to reach down and touch his shoulder, but Aaron said, "He's a dead'un! Come on, it ain't too far!"

They passed between the miserable clapboard shacks and came upon a wide field covered with gray snow. Here and there the frozen body of a human being or an animal lay contorted on the ground. "Come on!" Aaron called, jumping up and down impatiently. He'd been born amid death, had seen so much of it that it was a commonplace sight. He stepped over a woman's corpse and continued down a gently sloping hill to the large pond that over the years had drawn hundreds of wanderers to the settlement of Mary's Rest.

"There 'tis," Aaron said when Swan reached him. He pointed.

About a hundred feet away was what had indeed been a very large pond, nestled in the midst of dead trees. Swan saw that maybe an inch of yellow-green water remained right at its center, and all around was cracked, nasty-looking yellow mud.

And in that mud were dozens of half-buried human and animal skeletons, as if they'd been sucked down as they tried to get the last of that contaminated water. Crows perched on the bones, waiting. Heaps of frozen human excrement and garbage lay in the mud as well, and the smell that wafted from that mess where a pond used to be turned Swan's stomach. It was as rank as an open sore or an unwashed bathroom bucket.

"This is 'bout as close as you can stand without gettin' sick," Aaron said, "but I wanted you to see it. Ain't it a peculiar color?"

"My God!" Swan was fighting the urge to throw up. "Why doesn't somebody clean that up?"

"Clean what up?" Aaron asked.

"The pond! It wasn't always like that, was it?"

"Oh, no! I 'member when the pond had water in it. Real drinkin' water. But Mama says it just gave out. Says it couldn't last forever, anyway."

Swan had to turn away from the sight. She looked back the

way they'd come and could make out a solitary figure on the hill, scooping dirty snow into a bucket. Melting the gray snow for water was a slow death, but it was far better than the poisonous pond. "I'm ready to go back now," she told him, and she started walking slowly up the hill, probing before her with Crybaby.

Once over the hill, Swan almost tripped over a body in her path. She stopped, looking down at the small form of a child. Whether it had been a boy or girl she couldn't tell, but the child had died lying on its stomach, one hand clawing at the earth and the other frozen into a fist. She stared at those little hands, pallid and waxy against the snow. "Why are these bodies out here?" she asked.

"'Cause this is where they died," he told her, as if she was the dumbest old gourdhead in the whole world.

"This one was trying to dig something up."

"Roots, prob'ly. Sometimes you can dig roots up out of the ground, sometimes you cain't. When we can find 'em, Mama makes a soup out of 'em."

"Roots? What kind of roots?"

"You sure ask a lot of questions," he said, exasperated, and he started to walk on ahead.

"What kind of roots?" Swan repeated, slowly but firmly.

"Corn roots, I reckon!" Aaron shrugged. "Mama says there used to be a big ol' cornfield out here, but everythin' died. Ain't nothin' left but a few roots—if a body's lucky enough to find 'em. Come on, now! I'm cold!"

Swan looked out across the barren field that lay between the shacks and the pond. Bodies lay like strange punctuation marks scrawled on a gray tablet. The vision in her eye faded in and out, and whatever was under the the thick crust of growths burned and seethed. The child's white, frozen hands took her attention again. Something about those hands, she thought. Something . . . but she didn't know what.

The smell of the pond sickened her, and she followed Aaron toward the shacks again.

"Used to be a big ol' cornfield out here," Aaron had said. "But everythin' died."

She pushed snow away from the ground with Crybaby. The

earth was dark and hard. If any roots remained out here, they were far beneath the crust.

They were still winding their way through the alleys when Swan heard Mule neigh; it was a cry of alarm. She quickened her pace, stabbing ahead of her with the dowsing rod.

When they came out of the alley next to Glory Bowen's shack, Swan heard Mule make a shrill whickering sound that conveyed anger and fear. She tilted her head to see what was happening and finally made it out: people in rags were swarming all over the wagon, tearing it apart. They were shredding the canvas tent to pieces and fighting over the remnants, grabbing up blankets, canned food, clothes and rifles from the rear of the wagon and running with them. "Stop!" she told them, but of course they paid no attention. One of them tried to untie Mule from his harness, but the horse bucked and kicked so powerfully the scavenger was driven off. They were even trying to take the wheels off the wagon. "Stop it!" Swan shouted, stumbling forward. Someone collided against her, knocked her into the cold mud and almost stepped on her. Nearby, two men were fighting in the mud over one of the blankets, and the fight ended when a third man grabbed it and scuttled away.

The cabin's door opened. Josh had heard Swan's shout, and now he saw the Travelin' Show wagon being ripped apart. Panic shook him. That was all they had in the world! A man was running with a bundle of sweaters and socks in his arms, and Josh went after him but slipped in the mud. The scavengers scattered in all directions, taking away the last of the canvas, all the food, the weapons, blankets, everything. A woman with an orange keloid covering most of her face and neck tried to strip the coat off Swan, but Swan doubled up and the woman struck at her, screaming in frustration. When Josh got to his feet, the woman ran down one of the alleys.

Then they were all gone, and so were the contents of the Travelin' Show wagon—including most of the wagon itself.

"Damn it!" Josh raged. There was nothing left but the frame of the wagon and Mule, who was still snorting and bucking. We're up shit creek now, he thought. Nothing to eat, not even a damned *sock* left! "You okay?" he asked

Swan, going over to help her up. Aaron was standing beside her, and he reached out to touch her gourd of a head but drew his hand back at the last second.

"Yes." Her shoulder was just a little sore where she'd been struck. "I think I'm all right."

Josh gently helped Swan up and steadied her. "They took just about everything we had!" he fretted. In the mud lay a few items that had been left behind: a dented tin cup, a tattered shawl, a worn-out boot that Rusty had planned to mend and never got around to.

"You leave things sittin' out 'round here, they gonna get stole for sure!" Aaron said sagely. "Any fool knows that!"

"Well," Swan said, "maybe they need those things more than we do."

Josh's first impulse was an incredulous laugh, but he held it in check. She was right. At least they had good heavy coats and gloves, and they were wearing thick socks and sturdy boots. Some of those scavengers had been a few threads away from their Genesis suits—except this was surely as far from the Garden of Eden as a human could fall.

Swan walked around the wagon to Mule and settled the old horse down by calmly rubbing his nose. Still, he continued to make an ominous, worried rumbling.

"Better get inside," Josh told her. "Wind's picking up again."

She came toward him, then stopped when Crybaby touched something hard in the mud. She bent down carefully, groped in the mud and came up with the dark oval mirror that somebody had dropped. The magic mirror, she thought as she straightened up again. It had been a long time since she'd peered into it. But now she wiped the mud off on the leg of her jeans and held it up before her, grasping it by the handle with the two carved masks that stared in different directions.

"What's that thing?" Aaron asked. "Can you see y'self in there?"

She could only see the faintest outline of her head, and thought that indeed it did look like a swollen old gourd. She dropped her arm to her side—and as she did something flashed in the glass. She held it up again and turned so the mirror was facing in another direction; she hunted for the flash of light but couldn't find it. Then she shifted, turning a foot or so to the right, and caught her breath.

Seemingly less than ten feet behind her was the figure holding the glowing circle of light—close now, very close. Swan was still not quite able to make out the features. She sensed, however, that something was wrong with the face; it was distorted and deformed, but not nearly like her own. She thought that the figure might be a woman, just from the way whoever it was carried herself. So close, so close—yet Swan knew that if she turned around there would be nothing behind her but the shanties and alleys.

"What direction is the mirror facing?" she asked Josh.

"North," he answered. "We came in from the south. That way." He motioned in the opposite direction. "Why?" He could never understand what she saw when she looked into that thing. Whenever he asked, she would shrug her shoulders and put the mirror away. But the mirror had always reminded him of a verse his mother liked to read from the Bible: "For now we see in a glass darkly, but then face to face."

The figure with the glowing ring of light had never been so close before. Sometimes it had been so far away that the light was barely a spark in the glass. She didn't know who the figure was, or what the ring of light was supposed to be, but she knew it was someone and something very important. And now the woman was close, and Swan thought that she must be somewhere to the north of Mary's Rest.

She was about to tell Josh when the face with the leprous, parchment-like flesh rose up over her left shoulder. The monstrous face filled up the whole glass, its gray-lipped mouth cracking open in a grin, one scarlet eye with an ebony pupil emerging from its forehead. A second mouth full of sharp-edged teeth opened like a slash across its cheek, and the teeth strained forward as if to bite Swan on the back of the neck.

She turned so fast that the weight of her head almost spun her like a top.

Behind her, the road was deserted.

She lowered the mirror; she had seen enough for one day. If what the magic mirror showed her was true, the figure bearing the ring of light was very near.

But nearer still was the thing that reminded her of the Devil on Leona Skelton's tarot card.

Josh watched Swan as she went up the cinder block steps into Glory Bowen's shack, then looked north along the road. There was no movement but chimney smoke scattering before the wind. He regarded the wagon again and shook his head. He figured that Mule would kick the sauce out of anybody who tried to steal him, and there was nothing left to take. "That's all our food," he said, mostly to himself. "Every damned bit of it!"

"Oh, I know a place you can catch some big 'uns," Aaron offered. "You just gotta know where they are, and be quick to catch 'em."

"Quick to catch *what?*"

"Rats," the boy said, as if any fool knew that was what most of the people in Mary's Rest had been surviving on for the last few years. "That's what we'll be eatin' tonight, if you're stayin'."

Josh swallowed thickly, but he was no stranger to the gamy taste of rat meat. "I hope you've got salt," he said as he followed Aaron up the steps. "I like mine real salty."

Just before he reached the door, he felt the flesh at the back of his neck tighten. He heard Mule snort and whinny, and he looked toward the road again. He had the unnerving sensation of being watched—no, more than that. Of being *dissected*.

But there was no one. No one at all.

The wind whirled around him, and in it he thought he heard a squeaking sound—like the noise of wheels in need of grease. The sound was gone in an instant.

The light was quickly fading, and Josh knew this was one place he wouldn't walk the alleys at night even for a T-bone steak. He went into the shack and shut the door.

TEN
Seeds

The hand revealed / Swan and the big dude / A decent wish / The savage prince / Fighting fire with fire

Fifty-nine

Swan awakened from a dream. She'd been running through a field of human bodies that moved like stalks of wheat before the wind, and behind her advanced the thing with the single scarlet eye, its scythe lopping off heads, arms and legs as it sought her out. Only her head was too heavy, her feet weighted down by yellow mud, and she couldn't run fast enough. The monster was getting nearer, its scythe whistling through the air like a shriek, and suddenly she'd fallen over a child's corpse and she was looking at its white hands, one clawing the earth and the other clenched into a fist.

She lay on the floor of Glory Bowen's shack. Embers behind the stove's grate still cast a little light and a breath of heat. She slowly sat up and leaned against the wall, the image of the child's hands fixed in her mind. Nearby, Josh lay curled up on the floor, breathing heavily and deeply asleep. Closer to the stove, Rusty lay sleeping under a thin blanket, his head on the patchwork pillow. Glory had done a fine job of cleaning and stitching the wounds, but she'd said the next couple of days would be rough for him. It had been very kind of her to let them spend the night and share her water and a little stew. Aaron had asked Swan dozens of questions about her condition, what the land was like beyond Mary's Rest, and what all she'd seen. Glory had told Aaron to stop pestering her, but Swan wasn't bothered; the boy had a curious mind, and that was a rare thing worth encouraging.

Glory told them her husband had been a Baptist minister back in Wynne, Arkansas, when the bombs hit. The radiation of Little Rock had killed a lot of people in the town, and Glory, her husband and their infant son had joined a caravan of wanderers looking for a safe place to settle. But there were no safe places. Four years later, they'd settled in Mary's Rest, which at that time was a thriving settlement built around the pond. There'd been no minister or church in Mary's Rest, and Glory's husband had started building a house of worship with his own hands.

But then the typhoid epidemic came, Glory told them. People died by the score, and wild animals skulked in from the woods to gut the corpses. When the last of the community's stockpile of canned food gave out, people started eating rats, boiling bark, roots, leather—even the dirt itself—into "soup." One night the church had caught fire, and Glory's husband had died trying to save it. The blackened ruins were still standing, because nobody had the energy or will to build it back. She and her son had stayed alive because she was a good seamstress, and people paid her with extra food, coffee and such to patch their clothes. That was the story of her life, Glory had said; that was how she'd gotten to be an old woman when she was barely thirty-five.

Swan listened to the sound of the roving wind. Was it bringing the answer to the magic mirror's riddle closer? she wondered. Or was it blowing it further away?

And quite suddenly, as the wind faltered to draw another breath, Swan heard the urgent noise of a dog barking.

Her heart thudded in her chest. The barking ebbed away, was gone—then began to swell again, from somewhere very near.

Swan would know that bark anywhere.

She started to reach over and rouse Josh to tell him that Killer had found his way, but he snorted and muttered in his sleep. She let him alone, stood up with the aid of the dowsing rod and walked to the door.

The barking faded as the wind took a different turn. But she understood what it said: "Hurry! Come see what I've got to show you!"

She put on her coat, buttoned it up to her neck and slipped out of the shack into the tumultuous dark.

She couldn't see the terrier. Josh had unbridled Mule to let the horse fend for himself, and he'd wandered off to find shelter.

The wind came back, and with it the barking. Where was it coming from? The left, she thought. No, the right! She walked down the steps. There was no sign of Killer, and now the barking was gone, too. But she was sure it had come from the right, maybe from that alley over there, the same alley Aaron had taken her along to show her the pond.

She hesitated. It was cold out here, and dark except for the glow of a bonfire a few alleys away. Had she heard Killer's barking or not? she asked herself. It wasn't there now, just the wind shrilling through the alleys and around the shacks.

The image of the child's frozen hands came to her. What was it about those hands that haunted her? she wondered. It was more than the fact that they belonged to a dead child—much, much more.

She didn't know exactly when she made the decision, or when she took the first step. But suddenly she was entering the alley, questing with Crybaby before her, and she was walking toward the field.

Her vision blurred, her eye stinging with pain. She went blind, but she didn't panic; she just waited it out, hoping that this wasn't the time when her sight would go and not return. It came back, and Swan kept going.

She fell once over another corpse in the alley and heard an animal growling somewhere nearby, but she made it through. And then there was the field stretched before her, only faintly illuminated in the reflection of the distant bonfire. She began to walk across it, the odor of the poisonous pond thick in her nostrils, and hoped she remembered the way.

The barking returned, from off to her left. She changed her

direction to follow it, and she called, "Killer! Where are you?" but the wind snatched her voice away.

Step by step, Swan crossed the field. In some places the snow was four or five inches thick, but in others the wind had blown it away to expose the bare ground. The barking ebbed and faded, returned from a slightly different direction. Swan altered her course by a few degrees, but she couldn't see the terrier anywhere on the field.

The barking stopped.

So did Swan.

"Where are you?" she called. The wind shoved at her, almost knocked her down. She looked back at Mary's Rest, could see the bonfire and a few lanterns burning in windows. It seemed a long way off. But she took one more step in the direction of the pond.

Crybaby touched something on the ground right in front of her, and Swan made out the shape of the child's body.

The wind shifted. The barking came again—just a whisper now, from an unknown distance. It continued to fade, and just before it was gone Swan had a strange impression: that the sound no longer belonged to an old, weary dog. It had a note of youth in it, and strength, and roads yet to be traveled.

The sound was gone, and Swan was alone with the corpse of the child.

She bent down and looked at the hands. One clawing the earth, the other clenched into a fist. What was so familiar about that?

And then she knew: It was the way she herself had planted seeds when she was a little girl. One hand digging the hole, the other—

She grasped the bony fist and tried to pry it open. It resisted her, but she worked at it patiently and thought of opening a flower's petals. The hand slowly revealed what was locked in its palm.

There were six wrinkled kernels of corn.

One hand digging the hole, she thought, and the other nestling the seeds.

Seeds.

The child had not died digging for roots. The child had died trying to plant shriveled seeds.

She held the kernels in her own palm. Was there untapped life in them, or were they only cold bits of nothing?

"Used to be a big ol' cornfield out here," Aaron had told her. "But everythin' died."

She thought of the apple tree bursting into new life. Thought of the green seedlings in the shape of her body. Thought of the flowers she had grown in dry, dusty earth a long time ago.

"Used to be a big ol' cornfield out here."

Swan looked at the body again. The child had died in a strange posture. Why was the child lying on its stomach on the cold ground instead of curling up to save the last bit of warmth? She gently grasped the shoulder and tried to turn it over; there was a faint crackling noise as the ragged clothes unstuck from the ground, but the body itself was as light as a husk.

And underneath the body was a small leather pouch.

She picked it up with a trembling hand, opened it and reached in with two fingers—but she already knew what she'd find.

In the pouch were more dried kernels of corn. The child had been protecting them with body heat. She realized she would have done the same thing, and that she and the child might have had a lot in common.

Here were the seeds. It was up to her to finish the job the dead child had begun.

She scraped away snow and thrust her fingers into the dirt. It was hard and clayey, full of ice and sharp pebbles. She brought up a handful and worked warmth into it; then she put one kernel into it and did what she had done when she planted seeds in the dust of Kansas—she gathered saliva in her mouth and spat into her handful of dirt. She rolled it into a ball, kept rolling it until she felt the tingling running up through her backbone, through her arm and fingers. Then she returned the dirt to the ground, pressing it into the hole she'd scooped it from.

And that was the first seed planted, but whether it would grow in this tormented earth or not, Swan didn't know.

She picked up Crybaby, crawled a few feet away from the body and clawed up another handful of dirt. Either sharp ice or a stone cut her fingers, but she hardly noticed the pain; her mind was concentrated on the task. The pins-and-needles sensation was strengthening, starting to flow through her body in waves like power through humming wires.

Swan crawled ahead and planted a third seed. The cold was chewing down through her clothes, stiffening her bones, but she kept on going, scraping up a handful of dirt every two or three feet and planting a single seed. In some places the earth was frozen solid and as unyielding as granite, so she crawled on to another place, finding that the dirt cushioned beneath the snow was softer than the dirt where the covering snow had blown away. Still, her hands quickly became raw, and blood began to seep from cuts. Drops of blood mingled with the seeds and dirt as Swan continued to work, slowly and methodically, without pause.

She didn't plant any seeds near the pond, but instead turned back toward Mary's Rest to lay down another row. An animal wailed off in the distant woods—a high, shrill, lonely cry. She kept her mind on her work, her bloody hands searching through the snow to find pliable dirt. The cold finally pierced her, and she had to stop and huddle up. Ice was clogging her nostrils, her eye with its fragile vision almost frozen shut. She lay shivering, and it occurred to her that she'd feel stronger if she could sleep for a while. Just a short rest. Just a few minutes, and then she'd get back to work again.

Something nudged her side. She was dazed and weak, and she didn't care to lift her head to see what it was. She was nudged again, much harder this time.

Swan rolled over, angled her head and looked up.

A warm breath hit her face. Mule was standing over her, as motionless as if carved from gray-dappled stone. She started to lie back down again, but Mule nudged her in the shoulder with his nose. He made a deep rumbling sound, and the breath floated from his nostrils like steam from a boiler.

He was not going to let her sleep. And the warm air that came from his lungs reminded her of how very cold it was, and how close she'd been to giving up. If she lay there much longer, she would freeze. She had to get moving again, get her circulation going.

Mule nudged her more firmly, and Swan sat up and said, "Okay, okay." She lifted a blood-and-dirt-caked hand toward his muzzle, and Mule's tongue came out to lick the tortured flesh.

She started planting seeds from the leather pouch again as Mule followed along a few paces behind her, his ears pricking up and quivering at the approaching cries of animals in the woods.

As the cold closed in and Swan forced herself to keep working everything became dreamlike and hazy, as if she were laboring underwater. Every once in a while Mule's steamy breath would warm her, and then she began to sense furtive movement in the dark all around them, drawing closer. She heard the shriek of an animal nearby, and Mule answered with a husky grumble of warning. Swan kept pushing herself on, kept scraping through the snow to grip handfuls of dirt and replace them in the earth with seeds at their centers. Every movement of her fingers was an exercise in agony, and she knew the animals were being lured from the woods by the scent of her blood.

But she had to finish the job. There were still perhaps thirty or forty kernels left in the leather pouch, and Swan was determined to get them planted. The tingling currents coursed through her bones, continuing to grow stronger, almost painful now, and as she worked in the dark she imagined that she saw an occasional, tiny burst of sparks fly from the bloody mass of her fingers. She smelled a faint burned odor, like an electric plug beginning to overheat and short-circuit. Her face beneath the masklike crust of growths seethed with pain; when her vision would fade out, she would work for a few minutes in absolute blindness until her sight returned. She pushed herself onward—three or four feet, and one seed at a time.

An animal—a bobcat, she thought it was—growled somewhere off to the left, dangerously near. She tensed for its attack, heard Mule whinny and felt the pounding of his hooves against the earth as he galloped past her. Then the bobcat shrieked; there was the noise of turbulence in the snow—and, a minute or so later, Mule's breath warmed her face again. Another animal growled a challenge, off to the right this time, and Mule whirled toward it as the bobcat leapt. Swan heard a high squeal of pain, heard Mule grunt as he was struck; then there was the jarring of Mule's hooves against the ground—once, twice and again. He returned to her side, and she planted another seed.

She didn't know how long the attacks went on. She concentrated only on her work, and soon she came to the last five seeds.

At the first smear of light in the east, Josh sat up in the front room of Glory Bowen's shack and realized that Swan was gone. He called the woman and her son, and together they searched the alleys of Mary's Rest. It was Aaron who ran out to the field to look, and he came back yelling for Josh and his mama to come *quick*.

They saw a figure lying on the ground, huddled up on its side. Pressed close to it was Mule, who lifted his head and whinnied weakly as Josh ran toward them. He almost stepped on the crushed carcass of a bobcat with an extra clawed foot growing from its side, saw another thing that might have once been a bobcat lying nearby, but it was too mangled to tell for sure.

Mule's flanks and legs were crisscrossed with gashes. And in a circle around Swan were three more animal carcasses, all crushed.

"Swan!" Josh shouted as he reached her and dropped to his knees at her side. She didn't stir, and he took her frail body into his arms. "Wake up, honey!" he said, shaking her. "Come on now, wake up!" The air was bitterly cold, but Josh could feel the warmth that radiated from Mule. He shook her harder. "Swan! Wake up!"

"Oh, my Lawd Jesus," Glory whispered, standing just behind Josh. "Her . . . *hands.*"

Josh saw them too, and he winced. They were swollen, covered with dried black blood and dirt, the raw fingers contorted into claws. In the palm of her right hand was a leather pouch, and in her left palm was a single, withered kernel of corn mired in the dirt and blood. "Oh, God . . . *Swan* . . ."

"Is she dead, Mama?" Aaron asked, but Glory didn't answer. Aaron took a step forward. "She ain't dead, mister! Pinch her and wake her up!"

Josh touched her wrist. There was a weak pulse, but it wasn't much. A tear fell from the corner of his eye onto her face.

Swan drew a sharp breath and slowly released it in a moan. Her body trembled as she began to come up from a place that was very dark and cold.

"Swan? Can you hear me?"

A voice—muffled and far away—was speaking to her. She thought she recognized it. Her hands were hurting . . . oh, they were hurting so *much.* "Josh?"

The voice had been barely a whisper, but Josh's heart leapt. "Yes, honey. It's Josh. You just be still now, we're going to get you to where it's warm." He stood up with the girl in his arms and turned to the clawed-up, exhausted horse. "I'm going to find *you* a warm place, too. Come on, Mule." The horse struggled to his feet and began to follow.

Aaron saw Swan's dowsing rod lying in the snow and retrieved it. He prodded curiously at a dead bobcat with a second neck and head growing out of its belly, then he ran on after Josh and his mama.

Up ahead, Swan tried to open her eye. The lid was sealed shut. A viscous fluid leaked from the corner, and her eye burned so fiercely she had to bite her lip to keep from crying out. The other eye, long sealed, throbbed in its socket. She lifted a hand to touch her face, but her fingers wouldn't work.

Josh heard her whisper something. "We're almost there, honey. Just a few minutes more. You hang on, now." He knew she'd been very close to death out there in the open—and might still be. She spoke again, and this time he understood her, but he said, *"What?"*

"My eye," Swan said. She was trying to speak calmly, but her voice shook. "Josh . . . I've gone blind."

Sixty

Lying on her bed of leaves, Sister sensed movement beside her. She came up from sleep and clamped her hand like a manacle on somebody's wrist.

Robin Oakes was kneeling, his long brown hair full of feathers and bones and his eyes full of light. The colors of the glass circle pulsated on his sharp-boned face. He'd opened the satchel and was trying to slip the ring out of it. They stared at each other for a few seconds, and Sister said, *"No."* She put her other hand on the ring, and he let her have it.

"Don't get bent out of shape," he said tersely. "I didn't hurt it."

"Thank God. Who said you could go rummaging around in my bag?"

"I wasn't rummaging. I was looking. No big deal."

Sister's bones creaked as she sat up. Murky daylight was showing through the cave's entrance. Most of the young highwaymen were still asleep, but two of the boys were skinning a couple of small carcasses—rabbits? squirrels?—and another was arranging sticks to build the breakfast fire. At the rear of the cave, Hugh was sleeping near his patient, and Paul was asleep on a pallet of leaves. "This is important to me," she told Robin. "You don't know how important. Just leave it alone, okay?"

"Screw it," he said, and he stood up. "I was putting that weird thing *back,* and I was going to tell you about Swan and the big dude. But forget it, deadhead." He started to walk over and check on Bucky.

It took a few seconds for what the boy had said to register: "Swan. Swan and the big dude."

She hadn't told any of them about her dreamwalking. Hadn't said anything about the word "swan" and the hand prints burned into the trunk of a blossoming tree. How, then, could Robin Oakes know—unless *he* had gone dreamwalking, too?

"Wait!" she cried out. Her voice echoed like a bell within the cavern. Both Paul and Hugh were jolted from their sleep. Most of the boys awakened at once, already reaching for their guns and spears. Robin stopped in mid-stride.

She started to speak, couldn't find the words. She stood up and approached him, holding the glass circle up. "What did you see in this?"

Robin glanced over at the other boys, then back to Sister, and shrugged.

"You *did* see something, didn't you?" Her heart was pounding. The colors of the ring pulsated faster as well. "You did! You went dreamwalking, didn't you?"

"Dream*what?"*

"Swan," Sister said. "You saw that word written on the tree, didn't you? The tree that was covered with blossoms. And you saw the hand prints burned into the wood." She held the glass in front of his face. "You did, didn't you?"

"Uh-uh." He shook his head. "Not any of that stuff."

She froze, because she could see that he was telling the truth. "Please," she said. "Tell me what you saw."

"I . . . slipped it out of your bag about an hour ago, when I woke up," he said in a quiet, respectful voice. "I just wanted to hold it. Just wanted to look at it. I've never seen anything like it before, and after what happened with Bucky . . . I knew it was *special."* He trailed off, was silent for a few seconds as if mesmerized again. "I don't know what that thing is, but . . . it makes you *want* to hold it and look down inside it where all those lights and colors shine. I took it out of your bag, and I went over and sat down." He motioned toward his own bed of leaves on the far side of the cave. "I wasn't going to keep it very long, but . . . the colors started changing. They started making a picture—I don't know, I guess it sounds kind of crazy, right?"

"Go on." Both Paul and Hugh were listening, and the others were paying close attention as well.

"I just held it and kept watching the picture form, kind of like one of those mosaics they used to have on the walls of the orphanage chapel: If you looked at them long enough, you could almost swear they came alive and started moving. That's what this was like—only it suddenly wasn't just a picture anymore. It was *real,* and I was standing on a field covered with snow. The wind was blowing, and everything was kind of hazy—but damn, it was cold out there! I saw something lying on the ground; at first I thought it was a bundle of rags, but then I realized it was a person. And right next to it was a horse, lying down in the snow, too." He looked sheepishly over at the listening boys, then returned his gaze to Sister. "Weird, huh?"

"What else did you see?"

"The big dude came running across the field. He was wearing a black mask, and he passed about six or seven feet right in front of me. Scared the hell out of me, and I wanted to jump back, but then he'd gone on. I swear I could even see his footprints in the snow. And I heard him yell 'Swan.' I heard that as sure as I hear my own voice right now. He sounded scared. Then he knelt down beside that person, and it looked like he was trying to wake her up."

"Her? What do you mean, *her?*"

"A girl. I think he was calling her name: Swan."

A girl, Sister thought. A girl named Swan—that's who the glass ring was leading them to! Sister's mind was reeling. She felt faint, had to close her eyes for a moment to keep her balance; when she opened them again, the colors of the glass circle were pulsating wildly.

Paul had stood up. Though he'd ceased to believe in the

power of the ring before Hugh had saved the young boy, he was now almost trembling with excitement. It didn't matter anymore that he couldn't see anything in the glass; maybe that was because he was blind and would not look deeply enough. Maybe it was because he had refused to believe in anything much beyond himself, or his mind was locked to a bitter wavelength. But if this boy had seen a vision in the glass, if he'd experienced the sensation of "dreamwalking" that Sister talked about, then might they be searching for someone who really *was* out there somewhere? "What else?" he asked Robin. "Could you see anything else?"

"When I was going to jump back from that big dude in the black mask, I saw something on the ground almost in front of me. Some kind of animal, all crushed and bloody. I don't know what it was, but somebody had done a number on it."

"The man in the mask," Sister said anxiously. "Did you see where he came from?"

"No. Like I say, it was kind of hazy. Smoky, I guess. I could smell a lot of smoke in the air; and there was another smell—a sick kind of smell. I think there might have been a couple of other people there, too, but I'm not sure. The picture started fading and drifting apart. I didn't like that sick smell, and I wanted to be back here again. Then I was sitting over there with that thing in my hands, and that was all."

"Swan," Sister whispered. She looked at Paul. His eyes were wide and amazed. "We're looking for a girl named Swan."

"But where do we look? My God, a *field* could be anywhere—one mile away or a hundred miles!"

"Did you see anything else?" Sister asked the boy. "Any landmarks—a barn? A house? Anything?"

"Just a field. Covered with snow in some places, and in others the snow had blown away. Like I said, it was so real I could feel the cold. It was so real it was spooky . . . and I guess that's why I let you catch me putting that thing back in your bag. I guess I wanted to tell somebody about it."

"How are we supposed to find a field without landmarks?" Paul asked. "There's no way!"

"Uh . . . excuse me."

They looked over at Hugh, who was getting up with the aid of his crutch. "I'm really in the dark about all this," he said, once he'd gotten himself steadied. "But I know that what you believe you see in that glass you take to be a place that truly exists. I imagine I'm the last person in the world to understand such things—but it seems to me that if you're looking for that particular place, you might start with Mary's Rest."

"Why there?" Paul asked him.

"Because back in Moberly I had the opportunity to meet travelers," he replied. "Just as I met you and Sister. I assumed travelers might show some pity for a one-legged beggar—unfortunately, I was usually incorrect. But I remember one man who'd come through Mary's Rest; he was the one who told me the pond there had gone dry. And I remember . . . he said the air in Mary's Rest smelled *unclean.*" He turned his attention to Robin. "You said you smelled a 'sick' odor—and you also smelled smoke. Is that right?"

"Yeah. There was smoke in the air."

Hugh nodded. "Smoke. Chimneys. Fires for people trying to keep warm. I think the field you're searching for—if there *is* such a place—may be near Mary's Rest."

"How far is Mary's Rest from here?" Sister asked Robin.

"Seven or eight miles, I guess. Maybe more. I've never been there, but we've sure robbed a lot of people who were going in and out. That was a while back, though. Not so many travel this way anymore."

"There's not enough gas in the Jeep to make that distance," Paul reminded Sister. "I doubt if we'd make a mile."

"I don't mean seven or eight miles by road," Robin corrected. "I mean that far overland. It's southwest of here, through the woods, and the going's rough. Six of my men scouted a trail over there about a year ago. Two of them made it back, and they said there wasn't anything worth stealing in Mary's Rest. They'd probably rob *us* if they could."

"If we can't drive, we'll have to walk." Sister picked up her satchel and slipped the glass ring into it. Her hands were shaking.

Robin grunted. "Sister," he said, "I don't mean any

disrespect, but you're crazy. Seven miles on foot wouldn't be what I'd call a real fun thing to do. You know, we probably saved your lives stopping your Jeep like we did. You'd be frozen to death by now if we hadn't."

"We have to get to Mary's Rest—or at least *I* do. Paul and Hugh can decide for themselves. I've come a hell of a lot further than seven miles to get here, and a little cold's not going to stop me now."

"It's not just the distance, or the cold. It's what's out there in the deep woods."

"What?" Hugh asked uneasily, hobbling forward on his crutch.

"Oh, some real interesting wildlife. Things that look like they were hatched in some mad doctor's zoo. *Hungry* things. You don't want one of those things to catch you out in the woods at night."

"I should say not," Hugh agreed.

"I have to get to Mary's Rest," Sister said firmly, and her set expression told Robin her mind was made up. "All I need is some food, warm clothes and my shotgun. I'll make out okay."

"Sister, you won't make a mile before you get lost—or eaten."

She looked at Paul Thorson. "Paul?" she asked. "Are you still with me?"

He hesitated, glanced toward the gloomy light at the cave's entrance and then at the fire the boys were starting by rubbing two sticks together. Damn! he thought. I never *could* do that when I was a Cub Scout! It might not be too late to learn, though. Still, they'd come so far, and they might be so close to finding the answer they sought. He watched the fire spark and catch, but he'd already decided. "I'm with you."

"Hugh?" she prompted.

"I want to go with you," he said, "I really do. But I have a patient." He glanced at the sleeping boy. "I want to know what—and *who*—you find when you get to Mary's Rest, but . . . I think I'm needed here, Sister. It's been a long time since I've felt useful. Do you understand?"

"Yes." She'd already decided to talk Hugh out of going,

anyway; there was no way he could make the distance on one leg, and he'd only slow them down. "I do understand." She looked at Robin. "We'll want to be leaving as soon as we can get our gear together. I'll be needing my shotgun and the shells—if that's all right with you."

"You'll need more than that to make it."

"Then I'm sure you'll want to return Paul's gun and bullets to him, too. And we can use whatever food and clothes you can spare."

Robin laughed, but his eyes remained hard. "*We're* supposed to be the robbers, Sister!"

"Just give us back what you stole from us, then. We'll call it even."

"Anybody ever tell you you were crazy?" he asked.

"Yes. Tougher punks than you."

A faint smile spread slowly across his face, and his eyes softened. "Okay," he said, "you'll get your stuff back. I guess you'll need it more than us." He paused thoughtfully, then said, "Hold on," and he went over to his bed of leaves. He bent down and started going through a cardboard box full of tin cans, knives, watches, shoelaces, and other items. He found what he was looking for and returned to Sister. "Here," he said, placing something in her hand. "You'll need this, too."

It was a small metal compass that looked like it might have come from a CrackerJack box.

"It works, too," he told her. "At least, it worked when I took it off a dead man a couple of weeks ago."

"Thanks. I hope it's luckier for me than it was for him."

"Yeah. Well . . . you can have this, too, if you want it." Robin unbuttoned the brown coat from around his throat. Against his pallid skin he was wearing a tarnished little crucifix on a silver chain. He started to take it off, but Sister touched his hand to restrain him.

"That's all right." And she pulled her woolen muffler away from her neck to show him the crucifix-shaped scar that had been burned there in the Forty-second Street theater long before. "I've got my own."

"Yeah." Robin nodded. "I guess you do."

Their coats, sweaters and gloves were returned to Paul and Sister, along with their guns, bullets for Paul's Magnum and shells for Sister's shotgun. A can of baked beans and some dried squirrel meat wrapped up in leaves found their way into a duffel bag that was returned to Sister, along with an all-purpose knife and a bright orange woolen cap. Robin gave both of them wristwatches, and a search of another cardboard box of booty yielded three kitchen matches.

Paul siphoned the last of the gasoline from the Jeep's tank into a small plastic milk jug, and it barely wet the bottom. But the jug was securely sealed with tape and put down into the duffel bag, to be used to strengthen a fire.

It was as light as it was going to get outside. The sky was dingy, and there was no way to tell where the sun was. Sister's watch said ten twenty-two; Paul's said three thirteen.

It was time to go.

"Ready?" Sister asked Paul.

He looked longingly at the fire for a moment and then said, "Yeah."

"Good luck!" Hugh called, hobbling to the mouth of the cave as they started out. Sister lifted a gloved hand, then pulled her collar up around the muffler at her throat. She checked the compass, and Paul followed her toward the woods.

Sixty-one

"There it is." Glory pointed to the hulk of a gray-boarded barn half hidden within a grove of trees. Two other structures had collapsed, and from one of them protruded a crumbling red brick chimney. "Aaron found this place a while back," she said as Josh walked with her toward the barn and Mule tagged along. "Nobody lives out here, though." She motioned toward a well-worn trail that went past the decayed structures and deeper into the forest. "The Pit's not too far."

The Pit, as Josh understood it, was the community's burial ground—a trench into which hundreds of bodies had been lowered over the years. "Jackson used to say a few words over the dead," Glory said. "Now that he's gone, they just toss 'em in and forget 'em." She glanced at him. "Swan came mighty close to joinin' 'em last night. What'd she think she was doin' out there?"

"I don't know." Swan had lapsed into unconsciousness when they'd gotten her to the shack. Josh and Glory had cleaned her hands and bandaged them with strips of cloth, and they could feel the fever radiating from her. They'd left Aaron and Rusty to watch over her while Josh fulfilled his promise to find shelter for Mule, but he was half crazy with worry; without medicine, proper food or even decent drinking water, what hope did she have? Her body was so broken down with exhaustion that the fever might kill her. He remembered her last words to him before she'd faded away: "Josh, I've gone blind."

His hands gripped into fists at his sides. Protect the child, he thought. Sure. You've done a real fine job of that, haven't you?

He didn't know why she'd slipped out of the shack last night, but it was obvious she'd been digging in the hard earth. Thank God Mule had had the sense to know she was in trouble, or today they'd be taking Swan's body to the—

No. He refused to think about that. She'd get better. He knew she would.

They passed the rusted remains of a car—minus doors, wheels, engine and hood—and Glory pulled the barn's door open. It was dark and chilly inside, but at least the wind was blunted. Soon Josh's vision grew accustomed to the gloom. There were two stalls with a little straw on the floor and a trough in which Josh could melt some snow for Mule to drink. On the walls hung ropes and harness gear, but there were no windows an animal might crawl through. It seemed a safe enough place to leave him, and at least he'd be sheltered.

Josh saw what looked like a pile of junk on the other side of the barn and walked over to examine it. He found some broken-up chairs, a lamp without bulb or wiring, a small lawn mower and a coil of barbed wire. A mouse-eaten blue blanket covered more junk, and Josh lifted it away to see what was underneath.

"Glory," he said softly. "Come take a look."

She walked over beside him, and he ran his fingers across the cracked glass screen of a television set. "I haven't seen one of these in a while," he said wistfully. "I guess the ratings are pretty low these days, huh?" He punched the on–off button and started to turn through the channels, but the knob came off in his hand.

"Not worth a damn," Glory said. "Just like everything else."

The TV was supported on some sort of desk with rollers on it, and Josh picked up the set, turned it around and pulled the pressboard off to reveal the tube and the jungle of wires within. He felt about as dumb as a caveman, peering into a magic box that had once been a commonplace luxury—no, *necessity*—for millions of American homes. Without power, it was as useless as a stone—probably less so, really, because a stone could be used to kill rodents for the stewpot.

He set the TV aside, along with the other junk. It was going to take a smarter man than he to make juice run through wires and boxes show pictures that moved and spoke again, he mused. He bent down to the floor and found a box full of what looked like old wooden candlesticks. Another box held dusty bottles. He saw some pieces of paper scattered on the floor and picked up one. It was an announcement, and the faded red letters said *Antique Auction! Jefferson City Flea Market! Saturday, June 5! Come Early, Stay Late!* He opened his hand and let the announcement drift back to the floor and settle with a noise like a sigh amid the other pieces of yesterday's news.

"Josh? What's this thing?"

Glory was touching the desk with the rollers on it. Her hand found a small crank, and as she turned it there was the rattling noise of a chain moving over rusted gears. The rollers turned as achingly as old men revolving in their sleep. A number of rubber-cushioned pads were activated by the hand crank, coming down to press briefly against the rollers and then return to their original positions. Josh saw a small metal tray affixed to the other end of the desk; he picked up a few of the flea market announcements and put them in the tray. "Keep turning the crank," he said, and they watched as the rollers and pads grasped one piece of paper at a time, fed them through a slot into the depths of the machine and delivered them to another tray at the opposite end. Josh found a sliding panel, pushed it back and looked into an arrangement of more rollers, trays of metal type and a dried-up series of spongy surfaces that Josh realized must have once been ink pads.

"We've got us a printing press," he said. "How about that?

Must be an old knocker, but it's in pretty good shape." He touched the close-grained oak of the press's cabinet. "This was somebody's labor of love. Sure is a shame to let it sit out here and rot."

"Might as well rot here as anywhere else." She grunted. "That's the damnedest thing!"

"What is?"

"Before Jackson died . . . he wanted to start up a newspaper—just a little handout sheet. He said havin' some kind of town newspaper would make everybody feel like more of a community. You know, people would take more of an interest in everybody else instead of shuttin' themselves away. He didn't even know this thing was out here. 'Course, that was just a dream." She ran her hand across the oak next to Josh's. "He had a lot of dreams that died." Her hand touched his and quickly pulled away.

There was a moment of uncomfortable silence. Josh could still feel the heat of her hand against his own. "He must've been a fine man," he offered.

"He was. He had a good heart and a strong back, and he didn't mind gettin' his hands dirty. Before I met Jackson, I had a pretty rough life. I was full up with bad men and hard drinkin'. Been on my own since I was thirteen." She smiled slightly. "A girl grows up fast. Well, I guess Jackson wasn't afraid to get his hands dirty on *me,* 'cause I'd sure be dead if he hadn't turned me around. What about you? You have a wife?"

"Yes. An ex-wife, I mean. And two sons."

Glory turned the hand crank and watched the rollers work. "What happened to 'em?"

"They were in south Alabama. When the bombs hit, I mean." He drew a deep breath, slowly released it. "Down in Mobile. There's a naval station in Mobile. Nuclear submarines, all kinds of ships. *Was* a naval station there, at least." He watched Mule chomping at the straw on the floor. "Maybe they're still alive. Maybe not. I . . . I guess it's bad for me to think this, but . . . I kind of hope they died on the seventeenth of July. I hope they died watching television, or eating ice cream, or lying in the sun at the beach." His gaze found Glory's. "I just hope they died fast. Is that a bad thing to wish for?"

"No. It's a decent wish," Glory told him. And this time her hand touched his and did not retreat. Her other hand wandered up and gently brushed the black ski mask. "What do you look like under that thing?"

"I used to be ugly. Now I'm downright loathsome."

She touched the hard gray skin that sealed the right eyehole. "Does that stuff hurt?"

"Sometimes it burns. Sometimes it itches so much I can hardly stand it. And sometimes . . ." He trailed off.

"Sometimes what?"

He hesitated, about to tell her what he had never told either Swan or Rusty. "Sometimes," he said quietly, "it feels like . . . my face is changing. It feels like the bones are moving. And it hurts like hell."

"Maybe it's healin'."

He managed a weak smile. "Just what I need: a ray of optimism. Thank you, but I think I'm way beyond healing. These growths are about as hard as concrete."

"Swan's got the worst I've ever seen. She sounds like she can hardly draw a breath. Now, with that high fever she's runnin'—" She stopped, because Josh was walking toward the door. "You and she've been through a lot together, haven't you?" she asked.

Josh stopped. "Yes. If she dies, I don't know what I'll—" He caught himself, lowered his head and then lifted it again. "Swan won't die," he resolved. "She *won't*. Come on, we'd better get back."

"Josh? Wait—okay?"

"What is it?"

She worked the printing press's hand crank, rubbing her fingers against the smooth oak. "You're right about this thing. It's a shame for it to sit out here and rot."

"Like you said, here's as good a place as any."

"My shack would be a better place."

"Your shack? What do you want that thing for? It's useless!"

"Now, yes. But maybe not always. Jackson was right: It'd

do wonders for Mary's Rest to have some kind of newspaper —oh, not the kind people used to get thrown in their yards every afternoon, but maybe just a sheet of paper to tell folks who's bein' born, who's dyin', who's got clothes to spare and who needs clothes. Right now people who live across the alley from each other are strangers, but a sheet of paper like that might bring the whole town together."

"I think most people in Mary's Rest are more interested in finding another day's worth of food, don't you?"

"Yes. For now. But Jackson was a smart man, Josh. If he'd known this thing was sittin' here in a junkpile, he'd have toted it home on his back. I'm not sayin' I know how to write or anything—hell, I have a hard enough time speakin' right—but this thing might be a first step toward makin' Mary's Rest a real town again."

"What are you going to use for paper?" Josh asked. "And how about ink?"

"Here's paper." Glory picked up a handful of auction announcements. "And I've made dye from dirt and shoe polish before. I can figure out how to make ink."

Josh was about to protest again, but he realized a change had come over Glory; her eyes were excited, and their sparkle made her look five years younger. She has a challenge, he thought. She's going to try to make Jackson's dream come true.

"Help me," Glory urged. "Please."

Her mind was set. "All right," Josh answered. "You take the other end. This thing's going to be heavy."

Two flies lifted off from the top of the printing press and darted around Josh's head. A third sat motionlessly on the television set, and a fourth buzzed slowly just below the barn's roof.

The press was lighter than it looked, and getting it out of the barn was relatively easy. They set it down outside, and Josh went back in to tend to Mule.

The horse nickered nervously, walking around and around the stall. Josh rubbed his muzzle to calm him the way he'd seen Swan do so many times. He filled the trough with snow and put the blue blanket over Mule to keep him warm. A fly landed on Josh's hand, its touch stinging him as if the thing had been a wasp. "Damn!" Josh said, and he slapped his other hand down on it. A twitching, green-gray mess remained, but it still stung, and he wiped it off on his trousers.

"You'll be okay out here," Josh told the jittery horse as he rubbed its neck. "I'll check on you later, how about that?" As he closed the barn door and latched it he hoped he was doing the right thing leaving Mule out there alone. But at least this place—such as it was—would protect Mule from the cold and the bobcats. Mule would have to hold his own against the flies.

Together, Glory and Josh lugged the press down the road.

Sixty-two

Under a darkening sky, two figures struggled through a forest of dead pines where the wind had sculpted snowdrifts into barriers five feet high.

Sister kept close watch on the CrackerJack compass and pointed her nose toward the southwest. Paul followed at a few paces, carrying the duffel bag slung over his shoulder and watching their rear and flanks for the furtive movements of animals; he knew they were being tracked and had been tracked since they'd left the cave. He'd seen only quick glimpses of them, hadn't had time to tell what they were or how many, but he could smell the spoor of beasts. He kept the .357 gripped in his gloved right hand with his thumb on the safety.

Sister figured they had less than an hour of light left. They'd been traveling for almost five hours, according to the wrist-watch Robin had given her; she didn't know how many miles they'd covered, but the going was excruciating, and her legs felt like stiff lengths of timber. The effort of struggling across rocks and over snowdrifts had made her sweat, and now the sound of the ice in her clothes brought up the memory of Rice Krispies cereal—snap, crackle and pop! She remembered that her daughter used to like Rice Krispies: "Make it talk, Mama!"

She forced the ghosts of the past away. They had seen no sign of life but the things that prowled around them, watching them hungrily in the deepening twilight. When darkness fell, the beasts would get bolder. . . .

One step, she told herself. One step and then the next gets you where you're going. She said it mentally over and over again, while her legs continued to carry her like the laboring movement of a machine. She held her satchel close, and her left arm had cramped and locked in that position, but she could feel the outline of the glass ring through the leather, and she drew strength from it as surely as if it was her second heart.

Swan, she thought. Who are you? Where do you come from? And why have I been led to you? If indeed it was a girl named Swan that the dreamwalk path had brought her to, Sister had no idea what she'd say to the girl. Hello, she practiced, you don't know me, but I've come halfway across this country to find you. And I sure hope you're worth it, because Lord, I want to lie down and rest!

But what if there *was* no girl named Swan in Mary's Rest? What if Robin had been wrong? What if the girl was only passing through Mary's Rest and might be gone by the time they arrived?

She wanted to pick up the pace, but her legs wouldn't allow it. One step. One step and then the next gets you where you're going.

A scream from the woods to her left almost shocked her out of her boots. She whirled to face the noise, heard the scream become the shrill wail of a beast and then a muttering, chuckling noise like a hyena might make. She thought she saw a pair of greedy eyes in the gloom; they gleamed balefully before receding into the forest.

"We haven't got much more light," Paul told her. "We should find a place to camp."

She gazed toward the southwest. Nothing but a tortured landscape of dead pines, rocks and snowdrifts. It looked like a cold day in Hell. Wherever Mary's Rest was, they were not going to reach it today. She nodded, and they started searching for shelter.

The best they could find was a narrow niche in a hollow surrounded by rough-edged boulders. They pushed the snow away to expose the earth and form a three-foot-high snow wall circling them, then Paul and Sister went to work gathering dead branches to start a fire. Around them, shrill cries echoed from the woods as beasts began to gather like lords at a feast table.

They made a small pile of branches and ringed them with stones, and Paul dribbled a little gasoline on the wood. The first match he scraped across a stone flared, fizzled and went out. That left them with two. Darkness was falling fast.

"Here goes," Paul said tersely. He scraped the second match across the rock he was kneeling over, his other hand ready to cup the flame.

It flared, hissed and immediately began to die. He quickly held the weakening flame against a stick in the pile of branches, kneeling over it like a savage praying at the altar of a fire spirit.

"Catch, you little bastard," he whispered between clenched teeth. "Come on! *Catch!*"

The flame was all but gone, just a tiny glint dancing in the dark.

And then there was a *pop!* as a few drops of the gasoline caught, and flame curled up around the stick like a cat's tongue. The fire sputtered, crackled and began to grow. Paul added more gas.

A gout of flame leapt up, fire jumping from stick to stick. Within another minute they had heat and light, and they held their stiff hands toward the warmth.

"We'll get there in the morning," Paul said as they shared the dried squirrel meat. The stuff tasted like boiled leather. "I'll bet we've only got about another mile."

"Maybe." She pried the lid off the can of baked beans with the all-purpose knife and scooped some out with her fingers. They were oily and had a metallic taste but seemed okay. She gave the can to Paul. "I just hope this kiddie compass works. If it doesn't, we could be walking in circles."

He'd already considered that possibility, but now he shrugged his shoulders and scooped the beans into his mouth. If that compass was one hair off, he realized, they could have already missed Mary's Rest. "We haven't gone seven miles yet," he told her, though he wasn't even sure of that. "We'll know tomorrow."

"Right. Tomorrow."

She took first watch while Paul slept next to the fire, and she kept her back against a boulder with the Magnum on one side of her and the shotgun on the other.

Under its hard carapace of Job's Mask, Sister's face rippled with pain. Her cheekbones and jaw were throbbing. The searing pain usually passed within a few minutes, but this time it intensified to a point where Sister had to lower her head and stifle a moan. Again, for the seventh or eighth time in the last few weeks, she felt sharp, cracking jolts that seemed to run deep beneath the Job's Mask, down through the bones of her face. All she could do was clench her teeth and endure the pain until it passed, and when it was finally gone it left her shivering in spite of the fire.

That was a bad one, she thought. The pains were getting worse. She lifted her head and ran her fingers across the Job's Mask. The knotty surface was as cool as ice on the slopes of a dormant volcano, but beneath it the flesh felt hot and raw. Her scalp was itching maddeningly, and she put her hand under the hood of her parka to touch the mass of growths that encased her skull and trailed down the back of her neck. She longed to dig her fingers through the crust and scratch her flesh until it bled.

Slap a wig on my bald head, she thought, and I'd still look like a graduate of gargoyle school! She balanced precariously between tears and laughter for a few seconds, but the laughter won out.

Paul sat up. "Is it my watch yet?"

"No. Couple of hours to go."

He nodded, lay back down and was asleep again almost at once.

She continued to probe the Job's Mask. Feels like my skin's on fire underneath there—whatever skin I've got left, she thought. Sometimes, when the pain was acute and her flesh beneath the Job's Mask felt like it was boiling, she could almost swear that the bones shifted like the foundations of an unsteady house. She could almost swear that she felt her face changing.

A glimpse of movement on the right brought her attention back to the business of survival. Something made a deep, guttural barking noise off in the distance, and another beast replied with a sound like that of a baby crying. She laid the shotgun across her lap and looked up at the sky. Nothing but darkness up there, and a sensation of low, hanging clouds like the black ceiling of a claustrophobic's nightmare. She couldn't remember when she'd last seen the stars; maybe it had been on a warm summer's night, when she was living in a cardboard box in Central Park. Or maybe she'd stopped noticing the stars a long time before the clouds had blanked them out.

She missed the stars. Without them, the sky was dead. Without them, what was there to make a wish on?

Sister held her hands toward the fire and shifted against the boulder to get more comfortable. A hotel suite this was not, but her legs weren't aching so much now. She realized how tired she was, and she doubted she could have continued another fifty yards. But the fire felt good, and she had a shotgun across her lap, and she would blast hell out of anything that came within range. She put her hand on the satchel and traced the glass ring's outline. Tomorrow, she thought. Tomorrow we'll know.

She leaned her head against the rock and watched Paul sleeping. Good for you, she thought. You deserve it.

The fire's soft heat soothed her. The forest was silent. And Sister's eyes closed. Just for a minute, she told herself. It won't do any harm if I just rest for a—

She sat bolt upright. Before her, the fire was down to a few red embers, and the cold was slipping through her clothes. Paul was huddled up, still sleeping. Oh, Jesus! she thought as panic snapped at her. How long was I out? She was shivering, her joints throbbing with the cold, and she got up to add more branches to the fire. There were only a few small ones left, and as she knelt down and arranged them in the embers she sensed a quick, catlike movement behind her. The flesh tightened across the back of her neck.

And she knew with sickening certainty that she and Paul were no longer alone. Something was behind her, crouched on a boulder, and she'd left both weapons where she was sitting. She took a deep breath, made up her mind to move, turned and lunged for the shotgun. She picked it up and spun around to fire.

The figure sitting cross-legged atop the boulder lifted his gloved hands in mock surrender. A rifle lay across his knees, and he was wearing a familiar, patched brown coat with a cowl protecting his head.

"Hope you enjoyed your nap," Robin Oakes said.

"Whazzit?" Paul sat up, blinking. "Huh?"

"Young man," Sister said hoarsely, "I was about one second from sending you to a much warmer place than this. How long have you been sitting there?"

"Long enough so that you ought to be glad I don't have four legs. If one person goes to sleep, the other has to keep watch or you're both dead." He looked at Paul. "And by the time *you* woke up, you'd be bobcat meat. I thought you two knew what you were doing."

"We're okay." Sister took her finger off the trigger and put the weapon aside. Her insides felt like quivering jelly.

"Sure." He glanced over his shoulder and called toward the forest, "Come on in!"

Three bundled-up figures emerged from the woods and scrambled up onto the boulder with Robin. All of the boys carried rifles, and one of them lugged another of the canvas bags that Robin's highwaymen had stolen from Sister.

"You two didn't make such a good distance, did you?" Robin asked her.

"I thought we did damned fine!" Paul was shaking the last of the sleep out of his head. "I figure we've got about another mile in the morning."

Robin grunted disdainfully. "More like three, most likely. Anyway, I sat down and started thinking, back at the cave. I knew you'd make camp somewhere, probably screw that up, too." He appraised the boulders and the wall of snow. "You've got yourselves trapped in here. When that fire went down, the things in the woods would've jumped you from all sides. We saw a lot of them, but we stayed downwind and low to the ground, and they didn't see *us.*"

"Thanks for the warning," Sister said.

"Oh, we didn't come out here to *warn* you. We followed you to keep you from getting killed." Robin climbed down the boulder, and the other boys did the same. They stood around the fire, warming their hands and faces. "It wasn't hard. You left a trail that looked like a plow had gone through. Anyway, you forgot something." He opened the other duffel bag, reached into it and brought out the second jug of moonshine that Hugh had given Paul. "Here." He tossed it to Sister. "I think there's enough left for everybody to have a swig."

There was, and the moonshine's fire heated Sister's belly. Robin sent the three boys out to stand guard around the camp. "The trick is to make a lot of noise," Robin said after they'd gone. "They don't want to shoot anything, because the blood would drive the other animals crazy out there." He sat down beside the fire, pulled his hood back and took his gloves off. "If you want to sleep, Sister, you'd better do it now. We'll have to relieve them on watch before light."

"Who put you in charge?"

"I did." The firelight threw shadows in the hollows of his face, glinted off the fine hairs of his beard. His long hair, still full of feathers and bones, made him look like a savage prince. "I've decided to help you get to Mary's Rest."

"Why?" Paul asked. He was wary of the boy, didn't trust him worth a damn. "What's in it for you?"

"Maybe I want some fresh air. Maybe I want to travel." His gaze flicked toward Sister's satchel. "Maybe I want to see if you find who you're looking for. Anyway, I pay my debts. You people helped me with one of mine, and I owe you. So I'll get you to Mary's Rest in the morning, and we'll call it even, right?"

"Okay," Sister agreed. "And thank you."

"Besides, if you two get killed tomorrow, I want the glass

ring. You won't be needing it." He leaned against the boulder and closed his eyes. "You'd better sleep while you can."

A rifle shot echoed from the woods, followed by two more. Sister and Paul looked at each other uneasily, but the young highwayman lay motionless and undisturbed. The noise of rifle fire continued intermittently for another minute or so, followed by the angry shrieks of what sounded like several animals—but their cries were fading as they retreated. Paul reached for the moonshine jug to coax out the last drops, and Sister leaned back to contemplate tomorrow.

Sixty-three

"Fire! . . . Fire!"

The bombs were falling again, the earth erupting into flames, humans burning like torches under a blood-red sky.

"Fire! . . . Somethin's on fire!"

Josh shook loose from his nightmare. He could hear a man's voice shouting "Fire!" out in the street. At once he was on his feet and striding to the door; he threw it open, looked out and saw an orange glow reflected off the clouds. The street was empty, but Josh could hear the man's voice off in the distance, raising the alarm: "Fire! Somethin's on fire!"

"What is it? What's on fire?" Glory's face was stricken as she peered out the door beside him. Aaron, who could not be separated from Crybaby, pushed between them to see.

"I don't know. What's over in that direction?"

"Nothin'," she said. "Just the Pit, and—" She stopped suddenly, because both of them knew.

The barn where Josh had left Mule was on fire.

He pulled his boots on, put on his gloves and his heavy coat. Glory and Aaron raced to bundle up as well. Red embers burned in the stove's grate, and Rusty was sitting up from his bed of rags; his eyes were still dazed, and cloth bandages were plastered to the side of his face and the wound at his shoulder. "Josh?" he said. "What's goin' on?"

"The barn's on fire! I locked the door, Rusty! Mule can't get out!"

Rusty stood up, but his legs were weak and he staggered against the wall. He felt like a deballed bull, and he was furious at himself. He tried again but still didn't have the strength to even get his damned boots on.

"No, Rusty!" Josh said. He motioned toward Swan, who lay on the floor under the thin blanket that Aaron had given up. "You stay with her!"

Rusty knew he'd collapse before he got ten paces from the shack. He almost wept with frustration, but he knew also that Swan needed to be watched over. He nodded and sank down wearily to his knees.

Aaron darted on ahead, and Josh and Glory followed as fast as they could. Josh found some of the speed he had once shown on the football field at Auburn University in making the two hundred yards between the shack and the barn. Other people were out in the street, running toward the fire as well—not because they wanted to extinguish it, but because they could get warm. Josh's heart almost cracked; over the roar of flames that covered all but the structure's roof, he could hear Mule's frantic cries.

Glory screamed, "Josh! *No!*" as he barreled at the barn door.

Swan said something in a soft, delirious voice, but Rusty couldn't make it out. She tried to sit up, and he put his hand on her shoulder to restrain her. Touching her was like putting his hand to the stove's grate. "Hold on," he said. "Easy now, just take it easy."

She spoke again, but her speech was unintelligible. He thought she said something about corn, though that was all he could even halfway understand. Now the remaining eyehole in the mask of growths was almost sealed over. She'd been fading in and out of consciousness since Josh had brought her in at daylight from the field, and she'd alternately shivered and thrashed free of the blanket. Glory had wound cloth bandages around Swan's raw hands and tried to feed her some watery soup, but there wasn't a thing any of them could do for her now except try to make her more comfortable. Swan was so far gone she didn't even know where she was.

She's dying, Rusty thought. Dying right in front of me. He eased her back down again, and he heard her say something that might have included "Mule."

"It's all right," Rusty told her, his own swollen jaw making speech difficult. "You just rest now, everythin's gonna be all right in the mornin'." He sure wished he could believe that. He'd come too far with Swan to watch her fade away like this, and he cursed his own weakness. He felt about as sturdy as a wet sponge, and his mama sure hadn't raised him to live on rat meat soup. The only way he could get that stuff down was to pretend it came off the bones of little bitty steers.

A loose board popped out on the shack's porch, beyond the closed door.

Rusty looked up. He expected either Glory, Aaron or Josh to enter—but how could that be? They'd just been gone a few minutes.

The door did not open.

Another board popped and whined.

"Josh?" Rusty called.

There was no reply.

But he knew someone was standing out there. He was too familiar with the noise the loose boards made when stepped on, and he'd already sworn he was going to find a hammer and nails somewhere when he got his strength back and tighten those bastards down before they drove him batty.

"Anybody there?" he called. He realized somebody might be coming to steal the few items Glory possessed: her needles, her cloth or even the furniture. Maybe the hand crank printing press that occupied a corner of the room. "I've got a gun in here!" he lied, and he rose to his feet.

There was no more sound of movement beyond the door.

He walked to it on unsteady legs. The door was unlatched.

He reached for the latch and he sensed a terrible, gnawing cold on the other side of the door. A *dirty* cold. He started to slip the latch home.

"Rusty," he heard Swan rasp.

The entire door suddenly crashed inward, tearing off its wooden hinges and catching him squarely on his bad shoulder. He cried out in pain as he was flung backward and to the floor halfway across the room. A figure stood in the doorway, and Rusty's first impulse was to leap to his feet to protect Swan; he got as far as his knees before the agony of his reopened shoulder wound made him pitch forward on his face.

The man walked in, a pair of muddy hiking boots clumping on the floor. His gaze swept the room, saw the wounded man lying in spreading blood, the thinner figure curled up and shivering, obviously near death. And there it was, over in the corner.

The printing press.

That wasn't a good thing, he'd decided when the flies had brought him back images and voices from all over Mary's Rest. No, not good at all! First you had a printing press, and then you had a newspaper, and after that you had opinions and people thinking and wanting to do things, and then . . .

And then, he thought, you were right back to the situation that had gotten the world where it was right now. Oh, no, not good at all! They had to be saved from making the same mistake twice. Had to be saved from *themselves.* And that was why he'd decided to destroy the printing press before anything was printed on it. That thing was as dangerous as a bomb, and they didn't even realize it! And that horse was dangerous, too, he'd reasoned; a horse made people think about traveling, and wheels, and cars—and that led right up to air pollution and wrecks, didn't it? They'd thank him for setting the barn on fire, because they could eat cooked horsemeat in just a little while.

He was glad he'd come to Mary's Rest. And just in time, too.

He'd seen them come to town in their Travelin' Show

wagon, had heard that big one hollering for a doctor. Some people just had no respect for a quiet, peaceful town. Well . . . respect was going to be taught. Right now.

His boots clumped toward Swan.

Josh hit the flaming barn door with the full force of two hundred and fifty pounds, Glory's scream still ringing in his head.

For a bone-jarring second he thought he was back on the football field and had run smack dab into one of those huge linebackers. He thought the door wasn't going to give, but then wood split and the barn door caved in, carrying him into the midst of an inferno.

He rolled away from burning timbers and got to his feet. Smoke churned before his face, and the awful heat almost crushed him. "Mule!" he shouted. He could hear the horse bucking and shrieking but couldn't see him. Flames leapt at him like spears, and fire was starting to fall like orange confetti from the roof. He charged toward Mule's stall, his coat beginning to smolder, and the smoke took him.

"My, my," the man said softly. He'd stopped just past the thin figure on the floor, his attention drawn to an object on the pine wood table. He reached out with a slender hand and picked up a mirror with two carved faces on its handle, each looking in a different direction. He intended to admire the new face he'd created, but the glass was dark. A finger traced the carved faces. What kind of mirror had a black glass? he wondered—and his new mouth twitched just a fraction.

This mirror gave him the same sensation as the ring of glass. It was a thing that should not be. What was its purpose, and what was it doing here?

He didn't like it. Not at all. He lifted his arm and smashed the mirror to pieces against the table, and then he twisted the double-faced handle and flung it aside. Now he felt so much better.

But there was another object on the table, too. A small leather pouch. He picked it up and shook its contents into his palm. A little kernel of corn, stained red with dried blood, fell out.

"What is *this?*" he whispered. A few feet away, the figure on the floor quietly moaned. He gripped the kernel in his hand and slowly turned toward the sound, his eyes red and gleaming in the low firelight.

His gaze lingered on the figure's bandaged, clawed hands. A swirl of heat shimmered around the man's right fist, and from within it there was a muffled *pop.* He opened his hand and pushed the bit of popcorn into his mouth, chewing thoughtfully on it.

He'd seen this figure yesterday, after he'd watched their wagon being torn apart. Yesterday the hands had not been bandaged. Why were they bandaged now? *Why?*

Across the room, Rusty lifted his head and tried to focus. He saw a tall, slender man in a brown parka approaching Swan. Saw him standing over her. Pain wracked him, and he was lying in a puddle of blood. Gonna pass out again, he knew. Gotta move . . . gotta move . . .

He began crawling through his blood.

His good eye almost blinded by the smoke, Josh saw a swirl of motion ahead. It was Mule—panicked, rearing and bucking, unable to find a way out. The blanket on his back was smoking, about to burst into flames.

He ran to the horse and was almost trampled under Mule's hooves as the horse frantically reared and came down again, twisting in one direction and then the other. Josh could only think of one thing to do: He lifted both hands in front of the horse's muzzle and clapped them together as hard as he could, like he'd seen Swan do at the Jaspin farm.

Whether the noise brought Swan to mind or just snapped his panic for a second, Mule stopped thrashing and stood steady, his eyes watering and wide with terror. Josh wasted no time; he grabbed Mule's mane and pulled him out of the stall, trying to lead him to the door. Mule's legs stiffened.

"Come on, you dumb fool!" Josh yelled, the heat scorching his lungs. He planted his boots in burning straw, his joints cracking as he hauled Mule forward. Pieces of flaming wood fell from above, striking him on the shoulders and hitting Mule's flanks. Cinders spun before his face like hornets.

And then Mule must have gotten a whiff of outside air, because he lunged so fast Josh only had time to throw his arms around the horse's neck. His boots were dragged across the floor as Mule powered through the flames.

They burst through the opening where the barn door had been, out into the cold night air with sparks trailing from Josh's burning coat and the flames in Mule's mane and tail.

The man in the brown parka stood looking at those bandaged hands. "What have y'all been up to while my back's been turned?" he asked in a deep-South drawl. The printing press was forgotten for the moment. A mirror that showed no reflection, a single kernel of corn, bandaged hands . . . those things bothered him, just like the glass ring did, because he didn't understand them. And there was something else, too; something about the figure on the floor. What was it? This is a nothing, he thought. A less-than-zero. A piece of shit passing through the sewage pipe of Mary's Rest.

But why did he sense something different about this figure? Something . . . *threatening.*

He lifted his right hand. Heat shimmered around the fingers; one of them burst into flame, and the flame spread. In another few seconds his hand was a glove of fire.

The solution to things he did not understand was very simple: Destroy it.

He began to reach down toward the growth-encrusted head.

"No."

It was a weak whisper. But the hand that clamped around the man's ankle still had strength in it.

The man in the brown parka looked at him incredulously, and by the light of the flaming hand Rusty saw his face: heavily seamed and weather-beaten, a thick gray beard, eyes that were so blue they were almost white. Touching the man sent freezing waves through Rusty's bones, and he wanted more than anything on earth to draw his hand back, but the cold shocked his nerves and kept him from passing out. Rusty said, "No . . . don't you touch Swan, you bastard."

He saw the man smile faintly; it was a pitying smile, but then it passed the point of pity.

The man reached down and clamped his burning hand to Rusty's throat.

And Rusty's neck was encircled with a noose of fire. The man lifted him off the floor as Rusty screamed and kicked, and the fire pumped out of that hand and arm like napalm, sizzling Rusty's hair and eyebrows. His clothes caught, and he realized at a cold center within his pain and panic that he was becoming a human torch—and that he had only seconds to live.

And then after him, it would be Swan's turn.

Rusty's body jerked and fought, but he knew he was finished. The smell of himself afire made him think of the greasy French fries at the Oklahoma state fair when he was a kid. The flame was going bone-deep now, and as his nerves began to sputter the pain locked up, as if a point of no return had been passed.

Mama said somethin', Rusty thought. Said . . . said . . .

Mama said fight fire with fire.

Rusty embraced the man with the burning sticks of his arms, entwining his fingers at the man's back. The fingers melded like chains, and Rusty thrust his flaming face into the man's beard.

The beard caught fire. The face bubbled, melting and running like a plastic mask, exposing a deeper layer the color of modeling clay.

Rusty and the man whirled around the room like participants in a bizarre ballet.

"Lord God!" shouted one of two men who were looking in, drawn by the open doorway on their jaunt to the burning barn. "Lord God A'mighty!" The second man screamed, backed up and fell on his rump in the mud. Other people were running over to see what was happening, and the man in the burning rags of a brown parka could not thrust the flaming dead man away from him, and his new disguise was ruined, and *they* were about to see his true face.

He gave a garbled roar that almost shook the cabin and ran through the doorway out into the midst of them. He was still roaring as he ran up the street on melting legs in the embrace of a charred cowboy.

Glory helped Josh pull out of his burning coat. His ski mask was smoking, too, and before she could think twice about it, she reached up and yanked it off.

Dark gray growths, some the size of Aaron's fists, almost completely covered Josh's face and head. Tendrils had interlocked around his mouth, and the only clear area except for his lips was a circle in the crust through which his left eye, now bloodshot from the smoke, stared at Glory. His condition wasn't as bad as Swan's, but it still made Glory gasp and retreat a step.

He had no time to apologize for not being a beauty. He ran for Mule, who was bucking wildly as other onlookers scattered, and grabbed up a handful of snow; he clutched Mule's neck and crushed out the flames in his mane. Then Glory had a handful of snow and was pressing it to the horse's tail, and Aaron had some, too, and many of the other men and women were scooping up snow and rubbing it against Mule's sides. A thin, dark-haired man with a blue keloid grabbed Mule's neck opposite Josh, and after a minute of struggle they got the horse calmed down enough to stop bucking.

"Thanks," Josh told the man. And then there was a roaring and a rush of heat, and the barn's roof fell in.

"Hey!" a woman standing closer to the road called out. "There's some kinda commotion back there!" She pointed toward the shacks, and both Glory and Josh could see people out in the street. Shouts and cries for help drifted to them.

Swan! Josh thought. Oh, God—I left Swan and Rusty alone!

He started to run, but his legs betrayed him and he went down. His lungs were grabbing for air, black motes spinning before his eyes.

Someone took his arm, started helping him up. A second person supported his other shoulder, and together they got

Josh to his feet. Josh realized Glory stood on one side of him, and on the other was an old man with a face like cracked leather. "I'm all right," he told them, but he had to lean heavily on Glory. She stood firm and started guiding him along the road.

A blanket had been thrown on the ground about thirty feet from Glory's shack. Smoke curled from under it. A few people stood around it, motioning and talking. Others were crowded around Glory's front door. Josh smelled burned meat, and his stomach clenched. "Stay here," he told Aaron. The boy stopped, Crybaby gripped in his hand.

Glory went with Josh into the shack. She put her hand over her mouth and nose. Hot currents still prowled back and forth between the walls, and the ceiling was scorched black.

He stood over Swan, trembling like a child. She had pulled her knees up to her chest, and now she was motionless. He bent down beside her, took one wrist and felt for her pulse. Her flesh was cold.

But her pulse was there—faint but steady, like the rhythm of a metronome that would not be stilled.

Swan tried to lift her head but had no strength. "Josh?" It was barely audible.

"Yes," he answered, and he pulled her to him, cradling her head against his shoulder. A tear scorched his eye and ran down along the growths on his cheek. "It's old Josh."

"I . . . had a nightmare. I couldn't wake up. He was here, Josh. He . . . he found me."

"Who found you?"

"Him," she said. "The man . . . with the scarlet eye . . . from Leona's pack of cards."

On the floor a few feet away were fragments of dark glass. The magic mirror, Josh knew. He saw Rusty's cowboy boots, and he wished to God that he didn't have to go outside and see what was smoking under that blanket in the mud.

"Swan? I've got to go out for a minute," he said. "You just rest, all right?" He eased her down and glanced quickly at Glory, who had seen the puddle of blood on the floor. Then Josh stood up and made himself go.

"We threw snow on him!" one of the onlookers said as Josh approached. "We couldn't get the fire out, though. He was too far gone."

Josh knelt down and lifted the blanket. Looked long and hard. The corpse was hissing, as if whispering a secret. Both arms had snapped off at the shoulders.

"I seen it!" another man offered excitedly. "I looked in through that door and seen a two-headed demon a-runnin' around and around in there! God A'mighty, I ain't never seen such a sight! Then Perry and me started hollerin', and that thing come a-runnin' right at us! Looked like it was fightin' itself! Then it split in two and the other one run that way!" He pointed up the street in the opposite direction.

"It was another man on fire," a third witness explained, in a calmer voice. He had a hooked nose and a dark beard, and he spoke with a Northern accent. "I tried to help him, but he turned up an alley. He was too fast for me. I don't know where the hell he went, but he couldn't have gotten too far."

"Yeah!" The second man nodded vigorously. "The skin was meltin' right offa him!"

Josh lowered the blanket and stood up. "Show me where he went," he told the man with the Northern accent.

A trail of burned cloth turned into an alley, continued for about forty feet, turned left at another alley and ended at a pile of ashy rags behind a shack. There was no corpse, and the footprints were lost in the ravaged ground.

"Maybe he crawled under one of these shacks to die," the other man said. "There's no way a human being could live through that! He looked like a torch!"

They searched the area for another ten minutes, even squeezing under some of the shacks, but there was no sign of a body. "I guess wherever he is, he died naked," the man said as they gave up the search and went back to the street.

Josh looked at Rusty again. "You dumb cowboy," Josh whispered. "You sure pulled a magic trick this time, didn't you?"

"He was here," Swan had said. "He found me."

Josh wrapped Rusty up in the blanket, lifted the remains in his arms and got to his feet.

"Take him to the Pit!" one of the men said. "That's where all the bodies go."

Josh walked to what was left of the Travelin' Show wagon and laid Rusty in it.

"Uh-uh, mister!" a husky woman with a red keloid covering her face and scalp scolded him. "That'll draw every wild animal for miles!"

"Let them come, then," Josh replied. He turned toward the people, swept his gaze across them and stopped at Glory. "I'm going to bury my friend at first light."

"Bury him?" A frail teen-age girl with close-cropped brown hair shook her head. "Nobody *buries* anybody anymore!"

"I'm going to bury Rusty," Josh told Glory. "At first light, in that field where we found Swan. It'll be hard work. You and Aaron can help me, if you like. If you don't want to, that's all right, too. But I'll be damned if I'll—" His voice cracked. "I'll be damned if I'll throw him into a pit!" He sat up on the wagon's frame beside the body to wait for daylight.

There was a long silence. Then the man with the Northern accent said to Glory, "Lady? Do you have any way to fix your door?"

"No."

"Well . . . I've got a few tools in my shack. They're not much. I haven't used them in a while, but . . . if you like, I'll take a shot at fixing your door."

"Thank you." Glory was stunned by the offer. It had been a very long time since anyone had offered to do *anything* in Mary's Rest. "I'd appreciate whatever you could do."

"If you're gonna stay out here in the cold," the woman with the red keloid told Josh, "you'd better get yourself a fire lit. Better build one right here on the road." She snorted. "Bury a body! That's the damnedest thing I ever heard of!"

"I got a wheelbarrow," another man offered. "I reckon I could run it up there and pluck some hot coals out of that fire. I mean . . . I got better things to do, but . . . sure would be a shame to let all those good hot coals go to waste."

"I sure would like a fire!" a short man with one eye missing piped up. "It's cold as hell in my shack! Listen . . . I've got some coffee grounds I've been saving. If somebody's got a tin can and a hot stove, I guess we could brew it up."

"Might as well. All this excitement's got me as jumpy as a flea on a griddle." The woman with the red keloid brought a small gold watch from the pocket of her coat, held it with loving reverence and squinted closely at the dial. "Four twelve. First light won't show for five hours yet. Yep, if you're gonna watch over that poor soul, you're gonna need a fire and some hot coffee. I got a coffee pot at my mansion. Ain't been used in a while." She looked at Glory. "We can use it now, if you like."

Glory nodded. "Yes. We can brew the coffee on my stove."

"I have a pickaxe and shovel," a gray-bearded man in a plaid coat and a tan woolen cap said to Josh. "Part of the shovel blade's broken off, but it'll do to bury your friend."

"I used to be a wood carver," someone else spoke up. "If you're going to bury him, you'll need a marker. What was his name?"

"Rusty." Josh's throat choked up. "Rusty Weathers."

"Well?" The feisty woman put her hands on her hips. "We got things to do, seems like. Let's quit shirkin' and get to workin'!"

Almost three miles away, Robin Oakes stood in the twilight at the campfire's edge where the three boys slept. He was armed with a rifle and had been carefully watching for the movement of animals too close to the fire. But now he stared toward the horizon, and he called out, "Sister! Sister, come over here!"

It was a minute or so before she made her way to him from her sentry post on the other side of the fire. "What is it?"

"There." He pointed, and she followed the line of his finger to see a faint orange glow in the sky above the seemingly endless expanse of forest. "I think that's Mary's Rest. Nice of them to start a fire and show us the way, huh?"

"It sure is."

"That's the direction we'll be headed when it gets light enough to see. If we keep a good pace, we ought to make it in a couple of hours."

"Good. I want to get there as fast as we can."

"I'll see to it." His sly smile promised a rough march.

Sister started to return to her area of patrol, but she had a sudden thought and stopped at the edge of the firelight. She took the CrackerJack compass from her pocket, lined herself up with the glow on the horizon, and checked the needle.

It was far enough off southwest that they might have bypassed Mary's Rest by six or seven miles. Sister realized that they'd been very close to being lost if Robin hadn't seen that glow in the sky. Whatever it was, she was thankful for it.

She continued her patrol, her eyes searching the darkness for any lurking beasts, but her mind was on a girl named Swan.

ELEVEN

Daughter of Ice and Fire

Thy passin' guest / The Empress / Things that could be / It's a man's world / The Job's Mask cracked / The kiss

Sixty-four

First light came shrouded in a dense fog that lay close to the alleys and shacks of Mary's Rest, and a funeral procession moved quietly through the mist.

Josh led the way, carrying Swan in his arms. She was protected from the chill by a thick sweater and coat, her head resting against Josh's shoulder. He was determined not to let her out of his sight again, for fear of whatever had come after her the night before and set Rusty ablaze. Man with a scarlet eye, Devil or demon—whatever it was, Josh was going to protect Swan with his final breath.

But she was both shivering and hot with fever, and Josh didn't know if he could save her from what was killing her from the inside out. He prayed to God that he wouldn't soon have to dig a second grave.

Glory and Aaron followed behind Josh, and right behind them the handyman with the Northern accent—whose name was Zachial Epstein—and the gray-bearded man in the plaid coat—Gene Scully—carried between them a crudely constructed pine wood box that resembled a child's coffin. All that remained of Rusty Weathers had fit inside it, and before the lid had been nailed shut Josh had put his cowboy boots in with him.

Others who'd watched over Rusty's body during the night followed as well, including the woman with the keloid-scarred face—an ex-carnival roustabout from Arkansas named Anna McClay—and the man who'd provided the coffee grounds, whose name was John Gallagher and who'd been a policeman in Louisiana. The teen-age girl with close-cropped brown hair had forgotten her last name and just went by Katie. The young man who'd been a wood carver in Jefferson City was named Roy Creel, and he limped along on a crooked left leg that had been badly broken and never properly set; in his arms he carried a pine wood plank that had RUSTY WEATHERS carved into it in scrolled letters. Bringing up the rear was Mule, who stopped every few yards to sniff the air and paw at the hard ground.

Fog shrouded the field and clung close to the earth, and the wind was still. The reek of the pond didn't seem so bad today, Josh thought—or maybe that just meant he was getting used to it. Walking through the mist was like entering a ghostly world where time had halted, and the place might have been the edge of a medieval settlement six centuries before. The only sounds were the crunching of boots in the snow, the rush of breath pluming from their mouths and nostrils and the distant cawing of crows.

Josh could barely see ten feet ahead. He continued up through the low-lying mist into the field for what he took to be about forty or fifty yards before he stopped. This was as good a spot as any, he decided, and a whole hell of a lot better than the Pit. "Right here will do," he told the others. He carefully laid Swan down a few feet away. Anna McClay was carrying the shovel and pickaxe; he took the shovel from her and scooped the snow away from a rectangular area a little larger than the coffin. Then he took the pickaxe and began to dig Rusty's grave.

Anna joined in the work, shoveling the earth to one side as Josh broke it loose. The first six or eight inches was cold and clayey, full of a network of thick roots that resisted Josh's pickaxe. Anna pulled the roots up and tossed them aside, to be boiled in soup. Beneath the top layer of earth the dirt became darker, crumbly and easier to move. Its rich odor reminded Josh, oddly, of a fudge cake his mother had baked and left to cool on the kitchen windowsill.

When Josh's shoulders got tired, John Gallagher hefted the pickaxe and took over, while Glory shoveled the dirt aside. And so they alternated the work like that for the next hour, digging the grave deep enough so that the wild animals wouldn't disturb it. When it was ready, Josh, John and Zachial lowered the coffin into the earth.

Josh looked down at the pine wood box. "Well," he said, quietly and resignedly, "I guess that's that. I wish there was a tree out here to bury you under, but there's not enough sunlight to throw shade, anyway. I remember you told me you dug graves for all your friends back at that train wreck. Well, I figured it was the least your friend could do for *you.* I think you saved Swan last night; I don't know from who—or *what*—but I'm going to find out. That I promise you." He lifted his gaze to the others. "I guess that's all I've got to say."

"Josh?" Glory had gone into the shack to get something from under her mattress before they'd come out here, and now she drew it from the folds of her coat. "This was Jackson's Bible," she told him, and she opened the dog-eared, battered old book. "Can I read something from it?"

"Yes. Please."

She found the part she was looking for, on a page that was crinkled and hardly legible anymore. "Lord," she began reading, "let me know my end, and what is the measure of my days; let me know how fleetin' my life is! Behold, Thou hast made my days a few handbreadths, and my lifetime is nothin' in Thy sight. Surely every man stands as a mere breath! Surely every man goes about as a shadow! Surely for nought are they in turmoil; man heaps up, and knows not who will gather."

She rested her hand on Aaron's shoulder. "And now, Lord, for what do I wait?" she read. "My hope is in Thee. Deliver me from all my transgressions. Make me not the scorn of the fool. I am dumb, I do not open my mouth; for it is Thou who hast done it. Remove Thy stroke from me; I am spent by the blows of Thy hand. When Thou dost chasten man with rebukes for sin, Thou dost consume like a moth what is dear to him; surely every man is a mere breath!"

Josh heard the crows cawing, way off in the distance. The mist was undisturbed by wind, and Josh could only see the immediate area around Rusty's grave.

"Hear my prayer, oh Lord, and give ear to my cry; hold not Thy peace at my tears! For I am thy passin' guest, a sojourner, like all my fathers. Look away from me, that I may know gladness, before I depart and be no more." Glory hesitated for a few seconds, her head bowed, and then she closed the Bible. "That was the 39th Psalm," she told Josh. "Jackson used to like for me to read it to him."

Josh nodded, stared down at the coffin a moment longer—then scooped up the first shovelful of earth and dropped it into the grave.

When the grave was filled and the dirt was packed tight, Josh tapped the pine wood marker into the ground. The young wood carver had done a good job on it, and it would last a while.

"Mite cold out here," Anna McClay said. "We ought to be getting back."

Josh gave the pickaxe and shovel to John Gallagher and walked over to where Swan lay sleeping in the folds of her coat. He bent down to pick her up, and he felt a chill breeze sweep past him. The walls of mist shifted and swirled.

He heard something rustle in the breeze.

A noise like leaves being disturbed, somewhere off through the mist to his right.

The breeze faltered and died, and the sound was gone. Josh stood up, staring in the direction from which it had come. There's nothing out here, he thought. This is an empty field.

"What is it?" Glory asked, standing beside him.

"Listen," he said softly.

"I don't hear anything."

"Come on!" Anna called. "You're gonna freeze your butts solid out here!"

The air moved again, a breath of cold wind slanting from a different angle across the field.

And then both Josh and Glory heard the rustling noise, and Josh looked at her and said, "What's *that?*"

She couldn't answer.

Josh realized he hadn't seen Mule for a while; the horse could be anywhere out on the field, hidden by the mist. He took a step toward the rustling noise, and as the wind ebbed the sound ebbed as well. But he kept walking, and heard Zachial shout, "Come on, Josh!" He continued on, and Glory followed with Aaron right at her side.

The wind turned. The rustling sound was getting nearer. Josh was reminded of a hot summer day when he was a boy, lying on his back in a field of high grass, chewing on a weed and listening to the wind sing like a harp.

The mist was tattering apart like old cloth. Josh vaguely made out Mule's shape through it, about fifteen or twenty feet ahead. He heard the horse whinny—and then Josh abruptly stopped in his tracks, because right in front of him was something wonderful.

It was a row of plants, all about two feet tall, and as the breeze stirred the mist away the long, slender fronds swayed and rustled together.

Josh reached down, gently running his fingers over one of the delicate stalks. The plant was a pale green, but scattered on the fronds were dark red splotches that almost resembled blood stains.

"My Lord," Glory breathed. "Josh . . . that's new corn growin'!"

And Josh remembered the dried kernel that had been stuck to the blood-caked palm of Swan's hand. He knew what she'd been doing out there in the cold and dark.

The wind picked up strength, shrilled around Josh's head and made the young cornstalks dance. It punched holes through the gray walls of mist, and then the mist began to lift, and in the next moment Josh and Glory could see most of the field around them.

They stood amid several irregular, weaving rows of pale green stalks, all about two feet high and all spotted with what

Josh realized could very well have been drops of Swan's blood, absorbed right into the dirt and the dormant roots like fuel into a thirsty engine. The sight of green life in that devastated, snow-swept field almost knocked Josh to his knees; it was like seeing color again after a long blindness. Mule was nibbling tentatively at one of the plants, and a few crows swirled over his head, cawing indignantly. He snapped at them, then chased them between the rows with the exuberance of a colt.

"I don't know what's inside that girl," Josh recalled Sly Moody saying, "but she's got the power of life!"

He shook his head, unable to find words. He reached out to the stalk in front of him and touched a small green nub that he knew was an ear of corn, forming in its protective sheath. There were four or five others just on the one stalk alone.

"Mister," Sly Moody had said, "that Swan could wake the whole land up again!"

Yes, Josh thought, his heart pounding. Yes, she can.

And now he understood at last the commandment that had come from PawPaw's lips back in the dark basement in Kansas.

He heard a holler and whoop, and he looked back to see John Gallagher running toward them. Behind him, Zachial and Gene Scully followed. Anna stood, staring with her mouth open, next to the teen-age girl. John fell down on his knees before one of the stalks and touched it with trembling hands. "It's alive!" he said. "The earth's still alive! Oh, God . . . oh, Jesus, we're going to have *food!*"

"Josh . . . how can . . . this *be?*" Glory asked him, while Aaron grinned and poked at a stalk with Crybaby.

He inhaled the air. It seemed fresher, cleaner, infused with electricity. He looked at Glory, and his deformed mouth smiled. "I want to tell you about Swan," he said, his voice shaking. "I want to tell everybody in Mary's Rest about her. She's got the power of life in her, Glory. She can wake the whole land up again!" And then he was running across the field toward the figure that lay on the ground, and he bent down and lifted her in his arms and squeezed her against him.

"She can!" he shouted. His voice rolled like thunder toward the shacks of Mary's Rest. "She *can!*"

Swan shifted drowsily. The slit of her mouth opened, and she asked in a soft, irritated voice, "Can *what?*"

Sixty-five

The wind had strengthened and was blowing through the forest from the southwest. It carried the aroma of woodsmoke, mingled with a bitter, sulphurous smell that made Sister think of rotten eggs. And then she, Paul, Robin Oakes and the three other highwaymen emerged from the forest onto a wide field covered with ashy snow. Ahead of them, lying under a haze of smoke from hundreds of stove pipe chimneys, were the close-clustered shacks and alleys of a settlement.

"That's Mary's Rest," Robin said. He stopped, gazing around at the field. "And I think this is where I saw Swan and the big dude. Yeah. I think it is."

Sister knew it was. They were close now, very close. Her nerves were jangling, and she wanted to run toward those shacks, but her aching, weary legs would not permit it. One step at a time, she thought. One step and then the next gets you where you're going.

They neared a mudhole full of skeletons. The sulphurous odor was coming off it, and they gave it a wide berth as they passed. But Sister didn't even mind that smell; she felt as if she were dreamwalking in real life, exhilarated and strong, her gaze set toward the smoke-shrouded shacks. And then she *knew* she must be dreaming, because she imagined she heard the skittering music of a fiddle.

"Look there," Paul said, and he pointed.

Off to their left was a gathering of what looked to be thirty or forty people, possibly more. They were dancing in the snow, doing old-fashioned clogging steps and square-dance spins around a bonfire. Sister saw musicians: an old man in a faded red cap and a fleece-lined coat, sawing away at a fiddle; a white-bearded black man seated on a chair, scraping a stone across the ribs of a washboard he held between his knees; a young boy plucking chords on a guitar; and a thick-set woman beating a cardboard box like a bass drum. Their music was rough, but it swelled like a raw-boned symphony across the field, inviting the dancers to clog and spin with greater abandon. Snow kicked from their heels, and Sister heard merry shouts and whoops over the music. It had been a long time since she'd heard music, and she'd never seen a sight like this before: They were having a hoedown in the midst of a wasteland.

But then Sister realized that it was not quite a wasteland, for beyond the bonfire and the dancers were several rows of small, pale green plants. Sister heard Paul say, awestruck, "My God! Something's *growing* again!"

They walked across the field toward the celebrants and passed what appeared to be a newly-dug grave. There was a pinewood marker with RUSTY WEATHERS carved into it. Sleep well, she thought—and then they were getting close to the bonfire, and some of the people stopped dancing to watch their approach.

The music faltered and ceased with a last fiddle whine. "How do," a man in a dark green coat said, stepping away from the woman he'd been dancing with. He was wearing a Braves baseball cap, and underneath its brim almost all of his face was scarred by an ugly brown keloid; but he was smiling, and his eyes were bright.

"Hello," Sister replied. The faces here were different from others she'd seen. They were hopeful, joyful faces, in spite of the scars and keloids that marred many, in spite of the protruding cheekbones and sunken eyes that spoke of long hunger, in spite of the pallid skin that had not felt the sun in seven years. She stared at the pale green plants, mesmerized by their motion as they swayed in the wind. Paul walked past her and bent over to reach toward one of them with a trembling hand, as if he feared the delicate wonder might evaporate like smoke.

"She says not to touch 'em," the black man who'd been scraping the washboard said. "She says to let 'em be, and they'll take care of themselves."

Paul drew his hand back. "It's been . . . a long time since I've seen anything growing," he said. "I thought the earth was dead. What *is* it?"

"Corn," another man told him. "Stalks just came up almost overnight. I used to be a farmer, and I thought the dirt wasn't fit to plant in, too. Thought the radiation and the cold had about finished it." He shrugged, admiring the green stalks. "I'm glad to be wrong. 'Course, they're not too strong yet, but anything that grows in *that* dirt—well, it's a miracle."

"She says to let 'em be," the black musician continued. "Says she can seed a whole crop field if we lets these first ones ripen, and we stands guard and keeps them crows away."

"She's sick, though." The husky woman, who had a vivid red keloid on her face, laid aside the cardboard box she'd been beating time to. "She's burnin' up with fever, and there ain't no medicine."

"She," Sister repeated. She heard herself speaking as if in a dream. "Who are you talking about?"

"The girl," Anna McClay said. "Swan's her name. She's in pretty bad shape. Got that stuff on her face even worse than *you* do, and she's blind to boot."

"Swan." Sister's knees were weak.

"She done this." The black musician motioned toward the young cornstalks. "Planted 'em with her own hands. Everybody knows it. That Josh fella's tellin' the whole town." He looked at Sister, grinned and showed a single gold tooth in the front of his head. "Ain't it *something?*" he said proudly.

"Where have you folks come from?" Anna asked.

"A long way off," Sister replied, close to tears. "A long, long way."

"Where's the girl now?" Paul took a few steps toward Anna McClay. His own heart was pounding and the faint, rich odor of the stalks had been sweeter than the smell of any whiskey he'd ever poured into a glass.

Anna pointed at Mary's Rest. "That way. In Glory Bowen's shack. It ain't too far."

"Take us there," Paul urged. "Please."

Anna hesitated, trying to read their eyes like she used to do with the marks strolling on the carny midway. Both of them were strong and steady, she decided, and furthermore they would take no shit. The gaunt boy with the long hair full of feathers and bones looked to be a real hell-raiser, and the other kids appeared pretty tough, too; all of them probably knew very well how to use the rifles they were carrying. She'd already seen that the man had a gun tucked down in the waistband of his trousers, and the woman most likely was packing iron as well. But both of them had a need in their eyes, too, like the glimmer of a fire that burned deep inside. Josh had told her to be wary of strangers who wanted to see Swan, but she knew it was not for her to deny that need. "Come on, then," she said, and she walked toward the shacks. Behind them, the fiddler warmed his hands at the fire and then began playing again, and the black man scraped merrily at his washboard as the celebrants danced.

They followed Anna McClay through the alleys of Mary's Rest. And, as Sister turned a corner about five or six paces behind the other woman, something shot out into her path from the mouth of another alley. She had to draw up sharply to keep from stumbling and falling, and suddenly she had a sensation of numbing cold that seemed to draw the breath from her lungs. She instinctively whipped the shotgun from its holster beneath her coat—and stuck it into the leering face of a man who sat in a child's red wagon.

He stared up at her through deep-set eyes, and he lifted one hand toward the satchel that Sister held under her arm. "Welcome," he said.

Sister was aware of a series of clicks, and the man's fathomless eyes moved to look past her. She glanced back and saw that Paul had his Magnum in his hand. Robin was aiming his rifle, and so were the other three boys. They all had a deadly bead on the man in the red wagon.

Sister stared into his eyes; he cocked his head to one side, the grin widening to show a mouthful of broken teeth. Slowly he withdrew his hand and laid it across the stumps of his legs.

"That's Mr. Welcome," Anna said. "He's crazy. Just push him to one side."

The man's gaze ticked between Sister's face and the satchel. He nodded. "Welcome," he whispered.

Her finger tightened on the shotgun's trigger. Tendrils of cold seemed to be sliding around her, gripping her, slithering down through her clothes. The shotgun's barrel was about eight inches from the man's head, and Sister was seized with an impulse to blow that hideous, grinning face away. But what would be under it? she wondered. Tissue and bone—or *another* face?

Because she thought she recognized the cunning glint in those eyes, like a beast patiently waiting for the moment to destroy. She thought she saw something of a monster who'd called himself Doyle Halland in them.

Her finger twitched, ready to fire. Ready to unmask the face.

"Come on," Anna said. "He won't bite you. Fella's been hangin' around here a couple of days, and he's crazy, but he ain't dangerous."

The man in the red wagon suddenly drew a lungful of air and released it in a quiet hiss between clenched teeth. He lifted his fist and held it up before Sister's face for a few seconds; then one finger protruded to form the barrel of an imaginary weapon aimed at her head. "Gun goes bang," he said.

Anna laughed. "See? He's a looney!"

Sister hesitated. Shoot him, she thought. Squeeze the trigger—just a little harder. You *know* who it is. Shoot him!

But . . . what if I'm wrong? The shotgun's barrel wavered.

And then her chance was gone. The man cackled, muttered

something in a singsong rhythm and pushed himself past her with his arms. He entered an alley to the left, and Sister stood watching the demented cripple go. He did not look back.

"Gettin' colder." Anna shivered, pulling her collar up. She motioned ahead. "Glory Bowen's shack is this way."

The man in the red wagon turned down another alley and pushed himself out of Sister's sight. She let out the breath she'd been holding, and the white steam floated past her face. Then she returned her shotgun to its sheath and followed the other woman again, but she felt like an exposed nerve.

Another bonfire was burning on the main street of Mary's Rest, casting warmth and light over twelve or fifteen people who stood around it. The ugliest, most swaybacked old horse Sister had ever seen was tied to a post on the front porch of one of the shacks; the horse was covered with a number of blankets to keep him warm, and his head was nodding as if he were about to fall asleep. Nearby, a small black boy was trying to balance a crooked stick on the ends of his fingers.

Two men, both armed with rifles, sat on the shack's cinder block front steps, talking and drinking hot coffee from clay mugs. Their attention turned from their quiet talk to Anna.

"Folks here say they want to see the girl," Anna told one of them, a man in a plaid coat and tan cap. "I think they're all right."

He'd seen their weapons, and now he rested his own rifle across his knees. "Josh said no strangers were allowed in."

Sister stepped forward. "My name's Sister. This is Paul Thorson, Robin Oakes, and I can vouch for the other boys. Now, if you'll tell me your name, we won't be strangers anymore, will we?"

"Gene Scully," he answered. "Are you folks from around here?"

"No," Paul said. "Listen, we're not going to hurt Swan. We just want to see her. We want to talk to her."

"She can't talk," Scully said. "She's sick. And I've been told not to let any strangers through that door."

"You need your ears cleaned out, mister?" Robin, smiling with cold menace, stood between Sister and Paul. "We've come a long way. We said we want to see the girl."

Scully rose to his feet, ready to swing the rifle's barrel up at them. Beside him, Zachial Epstein also nervously stood up. The silence stretched. And then Sister gritted her teeth and started to climb the steps, and if the men tried to stop her, she thought, she was going to blast both of them to hell.

"Hey, Anna!" Aaron called suddenly. "Come look at the magic!"

She glanced over at him. He was still playing with that dumb stick. "Later," she told him. Aaron shrugged and started swinging it like an imaginary sword. Anna returned to the problem at hand. "Listen, we don't need any more shit around here. And nobody needs to get riled or hurt, either. Gene, why don't you just go on in and ask Josh to come speak to these folks?"

"We want to see *Swan.*" Anger reddened Paul's face. "We're not going to be turned back, lady!"

"Who's Josh?" Sister asked.

"Fella who's been travelin' with the girl. Takin' care of her. Her guardian, I guess you'd say. Well? Do you want to state your business to him, or not?"

"Bring him out."

"Go get him, Gene." Anna took the rifle from him and immediately turned it on the strangers. "And now you folks can dump all that hardware in a neat pile next to the steps, if you please. You too, kiddies—I ain't your mama! Drop 'em!"

Scully started into the shack, but Sister said, "Wait!" She opened her satchel, attracting the direct interest of the rifle the other woman had, but she took care to move slowly, without threat. She reached past the glass ring into the bottom of the satchel, fished out what she was after and handed it up to Anna. "Here. Give this to Josh. It might mean something to him."

Anna looked at it, frowned and passed it back to Scully, who took it and went in.

They waited. "Some town you've got here," Robin said. "How much rent do the rats charge?"

Anna smiled. "You'll be glad we've got plenty of rats after you taste some cooked up in a stew, smartass."

"We were better off back in the cave," he told Sister. "At

least we had fresh air. This place smells like somebody's shit bucket over—"

The door opened, and a monster walked out. Gene Scully followed behind. Robin just stood and stared, his mouth agape, because he'd never seen anybody so ugly before. The big dude was easily the size of three regular men.

"Jesus," Paul whispered, and he couldn't help but be repelled. The man's single eye fixed on him for a few seconds, then moved to Sister.

She didn't budge. Monster or not, she'd decided, nobody was going to stop her from seeing Swan.

"Where did you find this?" Josh asked, holding up the object Gene Scully had given him.

"In the parking lot of what used to be a K-Mart. It was in a town in Kansas called—"

"Matheson," Josh interrupted. "I know the place, from a long time ago. This belonged to a friend. But . . . do I know *you?*"

"No. Paul and I have been traveling for years, searching for someone. And I think the person we've been led toward is in that house. Will you let us see her?"

Josh looked again at what he held in his hand. It was one of Leona Skelton's tarot cards, the colors faded, the edges curled and yellowed. The legend on the card said *THE EMPRESS.*

"Yes," Josh said. "But just you and the man." And he opened the door to let them enter.

Sixty-six

"You sure?" Glory asked as Josh shut the door. She was stirring a pot of root soup on the stove, and she eyed the two strangers cautiously. "I don't like the looks of 'em."

"Sorry," Paul told her. "I left my tuxedo at the cleaners this morning." The room smelled like sassafras, and the stove was putting out a lot of heat. A couple of lanterns were set in the room, and by their smoky light both Paul and Sister could see what appeared to be blood stains on the floor.

"We had some trouble here last night," Josh explained. "That's why we have to be so careful about strangers wanting to see Swan."

Sister went cold, in spite of the room's comfortable warmth. She was thinking of that grinning cripple in the child's red wagon. If it was *him,* he could be wearing any face. Any face at all. She wished she had that moment back, wished she'd blown the mask right off his skull to see what was hiding behind it.

Josh turned up a lantern's wick and examined the tarot card again. "So you found this in Matheson. Okay. But how did this card lead you here?"

"It wasn't the card that brought us. Tell me: Is there a tree somewhere that's in blossom, with Swan's name burned into the trunk? I remember smelling apples. Is it an apple tree in bloom?"

"Yes. But that's back about fifty or sixty miles from here! Did Sly Moody send you after us?"

She shook her head, reaching into the satchel. "This sent us here," she said, and she withdrew the glass circle.

The colors leaped and pulsed. Glory gasped, dropping her spoon as her hand fluttered to her mouth. The walls glittered with lights. Josh stared at it, transfixed by its beauty, and then he laid the Empress card down on the table.

"Who are you?" he asked softly. "Why are you looking for Swan—and where did you find that?"

Sister said, "I think we have a lot to talk about. I want to know everything about you, and everything about Swan. I want to hear everything that's happened to you, and I want to tell you our stories, too. But right now I have to see her. *Please.*"

With an effort, Josh pulled his gaze away from the glass ring and looked into Sister's face. Looked long and deep, saw the tribulations and hardships there; but he also recognized tenacity and a will of iron. He nodded and led Paul and Sister into the next room.

A single lantern backed with a shiny piece of tin hung on the wall, casting a muted golden glow. Swan lay on Glory's iron-framed cot, on the mattress that was stuffed with rags and papers. She was covered with a number of blankets that various people had donated, and her face was turned away from the light.

Josh walked to the bedside, lifted the blankets and gently touched Swan's shoulder. She was still burning up with fever, yet she shivered and held the blankets. "Swan? Can you hear me?"

Her breathing was harsh. Sister's hand found Paul's and clenched it. In her other hand, the shades of the glass ring had turned to silver and gold.

"Swan?" Josh whispered. "Someone's come to see you."

She heard his voice, summoning her back from a nightmare landscape where a skeleton on a skeletal horse reaped a human field. Pain shot through the nerves and bones of her face. "Josh?" she replied. "Rusty . . . where's Rusty?"

"I told you. We buried him this morning, out in the field."

"Oh. I remember now." Her voice was weak, drifting toward delirium again. "Tell them . . . to watch the corn. Keep the crows away. But . . . tell them not to touch it yet, Josh. Tell them."

"I have. They're doing what you say." He motioned Paul and Sister closer. "Someone's here to see you. They say they've come a long way."

"Who . . . are they?"

"A man and a woman. They're here right now. Can you speak to them?"

Swan tried to focus her mind on what he was saying. She could sense someone else in the room, waiting. And there was something more, too; Swan didn't know what it was, but she felt her skin tingling as if in anticipation of a touch. In her mind she was a child again, staring with fascination at the fireflies' lights as they glowed against the window screen.

"Yes," she decided. "Will you help me sit up?"

He did, propping a couple of pillows up to support her. As Josh stepped away from the cot Paul and Sister had their first view of Swan's growth-covered head. Both eyeholes were now sealed up, and there were only small slits over her nostrils and mouth. It was the most horrifying Job's Mask that Sister had ever seen, much worse even than Josh's, and she had to fight off a shudder. Paul flinched, wondering how she could breathe or eat through that hideous crust.

"Who's there?" Swan whispered.

"My name is . . ." She lost her voice. She was scared to death. Then she drew her shoulders back, pulled in a deep breath and stepped to the side of the cot. "You can call me Sister," she began. "There's a man named Paul Thorson with me. We've—" Sister glanced quickly at Josh, then back to the girl. Swan's head was cocked to one side, listening through a tiny hole at her ear. "We've been looking for you for a long time. Seven years. We missed you in Matheson, Kansas; I believe we probably missed you in a lot of places and never knew it. I found a doll that belonged to you. Do you remember it?"

Swan did remember. "My Cookie Monster. I lost it in Matheson. I used to love that thing when I was a little girl."

Sister had to listen hard to understand everything she was saying. "I wish I could've brought it to you, but it didn't survive the trip."

"That's all right," Swan said. "I'm not a little girl anymore." She suddenly lifted her bandaged right hand and felt in the air for the woman's face. Sister drew away, but then she realized that Swan wanted to know what she looked like. Sister gently grasped her slender wrist and guided the hand over her facial features. Swan's touch was as soft as smoke.

Her fingers stopped when they found the growths. "You've got it, too." Swan's fingers continued across Sister's left cheek, then down to her chin. "Feels like a cobblestone road."

"I guess so. A doctor friend of ours calls it 'Job's Mask.' He thinks what's in the air causes some people's skin to crust over. Damned if I can figure out why it just screws up the face and head, though." She reached out and touched the girl's forehead, then quickly jerked her hand back. Under the Job's Mask, Swan was running a fever that had almost scorched Sister's fingers. "Does it hurt?" Sister asked.

"Yes. It didn't used to hurt so much. but now . . . it's all the time."

"Yeah, mine, too. How old are you?"

"Sixteen. Josh keeps track of my birthday for me. How old are *you?*"

"I'm—" She couldn't recall. She hadn't kept up with her birthdays. "Let's see, I think I was in my forties on the seventeenth of July. I guess I might be in my fifties now. *Early* fifties, that is. I feel like I'm gaining on eighty."

"Josh said . . . you came a long way to see me." Swan's head was heavy, and she was getting very tired again. "Why?"

"I'm not sure," Sister admitted. "But we've been looking for you for seven years, because of *this.*" And she held the glowing ring with its single remaining spire up before Swan's face.

Swan's skin prickled. She sensed a bright light beating at her sealed-up eyeholes. "What is it?"

"I think . . . it's a lot of things, all rolled up into a circle of beautiful glass and filled with jewels. I found it on the seventeenth of July, in New York City. I think it's a ring of miracles, Swan. I think it's a gift . . . like a magic survival kit. Or a life ring. Maybe anybody could've found it, maybe I'm the only one who could have. I don't know. But I do know that it led Paul and me to you. I wish I knew why. All I can say is that . . . I think you're someone very special, Swan. I saw the corn growing out in that field, where nothing ought to be alive. I looked into this glass ring and I saw a tree in bloom, with your name burned into the wood." She leaned forward, her heart pounding. "I think there's work ahead of you. Very important work, enough to fill up a lifetime. After seeing that corn growing out there . . . I think I know what it is."

Swan was listening carefully. She didn't feel very special; she just felt weary, and the fever was pulling at her again, trying to drag her back to that awful place where the bloody scythe reaped a human field. And then what Sister had said dawned on her: "A ring of miracles . . . all rolled up into a circle of beautiful glass and filled with jewels."

She thought of the magic mirror and the figure she'd seen bearing a ring of light. That figure, she knew, had been the woman who now stood at her bedside, and what she'd been carrying had finally arrived.

Swan held out both hands toward the light. "May I . . . hold it?"

Sister glanced at Josh. He was standing behind Paul, and Glory had come from the other room. Josh didn't know what was going on, and all this ring of miracles talk was beyond him—but he trusted the woman, and he let himself nod.

"Here." Sister put it into Swan's hands.

Her fingers curled around the glass. There was heat in it, a heat that began to spread into her hands, through her wrists and forearms. Under the bandages, the raw skin of her hands had begun itching and stinging. *"Oh,"* she said, more in surprise than in pain.

"Swan?" Josh stepped forward, alarmed at the sound. The glass circle was getting brighter and pulsating faster. "Are you o—"

The ring flared like a golden nova. All of them were blinded for a few seconds as the room was lit up as if by the flaring of a million candles. The memory of the white-hot blast in front of PawPaw's grocery streaked through Josh's mind.

Now a searing pain coursed in Swan's hands, and her fingers seemed locked to the glass. The pain rippled through her bones and she started to cry out, but in the next instant the anguish had passed, and left in her mind were scenes beautiful beyond dreams: fields of golden corn and wheat, orchards where trees bent under the weight of fruit, meadows of flowers and verdant green forests stirred by a breeze. The images poured forth as if from a cornucopia, so vivid that Swan smelled the aromas of barley, apples, plums and cherry trees in full bloom. She beheld dandelions blowing in the wind, forests of oaks dripping acorns into the moss, maples running sap and sunflowers thrusting up from the earth.

Yes, Swan thought as the images continued to flood through her mind in brilliant patterns of color and light. My work.

I know what my work is now.

Josh was first to recover from the glare. He saw that Swan's hands were engulfed by golden fire, the flames licking up along her arms. She's burning up! he realized and, horrified, he shoved Sister aside and grabbed the fiery ring to pull it away from Swan.

But as soon as his fingertips touched the glass, he was flung backward with such force that he left his feet before crashing into the wall, narrowly missing breaking most of the bones in Paul's body. The air was forced from his lungs with a noise like a ruptured steam pipe, and he crumpled to the floor, dazed from the worst knock he'd taken since Haystacks Muldoon had thrown him from the wrestling ring in Winston-Salem eleven years before. Damn thing *repelled* me, he thought, when thinking was possible again. He tried to struggle up and realized that the flaming ring had been cool under his fingers.

Still half blinded, Sister saw the strange fire, too, saw it crawling up Swan's arms; it snapped like the uncoiling of a whip and began to wrap itself around the girl's head.

The fire—noiseless and without heat—had shrouded Swan's face and head before Josh could get up from the floor. Swan made no sound and lay motionless, but she could hear a sizzling over the wonderful scenes that kept swirling through her mind.

Sister was about to grasp the ring herself, but as she reached for it Josh charged toward the cot again, almost flung her through the wall, braced his legs and got ready to withstand the jolt as he clenched his fingers around the ring.

This time it came smoothly free from Swan's hands. As he turned to smash it against the wall he heard Sister scream "*No!*" and she was on him like a wildcat.

"Wait!" Paul shouted. "Look at her!"

Josh held Sister at arm's length and swiveled his head toward Swan.

The golden flames that covered her hands were going out. The bandages had turned black.

As they watched they saw the fire—or what had *appeared* to be fire—being drawn into the Job's Mask like liquid into a dry sponge. The flames rippled, flared, and then disappeared.

Sister wrenched the ring from him and backed out of his reach. He went to Swan's side, put his arms beneath her shoulders and lifted her up, supporting her head with one hand. "Swan!" His voice was frantic. "Swan, answer me!"

She was silent.

"You've killed her!" Glory shouted at Sister. "God A'mighty, you've killed her with that damned thing!" She rushed to the bedside, while Sister retreated against the far wall. Her mind was reeling, and the explosion of light still burned behind her eyes.

But Josh could feel Swan's heart beating like the wings of a captured bird against a cage. He rocked the girl in his arms, praying that this shock wouldn't be the final burden. He looked up fiercely at Sister and Paul. "Get them out of here!" he told Glory. "Call Anna! Tell her to lock them away somewhere! Get them out before I kill them my—"

Swan's hand drifted up, touched Josh's lips to silence him.

Sister stared at the glass ring; its colors had paled, and some of the trapped jewels had turned ebony, like little burned-up pieces of charcoal. But the colors were getting stronger again, as if drawing power from her own body. Glory grasped her arm to pull her from the room, but Sister jerked free. Then Glory ran out to summon Anna McClay, who came with the rifle, ready for business.

"Get them out!" Josh shouted. "And get that thing away from her!"

Anna started to reach for the ring. Sister's fist was faster; she struck the other woman with a noise like a hammer whacking a board, and Anna McClay went down with a bloody nose. Anna struggled to her feet and aimed the rifle point-blank at Sister's head.

"Stop it!" Swan said suddenly, her voice frail. She'd heard the shouts, the scuffling and the sound of the blow. The majestic scenes that had so ignited her imagination began to fade. "Stop it," she repeated. Strength was returning to her voice. "No more fighting."

"They tried to kill you with that thing!" Josh said.

"No, we didn't!" Paul protested. "We came here to see her, that's all! We weren't trying to hurt her!"

Josh ignored him. "Are you all right?" he asked Swan.

"Yes. Just tired. But Josh . . . when I held it . . . I saw wonderful things. *Wonderful* things."

"What things?"

"Things . . . that could be," she replied. "If I want them to be, if I work hard enough."

"Josh?" Anna was itching to put a bullet through the

scraggly old woman who'd decked her. She wiped her nose with the back of her hand. "You want me to lock 'em up somewhere?"

"No!" Swan said. "Leave them alone. They weren't trying to hurt me."

"Well, this bitch sure hurt *me!* I think my damned schnozz is busted!"

Josh eased Swan's head down onto the pillow. His face felt strange—itching and burning—where Swan's fingers had touched. "You sure you're okay?" he asked. "I don't want you to be—" And then he glanced at one of her hands, and his voice trailed off. "Don't try to hide it if . . . you're . . ."

The bandages, black and oily-looking, had come loose. Josh could see a glimpse of pink flesh.

He took her hand gently in his own and began to unwind the bandages. The cloth was stiff and started coming apart with little crackling sounds. Sister pushed the rifle barrel out of her face and walked past Anna to the side of the cot. Anna made no move to stop her, because she came forward to see as well.

With nervous fingers, Josh carefully peeled part of the black bandage away. It came off with some of Swan's injured skin adhered to it, and revealed underneath was bright pink, healing flesh.

"What is it?" Swan asked, breaking the silence. "What's wrong?"

He cracked part of the other bandage off. It crumbled like ashes between his fingers, and he saw pink, clean, unscarred skin across a section of Swan's palm. He knew that it should have taken at least a week for Swan's hands to scab over, and maybe a month for them to heal. He'd been most worried about her wounds getting infected, that maybe her hands would be scarred and ruined for the rest of her life. But now . . .

Josh pressed his finger against her pink palm. "Ow!" she said, pulling her hand away from him. "That's sore!" Her hands were stinging and tingling and as warm as if they'd been deeply sunburned. Josh was afraid to peel any more of the bandages off, not wanting to expose the tender skin. He looked up at Glory, who stood beside him, then over at Sister. His gaze fell to the gleaming glass ring in her protective grip.

A ring of miracles, she'd said.

And Josh believed it.

He stood up. "I think we've got a lot to talk about," he said.

"Yes," Sister agreed. "I believe we do."

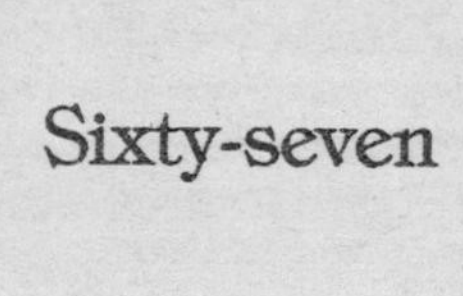

Sixty-seven

The shout of the Lord shook the trailer's walls, and the woman who lay on a bare mattress with a coarse blanket wrapped around her moaned in her tortured sleep. Rudy was crawling into her bed again, and he held an infant with a crushed head; she kicked at him, but his rotting mouth grinned. "Come on, Ssssheila," he chided her, his voice hissing through the blue-edged slash across his throat. "Is that how you treat an old friend?"

"Get away!" she screamed. "Get away . . . get *away!*"

But he was sliding up against her with slimy skin. His eyes had rolled back into his head, and decayed holes cratered his face. "Awwww," he said, "don't be like that, Sheila. We got high and happy too many times for you to kick me out of your bed. You let everybody *else* in these days, don't you?" He offered her the blue-skinned infant. "See?" he said. "I brought you a present."

And then the tiny mouth opened in that battered head and a wail came from it that made Sheila Fontana go rigid, her hands clamped to her ears and tears streaming from her wide-open, staring eyes.

The ghosts fragmented and whirled away, and Sheila was left with her own scream echoing within the filthy trailer.

But the shout of the Lord continued, this time pounding on the trailer's door. A voice from outside yelled, "Shut up, you crazy fool! You tryin' to wake up the fucking *dead?"*

Tears ran down her face, and she felt sick to her stomach; the trailer already smelled of vomit and stale cigarette smoke, and there was a bucket next to her mattress where she relieved herself during the night. She couldn't stop shaking, couldn't get enough air into her lungs. She fumbled for the bottle of vodka that she knew was there on the floor beside her bed, but she couldn't find it, and she wailed again with frustration.

"Come on, open the damned door!" It was Judd Lawry's voice, and he hammered at the door with the butt of his rifle. "He wants you!"

She froze, her fingers finally locked on the neck of the half-full bottle. He wants me, she thought. Her heart kicked. He wants me!

"You hear what I said? He sent me to get you. Come on, get your ass moving!"

She crawled out of bed and stood with the bottle in one hand and the blanket in the other. The trailer was cold, and red light came from a bonfire blazing outside.

"Speak, if you can understand English!" Lawry said.

"Yes," she told him. "I hear you. He wants me." She was shaking, and she dropped the blanket to take the top off the vodka bottle.

"Well, come on then! And he says for you to put on some *perfume* this time!"

"Yes. He wants me. He wants me." She drank from the bottle again, capped it and searched for her lantern and matches. She found them, got the lantern lit and placed it on her dressing table, next to the cracked mirror that hung on the wall. Atop the dresser was a forest of dried-up make-up bottles, lipsticks, bottles of scent that had long ago gone skunky, jars of cream and mascara applicators. Taped to the mirror were yellowed pictures of fresh-faced models clipped from ancient copies of *Glamour* and *Mademoiselle.*

She placed the vodka bottle next to the lantern and sat down in her chair. The mirror caught her face.

Her eyes resembled dull bits of glass sunken into a sickly, heavily lined ruin. Much of her hair had turned from black to a yellowish gray, and at her crown the scalp was beginning to show. Her mouth was tight and etched with deep lines, as if she'd been holding back a scream that she dared not release.

She peered into the eyes that looked back. Make-up, she decided. Sure. I need to use a little make-up. And she opened one of the bottles to smear the stuff on her face like a healing balm, her hands unsteady because she wanted to look pretty for the colonel. He'd been nice to her lately, had called for her several times, had even given her a few bottles of precious alcohol from a deserted liquor store. He wants me, she told herself as she scrawled lipstick across her mouth. The colonel used to prefer the other two women who'd lived in the trailer with Sheila, but Kathy had moved in with a captain and Gina had taken a .45 to bed one night. Which meant that Sheila was on her own in driving the pickup truck that hauled the trailer and earning enough gasoline, food and water to keep both the truck and herself going. She knew most of the other RLs—Recreation Ladies—who followed the Army of Excellence in their own convoy of trucks, cars and trailers; a lot of the women had diseases, some were young girls with ancient eyes, a few enjoyed their work, and most were searching for the "golden dream"—being taken in by an AOE officer who had plenty of supplies and a decent bed.

It's a man's world, Sheila thought. That had never been as true as it was now.

But she was happy, because being summoned to the colonel's trailer meant she wouldn't have to sleep alone and, for a few hours at least, Rudy couldn't come crawling into her bed with his grisly gift.

Rudy had been a kick in life. But in death he was a real drag.

"Hurry it up!" Lawry shouted. "It's cold out here!"

She finished her make-up and ran a brush through her hair. She didn't like to do that, though, because so much of her hair was falling out. Then she searched the many bottles of perfume for the right scent. Most of their labels had come off, but she found the distinctive bottle she wanted and sprayed perfume on her throat. She remembered an ad she'd seen in a *Cosmo* magazine a long time ago: "Every man alive loves Chanel Number 5."

She hurriedly pulled a dark red sweater over her sagging breasts, squeezed herself into a pair of jeans and put on her boots. It was too late to do anything about her fingernails; anyhow, they were all but bitten away. She shrugged into a fur coat that had belonged to Gina. One more peek in the mirror to check her make-up. He wants me! she thought, and then she blew the lantern out, went to the door, unbolted and opened it.

Judd Lawry, his beard cropped close to his jawline and a bandanna wrapped around his forehead, glared at her and laughed. "Jeez!" he said. "You ever heard of a movie called *The Bride of Frankenstein?"*

She knew not to answer him as she dug a key out of the fur coat and locked her door. He was always picking at her, and she hated his guts. Whenever she looked at him she heard the wail of a baby and the sound of a rifle butt striking innocent flesh. She walked right past him, in the direction of Colonel Macklin's silver Airstream command center on the western edge of what had been Sutton, Nebraska.

"You sure do smell nice," Lawry said as he followed her between the parked trailers, trucks, cars and pitched tents of the Army of Excellence. Firelight glinted off the barrel of the M-16 slung over his shoulder. "You smell like an open sore. When's the last time you took a bath?"

She couldn't remember. Bathing used up water, and she didn't have a lot of that to spare.

"I don't know why he wants *you,*" Lawry continued, walking right at her heels. "He could have a young RL, a pretty one. One who takes baths. You're a two-legged lice farm."

She ignored him. She knew he hated her because she'd never let him touch her, not even once. She'd taken on everybody who could pay her with gasoline, food, water, pretty trinkets, cigarettes, clothes or alcohol—but she wouldn't take on Judd Lawry if his prick gushed refined oil. Even in a man's world, a woman had her pride.

He was still ranting at her when she walked between two tents and almost into a squat, square trailer painted pitch black. She stopped abruptly, and Lawry almost barreled into her. His nagging ceased. Both of them knew what went on inside Roland Croninger's black trailer—the AOE's "interrogation center"—and being so close to it stirred in their minds the stories they'd heard of Captain Croninger's inquisition methods. Lawry remembered what Croninger had done to Freddie Kempka years ago, and he knew that the captain was best avoided.

Sheila regained her composure first. She walked past the trailer, its windows sealed with sheet metal, and on toward the colonel's command center. Lawry silently followed.

The Airstream trailer was hooked to the cab of a diesel truck surrounded by six armed guards. Spaced at intervals were fires that burned in oil drums. As Sheila approached, one of the guards rested his hand on the pistol beneath his coat.

"It's okay," Lawry said. "He's expecting her." The guard relaxed and let them pass, and they walked up a set of intricately carved wooden risers that led to the Airstream's closed door. The three-step staircase even had a bannister, into which was cut the grotesque faces of demons with lolling tongues, contorted nude human figures and deformed gargoyles. The subject matter was nightmarish, but the workmanship was beautiful, the faces and figures carved by a hand that knew blades, then sanded and polished to a high luster. Red velvet pads had been tacked down on the surface of each riser, as if on the steps to an emperor's throne. Sheila had never seen the staircase before, but Lawry knew it was a recent gift from the man who'd joined the AOE back in Broken Bow. It galled Lawry that Alvin Mangrim had already been made a corporal, and he wondered how Mangrim had gotten his nose chewed off. He'd seen the man working with the Mechanical Brigade and hanging around with a gnarled little dwarf he called "Imp," and Mangrim was another sonofabitch he wouldn't dare turn his back on.

Lawry knocked on the door.

"Enter," came Colonel Macklin's raspy voice.

They went in. The front room was dark but for the single oil lamp burning atop Macklin's desk. He was sitting behind the desk, studying maps. His right arm lay across the desktop, almost like a forgotten appendage, but the black-gloved palm of his new right hand was turned up, and the lamplight glinted on the sharp points of the many nails that pierced it.

"Thank you, Lieutenant," Macklin said, without lifting his leather-masked face. "You're dismissed."

"Yes, sir." Lawry shot a smirking glance at Sheila, then left the trailer and closed the door.

Macklin was calculating the rate of march between Sutton and Nebraska City, where he planned to lead the Army of Excellence across the Missouri River. But the supplies were dwindling by the day, and the AOE hadn't made a successful raid since the destruction of Franklin Hayes's army back in Broken Bow. Still, the ranks of the AOE continued to swell as stragglers from other dead settlements drifted in, seeking shelter and protection. The AOE had abundant manpower, weapons and ammunition, but the grease that slicked the wheels of forward movement was running out.

The ruins of Sutton had still been smoking when the AOE's advance armored cars pulled in just before full dark. All that was worth taking was already gone, even the clothes and shoes from the piles of dead bodies. There were signs that grenades and Molotov cocktails had been used, and at the eastern edge of the burning debris were the treadmarks of heavy vehicles and the footprints of soldiers marching off through the snow.

And Macklin had realized that there was another army—perhaps as large as or larger than the AOE—heading east right in front of them, looting settlements and taking the supplies that the Army of Excellence needed to survive. Roland had seen blood in the snow and reasoned that there would be wounded soldiers struggling to keep up with the main body. A small recon force might be able to capture some of those stragglers, Roland had suggested. They might be brought back and interrogated. Colonel Macklin had agreed, and Roland had taken Captain Braden, Sergeant Ulrich and a few soldiers out in an armored truck.

"Sit down," the colonel told Sheila.

She walked into the circle of light. A chair had been prepared for her, facing the colonel's desk. She sat down, edgy and not knowing what to expect. In the past, he'd always waited for her in his bed.

He continued to work on his maps and charts. He was dressed in his uniform with the Army of Excellence patch sewn over the breast pocket and four bars of gold-colored thread attached to each shoulder to signify his rank. Covering his scalp was a gray woolen cap, and the black leather mask obscured his face except for his left eye. She hadn't seen him without that mask for several years, and she didn't particularly care to. Behind Macklin was a rack of pistols and rifles, and a black, green and silver AOE flag was tacked neatly to the pine paneling.

He let her wait a few more minutes, and then he lifted his head. His frosty blue eye chilled her. "Hello, Sheila."

"Hello."

"Were you alone? Or did you have company?"

"I was alone." She had to listen hard to understand all his words. His speech had gotten worse since the last time she'd visited there, less than a week ago.

"Well," Macklin said, "sometimes it's good to sleep alone. You get more rest that way, don't you?" He opened a filigreed silver box that sat atop his desk. In it were about twenty precious cigarettes—not soggy butts or rerolled chewing tobacco, but the real thing. He offered the box to her, and she immediately took a cigarette. "Take another," he urged. She took two more. Macklin pushed a pack of matches across the desktop to her, and she lit up the first cigarette and inhaled it like true oxygen.

"Remember when we bluffed our way into here?" he asked her. "You, me and Roland? Remember when we bargained with Freddie Kempka?"

"Yeah." She'd wished a thousand times that she still had a

supply of cocaine and uppers, but that stuff was hard to come by these days. "I do."

"I trust you, Sheila. You and Roland are about the only ones I *can* trust." He pulled his right arm toward him and cradled it against his chest. "That's because we know each other so well. People who've been through so much together *should* trust each other." His gaze lifted from Sheila's face. He looked at the Shadow Soldier, who was standing behind her chair, just at the edge of the darkness. His eye shifted back to her again. "Have you been entertaining many officers lately?"

"A few."

"How about Captain Hewlitt? Sergeant Oldfield? Lieutenant Vann? Any of those?"

"I guess." She shrugged, and her mouth curled into a faint smile through the haze of smoke. "They come and go."

"I've heard things," Macklin said. "It seems that some of my officers—I don't know who—aren't very pleased with the way I'm running the Army of Excellence. They think we should plant roots, start a settlement of our own. They don't understand why we're moving east, or why we have to stamp out the mark of Cain. They can't see the grand scheme, Sheila. Especially the young ones—like Hewlitt and Vann. I made them officers against my better judgment. I should have waited to see what they were made of. Well, I know now. I believe they want to take my command away from me."

She was silent. Tonight there would be no screwing, just one of the colonel's sessions of raving. But that was fine with Sheila; at least Rudy couldn't find her here.

"Look at this," he said, and he turned one of the maps that he'd been working on toward her. It was an old, creased and stained map of the United States, torn from an atlas. The names of the states had been marked through, and large areas were outlined heavily in pencil. Substitute names had been scrawled in: "Summerland" for the area of Florida, Georgia, Alabama, Mississippi and Louisiana; "Industrial Park" for Illinois, Indiana, Kentucky and Tennessee; "Port Complex" for the Carolinas and Virginia; "Military Training" for the southwest, and also for Maine, New Hampshire and Vermont. The Dakotas, Montana and Wyoming were marked "Prison Area."

And across the entire map Macklin had written "AOE—America of Enlightenment."

"This is the grand scheme," he told her. "But to make it come true, we have to destroy the people who don't think like us. We have to wipe out the mark of Cain." He turned the map around and grazed the nails across it. "We have to stamp it out so we can forget what happened and put it behind us. But we've got to get ready for the Russians, too! They're going to be dropping paratroopers and landing invasion barges. They think we're dead and finished, but they're *wrong.*" He leaned forward, the nails digging into the scarred desktop. "We'll pay them back. We'll pay the bastards back a thousand times!"

He blinked. The Shadow Soldier was smiling thinly, his face streaked with camouflage paint under the brow of his helmet. Macklin's heart was hammering, and he had to wait for it to settle down before he could speak again. "They don't see the grand scheme," he said quietly. "The AOE has almost five thousand soldiers now. We have to move to survive, and we have to take what we need. We're not farmers—we're *warriors!* That's why I need you, Sheila."

"Need *me?* For what?"

"You get around. You hear things. You know most of the other RLs. I want you to find out whom I can trust among my officers—and who needs to be disposed of. Like I say, I don't trust Hewlitt, Oldfield or Vann, but it's nothing I can prove before a court-martial. And the cancer might run deep, very deep. They think that just because of *this*"—and he touched the black leather mask—"I'm not fit for command anymore. But this isn't the mark of Cain. This is different. This'll go away when the air gets clean again and the sun comes out. The mark of Cain won't go away until we destroy it." He angled his head to one side, watching her carefully. "For every name you can put on an execution list—and *verify*—I'll give you a carton of cigarettes and two bottles of liquor. How about it?"

It was a generous offer. She already had a name in mind; it started with an L and ended with a Y. But she didn't know if Lawry was loyal or not. Anyway, she sure would like to see him in front of a firing squad—but only if she could smash his brains out first. She was about to answer when someone knocked at the door.

"Colonel?" It was Roland Croninger's voice. "I've got a couple of presents for you."

Macklin strode to the door and opened it. Outside, illuminated by the firelight, was the armored truck that Captain Croninger and the others had gone out in. And chained to the rear fender were two men, both bloody and battered, one on his knees and the other standing straight and staring defiantly.

"We found them about twelve miles east, along Highway 6," Roland said. He was wearing his long coat, with the hood pulled up over his head. An automatic rifle was slung over his shoulder, and at his waist was a holstered .45. The dirty bandages still covered most of his face, but growths protruded like gnarled knuckles through spaces between them. The firelight burned red in the lenses of his goggles. "There were four of them at first. They wanted to fight. Captain Braden bought it; we brought back his clothes and guns. Anyway, that's what left of them." Roland's growth-knotted lips parted in a slick smile. "We decided to see if they could keep up with the truck."

"Have you questioned them?"

"No, sir. We were saving that."

Macklin walked past him, down the carved staircase. Roland followed, and Sheila Fontana watched from the doorway.

The soldiers who stood around the two men parted to make way for Colonel Macklin. He stood face to face with the prisoner who refused to fall in defeat, even though the man's knees were shredded and he had a bullet wound in his left shoulder. "What's your name?" Macklin asked him.

The man closed his eyes. "The Savior is my shepherd, I shall not want. He maketh me to lie down in green pastures. He leadeth me beside still waters, He restoreth my—"

Macklin interrupted him with a swipe of the nail-studded palm across the side of his face.

The man dropped to his knees, his slashed face lowered to the ground.

Macklin prodded the second man in the side with his boot. "You. Up."

"My legs. Please. Oh, God . . . my legs."

"Get *up!*"

The prisoner struggled to his feet. Blood streamed down both his legs. He looked at Macklin through horrified, dazed eyes. "Please," he begged. "Give me something for the pain . . . please . . ."

"You give me information first. What's your name?"

The man blinked. "Brother Gary," he said. "Gary Cates."

"That's good, Gary." Macklin patted his shoulder with his left hand. "Now: Where were you going?"

"Don't tell him anything!" the man on the ground shouted. "Don't tell the heathen!"

"You want to be a good boy, don't you, Gary?" Macklin asked, his masked face about four inches away from Cates's. "You want something to take your mind off the pain, don't you? Tell me what I want to know."

"Don't . . . don't . . ." the other man sobbed.

"It's over for you," Macklin stated. "It's finished. There's no need to make things more difficult than they have to be. Isn't that right, Gary? I'll ask you once more: Where were you going?"

Cates hunched his shoulders, as if afraid he might be struck down from above. He shivered, and then he said, "We were . . . trying to catch up with them. Brother Ray got shot. He couldn't make it on his own. I didn't want to leave him. Brother Nick's eyes were burned, and he was blind. The Savior says to leave the wounded . . . but they were my friends."

"The *Savior?* Who's that?"

"Him. The Savior. The true Lord and Master. He leads the American Allegiance. That's who we were trying to catch up with."

"No . . ." the other man said. "Please . . . don't tell . . ."

"The American Allegiance," Macklin repeated. He'd heard of them before, from wanderers who'd joined the AOE's fold. They were led, as he understood it, by an ex-minister from California who had had a cable television program. Macklin had been looking forward to meeting him. "So he calls himself the Savior? How many are traveling with him, and where are they headed?"

The fallen man sat up on his knees and began shrieking crazily, "The Savior is my shepherd, I shall not want! He maketh me to lie down in green pas—" He heard the click of Roland's .45 as its barrel pressed against his skull.

Roland did not hesitate. He squeezed the trigger.

The noise of the gun made Sheila jump. The man toppled over.

"Gary?" Macklin asked. Cates was staring down at the corpse, his eyes wide and one corner of his mouth twitching in a hysterical grin. "How many are traveling with the Savior, and where are they headed?"

"Uh . . . uh . . . uh," Cates stammered. "Uh . . . uh . . . three thousand," he managed to say. "Maybe four. I don't know for sure."

"They have armored vehicles?" Roland inquired. "Automatic weapons? Grenades?"

"All those. We found an Army supply center up in South Dakota. There were trucks, armored cars, machine guns, flamethrowers, grenades . . . everything, for the taking. Even . . . six tanks and crates of heavy ammunition."

Colonel Macklin and Roland looked at each other. The same thought flashed through their minds: Six tanks and crates of heavy ammunition.

"What kind of tanks?" The blood was pounding through Macklin's veins.

"I don't know. Big tanks, with big guns. But one of them wouldn't run right from the first. We left three others, because they broke down and the mechanics couldn't get them started again."

"So they've still got two?"

Cates nodded. He lowered his head in shame, could feel the Savior's eyes burning on the back of his neck. The Savior had three commandments: Disobey and Die; To Kill Is Merciful; and Love Me.

"All right, Gary." Macklin traced the other man's jawline with his finger. "Where are they going?" Cates mumbled something, and Macklin wrenched his head up. "I didn't hear you."

Cates's gaze skittered to the .45 Roland was holding, then back to the black-masked face with its single, cold blue eye. "To West Virginia," he said. "They're going to West Virginia. A place called Warwick Mountain. I don't know exactly where it is."

"West Virginia? Why there?"

"Because—" He trembled; he could feel the man with the bandaged face and the .45 just aching to kill him. "If I tell you, will you let me live?" he asked Macklin.

"We won't kill you," the colonel promised. "Tell me, Gary. *Tell me.*"

"They're going to West Virginia . . . because God lives there," the other man said, and his face folded with agony at betraying the Savior. "God lives on top of Warwick Mountain. Brother Timothy saw God up there, a long time ago. God showed him the black box and the silver key and told him how the world will end. And now Brother Timothy's leading the Savior to find God."

Macklin paused for a few seconds. Then he laughed out loud, its sound like the grunting of an animal. When he'd stopped laughing, he grasped the collar of Cates's shirt with his left hand and pressed the nails of his right against the man's cheek. "You're not among crazy religious fanatics now, my friend. You're among *warriors.* So stop the bullshitting and tell me the truth. *Now.*"

"I swear it! I swear it!" Tears rolled from Cates's eyes and through the grime on his face. "God lives on Warwick Mountain! Brother Timothy's leading the Savior to find him! I swear it!"

"Let me have him," Roland said.

There was a moment of silence. Macklin stared into Gary Cates's eyes and then drew his right hand away. Little dots of blood were rising from the man's cheek.

"I'll take good care of him." Roland holstered his .45. "I'll make him forget that pain in his legs. Then we'll have a nice talk."

"Yes." Macklin nodded. "I think that's a good idea."

"Unshackle him," Roland told the soldiers. They obeyed at once. His eyes gleamed with excitement behind the goggles. He was a happy young man. It was a hard life, yes, and sometimes he wished for a Pepsi and a Baby Ruth candy bar, or he craved a hot shower and then a good late-night war movie on TV—but those were all things that belonged to a past life. He was Sir Roland now, and he lived to serve the King in this never-ending game of King's Knight. He missed his computer, though; that was the only really bad thing about not having electricity. And sometimes he had a strange dream in which he seemed to be in an underground maze, at the King's side, and in that maze there were two tunnel trolls—a man and a woman—who had familiar faces. Their faces disturbed him and always brought him awake in a cold sweat. But those faces were not real; they were just dreams, and Roland was always able to go back to sleep again. He could sleep like the dead when his mind was clear.

"Help him walk," Roland ordered two of the soldiers. "This way," he said, and he led them in the direction of the black trailer.

Macklin prodded the corpse at his feet. "Clean it up," he told one of the guards, and then he stood facing the eastern horizon. The American Allegiance couldn't be very far ahead of them—maybe only twenty or thirty miles. They'd be loaded down with supplies from what had been a thriving community at Sutton. And they had plenty of guns, ammunition—and two tanks.

We can catch them, Macklin thought. We can catch them and take what they have. And I'll grind the Savior's face under my boot. Because nothing can stand before the Army of Excellence, and nothing can stop the grand scheme.

"God lives on Warwick Mountain," the man had said. "God showed him the black box and the silver key and told him how the world will end."

The crazy religious fanatics had to be destroyed. There was no room for their kind in the grand scheme.

He turned back toward the trailer. Sheila Fontana was standing in the doorway, and suddenly Macklin realized that all this excitement had given him an erection. It was a good erection, too. It promised to stay around awhile. He walked up the carved staircase with its bannister of demon faces, entered the trailer and shut the door.

Sixty-eight

"Sister! Sister, wake up!"

She opened her eyes and saw a figure standing over her. For a few seconds she didn't know where she was, and she instinctively tightened her grip around the leather satchel. Then she remembered: She was in Glory Bowen's shack, and she'd dozed off in the warmth of the stove. The last thing she recalled was listening to someone playing a flute at the bonfire outside.

Glory had awakened her. "Josh wants you!" she told Sister in a frightened voice. "Hurry! Somethin's happenin' to Swan!"

Sister stood up. Nearby, Paul had heard and was getting to his feet where he'd been sleeping on the floor. They followed Glory into the next room, where they saw Josh leaning over Swan. Aaron stood watching, wide-eyed, and holding onto the dowsing rod.

"What is it?" Sister asked.

"Her fever! She's burning up!" Josh took a cloth from a pail of melted snow and wrung it out. He began to rub the cold cloth over Swan's neck and arms, and he could swear he saw steam swirling up through the golden lamplight. He was afraid her entire body might suddenly hit the point of ignition and explode. "We've got to get her fever down!"

Paul touched Swan's arm and quickly drew his hand back as if he'd placed it against the stove's grate. "My God! How long's she been like this?"

"I don't know. She had a fever when I checked her about an hour ago, but it wasn't nearly this high!" He put the cloth into the cold water again, and this time he applied it to Swan's flesh without wringing it out. Swan trembled violently; her head thrashed back and forth, and she made a low, terrible moaning.

"She's dyin', Josh!" Aaron yelled. There were tears in his eyes. "Don't let her die!"

Josh put his hands into the cold water and rubbed it over Swan's burning skin. She was so hot inside, so terribly hot. He didn't know what to do, and he looked up at Sister. "Please," he said. "Help me save her!"

"Get her outside!" Sister was already reaching for Swan to help carry her. "We can cover her with snow!"

Josh put his arms underneath Swan and started to lift her. Swan thrashed, and her rebandaged hands clawed at the air. He got her up in his arms and supported her head against his shoulder. The heat radiating through her Job's Mask almost seared his skin.

He'd taken two strides when Swan cried out, shuddered and went limp.

Josh felt the fever break. Felt the terrible heat leave her body as if someone had opened the door of an oven right in his face. Felt it rise like a shroud of steam and cling to the ceiling a foot above his head.

She lay motionless in his arms, and Sister thought, She's dead. Oh, my God . . . Swan is dead.

Josh's knees almost buckled. "Swan!" he said, and his voice cracked. Her long, frail body was cooling. A tear almost burned him blind, and he released a sob that shook his bones.

Carefully, tenderly, he laid her down on the bed again. She lay like a crushed flower, her arms and legs asprawl.

Josh was afraid to pick up her wrist and feel for a pulse. Afraid that this time the spark of life would be gone.

But he did. Couldn't feel anything. He lowered his head for a few seconds. "Oh, no," he whispered. "Oh, no. I think she's—"

There was a faint tremor beneath his fingers.

And another. Then a third and a fourth—getting stronger.

He looked up at Swan's face. Her body shivered—and then there was an eerie noise that sounded like hard, dried clay cracking apart.

"Her . . . face," Paul whispered, standing at the foot of the bed.

A hairline crack crept along the Job's Mask.

It ran across where her forehead would be, zigzagging back over the nose, then down along the left cheek to the jawline. The single crack began to widen, became a fissure that gave birth to more cracks. Parts of the Job's Mask began to peel and flake off, like pieces of a huge scab that had finally healed over a deep and hideous wound.

Swan's pulse was wild. Josh let go of her wrist and stepped back, his eye so wide it looked about to burst from the surface of his own mask.

Sister said, "Oh—"

"—Lord," Glory finished. She grabbed Aaron, hugging him against her hip and putting a hand over his face to shield his eyes. He brushed it away.

The Job's Mask continued to break apart with quick little popping and crackling noises. Swan lay still except for the rapid rise and fall of her breathing. Josh started to touch her again but did not—because the Job's Mask suddenly cracked into two halves and fell away from Swan's face.

No one moved. Paul released his breath. Sister was too stunned to do anything but stare.

Swan was still breathing. Josh reached up, took the lantern from its wall hook and held it over Swan's head.

She had no face. Down amid the cracked, clayey fragments of Job's Mask, Swan's features had been wiped white and smooth as candle wax, except for two small nostril holes and a slit over her mouth. With a trembling hand, Josh ran his fingers across where her right cheek should be. They came away coated with a slick, whitish substance that had the consistency of petroleum jelly. And underneath the jellylike stuff was a glimpse of pale, faintly pink flesh.

"Sister," he said quickly, "will you hold this?" He gave her the lantern, and she saw what was in the cavity and almost swooned. "Hold it steady, now," he said as he took the cloth from the bucket of snow water. Then, slowly and carefully, he began to clean the jelly away.

"My God!" Josh's voice shook. "Look at this! *Look!*"

Glory and Paul came forward to see, and Aaron stood on his tiptoes.

Sister saw. She picked aside a fragment of the Job's Mask and touched a lock of Swan's hair. It was darkened by the slick jelly that covered it, but it shone with deep gold and red highlights. It was the most beautiful hair she'd ever seen, and it was growing strong and thick from Swan's scalp.

"Aaron!" Josh said. "Go get Anna and Gene! Hurry!" The boy darted out. As Josh continued to clean the film away Swan's features began to emerge.

And then he looked down at her face and touched her forehead. Her fever was gone, and her temperature felt near normal. Her eyes were still closed, but she was breathing just fine, and Josh decided to let her sleep.

"What the hell's the ruckus?" Anna McClay asked as she came in.

"This," Josh said softly, and he stepped back so Anna could see.

She stopped as if she'd hit a wall, and the eyes in her tough old face filled with tears.

Sixty-nine

"Here y'go, fellas! Breakfast time!"

Robin Oakes snorted with disinterest as Anna McClay brought a pot of soup and some bowls out on the front porch. He and the three other young highwaymen had spent the night sleeping by the bonfire, along with six or seven other people who were keeping watch on Glory's shack. It was another dark, cold morning, and small flakes of snow were whirling before the wind.

"Well, come on!" Anna urged. "You want breakfast or not?"

Robin stood up, his muscles stiff, and walked past the horse that was tied to the porch's support post. Two blankets were laid across Mule's back and shoulders, and he was close enough to the warmth of the bonfire that he was in no danger of frostbite. The other boys followed Robin, and a few other people stirred and came over to be fed as well.

Anna ladled the soup out into a bowl for him. He wrinkled his nose. "This junk again? Didn't we have this for *dinner?*"

"Sure did. You'll have it for lunch, too, so you'd better like it."

Robin restrained the urge to throw the stuff out on the

ground. He knew it was made of boiled roots, with a few shreds of good old wholesome rat meat. Now even the food in the orphanage cafeteria seemed like it had been manna from Heaven, and he would have walked to China if he knew he could get a Burger King Whopper there. He moved out of the chow line so the next person could get his dose, tilted the bowl to his mouth and drank. He'd had a miserable night, jumpy and restless, and had finally grabbed a few hours of sleep in spite of an old man who'd sat by the fire playing a flute. Robin would have thrown a boot at him, but some of the others seemed to actually *enjoy* that dumb music, and Robin had seen the old man's face glow in the firelight as he trilled notes into the air. Robin remembered what heavy metal had used to sound like: crashing, strutting guitar chords and a thunder of drums as if the world was about to blow up. That used to be his kind of music—but it dawned on him that the world really *had* blown up. Maybe it was time for peace now, he thought. Peace in action, words and music, too.

Damn! he told himself. I must be getting *old!*

He had awakened once, sometime in the night. He'd sat up, stiff and cranky, to find a warmer place, when he'd seen the man standing over on the other side of the fire. Just standing there, his dirty coat sweeping around him in the wind, and staring at Glory's shack. Robin didn't remember what the man's face had looked like, but the man had prowled slowly through the sleeping figures, approaching to within twenty feet of the shack's porch. Anna and Gene sat on the steps, armed with rifles and guarding the door, but they were talking to each other and didn't pay any attention. Robin recalled that Gene had shivered and drawn his collar up around his neck, and Anna had blown into her hands as if caught by a sudden, sneaking chill.

The man had turned and walked purposefully away. It was the stride of a man who had things to do and places to go. And maybe that was why Robin remembered him. But then Robin had shifted his position, laid his head back down and slept until awakened by cold bits of snow on his eyelids.

"When do we get our guns back?" he asked her.

"Not until Josh says so."

"Listen, lady! Nobody takes my gun away from me! I want it back!"

She smiled at him indulgently. "You'll get it. When Josh says so."

"Hey, Anna!" Aaron called from a little further down the road. He was playing with Crybaby. "Can you come see the magic now?"

"Later!" she replied, and she went back to ladling out the root and rat meat concoction. She even began to whistle as she worked—one of her favorite tunes, "Bali Ha'i" from *South Pacific*.

Robin knew there was no way to get his rifle back except to storm the shack. Neither he nor the other boys had been allowed inside since they'd gotten there, and Robin was getting pissed. "What the hell are *you* so happy about?" he snapped.

"Because," she answered, "this is a great and glorious morning. So glorious that not even a punk like you can get under my skin. See?" And she flashed him a quick grin that showed all of her front teeth.

"What's so great and glorious about it?" He flung out the rest of his soup. "Looks about the same to me—dark and cold." But he'd noted that her eyes were different; they were clear and excited. "What's going on?"

Sister came outside, with the leather satchel that never left her. She drew in a breath of cold air to clear her head, because she'd been up and watching over Swan, along with the others, since well before dawn. "Can I help you?" she asked Anna.

"Naw, I got it. That's the last one." She ladled soup into the final bowl. All but Robin had returned to the bonfire to eat their meals. "How is she?"

"Still the same." Sister stretched and heard her old joints pop and click. "She's breathing fine, and her fever's gone—but she's still the same."

"What's going on?" Robin demanded.

Anna took his empty bowl from him and dropped it into the pot. "When Josh wants you to know, he'll tell you. And everybody else, too."

Robin looked at Sister. "What's wrong with Swan?" he asked in a quieter voice.

Sister glanced quickly at Anna, then back to the young man. He was awaiting an answer, and she thought he deserved one. "She's . . . changed."

"Changed? Into *what?* A frog?" He smiled, but Sister didn't return it, and he let the smile slip away. "Why don't I get to see her? I'm not going to attack her or anything. Besides, I'm the one who saw her and the big dude in that glass thing. If it wasn't for me, you wouldn't be here. Doesn't that make me rate anything?"

Anna said, "When Josh says you—"

"I'm not talking to you, Big Mama!" Robin interrupted, and his cool, level gaze bored right into her skull. She flinched just a fraction, then returned his stare full-force. "I don't give a damn what Josh says or wants," he continued, unshaken. "I should be able to see Swan." He motioned to the leather satchel. "I know you believe that glass ring guided you here," he told Sister. "Well, did you ever stop to think that maybe it guided *me* here, too?"

That idea gave her food for thought. He might be right. Besides herself, he was the only person who'd seen a vision of Swan in the depths of the glass circle.

"How about it?" he asked.

"All right," she decided. "Come on."

"Hey! Don't you think we ought to ask Josh first?"

"No. It's okay." She went to the door and opened it.

"Why don't you comb that hair?" Anna told him as he came up the steps. "It looks like a freakin' bird's nest!"

He smiled sourly at her. "Why don't you *grow* some hair? Like on your face." And then he walked past Sister and into the shack.

Before she went in, Sister asked Anna if Gene and Zachial had found the cripple in the child's red wagon. Anna said they hadn't reported back yet, that they'd been gone for about two hours and that she was getting worried about them. "What do you want with him?" she asked. "He's crazy in the head, is all."

"Maybe so. And maybe he's crazy like a fox, too." And

then Sister entered the shack while the other woman went to collect the empty soup bowls.

"Hey, Anna!" Aaron called. "Will you come see the magic *now?"*

Inside the shack, Paul had shown an interest in the printing press and had taken some of it apart, and he and Glory were cleaning the gears and rollers with ashes. She looked warily at Robin as he walked to the stove and warmed his hands, but Paul said, "He's all right," and she returned to work.

Sister motioned for Robin to follow. They started into the next room, but Josh's bulk suddenly blocked the doorway. "What's he doing in here?"

"I invited him. I told him he could see Swan."

"She's still asleep. Either she was awfully exhausted, or . . . there's something still wrong with her." He angled his head so his eye was aimed at Robin. "I don't think it's a good idea for him to go in."

"Come on, man! What's the big mystery? I just want to see what she looks like, that's all!"

Josh ignored him but did not move from the doorway. He turned his attention to Sister. "Aren't Gene and Zachial back yet?"

"No. Anna says she's getting worried. I am, too."

Josh grunted. He, too, was deeply concerned. Sister had told him about the man with the flaming hand in the Forty-second Street theater, and about her meeting with Doyle Halland in New Jersey. She'd told him about the man who was bicycling on the Pennsylvania highway with a pack of wolves jogging at his heels, and who'd just missed her at the rescue station of Homewood. He could change his face and his body, too, she'd said. He could appear to be anyone, even a cripple. That would be a good disguise, she'd told Josh, because who would expect that a crippled man was as dangerous as a mad dog among sheep? What she couldn't figure out, though, was how he'd tracked her down. Had he decided to settle here and been waiting for her or for somebody who might have seen the glass ring? Anna had said that Mr. Welcome had only been there a couple of days, but then again he could have been living in Mary's Rest in any number of disguises. However and whenever he'd arrived, Mr. Welcome had to be found, and Gene and Zachial had gone looking for him armed to the teeth.

"He was here," Josh remembered Swan saying. "The man with the scarlet eye."

"Should we send somebody to find them?" Sister asked.

"What?" He came back from his thoughts.

"Gene and Zachial. Should we start looking for them?"

"No, not yet." He'd wanted to go with them, but Glory had grasped his sleeve and said he needed to stay near Swan. She knows what he is, Josh had thought. And maybe she was trying to save his life, too. "The man with the scarlet eye," he said softly.

"Huh?" Robin frowned, not knowing if he'd heard correctly.

"That's what Swan calls him." He did not tell the boy that the lettering on that particular tarot card had read THE DEVIL.

"Riiiight," Robin scoffed. "You two must have some strong medicine stashed around here, big dude."

"I wish." Josh decided that Robin was okay—a little rough around the edges, of course, but wasn't everybody these days? "I'm going to get a cup of coffee. You can go in, but you can only stay for two minutes. Understand?" He waited until the boy nodded, and then he went to the front room. The entrance to where Swan lay sleeping was unblocked.

But Robin hesitated. His palms were clammy. By the lamplight, he could make out a figure lying on the cot. A blanket was pulled up to her chin, but her face was averted, and he couldn't see it.

"Go on," Sister told him.

I'm scared shitless! he realized. "What did you mean, 'she's changed'? Is she . . . y'know . . . messed up?"

"Go in and see for yourself."

His feet refused to budge. "She's pretty important, isn't she? I mean, if she made the corn start growing again, she must really be somebody special. Right?"

"You'd better go in. You're wasting your two minutes."

She gave him a shove, and he entered the bedroom. Sister followed him.

Robin walked to the side of the bed. He was as nervous as if he was about to get his hands whacked by one of the nuns for throwing spitballs.

He saw a spill of golden hair on the patchwork pillow. It shone in the lamplight like newly mown hay, but it was flecked here and there with hints of red.

His knees bumped the edge of the bed. He was entranced by that hair. He'd forgotten what clean hair looked like.

And then she shifted position under the blanket and turned onto her back, and Robin saw her face.

She was still sleeping, her features peaceful. Her hair flowed back like a mane from her high, unlined forehead, and streaks of red coursed through the hair at her temples like flames in a yellow field. She had an oval-shaped face, and she was . . . yes, Robin thought. *Yes.* She was beautiful. The most beautiful girl he'd ever seen.

Reddish-blond brows made crescents over her closed eyes. She had a straight, elegant nose and sharp cheekbones, and in her chin was a small star-shaped cleft. Her skin was very pale, almost translucent; its hue reminded Robin of what the moon had looked like on a clear summer night in the world that used to be.

Robin's gaze wandered over her face—but timidly, like someone exploring a lovely garden where there is no path. He wondered what she'd look like awake, what color her eyes would be, what her voice would sound like, how her lips would move. His eyes couldn't get enough of her. She looked like the daughter of a marriage between ice and fire.

Wake up, he thought. Please wake up.

She lay sleeping and still.

But something awakened within himself.

Wake up. Wake up, Swan, he wished. Her eyes remained closed.

A voice jarred his rapture. "Josh! Glory! Come out here and look at this!" It was that old bat Anna, he realized. Calling from the front door.

He returned his attention to Swan.

"Let me see what's going on," Sister said. "I'll be right back." She left the room, but Robin had hardly heard her.

He reached out to touch Swan's cheek but stopped himself. He didn't feel clean enough to touch her. His clothes were tattered and stiff with sweat and grime, and his hands were dirty. Anna was right about his hair looking like a bird's nest. Why the hell had he ever wanted to braid feathers and bones in his hair? he wondered. It had been something to do, he guessed, and at the time he'd thought it was pretty cool. Now he just felt dumb.

"Wake up, Swan," he whispered. There was still no response. A fly suddenly dropped down, hovering above her face, and Robin snatched it in his fist and crushed it against his leg because a filthy thing like that had no business in here with her. The insect stung his skin just a little bit, but he barely noticed.

He stood staring down at her face and thinking of all the things he'd ever heard about love. Man! he thought. The guys sure would howl if they could see me right now!

But she was so beautiful that he thought his heart might crack.

Sister would be back at any second. If he was going to do what he yearned to, he would have to do it fast.

"Wake up," he whispered again, and when she still didn't move he lowered his head and lightly kissed the corner of her mouth.

The warmth of her lips under his own shocked him, and he caught the aroma of her skin like a faint breeze through a peach orchard. His heart was hammering like a heavy metal drumbeat, but he let the kiss linger. And linger. And linger.

Then he ended it, scared to death that Sister or one of the others would barge in. That big dude would boot him so high and far he could hitch a ride on a satellite, if any of those were still up th—

Swan moved. Robin was sure of it. Something had moved —an eyebrow, the corner of her mouth, maybe a twitch of the cheek or jaw. He leaned over her, his face only a few inches from hers.

Her eyes opened without warning.

He was so startled he jerked his head back, as if she were a statue coming to life. Her eyes were dark blue, flecked with red and gold, and their colors made him think of the glass ring. She sat up, one hand fluttering to her lips where the kiss had lingered, and then Robin saw her pale cheeks bloom vivid pink.

She lifted her right hand, and before Robin could think to duck, a stinging slap was delivered to the side of his face.

He staggered back a few feet before he caught himself. His own cheek was reddening now, but he managed a goofy grin. He could think of nothing better to say than "Hi."

Swan stared at her hands. Touched her face. Ran her fingers along her nose, across her mouth, felt the ridges of her cheekbones and the line of her jaw. She was shaking and about to cry, and she didn't know who the boy with feathers and bones in his hair was, but she'd hit him because she'd thought he was about to attack her. Everything was confused and crazy, but she had a face again, and she could see clearly through both eyes. She caught a glint of reddish gold from the corner of her eye, and she took a long strand of her own hair between her fingers. She stared at it as if she wasn't sure what the stuff was. The last time she'd had hair, she remembered, was on the day she and her mama had walked into that dusty grocery store in Kansas.

My hair used to be pale blond, she recalled. Now it was the color of fire.

"I can see!" she told the boy as tears slid down her smooth cheeks. "I can see again!" Her voice, without the Job's Mask pressing at her mouth and nostrils, was different, too; it was the soft, smoky voice of a girl on the edge of being a woman—and now her voice strained with excitement as she called, "Josh! *Josh!*"

Robin ran out to get Sister, with the image of the most beautiful girl he'd ever seen stamped like a cameo into his brain.

But Sister wasn't in the front room. She was standing at the foot of the porch steps, along with Glory and Paul.

Josh and Anna stood on either side of Aaron, about

thirty-five feet from the porch and almost dead center in the road.

Aaron was the focus of rapt attention. "See?" he crowed. "I told you it was magic! You just gotta know how to hold it!"

The two small branches that jutted off at opposite angles from Crybaby were balanced on the tips of Aaron's forefingers. The dowsing rod's other end was going up and down, up and down like the action of a pump. Aaron grinned proudly at his magic trick, all eyes and shining teeth, as more people gathered around.

"I do believe you might've found us a well," Josh said wonderingly.

"Huh?" Aaron asked as Crybaby continued to point the way to fresh water.

At the steps, Sister felt a hand grip her shoulder. She turned and saw Robin standing there. He was trying to speak, but he was so flustered he couldn't get the words out. She saw the splayed red handprint on his cheek, and she was about to push him aside and run into the shack when Swan came through the doorway, the blanket wrapped around her tall, thin body and her legs as uncertain as a fawn's. She squinted and blinked in the dim gray light.

Sister could have been knocked over by a snowflake, and then she heard Robin whisper, *"Oh,"* as if he'd been physically struck—and she knew.

Anna looked up from the bobbing dowsing rod. Josh turned around and saw what the others had already seen.

He took one step, a second and a third, and then he broke into a run that would have bowled even Haystacks Muldoon flat on his back. The people who'd gathered around scrambled out of his way.

He bounded up the steps, and Swan was already reaching out for him and just about to fall. He swept her off her feet before she tumbled, and he squeezed her to his chest and thought, Thank God, thank God my daughter's come back!

He sank his deformed head against her shoulder and began to cry—and Swan heard it not as a hurting sound this time, but as a song of new-found joy.

TWELVE
True Faces

Mr. Caidin's son / A visit with the Savior / A lady / Storming the fortress / The lair

Seventy

Swan walked amid the rows of green and growing cornstalks as flurries of snow hissed upon the bonfires. Josh and Sister walked on either side of her, and they were flanked by two men with rifles who kept a sharp lookout for bobcats—or any other kind of predator.

It had been three days since Swan's awakening. Her slender body was warmed by a patchwork coat of many colors that Glory had sewn for her, and her head was protected by a white knit cap, one of dozens of gifts that the grateful people of Mary's Rest left for her on Glory's front porch. She couldn't use all the coats, gloves, pairs of socks and caps that were offered, so the excess clothing went into cardboard boxes to be distributed among those whose clothes were almost worn out.

Her intense, dark blue eyes with their flecks of red and gold took in the new cornstalks, which were now about four feet tall and beginning to turn a darker green. Around the edges of her cap, Swan's hair flowed back like flames. Her skin was still very pale, but her cheeks were reddened by the chill wind; her face was bony, in need of food and filling out, but that would come later. Right now all that occupied her attention was the corn.

Bonfires burned across the field, and volunteers from Mary's Rest watched around the clock to keep away the bobcats, crows and whatever else might try to destroy the cornstalks. Every so often another group of volunteers would come with buckets and dippers to offer fresh water from the new well that the pickaxes and shovels had hit two days before. The water's taste blossomed the memories of all who sipped it, reminding them of things half forgotten: the smell of clean, cold mountain air; the sweetness of Christmas candy; fine wine that had sat in a bottle for fifty years awaiting appreciation; and dozens of others, each unique and part of a happier life. Water was no longer melted from the radioactive snow, and people were already beginning to feel stronger, their sore throats, headaches and other ailments starting to fade.

Gene Scully and Zachial Epstein had never returned. Their bodies were still missing, and Sister was certain they were dead. And certain also that "the man with the scarlet eye" was still somewhere in Mary's Rest. Sister kept her leather satchel in a tighter grip than ever, but now she wondered if he'd lost interest in the ring and had shifted his attention to Swan.

Sister and Josh had talked about what kind of creature the man with the scarlet eye might be. She didn't know if she believed in a horned and fork-tailed Devil, but she knew well enough what Evil was. If he'd searched for them for seven years, that meant he didn't know *everything*. He might be cunning, and maybe his intuition was razor-sharp, and maybe he could change his face as he pleased and burst people into flame with a touch, but he was flawed and dumb. And maybe his greatest weakness was that he thought himself so damned much smarter than human beings.

Swan paused in her inspection, then approached one of the smaller cornstalks. Its fronds were still speckled with the dark red spots of blood her hands had shed. She took off one of her gloves and touched the thin stalk, felt the prickling sensation that began at her feet, moved up her legs to her spine, then through her arm and fingers into the plant like a low current of electricity. She'd thought of that sensation as normal ever since she was a child; but now she wondered if her entire body wasn't, in a way, like Crybaby—she was receptive to and drew up power from the battery of the earth and could direct it through her fingers into seeds, trees and plants. Maybe it was a whole lot more, and maybe she could never really understand what it was, but she could close her eyes and see again the wonderful scenes that the glass ring had shown her, and she knew what she must devote the rest of her life to doing.

At Swan's suggestion, rags and old papers had been bundled around the bases of the stalks, to keep the new roots as warm as possible. The hard dirt had been broken up with shovels and holes dug every four or five feet between the rows; into these holes clean water was poured, and if you listened hard and the wind was still, you could hear the earth gasping as it drank.

Swan went on, stopping every so often to touch one of the stalks or bend down and knead the dirt between her fingers. It felt like sparks were jumping off her hands. But she was uncomfortable having so many people around her all the time—especially the men with the rifles. It was weird having people watch you and want to touch you and give you the clothes right off their backs. She'd never felt special, and she didn't feel special now, either. Being able to make the corn grow was just something she could do, like Glory could sew the patchwork coat and Paul could make the little printing press work again. Everybody had a talent, and Swan knew that this was hers.

She walked on a few more feet, and then she knew someone was staring at her.

She turned her head to look back toward Mary's Rest, and she saw him standing across the field, his shoulder-length brown hair blowing in the wind.

Sister followed Swan's line of sight and saw him, too. She knew Robin Oakes had been following them all morning, but he wouldn't come any closer. In the past three days he'd declined any offer to enter Glory's shack; he was content to sleep by the bonfire, and Sister noted with interest that he'd cleaned all the feathers and animal bones out of his hair. Sister glanced at Swan and saw her blush before she turned quickly away. Josh was occupied with watching the woods for bobcats, and he didn't notice the little drama. Just like a man, Sister mused. He can't see the forest for the trees.

"They're doing fine," Swan told Sister, to take her mind off Robin Oakes. Her voice was nervous and a little higher-pitched, and underneath the crust of her Job's Mask, Sister smiled. "The fires are keeping the air warmer out here. I think the corn's doing just fine."

"I'm glad to hear it," Sister answered.

Swan was satisfied. She went around to every bonfire, speaking to the volunteers, finding out if anyone needed to be replaced, if they wanted water or any of the root soup that Glory, Anna or one of the other women was always cooking up. She made sure to thank them for helping watch the field and chase the circling crows away. Of course, the crows needed to eat, too, but they'd have to find their own food somewhere else. Swan noticed a teen-age girl who had no gloves, and she gave her her own pair. Dead skin was still flaking off Swan's palms, but otherwise her hands had healed.

She stopped at the plank of wood that marked Rusty's grave. She still didn't remember anything of that night but her dream of the man with the scarlet eye. There had been no time to tell Rusty what he'd meant to her and how much she'd loved him. She remembered Rusty making red balls appear and disappear as part of the Travelin' Show's magic act and earning an old can of beans or fruit cocktail for his work. The earth had him now, had folded strong arms around him so that he would sleep long and undisturbed. And his magic was still alive—in her, in Josh, and in the green stalks that swayed in the wind with the promise of life yet to be.

Swan, Josh and Sister walked back across the field, accompanied by the two armed guards. Both Swan and Sister noted that Robin Oakes had already slipped away. And Swan felt a twinge of disappointment.

Children hopped and jumped around Swan as they continued through the alleys toward Glory's shack. Sister's heart pounded as she watched every alley they passed for a sudden, snakelike movement—and she thought she heard the squeak of red wagon wheels somewhere nearby, but the sound faded, and she wasn't sure if it had been there at all.

A tall, gaunt man with pale blue keloids burned diagonally across his face was waiting for them, standing at the foot of the steps talking to Paul Thorson. Paul's hands were stained dark brown from the mud and dyes he and Glory were mixing, to be used as ink for the bulletin sheet. There were dozens of people in the street and around the shack who'd come to catch a glimpse of Swan, and they made a path for her as she approached the waiting man.

Sister stepped between them, tense and ready for anything. But she caught no repulsive, dank wave of cold coming off him—just body odor. His eyes were almost the same color as the keloids. He wore a thin cloth coat, and his head was bare; tufts of black hair stuck up on a burn-scarred scalp.

"Mr. Caidin's been waiting to see Swan," Paul said. "He's all right." Sister immediately relaxed, trusting Paul's judgment. "I think you should listen to what he says."

Caidin turned his attention to Swan. "My family and I live over there." He motioned in the direction of the burned-out church. He had a flat Midwestern accent, and his voice was shaky but articulate. "My wife and I have three boys. The oldest is sixteen, and up until this morning he had the same thing on his face that I understand you did." He nodded toward Josh. "Like that. Those growths."

"The Job's Mask," Sister said. "What do you mean, 'up until this morning'?"

"Ben was running a high fever. He was so weak he could hardly move. And then . . . early this morning . . . it just cracked open."

Sister and Swan looked at each other.

"I heard that yours did the same thing," Caidin continued. "That's why I'm here. I know a lot of people must be wanting to see you, but . . . could you come to my place and look at Ben?"

"I don't think there's anything Swan can do for your son," Josh said. "She's not a doctor."

"It's not that. Ben's fine. I thank God that stuff cracked open, because he could barely draw a breath. It's just that—" He looked at Swan again. "He's *different,*" Caidin said softly. "Please, come see him. It won't take very long."

The need in the man's face moved her. She nodded, and they followed him along the street, into an alley past the charred ruins of Jackson Bowen's church and back through a maze of shacks, smaller shanties, piles of human waste and debris and even cardboard boxes that some people had fastened together to huddle in.

They waded through a muddy, ankle-deep pool and then went up a pair of wooden steps into a shack that was even smaller and draftier than Glory's. It only had one room, and as insulation old newspaper and magazine pages had been nailed up all over the walls until there was no space not covered by yellowed headlines, type and pictures from a dead world.

Caidin's wife, her face sallow in the light of the room's single lantern, held a sleeping infant in her thin arms. A boy about nine or ten years old, frail and frightened-looking, clutched at his mother's legs and tried to hide when the strangers entered. The room held a couch with broken springs, an old crank-operated washing machine, and an electric stove—an antique, Josh thought—in which chips of wood, embers and trash yielded a cheerless fire and little warmth. A wooden chair sat next to a pile of mattresses on the floor, where the eldest Caidin boy lay under a coarse brown blanket.

Swan approached the mattresses and looked down into the boy's face. Pieces of the Job's Mask lay like broken gray pottery around his head, and she could see the slick, jellylike stuff clinging to the inside of the fragments.

The boy, his face white and his blue eyes still bright from fever, tried to sit up, but he was too weak. He pushed thick, dark hair back from his forehead. "You're *her,* aren't you?" he asked. "The girl who started the corn growing?"

"Yes."

"That's really great. You can use corn a lot of different ways."

"I guess so." Swan examined the boy's features; his skin was smooth and flawless, almost luminescent in the lantern's light. He had a strong, square jawline and a thin-bridged nose that was slightly sharp at the end. Overall, he was a handsome boy, and Swan knew he would grow up to be a handsome man, if he survived. She couldn't understand what Caidin had wanted her to see.

"Sure!" This time the boy did sit up, his eyes glittering and excited. "You can fry it and boil it, make muffins and cakes, even squeeze oil out of it. You can make whiskey from it, too. I know all about it, because I did a science project on corn back at my elementary school in Iowa. I won first prize at the state fair." He paused, and then he touched the left side of his face with a trembling hand. "What's *happened* to me?"

She looked over at Caidin, who motioned for her, Josh and Sister to follow him outside.

As Swan started to turn away from the mattresses a headline on a newspaper plastered to the wall caught her eye: ARMS TALKS CRASH AS 'STAR WARS' GETS A-OK. There was a photograph of important-looking men in suits and ties, smiling and lifting their hands in some kind of victory celebration. She didn't know what it was all about, because none of those men were familiar to her. They looked like very satisfied men, and their clothes looked clean and new, and their hair was perfectly in place. All of them were clean-shaven, and Swan wondered if any of them had ever squatted down over a bucket to use the bathroom.

Then she went out to join the others.

"Your son's a fine-looking boy," Sister was telling Caidin. "You ought to be glad."

"I am glad. I'm thankful to God that stuff's off his face. But that's not the point."

"Okay. What is?"

"That's *not* my son's face. At least . . . that's not what he used to look like before he got that damned stuff on him."

"Swan's face was burned when the bombs hit," Josh said. "She doesn't look like she did then, either."

"My son wasn't disfigured on the seventeenth of July," Caidin replied calmly. "He was hardly hurt at all. He's always been a good, fine boy, and his mother and I love him very much, but . . . Ben was born with birth defects. He had a red birthmark that covered the entire left side of his face. The doctors called it a port-wine stain. And his jaw was malformed. We had a specialist operate on him in Cedar Rapids, but the problem was so severe that . . . there wasn't much to hope for. Still, Ben's always had guts. He wanted to go to a regular school and be treated like anybody else, no better and no worse." He looked at Swan. "The color of his hair and eyes are the same as they always were. The shape of his face is the same. But the birthmark's gone, and his jaw isn't deformed anymore, and . . ." He trailed off, shaking his head.

"And what?" Sister prompted.

He hesitated, trying to find the words, and then he lifted his gaze to hers. "I used to tell him that real beauty is deeper than skin. I used to tell him that real beauty is what's inside, in the heart and soul." A tear trickled down Caidin's right cheek. "Now Ben . . . looks like I always *knew* he did, deep down inside. I think that now . . . the face of his soul is showing through." His own visage was stretched between laughing and crying. "Is that a crazy thing to think?"

"No," Sister answered. "I think it's a wonderful thing. He's a handsome boy."

"Always was," Caidin said, and this time he let himself smile.

The man returned to his family, and the others walked back through the muddy maze to the road. They were quiet, each occupied by private thoughts: Josh and Sister reflecting on Caidin's story, wondering if and when their own Job's Masks might reach the point where they began to crack—and what might be revealed underneath; and Swan remembering something that Leona Skelton had told her a long time ago: "Everybody's got two faces, child—the outside face and the inside face. A face under the face, y'see. It's your true face, and if it was flipped to the outside, you'd show the world what kind of person you are."

"Flipped to the outside?" Swan recalled asking. "How?"

And Leona had smiled. "Well, God hasn't figured a way to do that yet. But He will. . . ."

"The face of his soul is showing through," Mr. Caidin had said.

"But He will. . . ."

". . . face of his soul . . ."

"But He will. . . ."

"Truck's comin' in!"

"Truck's comin'!"

Approaching along the road was a pickup truck, its sides and hood pitted with rust. It was coming at a crawl, and around it surged a tide of people, hollering and laughing. Josh imagined it had been a long time since most of them had seen a car or truck that still actually ran. He put his hand on Swan's shoulder, and Sister stood behind them on the roadside as the truck rumbled toward them.

"Here she is, mister!" a boy shouted, scrambling up onto the front fender and hood. "She's right here!"

The truck came to a stop, trailing a wake of people. Its engine sputtered, popped and backfired, but the vehicle might have been a shiny new Cadillac from the way folks were rubbing the rust-eaten metal. The driver, a florid-faced man wearing a red baseball cap and clenching the stub of a real cigar between his teeth, looked warily out his window at the excited crowd, as if he wasn't quite sure what kind of madhouse he'd driven into.

"Swan's right here, mister!" the boy on the hood said, pointing at her. He was talking to the man on the passenger side.

The passenger's door opened, and a man with curly white hair and a long, untrimmed beard leaned out, craning his neck to see who the boy was pointing to. His dark brown eyes, set in a tough, wrinkled old face, searched the crowd. "Where?" he asked. "I don't see her!"

But Josh knew who the man had come to find. He raised his arm and said, "Swan's over here, Sly."

Sylvester Moody recognized the huge wrestler from the Travelin' Show—and realized with a start exactly why he'd worn that black ski mask. His gaze moved to the girl who stood beside Josh, and for a moment he could not speak. "Sweet dancin' Jesus!" he finally exclaimed, as he stepped out of the truck.

He hesitated, still not sure it was her, glanced at Josh and saw him nod. "Your *face,*" Sly said. "It's all . . . healed up!"

"It happened a few nights ago," Swan told him. "And I think other people are starting to heal up, too."

If the wind had been blowing any harder, he might have keeled flat over. "You're beautiful," he said. "Oh, Lord . . . you're *beautiful!*" He turned toward the truck, and his voice quavered; "Bill! This here's the girl! This is Swan!" Bill McHenry, Sly's nearest neighbor and owner of the truck, cautiously opened his door and got out.

"We had a hell of a time on that road!" Sly complained. "One more bump and my ass would've busted! Lucky we brought along extra go-juice, or we'da been walkin' the last twenty miles!" He glanced around for someone else. "Where's the cowboy?"

"We buried Rusty a few days ago," Josh said. "He's in a field not too far from here."

"Oh." Sly frowned. "Well, I'm sorry to hear that. I'm awful sorry. He seemed like a decent fella."

"He was." Josh tilted his head, peering at the truck. "What are you doing here?"

"I knew you folks were goin' to Mary's Rest. That's where you said you were headed when you left my place. I decided to come visit."

"Why? It's at least fifty miles of bad road between here and your house!"

"Don't my achin' ass know it! God A'mighty, I'd like to sit on a nice soft pillow." He rubbed his sore rump.

"It's no pleasure trip, that's for sure," Josh agreed. "But you knew that before you started. You didn't say why you came all that way."

"No." His eyes sparkled. "I don't reckon I did." He gazed at the shacks of Mary's Rest. "Lord, is this a town or a toilet? What's that awful smell?"

"You stay around long enough, you'll get used to it."

"Well, I'm just here for one day. One day's all I need to pay my debt."

"Debt? What debt?"

"What I owe Swan, and you for bringin' Swan to my door. Throw it back, Bill!"

And Bill McHenry, who'd gone around to the rear of the truck, pulled back a canvas tarpaulin that covered the truck's bed.

It was piled full of small red apples, perhaps two hundred or more of them.

At the sight of the apples, there was a collective gasp that went back like a wave over the gathered onlookers. The smell of fresh apples sweetened the air. Sly started laughing, laughing fit to bust, and then he climbed up into the truck's bed and picked up a shovel that was lying there.

"I brought you some apples from my tree, Swan!" Sly yelled, his face split by a smile. "Where do you want 'em?"

She didn't know what to say. She'd never seen so many apples outside of a supermarket before. They were bright red, and each one about the size of a boy's fist. She just stood staring at them, and she figured she must look like a dumb fool—but then she knew where she wanted the apples to go. "Out there," she said, and she pointed to the people crowding around the tailgate.

Sly nodded. "Yes ma'am," he said, and then he dug the shovel into the pile of apples and let them fly over the heads of the crowd.

Apples rained from the sky, and the starving people of Mary's Rest snatched them as they fell. Apples bounced off their heads, shoulders and backs, but no one cared; there was a roar of voices as other people ran from the alleys and shacks to grab an apple, and they were dancing in the showers of apples, capering and hollering and clapping their hands. Sly Moody's shovel kept working as more and more people came flooding out of the alleys, but there was no fighting for the precious delicacies. Everyone was too intent on getting an apple, and as Sly Moody kept throwing them into the air the pile hardly seemed to have been dented. Sly grinned deliriously, and he wanted to tell Swan that two days before he'd awakened to find his tree burdened down with hundreds of apples, the branches dragging on the ground. And as soon as those were picked there were already new buds bursting open, and the whole incredibly short cycle was going to be repeated. It was the most amazing, miraculous thing he'd ever seen in his life, and that single tree looked healthy enough to produce hundreds more apples—maybe *thousands*. He and Carla had already filled their buckets to overflowing.

Every time Sly's shovel tossed the apples there was a roar of whooping and laughing. The crowd surged in all directions as apples bounced off them and rolled on the ground. Swan, Sister and Josh were jostled and pushed apart, and suddenly Swan felt herself being carried along with the crowd's momentum like a reed in a river. "Swan!" she heard Sister shout, but she was already at least thirty feet from Sister, and Josh was doing his best to plow through the people without hurting anyone.

An apple hit Swan's shoulder, fell to the ground in front of her and rolled a few feet. She bent to pick it up before she was swept away again, and as her fingers closed on it someone in a pair of scuffed brown boots stepped to within three feet of her.

She felt cold. A gnawing, bone-aching cold.

And she knew who it was.

Her heart hammered. Panic skittered up her spine. The man in the brown boots did not move, and people were not jostling him; they avoided him, as if repelled by the cold. Apples continued to fall to the ground, and the crowd surged, but nobody picked up the apples that lay between Swan and the man who watched her.

Her first, almost overwhelming impulse was to cry for help from Josh or Sister—but she knew he expected that. As soon as she stood up and opened her mouth, the burning hand would be on her throat.

She didn't know exactly what she was going to do, but she was so scared she was about to wet herself. And then she clenched her teeth and slowly, gracefully, stood up with the apple gripped in her hand. She looked at him, because she wanted to see the face of the man with the scarlet eye.

He was wearing the mask of a skinny black man, wearing jeans and a Boston Celtics T-shirt under an olive-green coat. A red scarf was wrapped around his neck, and his piercing, terrible eyes were pale amber.

Their stares locked, and Swan saw a silver tooth flash in the front of his mouth when he grinned.

Sister was too far away. Josh was still fighting the crowd. The man with the scarlet eye stood three feet away, and to Swan it seemed that everyone was swirling around them in nightmarish slow motion, that she and the man stood alone in a trance of time. She knew she must decide her own fate, because there was no one else to help her.

And she was aware of something else in the eyes of the mask he was wearing, something beyond the cold, lizardlike sheen of evil, something deeper . . . and almost human. She remembered seeing the same thing in the eyes of Uncle Tommy the night he'd crushed her flowers, back in the Kansas trailer park seven years ago; it was something wandering and longing, forever locked away from the light and maddened like a tiger in a dark cage. It was dumb arrogance and bastard pride, stupidity and rage stoked to atomic power. But it was something of a little boy, too, wailing and lost.

Swan knew him. Knew what he'd done and what he would do. And in that moment of knowledge she lifted her arm, reached out her hand toward him—and offered him the apple.

"I forgive you," she said.

His grin went crooked, like the reflection in a mirror abruptly shattered.

He blinked uncertainly, and in his eyes Swan saw fire and savagery, a core of pain past human suffering and so furious that it almost ripped her own heart to shreds. He was a scream wrapped up in straw, a little, weak, vicious thing gnashing inside a monstrous façade. She saw what he was made of, and she knew him very well.

"Take it," she told him, and her heart was beating wildly, but she knew he'd be on her at the first smell of fear. "It's time."

The grin faded. His eyes ticked from her face to the apple and back again like a deadly metronome.

"Take it," she urged, the blood pounding so hard in her head she couldn't hear herself.

He stared into her eyes—and Swan felt him probe her mind like a freezing ice pick. Little cuts here and there, and then a dark examination of her memories. It was as if every moment of her life was being invaded, picked up and soiled with dirty hands, tossed aside. But she kept her gaze steady and strong, and she would not retreat before him.

The apple snagged his attention again, and the cold ice pick jabbing within Swan's mind ceased. She saw his eyes glaze over and his mouth open, and from that mouth crawled a green fly that weakly spun around her head and fell into the mud.

His hand began to rise. Slowly, very slowly.

Swan didn't look at it, but she sensed it rising like the head of a cobra. She was waiting for it to burst into flame. But it did not.

His fingers strained for the apple.

And Swan saw that his hand was trembling.

He almost took it.

Almost.

His other hand shot out and grabbed his own wrist, wrenched his arm back and pinned the offending hand underneath his chin. He made a gasping, moaning noise that sounded like wind through the battlements of Hell's castles, and his eyes almost bulged from his skull. He shrank backward from Swan, his teeth gritted in a snarl, and for an instant he lost control: one eye bleached to blue, and white pigment streaked across the ebony flesh. A second mouth, full of shiny white nubs, gaped like a scar across his right cheekbone.

In his eyes was hatred and fury and longing for what could never be.

He turned and fled, and with his first running stride the trance of time broke and the crowd was whirling around Swan again, grabbing up the last of the apples. Josh was just a few feet away, trying to get through to protect her. But it was all right now, she knew. She needed no more protection.

Someone else plucked the apple from her hand.

She looked into Robin's face.

"I hope this one's for me," he said, and he smiled before he bit into it.

He ran through the muddy alleys of Mary's Rest with his hand trapped beneath his chin, and where he was going he didn't know. The hand tensed and shivered, as if trying to fight free with a will of its own. Dogs scattered out of his path, and then he tripped over debris and went down in the mud, got up and staggered on again.

And if anyone had seen his face, they would have witnessed a thousand transformations.

Too late! he screamed inwardly. Too late! Too late!

He'd planned to set her afire, right there in the midst of them, and laugh as he watched her dance. But he'd looked into her eyes and seen forgiveness, and he could not stand up to such a thing. Forgiveness, even for *him*.

He'd started to take the apple; for a brief instant, he'd *wanted* it, like taking the first step along a dark corridor that led back to light. But then the rage and pain had flared within him, and he'd felt the very walls of the universe warp and the wheels of time start to clog and lock. Too late! Too late!

But he needed no one and nothing to survive, he told himself. He had endured and would endure, and this was his party now. He had always walked alone. Always walked alone. Always walked—

A scream echoed from the edge of Mary's Rest, and those who heard it thought it sounded like someone being flayed alive.

But most of the people were busy collecting apples, shouting and laughing as they ate, and they did not hear.

Seventy-one

A ring of torches lit the night, burning around the perimeter of a huge parking lot fifteen miles south of the ruins of Lincoln, Nebraska. At the center of the parking lot was a complex of brick buildings connected by sheltered walkways, and with skylights and ventilators set in their flat roofs. In the side of one of the buildings that faced Highway 77 South were rusted metal letters that read GREENBRI R SHOP IN MALL.

On the western edge of the parking lot, a Jeep's lights flashed twice. About twenty seconds later, there was an answering double flash of headlights from a pickup truck with an armored windshield, parked near one of the entrances to the mall.

"There's the signal," Roland Croninger said. "Let's go."

Judd Lawry drove the Jeep slowly across the parking lot, aiming at the headlights that grew closer as the pickup truck approached. The tires jarred roughly over bricks, pieces of metal, old bones and other debris that littered the snow-slick concrete. In the seat behind Roland was a soldier with an automatic rifle, and Lawry wore a .38 in a shoulder holster, but Roland was unarmed. He watched the range between the two vehicles steadily decrease. Both the Jeep and the truck were flying white pieces of cloth from their radio antennas.

"They'll never let you out of there alive," Lawry said, almost casually. He glanced quickly over at Captain Croninger's bandage-wrapped face, cowled by the hood of his coat. "Why'd you volunteer for this?"

The cowled face slowly swiveled toward Lawry. "I like excitement."

"Yeah. Well, you're about to get it . . . *sir.*" Lawry negotiated the Jeep past the hulk of a burned-out car and tapped the brakes. The pickup truck was about fifty feet away and beginning to slow down. The vehicles stopped thirty feet apart.

There was no movement from the truck. "We're waiting!" Roland shouted out his window, the breath steaming through his gnarled lips.

The seconds ticked past with no response. And then the passenger door opened and a blond man wearing a dark blue parka, brown trousers and boots got out. He stepped a few paces away from the door and leveled a shotgun at the Jeep's windshield.

"Steady," Roland cautioned as Lawry started to reach for his .38.

Another man got out of the truck and stood beside the first. He was slight and had close-cropped dark hair, and he lifted his hands to show he was unarmed. "Okay!" the one with the shotgun shouted, getting edgy. "Let's make the trade!"

Roland was afraid. But he'd learned long before how to push the child Roland away and summon forth the Sir Roland in himself: the adventurer in service to the King, the King's will be done, amen. His palms were wet inside his black gloves, but he opened the door and got out.

The soldier with the automatic rifle followed him and stood off to the side a few feet, aiming at the other armed man.

Roland glanced back at Lawry, making sure the fool wasn't going to fuck this up, and then he began walking to the truck. The dark-haired man started walking to the Jeep, his eyes darting and nervous. The two figures passed, neither one looking at the other, and the man with the shotgun grabbed Roland's arm about the same time as the AOE soldier pushed his captive against the Jeep's side.

Roland was made to lean against the truck, spread his arms and legs and submit to a search. When it was over, the man spun him around and pressed the snout of the shotgun underneath his chin. "What's wrong with your face?" the man demanded. "What's under those bandages?"

"I was burned pretty bad," Roland answered. "That's all."

"I don't like it!" The man had lank, thinning blond hair and fierce blue eyes, like a maniac surfer-boy. "Imperfection is Satan's work, praise the Savior!"

"The trade's been done," Roland said. The American Allegiance hostage was already being shoved into the Jeep. "The Savior's waiting for me."

The man paused, jittery and uncertain. And then Lawry began to back the Jeep up, clinching the deal. Roland didn't know if that was smart or stupid.

"Get in!" The American Allegiance soldier hustled him into the truck's cab, where Roland sat squeezed between him and the heavyset, black-bearded driver. The truck veered across the parking lot and turned back toward the mall.

Through the narrow view slit in the armored windshield, Roland saw the headlights pick out more vehicles protecting the American Allegiance's fortress: an armored truck with BRINK's still barely legible on its side, a Jeep with a mounted machine gun in the rear seat, a tractor-trailer rig with dozens of gunports—each showing a rifle or machine gun barrel—cut into the long metal trailer; a postman's truck with a metal mesh turret on top; more cars and trucks, and then the vehicle that put a lump like a hen's egg in Roland's throat—a low-slung, wicked-looking tank covered with multicolored graffiti that said things like THE LOVE BUG and THE SAVIOR LIVES! The tank's main cannon, Roland noted, was aimed in the general direction of Colonel Macklin's Airstream trailer, where the King was now incapacitated, suffering from a fever that had struck him down the previous night.

The truck passed between the tank and another armored

car, went over the curb and continued up a ramp for the handicapped, entering the mall through the dark, open space where glass doors had once been. The headlights illuminated a wide central mall area, with stores on either side that had been looted and wrecked a long time before. Soldiers with rifles, pistols and shotguns waved the truck on, and hundreds of lanterns were burning in the central corridor and in the stores, casting a flickering orange glow—like the light at a Halloween party—throughout the building. And Roland saw hundreds of tents set up as well, cramped into every possible space except for a path along which the truck traveled. Roland realized that the whole American Allegiance had set up camp inside the shopping mall, and as the truck turned into a larger, skylighted atrium he heard singing and saw the glare of a fire.

Perhaps one thousand people were jammed into the atrium, clapping their hands rhythmically, singing and swaying around a large campfire, the smoke whirling up through the skylight's broken glass. Almost all of them had rifles slung over their shoulders, and Roland knew that one reason the Savior had invited an AOE officer here was to display his weapons and troops. But the reason Roland had accepted the courier's invitation was to find a weak spot in the Savior's fortress.

The truck did not enter the atrium, but continued along another corridor that branched off from it, again lined with looted stores now filled with tents, drums of gasoline and oil, what looked like cases of canned food and bottled water, clothes, weapons and other supplies. The truck stopped in front of a store, and the blond man with the shotgun got out and motioned for Roland to follow. Roland saw the broken fragments of a sign that had once said B. DALTON BOOKSELLERS over the entrance before he walked into the store.

Three lanterns burned on the cashier's desk, where both registers had been battered into junk. The walls of the store were scorched, and Roland's boots crunched over the skeletons of charred books. Not a volume remained on the shelves or display tables; everything had been piled up and set afire. More lanterns glowed back at the store's information desk, and the man with the shotgun pushed Roland toward the closed door of the stockroom, where another American Allegiance soldier with an automatic rifle stood at attention. As Roland approached, the soldier lowered his rifle and clicked the safety off. "Halt," he said. Roland stopped.

The soldier rapped on the door.

A short, bald man with narrow, foxlike features peered out. He smiled warmly. "Hello, there! He's almost ready to see you. He wants to know your name."

"Roland Croninger."

The man pulled his head back into the room and closed the door again. Then, abruptly, it opened, and the bald man asked, "Are you Jewish?"

"No." And then the hood of Roland's coat was yanked back.

"Look!" the man with the shotgun said. "Tell him they sent us somebody with a *disease!*"

"Oh. Oh, dear." The other one looked fretfully at Roland's bandaged face. "What's wrong with you, Roland?"

"I was burned, back on the seven—"

"He's a fork-tongued *liar,* Brother Norman!" The shotgun's barrel pressed against the hard growths on Roland's skull. "He's got the Satan Leprosy!"

Brother Norman frowned and made a clicking sound of sympathy with his lips. "Wait one minute," he said, and again he disappeared into the stockroom. He returned, approached Roland and said, "Open your mouth, please."

"What?"

The shotgun nudged his skull. "Do it."

Roland did. Brother Norman smiled. "That's good. Now stick out your tongue. My, my, I believe you need a new toothbrush!" He placed a small silver crucifix on Roland's tongue. "Now keep that inside your mouth for a few seconds, all right? Don't swallow it!"

Roland drew the crucifix in on his tongue and closed his mouth. Brother Norman smiled cheerfully. "That crucifix was blessed by the Savior," he explained. "It's very special. If you have corruption in you, the crucifix will be black when you open your mouth again. And if it *is* black, Brother Edward will blow your brains out."

Roland's eyes widened momentarily behind the goggles.

Perhaps forty seconds crept by. "Open up!" Brother Norman announced in a merry voice.

Roland opened his mouth, slowly stuck his tongue out and watched the other man's face for a reaction.

"Guess what," Brother Norman said. He took the crucifix from Roland's tongue and held it up. It was still bright silver. "You passed! The Savior will see you now."

Brother Edward gave Roland's skull a final shove for good measure, and Roland followed Brother Norman into the stockroom. Sweat was trickling down Roland's sides, but his mind was calm and detached.

Illuminated by lamplight, a man with brushed-back, wavy gray hair sat in a chair before a table, being attended to by another man and a young woman. There were two or three other people in the room, all standing back beyond the light's edge.

"Hello, Roland," the gray-haired man in the chair said gently, a smile twisting the left side of his mouth; he was holding his head very still, and Roland could only see his left profile—a high, aristocratic forehead, a strong and hawklike nose, a straight gray brow over a clear azure eye, clean-shaven cheek and jaw and a chin as powerful as a mallet. Roland thought he was probably in his late fifties, but the Savior seemed in robust health, and his face was unmarred. He was wearing a pin-striped suit with a vest and a blue tie, and he looked ready to preach before the cameras on one of his cable TV telecasts—but on closer observation Roland saw well-worn patches here and there at stress points on the coat, and leather pads had been sewn onto the knees. The Savior was wearing hiking boots. Around his neck, dangling down in front of his vest, were maybe twelve or fifteen silver and gold crucifixes on chains, some of them studded with precious stones. The Savior's sturdy hands were decorated with half a dozen glittering diamond rings.

The man and young woman attending him were working on

his face with pencils and powder applicators. Roland saw an open make-up case on the table.

The Savior lifted his head slightly so the woman could powder his neck. "I'm going before my people in about five minutes, Roland. They're singing for me right now. They have voices like angels, don't they?" Roland didn't answer, and the Savior smiled faintly. "How long has it been since you've heard music?"

"I make my own," Roland replied.

The Savior tilted his head to the right as the man penciled his eyebrow. "I like to look my best," he said. "There's no excuse for a shabby appearance, not even in this day and age. I like for my people to look at me and see confidence. And confidence is a good thing, isn't it? It means you're strong, and you can deal with the traps Satan lays for you. Oh, Satan's very busy these days, Roland—yes, he is!" He folded his hands in his lap. "Of course, Satan has many faces, many names—and one of those names might be *Roland*. Is it?"

"No."

"Well, Satan's a liar, so what did I expect?" He laughed, and the others laughed, too. When he was through laughing, he let the woman rub rouge onto his left cheek. "All right, Satan—I mean, *Roland*—tell me what you want. And tell me why you and your army of demons have been following us for the last two days, and why you've now encircled us. If I knew anything about military tactics, I might think you were about to lay siege. I wouldn't like to think that. It might disturb me, thinking of all the poor demons who were about to die for their Master. Speak, Satan!" His voice snapped like a whip, and everybody in the room jumped but Roland.

"I'm Captain Roland Croninger of the Army of Excellence. Colonel James Macklin is my superior officer. We want your gasoline, oil, food and weapons. If you give those to us within six hours, we'll withdraw and leave you in peace."

"You mean leave us in *pieces,* don't you?" The Savior grinned and almost turned his face toward Roland, but the woman was powdering his forehead. "The Army of Excellence. I think I've heard of you. I thought you were in Colorado."

"We moved."

"Well, I guess that's what armies do, isn't it? Oh, we've met 'armies' before," he said, slurring the word with disgust. "Some of them wore little uniforms and had little pop-guns, and all of them crumpled like paper dolls. No army can stand before the Savior, Roland. You go back and tell your 'superior officer' that. Tell him I'll say a prayer for both your souls."

Roland was about to be dismissed. He decided to try another tactic. "Who are you going to pray to? The god on top of Warwick Mountain?"

There was silence. The two make-up artists froze, and both of them looked at Roland. He could hear the Savior's breathing in the quiet.

"Brother Gary's joined us," Roland continued calmly. "He's told us everything—where you're going and why." Under Roland's persuasion in the black trailer, Gary Cates had repeated his tale of God living atop Warwick Mountain, West Virginia, and something about a black box and a silver key that could decide whether the earth lived or died. Even the grinding wheel hadn't changed the man's story. True to his word, Macklin had spared Brother Gary's life, and Brother Gary had been skinned and hung by his ankles from a flagpole in front of Sutton's post office.

The silence stretched. Finally, the Savior said softly, "I don't know any Brother Gary."

"He knows you. He told us how many soldiers you have. He told us about the two tanks. I've seen one of them, and I guess the other is around back somewhere. Brother Gary's a real fountain of information! He told us about Brother Timothy leading you to Warwick Mountain to find God." Roland smiled, showing bad teeth between the folds of his bandages. "But God's closer than West Virginia. Much closer. He's right out there, and he's going to blast you to Hell in six hours if we don't get what we want."

The Savior was sitting very still. Roland saw him tremble.

Saw the left side of his mouth twitch and his left eye begin to bulge, as if shoved forward by a volcanic pressure.

The Savior shoved the two make-up artists aside. His head swiveled toward Roland—and Roland saw both sides of his face.

The left side was perfect, brightened by rouge and smoothed with powder. The right side was a nightmare of scar tissue, the flesh gouged out by a terrible wound and the eye white and dead as a river pebble.

The Savior's living eye fixed on Roland like Judgment Hour, and as he stood up he grabbed the chair and flung it across the room. He advanced on Roland, the little crucifixes jingling around his neck, and lifted his fist.

Roland stood his ground.

They stared at each other, and there was a great, empty silence like that before the clash of an irresistible force and an immovable object.

"Savior?" a voice spoke. "He's a fool, and he's trying to bait you."

The Savior wavered. His eye blinked, and Roland could see the wheels turning in his head, trying to connect and make sense of things again.

A figure stepped out of the gloom to Roland's right. It was a tall, frail-looking man in his late twenties with slicked-back black hair and wire-rimmed glasses over deep-socketed brown eyes. A burn scar zigzagged like a lightning bolt from his forehead to the back of his skull, and along its route the hair had turned white. "Don't touch him, Savior," the man urged quietly. "They have Brother Kenneth."

"Brother Kenneth?" The Savior shook his head, uncomprehending.

"You sent Brother Kenneth as a trade for this man. Brother Kenneth is a good mechanic. We don't want him harmed, do we?"

"Brother Kenneth," the Savior repeated. "A good mechanic. Yes. He's a good mechanic."

"It's almost time for you to go on," the man said. "They're singing for you."

"Yes. Singing. For me." The Savior looked up at his fist, hanging in the air; he opened it and let his arm fall back to his side. Then he stood staring at the floor, the left corner of his mouth twitching in an on-again, off-again grin.

"Dear me, dear me!" Brother Norman fretted. "Let's finish the job now, kiddies! He's on presently, and we want him to look confident!"

A couple of other people emerged from the shadows, took the Savior's arms and turned him around like a marionette so the make-up artists could finish.

"You're a foolish, stupid heathen," the man with the eyeglasses said to Roland. "You must want to die very much."

"We'll see who lives and dies when six hours are up."

"God *is* on Warwick Mountain. He lives up near the top, where the coal mines are. I've seen him. I've *touched* him. My name is Brother Timothy."

"Good for you."

"You can go with us, if you like. You can join us and go to find God and learn how the wicked will die at the final hour. He'll still be there, waiting for us. I know he will."

"When's the final hour going to be?"

Brother Timothy smiled. "That only God knows. But he showed me how the fire will rain from Heaven, and in that rain even Noah's Ark would drown. In the final hour all the imperfection and wickedness will be washed clean, and the world will be fresh and new again."

"Right," Roland said.

"Yes. It *is* right. I stayed with God for seven days and seven nights, up on Warwick Mountain, and he taught me the prayer that he will speak at the final hour." Brother Timothy closed his eyes, smiling beatifically, and began to recite: "Here is Belladonna, the Lady of the Rocks, the lady of situations. Here is the man with three staves, and here the Wheel, and here is the one-eyed merchant, and this card, which is blank, is something he carries on his back which I am forbidden to see. I do not find The Hanged Man. Fear death by water." And when he opened his eyes they glistened with tears.

"Get that Satan out of here!" the Savior croaked. "Get him *out!*"

"Six hours," Roland said, but in his mind the prayer for the final hour echoed like the memory of a funeral bell.

"Get thee behind me, Satan; get thee behind me, Satan; get thee behind me, Sa—" the Savior intoned, and then Roland was taken out of the stockroom and delivered to Brother Edward again for the return trip.

Roland impressed everything he saw on his mind to report back to Colonel Macklin. He'd discovered no obviously weak areas, but once he sat down to draw a map of what he'd seen, maybe one would become apparent.

The ritual of the headlights was repeated. Roland was returned to the Jeep, and again he and Brother Kenneth passed without looking at each other. Then he was in the Jeep and breathing easily once more as Judd Lawry drove toward the fires of the AOE's camp.

"Have fun?" Lawry asked him.

"Yeah. Get me to the Command Center fast." I do not find the Hanged Man, Roland thought. God's prayer for the final hour was somehow familiar to him—but it wasn't a prayer. No. It was . . . it was . . .

There was some kind of activity around the colonel's trailer. The guards were out of formation, and one of them was hammering at the door with the butt of his rifle. Roland leapt out of the Jeep as it slowed down, and he ran toward the trailer. "What's going on?"

One of the guards hastily saluted. "The colonel's locked himself in, sir! We can't get the door open, and . . . well, you'd better hear it for yourself!"

Roland went up the steps, pushed the other guard aside and listened.

The sound of breaking furniture and shattering glass came through the Airstream's metal door. Then there was a barely human wailing that sent a shiver creeping up even Roland Croninger's spine.

"Jesus!" Lawry said, blanching. "There's some kind of animal in there with him!"

The last time Roland had seen him, the colonel was

immobile on his cot and burning up with fever. "Somebody was supposed to be with him at all times!" Roland snapped. "What happened?"

"I just stepped out for about five minutes to have a smoke!" the other guard said, and in his eyes was the fearful knowledge that he would have to pay dearly for that cigarette. "It was just five minutes, sir!"

Roland hammered on the door with his fist. "Colonel! Open up! It's Roland!"

The noise became a guttural grunting that sounded like a bestial equivalent of sobs. Something else shattered—and then there was silence.

Roland beat on the door again, stepped back and told the guard to get it open if he had to blast it off its hinges.

But someone else walked calmly up the steps, and a hand gripping a thin-bladed knife slid toward the door's lock.

"Mind if I give it a try, Captain?" Air whistled through the hole where Alvin Mangrim's nose had been.

Roland detested the sight of him, and also of that damned ugly dwarf who stood jumping up and down a few feet away. But it was worth a shot, and Roland said, "Go ahead."

Mangrim inserted the blade into the door's keyhole. He began to twist the knife back and forth, a hair at a time. "If he's got the bolts thrown, this won't do much good," he said. "We'll see."

"Just do what you can."

"Knives know my name, Captain. They speak to me and tell me what to do. This one's talking to me right now. It says, 'Easy, Alvin, real easy does the trick.'" He gently swiveled the blade, and there was a *click!* as the lock popped open. "See?"

The bolts had not been thrown, and the door opened.

Roland entered the darkened trailer, with Lawry and Mangrim right behind him. "We need some light!" Roland shouted, and the guard who'd sneaked a cigarette popped the flame up on his lighter and gave it to him.

The front room was a shambles, the map table overthrown and the chair broken to pieces, the rifles pulled off the wall rack and used to shatter lanterns and more furniture. Roland went into the bedroom, which was equally wrecked. Colonel Macklin was not there, but the lighter's flame showed what looked at first like fragments of gray pottery lying all over the sweat-damp pillow. He picked one up and examined it, couldn't quite figure out what it was; but some kind of white jellylike stuff got on his fingers, and Roland flung the thing aside.

"He's not back here!" Lawry yelled from the other end of the trailer.

"He's got to be somewhere!" Roland shouted back, and when his voice faded away he heard something.

The sound of whimpering.

Coming from the bedroom closet.

"Colonel?" The whimpering stopped, but Roland could still hear rapid, frightened breathing.

Roland walked to the closet, put his hand on the knob and started to turn it.

"Go away, damn you!" a voice thundered from behind the door.

Roland froze. That voice was a nightmarish mockery of Colonel Macklin's. It sounded as if he'd been gargling with razor blades. "I . . . have to open the door, Colonel."

"No . . . no . . . please go away!" Then there was that guttural grunting again, and Roland realized he was crying.

Roland's spine stiffened. He hated it when the King sounded weak. It wasn't the proper way for a king to behave. A king should never show weakness, *never!* He twisted the doorknob and pulled the closet door open, holding the lighter up to see what was inside.

Roland saw and screamed.

He backpedaled, still screaming, as the beast within the closet—the beast wearing Colonel Macklin's uniform and even the nail-studded hand—crawled out and, grinning crazily, began to stand up.

The crust of growths was gone from the colonel's face and head, and as Roland retreated across the room he realized the cracked pieces of it were lying over on the pillow.

Macklin's face had turned inside out. The flesh was bone-white, the nose had collapsed inward; the veins, muscles and knots of cartilage ran on the surface of his face, twitching and quivering as he opened those awful jaws to laugh with a shriek like fingernails on a chalkboard. His teeth had curved into jagged fangs, and his gums were mottled and yellow. The veins on his face were as thick as worms, lacing and intertwining across his bony cheeks, beneath the sockets of his stunned and staring ice-blue eyes, across his forehead and back into his thick, newly grown mat of graying hair. It looked as if the entire outer layer of facial flesh had either been peeled back or rotted away, and exposed was something as close to a living skull as Roland had ever seen.

He was laughing, and the hideously exposed jaw muscles jerked and quivered. The veins writhed as the pressure of blood filled them up. But as he laughed his eyes swam with tears, and he began to slam his nail-studded hand against the wall again and again, dragging the nails down through the cheap paneling.

Lawry and Mangrim had entered the room. Lawry stopped short when he saw the monster in Colonel Macklin's clothes, and he reached for his .38, but Roland grabbed his wrist.

Mangrim just smiled. "Far *out*, man!"

Seventy-two

Sister was dreaming of the sun. It burned hot in a dazzling blue sky, and she could actually see her shadow again. The sun's royal heat played on her face, settled into the lines and cracks and seeped down through her skin into her bones. Oh, Lord! she thought. It feels so good not to be cold anymore, and to see the blue sky, and your own shadow looking up at you! The summer day promised to be a scorcher, and Sister's face was already sweating, but that was all right, too. To see the sky no longer somber and overcast was one of the happiest moments of her life, and if she had to die she asked God to let it be in sunshine.

She stretched her arms up toward the sun and cried aloud with joy because the long, terrible winter was finally over.

Sitting in a chair next to the bed, Paul Thorson thought he heard Sister say something—just a drowsy whisper. He leaned forward, listening, but Sister was silent. The air around her seemed to ripple with heat, though the wind was shrilling outside the shack's walls and the temperature had fallen to well below zero just after dark. That morning, Sister had told Paul that she'd felt weak, but she'd kept going all day until the fever finally struck her down; she'd collapsed on the porch and had been sleeping, fading in and out of delirium, for about six hours.

In her sleep, though, Sister kept the leather satchel with the glass ring inside locked between her hands, and even Josh couldn't loosen her grip. Paul knew she'd come too far with the glass ring, had watched over it and protected it from harm for too long; she wasn't yet ready to give it up.

Paul had presumed that finding Swan meant the end of the dreamwalk path. But in the morning he'd watched Sister peer into the depths of the glass, just as she had done before they'd reached Mary's Rest. He'd seen the lights glitter in her eyes, and he knew her stare: The ring had taken her away again, and she was dreamwalking somewhere beyond Paul's realm of senses and imagination. Afterward, when Sister had come back—and it was over in about fifteen or twenty seconds—she shook her head and wouldn't talk about it. She had returned the glass circle to the satchel and hadn't looked into it again. But Paul had seen that Sister was troubled, and he knew that this time the dreamwalk path had taken a dark turn.

"How is she?"

Swan was standing a few feet behind him, and how long she'd been there he didn't know. "About the same," he said. "As hot as a four-alarm fire."

Swan approached the bed. She was familiar by now with the symptoms. In the two days since Sylvester Moody had brought his gift of apples, she and Josh had seen eight other people with Job's Mask who'd drifted into feverish, comalike sleep. When the growths had cracked open from the faces of seven of them, their skin was unmarked, their faces back to—or *better* than—what they'd been before. But the eighth one had been different.

It was a man named DeLauren, who lived alone in a small shed on the eastern edge of Mary's Rest. Josh and Swan had been summoned by a neighbor, who'd found DeLauren lying on the shed's dirty floor, unconscious and feverish. Josh had picked the man up and carried him across the shed to his mattress—and Josh's weight had popped open a floorboard. As Josh knelt to press the board back, he'd smelled the odor of decaying flesh and seen something wet and gleaming down in the gloom. He'd reached into the hole and brought up a severed human hand with most of the fingers gnawed away.

And at that moment DeLauren's face had cracked open, revealing something black and reptilian underneath. The man had sat up, screaming, and as he'd realized his hoard of food had been discovered he'd crawled across the floor, snapping at Josh with sharp little fangs. Swan had looked away before the rest of the man's Job's Mask had cracked apart, but Josh had grabbed him by the back of his neck and flung him head first through the door. Their last sight of DeLauren was as he fled toward the woods, clutching his hands to his face.

There was no way to tell how many bodies had been torn apart and hidden under the shed's floorboards, or who the people had been. DeLauren's shocked neighbor said he'd always been a quiet, soft-spoken man who wouldn't have hurt a fly. At Swan's suggestion, Josh had set fire to the shed and burned it to the ground. On returning to Glory's shack, Josh had spent the better part of an hour scrubbing his hands until he got the slime of DeLauren off his skin.

Swan touched the Job's Mask that covered the lower half of Sister's face and clung to her skull. It, too, was hot with fever. "What do you think she looks like, deep inside?" Swan asked Paul.

"Huh?"

"Her real face is about to show through," Swan said, and her dark blue eyes with their glints of many colors met his own. "That's what's underneath the Job's Mask. The face of a person's soul."

Paul scratched his beard. He didn't know what she was talking about, but when she spoke he listened to her, just like everybody else did. Her voice was gentle, but it conveyed a power of thought and command that was far older than her years. Yesterday he'd worked out in the field with some of the others, helping to dig holes and watching Swan plant the apple cores she'd gathered after the big apple-eating festival. She'd explained carefully exactly how deep the holes should be, and how far apart; then, as Josh had followed along behind her with a wheelbarrow full of apple cores, Swan had picked up handfuls of dirt, spat into them, and rubbed the dirt all over each core before placing them in the ground and covering them. And the crazy thing about it was that Swan's presence had made Paul want to work, though digging holes in the cold ground was not his idea of how to spend the day. She'd made him want to dig each hole as precisely as possible, and a single word of praise from her put energy in him like a charge into a weakening battery. He'd watched the others, too, and seen that she had the same effect on them. He believed that she could grow apple trees from each seed-filled core that went into the ground, and he was proud to dig holes for her until Gideon's trumpet blared New Orleans jazz. He believed in *her*, and if she said that Sister's real face was about to show through, he believed that, too.

"What do you think she looks like, deep inside?" Swan asked him again.

"I don't know," he finally replied. "I never met anyone with as much courage. She's one hell of a woman. A *lady,"* he said.

"Yes, she is." Swan looked at the knotty surface of the Job's Mask. Soon, she thought. Very soon. "She'll be all right," she said. "Do you need to get some rest?"

"No, I'm going to stay here with her. If I get sleepy, I can stretch out on the floor. Everybody else asleep?"

"Yes. It's late."

"I guess so. You'd better get some sleep yourself."

"I will. But when it happens, I'd like to see her."

"I'll call you," Paul promised, and then he thought he heard Sister say something again, and he leaned forward to hear. Her head slowly moved back and forth, but she made no other sounds, and she lay still again. When Paul looked up, Swan had gone.

Swan was too keyed-up to sleep. She felt like a child again on the night before Christmas. She went through the front room, where the others slept on the floor around the stove, and then opened the door. Cold wind swept in, fanning the stove's coals. Swan quickly stepped out, hugging her coat around her shoulders, and closed the door behind her.

"Mighty late for you to be up," Anna McClay said. She was

sitting on the porch steps next to an ex-Pittsburgh steelworker named Polowsky, and both of them were wearing heavy coats, caps and gloves and armed with rifles. At dawn, another pair of guards would take over for a few hours, and the rotating shifts continued all day and night. "How's Sister doin'?"

"No change yet." Swan looked at the bonfire that burned in the middle of the road. The wind whipped through it, and a shower of red sparks wheeled into the sky. About twenty people were sleeping around the bonfire, and several more were sitting up, staring into the flames or talking to one another to pass the night. Until she knew where the man with the scarlet eye was, Sister had demanded that the shack be guarded at all times, a demand to which Josh and the others had readily agreed. The volunteers also stayed around the bonfires in the field all night, watching the cornstalks and the new area where the apple cores had been planted.

Swan had told Josh and Sister about facing the man with the scarlet eye in the crowd that day, and she thought that maybe—just a little bit—she understood why he struck out to cause such suffering in human beings. She knew also that he'd almost taken the apple, but at the last second his unthinking rage and pride had won. And she'd seen that he hated her and hated himself for wanting to take a step beyond what he was; but he'd been afraid of her, too, and as she'd watched him stagger away Swan had realized that forgiveness crippled evil, drew the poison from it like lancing a boil. What might have happened if he'd taken the apple she didn't know, but the moment was gone. Still, she didn't fear the man with the scarlet eye as she had before, and since that day she hadn't been looking over her shoulder to see who was coming up from behind.

She walked to the corner of the porch, where Mule was hitched to the support post. The horse was kept warm by several blankets, and there was a pail of spring water for him to drink from. Finding food for him was a problem, but Swan had saved him a dozen apple cores and was feeding him those, as well as roots and some straw that had been stuffed inside Mr. Polowsky's mattress. He liked horses and had offered to help feed and water Mule. The horse didn't generally take to strangers, but he seemed to accept Mr. Polowsky's attention with a minimum of crankiness.

Mule's head had been drooping, but his nose twitched as he caught Swan's aroma, and instantly his head came up, his eyes open and alert. She scratched between his eyes and then down at the soft, velvety skin of his muzzle, and Mule nibbled at her fingers with unabashed delight.

Swan suddenly looked over toward the fire and saw him standing there, silhouetted by flames and sparks. She couldn't see his face, but she could feel him staring at her. Her skin broke out in goose bumps under her patchwork coat, and she quickly looked away, concentrating only on rubbing Mule's muzzle. But her eyes slid back toward Robin, who had come a few feet closer to the porch's edge. Her heart boomed like a kettle drum, and again she looked away. From the corner of her eye, she watched him approach, then stop and pretend to be examining something on the ground with the toe of his boot.

It's time to go back in now, she told herself. Time to check on Sister again.

But her legs didn't want to move. Robin was coming nearer, and then he stopped again and peered out beyond the fire as if something else had taken his attention. He shoved his hands into the pockets of his coat, seemed to be trying to decide whether to return to the bonfire's warmth or not. Swan didn't know if she wanted him to come closer or go away, and she felt as jumpy as a grasshopper on a hot rock.

Then he took another step forward. His mind was made up.

But Swan's nerve broke, and she started to turn away and go back inside.

Mule decided the issue by choosing that instant to playfully clamp his teeth on Swan's fingers, holding her prisoner for the few seconds it took Robin to reach her.

"I think your horse must be hungry," he said.

Swan pulled her fingers free. She started to turn away again, her heart pounding so strongly that she was certain he must hear it, like distant thunder over the horizon.

"Don't go." Robin's voice softened. "Please."

Swan stopped. She thought he didn't resemble at all the movie stars in the magazines her mother used to read, because there was nothing clean-cut and Hollywood-handsome about him; he looked nothing like the well-scrubbed teen-age boys in the soap operas Darleen Prescott had watched. His face, for all its hard lines and angles, was young, but his eyes were old. They were the color of ashes but looked capable of fire. She met his gaze, saw that he'd loosened his mask of toughness. His eyes were soft—maybe even tender—as he stared up at her.

"Hey!" Anna McClay said. "You go on about your business. Swan doesn't have time for you."

His tough mask tightened again. "Who made you her keeper?"

"Not keeper, smartass. *Protector.* Now, why don't you just be a good little boy and go on—"

"No," Swan interrupted. "I don't need a keeper, or a protector. Thank you for being concerned about me, Anna, but I can take care of myself."

"Oh. Sorry. I just thought he was botherin' you again."

"He's not bothering me. It's all right. Really."

"You *sure?* I used to see his type strollin' the midway, lookin' for pockets to pick."

"I'm sure," Swan replied. Anna gave Robin another warning glare, then returned to her conversation with Mr. Polowsky.

"That's telling her," Robin said, smiling gratefully. "It's about time she got her butt kicked."

"No, it's not. You might not like Anna, and she sure doesn't like you, but she's doing what she thinks is best for me, and I appreciate that. If you *were* bothering me, I would let her run you off."

Robin's smile faded. "So you think you're better than everybody else?"

"No, I didn't mean it like that." Swan felt flustered and nervous, and her tongue was getting tangled between her thoughts and her words. "I just meant . . . Anna is right to be careful."

"Uh-huh. So am I bothering you by being friendly?"

"You were a little too friendly when you came into the shack and . . . and woke me up that way," she replied crisply. She could feel her face reddening, and she wanted to go back to the beginning and start the conversation all over again, but it was out of control now, and she was half scared and half angry. "And I wasn't *offering* you that apple the other day, either!"

"Oh, I get it. Well, *my* feet are on solid ground. They're not up on a pedestal like some people's are. And maybe I couldn't help it that I kissed you, and maybe when I saw you standing there with an apple in your hand and your eyes big and wide I couldn't help but take it, either. When I first saw you, I thought you were okay; I didn't know you were a stuck-up little princess!"

"I'm *not!*"

"No? Well, you act like one. Listen, I've been around! I've met a lot of girls! I know stuck-up when I see it!"

"And—" Stop! she thought. Stop right now! But she couldn't, because she was scared inside, and she didn't dare let him know how much. "And *I* know a crude, loudmouthed . . . *fool* when I see one!"

"Yeah, I'm a fool, all right!" He shook his head and laughed without humor. "I'm sure a fool for thinking I might like to get to know the ice princess better, huh?" He stalked away before she could reply.

All she could think to say was, "Don't bother me again!" Instantly she felt a pang of pain that sliced her open from head to toe. She clenched her teeth to keep from calling him. If he was going to act like a fool, then he was one! He was a baby with a bad temper, and she wanted nothing more to do with him.

But she knew also that a kind word might call him back. One kind word, that was all. And was that so hard? He'd misunderstood her, and maybe she'd misunderstood him as well. She felt Anna and Mr. Polowsky watching her, and she sensed that Anna might be wearing a faint, knowing smile. Mule rumbled and exhaled steam into Swan's face. Swan pushed aside her swollen pride and started to call Robin, and as she opened her mouth the shack's door opened and Paul Thorson said excitedly, "Swan! It's happening!"

She watched Robin walking toward the bonfire. And then she followed Paul into the shack.

Robin stood at the edge of the fire. Slowly, he balled up a fist and placed it against his forehead. "Dumb, dumb, dumb, *dumb!*" he said as he hit himself in the head. He still didn't know what had happened; he just knew he'd been scared to death even speaking to someone as beautiful as Swan. He'd wanted to impress her, but now he felt like he'd just walked barefoot through a cow pasture. "Dumb, dumb, dumb!" he kept repeating. Of course, he hadn't met a lot of girls; in fact, he hardly had met *any* girls. He didn't know how to act around them. They were like creatures from another planet. How did you talk to them without . . . yeah, without coming off like a loudmouthed fool—which was exactly what he knew he was.

Well, he told himself, everything's sure messed up now! He was still shaking inside, and he felt sick down in the pit of his stomach. And when he shut his eyes he could still see Swan standing before him, as radiant as the most wonderful dream he'd ever known. Since the first day he'd seen her, lying asleep on the bed, he hadn't been able to get her out of his mind.

I love her, he thought. He'd heard about love, but he'd had no idea love made you feel giddy and sick and shaky all at the same time. I love her. And he didn't know whether to shout or cry, so he just stood staring into the flames and seeing nothing but Swan's face.

"I believe I just heard two arrows hit a couple of rear ends," Anna told Mr. Polowsky, and they looked at each other and laughed.

Seventy-three

The man with a face like a skull stood up in his Jeep and lifted an electric bullhorn. His jagged teeth parted, and he bellowed, "Kill them! Kill! Kill! *Kill!*"

Macklin's roar mingled with the shout of engines firing and was finally drowned out by the thunder of machinery as more than six hundred armored cars, trucks, Jeeps and vans began to move across the parking lot toward the Savior's fortress. Dawn's gray light was further dirtied by banners of drifting smoke, and fires burned on the parking lot, consuming the two hundred vehicles that had been wrecked or destroyed during the first two assault waves. The broken bodies of AOE soldiers lay dead or dying on the cracked concrete, and there were new screams of agony as the wheels of the third wave rolled over the wounded.

"Kill them! *Kill them all!*" Macklin continued to shout through the bullhorn, waving the monster machines on with his black-gloved right hand. The nails protruding from its palm glinted with the fires of destruction.

Hundreds of soldiers, armed with rifles, pistols and Molotov cocktails, moved on foot behind the advancing vehicles. And in a semicircle around the shopping mall, three densely packed rows of American Allegiance trucks, cars and vans awaited the onslaught, just as they'd waited for and repulsed the previous two. But piles of Allegiance dead littered the parking lot as well, and many of their vehicles blazed, still exploding as the gas tanks ruptured.

Flames leaped, and bitter smoke filled the air. But Macklin looked toward the Savior's fortress and grinned, because he knew the Allegiance could not stand before the might of the Army of Excellence. They would fall—if not in the third attack, then in the fourth, or fifth, or sixth, or seventh. The battle was winnable, Macklin knew. Today he would be the victor, and he would make the Savior kneel and kiss his boot before he smashed the Savior's face.

"Closer!" Macklin shouted to his driver, and Judd Lawry flinched. Lawry couldn't stand to look at Macklin's face, and as he drove the Jeep nearer to the advancing line of vehicles he didn't know whom he feared most: the leering, ranting *thing* that Colonel Macklin had become, or the American Allegiance sharpshooters.

"Onward! Onward! Keep moving!" Macklin commanded the soldiers, his eyes sweeping the ranks, watching for any signs of hesitation. "They're about to break!" he shouted. "Onward! Keep going!"

Macklin heard a horn blare and looked back to see a bright red, rebuilt Cadillac with an armored windshield roaring across the lot, weaving through and around other vehicles to get to the front. The driver had long, curly blond hair, and a dwarf was crouched up in the Cadillac's roof turret where the snout of a machine gun protruded. "Closer, Lieutenant!" Macklin ordered. "I want a front row seat!"

Oh, Jesus! Lawry thought. His armpits were sweating. It was one thing to attack a bunch of farmers armed with shovels and hoes, and something else entirely to storm a brick fortress where the fuckers had heavy artillery!

But the American Allegiance held their fire as the AOE's trucks and vans rolled steadily forward.

Macklin knew all his officers were in place, leading their battalions. Roland Croninger was on the right, in his own command Jeep, urging two hundred men and more than fifty armored vehicles into battle. Captains Carr, Wilson and Satterlee, Lieutenants Thatcher and Meyers, Sergeants McCowan, Arnholdt, Benning and Buford—all of his trusted officers were in their places, and all of them had their minds fixed on victory.

Breaking through the Savior's defenses was a simple matter of discipline and control, Macklin had concluded. It didn't matter how many AOE soldiers died, or how many AOE vehicles exploded and burned—this was a test of his personal discipline and control. And he swore that he'd fight to the last man before he let the Savior beat him.

He knew that he'd gone a little crazy when that stuff had cracked open, when he'd picked up a lantern and looked into a mirror at himself, but he was all right now.

Because, after his madness had passed, Colonel Macklin had realized he now wore the face of the Shadow Soldier. They were one and the same now. It was a miracle that told Macklin God was on the side of the Army of Excellence.

He grinned and roared, "Keep moving! Discipline and control!" through the bullhorn in the voice of a beast.

Another voice spoke. It was a hollow-sounding *boom!*, and Macklin saw the flash of orange light by the mall's barricaded entrance. There was a high shrieking noise that seemed to pass right over Macklin's head. About seventy yards behind him, an explosion threw up pieces of concrete and the twisted metal of an already-wrecked van. "Onward!" Macklin commanded. The American Allegiance might have tanks, he thought, but they didn't know shit about shell trajectories. Another round whistled through the air, exploding back in the encampment. And then there was a ripple of fire along the massed defenses of the American Allegiance, and bullets struck sparks from the concrete and ricocheted off the armored vehicles. Some of the soldiers fell, and Macklin shouted, "Attack! Attack! *Open fire!*"

The order was picked up by other officers, and almost at once the machine guns, pistols and automatic rifles of the Army of Excellence began to stutter and crack, aiming a barrage at the enemy's defensive line. The AOE's lead vehicles lunged forward, gathering speed to smash through to the mall. A third tank shell exploded in the parking lot, throwing a plume of smoke and rubble and making the ground tremble. And then some of the Allegiance's heavy vehicles were gunning forward, their engines screaming, and as the trucks and armored cars of both armies slammed together there was a hideous cacophony of shrieking tires, bending metal and ear-cracking explosions.

"Attack! Kill them all!" Macklin kept shouting at the advancing soldiers as Judd Lawry jinked the wheel back and forth to avoid corpses and wrecked hulks. Lawry's eyes were about to pop from his head, beads of cold sweat covering his face. A bullet glanced off the edge of the windshield, and Lawry could feel its vibration like the snap of a tuning fork.

Machine gun fire zigzagged across the parking lot, and half a dozen AOE soldiers spun like demented ballet dancers. Macklin threw aside the bullhorn, wrenched his Colt .45 from his waist holster and shot at Allegiance soldiers as they stormed over the defensive line into the maelstrom of bodies, skidding vehicles, explosions and burning wrecks. So many cars and trucks were slamming together, backing up and charging one another again that the parking lot resembled a gargantuan demolition derby.

Two trucks crashed right in front of the Jeep, and Lawry hit the brakes and twisted the wheel at the same time, throwing the Jeep into a sideswiping skid. Two men were struck down beneath its wheels, and whether they were AOE or Allegiance soldiers Lawry didn't know. Everything was confused and crazy, the air full of blinding smoke and sparks, and over the screaming and shouting Judd Lawry could hear Macklin laughing as the colonel fired at random targets.

A man with a pistol was suddenly framed in the Jeep's headlights, and Lawry ran him down. Bullets thunked against the Jeep's side, and to the left an AOE car exploded, sending its driver tumbling through the air, still gripping a fiery steering wheel.

Between the crashing and skidding vehicles, the infantrymen were locked in savage hand-to-hand combat. Lawry swerved to avoid a burning truck. He heard the shrill whistle of an approaching shell, and his groin shriveled. As he screamed, "We gotta get out of here!" he twisted the wheel violently to the right and sank his foot to the floorboard. The Jeep surged forward, running over two soldiers grappling on the concrete. A tracer bullet whacked into the Jeep's side, and Lawry heard himself whimper.

"Lieutenant!" Macklin shouted. "Turn the Jeep back—"

And that was all he had time to say, because the earth suddenly shook, and there was a blinding, white-hot blast about ten feet in front of the Jeep. The vehicle shuddered and reared up on its back tires like a frightened horse. Macklin heard Lawry's strangled scream—and then Macklin jumped for his life as the scorching shock wave of the explosion hit him and almost ripped the uniform off his body. He struck the concrete on his shoulder and heard the shriek of tires and the crash of the Jeep as it was flung into another car.

The next thing he knew, Macklin was on his feet, his uniform and coat hanging in tatters around him, and he was looking down at Judd Lawry. The man was sprawled on his back amid the wreckage of the Jeep, and his body was twitching as if he were trying to crawl to safety. Judd Lawry's head had been smashed into a misshapen mass of gore, and his broken teeth were clicking together like castanets.

Macklin had his gun in his left hand. The false right hand with its palmful of nails was still attached to the wrist by strong adhesive bandages. Blood was streaming down his right arm and dripping down the black-gloved fingers to the concrete. He realized he'd scraped his arm open from shoulder to elbow, but other than that he seemed to be okay. The soldiers swirled around him, fighting and firing, and a bullet dug up a chunk of parking lot about four inches from his right boot. He looked around, trying to figure out how to get back to the AOE's camp; without transportation, he was as helpless as the lowest infantryman. There was so much screaming, shouting and gunfire that Macklin couldn't think. He saw a man pinning an AOE soldier to the ground, repeatedly stabbing him with a butcher knife, and Macklin pressed the .45's barrel against the man's skull and blew his brains out.

The shock of the recoil thrumming up his arm and the sight of the body keeling over cleared the haze out of Macklin's head; he knew he had to get moving or he would be just as dead as the Allegiance soldier in front of him. He heard another shell coming down, and terror clutched the back of his neck. Ducking his head, he started running, avoiding the knots of fighting men and leaping over sprawled and bleeding bodies.

The explosion rained pieces of concrete down on him. He tripped, fell, crawled frantically behind the shelter of an overturned AOE armored car. Waiting for him was a body with most of the face shot away. Macklin thought it might have been Sergeant Arnholdt. Shaken, the colonel took the clip from his .45 and replaced it with a fresh one. Bullets whined off the armored car, and he crouched against the concrete, trying to find enough courage to continue his race back to the encampment.

Over the tumult, the cries of "Retreat! Retreat!" reached him. The third assault had failed.

He didn't know what had gone wrong. The Allegiance should have broken by now. But they had too many men, too many vehicles, too much firepower. All they had to do was sit tight in that damned mall. There had to be a way to get them out. There *had* to be!

Trucks and cars started racing across the parking lot, heading away from the mall. Soldiers followed them, many hobbling and wounded, stopping to fire a few shots at their pursuers and then stagger on. Macklin forced himself to get up and run, and as he broke from cover he felt a tug at his coat and knew a bullet had passed through. He squeezed off four wild shots without aiming, and then he fled with the rest of his Army of Excellence as machine gun bullets marched across the concrete and more men died around him.

When Macklin made it back to camp, he found Captain Satterlee already getting reports from the other surviving officers, and Lieutenant Thatcher was assigning scouts to guard the perimeter against an Allegiance counterattack. Macklin climbed on top of an armored car and stared at the parking lot. It looked like a slaughterhouse floor, hundreds of bodies lying in heaps around the burning wreckage. Already the Allegiance scavengers were running amid the corpses, gathering weapons and ammunition. From the direction of the mall he heard cheers of victory.

"It's not over!" Colonel Macklin roared. "It's not over yet!" He fired the rest of his bullets at the scavengers, but he was shaking so much he couldn't aim worth a damn.

"Colonel!" It was Captain Satterlee. "Do we prepare another attack?"

"Yes! Immediately! It's not over yet! It's not over until I *say* it's over!"

"We can't take another frontal assault!" another voice contended. "It's suicide!"

"What?" Macklin snapped, and he looked down at whoever dared to question his orders. It was Roland Croninger, his coat spattered with blood. It was someone else's blood, though, because Roland was unhurt, the dirty bandages still wrapped around his face. Blood streaked the lenses of his goggles. "What did you say?"

"I said we can't stand another frontal assault! We've probably got less than three thousand men able to fight! If we run head on into those guns again, we'll lose another five hundred, and we still won't get anywhere!"

"Are you saying we don't have the *willpower* to break through—or are you speaking for yourself?"

Roland drew a deep breath, tried to calm down. He'd never seen such slaughter before, and he'd be dead right now if he hadn't shot an Allegiance soldier at point-blank range. "I'm saying we've got to think of another way into that mall."

"And I say we attack again. Right *now*, before they can organize their defenses again!"

"They never were *disorganized*, damn it!" Roland shouted.

There was silence except for the moaning of the wounded and the crackle of flames. Macklin stared fiercely at Roland. It was the first time Roland had ever dared to shout at him, and there he was, disputing Macklin's orders in front of the other officers.

"Listen to me," Roland continued, before the colonel or anyone else could speak. "I think I know a weak spot in that fortress—more than one. The skylights."

Macklin didn't answer for a moment. His gaze burned balefully at Roland. "The skylights," he repeated. "The skylights. They're on the *roof*. How do we get to the fucking roof? Fly?"

Laughter interrupted their argument. Alvin Mangrim was leaning against the crumpled hood of the red Cadillac. Steam hissed from the cracked radiator. Bullet holes pocked the metal, and rivulets of blood had leaked from the turret's view slit. Mangrim grinned, his forehead gashed by metal splinters. "You want to get to that roof, Colonel? I can put you there."

"How?"

He held up his hands and wiggled his fingers. "I used to be a carpenter," he said. "Jesus was a carpenter. Jesus knew a lot about knives, too. That's why they crucified him. When I was a carpenter, I used to build dog houses. Only they weren't just ordinary old dog houses—oh, no! They were castles, like the knights used to live in. See, I used to read books about castles and shit like that, 'cause I wanted those dog houses to be real special. Some of those books said interesting things."

"Like what?" Roland asked impatiently.

"Oh . . . like how to get to roofs." He turned his attention to Colonel Macklin. "You get me some telephone poles, barbed wire and good sturdy lumber, and let me take a few of these wrecked cars apart. I'll put you on that roof."

"What are you planning on building?"

"Creating," Mangrim corrected. "Only it'll take me a while. I'll need help—as many men as you can spare. If I can get the right parts, I can finish it in three or four days."

"I asked you what you were planning on building."

Mangrim shrugged and dug his hands into his pockets. "Why don't we go to your trailer, and I'll draw you a picture. Might be some spies hanging around here."

Macklin's gaze ran the length of the Savior's fortress. He

watched the scavengers shooting some of the wounded AOE soldiers, then stripping the bodies. He almost screamed with frustration.

"It's not over," he vowed. "It's not over until I *say* it is." And then he climbed down from the armored car and said to Alvin Mangrim, "Show me what you want to build."

Seventy-four

"Yes," Josh said. "I think we can build it back." He felt Glory's arm clinging to him, and she leaned her head against his shoulder.

He put his arm around her, and they stood together next to the burned-out ruins of the church. "We can do it," he said. "Sure we can. I mean . . . it won't be tomorrow, or next week . . . but we can do it. It probably won't look like it used to, and it might be worse than it was—but it might be *better*, too." He squeezed her gently. "Okay?"

She nodded. "Okay," she said, without looking at him, and her voice was choked with emotion. Then she lifted her tear-streaked face. Her hand came up, and her fingers slowly moved across the surface of his Job's Mask. "You're . . . a beautiful man, Josh," she said softly. "Even now. Even like this. Even if it never cracked open, you'd still be the most beautiful man I've ever known."

"Oh, I'm not so hot. I never *was*. You should've seen me when I used to wrestle. Know what my name was? Black Frankenstein. I'd sure fit the bill now, wouldn't I?"

"No. And I don't think you ever did." Her fingers traced

the hard ridges and ravines, and then she let her hand drift down again. "I love you, Josh," she said, and her voice trembled, but her copper-colored eyes were steady and true.

He started to reply, but he thought of Rose and the boys. It had been so long. So long. Were they wandering somewhere, searching for food and shelter, or were they ghosts that only lived in his memories? It was torture not knowing whether they were dead or alive, and as he looked into Glory's face he realized he would probably never know. Would it be heartless and disloyal to cut out the hope that Rose and his sons might be alive—or was it just being realistic? But he was sure of one thing: He wanted to stay in the land of the living, instead of roaming the vaults of the dead.

He put his arms around Glory and held her tight. He could feel the sharpness of her bones through her coat, and he longed for the day when the harvest would be gathered.

He longed also to be able to see through both eyes, and to be able to breathe deeply again. He hoped his Job's Mask would crack soon, like Sister's had last night, but he was afraid as well. What would he look like? he wondered. What if it was the face of someone he didn't even know? But for now he felt fine, not even a trace of fever. It was the only time in his life he'd ever *wanted* to be laid low.

Josh saw something lying on the ground in a frozen puddle about four feet away. His stomach clenched, and he said quietly, "Glory? Why don't you go on back home now? I'll be along in a few minutes."

She pulled back, puzzled. "What is it?"

"Nothing. You just go on. I'm going to walk around for a little while and try to figure out how we can put this place back together."

"I'll stay with you."

"No," he said firmly. "Go home. I want to be by myself for a while. All right?"

"All right," she agreed. She started back to the road, then turned to him again. "You don't have to say you love me," she told him. "It's okay if you don't. I just wanted you to know what I was feelin'."

"I do," he said, his voice strained and tight. Glory's gaze lingered on him for a few more seconds, and then she started home.

When she was gone, Josh bent down and grasped what was lying in the puddle. The ice cracked as he pulled it free.

It was a piece of plaid wool, blotched with dark brown stains.

Josh knew what it was from.

Gene Scully's coat.

He gripped the bloody cloth in his hand and straightened up. Tilting his head to one side, he searched the ground around him. Another fragment of plaid cloth lay a few feet away, deeper into the alley that ran alongside the ruins. He picked that one up, too, and then he saw a third and a fourth fragment, both bloodstained, ahead of him. Little pieces of Gene Scully's coat lay scattered like plaid snow all over the ground.

An animal got him, Josh thought. Whatever it was must have torn him to shreds.

But he knew no animal had gotten Gene Scully. It had been a different kind of beast, maybe masquerading as a cripple in a child's red wagon, or as a black man with a silver tooth in the front of his mouth. Scully had either found the man with the scarlet eye—or had *been* found.

Go get help, Josh told himself. Go get Paul and Sister, and for God's sake find a rifle! But he kept following the little bits of plaid coat as his heart pumped violently and his throat went dry. There was other trash on the ground, and as Josh went deeper into the alley a rat the size of a Persian cat waddled in front of him, gave him a beady-eyed glare and then squeezed into a hole. Josh heard little squeakings and rustlings all around him, and he knew this part of Mary's Rest was infested with vermin.

He saw frozen splatters of blood on the ground. He followed them for about fifteen more feet and stopped at a circular piece of tin that lay up against the rough brick foundations of the ruined church. More frozen blood streaked the tin, and Josh could see other bits of shredded plaid around his boots. He put his foot against the piece of tin, which was about the size and shape of a manhole cover, drew a breath and slowly let it out. Then, abruptly, he shoved the tin aside and leaped back.

Exposed underneath it was a hole burrowed down below the church's foundations. A cold, sour reek rose from it that made his flesh crawl.

Found you, was Josh's first thought.

His second was: Get the hell out of here! Run, you flat-footed fool!

But he hesitated, staring at the hole.

There was no sound from within, no movement. It's empty! Josh realized. He's gone!

He took a tentative step toward the hole. Then a second, and a third. He stood over it, listening. Still no sound, no movement.

The lair was empty. The man with the scarlet eye had gone. After Swan had faced him down, he must have left Mary's Rest. "Thank God!" Josh whispered.

There was a rustling behind him.

Josh whirled around, his arms up to ward off a blow.

A rat sat atop a cardboard box, baring its teeth. It began to squeal and chatter like an irate landlord.

Josh said, "Be quiet, you little bas—"

Two hands—one black, one white—shot out of the hole and grasped Josh's ankles, jerking him off his feet. Josh had no time to cry out before he slammed to the ground, the air whooshing from his lungs. Dazed, he tried to scrabble free, tried to dig his fingers into the frozen earth around the hole, but the hands gripped his ankles like iron bands and began to draw him into the depths.

Josh was halfway into the hole before he fully registered what had happened. He started fighting, thrashing and kicking, but the fingers only tightened. He smelled burning cloth, twisted his body and saw blue flames dancing over the man's hands. Josh's skin was beginning to scorch, and he felt the man's hands wet and oozing like wax gloves melting.

But in the next second the flames weakened and went out. The man's hands were freezing cold again, and they yanked Josh down into darkness.

The hands left his ankles. Josh kicked, felt his left boot connect. A cold, heavy form fell on him—more like a sack of ice than a body. But the knee that pressed against his throat was solid enough, trying to crush his windpipe. Blows that almost broke his bones smashed into his shoulders, chest and rib cage. He got his hands up around a clammy throat and dug his fingers into what felt like cold putty. The thing's fists pounded his head and face but couldn't inflict damage through the Job's Mask. Josh's brain was rattled in his skull, and he was close to passing out. He knew he had two choices: fight like hell or die.

He struck out with his right fist, his knuckles flattening against the angular line of a jawbone, and instantly he brought his left fist around to crash it into the man's temple. There was a grunt—more of surprise than of pain—and the weight was off Josh. He struggled to his knees, his lungs dragging in air.

A freezing arm snaked around his throat from behind. Josh reached back, grabbed the fingers and twisted them at a vicious angle; but what had been bones a second before was now like coathanger wire—it would bend but would not break. With sheer strength, Josh lifted himself up from the floor and hurled himself backward, catching the man with the scarlet eye between himself and the church's foundation wall of rough bricks. The freezing arm slithered away, and Josh tried to scurry out of the hole.

He was caught and hauled down again, and as they fought in the dark like animals Josh saw the man's hands flicker, about to burst into flames—but they wouldn't catch, as if something had gone haywire with his ignition switch. Josh smelled an odor halfway between a struck match and a melting candle. But he kicked into the man's stomach and knocked him back. As Josh got to his feet again a blow hammered across his shoulder, almost dislocating his arm, and flung him onto his face in the dirt.

Josh twisted around to face him, his mouth bleeding and his strength running out fast. He saw the flicker of fire, and then both the man's hands grew flame again. By their blue light, he could see the man's face—a nightmare mask, and in it a gibbering, elastic mouth that spat dead flies like broken teeth.

The flaming hands came toward Josh's face, and suddenly one of them sputtered and went out like a live coal doused with water. The other hand began to burn out as well, little tongues of fire rippling along the fingers.

Something lay beside Josh in the dirt. He saw a bloody pile of flesh and twisted bones, and around it a number of coats, pairs of pants, sweaters, shoes and hats. Nearby was a child's red wagon.

Josh looked back at the man with the scarlet eye, who had also been Mr. Welcome. The burning hand was almost extinguished, and the man stared at the dying flame with eyes that in a human face might have been called insane.

He's not as strong as before, Josh realized.

And Josh lunged for the wagon, picked it up and smashed it into the thing's face.

There was a unholy bellow. The last of the flame went out as the man staggered back. Josh saw gray light and crawled for the hole.

He was about three feet from it when the crumpled red wagon was slammed down across the back of his head. Josh had a second to remember being thrown from a ring in Gainesville, and how it felt to hit a concrete floor, and then he lay still.

He awakened—how much later it was he didn't know—to the sound of high-pitched giggling. He couldn't move, and he thought every bone in his body must have snapped.

The giggling was coming from ten or fifteen feet away. It faded out, replaced by a snorting noise that became a language of some kind—German, Josh thought it might be. He made out fragments of other tongues—Chinese, French, Danish, Spanish and more dialects that tumbled out one after the other. Then the harsh, awful voice began to speak in English, with a deep Southern drawl: "Always walked alone . . . always walked alone . . . always . . . always . . ."

Josh mentally explored his body, probing to find out what worked and what didn't. His right hand felt dead, maybe broken. Bands of pain throbbed at his ribs and across his shoulders. But he knew he'd been lucky; the blow he'd just survived might have crushed his skull if the Job's Mask hadn't been so thick.

The voice changed, skittering into a singsong dialect Josh couldn't understand, then returned to English with a flat Midwestern accent: "The bitch . . . the bitch . . . she'll die . . . but not by my hand . . . oh, no . . . not by my hand . . ."

Josh slowly tried to turn his head. Pain shot through his spine, but his neck still worked. He gradually got his head turned toward the raving thing crouched in the dirt on the other side of the lair.

The man with the scarlet eye was staring at his right hand, where weak blue flames popped along the fingers. The man's face was hung between masks. Fine blond hair mingled with coarse black, one eye was blue and the other brown, one cheekbone sharp and the other sunken. "Not by my hand," he said. "I'll make *them* do it." His chin lengthened, sprouted a black stubble that turned into a red beard within seconds and just as quickly disappeared again into the writhing matter of his face. "I'll find a way to make *them* do it."

The man's hand trembled, began to curl into a tight fist, and the little blue flames went out.

Josh gritted his teeth and started crawling for the gray light at the top of the hole—slowly and painfully, an inch at a time. He stiffened when he heard the man's voice again, singing in a whisper, "Here we go 'round the mulberry bush, mulberry bush, mulberry bush; here we go 'round the mulberry bush, so early in the . . ." It trailed off into muttered gibberish.

Josh pushed himself forward. Closer to the hole. Closer.

"Run," the man with the scarlet eye said, in a thin and weary voice. Josh's heart pounded, because he knew the monster was speaking to him in the darkness. "Go on. Run. Tell her I'll make a human hand do the work. Tell her . . . tell her . . ."

Josh crawled upward toward the light.

"Tell her . . . I've always walked alone."

And then Josh pulled himself out of the hole, quickly

drawing his legs up after him. His ribs were killing him, and he was fighting to stay conscious, but he knew he had to get away or he was dead meat.

He kept crawling as rats scurried around him. A bitter cold had leeched to his bones, and he expected and dreaded the grip of the man with the scarlet eye, but it didn't come. Josh realized his life had been spared—either because the man with the scarlet eye was weakened, or because he was worn out, or because he wanted a message sent to Swan.

Tell her I'll make a human hand do the work.

Josh tried to stand but fell on his face again. It was another minute or two before he could find the strength to heave himself to his knees, and then he was finally able to stand up like a tottering, decrepit old man.

He staggered along the alley to the road and started walking toward the bonfire that burned in front of Glory's shack. But before he made it, his strength gave out; he toppled like a redwood to the ground, and he did not see Robin and Mr. Polowsky running toward him.

THIRTEEN
A Five-Star General

The Waste Land / Roland's prize / What the Junkman saw / Friend / Swan's decision / Robin being cool / Bitter ashes / The tide of death and destruction / Iron claws / The masters of efficiency

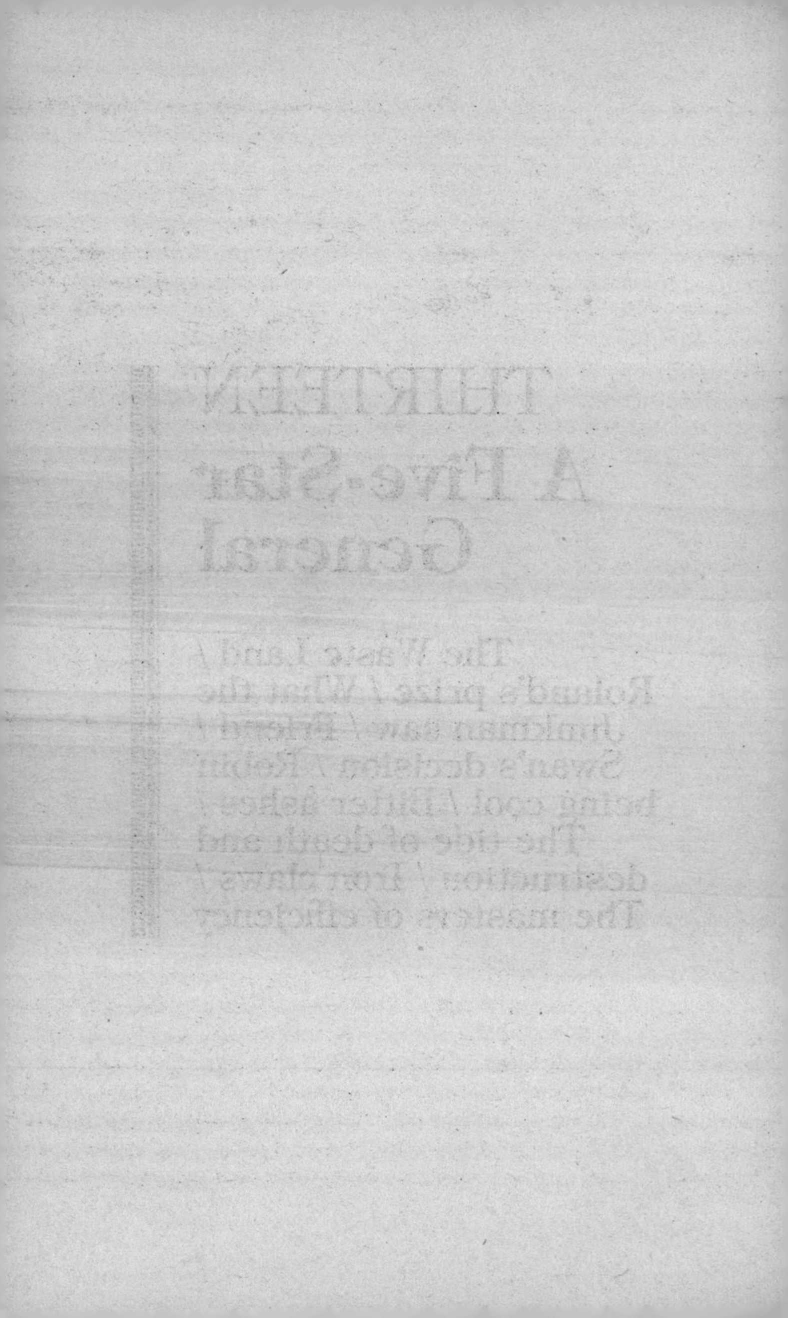

Seventy-five

Roland Croninger lifted a pair of binoculars to his goggled eyes. Snow was whirling through the freezing air and had already covered most of the corpses and wrecked vehicles. Fires were burning around the mall's entrance, and he knew the Allegiance soldiers were keeping watch as well.

He heard the slow rumble of thunder up in the clouds, and a spear of blue lightning streaked through the snow. He swept his gaze across the parking lot, and his binoculars revealed a frozen hand reaching from a mound of snow, a pile of bodies locked together in icy death, the gray face of a young boy staring at the dark.

The wasteland, Roland thought. Yes. The wasteland.

He lowered the binoculars and leaned against the armored car that shielded him from sniper fire. The sound of hammers at work was carried past him by the wind. The wasteland. That's what God's prayer for the final hour was about. He'd been trying to remember where he'd heard it before, only it hadn't been a prayer then, and it wasn't Sir Roland who'd heard it. It was a memory from the child Roland's mind, but it wasn't a prayer. No, not a prayer. It had been a *poem.*

He'd awakened that morning on the bare mattress in his black trailer and thought of Miss Edna Merritt. She was one of those spinster English teachers who must have been born looking sixty years old. She'd taught Advanced Freshman English back in Flagstaff. As Roland had sat up on his mattress he'd seen her standing beside the hand-crusher, and she was holding an open copy of *The New Oxford Book of English Verse.*

"I am going to recite," Miss Edna Merritt announced, in a voice so dry it made dust seem damp. And, cutting her eyes left and right to make sure the Advanced Freshman English class was attentive, she'd begun to read: "Here is Belladonna, the Lady of the Rocks,/ The lady of situations./ Here is the man with three staves, and here the Wheel,/ And here is the one-eyed merchant, and this card,/ Which is blank, is something he carries on his back,/ Which I am forbidden to see. I do not find/ The Hanged Man. Fear death by water." And when she'd finished, she'd announced that the entire class was going to do a reasearch paper on some facet of T. S. Eliot's "The Waste Land," a small portion of which she had just recited.

He'd made an A on the term paper, and Miss Edna Merritt had written in red on the title page, "Excellent—Shows interest and intelligence." He'd thought that it showed he was a superfine bullshitter. Bet old Miss Edna's down to the bones by now, Roland mused as he stared across the parking lot. Bet the worms ate her from the inside out.

Two possibilities intrigued him. One, that Brother Timothy was crazy and had been leading the American Allegiance to West Virginia in search of a fever dream; and two, that there *was* somebody on Warwick Mountain who called himself God and spouted poetry. Maybe he had some books up there or something. But Roland recalled a puzzling thing that Brother Gary had said, back in Sutton: "God showed him the black box and the silver key and told him how the world will end."

The black box and the silver key, Roland thought. What did that mean?

He let the binoculars dangle on their strap around his neck, and he listened to the music of hammering. Then he turned around to look beyond the encampment, where Alvin Mangrim's creation was being constructed by the light of bonfires about a mile away, and out of the line of sight of Allegiance sentries. The work had been going on for three days and three nights, and Colonel Macklin had supplied everything that Mangrim needed. Roland couldn't see it through the heavy snowfall, but he knew what it was. It was a damned simple thing, but he wouldn't have thought of it, and even if he had, he wouldn't have known how to put one together. He didn't like or trust Alvin Mangrim, but he had to admit that Mangrim had brains. If such a thing was good enough for a medieval army, it was certainly good enough for the Army of Excellence.

Roland knew the Savior must be getting jittery by now, wondering when the next attack would come. They must be in there singing their chants good and loud by—

Searing pain tore through Roland's face, and he pressed his palms against the bandages. A shuddering moan escaped his lips. He thought his head was going to explode. And then, beneath his fingers, he felt the growths under the bandages move and swell outward, like pressure seething below the crust of a volcano. Roland staggered with pain and terror as the entire left side of his face bulged outward, almost ripping the bandages loose. Frantically, he pressed his hands against his face to keep it from coming apart. He thought of the cracked fragments on the King's pillow, and what had been revealed beneath, and he whimpered like a child.

The pain ebbed. The movement of the bandages stopped. And then it was over, and Roland was all right. His face hadn't cracked apart. He was all right. This time the pain hadn't lasted as long as usual, either. What had happened to Colonel Macklin was a freak thing, Roland told himself. It wouldn't happen to him. He was content to wear these bandages for the rest of his life.

He waited until he'd stopped shaking. It wouldn't do for anyone to see him that way. He was an officer. Then he began walking briskly across the camp toward Colonel Macklin's trailer.

Macklin was seated behind his desk, going over reports

from Captain Satterlee about how much fuel and ammunition remained. The supplies were rapidly dwindling. "Come in," he said when Roland knocked at the door. Roland entered, and Macklin said, "Close the door."

Roland stood before his desk, waiting for him to look up—but dreading it, too. The skeletal face, with its jutting cheekbones, exposed veins and muscles made Macklin look like walking death.

"What do you want?" Macklin asked, busy with his merciless figures.

"It's almost ready," Roland said.

"The machine? Yes. What about it?"

"We'll attack when it's finished, won't we?"

The colonel put aside his pencil. "That's right. If I can have your *permission* to attack, Captain."

Roland knew he was still stung from their disagreement. It was time now to mend the rift, because Roland loved the King—and also because he didn't want Alvin Mangrim to be in the King's favor and himself cast out in the cold. "I . . . want to apologize," Roland said. "I spoke out of turn."

"We could've broken them!" Macklin snapped vengefully. "One more attack was all we needed! We could've broken them right then and there!"

Roland kept his eyes lowered in submission, but he knew damned well that another frontal attack would only have slaughtered more AOE soldiers. "Yes, sir."

"If anybody else had spoken to me like that, I would've shot them down on the spot! You were *wrong,* Captain! Look at these goddamned figures!" He shoved the papers at Roland, and they flew from the desk. "Look how much gasoline we've got left! Look at the ammunition inventory! You want to see how much *food* we have? We're sitting here starving, and we could've had the Allegiance's supplies three days ago! *If* we'd attacked *then!*" He slammed his black-gloved hand down on the desk, and the oil lantern jumped. "And it's your fault, Captain! Not mine! I wanted to attack! I have *faith* in the Army of Excellence! Go on! Get out!"

Roland didn't move.

"I gave you an order, Captain!"

"I have a request to make," Roland said quietly.

"You're in no position to make requests!"

"I'd like to request," Roland continued doggedly, "that I lead the first assault wave when we break through."

"Captain Carr's leading it."

"I know you gave him permission. But I'd like to ask you to change your mind. I want to lead the first wave."

"It's an honor to lead an assault wave. I don't think you're deserving of an honor, do you?" He paused and then leaned back in his chair. "You've never asked to lead an assault wave before. Why now?"

"Because I want to find someone, and I want to capture him alive."

"And who might that be?"

"The man who calls himself Brother Timothy," Roland replied. "I want him alive."

"We're not taking prisoners. They're all going to die. Every one."

"The black box and the silver key," Roland said.

"What?"

"God showed Brother Timothy the black box and the silver key and told him how the world will end. I'd like to know more about what Brother Timothy says he saw on that mountaintop."

"Have you lost your mind? Or did they brainwash you when you went in there?"

"I agree that Brother Timothy is probably insane," Roland said, keeping his composure. "But if he's not—then who's calling himself God? And what's the black box and the silver key?"

"They don't exist."

"Probably not. There might not even be a Warwick Mountain. But if there is . . . Brother Timothy could be the only one who knows how to find it. I think capturing him alive might be worth the effort."

"Why? Do you want the Army of Excellence to go looking for God, too?"

"No. But I want to lead the first assault wave, and I want Brother Timothy taken alive." Roland knew it sounded like an order, but he didn't care. He stared fixedly at the King.

There was silence. Macklin's left hand squeezed into a fist, then slowly unclenched. "I'll think about it."

"I'd like to know right now."

Macklin leaned forward, his mouth curved into a thin and terrible smile. "Don't push me, Roland. I won't stand to be pushed. Not even by you."

"Brother Timothy," Roland said, "is to be taken alive. We can kill everyone else. But not him. I want him able to answer questions, and I want to know about the black box and the silver key."

Macklin rose like a dark cyclone slowly unfurling. But before he could answer, there was another knock at the trailer's door. "What is it?" Macklin shouted.

The door opened, and Sergeant Benning came in. He immediately felt the tension. "Uh . . . I've brought a message from Corporal Mangrim, sir."

"I'm listening."

"He says it's ready. He wants you to come see it."

"Tell him I'll be there in five minutes."

"Yes, sir." Benning started to turn away.

"Sergeant?" Roland said. "Tell him *we'll* be there in five minutes."

"Uh . . . yes, sir." Benning glanced quickly at the colonel and then got out as fast as he could.

Macklin was filled with cold rage. "You're walking close to the edge, Roland. Very close."

"Yes, I am. But you won't do anything. You can't. I helped you build all this. I helped you put it together. If I hadn't amputated your hand in Earth House, you'd be dust by now. If I hadn't told you to use the drugs to trade with, we'd still be dirtwarts. And if I hadn't executed Freddie Kempka for you, there'd be no Army of Excellence. You ask my advice, and you do what I say. That's how it's always been. The soldiers bow to you—but *you* bow to me." The bandages tightened as

Roland smiled. He'd seen the flicker of uncertainty—no, of *weakness*—in the King's eyes. And he realized the truth. "I've always kept the brigades operating for you, and I've even found the settlements for us to attack. You can't even allocate the supplies without going to pieces."

"You . . . little bastard," Macklin managed to say. "I should . . . have you . . . shot. . . ."

"You won't. You used to say I was your right hand. And I believed it. But that was never true, was it? You're *my* right hand. I'm the real King, and I've just let you wear the crown."

"Get out . . . get out . . . get out . . ." Macklin felt dizzy, and he grabbed the edge of the desk to steady himself. "I don't need you! I never did!"

"You always did. You do now."

"No . . . no . . . I don't . . . I don't." He shook his head and looked away from Roland, but he could still feel Roland's eyes on him, probing to his soul with surgical precision. He remembered the eyes of the skinny kid who'd been sitting in Earth House's Town Hall during the newcomers' orientation, and he remembered seeing something of himself in them—determined, willful and, above all, cunning.

"I'll still be the King's Knight," Roland said. "I like the game. But from now on, we won't pretend it's you who makes the rules."

Macklin suddenly lifted his right arm and started to swipe the nail-studded palm across Roland's face. But Roland didn't move, didn't flinch. Macklin's skeletal face was twisted with rage, and he trembled but did not deliver the blow. He made a gasping sound, like a punctured balloon, and the room seemed to spin crazily around him. In his mind he heard the hollow, knowing laughter of the Shadow Soldier.

The laughter went on for a long time. And when it was over, Macklin's arm dropped to his side.

He stood staring at the floor, his mind on a filthy pit where only the strong survived.

"We should go see Mangrim's machine now," Roland

suggested, and this time his voice was softer, almost gentle. The voice of a boy again. "I'll give you a ride in my Jeep. All right?"

Macklin didn't answer. But when Roland turned and walked to the door, Macklin followed like a dog humbled by a new master.

Seventy-six

Headlights darkened, three rows of Army of Excellence vehicles moved slowly across the parking lot as howling winds blew snow in blinding crosscurrents. Visibility was cut to nine or ten feet in all directions, but the blizzard had given the AOE a chance to clear some of the debris off the parking lot with two of its three bulldozers. They'd shoved the frozen corpses and twisted metal into huge heaps on either side of what the AOE infantrymen now called "Death Valley."

Roland rode in his Jeep at the center of the first row, with Sergeant McCowan behind the wheel. Under his coat he wore a shoulder holster with a .38 in it, and at his side was an M-16. On the floorboard, behind his right boot, were a flare gun and two red flares.

He knew it was going to be a very good day.

Soldiers rode on the hoods, trunks and fenders of the vehicles, adding weight to help traction. Behind the advancing waves followed twelve hundred more AOE soldiers. Captain Carr controlled the left flank, and on the far side of Roland's Jeep Captain Wilson was in command of the right. Both of them, along with the other officers involved in Operation Crucify, had gone over the plans with Roland several times, and Roland had told them exactly what he expected. There was to be no hesitation when the signals were given, and the maneuvers had to be done precisely as Roland had outlined. There was to be no retreat, Roland had told them; the first man who shouted a retreat was to be shot on the field. And as the orders were given and the plan gone over again and again Colonel Macklin had sat silent behind his desk.

Oh, yes! Roland thought, delirious with a keen mingling of excitement and fear. It's going to be a good day!

The vehicles continued to advance, foot by foot, the noise of their engines covered by the shriek of the wind.

Roland wiped snow from his goggles. Down the first line of trucks and cars, soldiers began to slide off the hoods and fenders and scrabble forward on their hands and knees across the snow. They were members of the Recon Brigade that Roland had organized—small, fast men who could get up close to the Allegiance defensive line without being seen. Roland strained forward in his seat, watching for the Allegiance's bonfires. Even now, he knew, the Recon Brigade soldiers were taking up positions on the far left and right flanks, and they would be the first to open fire when the signals were given. If the Recon Brigade successfully drew enemy attention to the far left and far right of the defensive line, there might be a hole of confusion right in the center—and it was there that Roland planned to pierce.

Orange light flickered ahead—firelight, glowing from one of the bonfires on the defensive line. Roland cleared his goggles again, saw the glint of another bonfire to the left and maybe thirty yards away. He picked up the flare gun and loaded one flare into the breech. Then, with the second flare in his gloved left hand, he stood up in the Jeep and waited for the assault wave to close another five yards.

Now! Roland decided, and he aimed the flare gun just over the windshields of the vehicles on the left flank. He squeezed the trigger, and the gun coughed; the brilliant crimson flare streaked away, and the first signal had been delivered. The vehicles on the left side began to pivot, the entire line veering further left. Roland quickly reloaded and delivered the second signal on the right flank. The vehicles on that side slowed and began to veer to the right.

Sergeant McCowan, too, cut the wheel to the right side. The tires skidded over the snow for a few seconds before they responded. Roland was counting the time down: *eight . . . seven . . . six . . .*

He saw quick white flashes of gunfire from the far left flank, right up on the Allegiance's defensive line, and he knew the Recon Brigade on that side had gone to work.

. . . five . . . four . . .

Gunfire erupted on the far right flank. Roland saw sparks fly as bullets ricocheted off metal.

. . . three . . . two . . .

On the left side, the AOE vehicles suddenly turned on their headlights, the blinding shafts of light spearing through the snow and into the eyes of the Allegiance sentries not more than ten yards away. A fraction of a second later, the headlights on the right side came on. Machine-gun bullets, fired in blind panic by a sentry, threw up plumes of snow six feet in front of Roland's Jeep.

. . . one, Roland counted.

And the massive thing—half machine and half a construction from a medieval nightmare—that had been following thirty feet behind the command Jeep suddenly roared forward, its treads flattening corpses and debris, its steel scoop raised to shield against gunfire. Roland watched the huge war machine as it swept past, gaining speed, heading for the center of the enemy's defenses. "Go!" Roland shouted. "Go! *Go!*"

Mangrim's brainchild was powered by the third bulldozer, its driver inside an armor-plated cab; but towed by steel cables behind the bulldozer was a wide wooden platform with truck axles and wheels attached. Rising from the platform was an intricate wooden framework, made from sturdy telephone poles bolted and lashed together to support a central staircase that ascended more than seventy feet into the air. The stairs had been taken from houses in the dead residential district around the shopping center. The long staircase curved slightly forward at the pinnacle and ended in a ramp that could be unhinged and dropped outward like the drawbridge of a castle. Barbed wire and scavenged pieces of metal from wrecked cars covered the outside surfaces, with gunports cut here and there on several of the staircase landings. To help support the weight, some of the telephone poles had been driven onto iron spikes bolted to the bulldozer, and they thrust upward to hold the war machine steady.

Roland knew what it was. He'd seen pictures of them in books.

Alvin Mangrim had built a siege tower, like medieval armies had used to storm fortified castles.

And then the bulldozer's upraised scoop crashed into a mailman's armored truck that was covered with graffiti like LOVE THE SAVIOR and KILL IN THE NAME OF LOVE and began to shove it backward, out of the defensive line. The mailman's truck slammed into a car, and the car was crushed between it and an armored Toyota van as the bulldozer pressed forward, its engine screaming and the treads throwing back wakes of snow. The siege tower shivered and creaked like arthritic bones, but it was built strong, and it held.

Gunfire flared from the left and right flanks of the Allegiance's defenses, but the soldiers who manned the center were forced back in confusion, some of them being crushed to death at once as the bulldozer came powering through. Through the hole the bulldozer had opened rushed a swarm of shouting AOE infantrymen, dealing out more death from their guns. Bullets whined and sparked off metal, and further down the line a gas tank was hit and exploded, lighting up the battleground with a hellish glare.

The bulldozer pushed the wreckage aside and kept going. When its steel shovel slammed against the fortress's wall, the driver cut his engine and locked the brakes. A truck loaded with soldiers and ten drums of gasoline roared through the hole the bulldozer and siege tower had broken open and skidded to a stop alongside. As other infantrymen supplied a covering fire, some of the soldiers began to unload the gasoline drums while the rest, who carried coils of rope, ran to the siege tower and started up the steps. At the top, they unlocked the ramp and shoved it forward; on the underside of the ramp were hundreds of long nails, which dug into the snow on the mall's roof as the ramp fell into place. Now there was a seven-foot-long wooden bridge connecting the tower and the roof. One by one the soldiers ran across it, and once on the roof they began to drop the ends of their ropes to the men who were rolling the gasoline drums against the wall. The ropes were already looped and knotted, and as one was slipped around the end of a drum another was tied to the other end. The drums of gasoline were hauled up to the roof, one after the other, in quick succession.

More soldiers streamed up the siege tower, took their places at the gunports and fired down at the mass of Allegiance infantry, who were retreating toward the mall's entrance. And then the soldiers on the rooftop began to roll the gasoline drums through the central skylight and down into the densely-packed midst of the American Allegiance, many of whom had been sleeping and still didn't know what was going on. As the drums hit bottom the soldiers took aim and fired with their rifles, puncturing the drums and spewing gasoline into the air. The bullets threw sparks, and with a tremendous *whump!* the gasoline ignited.

Standing up in his Jeep, Roland saw flame leap into the night through the shattered skylight. "We've got them!" he shouted. "Now we've got them!"

Beneath the skylight, in the shopping mall's crowded atrium, men, women and children were dancing to Roland Croninger's tune. More gasoline drums plummeted through the skylight, exploding like napalm bombs in the conflagration. Within two minutes the entire floor of the atrium was awash with blazing gasoline. Hundreds of bodies were charring as hundreds more tried to fight free, trampling their brothers and sisters, clawing for a breath of air in the firestorm.

Now the rest of the Army of Excellence vehicles were crashing into the Allegiance's defensive line, and the air burned with bullets. A flaming figure ran past Roland's Jeep and was broken like a straw doll beneath the wheels of an oncoming truck. The Allegiance soldiers were panicking, not knowing which way to run, and the ones who tried to fight were slaughtered. Smoke was streaming from the mall's entrance, and still the men on the rooftop continued to drop the gasoline drums. Roland heard the explosions even over the screams and gunfire.

Army of Excellence soldiers were breaking into the mall. Roland picked up his M-16 and jumped from the Jeep, running through the confusion of bodies toward the entrance. A tracer bullet streaked past his face, and he tripped and fell over mangled bodies, but he got up again and kept going. His gloves had turned crimson, and somebody's blood covered the front of his coat. He liked the color; it was the color of a soldier.

Inside the mall he was surrounded by dozens of AOE infantry who were shooting at enemy soldiers in the stores. Gray smoke churned through the air, and people on fire came running down the corridor, but most of them crumpled before they got very far. The floor shook with the blasts as the final gasoline drum blew, and Roland felt a sickening wave of heat from the atrium ahead. He smelled the intoxicating reek of burning flesh, hair and clothes. More explosions jarred the floor, and Roland thought it must be the Allegiance's ammunition going off. Allegiance soldiers started throwing aside their guns and coming out of the stores, begging for mercy. They received none.

"You! You! And you!" Roland shouted, pointing out three soldiers. "Follow me!" He raced in the direction of the bookstore.

The atrium was a solid mass of flame. The heat was so terrible that the hundreds of corpses were beginning to liquefy, oozing and melting together. Searing winds screamed around the walls. Roland's coat was smoking as he ran past the atrium into the corridor that led to the bookstore. The three soldiers followed right behind.

But Roland suddenly stopped, his eyes widening with terror.

One of the Allegiance's tanks—the Love Bug—was parked in front of the B. Dalton store.

The soldier behind him said, "Oh Je—"

The tank's main cannon fired; there was an ear-cracking boom that blew the rest of the glass from the store's windows. But the cannon's elevation was too high, and the shell's hot wake threw Roland and the other men to the ground as it passed four feet overhead. It pierced the roof at the end of the corridor without exploding and blasted like a thunderclap about fifty feet in the air, killing most of the soldiers who had dropped the gasoline drums.

Roland and the soldiers opened fire, but their bullets pinged harmlessly off armor. The tank jerked forward, began to grind toward them and then stopped, backed up and started turning to the right. Its turret began to rotate, and then the cannon went off again, this time knocking a truck-sized hole through the brick wall. There was a noise of gears grinding and stripping, and with a backfire that gouted gray smoke the multimillion-dollar machine shuddered and stopped.

Either the driver doesn't know what he's doing, Roland thought, *or the tank's a lemon!*

The hatch opened. A man popped up with his arms raised. "Don't shoot!" he shouted. "Please don't—"

He was interrupted by the force of bullets passing through his face and neck, and he slithered back into the tank.

Two Allegiance soldiers with rifles appeared at the B. Dalton entrance and started shooting. The AOE infantryman to Roland's right was killed, but in another few seconds the firefight was over and the two Allegiance men lay riddled. The way into the bookstore was clear.

Roland dove to the floor as a shot rang out, closely followed by a second. The other two men fired repeatedly into the gloom at the back of the store, but there was no more enemy resistance.

Roland kicked the storeroom door open and leapt to one side, ready to fill the room with bullets if any more soldiers were in there guarding the Savior.

But there was no movement, no sound.

A single oil lantern glowed within the storeroom. His rifle ready, Roland darted in and crouched on the floor.

The Savior, wearing a lime-green coat and beige slacks with patched knees, was sitting in his chair. His hands gripped the armrests. His head was tilted back, and Roland could see the fillings in his molars.

Blood was trickling from a bullet hole between his eyes. A second bullet hole was black and scorched against the lime-green coat over his heart. As Roland watched, the Savior's hands suddenly opened and closed in a convulsion. But he was dead. Roland knew very well what a dead man looked like.

Something moved just beyond the light.

Roland aimed his rifle. "Come out. Now. Your hands above your head."

There was a long pause, and Roland almost squeezed off a few rounds—but then the figure stepped into the light, hands upraised. In one hand was a .45 automatic.

It was Brother Timothy, his face ashen. And Roland knew he'd been right; he was sure the Savior wouldn't let Brother Timothy very far from his side.

"Drop the gun," Roland ordered.

Brother Timothy smiled faintly. He brought his hands down, turned the .45's barrel toward his own temple and squeezed the trigger.

"No!" Roland shouted, already moving forward to stop him.

But the .45 clicked . . . and clicked . . . and clicked.

"I was supposed to kill him," Brother Timothy said as the .45 continued clicking on an empty clip. "He told me to. He said the heathen had won, and that my last act was to deliver him from the hands of the heathen . . . and then to deliver myself. That's what he told me. He showed me where to shoot him . . . in two places."

"Put it down," Roland said.

Brother Timothy grinned, and a tear streaked from each eye. "But there were only two bullets in the gun. How was I supposed to deliver myself . . . if there were only two bullets in the gun?"

He continued clicking the trigger until Roland took the gun, and then he sobbed and crumpled to his knees.

The floor shook as the atrium's roof, weakened by the flames, seven years of neglect and the tons of water from melted snow, collapsed onto the burning corpses. Most of the gunfire had stopped. The battle was almost over, and Roland had won his prize.

Seventy-seven

One afternoon, as new snow drifted across Mary's Rest, a panel truck with a sagging suspension entered town from the north. Its backfiring engine immediately made it the center of attention—but new people were coming in almost every day now, some in beat-up old cars and trucks, some in horse-drawn wagons, and most on foot, with their belongings in cardboard boxes or suitcases, so newcomers didn't draw the curiosity they once had.

Painted in big red letters on both sides of the truck was THE JUNKMAN. The driver's name was Vulcevic, and he and his wife, two sons and daughter had been following the pattern of a new society of wanderers—staying in a settlement long enough to find food and water and rest and then realizing there must be a better place somewhere else. Vulcevic was a former bus driver from Milwaukee who'd been laid low with a flu bug the day his city was destroyed, and whether that was good fortune or bad he still hadn't decided.

For the past two weeks he'd been hearing rumors from people they'd met on the road: Ahead was a town called Mary's Rest, and in that town there's a spring with water as sweet as the Fountain of Youth's. They've got a cornfield there, and apples fall from the sky, and they've got a newspaper and they're building a church.

And in that town—so the rumors had gone—there's a girl named Swan who has the power of life.

Vulcevic and his family had the dark hair, eyes and olive complexions of generations of gypsy blood. His wife was particularly attractive, with a sharply chiseled, proud face, long back hair streaked with gray, and dark brown eyes that seemed to sparkle with light. Less than a week before, the helmet of growths that had covered her face and head had cracked open, and Vulcevic had left a lantern burning for the Virgin Mary in the midst of a snow-shrouded forest.

As Vulcevic drove deeper into town he did indeed see a waterhole, right out in the middle of the road. A bonfire burned just past it, and further along the road people were reconstructing a clapboard building that might have been a church. Vulcevic knew this was the place, and he did what he and his family had done in every settlement they'd come across: He stopped the truck in the road, and then his two boys opened the truck's sliding rear panel and started hauling out the boxes full of items for sale or trade, among which were many of their father's own inventions. Vulcevic's wife and daughter set up tables to display the goods on, and by that time Vulcevic had an old megaphone to his lips and had started his salesman's spiel: "Come on, folks, don't be shy! Step right up and see what the Junkman's brought you! Got handy appliances, tools and gadgets from all across the country! Got toys for the kiddies, antiques from a vanished age, and my own inventions specially designed to aid and delight in this modern age—and God knows we all need a little aid and delight, don't we? So step right up, come one, come all!"

People began to crowd around the tables, gawking at what the Junkman had brought: gaudy women's clothing, including spangled party dresses and color-splashed bathing suits; high-heeled shoes, penny loafers, saddle oxfords and jogging sneakers; men's short-sleeved summer shirts by the boxful, most of them still with their department store tags; can openers, frying pans, toasters, blenders, clocks, transistor radios and television sets; lamps, garden hoses, lawn chairs, umbrellas and bird feeders; yo-yos, hula hoops, boxed games like Monopoly and Risk, stuffed teddy bears, little toy cars and trucks, dolls and model airplane kits. Vulcevic's own inventions included a shaving razor that ran on the power of wound-up rubber bands, eyeglasses with little rubber-band-powered windshield wipers on the lenses, and a small vacuum cleaner run by a rubber-band-operated motor.

"What'll you take for this?" a woman asked, holding up a glitter-covered scarf.

"Got any rubber bands?" he inquired, but when she shook her head he told her to go home and bring back what she had to trade, and maybe they could do business.

"I'll trade for whatever you've got!" he told the crowd. "Chickens, canned food, combs, boots, wristwatches—you bring 'em and let's deal!" He caught a fragrant aroma in the air and turned to his wife. "Am I going crazy," he asked her, "or do I smell apples?"

A woman's hand took an object off the table in front of Vulcevic. "That's a one-of-a-kind item right there, lady!" Vulcevic said. "Yes, ma'am! You don't see craftsmanship like that anymore! Go ahead! Shake it!"

She did. Tiny snowflakes flew over the roofs of a town within the glass ball she held.

"Pretty, huh?" Vulcevic asked.

"Yes," the woman answered. Her pale blue eyes watched the glittery flakes fall. "How much is it?"

"Oh, I'd say two cans of food at least. But . . . since you like it so much . . ." He paused, examining his potential customer. She was square-shouldered and sturdy, and she looked like she could spot a lie a mile off. She had thick gray hair trimmed just above her shoulders and brushed back from a widow's peak at her forehead. Her skin was smooth and unlined, like a newborn baby's, and it was hard to judge how old she was. Maybe her hair was prematurely gray, Vulcevic thought—but then again, something about her eyes was old, as if they'd seen and remembered a lifetime of struggle. She was a handsome woman, with even, lovely features—a regal look, Vulcevic decided, and he imagined that before the seventeenth of July she might have worn furs and diamonds and had a mansionful of servants. But there was kindness in her face, too, and he thought in the next second that maybe she'd been a teacher, or a social worker, or maybe a missionary. She held a leather satchel securely under her other arm. A businesswoman, Vulcevic thought. Yeah. That's what she used to be. Probably owned her own business. "Well," he said, "what have you got to trade, lady?" He nodded toward the satchel.

She smiled slightly, her eyes meeting his. "You can call me Sister," she said. "And I'm sorry, but I can't give up what I've got in here."

"Can't hold onto things forever," Vulcevic said, with a shrug. "Got to pass them along. That's the American way."

"I guess so," Sister agreed, but she didn't loosen her grip on the satchel. She shook the glass ball again and watched the snowflakes whirl. Then she returned it to the table. "Thank you," she said. "I'm just looking."

"Well, now!" Someone beside her reached into a box and lifted out a tarnished stethoscope. "Talk about relics!" Hugh Ryan hooked it around his neck. "How do I look?"

"Very professional."

"I thought so." Hugh couldn't help but stare at her new face, though he'd seen it often enough in the last two days. Robin had taken a few men back to the cave after Hugh and the rest of the boys and had brought all of them to live in Mary's Rest. "What'll you take for this?" Hugh asked Vulcevic.

"A valuable thing like that . . . it depends. You know, I might run into a doctor someday who really would need it. I can't be selling that to just anybody. Uh . . . what'll you trade for it?"

"I think I can get you a few rubber bands."

"Sold."

A giant figure stepped beside Sister, and Vulcevic looked up at a gnarled, growth-covered face as Hugh moved away. He flinched only a little bit, because he was used to such sights. The giant's arm was in a sling, and his broken fingers were bandaged and splinted with Popsicle sticks, courtesy of the town's new physician.

"How about this?" Josh asked Sister, holding up a long black dress covered with shining spangles. "Do you think she'd like it?"

"Oh, yes. She'd look great at the next opera opening."

"I think Glory would like it," he decided. "I mean . . . even if she didn't, she could use the material, couldn't she? I'll take this," he told Vulcevic, laying the dress across the table. "And this, too." He picked up a green plastic toy tractor.

"Good choice. Uh . . . what've you got to trade?"

Josh hesitated. Then he said, "Wait a minute. I'll be right back," and he walked toward Glory's shack, limping on his left leg.

Sister watched him go. He was as strong as a bull, but the man with the scarlet eye had almost killed him. He had a badly sprained shoulder, a bruised left kneecap, three broken fingers and a fractured rib, and he was covered with abrasions and cuts that were still healing. Josh was very lucky to be alive. But the man with the scarlet eye had vacated his lair under the burned-out church; by the time Sister had gotten there, along with Paul, Anna and a half-dozen men with rifles and shotguns, the man had gone, and though the hole had been watched around the clock for four days, he had not returned. The hole had been filled up, and work was proceeding on rebuilding the church.

But whether he'd left Mary's Rest or not Sister didn't know. She remembered the message Josh had brought back: "I'll make a human hand do the work."

People pushed in around her, examining the items as if they were fragments of an alien culture. Sister browsed through the stuff—junk now, but years ago things no household would have been without. She picked up an egg timer and let it fall back into the box along with rolling pins, cookie molds and kitchen tools. A multicolored cube lay on the table, and she recalled that such things had been known as Rubik's Cubes.

She picked up an old calendar illustrated with a pipe-smoking fisherman flycasting into a blue stream.

"That's only eight years old," Vulcevic told her. "You can figure out the dates from it if you count backwards. I like to keep up with the days, myself. Like today—it's the eleventh of June. Or the twelfth. Anyway, one or the other."

"Where'd you get all this?"

"Here and there. We've been traveling for a long time. Too long, I guess. Hey! Interested in a nice silver locket? See?" He flipped it open, but Sister glanced quickly away from the small yellowed photo of a smiling little girl inside it. "Oh," Vulcevic said, and he knew his salesmanship had gotten away from him. "Sorry." He closed the locket. "Maybe I shouldn't sell this, huh?"

"No. You should bury it."

"Yeah." He put it away and regarded the low, dark snow clouds. "Some morning in June, huh?" He gazed around at the shacks while his two sons dealt with the customers. "How many people live here?"

"I'm not sure. Maybe five or six hundred. New people are coming in all the time."

"I guess so. Looks like you've got a good water supply here. The houses aren't so bad. We've seen plenty worse. Know what we heard on the road coming here?" He grinned. "You've got a big cornfield, and apples fall out of the sky. Isn't that the funniest thing you've ever heard?"

Sister smiled.

"And there's supposed to be a girl here, named Swan or something like that, who can make crops grow. Just touch the dirt and they spring up! How about that? I tell you, the whole country would be dead if it wasn't for imagination."

"Are you planning on staying here?"

"Yeah, for a few days, at least. It looks okay. I'll tell you, we wouldn't go north again—no, ma'am!"

"Why? What's north?"

"Death," Vulcevic said; he scowled, shook his head. "Some people have gone off their rockers. We heard that there's fighting going on up north. There's some kind of damned *army* up there, just this side of the Iowa line. Or what *used* to be Iowa. Anyway, it's damned dangerous to go north, so we're heading south."

"An army?" Sister remembered Hugh Ryan telling her and Paul about the Battlelands. "What kind of army?"

"The kind that *kills* you, lady! You know, men and guns. Supposed to be two or three thousand soldiers on the march up there, looking for people to kill. I don't know what the hell they're doing. Little tin bastards! Crap like that got us in the mess we're in!"

"Have you seen them?"

Vulcevic's wife had been listening, and now she stepped to her husband's side. "No," she told Sister, "but we saw the lights of their fires one night. They were in the distance, like a burning city. Right after that we found a man on the road—all cut up and half dead. He called himself Brother David, and he told us about the fighting. He said the worst of it was near Lincoln, Nebraska, but that they were still hunting down the Savior's people—that's what he said, and he died before we could make sense of it. But we turned south and got out of there."

"You'd better pray they don't come through here," Vulcevic said to Sister. "Little tin bastards!"

Sister nodded, and Vulcevic went over to dicker with somebody about a wristwatch. If an army was indeed on the march this side of the Iowa line, it meant they might be within a hundred miles of Mary's Rest. My God! she thought. If two or three thousand "soldiers" swept into Mary's Rest, they'd smash it to the ground! And she thought also of what she'd been seeing lately in the glass ring, and she went cold inside.

Almost at the same instant, she felt a frigid wave of—yes, she thought—of *hatred* wash over her, and she knew *he* was behind her, or beside her, or somewhere very near. She felt his stare on her, like a claw poised at the back of her neck. She whirled quickly around, her nerves screaming an alarm.

But all the people around her seemed interested only in what lay on the tables or in the boxes. There was no one staring at her, and now the frigid wave seemed to be ebbing, as if the man with the scarlet eye—wherever and whoever he was—had begun to move away.

Still, his cold presence lingered in the air. He was close . . . somewhere very close, hidden in the crowd.

She caught a sudden movement to her right, sensed a figure reaching for her. A hand was outstretched, about to touch her face. She turned and saw a man in a dark coat, standing too close for her to escape. She cringed backward—and then the man's slender arm glided past her face like a snake.

"How much for this?" he asked Vulcevic. In his hand was a little windup toy monkey, chattering and banging two small cymbals together.

"What do you have?"

The man dug out a pocketknife and handed it over. Vulcevic examined it closely, then nodded. "It's yours, friend." The other man smiled and gave the toy to a child who stood beside him, waiting patiently.

"Here," Josh Hutchins said as he came through the crowd back to the table. In his good hand he was carrying something wrapped up in brown cloth. "How about this?" He put the cloth down on the table, next to the spangled black dress.

Vulcevic opened the cloth and stared numbly at what was inside. "Oh . . . my God," he whispered.

Lying in front of him were five ears of golden corn.

"I figured you might want one for each of you," Josh said. "Is that all right?"

Vulcevic picked one of them up as his wife stared spellbound over his shoulder. He smelled it and said, "It's *real!* My God, this is real! It's so fresh I can still smell the earth on it!"

"Sure. We've got a whole field of corn growing not too far from here."

Vulcevic looked as if he might keel over.

"Well?" Josh asked. "Do we have a deal or not?"

"Yes. Yes. Sure! Take the dress! Take whatever you want. My God! This is *fresh* corn!" He looked over at the man who wanted the wristwatch. "Take it!" he said. "Hell, take a handful! Hey, lady! You want that scarf? It's yours! I can't . . . I can't *believe* this!" He touched Josh's good arm as Josh carefully picked up Glory's new dress. "Show me," he begged. "Please show me. It's been so long since I've seen anything growing! *Please!*"

"All right. I'll take you out to the field." Josh motioned for him to follow.

"Boys! Watch the merchandise!" Vulcevic told his sons. And then he looked around at the faces of the crowd, and he said, "Hell! Give them whatever they want! They can have any of it!" He and his wife and daughter started following Josh out to the field, where the golden corn was ripening by the basketful.

Shaken and nervous, Sister was still aware of the cold presence. She began walking back to Glory's house, holding the satchel tightly under her arm. She still felt as if she were being watched, and if he was indeed out there somewhere, she wanted to get into the house and away from him.

She was almost at the porch when she heard a shouted *"NO!"* and, an instant later, the noise of the truck's engine roaring to life.

She whirled around.

The Junkman's truck was backing up, running over the tables and smashing the boxes of merchandise. People screamed and fled out of its path. Vulcevic's two sons were trying to climb up to get at the driver, but one of them stumbled and fell and the other wasn't quick enough. The truck's tires ran over a woman who had fallen to the ground, and Sister heard her back break. A child was in the way but was pulled to safety as the truck roared backward along the road. Then the truck swerved and veered, crashing into the front of another shack, and it started to turn around. The tires threw snow and dirt as the vehicle lurched forward, backfired and sped along the road out of Mary's Rest, heading north.

Sister got her feet moving, running to help some of the people who had fallen and narrowly missed being crushed. The Junkman's delights, antiques and inventions lay all over the street, and Sister saw things flying out of the rear of the truck as it rocketed away, skidded around a curve and went out of sight.

"He stole my dad's truck!" one of Vulcevic's sons was shouting, almost hysterical. "He stole my dad's truck!" The other boy ran off to get his father.

Sister had a feeling of dread that hit her in the stomach like a punch. She ran to the boy's side and grabbed his arm. He was still stunned, tears of anger streaming from his dark eyes. "Who was it?" she asked him. "What'd he look like?"

"I don't know! His face . . . I don't know!"

"Did he say anything to you? Think!"

"No." The boy shook his head. "No. He just . . . was there. Right in front of me. And . . . and I saw him *smile*. Then he picked them up and ran to the truck."

"Picked them up? Picked *what* up?"

"The corn," the boy said. "He stole the corn, too."

Sister released his arm and stood staring along the road. Staring toward the north.

Where the army was.

"Oh, my God," Sister said hoarsely.

She held the leather satchel in both hands and felt the circle of glass within it. For the last two weeks she'd gone dream-walking in a nightmare land, where the rivers ran with blood and the sky was the color of open wounds and a skeleton on a skeletal horse reaped a field of humanity.

"I'll make a human hand do the work," he'd promised. *"A human hand."*

Sister looked back at Glory's house. Swan was standing on the porch, wearing her patchwork coat of many colors, her gaze also directed to the north. Then Sister started walking toward her to tell her what had happened and what she feared was *about* to happen when the man with the scarlet eye reached that army and showed them the fresh corn. When he told them about Swan and made them understand that a march of a hundred miles was nothing to find a girl who could grow crops out of dead earth.

Enough crops to feed an army.

Seventy-eight

"Bring him in," Roland Croninger ordered.

The two sentries escorted the stranger up the steps to Colonel Macklin's trailer. Roland saw the stranger's left hand caress one of the demonic faces carved into the wood; in his right hand, the stranger carried something wrapped in brown cloth. Both sentries had their pistols pointed at the stranger's head, because he refused to give up the package, and he'd already snapped the arm of one soldier who'd tried to take it from him. He'd been stopped two hours before by a sentry on the southern edge of the AOE's camp and immediately taken to Roland Croninger for questioning. Roland had taken one look at the stranger and realized that he was an extraordinary man; but the stranger had refused to answer any questions, saying that he'd speak only to the army's leader. Roland couldn't get the package away from him, and no badgering or threats of torture made any impression on the stranger. Roland doubted that any man who wore nothing but faded jeans, sneakers and a brightly colored, summery short-sleeved shirt in freezing weather would be bothered very much by torture.

Roland stepped aside as they brought the man in. Other armed guards stood around the room, and Macklin had summoned Captains Carr and Wilson, Lieutenant Thatcher, Sergeant Benning and Corporal Mangrim. The colonel sat behind his desk, and there was a chair at the center of the room reserved for the stranger. Next to it was a small table on which rested a burning oil lamp.

"Sit down," Roland said, and the man obeyed. "I think all of you can see for yourselves why I wanted you to meet this man," Roland said quietly, the lamplight sparking red in his goggles. "This is exactly what he was wearing when he was found. He says he won't talk to anybody but Colonel Macklin. Okay, mister," he told the stranger. "Here's your chance."

The stranger glanced around the room, examining each man in turn. His gaze lingered a bit longer on Alvin Mangrim.

"Hey!" Mangrim said. "I know you from somewhere, don't I?"

"It's possible." The stranger had a hoarse, raspy voice. It was the voice of someone just overcoming an illness.

Macklin studied him. The stranger looked to be a young man, maybe twenty-five or thirty. He had curly brown hair and a pleasant blue-eyed face, and he was beardless. On his shirt were green parrots and red palm trees. Macklin hadn't seen a shirt like that since the day the bombs fell. It was a shirt made for a tropical beach, not for a thirty-degree afternoon. "Where the hell did you come from?" Macklin asked him.

The young man's eyes found his. "Oh, yes," he said. "You'd be in charge, wouldn't you?"

"I asked you a question."

"I've brought you something." The young man suddenly tossed his present toward Macklin's desk, and at once two guards were sticking rifle barrels in his face. Macklin cringed, had a mental image of a bomb ripping him apart and started to dive to the floor—but the package hit the desktop and came open.

What was inside rolled over his maps of Missouri.

Macklin was silent, staring at the five ears of corn. Roland crossed the room and picked one of them up, and a couple of the other officers crowded around as well.

"Get those out of my face," the young man told the guards, but they hesitated until Roland ordered them to lower their rifles.

"Where'd you get these?" Roland demanded. He could still smell the dirt on the ear of corn in his hand.

"You've asked me enough questions. Now it's my turn. How many men are out there?" He nodded toward the trailer's wall, beyond which sprawled the camp and its dozens of bonfires. Neither Roland nor the colonel answered him. "If you're going to play games with me," the stranger said, smiling thinly, "I'll take my toys and go home. You don't really want me to do that, do you?"

It was Colonel Macklin who finally broke the silence. "We've . . . got about three thousand. We lost a lot of soldiers back in Nebraska."

"All those three thousand are able-bodied men?"

"Who *are* you?" Macklin asked. He was very cold, and he noted Captain Carr blowing into his hands to warm them.

"Are those three thousand able to fight?"

"No. We've got about four hundred sick or wounded. And we're carrying maybe a thousand women and children."

"So you've only got sixteen hundred soldiers?" The young man clenched the chair's armrests. Macklin saw something change about him, something almost imperceptible—and then he realized the young man's left eye was turning brown. "I thought this was an *army*, not a boy scout troop!"

"You're talking to officers of the Army of Excellence," Roland said, quietly but menacingly. "I don't give a shit who you—" And then he saw the brown eye, too, and his throat seized up.

"Some great army!" the other man sneered. "Fucking great!" His complexion was reddening, and his jowls seemed to be swelling up. "You've got a few guns and trucks, and you think you're *soldiers?* You're *shit!*" He almost screamed it, and the single blue eye bled pallid gray. "What's your rank?" he asked Macklin.

Everyone was silent, because they'd seen, too. And then Alvin Mangrim, smiling and cheerful and already in love with the stranger, said, "He's a colonel!"

"A colonel," the stranger echoed. "Well, Colonel, I think the time has come for the Army of Excellence to be led by a five-star general." A streak of black rippled through his hair.

Alvin Mangrim laughed and clapped his hands.

"What are you feeding your sixteen hundred soldiers?" The stranger stood up, and the men around Macklin's desk retreated, bumping into one another. He snapped his fingers when Macklin didn't reply fast enough. "*Speak!*"

Macklin was dumbfounded. No one but the Cong guards at the prison camp a lifetime ago had ever dared to speak to him like this. Ordinarily he would have slashed the offender to shreds for this kind of disrespect, but he could not argue with a man who had a face like a molting chameleon and wore a short-sleeved shirt when others were shivering in fleece-lined overcoats. He felt suddenly weakened, as if this young stranger was sucking the energy and willpower right out of him. The stranger commanded his attention like a magnet, and his presence filled the room with waves of cold that had begun to crisscross like frigid tides. He looked around for some kind of help from the others but saw that they were mesmerized and impotent, too—and even Roland had backed away, his fists clenched at his sides.

The young stranger lowered his head. He remained that way for about thirty seconds. When he lifted his face again, it was pleasant, and both eyes were blue once more. But the black streak remained in his curly brown hair. "I'm sorry," he said, with a disarming smile. "I'm not myself today. Really, though, I'd like to know: What are you feeding your troops?"

"We . . . we captured some canned food . . . from the American Allegiance," Macklin said at last. "Some cases of canned soup and stew . . . some canned vegetables and fruit."

"How long will that supply last? A week? Two weeks?"

"We're marching east," Roland told him, getting himself under control. "To West Virginia. We'll raid other settlements on the way."

"To West Virginia? What's in West Virginia?"

"A mountain . . . where God lives," Roland said. "The black box and the silver key. Brother Timothy's going to lead us." Brother Timothy had been tough, but he'd cracked under Roland's attentions in the black trailer. According to Brother Timothy, God had a silver key that he had inserted into a black box, and a doorway had opened in solid stone. Within Warwick Mountain—so Brother Timothy had said—were corridors and electric lights and humming machines that made spools of tape spin around, and the machines had spoken to God, reading off numbers and facts that had been way over Brother Timothy's head. And the more Roland had thought about that story, the more he'd come to believe a very interesting thing: that the man who called himself God had shown Brother Timothy a roomful of mainframe computers still hooked up to a power source.

And if there *were* mainframe computers still in operation under Warwick Mountain, West Virginia, Roland wanted to find out why they were there, what information they held—and why somebody had made sure they'd keep functioning even after a total nuclear holocaust.

"A mountain where God lives," the stranger repeated. "Well. I'd like to see that mountain myself." He blinked, and his right eye was green.

No one moved, not even the guards with the rifles.

"Look at the corn," the stranger urged. "Smell it. It's fresh, picked right off the stalk a couple of days ago. I know where there's a whole field of corn growing—and pretty soon there'll be apple trees growing there, too. Hundreds of them. How long has it been since any of you tasted an apple? Or cornbread? Or smelled corn frying in a pan?" His gaze crept around the circle of men. "I'll bet way *too* long."

"Where?" Macklin's mouth was watering. "Where's the field?"

"Oh . . . about a hundred and twenty miles south of here. In a little town called Mary's Rest. They've got a spring there, too. You can fill up your bottles and kegs with water that tastes like sunshine." His eyes of different colors glinted, and he walked to the edge of Macklin's desk. "There's a girl who lives in that town," the young man said; he planted his palms on the desk and leaned forward. "Her name is Swan. I'd like you to meet her. Because *she's* the one who made that corn grow out of dead earth, and she planted apple seeds, and they're going to grow, too." He grinned, but there was rage in it, and dark pigment rose like a birthmark across his cheek. "She can make crops grow. I've seen what she can do. And if *you* had her—then you could feed your army while everybody else starved. Do you see what I mean?"

Macklin shivered from the cold that came off the man's body, but he couldn't look away from those gleaming eyes. "Why . . . are you telling me this? What's in it for you?"

"Oh . . . let's just say I want to be on the winning team." The dark pigment disappeared.

"We're marching to Warwick Mountain," Roland contended. "We can't go a hundred and twenty miles out of our way—"

"The mountain will *wait,*" the stranger said softly, still staring at Macklin. "First I'll take you to get the girl. Then you can go find God, or Samson and Delilah, if you want to. But first the girl—and the food."

"Yes." Macklin nodded, his eyes glazed and his jaw sagging. "Yes. First the girl and the food."

The young man smiled, and slowly his eyes became the same shade of blue. He was feeling so much better now, so much stronger. Fit as a fiddle! he thought. Maybe it was being here, among people he sensed had the right ideas. Yes, war was a good thing! It trimmed the population and made sure only the strong survived, so the next generation would be better. He'd always been an advocate of the humane nature of war. Maybe he was also feeling stronger because he was away from that girl. That damned little bitch was tormenting those poor souls in Mary's Rest, making them believe their lives were worth living again. And that sort of deception would not be tolerated.

He picked up the map of Missouri with his left hand and held it up before him while his right hand snaked down behind it. Roland saw a blue wisp of smoke rise and smelled a burning candle. And then a scorched circle began to appear on the map, about a hundred and twenty miles south of their present position. When the circle was complete, the stranger let the map slide back onto the desk in front of Macklin; his right hand was clenched into a fist, and a haze of smoke hung around it.

"That's where we're going," he said.

Alvin Mangrim beamed like a happy child. "Right on, bro!"

For the first time in his life, Macklin felt faint. Something had spun out of control; the gears of the great war machine that was the Army of Excellence had begun to turn of their own accord. He realized in that moment that he didn't really care about the Mark of Cain, or about purifying the human race, or about rebuilding to fight the Russians. All that had been what he'd told the others, to make them believe the AOE had a higher cause. And make himself believe it, too.

Now he knew all he'd ever wanted was to be feared and respected again, like he'd been when he was a younger man fighting in foreign fields, before his reflexes had slowed down. He'd wanted people to call him "sir" and not have a smirk in their eyes when they did it. He wanted to be somebody again, instead of a drone locked in a flabby bag of bones and dreaming of the past.

He realized he'd crossed a point of no return somewhere along the current of time that had swept him and Roland Croninger out of Earth House. There was no going back now—no going back ever.

But part of him, deep inside, suddenly screamed and cowered in a dark hole, waiting for something fearsome to come lift the lid and offer him food.

"Who are you?" he whispered.

The stranger leaned forward until his face was only inches from Macklin's. Deep in the man's eyes, Macklin thought he saw slits of scarlet.

The stranger said, "You can call me . . . Friend."

Seventy-nine

"They're going to come," Sister said. "I know they are. My question is: What are we going to do when they get here?"

"We shoots their damned heads off!" a skinny black man said, standing up from the rough-hewn bench. "Yessir! We gots us enough guns to make 'em turn tail!"

"Right!" another man agreed, on the other side of the church. "We're not gonna let the bastards come in here and take whatever they want!"

There was a murmur of angry agreement in the crowd of more than a hundred people who'd jammed into the half-built church, but many others shouted a dissent. "Listen!" a woman said, rising from her seat. "If what she says is true, and there are a couple of thousand soldiers on the way here, we're crazy to think we can stand up to them! We've got to pack up whatever we can carry and get—"

"No!" a gray-bearded man thundered from the next row. He stood up, his face streaked with burn scars and livid with rage. *"No,* by God! We stay *here,* where our homes are! Mary's Rest didn't used to be worth spit on a griddle, but look at it now! Hell, we've got a *town* here! We're buildin' things back!" He looked around at the crowd, his eyes dark and furious. About eight feet over his head oil lamps hung from the exposed rafters and cast a muted golden light over the assembly; smoke from the lanterns rose up into the night, because there was no roof yet. "I got a shotgun that says me and my wife are gonna stay right here," he continued. "And we're gonna die here, if we have to. We ain't runnin' from nobody no more!"

"Wait a minute! Just everybody hold on, now!" A big-boned man in a denim jacket and khaki trousers stood up. "What's everybody goin' crazy for? This woman tacks up these things"—he held up one of the crudely printed bulletin sheets that said Emergency Meeting Tonight! Everybody Come!—"and we all start jabberin' like a bunch of idiots! So she stands up there at the front and says some kind of damned army is gonna be marchin' through here in . . ." He glanced at Sister. "How long did you say it'd be?"

"I don't know. Three or four days, maybe. They've got trucks and cars, and they're going to be moving fast once they get started."

"Uh-huh. Well, you get up there and start on about an army comin' this way, and we all shit our britches. How do you *know* that? And what are they after? I mean, if they want to fight a war, they sure could find a better place! We're all Americans here, not Russkys!"

"What's your name?" Sister asked him.

"Bud Royce. That is, *Captain* Bud Royce, ex-Arkansas National Guard. See, I know a little about armies myself."

"Good. Captain Royce, I'll tell you exactly what they're after—our crops. And our water, too, most likely. I can't tell you how I know so you'd understand it, but I do know they're coming, and they're going to tear Mary's Rest to the ground." She held the leather satchel, and within it was the glass circle that had taken her dreamwalking on a savage landscape where the skeleton on his mount of bones held sway. She looked at Swan, who sat beside Josh in the front row and was listening carefully, and then back to Bud Royce. "Just believe it. They're going to be here soon, and we'd better decide right *now* what to do."

"We fight!" a man at the back shouted.

"How can we fight?" an old man who supported himself on a cane asked in a quavering voice. "We can't stand up against an army. We'd be fools to even try such a thing!"

"We'd be damned cowards if we didn't!" a woman said, over on the left.

"Yeah, but better live cowards than dead heroes," a young, bearded man sitting behind Josh contended. "I'm getting *out!*"

"That's a crock of buttered bullshit!" Anna McClay roared, standing up from her bench. She put her hands on her wide hips and regarded the crowd, her upper lip curled in a sneer. "God A'mighty, what's the point of livin' if you don't fight for what you hold dear? We work our butts to the bone cleanin' this town up and buildin' this church back, and we're gonna run at the first sniff of real trouble?" She grunted and shook her head in disgust. "I remember what Mary's Rest used to be—and most of you folks do, too. But I see what it is now, and what it *can* be! If we were to run, where would we go? Some other hole in the ground? And what happens when that damned army decides to come marchin' in our direction again? I say if we run once, we're as good as dead anyway—so we might as well go down fightin'!"

"Yeah! That's what I say, too!" Mr. Polowsky added.

"I've got a wife and kids!" Vulcevic said, his face stricken with fear. "I don't want to die, and I don't want them to die either! I don't know anything about fighting!"

"It's time you learned, then!" Paul Thorson stood up and walked along the aisle to the front. "Listen," he said, standing beside Sister, "we all know the score, don't we? We know where we used to be, and we know where we are now! If we give up Mary's Rest without a fight, we'll all be wanderers again, and we'll know we didn't have the guts to even *try* to keep it! I, for one, am pretty damned lazy. I don't want to go on the road again—and so I'm sticking right here."

As the people shouted out their opinions Sister looked at Paul and smiled faintly. "What's this? Another layer on the shitcake?"

"No," he said, his eyes electric blue and steely. "I believe my cake's about baked, don't you?"

"Yes, I guess it is." She loved Paul like a brother, and she'd never been prouder of him. And she'd already made her own decision—to stay and fight while Josh got Swan to safety, a plan that Swan didn't yet know about.

Swan was listening to the tumult of voices, and in her mind was something she knew she should stand up and say. But there were so many people crowded in there, and she was still shy about speaking before strangers. Still, the thought was important—and she knew she had to speak her mind before the chance passed. She drew a deep breath and stood up. "Excuse me," she said, but her voice was drowned out by the cacophony. She walked to the front, stood beside Paul and faced the crowd. Her heart was fluttering like a little bird, and her voice trembled as she said, just a little louder, "Excuse me. I want to—"

The tumult started to die down almost at once. In another few seconds there was silence but for the wail of the wind around the walls and the crying of an infant at the back of the church.

Swan looked out at all of them. They were waiting for her to speak. She was the center of attention, and it made her feel as if ants were running up and down her backbone. At the back of the church, more people pressed around the door, and maybe two hundred others were assembled out in the road, hearing what was said as it was passed back through the crowd. All eyes were on Swan, and she thought for a second that her throat had closed up. "Excuse me," she managed, "but I'd like to say something." She hesitated, trying to arrange her thoughts. "It . . . it seems to me," she began tentatively, "that we're all worried about whether we're going to be able to fight the soldiers off or not . . . and that's the wrong thing to be thinking of. If we have to fight them here, in Mary's Rest, we're going to lose. And if we run, and leave everything to them, they'll destroy it all—because that's what armies do." She saw Robin standing over on the right side of the church, surrounded by several of his highwaymen. Their eyes met and held for a few seconds. "We can't win if we fight," Swan continued, "and we can't win if we run, either.

So it seems to me that what we should be doing is thinking about *stopping* them from getting here."

Bud Royce laughed harshly. "How the hell do we stop an army if we don't fight 'em?"

"We make it cost too much for them to get here. They might decide to turn back."

"Right." Royce smiled sarcastically. "What do you suggest, missy?"

"That we turn Mary's Rest into a fort. Like the cowboys used to do in the old movies, when they knew the Indians were coming. We build walls around Mary's Rest; we can use dirt, fallen trees, sticks—even the wood from this place. We can dig ditches out in the forest and cover them over with brush for their trucks to fall into, and we can block the roads with logs so they'll have to use the woods."

"Ever heard of infantry?" Royce asked. "Even if we did build traps for their vehicles, the soldiers would still crawl right over the walls, wouldn't they?"

"Maybe not," Swan said. "Especially if the walls were covered with ice."

"Ice?" A sallow-faced woman with stringy brown hair stood up. "How are we supposed to conjure up ice?"

"We've got a spring," Swan reminded her. "We've got buckets, pails and washtubs. We've got horses to pull wagons, and we've got three or four days." Swan walked up the aisle, her gaze moving from face to face. She was still nervous, but not so much now, because she sensed that they wanted to listen. "If we start working right now, we could build a wall around Mary's Rest, and we could figure out a system to get the water to it. We could start pouring water onto the wall even before it's finished, and as cold as it is, it wouldn't take long for the water to freeze. The more water we use, the thicker the ice. The soldiers won't be able to climb over."

"No way!" Royce scoffed. "There's no damned time to do a job like that!"

"Hell, we gots to try!" the skinny black man said. "Ain't no choice!"

Other voices rose and fell, and arguments sparked. Sister

started to shout them down, but she knew it was Swan's moment, and it was Swan they wanted to hear.

When Swan spoke again, the arguments ceased. "You could help more than anybody," she said to Bud Royce. "Since you were a captain in the National Guard, you could figure out where to put the ditches and traps. Couldn't you?"

"That'd be the easy part, missy. But I don't *want* to help. I'm getting the hell out of here at first light."

She nodded, staring at him serenely. If that was his choice, so be it. "All right," she said, and she looked again at the crowd. "I think whoever wants to go should leave tomorrow morning. Good luck to all of you, and I hope you find what you're searching for." She glanced again at Robin; he felt a thrill of excitement course through him, because her eyes seemed to be aflame. "I'm staying," she said. "I'm going to do what I can to stop the soldiers from destroying what we've done—all of us, each and every one. Because it wasn't just *me* who grew the corn; it was everybody. I put the seeds in the ground and covered them with dirt, but somebody else built the bonfires that kept the dirt and the air warm. Other people kept the bobcats and crows away, and more people picked the corn. How many of you helped dig the spring out? Who helped gather the apple cores and worked to put this building back together?"

She saw they were all listening, even Bud Royce, and she had the sensation of drawing strength from them. She kept going, powered by their belief. "It wasn't just me. It was everybody who wanted to build things back again. Mary's Rest isn't just a bunch of old shacks full of strangers anymore; people know each other, and work together, and take an interest in the hardships everybody else has, because we know we're not so different from one another. We all know what we've lost—and if we give it up and run, we'll lose it all over again. So I'm staying right here," she said. "If I live or die, that's all right, because I've decided to stop running." There was a silence. "That's all I've got to say." She went back to sit beside Josh. He put a hand on her shoulder and felt her trembling.

The silence stretched. Bud Royce was still on his feet, but his eyes weren't as hard as they had been, and his forehead was creased with thought.

Sister didn't speak either. Her heart swelled with pride for Swan, but Sister knew full well that the army wasn't coming just for the crops and the fresh water. They were coming for Swan, too. The man with the scarlet eye was leading them there, and he was going to use the human hand to crush her.

"Walls covered with ice," Royce mused aloud. "That's the craziest thing I've ever heard of. Hell . . . it's so crazy, it might just work. *Might,* I said. It won't stop the soldiers very long, if they want to come over bad enough. Depends on what kind of weapons they've got. We break enough suspensions and axles in vehicle traps, and they might think twice."

"Then it can be done?" Sister asked.

"I didn't say that, lady. It'd be a mighty big job, and I don't know if we've got the manpower to do it."

"Manpower, my ass!" Anna McClay told him. "What about *woman*power? And we've got plenty of kids who can work, too!" Her rowdy voice drew shouts of assent.

"Well, we wouldn't need too many people and guns to hold the walls," Royce said, "especially if we leveled the woods and didn't leave those bastards any cover. We don't want 'em sneakin' up on us."

"We can fix it so they won't," a small voice said. A brown-haired boy of about ten or eleven stood up on the bench. He'd filled out since Sister had seen him last, and his cheeks were windburned. She knew that under his coat there would be a small round scar just below his heart. Bucky said, "If they're north of here, we can take a car and go find 'em." He drew a long-bladed knife from the folds of his coat. "It wouldn't be nothin' to hide in the woods and pop a few of their tires when they wasn't lookin'."

"It sure would help," Royce agreed. "Anything we can do to slow 'em down would give us more time to dig and build. Wouldn't be a bad idea to post lookouts about fifty miles up the road, either."

"I doubt you've had much time behind a wheel," Paul told

Bucky. "If I can get a car that doesn't sound like an elephant in heat, I'll do the driving. I've had a little experience in hunting wolves."

"I've got an axe!" another man said. "It ain't too sharp, but it'll get the job done!"

Other people stood up, volunteering. "We can tear down some of the empty shacks and use that wood, too!" a Hispanic man with a pale violet keloid on his face suggested.

"Okay, we'll have to round up all the saws and axes we can find," Bud Royce told Sister. "Jesus, I guess I always was half nuts! I might as well go the whole shell! We'll have to assign the work details and thrash out the schedules, and we'd better get started right now."

"Right," Sister said. "And everybody who doesn't want to help should leave and stay out of the way, starting this minute."

About fifteen people left—but their places were instantly filled by others from outside.

As the crowd settled down again Sister glanced at Swan and saw the determination in her face. She knew that Swan had, indeed, made her decision—and she knew also that Swan was not going to be persuaded to flee Mary's Rest and leave everyone else there to face the soldiers.

So, Sister thought, we take it one step at a time. One step and then the next gets you where you're going.

"We know what we have to do," she told the crowd. "Let's get to work and save our town."

Eighty

The hurting sound echoed through the freezing air, and Swan flinched. She pulled back on the rope bridle, checking Mule to a walk, and steam burst from Mule's nostrils as if he, too, had heard and been disturbed by the noise. More hurting sounds came to her, like the quick, high whine of notes played on a steel guitar, but Swan knew she had to endure them.

They were the sounds of living trees being chopped down, to be added to the four-foot-high wall of logs, brush and dirt that encircled Mary's Rest and the crop field.

Over the hurting sounds, Swan heard the steady chipping of axes at work. She said, "Go on, Mule," and she guided the horse along the wall, where dozens of people were piling up more brush and timbers. All of them looked up and paused for a second as she passed, then returned to work with renewed urgency.

Bud Royce had told her, Sister and Josh that the wall needed to be at least six feet tall before the water was poured onto it—but time was getting short. It had taken over twenty hours of nonstop, backbreaking labor to get the wall to its present height and circumference. Out on the rapidly receding edge of the forest, work crews headed by Anna McClay,

Royce and other volunteers were busy digging a network of trenches, then hiding them under a latticework of sticks, straw and snow.

Ahead of her was a group of people packing stones and dirt into chinks in the wall, their breath wisping up into the air. Among them was Sister, her hands and clothes grimy, her face reddened by the cold. A length of sturdy twine was draped around her neck and looped to the handle of the leather satchel. Nearby, Robin was unloading another wheelbarrow full of dirt. Swan knew he'd wanted to go with Paul, Bucky and three other young highwaymen when they'd headed north the day before in a gray Subaru, but Sister had told him they needed his muscle on the wall.

Swan reined Mule in and got off. Sister saw her and scowled. "What're you doing out here? I thought I told you to stay in the shack."

"You did." Swan scooped up a double handful of dirt and jammed it into a chink. "I'm not going to stay there while everybody else works."

Sister lifted her hands to show Swan. They were crisscrossed by bleeding gashes, made by small, sharp-edged stones. "You've got to save your hands for better things. Go on, now!"

"Your hands will heal. So will mine." Swan packed more dirt and rocks into a hole between two logs. About twenty yards away, a number of men were wrestling more logs and brush into position as the wall grew higher.

Robin looked up at the low, ugly sky. "It'll be dark in another hour. If they're anywhere near, we might be able to see their fires."

"Paul'll let us know if they're getting close." She hoped. She knew that Paul had volunteered for a very dangerous job; if the soldiers caught him and the boys, they were as good as dead. She glanced at Swan, her fear for Paul nagging at her. "Go on, Swan! There's no need for you to be out here tearing your hands up!"

"I'm not *different,* damn it!" Swan suddenly shouted, straightening up from her work. Her eyes flashed with anger, and crimson burst in her cheeks. "I'm a person, not . . . not some piece of glass on a damned shelf! I can work as hard as anybody, and you don't need to make it easy on me!"

Sister was amazed at Swan's outburst and aware that the others were watching as well.

"I'm sorry," Swan said, calming down, "but you don't have to shut me away and protect me. I can take care of myself." She looked around at the others, at Robin, and then her gaze returned to Sister. "I know why that army's coming here, and I know who's bringing them. It's *me* they want. It's because of me the whole town's in danger." Her voice cracked, and her eyes teared up. "I want to run. I want to get away, but I know that if I do, the soldiers will still come. They'll still take all the crops, and they won't leave anybody alive. So there's no need to run—but if everybody here dies, it's because of me. *Me*. So please let me do what I can."

Sister knew Swan was right. She, Josh and the others had been treating Swan like a fragile piece of porcelain, or like . . . yes, she thought, like one of those sculptures back in the Steuben Glass shop on Fifth Avenue. All of them had focused on Swan's gift of stirring life from dead earth, and they'd forgotten that she was just a girl. Still, Sister feared for Swan's hands, because those were the instruments that might yet make life bloom from the wasteland—but Swan was strong-minded and tough far beyond her years, and she was ready to work.

"I wish you'd find a pair of gloves, but I guess those are hard to come by." Sister's own pair had already worn out. "Well," she said, "let's get to work, then. Time's wasting." She returned to her task.

A pair of tattered woolen gloves was held up before Swan's face.

"Take them," Robin urged. His own hands were now bare. "I can always steal some more."

Swan looked into his eyes. Behind his tough mask there was a spark of gentle kindness, as if the sun had suddenly glinted through the snow clouds. She motioned toward Sister. "Give them to her."

He nodded. His heart was racing, and he thought that if he did something stupid this time he would crawl in a hole and just cover himself over. Oh, she was so beautiful! Don't do something stupid! he warned himself. Be cool, man! Just be cool!

His mouth opened.

"I love you," he said.

Sister's eyes widened. She straightened up from her work and turned toward Robin and Swan.

Swan was speechless. Robin wore a horrified grin, as if he realized his vocal cords had worked with a will of their own. But now those words were out in the air, and everybody had heard.

"What . . . did you say?" Swan asked.

His face looked like he'd been weaned on ketchup. "Uh . . . I've got to get some more dirt," he mumbled. "Out in the field. That's where I get the dirt. You know?" He backed toward the wheelbarrow and almost fell into it. Then he wheeled it rapidly away.

Both Sister and Swan watched him go. Sister grunted. "That boy's *crazy!*"

"Oh," Swan said softly, "I hope not."

And Sister looked at her and knew. "I imagine he might need some help with the dirt," Sister suggested. "I mean, somebody really ought to help him. It'd be faster if two people worked together, don't you think?"

"Yes." Swan caught herself and shrugged. "I guess so. Maybe."

"Right. Well, you'd better go on, then. We can take care of the work here."

Swan hesitated. She watched him walking toward the field and realized she knew very little about him. She probably wouldn't care for him at all if she got to know him. No, not at all!

And she was still thinking that when she took Mule's reins and started walking after Robin.

"One step at a time," Sister said quietly, but Swan was already on her way.

* * *

Josh had been hauling logs for eight hours straight, and his legs were about to give out as he staggered to the spring for a dipper of water. Many of the children, including Aaron, had the responsibility of carrying buckets of water and dippers around to the work crews.

Josh drank his fill and returned the dipper to its hook on the large barrel of water that stood next to the spring. He was weary, his sprained shoulder was killing him, and he could hardly see anything through the slit of his Job's Mask; his head felt so heavy it took tremendous effort just to keep it from lolling. He'd forced himself to haul wood over the objections of Sister, Swan and Glory. Now, though, all he wanted to do was lie down and rest. Maybe an hour or so, and then he'd feel good enough to get back to work—because there was still so much to be done, and time was running out.

He'd tried to talk Glory into taking Aaron and leaving, maybe hiding in the woods until it was over, but she was determined to stay with him. And Swan, too, had made up her mind. There was no use trying to change it. But the soldiers were going to come, and they wanted Swan, and Josh knew that this time he was powerless to protect her.

Underneath the Job's Mask, pain tore through his face like an electric shock. He felt weak, close to passing out. Just an hour's rest, he told himself. That's all. One hour, and then I can get back to work, broken fingers and busted ribs or not. Good thing that face-changing bastard gave up! I would've killed him!

He started walking toward Glory's shack, his legs like dragging lengths of lead. Man! he mused. If those fans could see old Black Frankenstein now, they'd really hoot and holler!

He unbuttoned his coat and loosened his sweat-damp shirt collar. The air must be getting warmer, he thought. Sweat was running down his sides, and the shirt was stuck to his chest and back. Lord! I'm burning up!

He stumbled and almost fell going up the steps, but then he was inside the shack and peeled his coat off, letting it slip to the floor. "Glory!" he called out weakly, before he remembered that Glory was out digging trenches with one of the work crews. "Glory," he whispered, thinking about how her amber eyes had lit up and her face had shone like a lamp in the dark when he'd given her the spangle-covered dress. She'd hugged it to herself, had run her fingers all over it, and when she'd looked at him again he'd seen a tear stealing down her cheek.

In that instant he'd wanted to kiss her. Had wanted to press his lips against hers and nuzzle her cheek with his own—but he couldn't, not with this damned shit all over his face. But he'd peered at her through the narrowing slit of his one good eye, and it had come to him that he had forgotten what Rose looked like. The faces of the boys, of course, remained in his mind as clearly as snapshots—but Rose's face was fading away.

He'd given Glory the dress because he'd wanted to see her smile—and when she *had* smiled, it was like a glimpse of another, better world.

Josh lost his balance and stumbled against the table. Something fluttered to the floor, and he bent over to pick it up.

But suddenly his entire body seemed to give way like a house of cards, and he fell forward onto the floor. The entire shack trembled with the crash.

Burning up, he thought. Oh, God . . . I'm burning up. . . .

He had something between his fingers. The thing that had fluttered down off the table. He held it closer to his eye and made out what it was.

The tarot card, with the young woman seated against a landscape of flowers, wheat and a waterfall. The lion and the lamb lay at her feet, and in one hand she grasped a shield with a phoenix on it, rising in flame from the ashes. On her head was what looked like a glass crown, shining with light.

"The . . . Em . . . press," Josh read.

He stared at the flower, looked at the glass crown and then at the young woman's face. Looked closely and carefully as fever seemed to surge through his head and body like the opening of volcanic floodgates.

Have to tell Sister, he thought. Have to tell Sister . . . that the glass ring in her bag . . . is a crown. Have to show her this card . . . because Swan and the Empress . . . have the same face. . . .

And then the fever seared all thoughts from his mind, and he lay motionless, with the tarot card clenched in his hand.

Eighty-one

On the fourth night, fire burned in the sky.

Robin saw it as he filled buckets and barrels full of water to be loaded onto wagons and carried out to the wall. Every possible container, from plastic pails to washtubs, was being utilized, and the workers around the spring had no sooner filled one wagon or truck than another pulled up to accept a load.

Robin knew that the light glowing off the bellies of low clouds to the north was coming from the torches and bonfires of the army's camp, maybe fifteen miles away. They would reach Mary's Rest the next day, and the glaze of ice that now covered the completed seven-foot-high wall had to be thickened in these last hours with an all-out effort. His shoulders ached, and every pail, bucket and pot that he dipped in the spring felt as if it weighed fifty pounds, but he thought of Swan and he kept working. She'd caught up with him that day and walked at his side, and she helped him with the dirt just like any ordinary person. Their hands had been cut and callused just the same, and as they'd worked Robin had told her all about himself, about the orphanage and his years with the highwaymen. Swan had listened to him without judgment, and when he was finished with his story she'd told him her own.

He didn't mind the pain in his body, had pushed aside the weariness like an old blanket. All he had to do was think of Swan's face, and he was recharged with new strength. She had to be protected, like a beautiful flower, and he knew he would die for her, if that was how it had to be.

He saw the same strength in the other faces, too, and realized that everyone was pushing far beyond their limits. Because they all knew, as he did, that tomorrow was the hinge of the future.

Glory stood on her porch, staring toward the north, and put her hand on Aaron's shoulder.

"I'm gonna give 'em a knock!" Aaron vowed, swinging Crybaby like a bludgeon.

"You're gonna stay in the house tomorrow," she told him. "Do you understand me?"

"I wanna be a soldier!" he protested.

She gripped his shoulder hard and spun him around. "No!" she said, her amber eyes furious. "You want to learn how to kill, and take what belongs to other folks? You want to make your heart like a stone, so you can stomp people down and think it's *right?* Boy, if I thought you were gonna grow up that way, I'd bust your head open right this minute! So don't you ever, *ever* say you want to be a soldier! You hear me?"

Aaron's lower lip trembled. "Yes, ma'am," he said. "But . . . if there ain't any *good* soldiers, how do you keep the *bad* soldiers from winnin'?"

She couldn't answer him. His eyes searched hers. Was it always going to be true, she wondered, that soldiers marched the land under different flags and leaders? Was there never really any end to war, no matter who won? And there her own son stood before her, asking the question.

"I'll think about it," she said, and that was the best she could do.

She looked out along the road to where the church had been. It was gone now, the wood used to fortify the wall. All the guns, axes, shovels, picks, hoes, knives—anything and everything that could be used as weapons—had been counted and distributed. There wasn't much ammunition to go around. The Junkman had even offered to make "supersonic slingshots" if enough rubber bands could be found.

Paul Thorson and the boys had not returned, and Glory doubted they ever would.

She went inside, back to the room where Josh lay on the bed in a feverish coma. She looked down at the gnarled Job's Mask and knew that beneath it was Josh's true face.

In his hand was a tarot card. His fingers gripped The Empress so tightly that none of them, not even Anna, had been able to pry his hand open. She sat down beside him and waited.

At the northern rim of the wall, one of the lookouts who perched atop a jerry-built ladder suddenly shouted, "Somebody's comin'!"

Sister and Swan, working together to pour water over their section of the wall, heard the cry. They hurried over to the lookout's station.

"How many?" Sister asked. They weren't ready yet! It was too soon!

"Two. No. Wait. Three, I think." The lookout cocked his rifle, trying to see through the dark. "Two on foot. I think one of them's carrying the third. It's a man and two kids!"

"Oh, God!" Sister's heart leapt. "Bring a ladder!" she called to the next lookout along the wall. "Hurry!"

The second ladder was lowered over the other side. First up was Bucky, his face streaked with dried blood. Sister helped him down, and he put his arms around her neck and clung tightly.

Paul Thorson came over, a three-inch-long gash in the side of his head, his eyes circled with gray shock. He was carrying over his shoulder one of the boys who'd helped Sister and himself make the trip to Mary's Rest. The boy's right arm was covered with dried blood, and bullet holes had marched across his back.

"Get him to the doctor's house!" Sister told another woman, giving Bucky over to her. The small boy made a soft whimpering sound, nothing more.

Paul set his feet on the ground. His knees gave out, but

Sister and Swan caught him before he fell. Mr. Polowsky and Anna were running toward them, followed by several others.

"Take him," Paul rasped. His beard and hair were full of snow, his face lined and weary. Polowsky and the lookout eased the boy off Paul's shoulder, and Sister could tell the boy was frozen almost stiff. "He'll be okay!" Paul said. "I told him I'd get him back!" He touched the cold blue face. "Told you, didn't I?"

They took him away, and Paul shouted after them, "You be careful with him! Let him sleep if he wants to!"

One of the other men uncapped a flask of hot coffee and gave it to Paul. He started drinking it so frantically that Sister had to restrain him, and he winced with pain as the hot liquid spread warmth through his bones.

"What happened?" Sister asked. "Where're the others?"

"Dead." Paul shivered, drank more coffee. "All dead. Oh, Jesus, I'm freezing!"

Someone brought a blanket, and Swan helped wrap him up. They led him to a nearby bonfire, and he stood for a long while getting the blood circulating in his hands again.

Then he told them the story: They'd found the army's camp on the second day out, about sixty miles north of Mary's Rest. The boys were born stalkers, he said; they'd been able to creep into camp and take a look around, and while they were there they'd punctured a few of the trucks' tires. But there were a lot of cars and trucks, Paul said, and most of them were covered with metal plate and had gun turrets. There were soldiers all over the place, carrying machine guns, pistols and rifles. The boys had gotten out all right, and they and Paul had kept in front of the army as it advanced the next day.

But tonight something had gone wrong. There were flares and gunshots, and only Bucky and the other boy had gotten back.

"We were trying to get away in the car," Paul said, his teeth still chattering. "We'd made it to about seven or eight miles from here. All of a sudden the woods were full of them. Maybe they'd been tracking us all day, I don't know. A machine gun went off. Bullets hit the engine. I tried to get off the road, but the car was finished. We ran. I don't know how long they kept after us." He stared into the fire, his mouth working for a moment but making no sounds. "They kept after us," he said finally. "I don't know who they are, but they know their business." He blinked heavily and looked at Sister. "They've got a lot of guns. Flares, maybe grenades, too. A lot of guns. You tell 'em to be easy with that kid. He's tired. I told him I'd get him back."

"You did get him back," Sister said gently. "Now I want you to go to Hugh's house and rest." She motioned Anna over to help him. "We're going to need you tomorrow."

"They didn't take it," Paul said. "I wouldn't let them kill me and get it."

"Get what?"

He smiled wanly and touched the Magnum lodged in his belt. "My old buddy."

"Go on, now. Better get some rest, okay?"

He nodded and allowed Anna to help him stagger away.

Sister suddenly lunged up the ladder, and her face filled with blood as she shouted toward the north, "Come on, you fucking killers! *Come on!* We see what you do to children! Come on, you sonofabitching cowards!" Her voice cracked and gave out, and then she just stood at the top of the ladder with steam bellowing from her mouth and nostrils and her body shaking like a lightning rod in a tempest.

The freezing wind blew into her face, and she thought she smelled bitter ashes.

There was no use standing up here and raving like a . . . like a New York City bag lady, she told herself. No; there was still a lot of work to be done, because the soldiers were going to be there very soon.

She descended the ladder, and Swan touched her arm. "I'm all right," Sister said hoarsely, and both of them knew Death was on its way, grinning like a skull and slashing down everything in its path.

They returned to their places in the wall and went back to work.

Eighty-two

The day came.

Somber light revealed the finished wall, glazed with three inches of ice and studded here and there with sharp wooden stakes, that encircled Mary's Rest and the crop field. Except for the occasional howling of dogs, the town was silent, and there was no movement on the stump-stubbled land that lay between the wall and the forest's edge forty yards away.

About two hours after dawn, a single shot rang out, and a sentry on the eastern section of the wall toppled off his ladder, a bullet hole in his forehead.

The defenders of Mary's Rest waited for the first attack—but it did not come.

A lookout at the western section of the wall reported seeing movement in the woods, but she couldn't tell how many soldiers there were. The soldiers slipped back into the forest, and there was no gunfire.

An hour after that, another lookout on the eastern side passed the word that he heard what sounded like heavy machines in the distance, moving through the forest and getting closer.

"Truck's coming!" one of the sentries on the northern section cried out.

Paul Thorson climbed up a ladder and looked for himself. He heard the scratchy, weirdly merry sound of recorded calliope music. What appeared to be an armored Good Humor truck with two loudspeakers mounted on its cab, an armored windshield and a sheet metal gun turret rumbled slowly along the road from the north.

The music stopped, and as the truck continued to move forward a man's voice boomed from the two speakers: "People of Mary's Rest! Listen to the law of the Army of Excellence!" The voice echoed over the town, over the field where the corn was growing and the new apple trees were taking root, over the foundations where the church had stood, over the bonfires and over the shack where Josh lay sleeping. "We don't want to kill you! Every one of you who wants to join us is welcome! Just come over that wall and join the Army of Excellence! Bring your families, your guns and your food! We don't want to kill any of you!"

"Riiiight," Paul muttered under his breath. He had his Magnum cocked and ready.

"We want your crops," the voice commanded from the speakers as the Good Humor truck rumbled nearer to the north wall. "We want your food and a supply of water. And we want the girl. Bring us the girl called Swan, and we'll leave the rest of you in peace. Just bring her to us, and we'll welcome you with loving, open—*oh, shit!*"

And at that instant the vehicle's front tires plunged into one of the hidden trenches, and as the rear tires spun in empty air the truck turned on its side and crashed into the ditch.

There was a shout of victory from the other sentries. A minute later, two men scrambled up from the trench and began running in the direction from which they'd come. One of them was limping, unable to keep up, and Paul aimed the Magnum at the center of his spine.

He wanted to pull the trigger. Knew he should kill the bastard while he had the chance. But he didn't, and he watched as both of the soldiers disappeared into the woods.

A machine gun chattered off to the right. Bullets zigzagged

across the wall, cracking through the ice and thunking into the logs and dirt. Paul ducked his head, heard shouting from the eastern section, then the noise of more gunfire, and he knew the first attack had begun. He dared to lift his head, saw about forty more soldiers taking cover at the edge of the woods. They opened fire, but their bullets couldn't penetrate the wall. Paul kept his head down and held his fire, waiting for a chance to tag one of them when they started across the open ground.

On the eastern side of Mary's Rest, the sentries saw a wave of perhaps two hundred soldiers coming out of the forest. The AOE infantry shouted and surged forward—and then they began tumbling into the network of hidden trenches, many of them breaking their ankles and legs as they hit bottom. The sentries, all armed with rifles, picked off their targets at random. Two of the sentries were shot and fell, but as soon as they hit the ground others were climbing up the ladders to take their places.

The AOE soldiers, their formation in disarray and men falling everywhere, began to turn back for the cover of the woods and toppled into more ditches and pits. The wounded were crushed under the boots of their companions.

At the same time, more than five hundred soldiers burst from the forest on the western edge of Mary's Rest, along with dozens of armored cars, trucks and two bulldozers. As they rushed forward in a shouting mass the trenches opened under their feet. One of the bulldozers plunged down and overturned, and an armored car following right behind hit the bulldozer and exploded in a red fireball. Several of the other vehicles were snagged on tree stumps and unable to go either forward or backward. Scores of men tumbled into the ditches, breaking their bones. The lookouts fired as fast as they could select targets, and AOE soldiers fell dead in the snow.

But most of the soldiers and vehicles kept coming, storming the western section of the wall, and behind them was a second wave of another two hundred troops. Machine gun, rifle and pistol fire began to chip at the wall, but still the bullets were turned aside.

"Step up and open fire!" Bud Royce shouted.

And a line of men and women stepped up on the two-foot-high bank of dirt that had been built along the wall's base, aimed their guns and started shooting.

Anna McClay ran along the wall, shouting, "Step up and give 'em hell!"

A blaze of gunfire erupted along the western wall, and the first wave of AOE soldiers faltered. The second wave crashed into them, and then the vehicles were running men down as they scattered. Officers in armored cars and Jeeps shouted commands, but the troops were panicked. They fled toward the forest, and as Captain Carr stood up in his Jeep to order them back, a bullet pierced his throat and slammed him to the ground.

The attack was over in another few minutes as the soldiers drew back deeper in the woods. Around the walls, the wounded crawled on the ground and the dead lay where they'd fallen. A victorious shout rang up from the defenders along the western wall, but a figure on horseback called out, "No! Stop it! *Stop it!*"

Tears were streaming down Swan's cheeks, and the gunfire still echoed in her head. "Stop it!" she shouted as Mule reared with her and pawed the air. She wheeled the horse toward Sister, who stood nearby with her sawed-off shotgun. "Make them stop!" Swan said. "They just *killed* other people! They shouldn't be glad about that!"

"They're not glad about killing other people," Sister told her. "They're just glad *they* weren't killed." She motioned toward a man's corpse that lay ten feet away, shot through the face. Someone else was already taking the dead man's pistol and bullets. "There're going to be more of those. If you can't take what you see, you'd better get inside."

Swan looked around. A woman was sprawled on the ground, moaning as another woman and man bound up her bullet-shattered wrist with strips torn from a shirt. A few feet away, a dark-haired man lay contorted and dying, coughing up blood as other people tried to comfort him. Swan flinched with horror, her eyes returning to Sister.

Sister was calmly reloading her shotgun. "You'd better go," she suggested.

Swan was torn; she knew she should be out there with the people who were fighting to protect her, but she couldn't stand watching the death. The noise of gunfire was a thousand times worse than all the hurting sounds she'd ever experienced.

But before she could decide to go or stay, there was the throaty growl of an engine beyond the wall. Someone shouted, "Jesus Christ! Look at *that!*"

Sister hurried to the wall, and stepped up on the mound of dirt.

Just emerging from the forest, about twenty yards to Sister's left, was a tank. Its wide treads crunched over the wounded and dead alike. The snout of its gun was aimed directly at the wall. And dangling all over the tank, like grotesque hood ornaments, were human bones tied to wires —legs, arms, rib cages, hip bones, vertebrae and skulls, some still bearing scalps. The tank stopped right at the edge of the woods, its engine idling like a beast's snarl.

The tank's hatch popped open. A hand emerged waving a white handkerchief.

"Hold your fire!" Sister told the others. "Let's see what they want first!"

A helmeted head came up; the face was bandaged, the eyes covered with goggles. "Who's in charge over there?" Roland Croninger called toward the row of faces he could see, like disembodied heads perched atop that damned wall.

Some of the others looked at Sister; she didn't want the responsibility, but she guessed she was it. "I am! What do you want?"

"Peace," Roland replied. He glanced at the bodies on the ground. "You people did a pretty good job!" He grinned, though inwardly he was shrieking with rage. Friend had said nothing about trenches and a defensive wall! How the hell had these goddamned farmers put together such a barricade? "Nice wall you've got there!" he said. "Looks pretty sturdy! Is it?"

"It'll do!"

"Will it? I wonder how many rounds it would take to knock a hole through it and blow you to Hell, lady."

"I don't know!" Sister had a rigid smile on her face, but sweat was running down her sides, and she knew they had no chance at all against that monstrous machine. "How much time do you have?"

"A lot! All the time in the world!" He patted the cannon's snout. It was too bad, he thought, that there were no shells for the cannon—and even if there were, none of them would know how to load and fire it. The second tank had broken down only a few hours out of Lincoln, and this one had to be driven by a corporal who'd once made his living hauling freight through the Rocky Mountains in a tractor-trailer rig; but even *he* couldn't keep control of the big bastard all the time. Still, Roland liked riding in it, because the inside smelled like hot metal and sweat, and he could think of no better warhorse for a King's Knight. "Hey, lady!" he called. "Why don't you people give us what we want, and nobody else will get hurt! Okay?"

"It looks to me like you're the ones getting hurt!"

"Oh, *this* little scrape? Lady, we haven't started yet! This was just an exercise! See, now we know where your trenches are! Behind me are a thousand soldiers who'd really like to meet all you fine people! Or I might be wrong: They could be over on the other side, or circling down to the south! They could be anywhere!"

Sister felt sick. There was no way to fight against a tank! She was aware of Swan standing beside her, peering over the wall. "Why don't you just go on about your business and leave us alone?" Sister asked.

"Our business won't be done until we've gotten what we came for!" Roland said. "We want food, water and the girl! We want your guns and ammunition, and we want them *now!* Do I make myself clear?"

"Perfectly," she answered—and then she lifted her shotgun and squeezed the trigger.

The distance was too great for an accurate shot, but pellets rang off Roland's helmet as he ducked his head through the hatch. The white handkerchief was riddled with buckshot, and a half-dozen pellets had punctured his hand. Cursing and shaking with rage, Roland fell down into the bowels of the tank.

The back of Sister's neck crawled. She tensed, waiting for the first blast of the cannon—but it didn't come. The tank's engine revved, and the vehicle backed over the bodies and tree stumps toward the woods again. Sister's nerves didn't stop jangling until the tank had moved out of sight in the underbrush, and only then did she realize that something must be wrong with the tank; otherwise, why hadn't they just blown a hole right through the wall?

A red flare shot up into the sky from the western woods and exploded over the cornfield.

"Here they come again!" Sister shouted grimly. She glanced at Swan. "You'd better get out of here before it starts."

Swan looked along the wall at the others who stood ready to fight, and she knew where she should be. "I'll stay."

Another flare rose from the eastern woods and burst like a smear of blood against the sky.

Gunfire swept the western wall, and Sister grabbed Swan to pull her behind cover. Bullets slammed against the logs, chips of ice and splinters spinning through the air. About twenty seconds after the first barrage had begun, the AOE soldiers massed in the forest on the eastern side of Mary's Rest started firing, their bullets doing no major damage but keeping the defenders' heads down. The shooting continued, and soon bullets were blasting chinks in the walls, some of them ricocheting off the ground, but others hitting flesh.

And on the southern perimeter, the defenders saw more armored cars and trucks emerge from the forest, along with fifty or sixty soldiers. The Army of Excellence rushed the wall. Hidden trenches stopped several vehicles and toppled twenty or more men, but the rest of them kept coming. Two trucks got through the maze of ditches and tree stumps and crashed into the logs. The entire southern section of the wall trembled, but it held. Then the soldiers had covered the open ground and reached the wall, trying to climb over it; their fingers couldn't grip the ice, and as they slipped back the defenders fired on them point-blank. Those without guns swung axes, picks and sharpened shovels.

Mr. Polowsky climbed up on a dead sentry's ladder, firing his pistol as fast as he could aim. "Drive them back!" he shouted. He took aim at an enemy soldier, but before he could pull the trigger a rifle bullet plowed into his chest and a second caught him in the side of the head. He fell off the ladder, and at once a woman plucked the pistol from his hand.

"Fall back! Fall back!" Lieutenant Thatcher commanded as bullets whined around his head and soldiers were wounded and killed on every side. Thatcher didn't wait for the others to obey; he turned and ran, and with his third stride a .38 slug hit him in the small of his back and propelled him into a ditch on top of four other men.

The charge had been broken, and the soldiers retreated. They left their dead behind.

"Hold your fire!" Sister shouted. The shooting died away, and in another minute it ceased over on the eastern wall as well.

"I'm out of bullets!" a woman with a rifle said to Sister, and further down the line there were more calls for ammunition—but Sister knew that once the bullets everyone had for his own weapons were gone, there would be no more. They're baiting us, she thought. Getting us to waste ammunition, and when the guns were useless they would storm the walls in a tide of death and destruction. Sister had six more shells for her own shotgun, and that was all.

They're going to break through, she realized. Sooner or later, they're going to break through.

She looked at Swan and saw in the girl's dark eyes that Swan had reached the same conclusion.

"They want *me,*" Swan said. The wind blew her hair around her pale, lovely face like the fanning of brilliant flames. "No one else. Just me." Her gaze found one of the ladders that leaned against the wall.

Sister's arm shot out; her hand caught Swan's chin and pulled her head back around. "You get that out of your mind!" Sister snapped. "Yes, they want you! *He* wants you!

But don't you think for one minute that it would be over if you went out to them!"

"But . . . if I went out there, maybe I could—"

"You could *not!*" Sister interrupted. "If you went over that wall, all you'd be doing is telling the rest of us that there's nothing worth fighting for!"

"I don't . . ." She shook her head, sickened by the sights, sounds and smell of war. "I don't want anyone else to die."

"It's not up to you anymore. People are going to die. *I* may be dead before the day's over. But some things *are* worth fighting and dying for. You'd better learn that right here and now, if you're ever going to lead people."

"Lead people? What do you mean?"

"You really don't know, do you?" Sister released Swan's chin. "You're a natural-born leader! It's in your eyes, your voice, the way you carry yourself—everything about you. People listen to you, and they believe what you say, and they *want* to follow you. If you said everyone should put down their guns right this minute, they'd do it. Because they know you're somebody very special, Swan—whether you want to believe that or not. You're a leader, and you'd better learn how to act like one."

"Me? A leader? No, I'm just . . . I'm just a *girl.*"

"You were born to lead people, and to teach them, too!" Sister affirmed. "*This* says you were." She touched the outline of the glass ring in the leather satchel. "Josh knows it. So does Robin. And *he* knows you were, just like I do." She motioned out beyond the wall, where she was certain the man with the scarlet eye must be. "Now it's time you accepted it, too."

Swan was puzzled and disoriented. Her childhood in Kansas, before the seventeenth of July, seemed like the life of another person a hundred years ago. "Teach them *what?*" she asked.

"What the future can be," Sister answered.

Swan thought of what she'd seen in the circle of glass: the green forests and meadows, the golden fields, the fragrant orchards of a new world.

"Now get on that horse," Sister said, "and ride around the

walls. Sit up tall and proud, and let everybody see you. Sit like a *princess,*" she said, drawing her own self up straight, "and let everybody know there's still something worth dying for in this damned world."

Swan looked at the ladder again. Sister was right. They wanted her, yes, but they wouldn't stop if they had her; they'd just keep killing, like rabid dogs in a frenzy, because that was all they understood.

She walked to Mule's side, grasped the rope reins and swung up onto his back. He pranced around a little bit, still unnerved by the uproar, and then he settled down and responded to Swan's touch. She urged him forward with a whisper, and Mule began to canter along the wall.

Sister watched Swan ride away, her hair streaming behind her like a fiery banner, and she saw the others turn to look at her as well, saw them all stand a little straighter, saw them check their guns and ammunition after she'd passed by. Saw new resolve in their faces, and knew that they would all die for Swan—and their town—if it came to that. She hoped it would not, but she was certain the soldiers would return stronger than ever—and right now, at least, there was no way out.

Sister reloaded her shotgun and stepped back up on the dirt bank to await the next attack.

Eighty-three

With darkness came the bone-numbing cold. The bonfires chewed up wood that had been the walls and roofs of shacks, and the defenders of Mary's Rest warmed themselves, ate and rested in hour-long shifts before they returned to the wall.

Sister had four shells left. The soldier she'd killed lay about ten feet from the wall, the blood icy and black around what had been his chest. On the northern perimeter, Paul was down to twelve bullets, and during one brief skirmish just before dark the two men who'd been fighting on either side of him had been killed. A ricocheting slug had driven wood splinters into Paul's forehead and right cheek, but otherwise he was okay.

On the eastern side of Mary's Rest, Robin counted six shells left for his rifle. Guarding that section of the wall, along with Robin and about forty other people, was Anna McClay, who'd long ago run out of bullets for her own rifle and now carried a little .22 pistol she'd taken from a dead man.

The attacks had continued all day, with lulls of an hour or two in between. First one side of the barricade would be hammered at, then another sprayed with gunfire. The wall was still holding strong, and it deflected most of the fire, but bullets were knocking chinks between the logs and occasionally hitting someone. Bud Royce's knee had been shattered by a rifle bullet that way, but he was still hobbling around on the southern edge, his face bleached with pain.

The word had gone out to save ammunition, but the supply was dwindling, and the enemy seemed to have enough to waste. Everyone knew that it was just a matter of time before the walls were stormed by massive force—but the question was: On what side would it come?

All this Swan knew as she rode Mule across the cornfield. The heavy-laden stalks swayed as the wind hissed through them. In a clearing ahead was the largest of the bonfires, around which fifty or sixty people rested and ate hot soup ladled from steaming wooden buckets. She was on her way to check on the many wounded who'd been taken to shelter inside the shacks for Dr. Ryan to help, and as she passed the bonfire a silence fell over the people who'd gathered around it.

She didn't look at any of them. She couldn't, because—even though she knew Sister was right—she felt as if she'd signed their death warrants. It was because of her that people were being killed, wounded and maimed, and if being a leader meant having to take that kind of burden, it was too heavy. She didn't look at them, because she knew that many of them would be dead before daylight.

A man shouted, "Don't you worry! We won't let the bastards in!"

"When I run out of bullets," another man vowed, "I'll use my knife! And when that breaks, I've still got *teeth!*"

"We'll stop 'em!" a woman called. "We'll turn 'em back!"

There were more shouts and calls of encouragement, and when Swan finally did look toward the bonfire, she saw the people watching her intently, some silhouetted by the flame and others illuminated by it, their eyes full of light and their faces strong and hopeful.

"We ain't afeared to die!" another woman said, and other voices agreed with her. "It's quittin' that scares the tar outta me, and by God, I ain't a quitter!"

Swan reined Mule in and sat staring at them. Her eyes filled with tears.

The skinny black man who'd been so vehement at the town meeting approached her. His left arm was bound up with bloody cloth, but his eyes were fierce and courageous. "Don't you cry, now!" he scolded her softly, when he got close enough. "It ain't for you to be cryin'. Lord, no! If *you* ain't strong, who's gonna be?"

Swan nodded and wiped her eyes with the back of her hand. "Thank you," she said.

"Uh-uh! Thank *you.*"

"For what?"

He smiled wistfully. "For lettin' me hear that sweet music again," he said, and he nodded toward the cornfield.

Swan knew what music he meant, because she could hear it, too: the wind moving between the rows and stalks like fingers brushing harp strings.

"I was born right close to a cornfield," he said. "Heard that music at night, just before I slept, and first thing in the mornin' when I woke up. Didn't think I'd ever hear it again, after them fellas messed everythin' up." He looked up at Swan. "I ain't afraid to die now. Uh-uh! See, I always figured it's better to die on your feet than live on your knees. I'm ready—and that's my choice. So don't you worry 'bout nothin'! Uh-uh!" He closed his eyes for a few seconds, and his frail body seemed to sway to the rhythm of the corn. Then he opened them again, and he said, "You take care now, hear?" He returned to the bonfire, offering his hands to the heat.

Swan urged Mule forward, and the horse trotted across the field. As well as looking in on the wounded, Swan wanted to check on Josh; the last time she'd seen him, early that morning, he'd still been deep in a coma.

She was almost across the field when bright flashes of light leaped over the eastern wall. Flames gouted, and mingled with the blasts was the high sewing-machine chatter of guns. Robin was on that side of the wall, she realized. She cried out, "Go!" and flicked the reins. Mule took off at a gallop.

Behind her, at the western wall, Army of Excellence infantry and vehicles were surging from the woods. "Hold your fire!" Sister warned, but the people around her were already shooting, wasting ammunition. And then something hit the wall about fifteen yards away, and flames leapt, fire rippling over the icy glaze. Another object struck the wall a few yards closer; Sister heard glass shatter, and she smelled gasoline an instant before a burst of orange flame dazzled her. Bombs! she thought. They're throwing bombs at the wall!

People were shouting and firing in a bedlam of noise. Bottles full of gasoline, with wicks of flaming cloth jammed down into them, sailed over the wall and exploded amid the defenders. Glass broke almost at Sister's feet, and she instinctively flung herself to the ground as a sheet of fiery gasoline spewed in all directions.

On the eastern side, dozens of Molotov cocktails were being thrown over the wall. A man near Robin screamed as he was hit by flying glass and covered with flames. Someone else threw him to the ground, tried to put out the fire with snow and dirt. And then, through the maelstrom of leaping flames and explosions, machine gun, pistol and rifle bullets hit the wall so hard the logs jumped, and slugs ricocheted through gaps between them.

"Let 'em have it!" Anna McClay thundered. The orange firelight showed her *hundreds* of soldiers between the wall and the forest, crawling forward, ducking into trenches, hiding behind wrecked vehicles and then firing or flinging their homemade bombs. As others around her fell back to get away from the flames, she shouted, "Stay where you are! Don't run!" A woman to her left staggered and went down, and as Anna turned to retrieve the wounded woman's gun a rifle bullet zipped through a hole in the wall and hit her in the side, knocking her to her knees. She tasted blood in her mouth and knew she'd bought the farm this time, but she stood up with a gun in each hand and lurched to the wall again.

The storm of bombs and gunfire rose in intensity. A section of the wall was aflame, the wet wood popping and smoking. As bombs burst on all sides and glass fragments whirled through the turbulent air Robin kept his position at the wall, firing over it at the advancing soldiers. He hit two of them, and then a bomb exploded on the other side of the wall right in front of him. The heat and flying glass drove him back, and he tripped over the body of a dead man behind him.

Blood streamed down his face from a gash at his hairline, and his skin felt seared. He wiped blood out of his eyes, and then he saw something that drove a freezing bolt of fear into his stomach.

A metal claw attached to a heavy rope suddenly flew over the wall. The rope was drawn taut, and the tongs of the crude grappling hook dug between the logs. Another hook came over, lodging nearby; a third grappling hook was thrown, but it didn't find a purchase and was rapidly reeled back to be tossed again. A fourth and a fifth grappling hook dug into the wall, and the soldiers started hauling at the ropes.

Robin realized at once that the entire section of the wall, already weakened by bullets and flames, was about to be pulled down. More grappling hooks were coming over, their tongs jamming tightly between the logs, and as the ropes went taut the wall cracked like a rib cage being torn apart.

He scrambled to his feet, ran toward the wall and grabbed one of the hooks, trying to wrench it loose. A few yards away, a husky, gray-bearded man was hacking at one of the ropes with an axe, and beside him a slim black woman was sawing at another rope with a butcher knife. Still the bottle bombs exploded along the wall, and more grappling hooks strained.

To the right of Robin's position, Anna McClay had emptied both of her guns, and now she saw the grappling hooks and ropes coming over the wall. She turned, looking for another weapon, heedless of the bullet in her side and a second in her right shoulder. Rolling a dead man over, she found a pistol, but there was no ammunition for it; then she discovered a meat cleaver that someone had dropped, and she used it to slash at the ropes. She cut through one and had almost severed a second when the top three feet of the wall was pulled down in a crash of logs and flames. A half-dozen soldiers rushed at her. "No!" she screamed, and she flung the cleaver at them. A fusillade of machine gun bullets spun her around in a macabre pirouette. As she fell to the ground her last thought was of a carnival ride called the Mad Mouse, its little rattling car rocketing around a bend in the tracks and taking off into the night sky, up and up with the fiery lights of the carnival burning in the earth below her and the wind whistling past her ears.

She was dead before she came down.

"They're breaking through!" Robin heard someone shout —and then the wall in front of him collapsed with a noise like a human groan, and he was standing exposed in a space that a tractor-trailer truck could have driven through. A wave of soldiers was coming right at him, and he leapt aside an instant before bullets tore through the air.

He aimed his rifle and shot the first soldier who rushed through. The others scurried back or hit the ground as Robin blasted away at them—and then his rifle was empty, and he couldn't see the soldiers anymore for the smoke that whirled off the burning logs. He heard more cracks and groans as other sections of the wall were pulled down, and flames leapt high as the bombs exploded. He was aware of figures running all around him, some of them firing and falling. "Kill the sonsofbitches!" he heard a man shout off to the left, and then a figure in a grayish-green uniform ran out of the haze. Robin planted his feet, turned the rifle around to use it like a club and struck the soldier in the skull as the man passed him. The soldier fell, and Robin discarded his rifle in favor of the other man's .45 automatic.

A bullet sang past his head. Twenty feet away a bottle bomb exploded, and a woman with burning hair, her face a mask of blood, staggered out of the smoke; she fell before she got to Robin. He aimed at the figures flooding over the broken wall, firing the rest of the .45's clip. Machine gun bullets plowed across the ground a few feet from him, and he knew there was nothing more he could do there. He had to get away, to find another place to defend from; the wall on the eastern side of Mary's Rest was being destroyed, and soldiers were pouring through the holes.

He ran toward town. Dozens of others were running as well, and the battlefield was littered with the bodies of the dead and wounded. Small bands of people had stopped to make their own desperate stands, but they were quickly shot down or scattered. Robin looked back and saw two armored cars coming through the smoke, their turret guns flashing fire.

"Robin! Robin!" someone was calling over the chaos. He recognized the voice as Swan's, and he knew she must be somewhere close.

"Swan!" he shouted. "Over here!"

She heard Robin's answer and wheeled Mule to the left, in the direction she thought his voice had come from. The smoke stung her eyes, made it almost impossible to see the faces of people until they were a few feet away. Explosions were still blasting just ahead, and Swan knew the enemy soldiers had broken through the eastern wall. She saw that people were wounded and bleeding, but they were stopping to turn and fire the last of their bullets; still others, armed only with axes, knives and shovels, ran forward to fight at close quarters.

A bomb exploded nearby, and a man screamed. Mule reared up on his hind legs and pawed the air. When he came down again, he kept sideslipping as if one half of him wanted to run in one direction and the other half the opposite way. "Robin!" she shouted. "Where are you?"

"Over here!" He still couldn't see her. He tripped over the corpse of a man whose chest was riddled with bullet holes; the dead man was grasping an axe, and Robin spent a few precious seconds working it loose from the hand.

When he stood up, he was face to face with a horse—and it was a toss-up as to who was most startled. Mule whinnied and reared again, wanting to break loose and run, but Swan quickly got him under control. She saw Robin's blood-smeared face and held out her hand to him. "Get on! Hurry!"

He grasped her hand and pulled himself up behind her. Swan kicked her heels into Mule's flanks, wheeled him toward town and let him run.

They came out of the thick smoke, and Swan suddenly reined Mule in. He obeyed, his hooves plowing into the ground. From this position, Swan and Robin could see fighting going on all around Mary's Rest; fires blazed on the southern side, and over on the west they saw soldiers streaming through huge holes in the wall, followed by more armored cars and trucks. The noise of gunfire, shouting and screaming was whipped back and forth in the wind—and at that instant Swan knew Mary's Rest had fallen.

She had to find Sister, and *fast.* Her face tight and strained and her teeth clenched with anger, Swan urged Mule forward.

Mule started running like a thoroughbred, his head held low and his ears laid back.

There was a high chattering noise, and hot currents of air seemed to sweep around her. Swan felt Mule shudder and heard him grunt as if he'd been kicked, and then Mule's legs went out from under him. The horse fell, throwing Robin free but trapping Swan's left leg under him. The breath was knocked out of Swan, and she lay stunned as Mule desperately tried to stand up. But Robin had already seen the bullet holes in Mule's belly, and he knew the horse was finished.

An engine growled. He looked up and saw a Chevy Nova with an armored windshield and a rooftop gun turret coming. He bent to Swan's side and tried to pull her free, but her leg was firmly pinned. Mule was still struggling to get up, steam and blood spraying from his nostrils, his sides heaving. His eyes were wide with terror.

The Chevy's gun turret fired, and bullets ripped across the ground dangerously near Swan. Robin realized with sickening certainty that he didn't have the strength to free her. The armored car's radiator grinned like a mouthful of metal teeth. Robin's grip tightened around the axe handle.

Swan grasped his hand. "Don't leave me," she said, dazed and unaware that Mule was dying on top of her.

Robin had already decided. He pulled free and sprinted toward the armored car.

"Robin!" she cried out, and then she lifted her head and saw where he was going.

He zigzagged as the turret's gun chattered again. Bullets kicked up snow and dirt at his heels. The Chevy veered toward him and away from Swan, just as he'd hoped it would. Move your lazy ass! he told himself as he dove to the ground, rolled and scrambled up again to throw off the gunner's aim. The Chevy picked up speed, steadily closing the range. He jinked to both sides, heard the machine gun speak and saw the hot streaks of slugs zip through the air. *Oh, shit!* he thought as a searing pain ripped across his left thigh; he knew he'd been tagged, but it wasn't too bad, and he kept going. The armored car followed him into the smoke.

On the northern perimeter, Paul Thorson and forty other men and women were surrounded by soldiers. Paul had only two bullets left, and most of the others had run out of ammunition a long time before; they wielded clubs, pickaxes and shovels and dared the soldiers to charge.

A Jeep pulled up behind the protective barrier of AOE infantry, and Colonel Macklin rose to his feet. His coat was draped over his shoulders, and the deep-set eyes in his skeletal face fixed on the group of defenders who'd been pushed back against the wall. "Is she with them?" he asked the man occupying the rear seat.

Friend stood up. He wore an Army of Excellence uniform and a gray cap pulled over his thin, dark brown hair; today his face was plain and nondescript, soulless and without character. His watery hazel eyes ticked back and forth for a few seconds. "No," he said finally, in a toneless voice, "she's not with them." He sat back down again.

"Kill them all," Macklin told the soldiers. Then he ordered his driver on as the Army of Excellence troops sprayed the trapped men and women with machine gun bullets. Among them, Paul squeezed off a shot and saw one of the soldiers stagger—and then he himself was hit in the stomach, and a second bullet broke his collarbone. He fell on his face, tried to get up and shivered as a third and fourth bullet hit his side and pierced his forearm. He pitched forward and lay still.

Three hundred yards away, the armored Chevy Nova was searching through the smoke, its turret gun firing at every hint of motion. The tires crunched over corpses, but one of the bodies that lay sprawled on the ground suddenly pulled in his arms and legs as the vehicle passed right over him.

When the armored car had cleared his body, Robin sat up and grasped the axe that had been hidden underneath him. He stood up, took three running strides and jumped onto the

Nova's rear fender. He kept going until he stood on the roof—and then he lifted the axe and smashed it down with all his strength on the sheet metal turret.

It crumpled inward, and the gunner tried to swivel his weapon, but Robin jammed it by placing his boot against the barrel. He battered down on the turret, his axe ripping through the sheet metal and slamming into the gunner's skull. There was a strangled cry of agony, and the driver put his foot down on the accelerator. As the Nova shot forward Robin was thrown off the roof to the ground; he'd lost his grip on the axe, and when he scrambled to his feet he could see the axe's handle still sticking rigidly up in the air, its business end about two inches deep in the gunner's head. Robin expected the car to come at him again, but the driver had panicked, veering erratically. The Nova kept going and disappeared in the smoke.

Mule was dying, steam rising from his nostrils and the bullet holes in his belly. Swan's head had cleared enough for her to realize what had happened, but she knew there was nothing she could do. Mule still twitched, as if trying to stand with willpower alone. Swan saw more soldiers coming, and she pulled at her leg, but it was jammed tight.

Suddenly someone bent down beside her and worked his arms under Mule's side. Swan heard the muscles and sinews crack in his shoulders as he heaved upward, supporting some of the horse's weight and easing the terrible pressure on Swan's leg.

"Pull yourself out!" he said, his voice strained with the effort. "Hurry!"

She wrenched at her leg and worked it a few more inches toward freedom. Then Mule shifted again, as if using his last strength to help, and with an effort that almost dislocated her thigh from its socket she pulled her leg out. The stinging blood immediately rushed back into it, and she gritted her teeth as the pain hit her.

The man withdrew his arms. His hands were blotched with white and brown pigment.

She looked up into Josh's face.

His skin had returned to its rich, dark umber color. He had

a short gray beard, and almost all of his tight cap of hair had turned white. But his nose, which had been broken so many times and been so misshapen, was straight-bridged and strong again, and the old scars of football and wrestling had been wiped clean. His cheekbones were high and sharp, as if chiseled from dark stone, and his eyes were a soft shade of gray that shone with the translucent wonder of a child.

She thought that, next to Robin, he was the most handsome man she'd ever seen.

Josh saw the soldiers coming, and adrenaline pumped through his body; he'd left Glory and Aaron in the house to search for Swan, and now he had to get all of them to safety. Where Sister was he didn't know, but he understood all too well that the soldiers were breaking through the walls on all sides of Mary's Rest, and soon they'd be in the alleys, setting the shacks on fire. He picked Swan up in his arms, his sprained shoulder and his ribs aflame with pain.

At that instant, Mule's body trembled and a burst of steam came from the horse's nostrils, pluming up into the sky like a tired soul finding release—and Josh knew that no beast of burden deserved rest as much as Mule. There would never be another horse as fine, or as beautiful.

Mule's eyes were already beginning to glaze over, but Swan understood that what Mule had been was already gone. "Oh . . ." she whispered, and then she was unable to speak.

Josh saw Robin running out of the smoke. "This way!" Josh shouted. Robin ran toward them, limping a little and holding his left thigh. But the soldiers had seen, too, and one of them started firing a pistol. A bullet plowed up dirt about four feet from Robin, and another whined past Josh's head.

"Come on!" Josh urged, and he started running toward town with Swan in his arms, his lungs working like a bellows in a metal forge. He saw another group of soldiers on the left. One of them shouted "Halt!" but Josh kept going. He looked quickly back to make sure Robin was following. Robin was right on his heels, wounded leg and all.

They were almost to the warren of alleys when four soldiers stepped into their path. Josh decided to barrel through them, but two of the men lifted their guns. He stopped, skidding in the mud and looking for a way out like a fox trapped by hounds. Robin whirled to the right—and about ten feet away were three more soldiers, one of them already leveling his M-16. More soldiers were approaching from the left, and Josh knew that within seconds they were going to be cut to pieces in a crossfire.

Swan was about to be killed in his arms. There was no way out now, and only one chance to save her—if indeed she *could* be saved. He had no choice, and no time to ponder the decision.

"Don't shoot!" he shouted. And then he had to say it, to keep the soldiers from firing: "This is Swan! This is the girl you're looking for!"

"Stand where you are!" one of the soldiers commanded, aiming a rifle at Josh's head. The other men formed a circle around Josh, Swan and Robin. There was a brief discussion among several of the soldiers, one of whom seemed to be in charge, and then two of the men headed off in opposite directions, obviously going to find someone else.

Swan wanted to cry, but she dared not let a tear show, not in front of these men. She kept her features as calm and composed as if sculpted from ice. "It's going to be okay," Josh said quietly, though the words sounded hollow and stupid. At least, for the moment, she was alive. "You'll see. We'll get out of this some—"

"No talking, nigger!" a soldier shouted, pointing a .38 in Josh's face.

He gave the man the best smile he could muster.

The noise of gunfire, explosions and screams still drifted over Mary's Rest like the residue of nightmares. Our asses are grass, Robin thought, and there wasn't a damned thing they could do about it. Two rifles and four pistols were aimed at him alone. He looked out toward the blazing eastern wall, then toward the west, way over beyond the cornfield, where trucks and armored cars seemed to be grouping to make camp.

In five or six minutes, one of the soldiers who'd left returned leading an old brown United Parcel Service truck in their direction. Josh was ordered to put Swan down, but she still had difficulty standing and had to lean against him. Then the soldiers conducted a thorough and rough body search. They let their hands linger on Swan's budding breasts; Josh saw Robin's face redden with anger, and he cautioned, "Be cool."

"What's this shit?" The tarot card that had been in the pocket of Josh's jeans was held up.

"Just a card," Josh replied. "Nothing special."

"Damn straight." The man tore it into fragments and let The Empress fall in pieces to the ground.

The rear door of the UPS truck was opened. Josh, Robin and Swan were shoved inside with thirty other people. When the door was slammed shut and bolted again, the prisoners were left in total darkness.

"Take 'em to the chicken coop!" the sergeant in charge ordered the driver, and the UPS truck carried away its new load of parcels.

Eighty-four

Swan clasped her hands over her ears. But she could still hear the terrible hurting sounds, and she thought her mind would crack before they stopped.

Out beyond the "chicken coop"—which was a wide circle of barbed wire surrounding the two hundred and sixty-two survivors, now prisoners—the soldiers were going through the cornfield, shearing the stalks off with machetes and axes or wrenching them up roots and all. The stalks were being piled up like corpses in the backs of trucks.

No bonfires were allowed within the coop, and the armed guards who stood around the wire were quick to fire warning shots that dissuaded people from huddling together. Many of the wounded were freezing to death.

Josh flinched at the laughter and singing of the troops in town. He looked toward the shacks with weary eyes and saw a large fire burning in the middle of the road, near the spring. Parked around Mary's Rest were dozens of trucks, armored cars, vans and trailers, and other bonfires blazed to keep the victors warm. Bodies were being stripped of clothes and left in macabre, frozen heaps. Trucks moved around collecting the clothes and guns.

Whoever the bastards were, Josh thought, they were masters of efficiency. They wasted nothing but human life.

There was the air of a wicked carnival over Mary's Rest, but Josh consoled himself with the fact that Swan was still alive. Also nearby, sitting as close as the guards would allow, were Glory and Aaron. She was shocked beyond tears. Aaron lay curled up, his eyes open and staring and the thumb of one hand jammed into his mouth. The soldiers had taken Crybaby and thrown it onto a bonfire.

Robin walked along the barbed wire like a caged tiger. There was only one way in or out, through a barbed wire gate the soldiers had hastily built. Off in the distance were more rapid gunshots, and Robin figured the bastards had found somebody still alive. He'd counted only six of his highway-men inside the coop, and two of them were badly wounded. Dr. Ryan, who'd survived an attack on his makeshift hospi-tal, had already told Robin those two were going to die. Bucky had made it, though he was sullen and would not speak. But Sister was missing, and that really twisted Robin's guts.

He stopped and stared across the wire at a guard. The man cocked his pistol, aimed it at Robin and said, "Move on, you piece of shit."

Robin grinned, spat on the ground and turned away. His groin crawled as he waited for the bullet to slam into his back. He'd seen prisoners shot down for no apparent reason other than to amuse the guards, and so he didn't breathe easily again until he'd gotten far away from the man. But he walked slowly; he wasn't going to run. He was through running.

Swan took her hands from her ears. The last of the hurting sounds were drifting away. The cornfield was a stubbled ruin, and the trucks rumbled away fat and happy as cockroaches.

She felt sick with fear, and she longed for the basement where she and Josh had been trapped such a long time ago. But she forced herself to look around at the other prisoners and to absorb the scene: the moaning and coughing of the wounded, the babbling of those who'd lost their minds, the sobbing and wailing of the death dirges. She saw their faces, their eyes dark and turned inward, all hope murdered.

They'd fought and suffered for her, and here she was sitting on the ground like an insect, waiting for a boot to smash down. Her fists clenched. Get up! she told herself. Damn it, get up! She was ashamed of her own frailty and weakness, and a spark of rage leapt within her as if thrown off by an iron wheel grinding flint. She heard two of the guards laughing. *Get up!* she screamed inwardly, and the rage grew, spread through her and burned the sick fear away.

"You're a leader," Sister had said, "and you'd better learn how to act like one."

Swan didn't want to be. Had never asked to be. But she heard an infant crying not too far away, and she knew that if there was to be a future for any of these people, it had to start right here . . . with her.

She stood up, took a deep breath to clear away the last cobwebs and walked among the other prisoners, her gaze moving left and right, meeting theirs and leaving the impression of a glimpse into a blast furnace.

"Swan!" Josh called, but she paid no attention and kept going, and he started to get up and go after her, but he saw how stiff her back was; it was a regal posture, full of confidence and courage, and now the other prisoners were sitting up as she passed them, and even the wounded were struggling to rise from the dirt. Josh let her go.

Her left leg was still stiff and aching, but at least it was unbroken. She, too, was aware of the energizing effect she was having on the others—but she did not know that around her they could have sworn they felt a radiance that briefly warmed the air.

She reached the crying infant. The child was held in the arms of a shivering man with a swollen, purple gash on the side of his head. Swan looked down at the child—and then she began to unbutton her coat of many colors and shrug out of it. She knelt down to wrap it around the man's shoulders and enfold the infant in it.

"You!" one of the guards shouted. "Get away from there!"

Swan flinched, but she kept at what she was doing.

"Get away!" a woman prisoner urged. "They'll kill you!"

A warning shot was fired. Swan arranged the folds of the

patchwork coat to keep the child warm, and only then did she stand up.

"Go back to where you were and sit down!" the guard ordered. He was holding a rifle braced against his hip.

Swan felt everyone watching her. The moment hung.

"I won't tell you again! Move your ass!"

God help me, she thought—and then she swallowed hard and started walking toward the barbed wire and the guard with the rifle. Immediately he lifted his weapon to a firing position.

"Halt!" another guard warned, off to the right.

Swan kept going, step after step, her eyes riveted to the man with the rifle.

He pulled the trigger.

The bullet whined past her head, and she knew it must have missed her by three inches or less. She stopped, wavered—and then took the next step.

"Swan!" Josh shouted, standing up. "Swan, don't!"

The guard with the rifle took a backward step as Swan approached. "The next one is right between your eyes," he promised, but the girl's merciless stare pierced him.

Swan stopped. "These people need blankets and food," she said, and she was surprised at the strength in her voice. "They need them *now*. Go tell whoever's in charge that I want to see him."

"Fuck you," the guard said. He fired.

But the bullet went over Swan's head, because one of the other guards had grabbed the rifle barrel and uptilted it. "Didn't you hear her *name*, dumb ass?" the second man asked. "That's the girl the colonel's looking for! Go find an officer and report!"

The first guard had gone pale, realizing how close he'd come to being skinned alive. He took off at a run toward Colonel Macklin's Command Center.

"I said," Swan repeated firmly, "that I want to see whoever's in charge."

"Don't worry," the man told her. "You'll get to see Colonel Macklin soon enough."

Another truck stopped over by the chicken coop's gate.

The rear door was unbolted and opened, and fourteen more prisoners were herded into the containment area. Swan watched them come in, some of them badly wounded and hardly able to walk. She went over to help—and an electric thrill shot through her, because she'd recognized one of the new arrivals.

"Sister!" she cried out, and she ran toward the dirty woman who'd stumbled through the gate.

"Oh, dear God, dear God!" Sister sobbed as she put her arms around Swan and held her. They clung together for a moment, silent, each just needing to feel the other's heart beating. "I thought you were dead!" Sister finally said, her vision blurred by tears. "Oh, dear God, I thought they'd killed you!"

"No, I'm all right. Josh is here, and so are Robin, Glory and Aaron. We all thought *you* were dead!" Swan pulled back to look at Sister. Her stomach clenched.

Burning gasoline had splattered onto the right side of Sister's face. Her eyebrow on that side had been burned off, and her right eye was almost swollen shut. Her chin and the bridge of her nose had both been gashed by flying glass. Dirt was all over the front of her coat, and the fabric was charred and torn. Sister understood Swan's expression, and she shrugged. "Well," she said, "I guess I was never meant to be pretty."

Swan hugged her again. "You're going to be okay. I don't know what I would've done without you!"

"You'd get along fine, just like you did before Paul and I showed up." She glanced around the area. "Where is he?"

Swan knew who she meant, but she said, "Who?"

"You know who. Paul." Sister's voice tightened. "He *is* here, isn't he?"

Swan hesitated.

"Where is he? Where's Paul?"

"I don't know," she admitted. "He's not here."

"Oh . . . my God." Sister clasped a dirt-caked hand to her mouth. She was dizzy, and this new blow almost finished her; she was weary and sick of fighting, and her bones ached as if her body had been snapped apart and rearranged. She'd retreated from the western wall as the soldiers overran it, had found a discarded butcher knife and killed one of them in hand-to-hand fighting, then had been forced across the field by a wave of attacking troops. She'd hidden under a shack, but when it was set afire over her head she'd had no choice but to surrender. "Paul," she whispered. "He's dead. I know he is."

"You don't know that! Maybe he got away! Maybe he's still hiding!"

"Hey, you!" the guard shouted. "Break it up and move on!"

Swan said, "Lean on me," and she started helping Sister back to where the others were. Josh was coming toward them, followed by Robin. And suddenly Swan realized that Sister no longer had the leather satchel. "The glass ring! What happened to it?"

Sister put a finger to her lips.

A Jeep roared up. Its two passengers were Roland Croninger, still wearing a helmet and with mud splattered across his bandaged face, and the man who called himself Friend. Both of them got out while the driver kept the engine idling.

Friend stalked along the wire, his brown eyes narrowed as he searched among the prisoners. And then he saw her, supporting an injured woman. "*There!*" he said excitedly, and he pointed. "That's her!"

"Bring the girl out," Roland told the nearest guard.

Friend paused, staring at the woman who leaned on Swan's shoulder. The woman's face was unfamiliar, and the last time he'd seen Sister she'd been disfigured. He thought he recalled seeing that woman the day he'd overheard the Junkman talking about the Army of Excellence, but he hadn't paid any attention to her. That was back when he was sick, and details had escaped him. But now he realized that, if indeed the woman *was* Sister, she no longer had that damned bag with the circle of glass in it.

"Wait!" he told the guard. "Bring that woman out, too! Hurry!"

The guard motioned for another to help him, and they entered the containment area with their rifles ready.

Josh was just about to reach out for Sister when the guards ordered Swan to halt. She looked over her shoulder at the two rifle barrels. "Come on," one of the men said. "You wanted to see Colonel Macklin? Here's your chance. You too, lady."

"She's hurt!" Josh objected. "Can't you see—"

The guard who'd spoken fired his rifle into the ground at Josh's feet, and Josh was forced back.

"Let's go." The guard prodded Swan with his rifle. "The colonel's waiting."

Swan supported Sister, and they were bracketed by the two guards as they were escorted to the gate.

Robin started after them, but Josh grabbed his arm. "Don't be stupid," Josh warned.

The boy angrily wrenched free. "You're just going to let them take her? I thought you were supposed to be her *guardian!*"

"I used to be. Now she'll have to take care of herself."

"Right!" Robin said bitterly. "What are we going to do, just *wait?*"

"If you have a better suggestion—and one that won't get a lot of people killed, including yourself and Swan—I'd just love to hear it."

Robin had none. He watched helplessly as Swan and Sister were herded toward the Jeep where the two men waited.

As they neared the Jeep, both Swan and Sister felt their skin crawl. Sister recognized the one with the bandaged face from her confrontation with the tank—and she knew the other as well. It was in his eyes, or his smile, or the way he cocked his head or held his hands in fists at his sides. Or maybe it was the way he trembled with excitement. But she knew him, and so did Swan.

He did not look at Swan. Instead, he strode forward and ripped the collar of Sister's coat away from her neck.

Exposed underneath was a brown scar in the shape of a crucifix.

"Your face is different," he said.

"So is yours."

He nodded, and she saw a quick glint of red deep in his

eyes, there and then gone like a glimpse of something monstrous and unknown. "Where is it?"

"Where is what?"

"The ring. The crown. Or whatever the fuck it is. Where?"

"Don't you know everything? You tell me."

He paused, and his tongue flicked across his lower lip. "You didn't destroy it. I know that fer sure, fer sure. You hid it somewhere. Oh, you think you're just a cutie-pie, don't you? You think you shit roses, just like—" He almost turned his head, almost let himself look at her, but he did not. The muscles of his neck were as taut as piano wires. "Just like *she* does," he finished.

"What crown?" Roland asked.

Friend ignored him. "I'll find it," he promised Sister. "And if I can't persuade you to help me, my associate Captain Croninger has a wonderful way with tools. Do you forgive me now?"

Swan realized he was speaking to her, though he still stared at Sister.

"I *said*, do you forgive me now?" When Swan didn't reply, his smile broadened. "I didn't think so. Now you have a taste of what hate is. How do you like it?"

"I don't."

"Oh," he said, not yet trusting himself to even glance at her, "I think you'll learn to enjoy the flavor. Shall we go, ladies?"

They got into the Jeep, and the driver headed toward Colonel Macklin's trailer.

Out by the broken northern wall, where flames still gnawed and trucks rumbled back and forth with their cargos of guns, clothing and shoes, a solitary figure found a group of corpses that the scavenger brigades hadn't yet gotten to.

Alvin Mangrim rolled the body of a dead man over and examined the ears and nose. The nose was too small, he decided, but the ears would do just fine. He withdrew a bloody butcher knife from a leather holder at his waist and went to work severing both the ears; then he dropped them into a cloth bag that hung around his shoulder. The bottom of it was soggy with blood, and inside it were more ears, noses and a few fingers he'd already "liberated" from other bodies. He was planning on drying the objects out and stringing them into necklaces. He knew Colonel Macklin would like one, and he thought it might be a good way to barter some extra rations. In this day and age a man had to use his mind!

He recalled a tune from a long time ago, part of a shadowy world. He remembered holding a woman's hand—a rough, hard and hateful hand, covered with calluses—and going to a theater to see a cartoon movie about a lovely princess who shacked up with seven dwarves. He'd always liked the tune that the dwarves whistled as they worked in the mine, and he began to whistle that song as he carved off a woman's nose and dropped it into the bag. Most of the music he was whistling went out through the hole where his own nose had been, and it occurred to him that if he found a nose the right size he could dry it and use it to plug the hole.

He went to the next corpse, which was lying on its face. The nose would probably be smashed, Alvin thought. But he grasped the corpse's shoulder and rolled it over anyway.

It was a man with a gray-streaked beard.

And suddenly the corpse's eyes opened, bright blue and bloodshot against the grayish-white flesh.

"Oh . . . *wow,*" Alvin Mangrim said.

Paul lifted his Magnum, pressed the barrel against the other man's skull and blew his brains out with the last bullet.

The dead man fell over Paul's body and warmed him. But Paul knew he was dying, and he was glad now that he'd been too gutless to put that gun against his own head and take the easy way out. He didn't know who the dead man was, but the bastard was history.

He waited. He'd lived most of his life alone, and he wasn't afraid to die alone. No, not afraid at all—because the fearsome thing had been getting to this point. It was a piece of cake from here on. The only thing he regretted was not knowing what had happened to the girl—but he knew that Sister was a tough old bird, and if she'd survived all this, she wasn't going to let any harm come to Swan.

Swan, he thought. Swan. Don't let them break you. Spit in

their eyes and kick their asses—and think sometimes of a Good Samaritan, okay?

He decided he was tired. He was going to rest, and maybe when he woke up it would be morning. It would be so wonderful to see the sun.

Paul went to sleep.

FOURTEEN
Prayer for the Final Hour

The master thief / Buried treasure / A feat of magic / The way out / The greatest power / Roland's good, long look / Realm of God / The machine / Swan's death knell / A place to rest / The vow

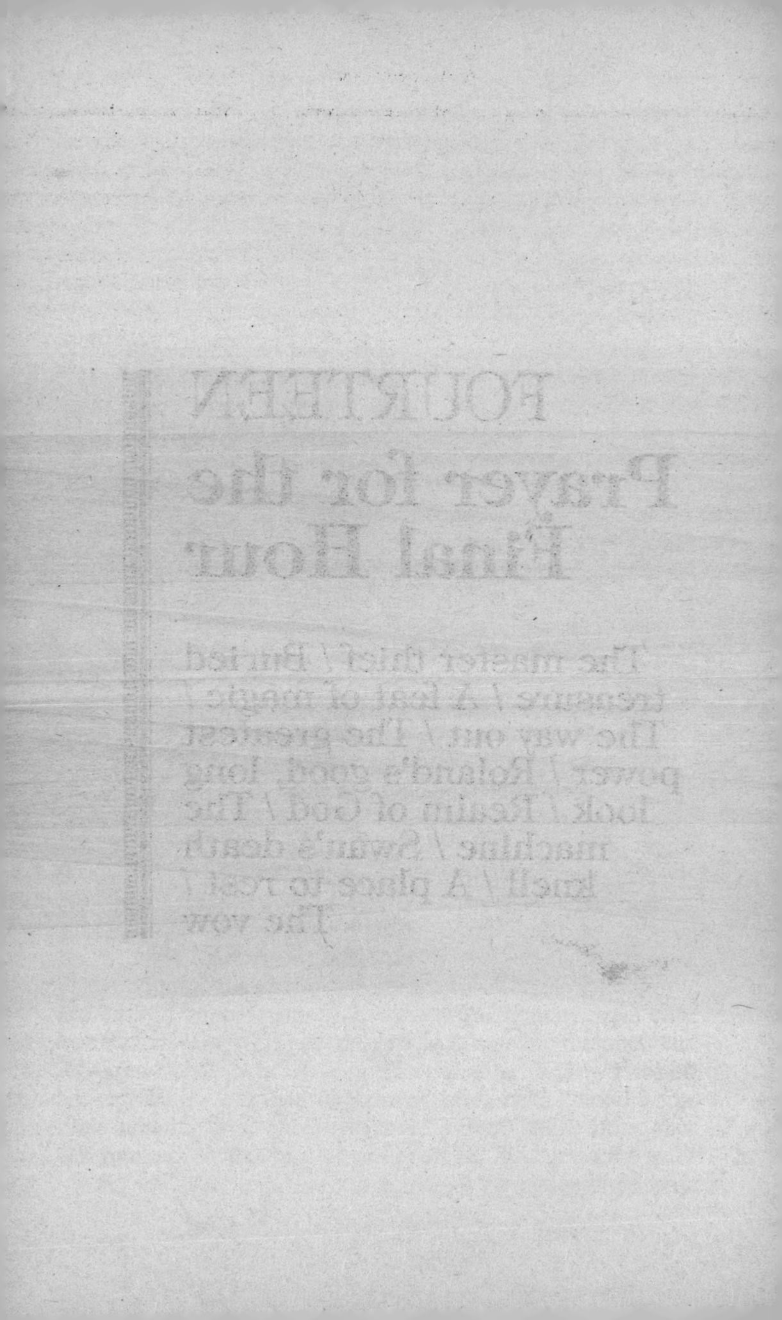

Eighty-five

Yellow lamplight fell upon the visage of Death, and in its presence Swan drew herself up tall and straight. Fear fluttered inside her ribs like a caged butterfly, but Swan met Colonel Macklin's gaze without cringing. He was the skeletal rider, Swan realized. Yes. She knew him, knew what he was, understood the ravenous power that drove him. And now he'd scythed down Mary's Rest, but his eyes were still hungry.

On the desk before Colonel Macklin was a piece of paper. Macklin lifted his right arm and slammed his hand down, impaling the casualty report on the nails. He pulled them loose from the scarred desktop and offered his palm to Swan.

"The Army of Excellence has lost four hundred and sixty-eight soldiers today. Probably more, when the reports are updated." He glanced quickly at the woman who stood beside Swan, then back to the girl. Roland and two guards stood behind them, and standing at Macklin's right was the man who called himself Friend. "Take it," Macklin said. "Look for yourself. Tell me if you're worth four hundred and sixty-eight soldiers."

"The people who killed those soldiers thought so," Sister spoke up. "And if we'd had more bullets, you'd still be outside the walls getting your butts kicked."

Macklin's attention drifted to her. "What's your name?"

"She's called Sister," Friend said. "And she's got something I want."

"I thought you wanted the girl."

"No. She's nothing to me. But *you* need her. You saw the cornfield for yourself; that's her work." He smiled vacantly at Sister. "This woman's hidden a pretty piece of glass that I'm going to have. Oh, yes! I'm going to find it, believe me." His eyes probed deeply into Sister's, down through flesh and bone to the storehouse of memory. The shadows of her experiences flew like startled birds within her mind. He saw the jagged ruins of Manhattan, and Sister's hands uncovering the circle of glass for the first time; he saw the watery hell of the Holland Tunnel, the snow-covered highway that wound through Pennsylvania, the prowling packs of wolves and a thousand other flickering images in the space of seconds. "Where is it?" he asked her, and at once he saw the image of an uplifted pickaxe in her mind, as if silhouetted by lightning.

She felt him picking at her brain like a master thief at a safe's lock, and she had to scramble the tumblers before he got in. She closed her eyes, squeezed them tightly shut and began to lift the lid of the most terrible thing, the thing that had sent her screaming over the edge and turned her into Sister Creep. The lid's hinges were rusted, because she hadn't looked inside it for a long time, but now she got the lid up and forced herself to see it, just as it had been that rainy day on the turnpike.

The man with the scarlet eye was blinded by a blue light spinning around, and he heard a male voice saying, "Give her to me, lady. Come on now, let me have her." The image cleared and strengthened, and suddenly he was holding a little girl's body in his arms; she was dead, her face smashed and distorted, and nearby was an overturned car with steam hissing from its radiator. On the bloody concrete a few feet away were fragments of glass and little bits of sparkle. "Give her to me, lady. We'll take care of her now," a young man in a yellow rain slicker was saying as he reached for the child.

"No," Sister said softly, painfully, deep within the awful moment, "I won't . . . let you . . . have her." Sister's voice sounded slurred and drunken.

He drew back, out of the woman's mind and memory. He resisted the urge to reach out and snap her neck. Either she was much stronger than he'd thought, or he was weaker than he knew—and he could feel that damned little bitch watching him, too! Something about her—her very *presence*—drained the power out of him! Yes, that was it! Her rampant evil was making him weak! One blow was all it would take; one quick blow to her skull, and it would all be over! He balled up his fist, and then he dared to look her in the face. *"What are you staring at?"*

She didn't answer. His face was fearsome, but it had a wet, plastic sheen. Then she said, as calmly as she could, "Why are you so afraid of me?"

"I'm not afraid!" he bellowed, and dead flies fell from his lips. His cheeks reddened. One of his brown eyes turned jet-black, and the bones shifted under his face like the rotten foundations of a papier-mâché house. Wrinkles and cracks shot from the corners of his mouth, and he aged twenty years in an instant. His red, wrinkled neck quivered as he pulled his gaze away from her and back to Sister. "Croninger!" he said. "Go get Brother Timothy and bring him here."

Roland left the trailer without hesitation.

"I could have someone shot every sixty seconds until you tell me." Friend leaned closer to Sister. "Who should we start with? That big nigger? How about the boy? Shall we just pick and choose? Draw straws, or names out of a hat? I don't give a shit. *Where'd you hide it?"*

Again, all he could see was a spinning blue light and the scene of an accident. A pickaxe, he thought. A pickaxe. He looked at the woman's dirty clothes and hands. And he knew. "You buried it, didn't you?"

There was no emotion on Sister's face. Her eyes remained tightly closed.

"You . . . *buried* . . . it," he whispered, grinning.

"What do you want with me?" Swan asked, trying to divert his attention. She looked at Colonel Macklin. "I'm listening," she prompted.

"You made the corn grow. Is that right?"

"The ground made the corn grow."

"*She* did it!" Friend said, turning away from Sister for the moment. "She put the seeds in the dirt and made them grow! Nobody else could've done that! The ground is *dead,* and she's the only one who can bring it back! If you take her with you, the Army of Excellence'll have all the food it needs! She could make a whole field grow from one ear of corn!"

Macklin stared at her. He didn't think he'd ever seen a girl as lovely as her—and her face was strong, very strong. "Is that right?" he repeated.

"Yes," she replied. "But I won't grow food for you. I won't grow crops for an army. There's no way you can force me."

"Yes, there is!" Friend hissed over Macklin's shoulder. "She's got friends out there! A big nigger and a boy! I saw them myself, just a little while ago! You bring them with us when we march, and she'll grow the crops to save their throats!"

"Josh and Robin would rather die."

"Would *you* rather they died?" He shook his head, and his other eye turned sea-green. "No, I don't think so."

Swan knew he was right. She couldn't refuse to help them if Josh's and Robin's lives were at stake. "Where are you marching to?" she asked tonelessly.

"Here!" Friend said. "Here's our Brother Timothy! He'll tell you!" Roland and Brother Timothy were just entering the trailer; Roland had a firm grip on the skinny man's arm, and Brother Timothy walked as if in a state of trance, his shoes shuffling along the floor.

Swan turned toward the two men and flinched. The new arrival's eyes were staring circles of shock, surrounded by deep purple. His mouth was half open, the lips gray and slack.

Friend clapped his hands together. "Simon says! Tell the little bitch where we're marching to, Brother Timothy!"

The man made a groaning, garbled sound. He shuddered, and then he said, "To . . . Warwick Mountain. To find God."

"Very good! Simon says! Tell us where Warwick Mountain is!"

"West Virginia. I was there. I lived with God . . . for seven days . . . and seven nights."

"Simon says! What does God have up on Warwick Mountain?"

Brother Timothy blinked, and a tear ran down his right cheek.

"Simon's about to get angry, Brother Timothy," Friend said sweetly.

The man whined; his mouth opened wider, and his head thrashed back and forth. "The black box . . . and the silver key!" he said, his words rushing and tangling together. "The prayer for the final hour! Fear death by water! Fear death by water!"

"Very good. Now count to ten."

Brother Timothy held up both hands in the lamplight. He began to count on his fingers. "One . . . two . . . three . . . four . . . five . . . six—" He stopped, puzzled.

And Swan had already seen that the other four fingers of his right hand had been chopped off.

"I didn't say 'Simon says,'" Friend told him.

The veins struck out from Brother Timothy's neck, and a pulse beat rapidly at his temple. Tears of terror filled his eyes. He tried to back away, but Roland's grip tightened on his arm. "Please," Brother Timothy whispered hoarsely, "don't . . . hurt me anymore. I'll take you to him, I swear I will! Just . . . don't hurt me anymore . . ." His voice was broken by sobbing, and he cringed as Friend approached.

"We won't hurt you." Friend stroked the other man's sweat-damp hair. "We wouldn't dream of it. We just wanted you to show these ladies what the power of persuasion can do. They'd be very stupid if they didn't do what we said, wouldn't they?"

"Stupid," Brother Timothy agreed, with a zombie grin. "Very stupid."

"Good dog." Friend patted the top of his head. Then he

returned to Sister's side, grabbed the back of her neck and twisted her head toward Brother Timothy; with his other hand he roughly forced one of her eyes open. "Look at him!" he shouted, and he shook her.

His touch spread unbearable cold through her body; her bones ached, and she had no choice but to look at the maimed man who stood before her.

"Captain Croninger has a very nice playroom." His mouth was right up against her ear. "I'm going to give you until dawn to remember where that trinket is. If your memory's still deficient, the good captain's going to start picking people out of the chicken coop to play games with him. And you're going to watch, because the first game will be to cut your eyelids off." His hand squeezed like a noose.

Sister was silent. The blue light continued to spin in her mind, and the young man in the yellow rain slicker kept reaching for the dead child in her arms.

"Whoever she was," he whispered, "I hope she died hating you."

Friend felt Swan watching him, felt her eyes probing to his soul, and he removed his hand before blind rage made him break the woman's neck. Then he could stand it no longer, and he whirled toward her. Their faces were about six inches apart. *"I'll kill you, bitch!"* he roared.

Swan used every shred of willpower to keep herself from shrinking back. She held his gaze like an iron hand trapping a snake. "No, you won't," she told him. "You said I didn't mean anything to you. But you were lying."

Brown pigment streaked across his pale flesh. His jaw lengthened, and a false mouth opened like a jagged wound in his forehead. One eye remained brown, while the other turned crimson, as if it had ruptured and gorged with blood. Smash her! he thought. Smash the bitch dead!

But he did not. *Could* not. Because he knew, even through the vile entanglement of his own hatred, that there was a power in her beyond anything he could understand, and something deep within him yearned like a diseased heart. He despised her and wanted to grind her bones—but at the same time he dared not touch her, because her fire might sear him to a cinder.

He backed away from her; his face became Hispanic, then Oriental, and finally it caught somewhere in mid-change. "You're going with us when we march," he promised. His voice was high and raspy, rising and tumbling through octaves. "We're going to West Virginia first . . . to find God." He sneered the word. "Then we're going to find you a nice farm with plenty of land. And we're going to get the seeds and grain for you, too. We'll find what you need in silos and barns along the way. We're going to build a big wall around your farm, and we'll even leave some soldiers to keep you company." The mouth in his forehead smiled, then sealed up. "And for the rest of your life you're going to be growing food for the Army of Excellence. You'll have tractors, reapers, all kinds of machines! And your own slaves, too! I'll bet that big nigger could really pull a plow." He glanced quickly at the two guards. "Go get that black bastard out of the chicken coop. And a boy named Robin, too. They can share Brother Timothy's quarters. You don't mind, do you?"

Brother Timothy grinned slyly. "Simon didn't say speak."

"Where can we put these two ladies?" Friend asked Colonel Macklin.

"I don't know. A tent, I guess."

"Oh, no! Let's at least give the ladies mattresses! We want them comfortable while they think! How about a trailer?"

"They can go into Sheila's trailer," Roland suggested. "She'll watch them for us, too."

"Take them there," Friend ordered. "But I want two armed guards on duty at that trailer's door. There will be no mistakes. Understood?"

"Yes, sir." He withdrew his pistol from its waist holster. "After you," he told Swan and Sister, and as they went out the door and down the carved steps Swan clenched Sister's hand.

Friend stood at the doorway and watched them go. "How long before dawn?" he asked.

"Three or four hours, I think," Macklin said. Swan's face remained impressed in Macklin's mind as clearly as a photograph. He ripped the casualty report off the nails in his palm; the numbers were organized by brigade, and Macklin tried to concentrate on them, but he couldn't get past the girl's face. He'd not seen such beauty in a long, long time; it was beyond sexual—it was *clean,* powerful and new. He found himself staring at the nails in his palm, and at the filthy bandages taped around his wrist. For an instant he could smell himself, and the odor almost made him puke.

He looked up at Friend in the doorway, and Macklin's mind suddenly cleared like clouds blown away by a scorching wind.

My God, he thought. I'm . . . in league with . . .

Friend turned his head slightly. "Is anything on your mind?" he inquired.

"No. Nothing. I'm just thinking, that's all."

"Thinking gets people in trouble. Simon says! Isn't that right, Brother Timothy?"

"Right!" the man chirped, and he clapped his mangled hands together.

Eighty-six

"I'm an entertainer," the woman who sat on a pile of dirty pillows in the corner suddenly said.

It was the first time she'd spoken since they'd been shoved into the filthy trailer more than a hour before. She'd just sat there and watched them as Swan lay on one of the bare mattresses and Sister paced the room.

"Do you two like to party?"

Sister stopped pacing, stared at her incredulously for a few seconds and then continued. There were nine steps from wall to wall.

"Well"—she shrugged—"if we're going to bunk together, we should at least know one another's names. I'm Sheila Fontana."

"Good for you," Sister muttered.

Swan sat up and regarded the dark-haired woman with closer scrutiny. By the light of the trailer's single kerosene lamp, Swan saw that Sheila Fontana was thin to the point of emaciation, her yellowish flesh drawn and sunken over her facial bones. The scalp showed at the crown of her head, and her black hair was dirty and lifeless. Around her on the floor was a scatter of empty food cans, bottles and other trash. The woman wore stained and dirty clothes under a heavy corduroy coat, but Swan had also seen that Sheila's fingernails, though broken and gnawed down to the quick, had been meticulously polished bright red. On first entering the trailer, Swan had noticed the dresser covered with make-up jars, tubes of lipstick and the like, and now she glanced over at the mirror where the clipped photographs of young, fresh-faced models were taped up. "I used to be an entertainer, too," Swan offered. "In the Travelin' Show, with Josh and Rusty. Mostly I just stayed in the wagon, though. Rusty was a magician—he could make things disappear and appear again, just like that." She snapped her fingers, lost in a memory of the past. She focused her attention on Sheila again. "What do you *do?*"

"A little of everything, honey." Sheila smiled, showing gray and shrunken gums. "I'm an RL."

"An RL? What's that?"

"Recreation Lady. I ought to be out on the stroll right now, too. A good RL can score till she's sore after a battle. It makes the men want to fuck."

"Huh?"

"She means she's a whore," Sister explained. "Jesus, it smells in here!"

"Sorry, I'm fresh out of Air-Wick. You can spray some of that perfume around, if you want." She motioned toward the gummy, dried-up bottles on the dresser.

"No, thank you." Sister broke her rhythm and strode to the door; she twisted the handle, opened the door and faced the two guards who were just outside.

Both of them held rifles. One of the guards said, "Get back in there."

"I'm just getting some fresh air. Do you mind?"

A rifle barrel was pushed against her chest. "Back *inside,*" the man ordered. He shoved her, and Sister slammed the door shut.

"Men are beasts," Sheila said. "They don't understand that a woman needs her privacy."

"We've got to get out of here!" Sister's voice quavered on the edge of panic. "If he finds it, he's going to destroy it—and if I don't let him find it, he's going to start executing people!"

"Find what?" Sheila drew her knees up against her chest.

"It's going to be dawn soon," Sister continued. "Oh, God!" She leaned against the wall, hardly able to stand. "He's going to find it! I can't stop him from finding it!"

"Hey, lady!" Sheila said. "Anybody ever tell you you were crazy?"

Sister was close to falling apart, Swan knew; she was, too, but she would not let herself think about what was ahead. "How long have you been with them?" Swan asked the dark-haired woman.

Sheila smiled thinly—a horrible smile on that emaciated, life-drained face. "Forever," she replied. "Oh, Christ, I wish I had some blow! Or pills. If I had just *one* Black Beauty, I'd slice that bastard into little-bitty pieces and fly high for a fucking week! You don't have any dope on you, do you?"

"No."

"I didn't think so. Nobody's got any. I guess it's all been smoked, snorted and popped by now. Oh, shit." She shook her head sadly, as if bemoaning the death of a lost culture. "What's your name, honey?"

"Swan."

Sheila repeated it. "That's a nice name. An unusual name. I used to know a girl named Dove. She was hitching a ride up near El Cerrito, and Rudy and I pulled—" She stopped. "Listen!" she whispered urgently. "Do you hear that?"

Swan heard some men laughing nearby, and in the distance were the sounds of gunshots.

"The baby!" Sheila's right hand went to her mouth. Her eyes were pools of darkness. "Listen! Can't you hear the baby crying?"

Swan shook her head.

"Oh . . . Jesus!" Sheila was almost choked with terror. "The baby's crying! Make it stop crying! Please!" She put her hands over her ears, and her body began to curl into a fetal shape. "Oh, God, please make it *stop!*"

"She's out of her mind," Sister said, but Swan got up from the mattress and approached the woman. "Better leave her alone," Sister warned. "She looks pretty far gone."

"Make it stop . . . make it stop . . . oh, Jesus, make it stop," Sheila was raving, curled up in the corner. Her face gleamed with sweat in the lamplight, and the woman's body odor almost repulsed Swan—but Swan stood over her and finally bent down at her side. She hesitated, then reached out to touch the other woman. Sheila's hand found Swan's and gripped it with painful pressure. Swan did not pull away.

"Please . . . make the baby stop crying," Sheila begged.

"There's . . . there's no baby here. There's no one here but us."

"I hear the crying! *I hear it!*"

Swan didn't know what kind of torment this woman had lived through, but she couldn't bear to watch her suffer. She squeezed Sheila's hand and leaned closer to her. "Yes," she said softly, "I hear the crying, too. A baby crying. Isn't that right?"

"Yes! Yes! Make it stop before it's too late!"

"Too late? Too late for what?"

"Too late for it to *live!*" Sheila's fingers dug into Swan's hand. "He'll kill it if it doesn't stop crying!"

"I hear it," Swan told her. "Wait, wait. The baby's stopping now. The sound's going away."

"No, it's not! I can still hear—"

"The sound's going *away,*" Swan repeated, her face only a few inches from Sheila's. "It's getting quieter now. Quieter. I can hardly hear it at all. Someone's taking care of the baby. It's very quiet now. Very quiet. The crying's gone."

Sheila drew a sharp, sudden breath. Held it for a few seconds, and let it out in a soft, agonized moan. "Gone?" she asked.

"Yes," Swan answered. "The baby's stopped crying. It's all over."

"Is . . . is the baby still alive?"

That seemed very important to her. Swan nodded. "Still alive."

Sheila's mouth was slack, and a thin thread of saliva broke

over the lower lip and trailed down into her lap. Swan started to work her hand free, but Sheila wouldn't let her go.

"You need some help?" Sister offered, but Swan shook her head.

Sheila's hand came up, very slowly, and the tips of her fingers touched Swan's cheek. Swan couldn't see the woman's eyes—just two dark craters in the chalky flesh. "Who are you?" Sheila whispered.

"Swan. My name is Swan. Remember?"

"Swan," Sheila repeated, her voice gentle and awed. "The baby . . . never stopped crying before. Never stopped crying . . . until it was dead. I never even knew if the baby was a boy or girl. It never stopped crying before. Oh . . . you're so pretty." Her dirty fingers moved across Swan's face. "So pretty. Men are beasts, you know. They take pretty things . . . and they make them ugly." Her voice cracked. She began to cry softly, her cheek resting against the girl's hand. "I'm so tired of being ugly," she whispered. "Oh . . . I'm so tired. . . ."

Swan let her cry, and she stroked the woman's head. Her fingers touched scabs and sores.

After a while, Sheila lifted her head. "Can . . . can I ask you something?"

"Yes."

Sheila wiped her eyes and snuffled her nose. "Will you . . . let me brush your hair?"

Swan stood up and helped Sheila to her feet; then she went to the dressing table and sat down before the mirror. Sheila took a tentative step after her, followed by another. She reached the dresser and picked up a brush that was clotted with hair. Then Sheila's fingers smoothed out Swan's mane and she began to brush it, long and slow, stroke after stroke.

"Why are you here?" Sheila asked. "What do they want with you?"

Her tone was hushed and reverent. Sister had heard it before, when other people in Mary's Rest had talked to Swan. Before the girl could answer, Sister said, "They're going to keep us here. They're going to make Swan work for them."

Sheila stopped brushing. "Work for them? Like . . . as an RL?"

"In a way, yes."

She paused for a few seconds, then continued slowly brushing Swan's hair. "Such a pretty thing," she whispered, and Sister saw her blink heavily, as if trying to grapple with thoughts that she'd rather shut out.

Sister knew nothing about the woman, but she watched the way Sheila gently used the brush, her fingers moving dreamlike through Swan's hair to loosen tangles. She saw how Sheila kept admiring Swan's face in the mirror, then hesitantly lifting her gaze to her own shriveled, worn-out features—and Sister decided to take a chance. "It's a shame," she said quietly, "that they're going to make her ugly."

The brush stopped.

Sister glanced quickly at Swan, who'd begun to realize what the older woman was trying; then Sister came up to stand behind Sheila. "Not all men are beasts," she said, "but *those* men are. They're going to use Swan and make her ugly. They're going to crush her and destroy her."

Sheila looked at Swan in the mirror and then at herself. She stood very still.

"You can help us," Sister said. "You can stop them from making her ugly."

"No." Her voice was weak and listless, like that of a weary child. "No, I . . . can't. I'm nobody."

"You can help us get out of here. Just talk to the guards. Get their attention and move them away from that door for one minute. That's all."

"No . . . no . . ."

Sister put her hand on the woman's shoulder. "Look at her. Go ahead. Now look at yourself." Sheila's eyes shifted. "Look what they've made you into."

"Ugly," Sheila whispered. "Ugly. Ugly. Ugly . . ."

"Please help us get away."

Sheila didn't reply for perhaps a minute, and Sister was afraid that she'd lost her. Suddenly the other woman began brushing Swan's hair again. "I can't," Sheila said. "They'd kill all of us. It wouldn't matter to them, because they like to use their guns."

"They won't kill us. The colonel doesn't want us hurt."

"They'd hurt *me*. Besides, where would you go? Everything's fucked up. There's no place to hide."

Sister cursed inwardly, but Sheila was right. Even if they did manage to escape the trailer, it would only be a matter of time before the soldiers caught them again. She looked at Swan in the mirror, and Swan shook her head a fraction to communicate the message that it was no use pursuing that tactic. Sister's attention fell on the glass bottles of perfume atop the dresser. Now she had very little to lose. "Sheila," she said, "you like pretty things, don't you?"

"Yes."

So far, so good. Here comes the kicker. "Would you like to see something that's *really* pretty?"

Sheila looked up. "What?"

"It's . . . a secret. A buried treasure. Would you like to see it?"

"I know all about buried treasure. Roland buried the stash. He killed the Fat Man, too."

Sister disregarded her raving and stuck doggedly to the point. "Sheila," she said in a confiding tone, "I know where the treasure's buried. And it's something that could help us. If you're a wh—an RL," she quickly amended, "the guards wouldn't stop you from leaving. Like you said, you ought to be on the stroll right now. But you've never seen anything as beautiful as this treasure is, and if you went where I said and brought it back here, you'd be helping Swan. Isn't that right, Swan?"

"Yes, that's right."

"It would have to be our secret, though," Sister continued, carefully watching Sheila's slack, emotionless face. "You couldn't let anybody know where you were going—and you couldn't let anybody see you digging it up or bringing it back here. You'd have to hide it under your coat. Could you do that?"

"I . . . don't know. I just did my nails."

"The buried treasure can stop them from making her ugly," Sister said, and she saw the thought register with slow power on the woman's face. "But it'll be our secret. Just between us roommates. Okay?" Still Sheila didn't answer, and Sister said, "Please help us."

Sheila stared at her reflection in the mirror. She hardly recognized the monster who peered back. The colonel didn't need her, she realized. Had never needed her, except to use and abuse. Men are beasts, she thought, and she remembered the colonel's map of a new America, with its sprawling gray Prison Area.

That was not a country she wanted to live in.

She put the brush down. She felt Swan watching her in the mirror, and Sheila knew she could not—*must* not—let them make such a beautiful thing as ugly as herself.

"Yes," she answered finally. "I'll help you."

Eighty-seven

"*Stop!*" he roared, and as the Jeep skidded in the plowed-up, icy mud of the ruined cornfield the man with the scarlet eye leapt over the vehicle's side and ran through the stubble.

I've got it now! he thought. It's mine! And whatever it is—ring of light, mystic gift or crown—I'm going to break it into bits right in front of her eyes!

The mud clung at his boots as he ran, and he tripped over the corn stubble and almost fell in his fury to get there.

Gray, murky light painted the clouds. In the wind he could smell fire and blood, and he stepped on the naked corpses in his way.

Oh, she thought she was so clever! he raged. So clever! Well, now she would understand that he was not to be denied, not to be fucked with; she would understand that it was still his party, after all the smoke had cleared and the bodies were counted.

At the first tinge of light, the guards had brought Sister to the colonel's trailer, and she'd been placed in a chair at the center of the room. He'd sat down in a chair before her, while Roland and Macklin had watched. And then he'd leaned his

Oriental face close to hers, and he'd said in a Southern drawl, "Where'd ya'll bury it?"

She'd gathered up her saliva and spat in his face—but that was all right! Oh, yes! That was just fine! He'd *wanted* her to fight him, to block her memory with that damned blue light spinning around, so he could press both hands against her cheeks until blood spurted from her nostrils. And then, through the haze of her pain, he'd seen the pickaxe in her mind again, had seen it uplifted and slammed down into the dirt. She'd tried to barricade herself behind the blue light again and blind him with it. But he was too fast for her, and he'd slipped into her mind with ease, since the little bitch wasn't there to distract him.

And there it was. There it was. The plank of wood that had RUSTY WEATHERS carved into it.

She'd buried the glass ring in the cowboy's grave.

He'd almost killed her when he saw it, but he wanted her alive to watch him break the glass to pieces. The grave was just ahead, in the clearing between the stubble and the rows of apple tree seedlings that had been scooped from the earth and loaded on another truck. He ran toward the area where he knew the cowboy had been buried. The ground under his boots had been chewed up by truck tires and the feet of soldiers, and the mud tried to grip and hold him.

He was in the clearing, and he looked around for the makeshift grave marker.

But it was not there.

Tire tracks interwove across the clearing like the plaid on the coat of the man he'd ripped apart. He looked in all directions and decided he was not yet in the correct place. He ran on about thirty more yards to the west, stopped and hunted again.

Nude corpses littered the clearing. He picked them up and flung them aside like broken dolls as he searched for any sign of the grave.

After about ten minutes of frenzied search, he found the grave marker—but it was lying flat and covered with mud. He got down on his knees and started clawing at the ground around the marker, digging the dirt up and throwing it behind him like a dog after a mislaid bone. His hands only found more dirt.

He heard voices and looked up. Four soldiers were prowling the field for anything the scavenger brigades might have missed. "You! Start digging!" he shouted at them—and they stared stupidly at him until he realized he'd spoken in Russian. "Dig!" he commanded, finding his English again. "Get down on your hands and knees and dig this whole fucking field up!"

One of the men ran. The other three hesitated, and a soldier called, "What are we digging for?"

"A bag! A leather bag! It's here somewhere! It's—" And then he abruptly stopped and gazed around at the muddy, ravaged clearing. Armored cars and trucks had been moving across it all night. Hundreds of soldiers had marched through the clearing and the cornfield. The marker might have been knocked down an hour, three hours or six hours earlier. It might have been dragged under the wheels of a truck, or kicked aside by the boots of fifty men. There was no way to tell where the grave had actually been, and frantic rage sizzled through him. He lifted his head and screamed with anger.

The three soldiers fled, tumbling over one another in their panic to get away.

The man with the scarlet eye picked up the nude corpse of a man by the neck and one stiff, outstretched arm. He swung it away, and then he kicked the head of another body like a football. He fell upon a third corpse and twisted its head until the spine snapped with a noise like off-key guitar strings. Then, still seething with rage, he got on all fours like an animal and searched for someone living to kill.

But he was alone with the dead.

Wait! he thought. *Wait!*

He sat up again, his clothes filthy and his shifting face splattered with black mud, and he grinned. He began to giggle, then to chuckle, and finally he laughed so loud that the few remaining dogs that slinked through the alleys heard and howled in response.

If it's lost, he realized, no one else can have it either! The earth's swallowed it up! It's gone, and *nobody* will ever find it again!

He kept laughing, thinking about how stupid he'd been. The glass ring was gone forever! And Sister herself was the one who'd thrown it away in the mud!

He felt a lot better now, a lot stronger and more clear-headed. Things had worked out just as they should. It was still his party, because the little bitch belonged to Macklin, the human hand had destroyed Mary's Rest and Sister had consigned her treasure to the black, unforgiving dirt—where it would lie forever next to a cowboy's charred bones.

He stood up, satisfied that the grave was lost, and began striding across the field to where his driver waited with the Jeep. He turned back for one last look, and his teeth glinted white against his mud-smeared face. It would take a feat of magic, he mused, to make that damned glass ring reappear—and *he* was the only magician he knew.

Now we march, he thought. We take the little bitch with us, and we take Sister, that big nigger and the boy, too, to keep her in line. The rest of the dogs can live in these miserable shacks until they rot—which won't be very long.

Now we go to West Virginia and Warwick Mountain. To find *God*. He smiled, and the driver who was waiting just ahead saw that awful, inhuman grimace and shuddered. The man with the scarlet eye was very eager to meet "God," very eager indeed. After that, the little bitch would go to her prison farm, and then . . . who knows?

He liked being a five-star general. It was a task he seemed particularly well suited for, and as he swept his gaze across the plain of heaped-up corpses he felt like the king of all he surveyed, and very much at home.

Eighty-eight

At the crash of the dinner gong, Josh started salivating like an animal.

The guard was beating on the truck's rear door with his rifle butt, signaling the three prisoners to move to the far end of their cell-on-wheels. Josh, Robin and Brother Timothy knew that noise very well. Robin had held out the longest, refusing to eat any of the watery gruel for four days—until Josh had held him down and force-fed him, and afterward, when Robin wanted to fight, Josh had knocked him flat and told him he was going to live whether he liked it or not.

"What for?" Robin had asked, aching to fight but too smart to charge the black giant again. "They're just going to kill us anyway!"

"I don't really give a crap whether you live or not, you pissant punk!" Josh had told him, trying to make the boy mad enough to stay alive. "If you'd been a man, you would've protected Swan! But they're not going to kill us today. Otherwise they wouldn't have wasted the food. And what about Swan? You're just going to give up and leave her to the wolves?"

"Man, you're a jive fool! She's probably already dead, and Sister, too!"

"No way. They're keeping Swan and Sister alive—and us, too. So from now on you'll eat, or by God, I'll shove your face in that bowl and make you suck it up your nostrils! Understand?"

"Big man," Robin had sneered, crawling away into his customary corner and wrapping his dirty, threadbare brown blanket around himself. But from that day on he'd eaten his food without hesitation.

The truck's metal rear door was perforated with thirty-seven small round holes—both Josh and Robin had counted them many times, and they had devised a mental connect-the-dots-type game with them—which let in dim gray light and air. They were useful peepholes, too, through which to see what was going on in the camp and the landscape they were passing over. But now the door was unbolted, and it slid upward on its rollers. The guard with the rifle—who Robin less-than-affectionately called Sergeant Shitpants—barked, "Buckets out!"

Two more guards stood by with guns aimed and ready as first Josh, then Robin and Brother Timothy brought their waste buckets out.

"Step down!" Sergeant Shitpants ordered. "Single file! Move it!"

Josh squinted in the hazy light of morning. The camp was gearing up to move again; tents were being packed up, vehicles being checked over and gassed up from drums on the back of supply trucks. Josh had noted that the number of gas drums was dwindling fast, and the Army of Excellence had left many broken-down vehicles behind. He looked around at the land as he walked about ten yards away from the truck and dumped his bucket into a ravine. Dense thicket and leafless woods lay on the far side of the ravine, and in the misty distance were snow-covered, hard-edged mountains. The highway they'd been traveling on led up into those mountains, but Josh didn't know exactly where they were. Time was jumbled and confused; he thought it had been two weeks since they'd left Mary's Rest, but he wasn't even sure of that. Maybe it was more like three weeks. Anyway, by this time they'd left Missouri far behind, he figured.

And Glory and Aaron as well. When the soldiers had come to take him and Robin out of the chicken coop, Josh had had time only to pull Glory against him and say, "I'll be back." Her eyes had looked right through him. "Listen to me!" he'd said, shaking her—and finally she'd let her mind return and had focused on the handsome black man who stood before her. "I'll be back. You just be strong, you hear? And take care of the boy as best you can."

"You won't be back. No. You won't."

"I *will!* I haven't seen you in that spangled dress yet. That's worth coming back for, isn't it?"

Glory had gently touched his face, and Josh had seen that she wanted desperately to believe. And then one of the soldiers had thrust a rifle barrel at his injured ribs, and Josh had almost doubled up with agony—but he'd forced himself to remain standing and to walk out of the chicken coop with dignity.

When the trucks, armored cars and trailers of the Army of Excellence had finally rolled out of Mary's Rest, about forty people followed on foot for a while, calling Swan's name, sobbing and wailing. The soldiers had used them for target practice until the last fifteen or so turned back.

"Returrrrn buckets!" Sergeant Shitpants thundered after Robin and Brother Timothy had emptied theirs. The three prisoners took their buckets back into the truck, and the sarge commanded, "Bowls ready!"

They brought out the small wooden bowls they'd all been given, and about that time a cast-iron pot arrived from the field kitchen. A bland soup made of canned tomato paste and fortified with crumbled saltines was ladled into the bowls; the menu was usually the same, delivered twice a day, except sometimes the soup had slivers of salt pork or Spam floating in it.

"Cups out!"

The prisoners offered their tin cups as another soldier poured water from a canteen. The liquid was brackish and oily—certainly not water from the spring. This was water from melted snow, because it left a film in the mouth, made the back of the throat sore and caused ulcers on Josh's gums. He knew there were big wooden kegs of springwater on the supply trucks, and he knew also that none of them would get a drop of it.

"Back up!" Sergeant Shitpants ordered, and as the prisoners obeyed the metal door was pulled down and bolted shut, and feeding time was over.

Inside the truck, each found his own space to eat in—Robin in his corner, Brother Timothy in another, and Josh toward the center. When he was finished, Josh pulled his tattered blanket around his shoulders, because the unlined metal interior of the truck's storage space always stayed frigid; then he stretched out to sleep again. Robin got up, pacing back and forth to burn off nervous energy.

"Better save it," Josh said, hoarse from the contaminated water.

"For what? Oh, yeah, I guess we're going to make our break today, huh? Sure! I'd really better save it!" He felt sluggish and weak, and his head ached so much he could hardly think. He knew it was a reaction to the water after his system had been cleaned out by the spring in Mary's Rest. But all he could do to keep from going crazy was move around.

"Forget trying to escape," Josh told him, for about the fiftieth time. "We've got to stay near Swan."

"We haven't seen her since they threw us in here! Man, there's no telling *what* the bastards have done to her! I say we've got to get out—and then we can help Swan get away!"

"It's a big camp. Even if we could get out—which we couldn't—how would we find her? No, it's best to stay right here, lay low and see what they've got planned for us."

"Lay *low?*" Robin laughed incredulously. "If we lay any lower we'll have dirt on our eyelids! I *know* what they've got planned! They're going to keep us in here till we rot, or shoot us on the side of the road somewhere!" His head pounded fiercely, and he had to kneel down and press his palms against his temples until the pain had passed. "We're dead," he rasped finally. "We just don't know it yet."

Brother Timothy slurped at his bowl. He licked the last of it from the sides; he had a patchy dark beard now, and his skin was as white as the lightning streak that marked his oily black hair. "I've seen her," he said matter-of-factly—the first utterance he'd made in three days. Both Josh and Robin were shocked silent. Brother Timothy lifted his head; one lens of his spectacles was cracked, and electrical tape held the glasses together on the bridge of his nose. "Swan," he said. "I've seen her."

Josh sat up. "Where? Where'd you see her?"

"Out there. Walking around one of the trailers. That other woman—Sister—was there, too. The guards were right behind them. I guess that was their exercise break." He picked up the tin cup and sipped the water as if it were liquid gold. "I saw them . . . day before yesterday, I think. Yes. Day before yesterday. When I went out to read the maps."

Josh and Robin moved around him, watching him with new interest. Lately the soldiers had been coming for Brother Timothy and taking him to Colonel Macklin's Command Center, where old maps of Kentucky and West Virginia were tacked to the wall. Brother Timothy answered questions from Captain Croninger, Macklin and the man who called himself Friend; he'd shown them the Warwick Mountain Ski Resort on the map, over in Pocahontas County, just west of the Virginia line and the dark crags of the Alleghenies. But that wasn't the place he'd found God, he'd told them; the ski resort lay in the foothills on the eastern side of Warwick Mountain, and God lived in the heights on the opposite side, way up where the coal mines were.

The best that Josh could determine from Brother Timothy's rambling, often incoherent tale was that he'd been in a van with either his family or another group of survivors, heading west from somewhere in Virginia. Someone was after them; Brother Timothy said their pursuers rode motorcycles and had chased them for fifty miles. The van either ran off the road or had a blowout, but they'd made it on foot to the shuttered Warwick Mountain Hotel—and there the motorcycle riders had trapped them, attacking with machetes, butcher knives and meat cleavers.

Brother Timothy thought he recalled lying in a snowdrift on his belly. Blood was all over his face, and he could hear thin, agonized screaming. Soon the screaming stopped, and smoke began to curl from the hotel's stone chimney. He ran and kept going cross-country through the woods; then he had found a cave large enough to squeeze his body into during the long, freezing night. And the next day he'd come upon God, who had sheltered him until the motorcycle riders stopped searching for him and went away.

"Well, what about her?" Robin prompted irritably. "Was she all right?"

"Who?"

"Swan! Was she okay?"

"Oh, yes. She seemed to be fine. A little thin, maybe. Otherwise A-OK." He sipped water and ran it over his tongue. "That's a word God taught me."

"Look, you crazy fool!" Robin grasped the collar of his grimy coat. "What part of the camp did you see her in?"

"I know where they're keeping her. In Sheila Fontana's trailer, over in the RL district."

"RL? What's that?" Josh asked.

"Red Light, I think. Where the whores are."

Josh pushed aside the first thought that came at him: that they were using Swan as a prostitute. But no, no; they wouldn't do that. Macklin wanted to use Swan's power to grow crops for his army, and he wasn't going to risk her getting hurt or infected with disease. And Josh pitied the fool who tried to force himself on Sister.

"You don't . . . think . . ." Robin's voice trailed off. He felt breathless and sick, as if he'd been kicked in the stomach, and if he saw any indication that Josh thought it might be true, he knew he was going to lose his mind in that instant.

"No," Josh told him. "That's not why she's here."

Robin believed it. Or wanted to, very badly. He let go of Brother Timothy's coat and crawled away, sitting with his back against the metal wall and his knees drawn up to his chest.

"Who's Sheila Fontana?" Josh asked. "A prostitute?"

Brother Timothy nodded and returned to slowly sipping his water. "She's watching them for Colonel Macklin."

Josh looked around their makeshift prison and felt the walls pressing in on him. He was sick of the cold metal, sick of the smell, sick of those thirty-seven holes in the door. "Damn! Isn't there *any* way out of here?"

"Yes," Brother Timothy replied.

That got Robin's attention again and brought him back from his memory of awakening Swan with a kiss.

Brother Timothy held up his tin cup. He ran a finger along a small, sharp edge that had broken loose from the handle. "This is the way out," he said softly. "You can use it on your throat, if you like." He drank the rest of the water and offered the cup to Josh.

"No, thanks. But don't let me stop *you.*"

Brother Timothy smiled slightly. He put the cup aside. "I would, if I were without hope. But I'm not."

"How about spreading the cheer around, then?" Robin said.

"I'm leading them to God."

Robin scowled. "Excuse me if I don't jump right up and dance."

"You would, if you knew what I do."

"We're listening," Josh prompted.

Brother Timothy was silent. Josh thought he was going to refuse to answer, and then the man leaned his back against the wall and said quietly, "God told me that the prayer for the final hour will bring down the talons of Heaven upon the heads of the wicked. In the final hour, all evil will be swept away, and the world will be washed clean again. God told me . . . he was going to wait on Warwick Mountain."

"Wait for what?" Robin asked.

"To see who won," Brother Timothy explained. "Good or Evil. And when I lead Colonel Macklin's Army of Excellence up Warwick Mountain, God will see for himself who the victors are. But he won't permit Evil to conquer. Oh, no." He shook his head, his eyes dreamy and blissful. "He'll see that it's the final hour, and he'll pray to the machine that calls down the talons of Heaven." He looked at Josh. "You understand?"

"No. What machine?"

"The one that speaks and thinks for hour after hour, day after day. You've never seen such a machine as that. God's army built it, a long time ago. And God knows how to use it. You wait, and you'll see."

"God doesn't really live on top of a mountain!" Robin said. "If there's anybody up there, it's just a crazy man who thinks he's God!"

Brother Timothy's head slowly swiveled toward Robin. His face was tight, his eyes steady. "You'll see. At the final hour, you'll see. Because the world will be washed clean again, and all that is will be no more. The last of the Good must die with the Evil. Must die, so the world can be reborn. You must die. And *you.*" He looked at Josh. "And me. And even Swan."

"Sure!" Robin scoffed, but the man's sincerity gave him the creeps. "I'd hate to be in your skin when old Colonel Mack finds out you've been jiving him along."

"Soon, young man," Brother Timothy told him. "Very soon. We're on Highway 60 right now, and yesterday we passed through Charleston." There hadn't been much left, only burned-out and empty buildings, a brackish contaminated river, and maybe two hundred people living in wood-and-clay hovels. The Army of Excellence had promptly taken all their guns, ammunition and clothing and their meager supply of food. The AOE had raided and destroyed five settlements since leaving Mary's Rest; none of them had given even the slightest resistance. "We'll keep following this highway to the junction of 219," Brother Timothy continued, "and then we'll turn north. There'll be a ghost town called Slatyfork within forty or fifty miles. I hid there for a while after I left God. I hoped he'd call me back, but he didn't. A road goes east from that town, up the side of Warwick Mountain. And that's where we'll find God waiting." His eyes shone. "Oh, yes! I know the way very well, because I always hoped to come back to him. My advice to both of you is to prepare yourselves for the final hour—and to pray for your souls."

He crawled away into his corner, and for a long time afterward Josh and Robin could hear him muttering and praying in a high, singsong voice.

Robin shook his head and lay down on his side to think.

Brother Timothy had left his tin cup behind. Josh picked it up and sat thoughtfully for a moment. Then he ran his finger along the handle's sharp edge.

It drew a fine line of blood.

Eighty-nine

"Please," Sheila Fontana said, touching Sister's shoulder. "Can I . . . hold it again?"

Sister was sitting on a mattress on the floor, drinking the vile soup that the guards had brought in a few minutes before. She looked over at Swan, who sat nearby with her own bowl of watery breakfast, and then she lifted the thin blanket that was draped across the lower end of the mattress; underneath, the mattress had been slashed open and some of the stuffing pulled out. Sister reached up into the hole, her fingers searching.

She withdrew the battered leather satchel and offered it to Sheila.

The other woman's eyes lit up, and she sat down on the floor the way children had once done on Christmas morning.

Sister watched as Sheila hurriedly unzipped the satchel.

Sheila reached into it, and her hand came out gripping the circle of glass.

Dark blue fire rippled through it, brightened for a few seconds and then faded away. The somber blue picked up Sheila's rapid heartbeat. "It's brighter today!" Sheila said, her fingers gently caressing the glass. Only one of the glass spikes remained. "Don't you think it's brighter today?"

"Yes," Swan agreed. "I think it is."

"Oh . . . it's pretty. So pretty." She held it out to Sister. "Make it be bright!"

Sister took it, and as her hand closed on its cool surface the jewels flared and fire burned along the embedded filaments.

Sheila stared at it, transfixed, and in its wonderful glow her face lost its hardness, the lines and cracks softening, the toil of the years falling away. She'd done just as Sister had said that first night. She'd gone out into the field and searched for the grave marker that said RUSTY WEATHERS. Trucks and armored cars were rolling over the field, and soldiers called mockingly to her, but none of them bothered her. At first she couldn't find the marker, and she'd wandered back and forth across the field in search of it. But she'd kept looking until she'd found it, still planted in the earth but leaning crazily to one side and all but ripped loose. Tire tracks had zigzagged all around it, and there was a dead man lying near it with most of his face shot away. She'd gotten down on her knees and begun to dig through the churned-up dirt. And then, finally, she'd seen the edge of the leather satchel sticking up, and she'd worked it loose. She had not opened the satchel but had hidden it up under her coat so no one would take it from her. Then she'd done the last thing that Sister had said: She'd pulled the marker out of the ground and had taken it far away from where it originally was, and there she'd left it lying in the mud.

And keeping the satchel in the folds of her heavy coat and hiding her muddy hands, she'd returned to her trailer. One of the guards had called out, "Hey, Sheila! Didja get paid, or was it another freebie?" The other one had tried to grab at her breasts, but Sheila had gotten inside and shut the door in his leering face.

"So pretty," Sheila whispered as she watched the jewels shine. "So pretty."

Sister knew that Sheila was entranced by the circle of glass, and she'd kept their secret very well. During the time they'd been together, Sheila had told Sister and Swan about her life before the seventeenth of July, and how she and Rudy had been attacked by Colonel Macklin and Roland Croninger in the dirtwart land, on the edge of the Great Salt Lake. She didn't hear the infant crying much anymore, and Rudy no longer crawled after her in her nightmares; whenever the baby did start to cry, Swan was always there, and she made the baby stop.

"So pretty," she whispered.

Sister stared at her for a moment—and then she snapped off the last glass spike. "Here," she said, and it rippled with bright emerald green and sapphire blue as she held it toward Sheila. The other woman just looked at it. "Take it," Sister offered. "It's yours."

"Mine?"

"That's right. I don't know what's ahead for us. I don't know where we'll be tomorrow—or a week from tomorrow. But I want you to have this. Take it."

Slowly, Sheila lifted her hand. She hesitated, and Sister said, "Go ahead." Then Sheila took it, and at once the colors darkened again to the somber blue. But down deep inside the glass there was a small ruby-red glint, like the flame of a candle. "Thank you . . . thank you," Sheila said, almost overcome. It didn't occur to her that it would have been worth many hundreds of thousands of dollars in the world that had used to be. She lovingly moved her fingers over the tiny red glint. "It'll get brighter, won't it?" she asked hopefully.

"Yes," Sister replied. "I think it will."

And then Sister turned her attention to Swan, and she knew it was time.

She remembered something the Junkman had told her, when he'd wanted to see what was inside the satchel: "Can't hold onto things forever. Got to pass them along."

She knew what the circle of glass was. Had known it for a long time. Now, with the last spire broken off, it was even more clear. Beth Phelps had known, long ago in the ruined church, when it had reminded her of the Statue of Liberty: "It could be a crown, couldn't it?" Beth had asked.

The man with the scarlet eye had realized, as well, when he'd asked her where it was: "The ring. The crown," he'd said.

The crown.

And Sister knew to whom that crown belonged. She'd known it ever since she'd found Swan in Mary's Rest and seen the new corn growing.

Can't hold onto things forever, she thought. But oh, she wanted to so very, very badly. The glass crown had become her life; it had lifted her off her feet and made her go on, one step at a time, through the nightmare land. She'd clung to the crown with the jealous fervor of a New York City bag lady, and she'd both shed and taken blood to protect it.

And now it was time. Yes. Now it was time.

Because for her the dreamwalk path had ended. When she looked into the glass, she saw beautiful jewels and threads of gold and silver, but nothing more. Her dreamwalking was done.

It was for Swan to take the next step.

Sister got up off the mattress and approached Swan, holding the shining circle of glass before her. Swan realized it was the image she'd seen in Rusty's magic mirror. "Stand up," Sister said, and her voice quavered.

Swan did.

"This belongs to you," Sister said. "It always belonged to you. I've just been its keeper." Her fingers traced a filament of platinum, and it sizzled within the glass. "But I want you to remember one thing, and hold it fast: If a miracle can make sand into something like this . . . then just think—just *dream* —of what people can be." And she placed the crown on Swan's head.

It was a perfect fit.

Golden light suddenly flared around the crown, receded and flared again. The brilliant glow made both Sister and Sheila squint, and down deep within the gold more colors bloomed like a garden in sunlight.

Sheila put a hand to her mouth; her eyes overflowed, and she began laughing and crying at the same time as the colors washed over her face.

Sister felt heat radiating from the glass, as startling and strong as if she'd caught a faceful of sun. It was getting so bright that she had to retreat a step, her hand rising to shield her eyes.

"What's happening?" Swan asked, aware of the brightness and a tingling sensation of warmth in her scalp. She was getting scared, and she started to take the crown off, but Sister said, "No! Don't touch it!"

The golden, fiery light had begun to ripple through Swan's hair. Swan stood as rigidly as if balancing a book on her head, scared to death but excited, too.

The golden light flared again, and in the next instant Swan's hair seemed to be on fire. The light was spreading over her forehead and cheeks in tendrils, and then Swan's face became a mask of light—a wonderful and terrifying sight that almost knocked Sister to her knees. The fierce glow spread over Swan's throat and neck and began to wind like golden smoke around her shoulders and arms, rippling down over her hands and around each finger.

Sister reached toward Swan; her hand entered the radiance and touched Swan's cheek—but it felt like armor plate, though she could still see the faint impression of Swan's features and the girl's eyes. Sister's fingers could not reach Swan's skin—not her cheeks, her chin, her forehead—not anywhere.

Oh, God, Sister thought—because she'd realized the crown was weaving an armor of light around Swan's body.

It had covered her almost to the waist. Swan felt as if she were standing at the center of a torch, but the warmth was not unpleasant, and she saw the fiery reflection on the walls and the faces of Sister and Sheila with vision only slightly tinged golden. She looked down at her arms, saw them ablaze; she curled her fingers, and they felt fine—no pain, no stiffness, no sense of anything around them at all. The light moved with her, cleaving to her flesh like a second skin. The fire had begun to crawl down her legs.

She moved, cocooned by light, to the mirror. The sight of what she was becoming was too much for her. She reached up, grasped the crown and lifted it off her head.

The golden glow faded almost at once. It pulsed . . . pulsed . . . and the armor of light evaporated like drifting mist.

Then Swan was as she'd been before, just a girl holding a ring of sparkling glass.

She couldn't find her voice for a minute. Then she held the crown to Sister, and said, "I . . . I think . . . you'd better keep it for me."

Slowly, Sister lifted her hand and accepted it. She returned the crown to the satchel and zipped it up. Then, moving like a sleepwalker, she pulled up the blanket and put the satchel back in the mattress. But her eyes still buzzed with golden fire, and as long as she lived she'd never forget what she'd just witnessed.

She wondered what might have happened if, as an experiment, she'd balled up her fist and tried to strike Swan in the face. She didn't want to suffer broken knuckles to find out. Would the armor have turned away the blade of a knife? A bullet? A bomb's shrapnel?

Of all the powers the circle of glass held, she knew that this was one of the greatest—and it had been saved for Swan alone.

Sheila held her own piece of the crown up before her face. The red glint was stronger; she was sure of it. She got up and hid that in the mattress, too.

And perhaps thirty seconds later, there was a loud banging at the door. "Sheila!" a guard called. "We're getting ready to move out!"

"Yeah," she answered. "Yeah. We're ready."

"Everything okay in there?"

"Yeah. Fine."

"I'll be driving the rig today. We'll be hitting the road in about fifteen minutes." A chain rattled as it was being fastened around the doorknob and across the door; then there was the solid click of a padlock. "Now you're nice and tight."

"Thanks, Danny!" Sheila said, and when the guard had gone Sheila knelt on the floor beside Swan and pressed the girl's hand against her cheek.

But Swan was lost in thought. Her mind had turned to the visions of green fields and orchards. Were those images of things that would be, or things that *could* be? Were they visions of the prison farm, the fields tended by slaves and stuttering machines, or were they places free of barbed wire and brutality?

She didn't know, but she understood that each mile they traveled brought her closer to the answer, whatever it was to be.

In Macklin's Command Center, preparations were being made to get underway. The fuel allocation reports from the Mechanical Brigade lay on his desk, and Roland stood next to Friend in front of the West Virginia map tacked to the wall. A red line marked their progress along Highway 60. Roland got as close to Friend as he could; he was tortured with fever, and the cold that came off the other man comforted him. Last night the pain in his face had almost driven him crazy, and he swore he'd felt the bones shift under the bandages.

"We're down to nine drums," Macklin said. "If we don't find any more gasoline, we're going to have to start leaving vehicles behind." He looked up from his reports. "That goddamned mountain road'll make the engines strain. They'll use more gas. I still say we give it up and go find fuel."

They didn't answer.

"Did you hear me? We've got to have more gas before we start up that—"

"What's wrong with 'Nel Macreen today?" Friend turned toward him, and Macklin saw with a start of horror that the man's face had changed again; the eyes were slits, the hair black and plastered down. His flesh was pale yellow—and Macklin was looking at a mask that took him back to Vietnam and the pit where the Cong guards had dropped their refuse on him. 'Nel Macreen gots a plobrem?"

Macklin's tongue had turned to lead.

Friend came toward him, his Vietnamese face grinning. "Onry plobrem 'Nel Macreen gots is gettin' us where we wants go." His accent changed from pidgin English back to a husky American voice. "So you get rid of the trucks and shit. So what?"

"So . . . we can't carry as many soldiers or supplies if we leave trucks behind. I mean . . . we're losing strength every day."

"Well, what do you say we do, then?" Friend pulled another chair toward him, turned it around and sat down with his arms crossed on the chair's back. "Where do we go to find gasoline?"

"I . . . don't know. We'll have to search for—"

"You don't know. And so far the towns you've raided were zero for gas, right? So you want to backtrack and fuck around until every truck and car is running on empty?" He cocked his head to one side. "What do *you* say, Roland?"

Roland's heart jumped every time Friend addressed him. The fever had slowed his mind, and his body felt sluggish and heavy. He was still the King's Knight, but he'd been wrong about something: Colonel Macklin was not the King, and neither was he his own King. Oh, no—the man who sat in the chair before Macklin's desk was the King. The undisputed, the one and only King, who did not eat or drink and whom he'd never seen either crap or piss either, as if he didn't have time for such mundane things.

"I say we keep going on." Roland knew many armored cars and trucks had already been left behind; the tank had broken down two days out of Mary's Rest, and several million dollars worth of Uncle Sam's machinery had been abandoned on the Missouri roadside. "We go on. We've got to find out what's on that mountain."

"Why?" Macklin asked. "What's it to us? I say we—"

"Silence," Friend commanded. The slitted Vietnamese eyes bored into him. "Must we go around about this again, Colonel? Roland feels that Brother Timothy saw an underground complex on Warwick Mountain, complete with an operating electrical supply and a mainframe computer. Now, why's the power still on up there, and what purpose does the complex serve? I agree with Roland that we should find out."

"There might be some gasoline up there, too," Roland added.

"Right. So going to Warwick Mountain might solve your problem. Yes?"

Macklin kept his gaze averted. In his mind he saw the girl's face again, achingly beautiful. He saw her face at night, when he closed his eyes, like a vision from another world. He could not stand his own smell when he awakened. "Yes," he answered, in a small, quiet voice.

"I kneeewww you'd see the light, brotha!" Friend said, in the high, careening voice of a Southern revival preacher.

A ripping noise made Friend's head swivel.

Roland was falling; he'd reached out for support and was taking half the map with him. He hit the floor.

Friend giggled. "Fall down go boom."

In that instant Macklin almost lunged forward and slammed the palm of his right hand into the monster's skull, almost drove the nails deep into the head of the beast that had taken his army from him and made him into a snuffling coward—but as the thought thrilled through him and he tensed for action, a small slit opened in the back of Friend's head, about four inches above the nape of the neck.

In the slit was a staring scarlet eye with a silver pupil.

Macklin sat very still, his lips drawn back from his teeth in a grimace.

The scarlet eye suddenly shriveled and disappeared, and Friend's head turned toward him again. He was smiling cordially. "Please don't take me for a fool," he said.

Something hit the roof of the Airstream trailer: *bump!* Then another: *bump bump!* Followed in the next few seconds by a bumping noise that seemed to sweep the length of the trailer and gently rock it from side to side.

Macklin got up on rubbery legs and went around the desk to the door. He opened it and stood looking out at golf ball-sized hail whirling down from the leaden sky, bumping and clattering on the windshields, hoods and roofs of the other vehicles parked around. Thunder echoed in the clouds like a bass drum in a barrel, and an electric-blue spear of lightning struck somewhere in the distant mountains. In the next minute the hail stopped, and sheets of black, cold rain began falling over the encampment.

A boot thrust out and hit him in the small of the back. He

lost his balance and tumbled down to the bottom of the steps, where the armed guards stared at him in stunned surprise.

Macklin sat up on his knees as the rain struck him in the face and crawled through his hair.

Friend stood in the doorway. "You're riding in the truck with the driver," he announced. "This is *my* trailer now."

"Shoot him!" Macklin bawled. "Shoot the bastard!"

The guards hesitated; one of them lifted his M-16 and took aim.

"You'll die in three seconds," the monster promised.

The guard wavered, looked down at Macklin and then looked at Friend again. He abruptly lowered the rifle and stepped back, rubbing rain from his eyes.

"Help the colonel out of the rain," Friend commanded. "Then spread the word: We're moving out in ten minutes. Anyone who's not ready will be left behind." He closed the door.

Macklin shrugged off help as he got to his feet. "It's mine!" he shouted. "You won't take it from me!"

The door remained shut.

"You won't . . . take it . . . from me," Macklin said, but no one was listening anymore.

Engines began to mutter and growl like awakening beasts. The smell of gasoline and exhaust was in the air, and the rain reeked of brimstone.

"You won't," Macklin whispered, and then he started walking toward the truck that hauled the Command Center as the rain beat down like hammer blows on his shoulders.

Ninety

The Army of Excellence left a trail of broken-down armored cars, trucks and trailers in its wake as it turned north onto Highway 219 and began to climb along the steep western ridge of the Allegheny Mountains.

The land was covered with dead forests, and an occasional ghost town crumbled alongside the ribbon of road. There were no people, but a scouting party in a Jeep pursued and shot two deer near the ruins of Friars Hill—and they came across something else that was worth reporting: an ebony, frozen lake. At its center was the tail section of a large aircraft jutting up from the depths. Two of the scouts started across the lake to investigate it, but the ice cracked under them, and they drowned crying for help.

Rain alternated with snow flurries as the Army of Excellence climbed past dead Hillsboro, Mill Point, Seebert, Buckeye and Marlington. A supply truck ran out of gas twelve feet from a rusted green sign that said Entering Pocahontas County, and the vehicle was pushed into a ravine to let the others pass.

The column was stopped three miles over the county line by a storm of black rain and hail that made driving impossible. Another truck went into the ravine, and a tractor-trailer rig choked on its last swallow of gasoline.

As the rain and hail battered down on the Airstream trailer's roof Roland Croninger awakened. He'd been flung into a corner of the room like a sack of laundry, and his first realization was that he'd messed his britches.

The second was that what looked like lumps of clay and torn, grimy bandages lay on the floor around his head.

He was still wearing the goggles. They felt very tight. His face and head throbbed, gorged with blood, and his mouth felt funny—kind of twisted.

My . . . face, he thought. My face . . . has changed.

He sat up. A lantern glowed on the desk nearby. The trailer shuddered under the storm.

And suddenly Friend knelt down in front of him, and a pale, handsome mask with close-cropped blond hair and ebony eyes peered curiously at him.

"Hi there," Friend said, with a gentle smile. "Have a nice sleep?"

"I . . . hurt," Roland answered. The sound of his voice made his skin creep; it had been a diseased rattle.

"Oh, I'm sorry. You've been sleeping for quite some time. We're just a few miles away from that town Brother Timothy told us about. Yes, you really got your beauty sleep, didn't you?"

Roland started to lift his hands to touch his new face, and his heartbeat deafened him.

"Let me," Friend said—and he held up one hand. In it was a broken piece of mirror.

Roland saw and his head jerked away. Friend's other hand shot out, cupping the back of Roland's neck. "Oh, don't be bashful," the monster whispered. "Take a good, long look."

Roland screamed.

Internal pressure had buckled the bones into hideous, protruding ridges and collapsed gullies. The flesh was sickly yellow, cracked and pitted like an atomic battleground. Red-edged craters had opened in his forehead and his right cheek, exposing the chalky bone. His hair had receded far back on his head and was coarse and white, and his lower jaw jutted forward as if it had been brutally yanked from its sockets. But the most terrible thing, the thing that made Roland begin to wail and gibber, was that his face had been twisted so that it was almost on the side of his head, as if his features had melted and dried hideously askew. In his mouth, the teeth had been ground down to stubs.

He flailed at Friend's hand, knocked the glass aside and scurried into the corner. Friend sat back on his haunches and laughed, while Roland gripped the goggles with both hands and tried to pull them off. The flesh tore around them, and blood ran down to his chin. The pain was too much; the goggles had grown into his skin.

Roland shrieked, and Friend shrieked with him in unholy harmony.

Finally, Friend snorted and stood up—but Roland grasped his legs and clung to him, sobbing.

"I'm a King's Knight," he gibbered. "King's Knight. Sir Roland. King's Knight . . . King's Knight . . ."

Friend bent down again. The young man was wasted, but he still had talent. He was actually a wonderful organizer of the last gasoline supplies and the food, and he'd made Brother Timothy sing like a castrato. Friend ran a hand through Roland's old-man hair.

"King's Knight," Roland whispered, burrowing his head into Friend's shoulder. Tumbling through his mind were scenes of Earth House, the amputation of Macklin's hand, the crawl through the tunnel to freedom, the dirtwart land, the murder of Freddie Kempka and on and on in a vicious panorama. "I'll serve you," he whimpered. "I'll serve the King. Call me Sir Roland. Yes, sir! I showed him, I showed him how a King's Knight gets even, yes, sir, yes, sir!"

"Shhhhh," Friend said, almost crooning. "Hush, now. Hush."

Finally, Roland's sobbing ceased. He spoke drowsily: "Do you . . . do you love me?"

"Like a mirror," Friend answered. And the young man said no more.

The storm slacked off within an hour. The Army of

Excellence struggled onward again, through the deepening twilight.

Soon the scout Jeep came back along the mountain road, and the soldiers reported to General Friend that there were clapboard buildings about a mile ahead. On one of those buildings was a faded sign that read *Slatyfork General Store.*

Ninety-one

They came at first light. Josh was awakened by the banging of a rifle butt on the truck's rear door, and he got up off the metal floor, his bones aching, to move back with Robin and Brother Timothy.

The door was unbolted and rolled up on its casters.

A blond man with ebony eyes stood looking in, flanked by two soldiers with rifles. He wore an Army of Excellence uniform with epaulets and what appeared to be Nazi medals and insignia on his chest. "Good morning, all!" he said cheerfully, and as soon as he spoke both Josh and Robin knew who he was. "How did we sleep last night?"

"Cold," Josh answered tersely.

"We'll have a heater for you on the plantation, Sambo." His gaze shifted. "Brother Timothy? Come out, please." He crooked an inviting finger.

Brother Timothy cringed, and the two soldiers came in to haul him out. Josh started to jump one of them, but a rifle barrel was thrust at him and the moment passed. He saw two Jeeps parked nearby, their engines rumbling. In one of them were three people: a driver, Colonel Macklin and a soldier with a machine gun; in the other was also a driver, another armed soldier, a slumped-over figure wearing a heavy coat and hood—and Swan and Sister, both thin and wan-looking.

"Swan!" Robin shouted, stepping toward the opening.

She saw him, too, and cried out, "Robin!" as she rose from her seat. The soldier grabbed her arm and pulled her down again.

One of the guards shoved Robin back. He rushed at the man, his face contorted with rage, and the soldier lifted his rifle butt to smash Robin's skull. Josh suddenly lunged out and caught the boy, holding him as he thrashed. The soldier spat on the floor, and when he stepped down from the truck the rear door was slid into place and bolted once more.

"Hey, you bastard!" Josh shouted, peering through one of the thirty-seven punctures. "Hey! I'm talking to *you*, creep-show!" He realized he was bellowing in his old wrestler's voice.

Friend shoved Brother Timothy toward the first Jeep and then turned regally.

"What do you need Swan and Sister for? Where are you taking them?"

"We're all going up Warwick Mountain to meet God," he answered. "The road's not good enough for anything heavier than the Jeeps. That satisfy the old negroid curiosity?"

"You don't need them! Why don't you leave them here?"

Friend smiled vacantly and strolled closer. "Oh, they're too valuable for that. Suppose some crafty old fox decided he wanted a little more power and snatched them away while we were gone? That wouldn't do." He started to return to the Jeep.

"Hey! Wait!" Josh called, but the man with the scarlet eye was already getting into the Jeep beside Brother Timothy. The two vehicles moved away and out of sight.

"Now what?" Robin asked him, still seething. "Do we just sit here?"

Josh didn't answer. He was thinking of something Brother Timothy had said: *"The last of the Good must die with the Evil. Must die, so the world can be reborn. You must die. And you. And me. And even Swan."*

"Swan won't come back," Robin said tonelessly. "Neither will Sister. You know that, don't you?"

"No, I don't." *"He'll pray to the machine that calls down the talons of Heaven,"* he remembered Brother Timothy saying. *"Prepare yourselves for the final hour."*

"I love her, Josh," Robin said. He grasped Josh's arm tightly. "We've *got* to get out of here! We've got to stop . . . whatever it is that's going to happen!"

Josh pulled free. He walked to the far corner of the cell and looked down.

On the floor beside Brother Timothy's bucket was the tin cup, with its sharp metal handle.

He picked it up and touched the ragged edge.

It was too small and awkward to use as a weapon, and Josh had already dismissed that possibility. But he was thinking of an old wrestling trick, something that was done with a hidden razor when the promoter wanted more "juice." It was a common practice, and it always made the violence look more real.

Now it might give the illusion of something else, as well.

He started to work.

Robin's eyes widened. "What the *hell* are you doing?"

"Be quiet," Josh cautioned. "Just get ready to start yelling when I say so."

The two Jeeps were about a quarter mile away, slowly climbing a winding, snow- and rain-slick mountain road. At one time the road had been paved, but the concrete had cracked and slid apart, and underneath was a layer of mud. The Jeeps' tires slipped, and the vehicles fishtailed as the engines roared for traction. In the second Jeep, Sister gripped Swan's hand. The hooded figure sitting in the front suddenly turned his head toward them—and they had a heart-stopping glimpse of his deathly yellow, cratered face. The goggled eyes lingered on Swan.

The drivers fought for every foot. To the right stood a low steel guard rail, and just beyond it was a rocky drop-off that fell seventy feet into a wooded ravine. Still the road ascended as the broken plates of concrete shifted beneath the Jeeps' wheels.

The road curved to the left and was blocked by an eight-foot-high chain link fence and gate. On the gate was a metal sign, surprisingly free of corrosion: WARWICK COAL MINING COMPANY. TRESPASSERS WILL BE PROSECUTED. Ten feet beyond the fence was a brick enclosure where a guard might once have stood duty. A sturdy-looking chain and padlock secured the gate, and Friend said, "Get that thing open" to the soldier with the machine gun. The man got out, walked to the gate and reached out to test the padlock before he blasted it off.

There was a sizzling like fat being fried in a pan. The soldier's legs began to boogie, with his hand sealed to the chain and his face bleached and grimacing. The machine gun chattered on its own, spraying bullets into the ground. His clothes and hair smoked, his face taking on a blue cast; then the muscle tension snapped the soldier backward, and he fell, still jerking and writhing, to the ground.

The smell of scorched flesh and electricity wafted through the air. Friend whirled around and clamped his hand to Brother Timothy's throat. "Why didn't you say it was an electric fence?" he bellowed.

"I . . . I didn't know! It was broken open the last time! God must've fixed it!"

Friend almost set him afire, but he could see that Brother Timothy was telling the truth. The electrified fence also told him that the power source, wherever it was, was still active. He released the man, got out of the Jeep and strode to the gate.

He reached through the chain link mesh and grasped the padlock. His fingers worked at it, trying to break it open. Both Swan and Sister saw his sleeve beginning to smoke, the flesh of his hand getting as soft as used chewing gum. The padlock resisted him, and he could feel the little bitch watching and sucking all the strength out of him. In a rage, he gripped the mesh with the fingers of both hands and wrenched at the gate like a child trying to break into a locked playground. Sparks popped and flew. For an instant he was outlined in an electric-blue glow, his Army of Excellence uniform smoking and charring, the shoulder epaulets bursting into flame. Then the gate's hinges gave way, and Friend hurled the gate aside.

"Didn't think I could, did you?" he shouted at Swan. His face had gone waxy, most of his hair and his eyebrows singed away. Her expression remained placid, and he knew it was a good thing she was going to a prison camp, because the bitch would have to be broken under a whip before she learned respect.

He had to concentrate harder than usual to get his oozing hands solid again. His epaulets were still burning, and he tore them away before he retrieved the dead soldier's machine gun and returned to the first Jeep. "Let's go," he ordered. Two fingers on his right hand remained scorched and twisted, and they would not reform.

The two Jeeps moved through the opening and continued up the mountain road, winding between dense stands of lifeless pines and hardwood trees.

They came to a second brick guard's station, where a rusted sign commanded Present Identification. Atop the structure was what appeared to be a small videotape camera.

"They had pretty tight security up here for a coal mine," Sister observed, and Roland Croninger growled, "No talking!"

The road emerged from the forest into a clearing; there was a paved parking lot, empty of cars, and beyond it stood a complex of one-story brick buildings and a larger, aluminum-roofed structure built right into the mountainside. Warwick Mountain continued upward about another two hundred feet, covered with dead trees and boulders, and at its peak Sister saw three rusted towers—antennas, she realized—that disappeared in the swirling gray clouds.

"Stop," Friend said. The driver obeyed, and a second later the other Jeep halted. He sat looking around the complex for a moment, his eyes narrowed and his senses questing. There was no movement, no life as far as he could see. The chilly wind blew across the parking lot, and thunder rumbled in the clouds. A black drizzle began to fall again. Friend said, "Get out" to Brother Timothy.

"What?"

"Get out," Friend repeated. "Walk ahead of us, and start calling him. *Go on!*"

Brother Timothy climbed out of the Jeep and started walking across the parking lot through the black rain. "God!" he shouted, and his voice echoed off the walls of the large metal-roofed building. "It's Timothy! I've come back to you!"

Friend got out and followed behind him a few yards, the machine gun resting on his hip.

"God! Where are you? I've come back!"

"Keep going," Friend told him, and the other man walked forward with the rain beating in his face.

Sister had been waiting for the right moment. Everyone's attention was fixed on the two men. The woods lay about thirty yards away, and if she could keep the rest of them busy, Swan might have a chance to make it; they wouldn't kill her, and if she could reach the woods, Swan might be able to escape. She squeezed Swan's hand, whispered, "Get ready" and tensed to slam her fist into the face of the guard at her side.

Brother Timothy shouted joyously, *"There he is!"*

She looked up. High above, a figure stood on the sloping aluminum roof.

Brother Timothy fell to his knees, his hands upraised and his face torn between terror and rapture. "God!" he called. "It's the final hour! Evil's won! Cleanse the world, God! Call down the talons of Hea—"

Machine gun bullets ripped across his back. He fell forward, his body still kneeling in an attitude of prayer.

Friend swung the smoking barrel up toward the roof. "Come down!" he ordered.

The figure stood motionlessly but for the billowing of a long, ragged coat around his thin body.

"I'll tell you once more," Friend warned, "and then we'll see what color God's blood is."

Still the figure hesitated. Swan thought the man with the

scarlet eye was going to shoot—but then the figure on the roof walked over near the edge, lifted a hatch and began to descend a metal-runged ladder bolted to the building's wall.

He reached the ground and walked to Brother Timothy, where he bent to examine the dead man's features. Friend heard him mutter something, and 'God' shook his gray-maned head in disgust. Then he stood up again, approached Friend and stopped about two feet away. Above the dirty, tangled mat of his gray beard, the man's eyes were sunken deep in purple craters, his flesh ivory and covered with intersecting cracks and wrinkles. A brown-ridged scar sliced across his right cheek, narrowly missing the eye, cutting through the thick eyebrow and up into the hairline, where it divided into a network of scars. His left hand, dangling from the folds of his overcoat, was brown and withered to the size of a child's.

"You bastard," he said, and with his right hand he slapped Friend across the face.

"Help!" Robin Oakes was shouting. "Somebody help! He's killing himself!"

Sergeant Shitpants emerged from a nearby trailer, cocked his .45 automatic and ran through the rain to the truck. Another guard with a rifle came from a different direction, and a third soldier followed.

"Hurry!" Robin yelled frantically, looking through one of the punctures. "Somebody help him!"

Sergeant Shitpants thrust the pistol's barrel up at Robin's face. "What's going on?"

"It's Josh! He's trying to kill himself! Open the door!"

"Right! Fuck that!"

"He's cut his wrists, you dumb-ass!" Robin told him. "He's bleeding all over the floor in here!"

"That trick was old in silent movies, you little prick!"

Robin pushed three fingers through one of the holes, and Sergeant Shitpants saw the crimson smear of blood all over them.

"He's slashed his wrists with a cup's handle!" Robin said. "If you don't help him, he's going to bleed to death!"

"Let the nigger die, then!" the guard with the rifle said.

"Shut up!" Sergeant Shitpants was trying to figure out what he should do. He knew the consequences if anything happened to the prisoners. Colonel Macklin and Captain Croninger were bad enough, but the new commander would cut off his balls and use them as hood ornaments.

"Help him!" Robin shouted. "Don't just stand there!"

"Step back from the door!" the other man ordered. "Go on! Get back, and if you make one move I don't like, I swear to God you're dead meat!"

Robin retreated. The door was unbolted and shoved upward about eight inches.

"Throw it out! The cup! Throw the damned thing out!"

A bloody tin cup was slid through the opening. The sergeant picked it up, felt the ragged metal edge and tasted the blood to make sure it was real. It was. "Damn it!" he raged, and he pushed the door up the rest of the way.

Robin stood at the back of the truck, away from the door. Curled on the floor near him was the body of Josh Hutchins, lying on his right side with his face averted. Sergeant Shitpants climbed into the truck, his gun aimed at Robin's head. The guard with the rifle climbed up as well, and the third man stayed on the ground with his pistol unholstered and ready. "Stay back and keep both hands up!" Sergeant Shitpants warned Robin as he approached the black man's body.

Blood gleamed on the floor. The sergeant saw blood all over the black man's clothes, and he reached down to touch one outthrust wrist; his own fingers came away bloody. "Jesus!" he said, realizing he was tailbone deep in trouble. He holstered his .45 and tried to turn the man over, but Josh was way too heavy for him. "Help me move him!" he told Robin, and the boy bent down to grasp Josh's other arm.

Josh gave a low, guttural groan.

And two things happened at once: Robin picked up the bucket of waste lying beside Josh's arm and hurled its contents into the face of the guard with the rifle, and Josh's body came to life, his right fist smashing into Sergeant Shitpants' jaw and snapping it crooked. The man gave a scream as his teeth tore into his tongue, and then Josh was wrenching the .45 out of its holster.

The blinded guard fired his rifle, and the bullet sang past Robin's head as the boy lunged at him, grabbing the rifle and kicking him in the groin. The third soldier fired at Josh, but the bullet hit Sergeant Shitpants in the back and drove him into Josh like a shield. Josh wiped the blood out of his eyes and shot at the soldier, but the man was already running through the rain shouting for help.

Robin kicked the guard again, tumbling him out of the truck to the ground. Josh knew they would only have a minute or so before the place was swarming with soldiers, and he started digging through Sergeant Shitpants' pockets, looking for the truck's key. Blood was streaming down his face from three slashes across his forehead, inflicted with the ragged edge of metal; he'd smeared his wrists with blood and gotten it all over his clothes to make it appear as if he'd cut his veins. In the wrestling ring, a small sliver of razor blade hidden in a bandage had often been drawn across the forehead to create a superficial but nasty-looking wound, and in this case the gore was needed for a similarly theatrical purpose.

Two soldiers were running toward the truck. Robin took aim and shot one of them down, but the other fell onto his stomach and crawled under a trailer. Josh couldn't find a key. "Look in the ignition!" he shouted, and he fired shots at random as Robin jumped to the ground and ran around to the truck's cab.

He opened the door and reached up to the dashboard, his fingers searching. There was no key in the ignition.

The soldier under the trailer squeezed off two shots that ricocheted dangerously around Josh, who flung himself flat. Another soldier opened up with an automatic rifle, over to the left. The air turned hot above Josh's head, and he heard bullets whack off the inside of the truck like hammers beating garbage can lids.

Robin searched under the seat and found nothing but empty cartridges. He opened the glove compartment. *There!* Inside was a tarnished key and a snub-nose .38. He fit the key into the ignition, turned it and jammed his foot down on the accelerator. The engine coughed and racketed, then roared to life, the entire truck quaking. He gaped at the gearshift. Shit! he thought; one thing he'd forgotten to tell Josh while they were planning their escape was that his experience in driving had been very limited. Still, he knew you had to press the clutch down to engage the gears. He did, and he forced the gearshift into first over the transmission's objections. Then he put his foot to the floor on the accelerator and let up suddenly on the clutch.

The truck shot forward as if it were rocket-powered. Josh was propelled to the edge of the truck's bed, and he kept himself from flying out by grabbing the upraised track of metal on which the door slid up and down.

Robin jammed the gearshift into second. The truck bucked like a wild stallion as it tore through the encampment, grazing a parked car and scattering a half-dozen soldiers who had been alerted by the noise. A bullet shattered the windshield and sent wasps of glass flying around Robin's head and face, but he shielded his eyes and kept going.

Robin shifted upward as the truck gained speed. Glass glittered in his tangled hair like wet diamonds. He reached over for the .38, popped its cylinder open and found it held four bullets. He veered past another parked vehicle, almost crashed into a trailer, and then the truck was out on the open road, speeding away from the camp. Just ahead was the turnoff to the right that Robin knew must lead up the side of Warwick Mountain; he could see the tracks of the Jeeps' tires in the mud as he slowed the truck enough to take the sharp turn. In the rear of the truck, Josh lost his grip and was battered against the opposite wall with bone-jarring force, and it occurred to him that this was surely going to be a day to remember.

But they had to reach Sister and Swan before the final hour—whatever and whenever that was. Robin was driving like hell up the mountain road, the tires skidding back and forth, the truck careening from one side of the road to the other. Josh hung on as best he could, and he saw sparks fly as the truck grazed the right-hand guard rail. A plate of concrete suddenly slipped out from under the rear tires, and the wheel tore itself from Robin's hands. The truck hurtled toward the cliff's edge.

He threw all his weight against the wheel to twist it around, his foot fighting the brake. The tires threw up plumes of mud, and the front fender dented the guard rail about six inches before the truck came to a stop.

Then he felt the tires starting to slide back over the broken concrete, mud and snow. He pulled up the emergency brake, but there was no traction to lock the tires. The truck slid in reverse, quickly gathering speed as Robin tried to jam the gearshift into first again. But he knew it was the end of the line; he opened the door, shouted "Jump!" and did so.

Josh didn't wait to be told twice. He jumped from the rear of the truck, hit the mud and rolled aside as the vehicle fishtailed past him.

It kept going, the front of the truck sliding around as if the vehicle was trying to spin in a circle—and then a Jeep carrying five Army of Excellence soldiers suddenly veered around the curve, heading uphill and going too fast to stop.

Josh saw the expression of stark terror on the driver's face; the soldier instinctively threw up his arms as if to hold back metal with muscle and bone. The runaway truck and the Jeep crashed together, and the truck's weight shoved the smaller vehicle through the guard rail and followed it over the cliff's edge like an anvil. Josh looked over the rail in time to see human bodies tumbling through space; there was a chorus of high screams, and then the bodies disappeared in the ravine, and either the Jeep or truck exploded in a burst of flame and black smoke.

Josh and Robin had no time to ponder how close they'd come to taking a one-way flight. Josh still gripped the automatic in his hand, and Robin had the .38 with four bullets in it. They would have to go the rest of the way on foot, and they had to hurry. Josh took the lead, his boots skidding over the tortured surface, and Robin followed him upward toward the realm of God.

Ninety-two

In the aftermath of the slap, Friend curled his hand into the man's collar, drawing him close. 'God' wore the dirty rags of a blue-checked shirt and khaki trousers under his coat. On his feet were leather moccasins, and he wore emerald-green socks. Sister realized that the unkempt, wild-eyed man would have fit right in among the street people of Manhattan before the seventeenth of July.

"I could hurt you," Friend whispered. "Oh, you don't know how I could hurt—"

The man gathered a mouthful of saliva and spat in Friend's waxy face.

Friend threw him to the ground and kicked him in the ribs. The man curled up, trying to protect himself, but Friend kept kicking him in a frenzy. He grasped 'God' by the hair and slammed his fist into the man's face, breaking his nose and splitting his lower lip open; then he hauled 'God' up again and held him for the others to see.

"Look at him!" Friend crowed. "Here's your God! He's a crazy old man who's got shit for brains! Go on, look at him!" He grasped the man's beard and angled his bloody face toward Swan and Sister. "He's nothing!" And as emphasis,

Friend drove his fist deep into the man's belly but held him upright even as his knees buckled. Friend started to strike him again—and a calm, clear voice said, "Leave him alone."

Friend hesitated. Swan was standing up in the second Jeep, the rain running through her hair and across her face. She couldn't bear to watch the old man being beaten, and she couldn't sit in silence. "Let him go," she said, and the man with the scarlet eye grinned incredulously. "You heard me. Take your hand off him."

"I'll do as I please!" he roared, and he laid his fingers alongside the man's cheek. His nails began to tear through the skin. "I'll kill him if I want!"

"No!" Roland protested. "Don't kill him! I mean . . . we've got to find the black box and the silver key! That's what we came here for! Then you can kill him!"

"You don't tell me what to do!" Friend shouted. "It's my party!" He shot a challenging glare at Colonel Macklin, who did nothing but sit and stare blankly ahead. Then Friend's gaze met Swan's, and their eyes locked.

For a second he thought he could see himself through her unflinching eyes: an ugly, hateful thing, a small face hidden behind an oversized Halloween mask like a cancer under gauze. *She knows me,* he thought; that fact made him afraid, just as he'd feared the glass ring when it went black in his grip.

And something else speared him, too. His memory of the offered apple, and his desire to accept it. Too late! Too late! He saw, just for an instant, who and what he was—and in that brief space of time he knew himself, too, in a way that he'd shoved aside a long, long time before. Self-loathing uncoiled within him, and suddenly he feared that he was going to see too much, and he would start to split at the seams, unravel like an old suit and blow away in the wind.

"Don't look at me!" he screamed, his voice shrill, and he lifted one hand to shield his face from hers. Behind his hand, his features churned like muddy water disturbed by a stone.

He could still feel her there, drawing the strength out of him like the sunlight drawing the wet from rotten timber. He flung 'God' to the ground, backed away and kept his face averted. Now the truth was coming back to him: It was not himself he should loathe, it was *her!* She was the ruin and enemy of all creation, because she—

Too late! Too late! he thought, still backing away.

—because she wanted to prolong the suffering and misery of humankind. She wanted to give them false hope and watch them writhe when it was wrenched away. She was—

Too late! Too late!

—the worst kind of Evil, because she masked cruelty with kindness and love with hate, and too late! too late! too—

"Late," he whispered, and he lowered his hand. He'd stopped retreating, and he realized then that Swan had gotten out of the Jeep and was standing over the gray-bearded old man. He saw the others watching, and he caught a thin, mocking smile on Macklin's skull of a face.

"Stand up," Swan told the old man. Her spine was rigid, her bearing proud, but inside her nerves were knotted with tension.

'God' blinked at her, wiped the blood from his nostrils and looked fearfully at the man who'd struck him.

"It's all right," Swan said, and she offered him her hand.

She's just a *girl!* Friend realized. She's not even worth a rape! And she'd like me to rape her, too, she'd like me to stick it in hard and grind up to my ankles!

'God' hesitated uncertainly—and then he put his hand into Swan's.

I'll rape her, Friend decided. I'll show her it's still my party! I'll show her *right fucking now!*

He advanced on her like a juggernaut, and every step he took made his crotch bulge larger. He was leering, and she saw that leer and knew what was behind it, and she waited for him without moving.

The hollow, booming echo of an explosion drifted from the distance. Friend stopped in his tracks. "What was that?" he shouted, to everyone and no one. "What was that?"

"Came from the road," one of the soldiers said.

"Well, don't sit there! Get off your ass and find out what it was! All of you! *Go!*"

The three soldiers left the Jeeps and ran across the parking lot. They disappeared around the heavily wooded bend, their weapons ready.

But Friend's weapon was shriveling. He could not look at the bitch without thinking of the apple, and he knew she'd planted some kind of evil, soul-destroying seed right in him, too. But it was still his party, and it was too late for turning back, and he would rape her and crush her skull when she was eighty years old and her fingers were worked to the bones.

But not today. Not today.

He aimed his machine gun at Sister. "Get out. You stand over there with the little bitch."

Swan let her breath out. His attention was on other things now, but he was still as dangerous as a mad dog in a butcher's shop. She helped the old man to his feet. He staggered, still hurting from the blow that had shattered his nose, and looked around at the malformed faces of Macklin and Roland. "It *is* the final hour, isn't it?" he asked Swan. "Evil's won. It's time for the final prayer, isn't it?"

She couldn't answer. He touched her cheek with spavined fingers. "Child? What's your name?"

"Swan."

He repeated it. "So young," he said sadly. "So young to have to die."

Roland got out of his Jeep, but Macklin stayed where he was, his shoulders stooped now that Friend was in control again. "Who are you?" Roland asked the old man. "What are you doing up here?"

"I'm God. I fell to earth from Heaven. We landed in water. The other one lived for a while, but I couldn't heal him. Then I found my way here, because I know this place."

"What's your power source?"

'God' extended a finger and pointed to the earth at his feet.

"Underground?" Roland asked. "Where? In the coal mine?"

'God' didn't reply but instead lifted his face toward the sky and let the rain beat down.

Roland drew his pistol from the holster at his waist, cocked it and placed it to the man's head. "You answer when I ask you a question, you old fuck! Where's that power coming from?"

The man's insane eyes met Roland's. "All right," he said, and he nodded. "A-OK. I'll show you, if you want to see."

"We do."

"I'm sorry, child," he told Swan. "Evil's won, and it's time for the final prayer. You *do* understand, don't you?"

"Evil hasn't won! Not everybody is like they are!"

"It's the final hour, child. I fell from Heaven in a whirlwind of fire. I knew what had to be done, but I waited. I couldn't make myself pray the last prayer. But now I can, because I see that the world has to be cleansed." He said to the others, "Follow me," and he started walking toward the large building with the metal roof.

"Colonel?" Friend prompted. "We're waiting for you."

"I'll stay here."

"You'll come with us." Friend swung the machine gun's barrel up at him. "Roland, take the colonel's pistol away from him, please."

"Yes, sir," Roland answered at once, and he approached Macklin. He held out his hand for the other man's weapon.

Colonel Macklin didn't move. The rain was falling harder, hammering on the Jeeps and streaming down Macklin's face.

"Roland," Macklin said in a strengthless voice, "we created the Army of Excellence together. Both of us. We're the ones who made plans for the new America, not . . . not that *thing* over there." He motioned toward Friend with his nail-studded right hand. "He just wants to destroy it all. He doesn't care about the Army of Excellence, or the new America, or feeding the troops. He doesn't care about the girl; all he wants to do is put her on that prison farm, out of his way. And he doesn't care about *you*, either. Roland . . . please . . . don't follow him. Don't do what he says." He reached out to touch Roland, but the young man stepped back. "Roland . . . I'm *afraid,*" Macklin whispered.

"Give me your gun." In that moment Roland despised the cringing dog who sat before him; he'd seen that weakness before, back when Macklin was delirious after his hand had been amputated, but now Roland knew the weakness went soul-deep. Macklin had never been a King, only a coward hiding behind a warrior's mask. Roland pressed the barrel of his own weapon against the colonel's head. "Give me your gun," he repeated.

"Please . . . think about what we've been through . . . you and me, together . . ."

"I have a new King now," Roland said flatly. He looked at Friend. "Should I kill him?"

"If you like."

Roland's finger tightened on the trigger.

Macklin knew death was very near, and its oily perfume energized him to action. His spine stiffened, and he sat up ramrod-straight. "Who do you think you *are?*" he said vehemently. "You're nothing! I was fighting for my life in a Viet Cong POW camp when you were shitting your diapers! I'm Colonel James B. Macklin, United States Air Force! I fought for my life and for my country, boy! Now you get that fucking gun away from my head!"

Roland faltered.

"Did you hear what I said, mister? If you want my weapon, you ask for it with the respect I deserve!" Every muscle in his body tightened as he waited for the gun to go off.

Still Roland didn't move. Friend laughed quietly, and 'God' was waiting for them about ten yards beyond Swan and Sister.

Slowly, Roland took the pistol away from Macklin's head. "Give . . . me your gun . . . *sir,*" he said.

Macklin removed it from his holster and flung it to the ground, and then he stood up and got out of the Jeep—but unhurriedly, at his own pace.

"Let's go, kiddies," Friend said. He motioned toward Swan and Sister with the machine gun, and they followed 'God' to the metal-roofed building.

Inside, it was apparent that the building was nothing more than a huge shed protecting the entrance to the Warwick Mountain coal mine. The floor was of hard-packed dirt, and a few naked light bulbs that hung from the ceiling gave off a dirty yellow illumination. Bundles of cables and wires lay around, as well as old pieces of steel track, piles of rotting timber and other bits of refuse that suggested Warwick Mountain had once boasted a thriving coal business. A steel stairway ascended to a series of catwalks, and at the far end of the building, where the structure abutted Warwick Mountain, was the dark square of the mine's entrance.

'God' led them up the stairway and along one of the catwalks to the mine shaft. A few light bulbs gave off a meager yellow glow within the mine, which slanted downward at a steep angle. Resting on tracks inside the shaft was a large wire mesh cage about six feet high and four feet wide, its wheels like those of a railroad car. Inside it were padded benches and straps to hold the riders in place. 'God' opened the rear of the cage and waited for them to enter it.

"I'm not getting in that damned thing!" Sister balked. "Where are you taking us?"

"Down there." 'God' pointed along the mine shaft, and the yellow light winked off something metallic in the sleeve of his blue-checked shirt. Sister realized the old man was wearing cuff links. He looked at Friend. "Isn't that where you want to go?"

"What's in there?" Roland asked, all his bluff and bluster gone.

"The power source you're looking for. And other things you might be interested in seeing. Do you want to go or not?"

"You get in first," Friend told him.

"A-OK." 'God' turned toward the rock wall, where there was a panel with two buttons on it, one red and the other green. He punched the green button, and the sound of humming machinery echoed up the shaft. Then he climbed into the cage, sat down on one of the benches and buckled himself in. "All aboard!" he said cheerfully. "We'll start moving in ten seconds."

Friend was the last one in. He crouched at the rear of the cage, his face averted from Swan's. The machinery got steadily louder, and then there were four clicks as the brakes on each wheel disengaged. The cage began to descend along the tracks, its speed restrained by a steel cable that had snapped taut and was reeling out behind it.

"We're going down more than three hundred feet," 'God' explained. "This used to be a working mine about thirty years ago. Then the United States government bought it. Of course, all this rock is reinforced with concrete and steel." He waved his arm at the walls and roof, and Sister saw the cuff link glitter again. Only this time she was close enough to see that it looked very familiar, and it had writing on it. "You'd be amazed to know what the engineers can do," he continued. "They put in ventilation ducts and air pumps, and even the light bulbs are supposed to last for seven or eight years. But they're starting to burn out now. Some of the same people who put this place together worked on Disney World."

Sister caught his sleeve and looked closer at the cuff link. On it was a very recognizable blue, white and gold emblem, and the much-polished lettering said: Seal of the President of the United States of America.

Her fingers had gone numb, and she let his arm go. He stared impassively at her. "What's . . . down in here?" she asked him.

"Talons," he said. "The talons of Heaven." They went through a long area where there were burned-out light bulbs, and when they approached the illumination again, the President's eyes burned with inner fever as he stared across the cage at Friend. "You want to see a power source?" he asked, his breath wisping out in the chilly air. "You will. Oh, yes; I promise you will."

In another minute the brakes engaged again and shrieked along the tracks as the conveyance shuddered and slowed. It bumped against a thick foam rubber barrier and stopped.

The President unbuckled his seat belt, opened the front section of the cage and stepped out. "This way," he said, motioning them on like a demented tour guide.

Roland shoved Swan ahead of him, and they entered a passageway that led off to the right of the tracks. Bulbs burned fitfully overhead, and suddenly the passageway ended at a wall of rough-edged rocks.

"It's blocked!" Roland said. "It's a dead end!"

But Friend shook his head; he'd already seen the small

black box embedded in the rock wall at about chest height. The upper half of the black box seemed to be some sort of display screen, while the bottom was a keyboard.

The President reached up to his throat with his good hand and lifted off a braided length of leather that had been hanging around his neck. On it were several keys—and the President chose one that was small and silver. He kissed it, and then he started to insert it into a lock in the black box.

"Hold it!" Friend said. "What does that thing do?"

"It opens the door," the man replied; he fit the key into the lock and twisted it to the left. Instantly, pale green letters appeared on the screen: HELLO! ENTER CODE WITHIN FIVE SECONDS. Swan and Sister watched as the President punched three letters on the keyboard: AOK.

CODE ACCEPTED, the screen replied. HAVE A NICE DAY!

Electric tumblers whirred, and there was the muffled sound of locks opening in rapid-fire succession. The false wall of rock cracked open like the door of a massive vault, hissing on hydraulic hinges. The President pulled it wide enough to admit them, and clean white light glowed from the room beyond. Roland started to reach up for the silver key, but the old man said, "No! Leave that alone! If it's disturbed while the door's open, the floor's electrified."

Roland's fingers stopped an inch away from the key.

"You go first." Friend shoved the man through the opening. Sister and Swan were pushed in. Macklin followed, then Roland and finally the man with the scarlet eye.

They all squinted in the bright light of a white-walled, antiseptic-looking chamber where six mainframe computers quietly conversed, their data tapes slowly turning behind windows of tinted glass. The floor was coated with black rubber, and there was the polite rumble of the air-purifying system drawing cleansed air through small metal grilles in the walls. At the center of the room, sitting atop a rubber-coated table and connected by thick bundles of cables to the mainframe computers, was another small black box with a keyboard, about the size of a telephone.

Roland was delirious at the sight of the machines. It had been so long since he'd seen a computer, he'd forgotten how beautiful they were; to him, the mainframes were the Ferraris of computers, pulsing brain matter squished into sleek plastic and metal skins. He could almost hear them breathing.

"Welcome to my home," the President said—and then he walked to a metal panel on the wall. There was a small lever that you could fit your finger into and pull upward on, and above it a little red plastic DANGER sign. He hooked his finger into the lever's notch and wrenched it up.

The door slammed shut, and instantly the electronic locks bolted themselves. On this side of the false wall was a sheet of stainless steel.

Swan and Sister had turned to face him. Friend had his finger on the machine gun's trigger, and Macklin stood staring numbly at the old man.

"There," the President said. "There." He stepped back from the metal panel, nodding with satisfaction.

"Open that door!" Macklin demanded, his flesh crawling. The walls were closing in on him, and this place was too much like Earth House. "I don't like to be shut up! Get that damned door open!"

"It's locked," the other man replied.

"Open it!" Macklin shouted.

"Please open it," Swan said.

The President shook his gray-maned head. "I'm sorry, child. Once you lock the door from in here, it's locked for good. I lied about the key. I just didn't want him to pull it out. See, you can open it from the inside if you have the silver key. But now the computer's locked it—and there's no way out."

"Why?" Sister asked, her eyes wide. "Why'd you lock us in here?"

"Because we're going to stay here until we die. The talons of Heaven are going to destroy all the evil . . . every bit of it. The world will be cleansed, and the world can begin again—fresh and new. You see?"

Colonel Macklin attacked the stainless steel door, hammering at it with his good hand. The insulation in the room soaked up the noise like a sponge, and Macklin couldn't even put a dent in the steel. The door had no handles, nothing to grab hold of. He turned on the old man and charged at him with his deadly right hand upraised for a killing blow.

But before Macklin reached him, Friend stopped the colonel with a short, sharp blow to the throat. Macklin gagged and fell to his knees, his eyes bright with terror.

"No," Friend said, like an adult chastising a naughty child. Then he lifted his gaze to the old man. "What *is* this place? What are these machines for, and where's the power coming from?"

"Those gather information from satellites." The President motioned toward the mainframes. "I know what space looks like. I've looked down on the earth. I used to believe . . . it was such a *good* place." He blinked slowly as the memory of falling through the flaming whirlwind again stirred like a recurrent nightmare. "I fell to earth from Heaven. Yes. I fell. And I came here, because I knew I was close to this place. There were two men here, but they're not here now. They had food and water, enough to last them for years. I think . . . one of them died. I don't know what happened to the other one. He just . . . went away." He paused for a moment, and then his mind cleared again. He stared at the black box on the rubber-coated table and approached it reverently. "This," he said, "will bring down the talons of Heaven."

"The talons of Heaven? What's that mean?"

"Talons," the President said, as if the other man should know. "Tactical Long Range Nuclear Sanitizer. Watch—and listen." He punched his code into the keyboard: AOK.

The mainframes began to spin their data tapes faster. Roland watched, fascinated.

A woman's voice—soft and seductive, as cool as balm on an open wound—filtered through speakers in the walls: "Hello, Mr. President. I'm waiting for your instructions."

The voice reminded Sister of a New York social worker who'd politely explained that there was no more room in the Women's Shelter on a freezing January night.

The President typed, *Here is Belladonna, the Lady of the Rocks, the lady of situations.*

"Here is the man with three staves, and here the wheel," the disembodied computer voice answered.

"Wow!" Roland breathed.

And here is the one-eyed merchant, and this card

"Which is blank, is something he carries on his back"

The President typed, *Which I am forbidden to see.*

"What are you doing?" Sister shouted, close to panic. Swan squeezed her hand.

I do not find The Hanged Man, the President typed into the black box.

"Fear death by water," the feminine voice replied. There was a pause, then: "Talons armed, sir. Ten seconds to abort."

He pressed two letters on the keyboard: *No.*

"Initial abort sequence denied. Talons firing procedure activated, sir." The voice was as cool as the memory of lemonade on a scorching August afternoon. "Talons will be in target range in thirteen minutes and forty-eight seconds." Then the computer voice was silent.

"What's happened?" Friend was keenly interested. "What'd you do?"

"In thirteen minutes and forty-eight seconds," the President said, "two satellites will enter the atmosphere over the North Pole and Antarctica. Those satellites are nuclear missile platforms that will each fire thirty twenty-five-megaton warheads into the ice caps." He glanced over at Swan and looked quickly away, because her beauty made him yearn. "The blasts will throw the earth off its axis and melt the ice. The world will be cleansed, don't you see? All the evil will be washed away by the talons of Heaven—and someday things will start over again, and they'll be good, like they used to be." His face wrinkled with pain. "We lost the war," he said. "We lost—and now we have to start all over again."

"A . . . Doomsday machine," Friend whispered, and a grin skittered across his mouth. The grin stretched into a laugh, and the eyes danced with malignant glee. "A Doomsday machine!" he shouted. "Oh, yes! The world *must* be cleansed! All the Evil must be washed away! Like *her!*" He pointed a finger at Swan.

"The last of the Good must die with the Evil," the President replied. "Must die, so the world can be reborn."

"No . . . no . . ." Macklin croaked, clutching at his bruised throat.

Friend laughed, and he directed his attention to Sister, though he really spoke to Swan. "I told you!" he crowed. "I told you I'd make a human hand do the work!"

The cool feminine voice said, "Thirteen minutes to detonation."

Ninety-three

Josh and Robin came upon the dead soldier at the broken-open gate, and Josh bent down beside the corpse. Robin heard a hissing, sputtering noise but couldn't figure out where it was coming from. He reached out to touch the chain link fence.

"No!" Josh said sharply—and Robin's fingers stopped just short of the metal mesh. "Look at this." Josh opened the dead man's right hand, and Robin could see the chain link design burned into the corpse's flesh.

They went through the opening where the gate had been, while the fence's broken connections hissed like a nest of vipers. It was raining harder, and gray sheets of water whipped through the dead trees on either side of the road. Both of them were drenched and shivering, and the torn-up surface beneath them alternately gripped their boots in mud and then skidded them over icy patches. They moved as fast as they could, because both of them knew that Swan and Sister were somewhere ahead, at the mercy of the man with the scarlet eye, and they sensed time ticking rapidly toward the final hour.

Coming around a curve, Josh stopped, and Robin heard him say, "Damn it!"

Three soldiers, all but obscured by the rain, were descending the road and heading right at them. Two of them saw Josh and Robin and stopped less than ten yards away; the third kept going a few more steps until he stopped as well and gaped stupidly at the two figures in front of him.

Perhaps four seconds passed, and Josh thought he and the others had frozen into lead-boned statues. He couldn't figure out what to do—and suddenly the choice was made for him.

Like two bands of rival gunfighters meeting on a street at high noon, they started shooting without taking aim, and the next few seconds were a blur of motion, nerve-frazzling panic and flashes of gunfire as bullets screamed toward their targets.

"Ten minutes to detonation," the voice announced, and it struck Sister that the woman who'd made that tape was probably long dead.

"Stop it," Swan said to the scarred man who'd once been the President of the United States. "Please." Her face was calm but for the rapid beating of a pulse at her temple. "You're wrong. Evil hasn't won."

The President was sitting on the floor, his legs crossed beneath him and his eyes closed. Colonel Macklin had gotten to his feet and was beating weakly at the steel door, while Roland Croninger walked amid the computers, babbling to himself about being a King's Knight and lovingly running his fingers over the mainframes.

"Evil doesn't win unless you let it," Swan said quietly. "People still have a chance. They could bring things back. They could learn to live with what they have. If you let this thing happen—then evil *will* win."

He was silent, like a brooding idol. Then he said, with his eyes still closed, "It used to be . . . such a beautiful world. I know. I saw it from the great dark void, and it was good. I know what it used to be. I know what it is now. Evil will perish in the final hour, child. All the world will be made clean again by the talons of Heaven."

"Killing everyone won't make the world clean. It'll just make *you* part of the Evil."

The President didn't move or speak. Finally, his mouth opened to say something, but then it closed again, as if the thought had submerged itself.

"Nine minutes to detonation," the voice of a dead woman said.

"Please stop it." Swan knelt beside the man. Her heart was pounding, and the cold claws of panic gripped the back of her neck. But she could also feel the man with the scarlet eye watching her, and she knew she must not give him the satisfaction of seeing her break. "There are people outside who want to live. Please"—she touched the thin shoulder of his withered arm—"please give them the chance."

His eyes opened.

"People can tell the difference between Good and Evil," Swan said. "Machines can't. Don't let these machines make the decision, because it's going to be the wrong one. If you can . . . please stop the machines."

He was silent, staring at her with dead, hopeless eyes.

"*Can* you?" she asked him.

He closed his eyes. Opened them again, and stared into hers. He nodded.

"How?"

"Codeword," he answered. "Codeword . . . ends the prayer. But . . . Evil must be destroyed. The world must be cleansed. Codeword can stop the detonation . . . but I won't speak it, because the talons of Heaven must be released. I won't speak it. I can't."

"You *can*. If you don't want to be part of the Evil, you have to."

His face seemed to be contorted from within by currents of pressure. For an instant Swan saw a flicker of light in the dark craters of his eyes and thought he was going to stand up, go to that keyboard and type in the codeword—but then the light died, and he was insane again. "I can't," he said. "Not even . . . for someone as beautiful as you."

The computer voice said: "Eight minutes to detonation."

Across the room, Friend waited for Swan to crack.

"The power source," Roland said, part of his mind comprehending what was about to happen and shunting it aside, another part repeating over and over that he was a King's Knight and that he had finally, at long last, come to the end of an arduous journey. But he was with the true King, and he was happy. "Where's the power source for all this?"

The President stood up. "I'll show you." He motioned toward another door on the far side of the chamber. It was unlocked, and he led Roland through. As the door opened Swan heard the roaring sound of water, and she went through to see what lay beyond it.

A passageway led to a concrete platform with a waist-high metal railing, which stood about twenty feet over an underground river. The water rushed from a tunnel along a concrete-lined spillway, dropped off a sloping embankment and turned a large electric turbine before it streamed away through another tunnel cut into solid rock. The turbine was connected by a network of cables to two electric generators that hummed with power, and the air smelled of ozone.

"Seven minutes to detonation," the voice echoed from the other chamber.

Roland leaned over the railing and watched the turbine going around. He could hear the crackling of power through the cables, and he knew that the underground river supplied an inexhaustible source of electricity—plenty to drive the computers, the lights and the electric fence.

"The miners found this river a long time ago," the President said. "That's why the complex was built here." He cocked his head, listening to the river's noise. "It sounds so *clean,* doesn't it? I knew it was here. I remembered, after I fell from Heaven. Fear death by water." He nodded, lost in his memories. "Yes. Fear death by water."

Swan was about to ask him to type in the codeword again—but she saw his blank expression, and she knew it was useless. There was a movement from the corner of her eye, and the grinning monster in a human mask came through the doorway onto the platform.

"God?" Friend called, and the President turned from the railing. "There's no other way to stop the satellites, is there?

You're the only one who could—if you wanted to. Isn't that right?"

"Yes."

"Good." Friend lifted the machine gun and fired a burst of bullets, the sound deafening in the cavernlike room. The slugs marched up the President's stomach and chest and knocked him back against the railing, where he clawed at the air and danced to the gun's deadly rhythm. As Swan put her hands to her ears she saw the bullets slam into the man's head and knock him off his feet. He toppled over the railing as Roland Croninger gave a scream of hysterical laughter. The machine gun choked on an empty clip, and the President hit the water and was swept into the tunnel and out of sight.

"Bang bang!" Roland shouted merrily, leaning over the blood-spattered railing. "Bang bang!"

Tears burned Swan's eyes. He was gone, and so was the last hope of halting the prayer for the final hour.

The man with the scarlet eye tossed the useless weapon over the railing into the water and left the platform.

"Six minutes to detonation," the voice echoed.

"Keep your head down!" Josh shouted. A bullet had just ricocheted off the tree Robin crouched behind. Josh fired across the road at the other two soldiers, but his shot went wild. The third soldier lay on the road, writhing in pain, his hands clenched around a stomach wound.

Josh could hardly see anything through the rain. A bullet had plucked at his sleeve as he dove for cover, and he thought he'd wet his pants, but he wasn't sure because he was already so wet; he didn't know, either, if he or Robin had shot the third soldier down. For a few seconds bullets had been whizzing past as thick as flies at a garbage men's convention. But then he'd leapt into the woods, and Robin had followed an instant later as a ricocheting slug grazed his left hand.

The two soldiers fired repeatedly, and both Josh and Robin stayed under cover. Robin finally dared to lift his head. One of the men was running to the left to reach higher ground. He wiped rain from his eyes, took careful aim and squeezed off his last two shots. The soldier grabbed at his ribs, spun like a top and fell.

Josh shot at the remaining man, who returned the fire and then leapt to his feet, sprinting wildly along the edge of the road toward the electrified fence. "Don't shoot!" he screamed. "Don't shoot!" Josh aimed at his back, had a clear and killing shot—but he held his fire. He'd never shot a man in the back—not even an Army of Excellence trooper—and he was damned if he'd start now. He let the man go, and in another moment he stood up and motioned Robin on. They started up the road again.

Sister closed her eyes as the voice announced five minutes to detonation. She was dizzy, and she reached out to the wall for support, but Swan grasped her arm and held her steady.

"It's finished," Sister rasped. "Oh, my God . . . everyone's going to die. It's finished." Her knees started to buckle, and she wanted to slide down to the floor, but Swan wouldn't let her.

"Stand up." Still the other woman's body sagged. "Stand up, damn it!" Swan said angrily, and she pulled her up. Sister looked blankly at her and felt the twilight haze that she'd lived in as Sister Creep beginning to close around her.

"Oh, let her fall," the man with the scarlet eye said, standing across the chamber. "You'll die all the same, whether you're on your knees or your feet. Do you wonder how it'll happen?"

Swan didn't give him the satisfaction of answering.

"I do," he went on. "Maybe the whole world'll split apart and go spinning off in pieces, or maybe it'll be as quiet as a gasp. Maybe the atmosphere'll rip like an old sheet, and everything—mountains, forests, rivers, what's left of cities—will be flung off like dust. Or maybe gravity'll smash everything flat." He crossed his arms and leaned casually against the wall. "Maybe it'll shrivel and burn, and only a cinder will be left. Well, nobody can live forever!"

"How about *you?*" she had to ask. "Can you live forever?"

He laughed, softly this time. "I *am* forever."

"Four minutes to detonation," the cool voice promised.

Macklin was crouched on the floor, breathing like an animal. As the four minute mark was passed a terrible, mournful moan came from his injured throat.

"There's your death knell, Swan," the man with the scarlet eye said. "Do you still forgive me?"

"Why are you so afraid of me? I can't do anything to hurt you."

He didn't reply for a few seconds, and when he spoke his eyes were fathomless. "Hope hurts me," he said. "It's a disease, and you're the germ that spreads it. We can't have disease at my party. Oh, no. It won't be allowed." He was silent, staring at the floor—and then a smile skittered across his mouth as the computer voice said, "Three minutes to detonation."

Rain smashed against the aluminum roof as Josh and Robin reached the long shedlike structure. They'd passed the Jeeps and the corpse of Brother Timothy, and now they saw the entrance to the mine shaft in the dim yellow light. Robin ran ahead up the steps and along the catwalk while Josh followed. Just before Josh got to the shaft, he heard a thunder of what sounded like baseball-sized hailstones slamming on the roof, and he thought the whole damned place was about to cave in.

But the din abruptly ceased, as if a mechanism had been switched off. It was so silent Josh could hear the shriek of the wind outside the walls.

Robin looked down the slanting mine shaft and saw the tracks. Some kind of conveyance was at the bottom. He looked around and found the metal plate with the red and green buttons; he pressed the red one, but nothing happened. A touch of the green button, and at once machinery rumbled in the walls.

The long metal cable that stretched down the tracks began to reel itself up.

"Two minutes to detonation."

Colonel James B. Macklin heard himself whimper. The

walls of the pit were closing around him, and from far away he thought he heard the Shadow Soldier laughing; but no, no—*he* had the face of the Shadow Soldier now, and he and the Shadow Soldier were one and the same, and if anyone was laughing, it was either Roland Croninger or the monster who called himself Friend.

He clenched his left fist and beat against the sealed door—and there, in the stainless steel, he saw the skull staring back.

In that instant he clearly saw the face of his soul, and he teetered on the edge of madness. He hammered at that face, trying to smash it and make it go away, but it did not. The frozen fields where dead soldiers lay heaped and broken moved through his mind in a grisly panorama. The smoldering ruins of towns, burning vehicles and charred bodies lay before him like an offering on the altar of Hades, and he knew in that moment what the legacy of his life would be, and where it had led him. He'd escaped from the pit in Vietnam, had left his hand in the pit in Earth House, had lost his soul in the pit carved into the dirtwart land, and now would lose his life in this four-walled pit. And instead of crawling from the mud and standing on his feet after the seventeenth of July, he'd chosen to wallow in filth, to live from pit to pit, while the greatest and most hideous pit of all opened within himself and consumed him.

He knew with whom he was in league. He *knew*. And he knew also that he was damned, and the final pit was about to close over his head.

"Oh . . . the waste . . . the waste," he whispered, and tears ran down from the staring eyes. "God forgive me . . . oh, God forgive me," he began to sob as the man who called himself Friend laughed and clapped his hands.

Someone touched Colonel Macklin's shoulder. He lifted his head. Swan did her best not to flinch from him, because there was a tiny flicker of light deep in his eyes, just as there'd been a small flame in Sheila Fontana's bit of glass.

For a soul-awakening instant, Macklin thought he saw the sun in her face, thought he saw all that the world *could* have been. Now all was lost . . . all was lost. . . .

"No," he whispered. The pit hadn't closed over him yet . . . not yet. And he rose to his feet like a king and turned toward the mainframe computers that were about to destroy the wounded world.

He attacked the nearest machine, battering frenziedly at it with his nail-studded palm, trying to shatter the smoked glass and get at the spinning data tapes. The glass cracked, but it was reinforced with tiny threads of metal and would not let his hand through. Macklin fell to his knees and started ripping at one of the cables on the floor.

"Roland!" Friend snapped. "Stop him—*now!*"

Roland Croninger stepped behind Macklin and spoke one word—"Don't!"—that went unheeded.

"Kill him!" Friend shouted, coming forward like a whirlwind before the nails in Macklin's palm tore through the rubber cable into the wiring.

The true King had spoken. Roland was a King's Knight, and he must follow the word of the King. He lifted his .45. His hand was shaking.

And then he fired two bullets into Colonel Macklin's back at point-blank range.

The colonel fell onto his face. His body twitched, and then he lay still.

"Bang bang!" Roland wailed. He tried to laugh, but the sound came out strangled.

"One minute to detonation."

Ninety-four

Friend smiled.

All was in hand. It had turned out to be a fine party, and now it was to be finished with a fireworks display. But the place to watch such a show was not here, in the basement seats. He saw that Sister and the little bitch were down on their knees, clinging together, because they knew it was almost finished. It was a pleasant sight, and he had nothing else to prove here.

"Fifty seconds," the countdown continued.

He let his gaze move over Swan's face. *Too late,* he thought, and he swept the weakness aside. Outside this place there would still be bands of people, more settlements to visit; the fireworks display might crack the world in an eye blink, or it might be a slow decay and consumption. He didn't fully understand all that nuclear shit, but he was always ready to party.

In any case, *she* would be here, out of his way. The glass ring, or crown, or whatever it was, was lost. Sister had given him a good run, but she was on her knees now, broken. "Swan?" he said. "Do you forgive me?"

She didn't know what she was going to say until she said it, but as she opened her mouth he put his finger to his lips and whispered, "Too late."

His already-charred uniform had begun to smoke. His face had started melting.

"Forty seconds," the computer's voice said.

The flame that was consuming the man with the scarlet eye was a cold burning. Both Sister and Swan shrank away, but Roland stood awed, his teeth chattering and his eyes gleaming behind the goggles.

False flesh sizzled away and laid open what was beneath the mask—but Swan averted her eyes at the last second, and Sister cried out and shielded her face.

Roland watched and saw a face that no human being had ever witnessed and lived to tell about.

It was a suppurating sore with reptilian eyes, a seething and diseased mass that pulsed and rippled with volcanic fury. It was a maddening glimpse into the end of time, at worlds afire and the universe in chaos, black holes yawning in the fabric of time and civilizations scorched to ashes.

Roland fell to his knees at the feet of the true King. He lifted his hands toward the cold flame and begged, "Take me with you!"

What might have been a mouth opened in that nightmarish, apocalyptic face, and the ancient voice answered, "I've always walked alone."

Freezing fire leapt out of the uniform and sizzled over Roland's head like a bolt of electricity. It slammed upward through a small air vent in the wall, leaving a hole in the metal grille that was at the same time burned and rimmed with dirty ice.

The empty Army of Excellence uniform, still molded in the shape of a man, collapsed to the floor, ice crackling in its folds.

"Thirty seconds," the seductive voice intoned.

Sister saw her chance and knew what she must do. She shrugged off the shock and lunged toward Roland Croninger.

Her fingers gripped the wrist of his gun hand. He looked up at her, now totally insane. She shouted, "Swan! Stop the machine!" and tried to wrench the gun loose, but his other fist struck her in the face. She hung onto his wrist with all her strength, and the young knight of an infernal king fought her in a maniacal frenzy, getting his arm around her throat and squeezing.

Swan started to help Sister, but Sister was buying them precious seconds, and she must do what she could to stop the countdown. She bent to the floor and tried to rip up one of the cables.

Roland released Sister's throat and slammed his fist into her mouth. His teeth snapped at her cheek, but she warded him off with an elbow and hung on. The gun fired, its bullet whining off the opposite wall. They fought for the weapon, and then Sister rammed her elbow into his chest and leaned forward, sinking her teeth into his thin wrist. He howled in pain; his fingers opened, and the gun fell to the floor. Sister reached for it, but Roland's hand gripped her face, and his fingernails dug toward her eyes.

Swan couldn't get the cable loose; it was sealed to the floor, and the rubber was too thick to tear through. She looked up at the black keyboard on the table at the room's center and remembered what the old man had said about a codeword. But whatever it was had died with him. Still, she had to *try*. She jumped over the fighting figures and reached the keyboard.

"Twenty seconds."

Roland clawed at Sister's face, but she twisted her head away, and her fingers closed on the butt of the gun. As she picked it up a fist hammered across the back of her neck, and she lost her grip.

Trying to clear her mind, Swan stood over the keyboard. She typed, *Stop*.

Roland broke free from Sister and scrambled after the gun. He got it and twisted to fire at Sister, but she was on him like a wildcat, grabbing his wrist again and pounding at his misshapen, bleeding face.

"Fifteen seconds," the countdown continued.

End, Swan typed, all her concentration on the letters.

Sister reared her arm back and smashed her fist into Roland's face. One of the goggles' lenses shattered, and he yelped with pain. But then he struck her a glancing blow on the temple, stunning her, and he flung her aside like a sack of straw.

"Ten seconds."

Oh, God, help me! Swan thought as panic shot through her, and she clenched her teeth to hold back a scream.

She typed, *Finish.*

"Nine . . ."

She would have only one more chance now. She couldn't waste it.

The prayer for the final hour, she thought. The *prayer.*

"Eight . . ."

The *prayer.*

Sister grabbed at Roland's arm again, still fighting for the gun. He jerked free, and she saw his hideous face grin as he squeezed the trigger. Once . . . twice . . .

The bullets pierced Sister's ribs and shattered her collarbone, and she was flung back to the floor as if she'd been kicked. Blood was in her mouth.

"Seven . . ."

Swan had heard the shots, but the answer was close, and she dared not turn her attention from the keyboard. What ended a prayer? What ended—

"Get away!" Roland Croninger roared, rising from the floor with blood running from his mouth and nostrils.

"Six . . ."

He aimed at Swan, started to pull the trigger.

Something pounded like judgment on the other side of the steel door, and Roland was distracted for a vital split second.

And suddenly Colonel Macklin rose, and with his last surge of life and strength he slammed the nail-studded right hand into Roland Croninger's heart. As Roland was struck the gun went off, and the bullet whistled inches over Swan's head.

"Five . . ."

The nails had plunged deep. Roland fell to his knees, the scarlet blood pumping around Colonel Macklin's rigid, black-gloved fingers. Roland tried to lift the gun again, shaking his head from side to side, but Macklin's weight drove him down, and he lay jittering on the floor. Macklin held him in what was almost a loving embrace.

"Four . . ."

Swan stared at the keyboard. What ended a prayer?

She knew.

Her fingers moved across the keys.

She typed, *Amen.*

"Three . . ."

Swan shut her eyes and waited for the next second to fall.

Waited.

And waited.

When the silken voice came through the speakers again, Swan almost jumped out of her skin: "Talons detonation holding at two seconds. What is your next command, please?"

Swan's legs were weak. She backed away from the keyboard and almost fell over the bodies of Colonel Macklin and Roland Croninger.

Roland sat up.

Blood bubbled in his lungs and drooled from his mouth, and his arm shot out and grasped Swan's ankle.

She wrenched it free, and his body sprawled again. The bubbling noise ceased.

She looked at Sister.

The woman was propped up against the wall; her eyes were watery, and a thin line of blood had spilled over her lower lip and clung to her chin. She pressed her hand against the wound in her abdomen and managed a tired, vague smile. "We kicked some ass, didn't we?" she asked.

Fighting back bitter tears, Swan knelt at her side. Again, there was a pounding on the other side of the door. "Better find out who it is," Sister said. "They're not going to go away."

Swan went to the door and pressed her ear against the line where the metal sealed to the stone. She could hear nothing for a moment—and then there was a muffled, distant voice: "Swan! Sister! Are you in there?"

It was Josh's voice, and he was probably yelling at the top

of his lungs, but she could barely hear him. "Yes!" she shouted. "We're here!"

"Shhhh!" Josh told Robin. "I think I hear something!" He bellowed: "Can you let us in?" Both of them had seen the black box with the silver key in the lock, but upon turning it to the left, Robin had been faced with a demand for a codeword that flickered off after five seconds.

It took a minute of shouting back and forth for Josh to understand what Swan was trying to tell him. He turned the key to the left and pressed AOK on the keyboard when the codeword demand came on.

The door unlocked and popped open, and Robin was the first one through.

He saw Swan standing before him like a dream, and he put his arms around her and held her tight, and he told himself that as long as he was alive he would never let her go. Swan clung to him, too, and for a moment their hearts beat as one.

Josh pushed past them. He'd seen Macklin and the other man on the floor—and then he saw Sister. Oh, no, he thought. There was too much blood.

He reached her with two long strides and bent beside her.

"Don't ask me where it hurts," she said. "I'm numb."

"What happened?"

"The world . . . got a second chance," she answered.

The computer's voice said, "What is your next command, please?"

"Can you stand up?" Josh asked Sister.

"I don't know. I haven't tried. Oh . . . I've made a mess here, haven't I?"

"Come on, let me help you up." Josh got her to her feet. She felt light, and she left blood all over Josh's hands.

"Are you going to be okay?" Robin asked her, supporting her other arm with his shoulder.

"That's about the stupidest question . . . I've ever heard." She was getting short of breath, and now the pain was lancing through her ribs. But it wasn't bad. Not bad at all for a dying old lady, she thought. "I'm going to be fine. Just get me out of this damned hole."

Swan paused over Macklin's body. The dirty tape had

unraveled from around his right wrist, and the hand with its nail-studded palm was almost severed from the arm. She ripped the rest of the tape away, then forced herself to work the long, bloody nails out of Roland Croninger's body. She stood up with the brutal hand clenched in her own blood-smeared fingers.

They left the chamber of death and machines. The seductive voice asked, "What is your next command, please?"

Swan turned the silver key to the right. The door sealed itself, and the locks clicked shut. She put the key in the pocket of her jeans.

And then they helped Sister into the mine shaft's car, and Robin pressed the green button on a metal wall plate next to the tracks before he climbed in. The noise of machinery grew, and the car rose toward the top of the shaft.

Sister lost all feeling in her legs as they were moving along the catwalk to the stairs. She clung tighter to Josh, who took more of her weight on him. Behind her she left a trail of blood, and now her breathing was forced and irregular.

Swan knew Sister was dying. She felt about to choke, but she said, "We'll get you well!"

"I'm not sick. I'm shot," Sister replied. "One step at a time," she said as Josh and Robin eased her down the stairs. "Oh, Lord . . . I feel like I'm about to pass out."

"Hold on," Josh told her sternly. "You can make it."

But her legs folded at the bottom of the stairs. Her eyelids fluttered, and she fought to stay conscious.

They left the aluminum-roofed building and started across the parking lot toward the Jeeps as the cold wind shrilled around them and the clouds hung low over the mountains.

Sister couldn't hold her head up anymore. Her neck was weak, and her skull felt as if it weighed a hundred pounds. One step, she urged herself. One step and then the next gets you where you're going. But the taste of blood was thick and coppery in her mouth, and she knew where her dragging steps were taking her.

Her legs locked.

She'd seen something there on the broken pavement before her. It was gone now. But what had it been?

"Come on," Josh said, but Sister refused to budge.

She saw it again. Just a brief glimpse and gone. "Oh, God!" she said.

"What is it? You hurting?"

"No! No! Wait! Just wait!"

They waited, while Sister's blood trickled to the pavement.

And there it was, a third time. Something Sister had not seen in a very long while.

Her shadow.

It was gone in an instant. "Did you see it? Did you?"

"See what?" Robin looked at the ground, saw nothing.

But in the next moment, it happened.

They all felt it.

Heat, like the rays of a searchlight behind the clouds, slowly sweeping across the parking lot.

Sister watched the ground—and as she felt the heat spread across her back and shoulders like a healing balm she saw her shadow take form on the pavement, saw the shadows of Josh and Swan and Robin all gathered around her own.

With a mighty effort, she lifted her head toward the sky, and the tears ran down her cheeks.

"The sun," she whispered. "Oh, dear God . . . the sun's coming out."

They looked up. The leaden sky was moving, plates of clouds colliding and ripping apart. "There!" Robin shouted, pointing. He was the first to see a patch of azure before the clouds closed up again.

"Josh! I want to go . . . up there!" She motioned to the peak of Warwick Mountain. "Please! I want to see the sun come out!"

"We've got to get some help for you before—"

She clenched his hand. "I want to go up there," she repeated. "I want to watch the sun come out. Do you understand me?"

Josh did. He hesitated, but only for a few seconds, because he knew time was short. He lifted her in his arms and started up the side of Warwick Mountain.

Swan and Robin followed as he climbed through the rough

terrain of boulders and dead, twisted trees, carrying Sister up toward the turbulent sky.

Swan felt the sun's touch on her back, saw the shadows of rocks and trees appear around her; she looked up and caught a hint of bright blue off to the left, and then the clouds sealed up. Robin grasped her hand, and they helped each other climb.

"Hurry!" Sister told Josh. "Please . . . hurry!"

Shadows scurried across the mountain. The wind was still cold and whipped violently, but the clouds were beginning to break up, and Josh wondered if that last storm hadn't been the final gasp of a seven-year winter.

"*Hurry!*" Sister pleaded.

They came out of the woods and into a small clearing near the peak. Rough-edged boulders were strewn about, and from this height there was a view to all points of the compass, the landscape around them fading into the mist.

"Here." Sister's voice was weakening. "Lay me down here . . . so I can see."

Josh gently put Sister on a bed of dead leaves, with her back molded into the smooth hollow of a boulder and her face turned toward the west.

The wind swirled around them, still carrying a bite. Dead branches snapped from the trees, and black leaves flew overhead like ravens.

Swan caught her breath as rays of golden light streamed through the western clouds, and for an instant the harsh landscape softened, its forlorn colors of black and gray turning to pale brown and reddish-gold. But just as quickly, the light was gone.

"Wait," Sister said, watching the advance of the clouds. Whirlwinds and eddies moved in them like tides and currents after a storm. She could feel her life quickly ebbing away, her spirit wanting to bolt out of her tired body, but she clung to life with the same dogged tenacity that had helped her carry the glass crown mile after rugged mile.

They waited. Above Warwick Mountain the clouds were drifting apart, slowly unlocking, and behind them were fragments of blue, connecting like the pieces of a huge jigsaw puzzle finally revealed.

"There." Sister nodded, squinting up as the light spread over the land and up the mountainside, over dead leaves and trees and boulders and onto her face. *"There!"*

Josh shouted with joy. Huge holes were breaking open in the clouds, and through them streamed a golden light as beautiful as a promise.

From down in the distant valleys and hollows below Warwick Mountain other cries of joy echoed from the hill-sides, where little communities of shacks had finally been touched by the sun. A car horn blew, followed by another and another, and the shouts grew and merged into a mighty voice.

Swan lifted her face up and let the wonderful, stunning warmth soak into her skin. She drew a long breath and smelled sweet, uncontaminated air.

The long twilight was ending.

"Swan," Sister rasped.

She looked down at Sister, saw her radiant with sunlight and smiling. Sister lifted her hand to Swan; she took it, grasped it tightly and knelt down beside her.

They looked at each other for a long time, and Swan put Sister's hand against her wet cheek.

"I'm proud of you," Sister said. "Oh, I'm so proud of you."

"You're going to be all right," Swan told her, but her throat was closing up, and a sob welled out. "You'll be fine as soon as we get you to—"

"Shhhhh." Sister ran her fingers over Swan's long, flame-colored hair. In the sunshine, it gleamed with the intensity of a bonfire. "I want you to listen to me, now. Listen close. Look at me, too."

Swan did, but Sister's face was blurred through the tears. Swan wiped her eyes.

"The summer's . . . finally come," Sister said. "There's no telling when winter will be back. You're going to have to work while you can. Work as hard and fast . . . as you can, while the sun's still shining. Do you hear me?"

Swan nodded.

Sister's fingers tightened around the girl's. "I wish I could go with you. I do. But . . . that's not how it's going to be. You and I . . . are going in different directions now. But that's all right." Sister's eyes sparkled, and she looked over at Robin. "Hey," she said. "Do you love her?"

"Yes."

"How about you?" she asked Swan. "Do you love him?"

"Yes," Swan said.

"Then . . . that's half the battle won right there. You two hold onto each other, and you help each other . . . and don't let anybody or anything pull you apart. You keep going, step after step . . . and you do the work that has to be done while it's still summertime." She turned her head, and squinted up at the black giant. "Josh?" she said. "You know . . . where you have to go, don't you? You know who's waiting for you."

Josh nodded. "Yes," he finally managed to say. "I know."

"The sun . . . feels so good," Sister said, looking up at it. Her sight was dimming, and she didn't have to squint anymore. "So good. I've come . . . a long way . . . and I'm tired now. Will you . . . find a place for me to rest up here . . . so I can lie close to the sun?"

Swan squeezed her hand, and Josh said, "We will."

"You're a good man. I don't think . . . even you knew how good you were. Swan?" Sister reached up with both hands and cupped them around Swan's beautiful face. "You listen to me. Do the work. Do it well. You can bring things back . . . even better than they were. You're a . . . natural-born leader, Swan . . . and when you walk, you hold yourself strong and proud . . . and . . . remember . . . how much I love you. . . ."

Sister's hands slipped away from Swan's face, but Swan caught and held onto them. The spark of life was almost gone.

Sister smiled. In Swan's eyes she could see the colors of the glass crown. Her mouth trembled and opened again.

"One step," she whispered.

And then she took the next.

They stayed around her as the sun warmed their backs and thawed out their muscles. Josh started to close Sister's eyes—but he didn't, because he knew how much she loved the light.

Swan stood up. She walked away from them and dug her hand into her pocket.

She brought out the silver key, and she climbed up on a boulder and walked to the edge of Warwick Mountain.

She stood with her head held high, staring into the distance. But she was seeing more armies of fighting and frightened men, more guns and armored cars, more death and misery that would still be lurking in the minds of men like a cancer waiting to be reborn.

She gripped the silver key.

Never again, she thought—and she flung the key as hard and as far as she could.

Sunlight winked off it as it fell through space. It bounced off the limb of an oak tree, hit the edge of a boulder, fell fifty more feet into a small green pond half hidden by underbrush. As it drifted through the water and into the leaves at the pond's bottom it stirred up several tiny eggs that had been hidden there for a long, long time. Shafts of sunlight stroked the pond and warmed the eggs, and the hearts of tadpoles began to beat.

Josh, Swan and Robin found a place to let Sister's body rest; it was not sheltered by trees or hidden in shade, but lay where the sun could reach it. They dug the grave with their hands and lowered Sister into the earth. When the grave was filled again, each of them said whatever was on his or her mind, and they ended with "Amen."

Three figures came down off the mountain.

Ninety-five

Sunlight had touched the camp of the Army of Excellence as well, and each man, woman and child there saw what was exposed.

Faces that had been hidden in twilight now emerged monstrous. The light hit the grotesque demons on the carved steps of the Central Command trailer, fell upon the trucks with their cargoes of bloodstained clothing, illuminated the black trailer where Roland Croninger had tortured in his quest for truth, and men who'd learned to live for the sight of blood and the sound of screams shrank back from that light as if pinpointed beneath the eye of God.

Panic ruled the mob. There were no leaders now, only followers, and some men fell to their knees and jabbered for forgiveness, while others crawled into the familiar darkness beneath the trailers and curled up there with their guns.

Three figures walked through the howling, sobbing mass of humanity, and many could not bear to look at the face of the girl with hair like fire. Others screamed for Colonel Macklin and the man they'd come to know as Friend, but they were not answered.

"Halt!" A young, hard-featured soldier leveled his rifle. Two other men stood behind him, and a fourth came out from behind a truck to aim his pistol at Josh.

Swan regarded each of them in turn and held herself tall

and proud, and when she took a step forward, all of the soldiers moved back except the man who'd spoken.

"Get out of our way," Swan said, as calmly as she could manage, but she knew the man was scared, and he wanted to kill somebody.

"Fuck you!" the young soldier sneered. "I'll blow your head off!"

She tossed something to his feet, into the steaming mud.

He looked down.

It was the black-gloved hand of Colonel Macklin, its palm and nails smeared with dried gore.

He scooped it up, and then he grinned crazily as the realization hit him. "It's *mine,*" he whispered. "It's mine!" His voice grew louder, more frantic. "Macklin's dead!" he shouted, and he lifted the hand for the others to see. "It's mine now! I'm in command! I've got the pow—"

He was shot through the forehead by the soldier with the pistol, and as the false hand fell to the mud the other men went after it, fighting like animals for the symbol of power.

But another figure leapt amid them, flinging first one man back and then another, tearing the gloved hand away and holding it in his own grasp. He stood up, and as his mud-smeared face swiveled toward Swan she saw the shock and hatred in his eyes; he was a brutal, dark-haired man in an Army of Excellence uniform—but there were bullet holes across the front of his shirt and dried blood around the heart. The face seemed to ripple for just a fraction of a second, and then the man lifted one dirty hand to either shield himself from the sun or ward off the sight of Swan.

Maybe it was him, she realized. Maybe he'd already put on a new skin and climbed into a corpse's clothes. She couldn't tell for sure, but if it was him, she had to answer the question he'd asked her down in the mine. "The machine's stopped, and the missiles aren't going to fire," she said. "Not ever."

He made a low, garbled noise and stepped back, still hiding his face.

"There won't be an end," Swan told him. "So yes, I do forgive you, because if it wasn't for you, we wouldn't have a second chance."

"Kill her!" the dark-haired man tried to shout, but his voice came out weak and sick. "Shoot her down!"

Josh stepped in front of Swan to protect her. The soldiers hesitated.

"I said kill her!" He lifted Macklin's hand, his face averted from Swan's. "I'm your master now! Don't let her walk out of here a—"

One of the soldiers fired at point-blank range.

The rifle bullet went into the dark-haired man's chest, and the impact staggered him. Another bullet hit him, and he tripped over the dead man and fell into the mud, and already the other soldiers were leaping onto him, fighting again for the nail-pierced hand. And now more soldiers were coming, drawn by the shots, and they saw the disembodied hand and threw themselves into the fight as well. "Kill her!" the dark-haired man demanded, but he was being pressed down into the mud under the thrashing bodies, and his voice was a high whine. "Kill the little bi—"

Someone had an axe and started hacking with it. The dark-haired man was down at the bottom of the pile, and over the curses and grunts of the fighting men, Swan heard him jibbering, "It's my party! It's my party!" She saw a boot mash his face into the mud.

Then the soldiers closed over him, and she could no longer see any part of him.

Swan went on. Josh followed, but Robin paused. Lying on the ground was another pistol. He started to reach down and retrieve it—but he caught himself and did not touch it. Instead, he shoved it deeper into the mud as he passed.

They went through the encampment, where soldiers ripped off their filthy, blood-caked uniforms and threw them into a huge bonfire. Trucks and armored cars roared past as men and women fled to destinations unknown. The shout, "The colonel's dead! Colonel Macklin's dead!" was carried over the camp, and more shots rang out as last quarrels were settled or suicide was chosen.

And, finally, they came to Sheila Fontana's trailer.

The guards had gone, and the door was unlocked. Swan opened it and found Sheila inside, sitting at her dresser before the mirror, looking at herself and holding the shard of glass.

"It's over," Swan said, and as Sheila stood up the piece of glass pulsed with light.

"I've . . . been waiting for you," Sheila told her. "I knew you'd come back. I . . . I prayed for you."

Swan walked toward her. She embraced the other woman, and Sheila whispered, "Please . . . please let me come with you. All right?"

"Yes," Swan answered, and Sheila grasped her hand and pressed it against her lips.

Swan went to the mattress, reached inside it and brought out the battered leather satchel. She could feel the shape of the crown in it, and she pulled it to her chest. She would protect it and carry it with her for the rest of her life, because she knew the man with the scarlet eye would be back. Maybe not today or tomorrow, maybe not even next year or the year after that—but someday, somewhere, he would slip from the shadows wearing a new face and a new name, and on that day she would have to be very careful and very strong.

She didn't know what other powers the crown held, didn't know where the dreamwalking would lead her, but she was ready to take the first step. And that step, she knew, would take her along a path she'd never imagined when she was a child, growing her flowers and plants in the trailer park dirt of Kansas a world and a lifetime away. But she was no longer a child, and the wasteland awaited a healing touch.

She pulled back from Sheila Fontana and turned toward Josh and Robin. She knew Sister was right: Finding someone you loved, and someone who loved you, was half the battle. And now she knew, as well, what she had to do to make the wonderful things she'd seen in the glass crown come true.

"I think . . . there are others who might want to go with us," Sheila said. "Other women . . . like me. And some of the men, too. They're not all bad men . . . they're just afraid, and they won't know what to do or where to go."

"All right," Swan agreed. "If they put down their guns, we'll welcome them."

Sheila left to gather the others, and she returned with two

bedraggled-looking RLs—one a heavily made-up, frightened teenager and the other a tough black woman with a red Mohawk haircut—and three nervous men, one of them wearing a sergeant's uniform. As a show of good faith, the ex-soldiers had brought knapsacks full of canned Spam, corned beef hash and soup, as well as canteens of fresh water from the spring in Mary's Rest. The black prostitute, whose name was Cleo—"short for Cleopatra," she announced dramatically—brought an assortment of gaudy rings, necklaces and trinkets that Swan had no use for, and the teen-age girl—"They call me Joey," she said, her dark hair all but obscuring her face—offered Swan her prized possession: a single yellow flower in a red clay pot that she'd somehow kept alive.

And as the light of the new day faded a truck with Josh at the wheel and carrying Robin, Swan, Sheila Fontana, the two RLs and the three men left the camp of the Army of Excellence, where a group of rampaging madmen had set fire to Colonel Macklin's trailer, and the last of the ammunition was exploding.

Long after Josh had driven away, the wolves began to come down from the mountains, and they silently circled the remnants of the Army of Excellence.

The night passed, and patches of stars came out. The truck, with one remaining headlight and not much gasoline, turned west.

In the darkness, Swan cried for a while with the memory of Sister, but Robin put his arm around her, and she leaned her head against the strength of his shoulder.

Josh thought of Mary's Rest and of the woman he hoped was still waiting for him with the boy at her side. Sheila Fontana slept the sleep of the innocent and dreamed of a beautiful face looking back at her from a mirror.

Sometime during the night, Cleo and one of the men jumped out of the truck with a knapsack full of food and water. Josh wished them good luck and let them go.

The stars faded. A thin red line crept across the eastern horizon, and Josh almost cried when the sun peeked back through the thinning clouds.

The truck coughed and ran out of gas about two hours after sunrise. They started off on foot, following the road that led westward.

And on the afternoon of that day, as the light slanted through the trees and the blue sky was dappled with white, slowly drifting clouds, they stopped to rest their legs. But Swan stood on the edge of the road looking down into a valley where three small shacks were clustered around the brown stubble of a field. A man in a floppy straw hat and a woman in overalls were working in that field with a shovel and hoe, and two small children were on their knees carefully planting seeds and grain from burlap sacks.

It wasn't a very large field. It was surrounded by withered trees—maybe pecan or walnut trees, Swan thought. But a sparkling stream of water meandered across the valley, and it occurred to Swan that it might be a trickle from the underground river that had powered the machines in Warwick Mountain.

Now, she thought, that same water could be used for life instead of death.

"I'll bet they're planting beans," Josh said, standing beside her. "Maybe squash or okra, too. What do you think?"

"I don't know."

He smiled faintly. "Yes, you do."

She looked at him. "What?"

"You *do* know," he replied. "You know you have to start somewhere. Even a field as small as that one."

"I'm going back to Mary's Rest with you. That's where I'm going to st—"

"No," Josh said, and his eyes were gentle but pained. Across his forehead were three gashes that would heal into scars and forever remind him of the old wrestling trick. "We don't have enough food and water left for us all to make it back to Mary's Rest. That's a long way from here."

"Not so far."

"Far enough," he said, and he motioned toward the valley. "You know, there's plenty of room down there for more crops. I imagine there are a lot of other shacks in these mountains, too. Plenty of people who haven't had fresh okra, beans or squash in a long time." His mouth watered at the thought. "Soul food," he said, and he smiled.

She watched the man, woman and children at work. "But . . . what about the people in Mary's Rest? What about my *friends?"*

"They made do before you got there. They'll make do until you get back. Sister was right. You need to work while it's summertime—and there's no telling how long that'll be. Maybe a month, maybe six. But the cold will come back. I just pray to God the next winter won't last as long."

"Hey! Hey up there!" The farmer had seen them, and he lifted his hand and waved. The woman and children paused in their work and looked up toward the road.

"It's time to make new friends," Josh said softly.

Swan didn't reply. She watched the man waving, and then she raised her own hand and waved back. The farmer said something to the woman and started up the winding trail that connected their land with the road.

"Start here," Josh told her. "Start now. I think that girl—Joey—might even be able to help you. Otherwise how could she have kept that flower alive so long?" His heart was aching, but he had to say it: "You don't need me anymore, Swan."

"Yes, I do!" Her lower lip trembled. "Josh, I'll always need you!"

"Bird's gotta fly," he said. "And even a swan has to spread her wings sometime. You know where I'll be—and you know how to get there."

She shook her head. *"How?"* she asked.

"Field by field," he said.

She reached for him, and he put his arms around her and held her tight.

"I love you . . . so much," Swan whispered. "Please . . . don't go yet. Just stay one more day."

"I wish I could. But if I did . . . I wouldn't leave. I have to go while I still know I want to."

"But—" Her voice cracked. "Who's going to *protect* you?"

He laughed then, but his laughter was mixed with tears. He

saw the farmer coming up the trail, and Robin was walking to meet him. The others had gotten to their feet again.

"No man was ever prouder of a daughter than I am of you," Josh whispered in her ear. "You're going to do wonderful things, Swan. You're going to set things right again, and long before you come back to Mary's Rest . . . I'll hear your name from travelers, and they'll say they know of a girl called Swan who's grown up to be a beautiful woman. They'll say she has hair like fire, and that she has the power of life inside her. And that's what you must return to the earth, Swan. That's what you must return to the earth."

She looked up at the black giant, and her eyes shimmered with light.

"Howdy!" the farmer in the straw hat said. He was skinny, but he already had a sunburn on his cheeks. Dirt clung to his hands. "Where you folks from?"

"The end of the world," Josh said.

"Yeah. Well . . . doesn't look like the world's gonna end *today*, does it? Nope! Maybe tomorrow, but surely not today!" He took off his hat, wiped his forehead with his sleeve and squinted up at the sun. "My Lord, that's a pretty thing! I don't think I've ever seen anything prettier—except my wife and kids, maybe." He held out his hand toward Robin. "Name's Matt Taylor."

"Robin Oakes." He shook the man's sturdy hand.

"You folks look like you could use a drink of water and sit a spell. You're welcome to come down, if you like. We ain't got much, but we're workin' at it. Just tryin' to plant some beans and okra while the sun's shinin'."

Swan looked past him. "What kind of trees are those?"

"What? Those dead ones? Well, sad to say, those used to be pecan trees. Used to just about break the branches down come October. And way over there"—he pointed toward another grove—"we used to have peaches in the spring and summer. 'Course, that was before everything went so bad."

"Oh," Swan said.

"Mr. Taylor, where's the nearest town from here?" Josh asked.

"Well, Amberville is just over the hill about three or four

miles. Ain't much there but a few shacks and about fifty or sixty people. Got a church, though. I ought to know: I'm *Reverend* Taylor."

"I see." Josh stared into the valley at the figures in the field and the grove of trees that he knew were not dead, only waiting for a healing touch.

"What's in the bag?" The reverend nodded toward the satchel Swan had set at her feet.

"Something . . . wonderful," Josh answered. "Reverend Taylor, I'm going to ask you to do something for me. I'd like for you to take these folks down to your house, and I'd like for you to sit yourself in a chair and listen to what . . . to what my daughter has to tell you. Will you do that?"

"Your *daughter?*" He frowned, puzzled, and looked at Swan. Then he abruptly laughed and shrugged. "Well, this has sure turned out to be a crazy world. Sure," he told Josh. "Everybody's welcome to come and sit a spell."

"It'll be a spell, all right," Josh replied. He went across the road and picked up one of the knapsacks full of food and a canteen of water.

"Hey!" Robin called. "Where're you going?"

Josh walked toward Robin; he smiled and grasped the young man's shoulder. "Home," he said, and then his expression went severe and menacing: one of his glowering masks from the wrestling ring. "You watch yourself, and you take care of Swan. She's very precious to me. Do you understand that?"

"Yes, sir, I do."

"Make sure you do. I don't want to come back this way to kick your butt to the moon." But he'd already seen how Robin and Swan looked at each other, how they walked close together and talked quietly, as if sharing secrets, and he knew he wouldn't have to worry. He slapped Robin on the shoulder. "You're okay, my friend," he said—and suddenly Robin put his arms around Josh, and they embraced each other. "You take care of yourself, Josh," Robin said. "And don't you ever worry about Swan. She's precious to me, too."

"Mister?" Reverend Taylor called. "Aren't you going down into the valley with us?"

"No, I'm not. I've got a ways to go yet, and I'd better get started. I want to make a couple of miles before dark."

The reverend paused, obviously not understanding, but he saw that the black giant did indeed intend to continue on his way. "Just a minute, then! Hold on!" He reached into the pocket of his canvas jacket, and his fingers came out with something. "Here," he said. "Take this to carry you on your way."

Josh looked at the little silver crucifix on a chain that Reverend Taylor was offering him.

"Take it. A wayfarer needs a friend."

"Thank you." He put the chain around his neck. "Thank you very much."

"Good luck. I hope you find what you're looking for when you get where you're going."

"I do, too." Josh started walking away, westward along the mountain road. He'd gone about ten yards when he turned back and saw Robin and Swan standing together, watching him go. Robin had his arm around her, and she was leaning her head on his shoulder.

"Field by field!" he called.

And then he was blinded by tears, and he turned away with the beautiful image of Swan burned forever in his mind.

She watched him until he was out of sight. Except for Robin, the others had already gone with Reverend Taylor down to his house in the valley. She gripped Robin's hand and turned her face toward the landscape of mountains and hollows, where dead trees waited to be awakened like restless sleepers. Off in the distance she thought she heard the high, joyful song of a bird—perhaps a bird just finding her wings.

"Field by field," Swan vowed.

The days passed.

And high up where Warwick Mountain's peak almost touched the blue sky, tiny seeds that had been scattered by the whirlwinds and stirred to life by the fingers of a girl with hair like flame began to respond to the sunlight and send out fragile green stems.

The stems searched upward through the dirt, pushed

through the surface and into the warmth, and there they bloomed into flowers—red and purple, bright yellow, snow-white, dark blue and pale lavender.

They glowed like jewels in the sunshine and marked the place where Sister lay sleeping.

Weeks passed, and the road lamed him.

His face was grayed with dust, but the knapsack was lighter on his bowed and weary back. He kept walking, one step after the next, following the road as it wound westward across the land.

Some days the sun was out in full force. Some days the clouds returned and the rain fell. But the rainwater was sweet on his tongue, and the storms never lasted very long. Then the clouds would scatter again, and the sun would shine through. At midday the temperature felt like the height of summer, which he realized it must be—at least by the calendar of the world that used to be—but the nights were frosty, and he had to huddle up for warmth in a roadside barn or house, if he was lucky enough to find shelter.

But he kept going, and he kept hoping.

He'd been able to trade food for matches along the way, and when he was out in the open at night he built fires to keep the night-things at bay. One night in western Kentucky he was awakened under a starry sky, and at first he didn't know what had jarred him—but then he listened, and he heard it.

The sound of whistling, fading in and out, as if from a great distance.

He knew he must be losing his mind or coming down with fever—but he thought the tune was "Here we go 'round the mulberry bush, the mulberry bush, the mulberry bush; here we go 'round the mulberry bush so early in the morrrrrning. . . ."

After that he looked for a house or barn to spend the night in.

On the road he saw signs of awakening: small green buds on a tree, a flock of birds, a patch of emerald-green grass, a violet growing from an ash heap.

Things were coming back. Very slowly. But they were coming back.

And not one day—and very few hours—passed that Josh didn't think of Swan. Thought of her hands working the dirt, touching seeds and grain, her fingers running over the rough bark of pecan and peach trees, stirring all things to life once again.

He crossed the Mississippi River on a flatbed ferryboat captained by a white-bearded old man with skin the color of that river's mud, and his ancient wife played the fiddle all the way across and laughed at Josh's worn-out shoes. He stayed with them that night and had a good dinner of beans and salt pork, and in the morning when he set out he found his knapsack heavier by one pair of soft-soled sneakers that were just a little too small, but fine once the toes were sliced open.

He entered Missouri, and his pace quickened.

A violent thunderstorm stopped him for two days, and he found shelter from the deluge in a small community called, laconically, All's Well, because there was indeed a well at the center of town. In the schoolhouse, he played poker against two teen-age boys and an elderly ex-librarian, and he wound up losing five hundred and twenty-nine thousand dollars in paper clips.

The sun came out again, and Josh went on, thankful that the card sharps hadn't taken his sneakers off his feet.

He saw green vines trailing through the gray woods on either side of the road, and then he rounded a bend and abruptly stopped.

Something was glittering, far ahead. Something was catching the light and shining. It looked like a signal of some kind.

He kept walking, trying to figure out what the sparkling was coming from. But it was still far ahead, and he couldn't tell. The road unreeled beneath his feet, and now he didn't even mind the blisters.

Something sparkled . . . sparkled . . . sparkled. . . .

He stopped again and drew in his breath.

Far up the dusty road he could see a figure. Two figures. One tall, one small. Two figures, waiting. And the tall one wore a long black dress with sparkles on the front that was catching the sunlight.

"Glory!" he shouted.

And then he heard her shout his name and saw her running toward him in the dress that she'd worn every day, day in and day out, in hopes that *this* would be the day he came home.

And it was.

He ran toward her, too, and the dust puffed off his clothes as he picked her up and crushed her to his body, and Aaron yelled and jumped around at their feet, tugging on the black giant's sleeve. Josh scooped Aaron up as well and held them both tightly in his arms as all of them surrendered to tears.

They went home—and there in the field beyond the houses of Mary's Rest were apple trees, loaded down with fruit, from saplings that the Army of Excellence had missed.

The people of Mary's Rest came out of their homes and gathered around Josh Hutchins, and by lamplight in the new church that was going up he told them everything that had happened, and when someone asked if Swan was ever coming back, Josh replied with certainty, "Yes. In time." He hugged Glory to him. "In time."

Time passed.

Settlements struggled out of the mud, built meeting halls and schoolhouses, churches and shacks, first with clapboard and then with bricks. The last of the armies found people ready to fight to the death for their homes, and those armies melted away like snow before the sun.

Crafts flourished, and settlements began to trade with one another, and travelers were welcome because they brought news from far away. Most towns elected mayors, sheriffs and governing councils, and the law of the gun began to wither under the power of the court.

The tales began to spread.

No one knew how they started, or from where. But her name was carried across the awakening land, and it held a power that made people sit up and listen and ask travelers what they'd heard about her, and if the stories were really true.

Because, more than anything, they wanted to believe.

They talked about her in houses and in schools, in town halls and in general stores. She's got the power of life in her! they said. In Georgia she brought back peach orchards and apple trees! In Iowa she brought back miles upon miles of corn and wheat! In North Carolina she touched a field, and flowers sprang forth from the dirt, and now she's heading to Kentucky! Or Kansas! Or Alabama! Or Missouri!

Watch for her! they said. Follow her, if you like, as many hundreds of others do, because the young woman called Swan has the power of life in her, and she's waking up the earth!

And in the years to come they would talk about the blooming of the wasteland, the cultivation projects and the work being done to dig canals for flatboat barges. They would talk about the day Swan met a boatload of survivors from the destroyed land that had been called Russia, and nobody could understand their language, but she talked to them and heard them through the miraculous jeweled ring of glass that she always carried close at hand. They would talk about the rebuilding of the libraries and the great museums, and of the schools that taught first and foremost the lesson learned from the awful holocaust of the seventeenth of July: *Never again.*

They would talk about the two children of Swan and Robin—twins, a boy and a girl—and about the celebration when thousands flocked to the city of Mary's Rest to see those children, who were named Joshua and Sister.

And when they would tell their own children the tale by candlelight in the warmth of their homes, on the streets where lamps burned under stars that still stirred the power to dream, they would always begin the tale with the same magic words:

"Once upon a time . . ."